A WolfGirl Novel

As Worlds Tilt

Tasneem Alam

An Imprint of Venom and Virtue House

Published in the United States by Venom and Virtue House, 2026

This is a work of fiction. While it may draw from historical events, mythologies, and religious traditions—these elements have been interpreted creatively for fictional purposes. Any names, characters, places, events or settings not explicitly historical are products of the author's imagination. Any resemblance to actual people, living or dead, are purely coincidental.

Cover Design by Tasneem Alam
Cover Art by Kristy P @thirdattemptt
Cover Typography Design by Tasneem Alam

ISBN: 979-8-9955442-1-0

DEDICATION

To those who feared their own darkness—not because it was evil, but because it was powerful enough to set them free

CONTENT WARNING

As Worlds Tilt contains mature themes, including graphic depictions and/or implications of:

- Violence
- Sexual content
- Manipulation
- Emotional and mental warfare
- Relationship trauma
- Coercion
- Blood
- Drugs
- Supernatural/witchcraft/religion
- Grief and loss of a child or loved one
- Death

Some scenes may be distressing to readers.

This story explores heavy themes and darker emotional experiences that may not be suitable for all audiences. Please read with care and prioritize your mental well-being.

For an immersive experience check out the author's Instagram for character and world aesthetics, guides, and much more!

AUTHOR'S NOTE

This is a dark paranormal fantasy romance intended for readers 18+.

This story is told through Rose's understanding of her world—and her understanding is incomplete. It is also told through Josh's trauma, his grief, and navigating right and wrong after that.

If at times the plot feels fragmented, withheld, or maddening, understand that you are experiencing the story exactly as they do.

Some truths are hidden for protection.
Some are hidden for control.

You will not be given every answer as their world is just beginning, and like life, sometimes the unknown is just that—unknown.
That is intentional.

If you prefer clean morality, immediate clarity, fully resolved endings, and a cute, innocent love story—this may not be your book.

But if you are willing to sit in uncertainty…to feel the frustration of being kept in the dark…and still be in the dark…to watch a woman discover and remember herself…

Welcome.
Trust the unraveling and turn the page.

~ Tasneem Alam

GUIDE

SHIFTER ROYALTY

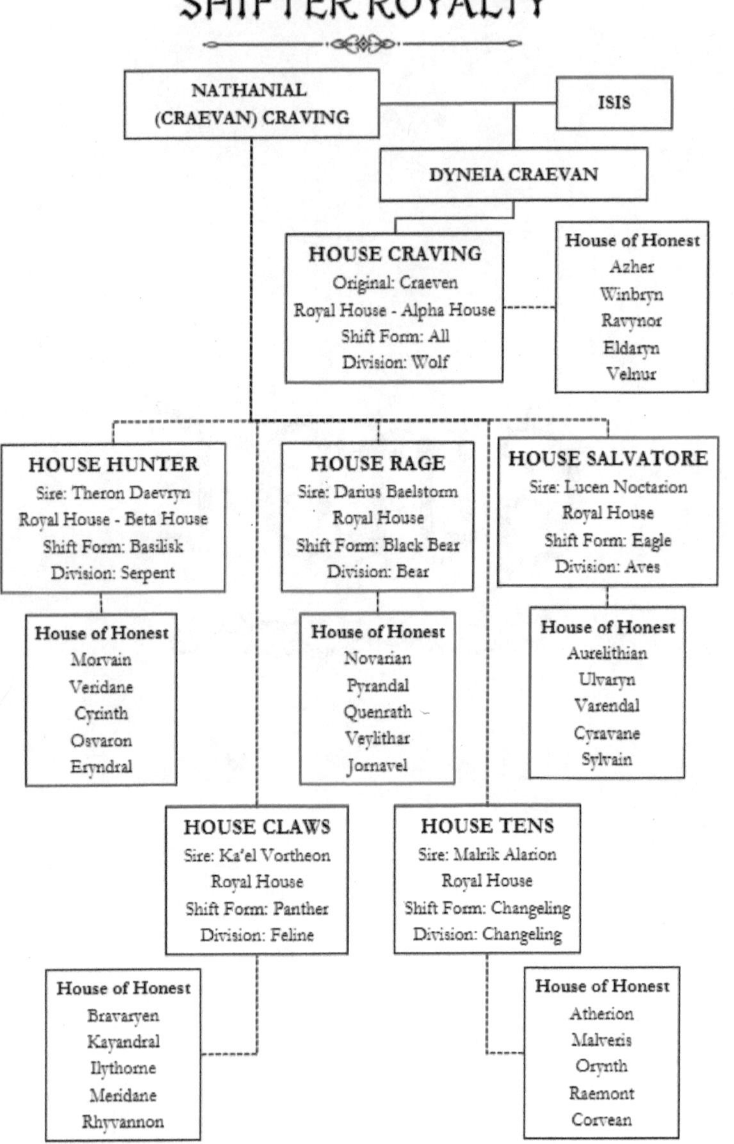

VAMPIRE ROYALTY

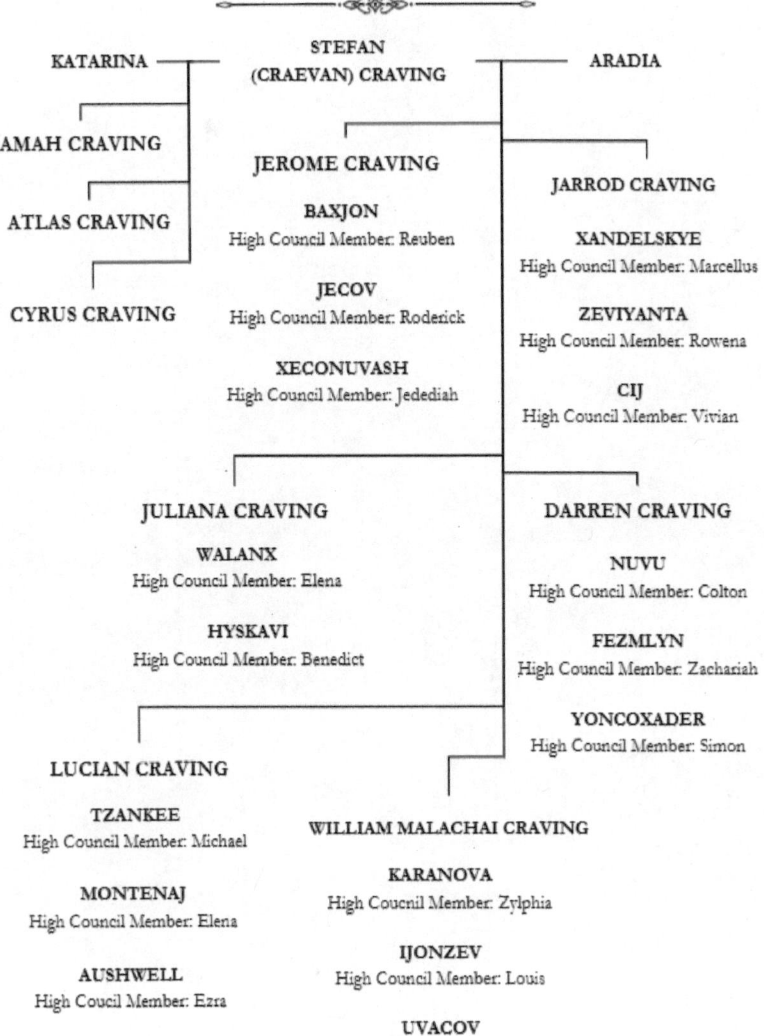

PART ONE

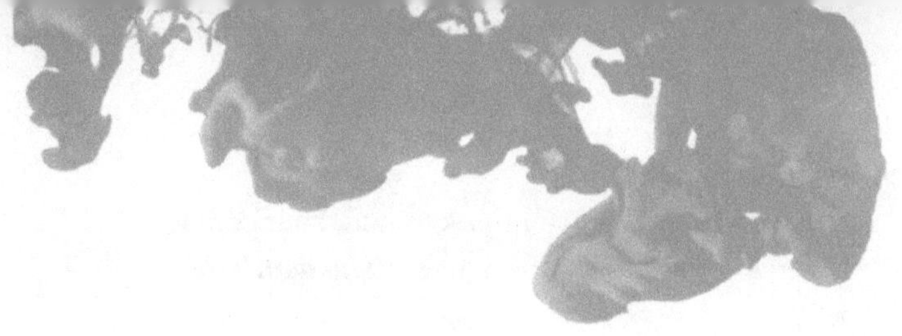

PROLOGUE

Rosella Craving
July 16

The father of shifters teleports me to Romania. I follow Nathanial Craving closely as he leads the way to a private study in the vampire castle. The world thinks all shifters and vampires stay in their respective territories and out of each other's way, but that's not true.

The brown leather couch is cool as I sit down while Nathanial pours us a drink. He hands the glass to me, saying, "Don't drink it yet."

I don't, but I do sniff it. Can never be too safe.

He sits down too, his leg pressed against mine comfortably. His arm comes around to rest on my hip. He's always at ease in Romania.

"They're here," I mumble as his eyes travel from my face to the door as it opens.

The vampire monarchs step inside. King Stefan is dressed in his usual regal attire—robes, crown, the whole nine yards. Queen Aradia is in a pretty shimmery silver dress, not fit for a queen. The dress shows off far more than I'd like to ever see of her. I never understood why she insists on dressing so provocatively.

Behind them is a boy I know all too well from the media—Zak Xandelskye. He's maybe sixteen, but he's already made a name for himself with public fights and trouble only spoiled heirs of the most powerful vampire royal families can get away with. He's dressed in custom-tailored black clothes, with a chain dangling from his neck. His short brown hair is a mess, and his caramel-brown eyes land on me immediately, sizing up the biggest threat in the room. At least he's not stupid.

The fourth *person* to walk in…makes my powers *angry*. My fingers, my skin—my entire being wants to retaliate and throw my walls up in defense—which obviously I do. The energy coming from the woman makes my heart race and my mouth dry.

"Remember," Nathanial's voice warns in my mind, ***"don't show***

any reaction to her."

"She won't touch me," I think to him, confidently.

"No, you're with me," he agrees. ***"She won't dare."***

She.

The woman in black from our childhood stories.

From head to toe, her dress reveals nothing as it trails behind her into the room. A thick black veil hides her face, her hands swallowed by long sleeves—nothing but a figure in black.

The Cursed One.

Lilith.

We are taught Mother Isis—Nathanial's wife—put Lilith to sleep and is in prayer to keep Lilith's magic subdued so she can't wake and cause world destruction again.

Obviously, that's not true. Nathanial has always taught me one thing—family stays together no matter which side of a war they're on.

Nathanial brings me closer to his side as he sits straighter. My shoulder is against his chest and I lean into him. Neither of us stand for our companions as they settle in.

The vampire boy eyes me with a bored expression as he drops into the armchair on my left side. He sits down before the King does.

No one would ever dare sit down before Nathanial unless he tells us to. I know the vampires have the same respect toward their monarchs—yet this kid…who the Hell does he think he is?

When our eyes meet, he narrows his caramel-brown ones.

The King follows in Nathanial's footsteps and pours the liquor. He throws his drink back first before bringing another glass over to Zak.

The *King* just served this kid—what the actual fuck is happening here? Consider my mind blown.

The Queen takes a seat across the coffee table on the other couch, smiling at Zak and me. "Now, now, children. Play nice. Zak, fix your face. Rose is a friend."

I can't take her seriously when she looks like she just walked off the front covers of Eternal Vogue. She was on it for their Summer Solstice edition. I guess some people would think the same of me. At least I had the decency to wear black today.

"This *is* my face," Zak says bluntly, and I smirk. Okay, he's funny.

"Let's get this shit over with," Nathanial announces to no one in particular.

"Over with?" Zak asks, frowning, "We're just getting started."

From the corner of my eyes, I track The Cursed One as she makes her way behind the couch Nathanial and I sit on and loom over Zak and me. She's so unnaturally tall that it's hard not to look at her. I don't give her any attention, but Zak openly watches her as she presents a dagger that looks homemade. The blade is rusted, and there are black stones on the hilt.

Zak takes the blade and hands it to Aradia, who is glaring at Nathanial.

"You might be in a rush, dear brother-in-law," she says coldly to him, "but you're demanding a lot from your favorite. She deserves the courtesy of a little fucking patience."

For a second, Nathanial is quiet, before his fingers brush my neck as he pushes my hair back and kisses the side of my head. It's not a wildly intimate move, but I feel exposed right now with the gesture. Everyone in this room, with the exception of Zak, know Nathanial for thousands of years. They know Isis for just as long, but no one has made any objections since Nathanial's introduced me.

He turns to Aradia and nods. "You're right," then he says to me, "humans aren't the only ones who are…sensitive to information. The supernatural, the underworld needs structure too. They need hope, a purpose to look forward to the next day. Something to fight for—so why not fight for a new world?"

Zak scoffs. He leans forward, rolling his eyes before saying, "Shit's been weird. I mean, look at you. You have gray eyes. You're Mated to another Warrior—shit that's not supposed to ever happen in our world, much less all happen to one person."

He gives me a once over in a way that I can only describe as disgust. Rude. Then his fangs extend and he bites into his wrist. He holds it out for me to see the black blood surfacing.

Vampire blood shows what element they are the strongest in—it usually correlates with their zodiac sign.

Zak's blood is black. The only vampires I ever heard of having black blood were from House Walanx. Is Zak a secret love child? Or a distant relative that somehow got lost?

We royals keep very close tabs on our bloodlines—it's highly unlikely.

"I'm not supposed to have black blood—yet here it is," he says. "You and I have a job to do, Mistress of Darkness."

I cross one leg over the other, keeping my expression blank.

"Do you see where I'm going with this?" he asks. I simply blink at him, causing him to glare at Nathanial. "Did you even tell her?"

"She's known all her life," Nathanial replies, his tone suggesting he doesn't care for Zak's.

I sigh heavily. "You're the body, I'm the soul. You're the physical. I'm the essence. I get it. You need my power." I face Nathanial and say to him, "I thought we were waking Isis."

"We will," he answers, caressing my hand with his fingertips. "We want to ensure this is the last time we have to wake her."

Zak takes a drink of his whiskey as Stefan brings over a golden goblet. Zak gives Aradia his arm before he turns to me, saying, "We're going to mix our blood and then we're going to drink it."

Aradia slashes his arm, letting his blood fall into the goblet.

"Drinking vampire blood will kill a shifter. It will kill me." I narrow my eyes. He's lost me now.

"Normally, yes vampire blood would kill you," Zak smirks, "but you're a little freak too, aren't you?"

I *really* hate that word.

"Zak," Nathanial warns.

I lean forward, making my hair fall around my shoulders as I look Zak in the eyes. "There isn't much that can kill me. Vampire blood will. Why would I exchange and drink blood with you? What are *your* powers?"

"Vampire blood won't kill you because your blood is poison itself. So, when we mix our blood, it cancels it out to put it simply." Zak keeps his focus only on me as Aradia finishes taking his blood. He flexes his arm as the wound closes. "My powers are above your clearance level, princess."

I laugh. Hard. Then I face Nathanial and say seriously, "I'm ready to leave. This kid actually thinks he's more powerful than me?"

"Not more…equivalent," Nathanial glares at Zak, who rolls his eyes.

"Spirit magic. That's my power, but it's more than that," Zak hesitates for the first time since we've been here.

Aradia's eyes go over to her big sister standing beside me. I see long, gloved fingers edging closer to me from my periphery and will myself not to react.

"Don't even think about touching her," Nathanial says in a bored tone, but the warning is clear in his voice.

Lilith hisses, retracting her hand. Zak smirks at that but hides it quickly. He meets my gaze and there's a hint of mischief in his eyes. Lilith is The Cursed One—the thing of nightmares, yet Zak's not scared. He's annoyed, more than anything.

"More than that how?" I ask Zak.

"I can access realms," he answers shortly.

"Uh huh…" I'm not going to rule it out. He was right earlier. Weird things have been happening in the underworld. "Why exactly do we need to do a blood exchange? Can't we just hold hands and do a ritual?"

"Blood is the lifeforce. It contains our magic," he gives me a blunt look. I know that. I'm not stupid.

"And what are you going to do with *my* magic? Why would I give it to you? Why would I agree to any of this?" I frown. I telepath Nathanial, ***"You never mentioned any of this in the years you've been training me."***

"Because our powers are incomplete without the other. And because you don't have a choice," Zak says like I'm an idiot. What the Hell exactly is his power?

"Zak," Nathanial scolds, before he takes over. He focuses all his attention on me, saying, "You're not giving him your power or your blood without getting something in return."

"What am I getting in return? Access to realms I don't care about? The earth is fucked up enough. I don't want another realm's drama." I cross my arms over my chest. I'm powerful in my own right, and once Josh and I complete our Mating bond, we'll be…legendary. Well, at least I will be. He's powerful but not like me.

"You're the Mistress of Darkness, love," Aradia chuckles softly as if that's an answer, "weren't you curious where your powers came from?"

We are taught our magic is drawn from the universe, but mine has always felt…internal. I've never felt like my powers came from an outside source—the darkness is and always has been a part of me. We're one and the same. I've always known where my power came from—me.

"Zak's going to open a gateway on Samhain. What comes through will only ever answer to you and him," Nathanial explains, finally getting to the point. "What comes through will help you retire Isis so you can be the next Eternal Queen. You'll become immortal, and Isis can step down." I know there are easier ways to become immortal—we have two vamps in the room right now—but I also know Isis is one of a kind. No one can do what she has done for the world. Replacing her is a challenge.

"Nature needs to be balanced, of course," Aradia adds, innocently. "I'm light and while everyone always thinks Lilith is the evil one, Isis…well," Aradia sighs, dramatically, "she just had to…compete with big sissy."

"Lilith is still…Lilith," Zak says as a warning not to underestimate The Cursed One, especially when she's in the room with us.

Aradia passes Nathanial the dagger, but he keeps his eyes on me. "The world isn't as simple as good and bad. The world, what keeps it turning, has always, and will always be in the gray, my little mistress," he says. I can't argue with that. Things are not always black and white. The gray is always forgotten.

Then, without waiting for my permission, Nathanial cuts my wrist open, letting my blood fall into the goblet.

Nathanial always gave me a choice. I always made the choice he preferred. Something about this makes him desperate enough to make the mistake of crossing me.

I don't get to question him or watch my own blood mix with Zak's. The study's door opens once again but Nathanial doesn't pause as I lift my gaze. The last person I ever expected to be here strides in—gray eyes locked on me.

1 CRAVENHOLD

Rosella Craving

July 19

The Luna sighs as she sinks deeper into the velvet cushions, one hand cradling her five-month-pregnant belly. She fans her flushed face with the other hand, muttering something about how her chair was not designed for pregnant women.

"I think you've just outgrown the throne, Eliza," I tease my sister-in-law, reaching to grab her blood glass before she knocks it over again.

"Outgrown?" she frowns, clipping her blonde hair up messily. "I don't like that word. I forbid you to use it again until after the babies."

Mariella Jornavel, one of my best friends, laughs from across the room, her knitting needles clicking softly. She arrived at Cravenhold a week ago to prepare for her first transformation. I'm glad we have each other right now, even if we'll go through the shift separately with our own Mates when the night comes. Warrior Antonio Rage is Mariella's Mate, and he's sweet to her. My friend will be in good hands.

"The chair fears the future Alpha." My friend winks, her golden-brown eyes sparkling. I always found it fascinating how her hair is the exact shade.

Eliza hums, closing her baby blue eyes.

"How would that work anyway? Would the next Alpha be the first baby that comes out?" Mariella asks Eliza before looking at me.

Twins do tend to run in the Craving family, but there haven't been twins in a long, long time. I shrug in response.

Eliza sighs. "I would assume that would be the case, unless they have to battle it out."

Mariella shudders. "That'd be terrible. Can you imagine brothers fighting each other for the title?"

"It's happened before," I say, though I'd never want that for my nephews.

I look at Eliza and grow cold. Her warm smile is still there, her cheeks glowing like an expecting Luna should, but I don't see *her* anymore. Her belly darkens like a storm cloud threaded with smoke.

It pulses black, with black veins and green venom spreading across her belly like poison.

My heart stops.

Inside the darkness, I glimpse two sparks. One steady—strong even. The other—smaller, struggling, choking.

Mariella and Eliza are laughing, but I can't concentrate. All I *feel* is corruption. All I see is darkness surrounding her babies.

The back of my throat burns with realization.

Everyone is hopeful Shane and Eliza's twins are blessed, not cursed. *I'm* hopeful, but every instinct in me screams something's wrong.

My reflection catches on Eliza's phone. My eyes are completely black, void of color. I quickly blink them away, changing them back to my gray irises, and focus on what Mariella's saying instead.

"How are you doing, Rose?" she asks me, causing Eliza's head to turn in my direction.

"Just another day before you shift!" Eliza grins at me, reaching for my hand. "Are you excited?"

"Of course…but more anxious," I tell them, warily.

"Don't worry, babe. He'll be here. I made Josh promise me and he can't defy his Luna." Eliza smirks and I laugh. My Mate has no choice but to be here by tomorrow night. If I die, he dies, and Beta Warrior Josh Hunter can never allow that to happen.

My brother, Shane, hasn't been home in over a month. He took his Beta with him, naturally, but they were supposed to be back days ago. Not to mention they're missing my birthday today.

Eliza adjusts uncomfortably and lets out a small groan.

"Are you okay?" I ask, quickly.

She waves me off, but her brow pinches in a way I recognize well. She's playing it down.

"Maybe you should lie down for a little bit, Eliza," Mariella suggests, slowly.

"The little princes are just practicing their Alpha challenge apparently," Eliza says with a grin. We give her a second as she breathes through the kicks before murmuring, "This is so annoying. I will hold this over Shane for the rest of his life. Fucking asshole."

Mariella and I stifle a laugh. Only the Luna can cuss out the Alpha Warrior and live to tell the tale.

"Yeah, yeah, laugh now. You, two, will be in the same position soon enough." Eliza rolls her blue eyes at us.

I highly doubt that. Josh can't stand being in the same room as me, which is another reason I'm anxious about tomorrow night. It'll be just him and I.

The Warriors are untouchable. They're the male descendants of Nathanial, the first shifter, and the five men he sired centuries ago. That's how it's always been. In House Craving, the firstborn son is crowned Alpha on his eighteenth birthday—just like my brother was six years ago.

The Hunter bloodline was bestowed the highest honor of being the Beta Warriors after the first sired, Theron Daevryn, was injured saving Nathanial's life. It's the birthright of the first-born Hunter son to serve as the Alpha Warrior's second in command.

The Hunters. The Claws. The Tens. The Salvatores. The Rages. And my family—the Cravings.

Together, we form the Warrior Pack. Six royal bloodlines. Six Houses.

Legacy isn't a choice, it's inheritance. Every generation is born into it—into service, into duty, into expectations that begin before we can even walk.

All Warriors shift into white wolves. That part never changes. But each House carries its own secondary form—its own mark of power. It's an honor the princes uphold with pride. The sons of these six families are marked at birth with gray eyes. It's their sign.

No other shifter has that trait.

Except me.

No one has been able to solve this mystery and tell me why I was born with gray eyes. Josh used to make fun of me and say I should've been born a boy when we were younger. As we got older and my breasts developed, he's reinvented his insults by calling me a freak of nature. It stings, because he's not wrong. A female has never had gray eyes, even in my bloodline.

That's not all.

Josh and my Mating bond is also out of the ordinary. Warriors' Mates, known as Crescents, are always chosen from the House of Honest—prominent shifter families sired by the royal houses. Their daughters are offered and chosen at the blood-tie ritual when a Warrior is two years old, their families bear witness to the creation of the Mating bond. Josh never bonded with any of the daughters from the

House of Honest. He was six when I was born and our parents saw the gold cord instantly snap into place for him—for me. There was no ceremony, no ritual, no blood-ties—nothing. It just happened.

Except Mating cords for Warriors isn't gold—it's red.

Our parents believed our Mating bond to be Divinely blessed and chosen since Josh never bonded with anyone else. It's all very strange because my Mate doesn't believe any of it.

A part of me wonders if he's purposefully waiting for the last second to come back. Why would the man who doesn't even acknowledge my existence care about easing my mind before the biggest night of my life?

"Don't go there," Eliza says gently, catching me in the act of spiraling. "He'll be here. The bond will make sure."

Ugh, the bond. The curse is what I call it.

"As it should!" Mariella comes to my defense. "Shame on the Alpha and Beta for not being back yet, knowing Rose is shifting tomorrow! She does not need that kind of stress."

"Don't worry. I already have an earful prepared for Shane," Eliza promises us. I smile. I do adore my sister-in-law. She's especially sassy while she's pregnant.

The doors to the Sunroom swing open and we turn to see none other than the Alpha stride in.

"Well, speak of the devil," I say to the ladies.

My brother is dressed in black leathers that cling to his large six-foot-three frame. A single pauldron juts sharply from his right shoulder while Dad's royal blue—also known as Warrior blue—cape flows from his left, and gold chains hang at his belt. His black hair is a little longer than usual, his jaw more scuffed, but there's that same easy grin that always gets him out of trouble. He looks every bit the picture of polished chaos.

Shane raises a brow as he saunters in. "What was that, Lady Mariella? Something about shaming your Alpha?"

Mariella fake gasps, clasping a hand over her mouth. "No, never. I was talking about Josh."

"Mmm," Shane drawls, walking past her, "so the Beta. You know he's less forgiving than I am."

Then he drops to one knee in front of Eliza like some rogue prince. I resist the urge to roll my eyes as he lowers his voice, taking her hand in his.

"I'm sorry, love. I know it was too long, but I kept my promise," he says, suggestively.

"You always do," Eliza mumbles, pretending to be angry but her eyes give everything away. She touches his scruffy cheek, saying, "You have to shave before tonight."

He presses a kiss into her palm before saying, "I have to shower. I miss my shower and you in it."

Mariella and I groan, but my chest twists and it's stupid how much I envy them. SoulMates who choose each other every day despite the Mating bond. Even when Shane drives her crazy, Eliza never doubts his love. Not for a second. They've always been this close. Shane is six years older than me and Eliza is three. I grew up watching them be in love. I don't remember them falling—they were just always *in love.*

It's ridiculous. And really cute.

When Shane finally turns those Warrior gray eyes toward me, I'm trying to school my expression. Looking into Shane's eyes is looking into my own—same striking gray. Same as Dad's.

He flashes a grin. "Happy birthday, baby thorn."

I roll my eyes at the nickname I can't seem to outgrow as I say, "I'm not a baby. I haven't been since I was sixteen."

The shifter world has our own legal age—which used to be fourteen but changed to sixteen two centuries ago. Sometimes I wish it didn't.

"Still a thorn in my ass though," he adds, pulling something out of his pocket. It's a small white box with a red ribbon. He tosses it to me. "For you."

I catch it and blink. "You got me something?"

Shane looks offended. "I'm not that bad of a brother."

"You missed my birthday," I point out.

He pretends to check his watch. "There's still plenty of hours before the day is over. I missed nothing. I got here before the party." He pokes at my rib, before nodding to the box. "Open it."

I lift the lid as Eliza and Mariella lean in closer to see too. There's a delicate gold key inside with two prongs.

"Wow, this will go great with this season's gowns," I say animatedly, raising a brow at him.

He rolls his eyes. "It's your Veyara key. Josh is supposed to give it to you but…I beat him to it."

Shane didn't beat him to it. My brother knows very well that Josh doesn't care about giving it to me, so he took it upon himself.

"What's it for?" I ask, swallowing the truth behind my brother's words. The key is heavier than it looks.

"You'll have to ask Josh," Shane shrugs. That's helpful. "Probably has something to do with being Lady of House Hunter," he adds, smiling with the same gentleness he'd used to braid my hair, tie my shoes, and sneak sweets into my room after hours. He's always taken such good care of me. He's my favorite person in the world, though being Josh's best friend made us grow apart over the years.

"Where's Josh?" Eliza asks Shane as I create an air pocket with my magic to put the key in for safekeeping and easy retrieval in the future.

Shane looks at his wife, pausing for just a second too long. "He went home to wind down," Shane looks back to me, "but he's here. He won't miss your first shift."

"Because you'll kill him?" I suggest sweetly, smiling.

"Because he's your Mate," Shane replies, smirking.

"No one wants a pig for a Mate," I retort.

"Wait, he went home? To Coilspire?" Eliza frowns. "He has to be at Rose's party tonight."

"No, not Coilspire. He's at court," Shane answers, looking between Eliza and me and sighing. "Will you two relax? It was a long ass mission. We're all tired."

He's right. He just got back and we're already grilling him. Mariella decides to stand up just then.

"Well on that note, we'll give the Alpha and Luna some privacy. Rose, we should probably head over to the bath house, anyway," Mariella says, gathering her knitting items.

I get up too, telling Shane and Eliza, "We'll see you tonight."

"Have fun!" Eliza grins at us as Mariella links arms with me, tugging me away.

When we step outside the room, we nearly collide with Daniya Claws, her long strawberry blonde braid swinging behind her as she texts frantically away. Everything Daniya does is fast—after all, she's a cheetah shifter.

"There you are!" Our best friend exclaims, her brown eyes wide with relief. "I was just coming to find you. The bath house is calling our names!"

"Eliza booked it out just for us," Mariella tells me, smiling.

For my birthday, I asked for a few hours of quiet with my best friends. I usually only see Mariella during festivities at court—but that'll change now. Mariella is here to stay until she has a baby.

All Crescents shift at Cravenhold. After their first shift, they're given an apartment here so their Warrior can properly court them until the blood-tie reunion. With the Mating bond complete, the couple is allowed to move in together. Once they have their first child, only then do they move to their Warrior family territories.

It's also to keep the Warrior Pack together while the power shifts from one generation to the next. To ensure the new Pack holds before anyone drifts too far from the seat of power. Strong brotherhood and all.

Daniya arches a perfect eyebrow. "The glam team has strict instructions from the Luna—something about soft colors and Moonlit goddess aesthetics to make the Beta feel guilty?"

I groan as Mariella snickers, telling her, "Sounds about right. Josh has it coming."

"Honestly, he should know better than to give you stress before your big night," Daniya rolls her eyes. "If Daniel pulled something like that, I would've canceled sex for a whole year."

She just shifted two full Moons ago and is Mated to Warrior Daniel Claws—the only Warrior who I can say I'm friends with. Daniel is the youngest in the Warrior Pack, having joined it two years ago. He and I became close due to his family living at court, because Daniel's mom is the High Priestess of shifterkind.

Mariella passes off her knitting bag to her assistant before asking Daniya, "And die for not getting Marked before the Claiming?"

Daniya scrunches her nose. "Mmm, maybe eleven months then. He's not worth dying over."

We laugh, continuing toward the exit of the Palace with our bodyguards shadowing silently. Their crisp black uniforms with the insignia of the House they represent. After tomorrow night, my protective detail will wear House Hunter's emblem.

Every Warrior and their Mate know the weight of the Claiming. If a Crescent isn't Marked within a year after her first shift, completing the Mating ritual, both she and her Warrior die. We're taught it's because Mating bonds are sacred, Divinely blessed—to not fulfill it is blatant disrespect to the Heavens above. If our Mates disrespect the Divine and don't claim us, the fates will—one way or another.

Most Warrior Mates are excited to complete their Mating rituals as soon as possible. Daniya already had her blood-tie reunion last month, making her officially the second Crescent Claws.

"I'm not even sure how a year is needed to complete the Mating ritual," Mariella comments, "it's damn near impossible to resist your Mate."

Daniya laughs, "Right! I don't know how those boys get anything done. I feel like whenever Daniel and I are together, all we do is fuck."

Mariella eyes her warily. "Girl, how are you not pregnant?"

Daniya just winks at Mariella. "I think the drugs help with that."

It's possible. There are street drugs that have been created to prevent pregnancies. It's frowned upon, especially amongst royalty since our sole purpose is to continue the lineage. Good on Daniya for doing what she wants.

I have nothing to contribute to this conversation, so I remain silent. Seems as though lately all anyone can talk about is sex, Mating, Marking, or babies.

As we step outside to get into the car waiting for us, the afternoon mid-July heat clings to my skin. The drive to the bath house is about twenty minutes, so I lean back into my seat and get comfortable, watching the old stone walls pass by, dripping in glossy green ivy curtains. With the windows down, the smell of honeysuckle and jasmine tangling together is so thick the air tastes like sugar. String lights are already strung between pavilions waiting to turn on as soon as the Sun disappears. Workers are hauling in the supplies for the Lammas feast, stacking them beside barrels of bloodwine and long tables.

Cravenhold is a town of its own—we have everything a person can need here. Shops, restaurants, entertainment, administration, even hotels and apartments, along with permanent residences for royal families and those who frequently visit.

"A little over a week left before Lammas," Daniya says, catching my gaze as I take in the preparations. "Nathanial wants it to be bigger than last year."

I smile at that. Nathanial Craving holds a special place in all of our hearts, but I'd like to think he and I have a stronger relationship. He's the father of shifters and from him comes the rest of us. But no one else has access to him like my brother and I do. Shane doesn't count since he's the Alpha. Dad told me Nathanial was the first to hold me, even before Mom, and we've been inseparable since. I've heard people say I'm his favorite.

Mariella loops her arm with mine, bringing me out of my thoughts. "You'd think it was a royal wedding with all the vendors coming in soon."

I laugh. "Might as well be. I heard they're flying in some glam specialists for the dinner performers."

My phone buzzes with a text and I glance at it to see that it's from my Mate.

Josh: *You sent a box of vipers to Mona Eryndral. What the fuck is wrong with you?*

"Josh just found out about the vipers," I tell the girls and Daniya bursts into laughter.

Mariella shudders. "I hate snakes, and I'd hate to be Mona Eryndral."

I laugh as I shoot back a reply.

Me: *Since she likes to fuck a snake so much, I sent some to keep her company until you got back :)*

Josh: *Fuck you*

He hates being called a snake.

Me: *Fuck you too, babe.*

Josh: *When are you going to grow up?*

Me: *She's lucky snakes showed up at her doorstep and not me. How's that for grown up?*

The bath house comes into view soon, the white stone building sparkling under the Sun. It's tucked behind a sacred grove and surrounded by tall cypress trees, just by the river and the Warrior's ritual site. Gold-edged windows catch the light. From this side of Cravenhold, you can barely hear the commotion of court life. It's a pocket of calm luxury.

The cars come to a stop and the bath house door swings open before we even reach it. A middle-aged woman in a maroon uniform greets us with a soft nod. "Your highnesses, we've been expecting you." She's in her fifties I'd say, with brown curls and soft green eyes.

Out of habit, I scan the woman first—her soul and body. The light around her chest feels warm and there's no sign of blackness or rot in her. When I blink, the woman's staring at me, blood drained from her face.

"Oh, please don't be afraid," Daniya laughs, waving the woman's concerns away. "Don't mind Rose. She's just checking to make sure you won't kill us during our self-care session."

Heat crawls up my cheeks. "I'm so sorry." I rush out to apologize to the woman, mortified by my action. "It's instincts. I know it's a huge violation…"

The woman chuckles in good-nature. "Hopefully I passed the test. Now, are you ladies going to come in or should I set up bath outside. I don't imagine the Elders will be too happy with that."

We laugh away the awkwardness and follow each other inside while our bodyguards secure the perimeter.

Mariella hooks her arm through mine, smirking. "I don't even know why you bother with bodyguards. You're a walking soul reader."

"I'm not a soul reader," I tell her, smiling.

Truth is, I don't really know what my powers are.

The scent of the bath house hits first along with the humidity from the steamy waters. Lavender, honeycomb, and sandalwood invade my senses. I inhale it in deeply. Soft instrumental music plays through the speakers as the space opens into a chamber of glowing blue pools. The waters are adorned with rose petals of various colors.

"Eliza reserved the whole space for us," Daniya sings, happily, seeing how empty it is.

"Yeah, there was no way we'd be here with…people." Mariella frowns at the thought. Clearly, I don't come here much. Last time I was here was for Azura Salvatore's blood-tie reunion prep and that was two years ago.

"This way, your highness," the woman leads the way. "My name is Matilda. If you need anything," she hands me a little bell, "feel free to ring it and I'll come running."

"It's lovely to meet you, Matilda," I say to her as she guides us behind a screen, where waiting robes in soft shades hang from golden hooks.

"Likewise, your highnesses," she smiles.

Attendants move around us gracefully, like they've been preparing for this all day—which they probably have been.

I peel off my clothes, handing them over to one of the attendants without much thought. Then I slip into one of the loose silk robes hanging on the wall, the fabric feels cool against my skin. I relish the moment, because the next few months will be filled with corsets and formalwear to celebrate the holidays coming up.

I check my phone before putting it away. Josh hasn't texted back.

Good. The fact that he even has my number is annoying.

I catch my reflection in the foggy glass as we walk through the steam-curtained hallway. My long black hair is thrown up into a bun, gray eyes tired—I haven't been sleeping much—and my skin is flushed from the heat in here. The robe falls just right over my curves as I tie the knot which emphasizes them more.

Mariella looks over her shoulder and shakes her head. "Why do you always look like you're in a perfume ad though?"

"I swear," Daniya agrees, "you look more like Luna Rosemary every day."

"No, Mom was way prettier," I disagree, and the girls just look at me like I'm insane. I let out a little laugh and say, "I wish she was here today."

That earns me sympathetic looks as Mariella weaves her arm through mine. "She'd be so proud and excited for your first shift."

I squeeze her arm, appreciative of the kind words as we go deeper before coming upon the private bath chamber. I follow my friends into the circular pool. We each slip in one at a time, robes discarded on the stone benches nearby. The heat of the water hits instantly, wrapping around my muscles, seeping in. I sink lower, my body stretches out, limbs feeling weightless.

Mariella lets out a dramatic groan beside me. "I could stay here forever."

"No one's stopping you," Daniya replies, tipping her head back and closing her eyes. "We have plenty of time before we have to get ready for the party."

I close my eyes too, and for a second, I pretend my mother's sitting behind me, brushing out my hair like she used to. She'd always hum a tune that she swore was a protection spell…makes me wonder why she wasn't humming it the night she and Dad died four years ago.

I was fourteen.

Shane won't talk about them, but I've caught him at the ritual ground lighting candles on Samhain. He goes out to the lake by himself on new Moon nights—something Dad and him used to do. He wears Dad's blue cape instead of his own. On Ostara, he fills our residential wing with Mom's favorite flowers—roses, of every color. Ostara was Mom's favorite holiday.

"I had my final fitting for my blood-tie reunion," Mariella tells us softly, breaking the silence.

"How exciting!" Daniya smiles brightly, reaching for her hand. "The light gray was actually such a gorgeous choice for us. I had my fitting yesterday."

"Thank you," Mariella replies. "These last-minute changes are a pain in the ass. Antonio obviously is no help."

"Eliza's already planning Rose's reunion," Daniya chuckles, "and my mom planned mine when I was five."

Mariella fans herself, stressing, "You really do have to start that early."

I don't really like thinking about my reunion. Things between Josh and I aren't great, but it's another milestone my parents won't be there for. It's one thing Josh and I have in common. He lost his parents too, just after he became the Beta Warrior six years ago.

2 HOME SWEET…NAH

Josh Hunter
July 19

I've never been more relieved to return to Cravenhold, even though I fucking hate being here. But a month-long mission dealing with felines and hunting Sisterhood of Sin Covens made me miss my own bed.

"Before you go," Shane starts and I almost groan out loud. Instead, I give him a death glare, and he hands me the stack of papers. "Sign these."

I glance at the papers quickly. It's basic reports from an old mission that I had already reviewed, but I sign everywhere the yellow tabs are. Strange it's printed and not on the tablet as usual. I sign warily, but not so much that he notices.

I hand them back and the asshole stops me again. "Josh?"

"What?" I nearly snap at him. Nearly.

Shane looks so much like his father as he pins me with his stern look. "You're going to the party tonight."

I clench my jaw. Of course, he's going to use his Alpha voice. I give him a mock smile. "Well, since you're going to be such a darling and ask so nicely, how can I say no?"

He smirks and pats my cheek like I'm his son or something. I slap his hand away and he chuckles. "I'll see you tonight then. Or we all answer to my wife."

"I'm going, but don't expect me to be nice," I warn him. Rose's stupid birthday party is a waste of my time.

"What the Hell was that stunt about Vanessa then?" Shane asks, frowning deeply. "Why ask her to be Rose's security?"

So he's not okay with having our best friend's Crescent back on duty. Tough.

I sigh heavily. "You know I don't fucking trust anyone. Including the security detail Rose already has. I trust Vanessa."

"Why's it matter?" he questions and I know what he's doing. He wants me to admit I care about his spoiled ass sister.

"You know why. Rose dies, I die. Vanessa protecting her gives her better odds. She's your sister and my Mate, someone's always going to come for her." It's not fucking rocket science. I shake my head, mad tired. "Can I go now, *Alpha?*"

"Don't be late," Shane replies, "and Josh?"

I swear to the Divine he's doing this shit on purpose now.

"Take a nap," he says with a smug smirk on his stupid face. I simply give my Alpha the finger before sliding into my car.

The drive is barely fifteen minutes from the armory to my house and I stride straight into my residence at Cravenhold. The second those heavy doors swing open, the black-and-green Hunter banner rises up the flagpole outside—serpent coiled tight around a wolf, both heads staring each other down.

The Beta is at court.

Inside, everything's exactly where I left it. My housekeeper's a goddamn ninja—it's always spotless, but nothing ever moves an inch. She knows I hate people fucking with my shit. On the bar cart, there's the crystal tumbler and the decanter calling my name. Nightthorn scotch, a House Tens vintage with that darker swirl of blood laced through it. Divine bless them for knowing how to make a drink that hits.

I pour a heavy double and knock it back in one go. The burn slides down my throat, scorching away the day's bullshit, loosening the knots in my shoulders. I pour another, and then head to the kitchen, pulling my phone out.

The screen lights up with the usual avalanche of crap—summons from court, invites to shit, social obligations…a couple emails about Antonio Rage's reunion fitting that I've been dodging. Apparently, that's *ASAP* too.

And of course, my serpent Lords want a Den meeting tomorrow morning. Naturally. Because nothing says relaxation like getting grilled by a room full of scaled assholes first thing.

My thumb stills at a notification from five hours ago.

Rose's birthday shoot.

It's followed by a text from the Luna.

> **Eliza:** *Doesn't she look hot?*

The text is attached to a picture and—fucking Hell—there's my Mate smiling back.

Rose.

She's in a blush-pink silk and lace dress that's a crime against my sanity. It hugs every sinful curve like it was sewn onto her, dipping low on those hips, sheer in spots that make my mouth go dry. The neckline outlines her tits flawlessly—full, perfect, the kind that can make a guy forget his own name. My eyes linger there longer than they should. Her black hair tumbles in waves around that heart-shaped face that's been living rent-free in my head all my life. Soft gray eyes daring me—anyone—to look away.

I don't. I can't.

My dick stirs, hardens way too fast, pressing against my black uniform pants like it's got a mind of its own.

Pure fucking torture. She's my Veyara. My Mate. And every primal instinct in me is screaming to hunt her down and claim her wherever the fuck that picture was taken, on camera, in front of the whole world. My dick is not picky right now—neither is our bond.

But no matter how gorgeous she looks, she's Rosella fucking Craving. If it were anyone else, things might've been different. But it's her.

I text Eliza back.

Me: *Stop.*

Bubbles pop up immediately. Of course. Eliza's phone is glued to her hand, the pregnancy leaving her with little to do these days except meddle.

Eliza: *You're so fucked, Josh. Even the Alpha won't be able to help you.*

Rose gets away with half the shit she does to the girls I fuck *because* Eliza protects her—not that Rose needs it. She's a fucking Craving—she gets away with everything because who's going to stop the first shifter's precious descendent and the Alpha's sister? Nobody with a survival instinct.

She never fails to irritate me with her ridiculous stunts. Her recent assault was a box of vipers to a girl who wasn't even in the papers. Whoever's feeding her intel needs a raise because the way she always knows exactly who I've been with within hours is creepy as Hell. My mind did go to my assistant, Camille, but she's not stupid. She wouldn't jeopardize her job or my favor to help my Mate.

The Elders are gonna chew my ass out for missing her birthday shoot. Those damn magazine spreads are just another royal checkbox, but we miss one and suddenly it's *disrespecting the bloodline.*

Whatever. Guess I have to be my father's son.

Rose hasn't thrown a fit over stuff like this since she got back from that Royal Tour. Part of me wonders what the fuck happened out there that turned the venom-spewing bitch into…whatever this quieter version is. The rest of me doesn't give a single damn. She's not starting wars in the hallways anymore, and I'll take the ceasefire.

Unless she's quiet because she's planning something far worse…shit, it's what I would do. Attack when my enemy least expects it, after making them think all is well. It's textbook psychological warfare.

Tonight isn't just another society gala, or ball Nathanial or the Elders want to throw. It's Rose's eighteenth. The whole supernatural world's going to be tuned in—paparazzi, gossip sites, every outlet and influencer waiting to drool over the Craving princess, the Alpha's little sister. The Beta's Veyara. It's gonna be a circus, and I already know the script. She'll glide in looking like a goddamn miracle, and every sucker in the room will eat it up. But I see the pretty packaging wrapped around a pitch-black heart, that no one else does.

Being chained to her, bound by a fucking gold cord everyone deems Holy, feels like a collar around my neck. I don't know how I'm expected to be her Mate. Everything is orchestrated to protect her—her name, her reputation as a Craving princess, and her title as the next Veyara.

I leave Eliza on read and head for the bedroom. My head of security, Cole, nods once from the hallway post—silent, always watching.

My muscles are screaming from the last three weeks of no sleep, blood on my hands, and endless negotiations with the Pride leaders and interrogations of witches. Felines though, are the biggest pain in the ass of all shifterkind. Thank fuck Devaughn was with us on that trip—those cats can't say no to their own king.

I strip in the bathroom, crank the rain head to scalding, and step under the spray. Marble walls fog up fast as water hammers my shoulders, working out the knots and rinsing away the dried blood I didn't quite get earlier. But no amount of soap scrubs out the heat crawling under my skin.

That picture's burned into my skull. Pink lace clinging to every dangerous curve that belongs to me. That soft, flirty smile aimed right at the camera like she knows exactly how to make a guy lose his mind. My cock's rock-hard, throbbing under the water like the shower itself is teasing me. I slam a palm against the tile, head dropped, jaw clenched so tight it aches.

Get it together, Hunter.

I'm supposed to hate her. And I hate that some fucked-up part of me can't.

Then I catch the soft footsteps, too light to be an intruder. The faintest whiff of vanilla cuts through the steam and I regain my composure.

"Couldn't wait, Beta?" Camille, my PA's voice purrs. Her shadow shifts behind the glass and I catch her outline before she walks into the shower.

I should tell her to get the fuck out. But tomorrow Rose shifts for the first time. Camille's here offering the one thing that can drown out the noise in my head for a few minutes.

Her hands slide around my waist first, cool palms pressing against my wet skin. Then her tits flatten against my back, soft and warm as lips graze my shoulder.

"You always come back wound so tight," she murmurs, breath hot against my neck as the spray mists her face and her fingers wrap around my dick. "Let me fix that for you."

I don't say a word. I spin her around and press her face against the glass. Her gasp is sharp but eager, nails dragging lightly across my tattooed arm as she braces herself.

I don't waste time. My hips thrust forward and I slide into her in one hard push from behind, water pounding around us. She moans loud, head tipping back against my shoulder, but the sound barely registers. My jaw locks tight. Every stroke is mechanical, chasing release and nothing else.

Her body shakes under me, thighs trembling, but my head's a fucking war zone. The bond claws at my chest the second I'm inside her—sharp, angry, yanking me backward toward Rose like a chain I can't snap. I grit my teeth and thrust harder, trying to drown it out, trying to fuck her out of my system for a few goddamn minutes.

Regular shifters can reject their Mate and walk away. Warriors don't get that luxury. I'm stuck with this golden noose for life.

I can't break the bond.

But I can break her heart.

I see it every time I do it on purpose—every time I skip her event, every time I let another female hang off my arm in public, every time

I don't show up for her like the other Warriors do for their Mates. The flash of pain she never learned to conceal in those soft gray eyes. The way her lips press tight like she's swallowing glass. I hate how much I notice it. Hate how much it twists something in my gut when I should be reveling in it.

Rose's innocent-looking face, her fucking sweet fruity floral scent, her *everything* floods my thoughts. Fuck. My grip on Camille tightens as the weight of my Mate crashes down on me. The bond throbs in my chest, hot and insistent, screaming that this isn't right, that *she's* the one I'm supposed to be buried inside not the blonde in front of me.

Fuck this bond. Fuck it straight to Hell.

I finish fast, pulling out of Camille. She turns and leans against the glass to catch her breath, tilting her head back and letting the water fall on her like she's in some steamy music video. She looks wrecked, flushed skin and satisfied sighs, but it does nothing for me.

I wash off and step out, not waiting for her. I wrap a towel around me, my chest feeling heavier as I rake a hand through my wet black hair.

I need to sleep. I need a drink and then I need to sleep.

"Josh?" Camille's voice cuts through my tiredness as I walk over to my dresser.

"Leave, Camille," I tell her without so much of a glance. I put on a pair of basketball shorts. "Get dressed. I need to sleep before the fucking party."

I walk around her to slide into my bed. My body instantly thanking me. Divine, I missed it.

I feel her staring at me as she puts her clothes on.

"You know," Camille starts as she buttons her crème-colored blouse. Why do women insist on *talking* after fucking?

I look over at her. She's a beautiful woman, no doubt about it. She's a serpent shifter—taller than Rose, slender where Rose has curves, blonde where Rose has jet-black hair, willing blue eyes where Rose's—I can't think about her eyes. Camille's just not my Mate. And there goes my fucking cock getting hard again at the mere thought of *her.*

"What?" I sigh, already knowing I'm not gonna like wherever this is going. I tuck one arm behind my head, the other resting on the old family name tattoo on my abs.

"You didn't confirm Rose's birthday gift," Camille says casual as Hell, like she's reminding me about a council meeting. It's a bitch-ass move.

My eyes flash—basilisk slits for half a second but I lock it down before I accidentally turn my PA into stone. She knows the rules. Known them for years.

Camille just rolls her light blue eyes. "She shifts tomorrow," she adds, quieter now, zipping her skirt. "What are you going to tell the Den?"

Crescents are almost always from the same animal division as the Warrior they're Mated to, unless the Warrior is a Craving or a Tens. Those two Houses can master any form with enough blood and sweat.

That's why every House throws their daughters at the baby Alpha—fair shot for Luna. Eliza just happened to already be wolf-born, so it lined up clean for Shane—keeping the wolves superior and the other Houses equal.

James Tens was the first changeling in generations to have a Mate who wasn't a changeling. It had been so long, people almost forgot that was possible for them. It's said that because changelings don't have an identity of their own, they're flexible with their Mating bond. No one knows why Vanessa was chosen by the Divine to be his Mate, and no one fucking cares anymore. Not like how the serpents did with my mother. It's still brought up even after her death.

Now, history is repeating with Rose and me. Even though I've known she's my Mate for eighteen years, I still looked for a serpent shifter who might've slipped through the cracks, to be my Veyara. Hoping some overlooked female would light up red for me. Praying the gold cord with Rose was a glitch, a mistake, anything but permanent. I needed proof Rose wasn't my Mate. Needed a way out and it helped that she wasn't a serpent.

But there's no defying the Divine and a Mating bond. It's sacred. It's our supreme law—the one we hold above all. I've spent the last four years spitting on that law every chance I had. No Mate in her right mind would forgive half the shit I've pulled.

But that's okay.

I can never forgive what Rose did either.

3 REST AND RELAXATION

Rosella Craving

July 19

Two hours pass in a blur of warmth and drifting conversations. I've lost track of how many times I drifted off and woke again to thinner steam or freshly refilled, sugar-rimmed blood glasses by the pool. At some point, someone braided my hair and wrapped it in a towel.

"Don't fall asleep during your facial this time," Daniya teases me as we walk down the hallway lined with crystals and carved wooden panels toward the lounge chambers. "Last time they had to shake you awake, and no one wants to shake a princess."

I laugh, remembering. "No promises."

The girls and I enter the dimly lit lounge with cushioned beds. Trays of chilled fruit and infused blood sit on low tables for us to replenish. There's a team of specialists waiting.

"We have only the best for you," Matilda assures us as we settle into our own treatment spaces. "It's not every day a Veyara turns eighteen," she tells me, smiling warmly. I return it.

Veyara—the title for the Beta's Mate. While the Luna is the face, the authority, the second to the Alpha just as the Beta is but with different responsibilities—the Veyara moves quietly, behind the scenes. She notices what others overlook, and mends what slips through the cracks. The Luna commands the room. The Veyara studies it. The Veyara has always been the silent weapon hidden in plain sight. The one people underestimate.

It's the role I'll be fully stepping into tomorrow.

The massage starts first. Then a layer of warm clay is painted over my face, cooling almost instantly. I lose track of the order after that. My hands soak while my feet are gently buffed—even though I will be running around barefoot in the forest tomorrow night.

But I'm slipping.

The bed beneath me is warm and smells like lilacs. The clay mask tightens just enough to remind me I have a face. My fingers twitch as someone paints them.

It's so relaxing.

My breathing slows as the noises start to fade and I let go.

A sharp, deep pain blooms low in my stomach, twisting and growing until it rips me out of the hazy calm I'd slipped into. My breath catches in my throat, and the Mating bond flares like someone just poured acid straight into my veins.

No. Not now. Not on my birthday.

"Can you get me a glass of blood?" I ask the attendant softly, my voice sweet and steady even as another wave of agony rolls through me. "I'm suddenly so parched. And…I'm so sorry, but lavender feels a little heavy right now. Do you have something lighter—like almond—for the face mask and scrubs instead?"

She nods kindly, used to royal whims. "Of course, Princess. I'll need a few minutes to mix a fresh batch."

"Take your time," I tell her, smiling through the burn. "No rush at all."

The moment the curtain closes behind her, my polite mask cracks. I curl forward, pressing both palms hard into my thighs to keep the darkness inside me from exploding outward. My magic writhes under my skin like black smoke, clawing to be free, to find the source of this pain and tear it apart. But I swallow the scream in my throat and lock it down.

Like a cruel movie projected straight into my head, I see everything through Josh's eyes.

Camille.

Josh is fucking our assistant. On my birthday.

I feel his pleasure spiking sharply, and it makes my stomach heave. Bile rises in my throat so fast I have to slap a hand over my mouth to keep from vomiting right here on the spa's pristine sheets.

His hate for me is blatantly clear when he's inside her on my eighteenth birthday the second he's home.

The ache twists in my chest until I think I might actually claw it out. But it's over quickly—ten minutes maybe. The pain starts to fade and I'm left hollow, like the bond itself is grieving for me.

I always know. It's a cruel little trick of being Mated—our bodies snitch on each other. When Josh touches himself, I feel the pulse of release, it's not painful—if anything it turns me on when he uses his hand—nothing like when he's with someone.

My body used to react more violently. In the beginning, it'd make me sick. Every time he disrespects the bond, it lashes out on me as if it's my fault. As the years went on, I've learned to…adapt. It's his all-nighters that are the most painful.

I hate that I can tell the difference. He's good at keeping his shields up, but sex has a way of tearing those down. And no matter how powerful Josh is, he isn't immune. Like he wasn't right now. Or maybe that's the bond's doing.

Well, he's home like Shane said he was.

I sigh heavily and lay back down as I wait for the attendant to return.

The shortcut from the bath house to my home in the Palace is past House Claws' residential estate—through their gardens. While all Warriors are white wolves—each House represents a different animal. House Claws, given their name, shift into panthers—majestic, stealthy, and absolutely terrifying.

They also, unrelated, have the prettiest gardens, filled with dahlias. Lady Tiara's touch is everywhere. It's the only residence that smells alive, always green, always blossoming no matter what time of the year. House Claws' flower is the black dahlia. Daniel had a sister named Dahlia though I don't remember much about her. She was older than us, and I was six when she disappeared.

Rumor has it, she ran away with a non-shifter lover, even before her transformation. No one's heard of her since. It makes me wonder what happened to her, if her Mate ever found her. Mates always find each other. If a female shifter comes upon her first transformation without a Mate, she dies. A Mate helps her complete the full transition. We're one soul and during the transformation our souls rejoin, becoming whole.

It's why Eliza was annoyed that Shane and Josh were gone so long. I knew Josh wouldn't risk me dying. Unlike regular shifters, Warriors are bound to their Mate's lifelines. So much is on the line for us—our lineage, bloodlines, powers, secrets.

As shifters, we can Mate with other shifters, even if they're not the same as our own. The stronger animal presents itself in the offspring. But Mating outside of our own supernatural faction is forbidden and punishable by death. It's probably why Dahlia ran away. Mating with someone who isn't a shifter results in human, non-magical, babies. It's scandalous for all parties. The worst thing we can do to our bloodlines is tainting it with human offspring.

Princess Dahlia's name has been wiped. There's no mention of her anywhere, almost as if she never existed. I know Elder Claws—Daniel's father—has the Royal Guard hunting her still, but I don't know how hard he truly wants to find his daughter knowing what awaits her if she's brought back. Because let's face it. If we wanted to find someone, we would.

I don't blame him.

No one really does. We turn our heads and let things be.

The Claws' gardens lead to a cobblestone path that takes me to the entrance of the underground tunnels, letting me avoid the traffic around court. My bodyguards hate it, but that's what all their training is for. There are certain tunnels with extra security which only allow members of the Royal Houses and the House of Honest to enter. All of our personnel staff are chosen from the House of Honest.

It's supposed to be an honor.

"Guess it was too much to ask for you to enjoy the safety of a vehicle, my lady?" Cristobal's tone is dry, but the quick glance he casts down the side corridor tells me he's only half joking. He's twenty-five, the younger of my two bodyguards, and from House Eldaryn.

I could've been driven back home, but Cravenhold is more exciting on foot, even if it makes me a few minutes late. It's always worth it.

I smirk over my shoulder. "What's the point of living in a fortress if we don't use the *secret* tunnels to get places."

Cristobal glances over at Franklin Velnur, my other bodyguard and Eliza's distant cousin. He's two years older than Cristobal. They have been my shadows since I was twelve and both are wolf shifters—my father was very specific when he chose them. I'm told I have a much larger detail, but Cristobal and Franklin are always visible to me.

The tunnel lights flicker on, activated by our motion. The walls look like stone to resemble the exterior of Cravenhold but touch them and you'll feel the reinforced panels and hidden layers of steel that always jam my phone. It's nice when one is trying to hide from, let's say, overbearing aunts, personal assistants, and asshole Mates.

The archways drip with carved vines, but every few feet, I catch sensors tucked into corners. Magic and machine, one of my favorite aspects of Cravenhold—where the old world meets the new.

It's another ten-minute walk to the Palace, weaving through the tunnels, before Franklin holds open a door for me. I step through it and into a hallway that connects the foyer to the kitchen.

My room sits at the far end of the residential wing, but I chose it for the view from my balcony. The moment I step inside, the velvet walls greet me—maroon and black with crème accents. My shelves are stacked floor-to-ceiling with books I've collected over the years. The fire crackles, reflecting off the chandelier at the center of the room.

The glam team is ready and waiting for me. They don't speak much—just move with efficiency to get me ready in time. Once my face and hair are done, I slip into the blush lace dress, before one of the girls adjusts the skirt appropriately. A small tiara is secured on the crown of my head while the rest of my jewelry is put on me.

When they're done, they pack everything and disappear through the doors.

For a moment, I stand there, breathing in the Chanel perfume and listening to the tick of the clock on the mantle. I still have half an hour before I need to make my appearance.

I pull open my black balcony doors, stepping out to feel the cool summer breeze that carries the scent of a bonfire lit somewhere. The stone bannisters stretch out to the length of my room. It's spacious enough for my reading swing and a sitting area for when I have friends over. The balcony is covered with greenery to give it more life. From here, I can see nearly everything—the glow of the entertainment plaza, the flickering lights of the shops and restaurants, the training grounds farther away, and the apartments nearby.

I lean into the stone edge, glancing toward the Hunter Residence to my right. The green and black banner flies high, waving with the assurance of a Mate not far.

Camille Osvaron, Josh's personal assistant and mine by default, is already two steps ahead, earpiece clipped in, tablet tucked under one arm as she texts away. I sit almost lazily in an armchair hidden in one of the alcoves, trying to just wait.

The herald's booming voice announces, "Alpha Warrior Shane Craving and Luna Eliza Craving."

"See you in a bit," Eliza winks at me before giving Camille a pointed look that needs no translation: get the Beta here.

The guests cheer and applaud as my brother and his wife step into the ballroom, regal as ever. Eliza chose a reddish maroon dress to match Shane's suit—the Craving House color. It's either the Warrior blue or Craving red for them. Shane's hand never leaves hers as the doors close behind them again.

I barely have a moment before Uncle Edward and Aunt Susan approach me. Uncle was always close to Shane and me. He's two years younger than my father was and looks so much like Dad with the same strong features, kind eyes, and jet-black hair—though Uncle's is long and almost always in a bun. Aunt Susan hates it. I think he wears it well. It gives him that wolfish rugged edge.

Uncle Edward is dressed in Craving red as well, and Aunt Susan chose a pinker option for her dress. Not as light as mine, rosier with maroon accents. Uncle greets me with a wink but Aunt Susan—she's always been carved of stone. She's tall, and beautiful with dark brown hair that's always perfectly in place, and chilling brown eyes. She's poised and has a smile plastered on her face, but it never quite reaches her eyes. She's nothing like Mom.

She gives me a once over before saying, "Don't slouch, dear. You're a princess. Chin up." I sit up instantly before her gaze cuts to Camille. "What's the hold up? Why is the birthday girl looking bored and not at her own party?"

Camille's professional mask doesn't slip. "The Beta is running late, Lady Susan. He should be here any moment."

Aunt Susan's eyes narrow as if Camille just offended her. "That's unacceptable and on Rose's birthday? What is he possibly doing? He already missed her photoshoot earlier."

I'd honestly forgotten about that. Josh was supposed to be there, standing next to me like a proper Mate for the official portraits and fashion magazines. But he didn't get back in time for it. That one wasn't entirely on him.

Uncle clears his throat, ever the peacemaker. "Is everything okay? Josh is never late to anything."

Camille answers him but I barely hear her as my skin tingles, and I already know my Mate has arrived.

4 BIRTHDAY BALL

Rosella Craving

July 19

Of the six Warrior families, House Hunter is the most daunting. They can shift into any serpent they choose, granting them dominion over all serpents. However, the basilisk is their primary form alongside the Warrior white wolf. Poison runs through their blood. Venom is in their bite. They have the power to paralyze, seduce, and kill with their slit, hypnotic eyes or their voice, making them the perfect protectors—the perfect Beta Warriors.

Josh Hunter doesn't even have to try. When he's in the room, it's hotter, heavier, charged with whatever energy he decides. People fold under his gaze, bend because what are you going to do? Cross a basilisk? He'll never let you live to tell the tale, and if by chance he does, better watch your back because serpents do not forgive—they're just biding their time.

The men in my family have raved about him for as long as I can remember. On the field, he's ruthless. In training, he's relentless. In politics, he's calculated. The greatest ally one could ever want—and the worst nightmare if crossed.

I've seen him freeze men with one look, then out of spite, shatter them—not even a body left for funeral rites. Josh Hunter is cruel. He can take whatever he wants—make you do whatever he wants with just his voice. He's always strategic, never truly out of control. Even when he looks reckless, every careless smile, every action—it's planned. Josh never loses control of it, or of himself.

He strides toward us with measured steps, every angle considered to attract attention. His gray eyes are sharp and cutting, missing nothing, framed by dark lashes that make them look even more threatening. His black hair is perfectly set, not a strand out of place. Strong cheekbones, a chiseled jaw, and that perfect mouth—lips curved in a way that can promise ruin or pleasure with the smallest tilt.

But Divine, have mercy, he looks infuriatingly good tonight. That black suit fits him to the exact measure of his sculpted body, showing off those broad shoulders and the stupidly perfect chest I'm not supposed to notice. The black Hunter emblem is pinned to the lapel of his jacket, a coiled snake at a stand-off with a wolf, both facing each other. I think about how that's the preface of our relationship. I also know that's not what the serpent and wolf represent, and the emblem really stands for the unity of the Warriors and Serpent Nation. The forest-green shirt beneath his jacket sets off the sharp black of his tie and slacks. A blush pink handkerchief is folded into the pocket of his jacket to match me—his stylist's touch. His polished shoes catch the chandelier light with every step. He adjusts one custom cufflink as he approaches, the motion deceptively casual.

He's perfection weaponized, built to seduce, command, and obliterate his victims—and he knows it.

And I totally didn't just check him out head to toe. Gross.

"I'm here," Josh says, his voice low, but we all hear him loud and clear. Don't get me started on that voice. It's smooth and deep, but not too deep, with a slight gravel to it that perks my ears and makes me wet so fast it's embarrassing. My knees grow weak and I have the urge to let out a moan from just hearing his voice. My body is the biggest traitor. It's worse because he's *not even trying*. I'm the last person he wants to seduce.

I rise instantly, gracefully, not caring for the invisible cord pulling at us. If he feels it too, he ignores it. Speaking of traitors, Camille flashes Aunt Susan a polite, victorious smile, and then the herald's voice carries across the marble floor.

"Elder Edward Craving and Lady Susan Craving."

Aunt Susan sweeps past us in a cloud of expensive perfume, but she pauses just long enough to lean toward Josh and hiss, "Of all nights, Josh, not tonight."

He meets her icy stare with one twice as cold. "I'm not your child, Susan. Don't dare scold me."

My breath catches. Aunt Susan is from a serpent House, therefore Josh has authority over her if it ever comes down to it.

I don't like him. I hate him, but fuck, something about a man with that much power who isn't afraid of anyone just…nope—no. NO. Josh Hunter is a pig—that's what his animal form should've been. He's not hot.

He's *not.*

Okay, he is, but I will never tell him that. Ever. Why would I? He has all the serpent women already telling him.

Uncle senses the tension because he gently touches my aunt's elbow and guides her toward the massive double doors. She goes without another word, chin high, but I can tell she's fuming.

And then…it's just us.

Josh looks annoyed after that interaction with my aunt as he comes to a stop beside me. He's close enough that his cologne hits me like a wave—sharp citrus and smoke, and this warm spice that always makes my head spin a little in the best way. It's *his* scent and my absolute weakness.

His lips curl, but the smile is anything but.

"Well, big night for a little freak like you," he murmurs, soft enough for only me to hear.

For as long as I can remember, I've been a target of his contempt. I'm six years younger than him, but somehow one day in my childhood I pissed him off and he hasn't let go of it since. For the life of me, I cannot pinpoint what it was. He won't enlighten me, saying he won't be having the same conversation repeatedly which doesn't even make sense—but like I said, Hunters are the least forgiving House.

It's frustrating, it's infuriating, and a little heartbreaking if I'm honest. No matter how much he despises me, he's my Mate. Which is probably the only reason I'm still alive, seeing how much he loves to hate me. No doubt if we weren't tied together, he would've killed me. He's said it before.

"Careful now, or I might accidentally take your breath away." I raise my chin slightly. I'm not flirting. My magic can do that.

His chuckle is low, dark, as his eyes drag over me slowly like he's deciding if he approves of my dress or not, but his cold gaze doesn't give anything away.

I roll my eyes. "What? Is it not slutty enough for you?"

The anger that sparks in his eyes is instant. My darkness stirs under my skin, ready if he snaps, shadows curling at the edges of my vision like they're eager to play.

"Keep talking and see how fast I shut you up," he says so low, it can only be meant for my ears.

Gosh…I scowl at him. "Why are you so angry all the time? Didn't you just fuck Camille in the shower?"

I'm spared from him lashing out when Camille's heels click sharply against the marble as she steps between us. Her expression is perfectly calm even though I know she's heard me.

"Are we ready?" she asks, voice smooth and unbothered. Shame is nonexistent these days, I suppose.

Josh doesn't even look at her, keeping his stone gaze on me as he says, "Yes."

It's scary how he can be so dismissive of her when he was just inside her.

Without hesitation, he holds his arm out to me. My pulse stutters, but I match his grace with my own, slipping my gloved hand lightly over his sleeve even if my entire body is singing and revolting at the same time. From a distance, it must look perfect. The Beta and his Veyara, poised and untouchable. But up close, the heat in his gaze is anything but kind.

The herald clears his throat, his voice echoing over the orchestra inside the ballroom. "Beta Warrior Josh Hunter and Her Royal Highness, Princess Rosella Craving."

My Veyara title, even though acknowledged in every right, isn't officially used until after the Veyara Gala—which is okay with me. I get to be just a princess for a little longer.

The doors open, the lights and sounds rushing out to meet us. The ballroom roars with applause as we step forward and descend the grand staircase. I keep a soft, practiced smile on my lips and wave delicately with my free hand.

"Why were you late?" I ask Josh quietly, voice sweet enough for anyone watching to think we're whispering sweet nothings. "You're never late."

He might not always show up, but when he does, he's always punctual. The sooner he arrives, the sooner he can leave.

"Like you said, I was fucking Camille in the shower," he replies and I resist the urge to clench my jaw and punch him in the face. When is he going to learn he can't lie to me?

"That was hours ago," I say through my gritted teeth.

He leans in and brushes a kiss to my temple for the flashing cameras. "And how do you know that for certain, freak?"

I tilt my head and give the people my shyest, sweetest laugh, the one that makes the tabloids call me *adorable* and *innocent*, making people feel sorry for me. I don't bother answering him. I know it irritates him to not know exactly what my secret weapon is. Why would I tell him?

We both continue giving the cameras and gossip columnists what they want as we're supposed to.

I hate this part but Divine help me, there's a tiny, sad part of me that drinks it in anyway. For these few minutes under the lights, I get to pretend my Mate is mine. That the arm around my waist isn't just for show. That the lips on my skin belong only to me. Being in front of cameras is the only time I get to remotely experience a sliver of what the other Mates have. Even if it's fake. I've always wanted that—so it's cruel that I have the unfortunate luck of having Josh fucking Hunter as my Divinely chosen.

It's pathetic, and I hate myself for loving it even a little.

Josh finally smiles charmingly at the photographers, telling them to enjoy the rest of their evening. Then, he steers me away with that gentle-but-firm grip that looks protective to everyone else. The second we're out of the cameras' sights he drops his hand. It's fine—those hands are disgusting and don't deserve to touch me anyway.

The ballroom always steals my breath when I'm inside it. The chandeliers' light reflects across the black and gold marble floor. The ceilings are impossibly high, every curve and carving in it is a masterpiece. Twin staircases mirror the one Josh and I descended from at the other end of the room—for the rest of the court to enter. Clusters of dark leather couches circle the low tables, candles flickering on them. Dark velvet drapes are pulled apart, framing the towering windows, letting the Moonlight in.

My brother lifts his glass to me in a small, private salute. It catches Nathanial's attention and he winks at me before going back to his conversation with Elder Rage. Nathanial sits between the Alpha and the Luna in a slightly larger throne. To his right, Eliza looks ever the beautiful Luna as she smiles and greets socialites.

The live orchestra plays classical music that blends in with the chatter of courtiers. It makes everything feel just a little more cinematic. The food looks too pretty to eat—towers of fruit, trays of meats carved to perfection along with various cheeses and sides, and desserts are lined up in elegant rows. The VelFlame champagne and Moon's Kiss elixir never stops flowing as servers glide by with flutes for the guests.

Every royal house is here, easily spotted, wearing their House colors and emblems. The House of Honest are here too. Nathanial and his Sires, sired five families each, resulting in thirty bloodlines that fall under shifter nobility. Siring became banned, and I can only imagine an exceptional human being granted that gift now under extraordinary circumstances.

Other prominent shifters are present as well, polished and perfect, dropping smiles and handshakes confidently, knowing they earned their spot here.

"For the love of anything you hold Holy, don't flash your eyes tonight," Josh tells me as he and I both reach for champagne flutes from a passing server. I don't dignify that with a response.

Our champagne isn't boring. A reddish gold powder—VelFlame—is added to it. The red color comes from dried blood. The mixture heightens sensuality and allure. It helps to dance easier in heels, that's for sure, but too much can have you hearing things that may not be real.

I catch Josh's gaze sliding across the room to Natalia Osvaron—Camille's ex-sister-in-law. Her platinum hair is swept up to show off that long, elegant neck dripping in diamonds, black dress clinging to every curve like it was painted on. She turns, meets his eyes, and he winks at her. Actually winks. Right in front of me.

I drop my gaze to the bubbles in my glass and tip the rest of the champagne back in one go, feeling it burn all the way down.

Disgusting. He's disgusting. First, Camille, and now he's already on the hunt.

Mariella comes up to us first as I set the empty flute on a passing tray and grab another before the server can even take two steps.

"That dress!" Mariella sighs dramatically, holding a coupe of Moon's Kiss—a shimmering silver alcoholic drink that makes its drinker glow and enhancing charm. It's great for conversations and very popular in high society, especially at events like tonight.

She leans into Antonio. They're both dressed in Rage House colors—black. I find it ironic that the happiest, sweetest girl I know is always dressed in black. Like Josh, Antonio sports his House emblem on the lapel of his jacket too—a blazing bear pawprint within a broken crown. I've wondered why a broken crown—maybe the bear stepped on it.

"Rose had seven dresses and they were all the same pink." Mariella tells Antonio and Josh.

The Beta does not give a fuck about my dresses but bless my best friend's heart for keeping the air light.

Antonio's thick black hair is freshly cut short, clearly for tonight.

He laughs and his gray eyes twinkle before he clinks his flute with mine. "Happy Birthday, Rosie. Excited for your shift tomorrow?"

"The *Veyara* is more than excited." Daniya winks at me as she and Daniel join us.

Only I notice how Josh stiffens slightly at the comment—at the title—but Daniel embraces me, pulling me right out of Josh's arm. "Happy Birthday, Princess!" Then he proceeds to plant a smooch on my forehead, making Daniya and Antonio laugh.

"Daniel, her makeup!" Mariella pulls him off, lightly smacking his arm. Daniel is grinning, running a hand over his light brown hair. He's dressed in a black and gold suit. The Claws House emblem pinned, a feline and wolf tail creating a circle and meeting in the middle to interlock upward. It's actually the cutest of all the emblems.

Daniel winks at his Beta. "Oh, loosen up. If you're not going to kiss her, don't get in the way of the rest of us. Some of us would love to have a threesome with Rose."

Daniel and Daniya's sexcapades are not a secret, but why on earth would he drag me into this, and that too, in front of Josh? I look at Daniya horrified, but she just laughs like he's the funniest thing in the world. Mates, I swear.

"By all means, she's yours." Josh rolls his eyes and while the others laugh, a pang shoots through my chest. He can say that so easily.

I clear my throat. "I should make my rounds. You guys have fun with your three and foursomes."

"What? No, don't run off!" Daniel reaches for my arm. "I was just teasing!"

"Were you, little brother?"

Devaughn Claws strolls up right on cue, whiskey in his hand, sandy hair falling into those Warrior eyes that always look like they're laughing at some secret joke. He's devastatingly handsome, wearing charm and danger in a single look.

Daniel's grin stays in place as his brother rolls his eyes. Then Devaughn looks at me, giving me a hug and a kiss on the cheek, saying, "Happy Birthday, Veyara," he pulls away, and adds, "heard you'll be on the front page of Eternal Vogue."

"What else is new?" Daniya fans herself, "It's exhausting having a hot best friend."

Devaughn raises his glass to Daniya, laughing, and I've never been more grateful for blush on my cheeks as I am now. I can't help it.

Devaughn is hot as fuck. He's happily Mated to one of the sweetest girls, but one can look right?

Devaughn takes a drink before patting Josh on the arm. Shane, Devaughn, and Warrior James Tens are the only people I've seen Josh close to. They're all a few months apart from each other.

I scan the crowd for Devaughn's Mate, Crystal, and catch her blue eyes as she makes her way through the crowds. Like Daniya, she's wearing a beautiful black and gold dress—the colors of House Claws. Her flowing gown does little to hide the small baby bump. She's four months along, and she glows with it. Devaughn and Crystal had their reunion a few months after Shane and Eliza.

Her blonde hair is wrapped up in a braided bun, showing off her diamonds. She's grinning as she joins our growing circle. Devaughn slips an arm casually around Crystal's waist, his thumb brushing against her hip with unconscious tenderness, making her involuntarily press into him. I focus back on Crystal's face, hating the jealous sting in my chest, not because she's with Devaughn, but because her Mate cares for her in a way that's second nature to him.

"Happy birthday, darling!" Crystal squeezes my hand, "You look absolutely stunning, doesn't she, Josh? I picked out the dress for tonight." Crystal beams proudly. One of her sisters is a well-known fashion designer in the supernatural world and my go-to designer. Crystal narrows her eyes on my Mate, before adding in a more threatening tone, "Say she looks stunning, Josh."

"She looks stunning in the dress you chose, Crystal." Josh complies without a glance my way.

Daniya actually rolls her eyes, and I love that my best friend is bold enough to do so in front of a basilisk shifter—but Josh could never hurt her, not without hurting Daniel.

"So, are we sneaking off later and going to Fang Gates?" Daniel asks, looking around the circle. Fang Gates is one of the five clubs in Cravenhold, but it's the only club that spikes their drinks in the most…euphoric way.

Antonio looks at Mariella, who shrugs, looking at me.

I shake my head. "Guys, I'm shifting tomorrow. I don't want to do that with a hangover."

"I don't like sensible Rose," Daniel mumbles, playfully, but Daniya, Daniel, and I already have plans.

No, it's not a threesome.

"Oh, here," Devaughn slips his hand into his jacket, before holding out his closed fist to me. I eye him, reaching out so he can slip a small bag into my hand.

Josh intercepts it, taking the bag and glaring at his best friend.

"What'd you give her?" Crystal asks, seeing Josh's reaction, humor sparking in her blue eyes as she nudges Devaughn with her elbow.

The smile he flashes is all teeth. "Just a little insurance for tomorrow."

My brows knit together, but before I can ask, Daniya gasps and in a hushed voice asks her brother-in-law, "Veins?!"

My head whips to look at Devaughn, impressed with the bold gesture, and the look on his face only confirms Daniya's suspicion. Josh pockets the drug as Antonio lets out a low whistle.

"How'd you even…where did you find that?" Daniel asks, blinking. I'm not sure if I hear praise or disappointment in his voice. Praise, because he asks, "What else do you have in your pharmacy collection?"

Devaughn wrinkles his nose, "I prefer apothecary, thank you very much."

"Rose will not be needing any of that," Josh says firmly, to my surprise.

Devaughn's expression flickers, and for a moment I see the boyish mischief in him that is so similar to Daniel's, but it hardens into something darker. Devaughn snorts, rolling his eyes. "Just a pinch enough to make tomorrow go smooth. You know what the first shift feels like."

"He's not wrong…" Daniya says, slowly, shuddering at the thought of her first shift. "It's the worst pain ever."

Devaughn turns to Mariella. "I have more, do you want it?"

"Devaughn!" Crystal scolds him as Mariella blinks, shaking her head no. It's not that we're above using drugs—Veins is just very dangerous. Antonio laughs, pressing his lips to Mariella's temple and I look away. I love how happy my friends are in their relationships, but it makes me sad for myself. I'm allowed to be both.

Josh turns back to Devaughn. His gray eyes are ice cold. "You know the side effects are lethal."

Silvervein—Veins—is a very rare, glittering powder that can be ingested or inhaled to dull the agony of a first shift, but the side effects are not worth it. It can cause incomplete shifts, shot nerves, or weaken a shifter's powers for the rest of their lives. Of course, those are extreme scenarios, it doesn't happen to everyone. Among the royals, it's a dirty little secret. Usually, Omegas use it to survive the shift—but if their Pack finds out—it's a big disgrace that can lead to exile.

It defeats the whole point of a first shift—survival of the fittest.

"You think I'd let Rose risk her life like that?" Josh's voice cuts through the tension. It's not my life he cares about risking, it's his.

Daniel comes to his brother's defense, telling Josh, "Well…you could administer it. Give her a small dose."

"Exactly," Devaughn agrees, before looking between Josh and me. "Done right, it will lessen the pain at night the way a Mate's touch is supposed to," his focus is on Josh now, "she'll need something to get through the night when you're not there."

Devaughn says it so casually, but the words hit harder than the champagne bubbles fizzing down my throat as I try not to choke on my sip. Josh goes absolutely still at Devaughn's clear implication. His jaw tightens until I think it might crack.

"Careful," Josh says, the threat clear in his voice.

Devaughn just shakes his head, almost sadly. "Veins will spare her the agony that you won't."

My stomach twists. Every word feels like it's being grated across my skin. A male Mate is very much part of a female Mate's transformation, but also part of the aftercare. Mates are meant to spend the night together after the female's shift to ease her pain—a pain that's only subsided by her Mate's release inside her.

Josh takes a slow step closer, his presence swallowing the space between him and Devaughn. They're both the same height, towering over Crystal and me. I glance at her and find her chewing on the inside of her cheek, nervously.

"Why don't you let me worry about what my Mate needs, Devaughn. I can assure you it's not your fucking concern," Josh says, lowly.

The humiliation burns my cheeks as my chest tightens. They're talking about me as if I'm not even standing here. As if *I* have no say in this.

I appreciate Devaughn looking out for me but it's…embarrassing. Why is he going out of his way to ensure my comfort after my shift when my own Mate won't? Veins is not an easy drug to get, even for us royals. I don't know how to feel about this.

Josh is radiating fury beside me, his shoulders tight like a predator about to strike. But he can't. Not here, and not tonight when every camera and socialite is waiting for something juicy to take place at my party.

5 ROMANCE IS DEAD

Rosella Craving

July 19

Josh takes a step back, letting the anger roll off him. "She'll be fine without drugs—and me."

Devaughn tips back his drink, appearing unconcerned, though the tick in his jaw betrays him. "Of course. You know what's best for your Mate, Josh."

Josh takes a threatening step toward Devaughn again as if he's going to hit him right here in the middle of the ballroom, but I move before I can stop myself. My chest presses against Josh's. I feel how fast his heart is pounding and how hot his skin is. I almost pull away, but his heated glare that was directed at Devaughn shifts to me. Surprise flashes across his violent gray eyes because I *never* voluntarily touch him, much less press myself up against him like this.

"Move," Josh orders me when he realizes why I'm in his space.

I place a light hand on his chest, and say over my shoulder to our friends, jokingly, "Maybe if I die of embarrassment from you all talking about my sex life, we won't have anything to worry about at all." I slip my hand down to Josh's. He watches my face with the same anger he had for Devaughn before his gaze falters to my lips and chest that's still pressed against him. Anyone else might think he's checking me out, but I know better. He unclenches his fist to let my fingers weave through his, instantly regulating his temperature to a normal degree.

"Let's get some air. I think the drinks are getting to me," I say to him.

Crystal jumps in and squeezes Devaughn's arm, her smile brittle. "Yeah…that's enough excitement to start the party. Your baby's hungry. Find me food."

I tug Josh with me before we slip through a side archway toward one of the private balconies overlooking the perfectly manicured gardens. Security nods in acknowledgement as we pass. Josh's hand is massive around mine and even with the tension, it's calming just to touch him.

The cool air out on the balcony is welcomed after all that energy. It's a starry night and the Moon glows almost full, eager for tomorrow.

Josh drops my hand the second we're alone and strides to the stone balustrade. His shoulders are drawn tight beneath his black blazer. I don't let my eyes linger too long, afraid he might smell my arousal if I do. Only male Mates can sense when their female counterparts crave them—no one else, thank the Divine. It's embarrassing enough.

I linger at the threshold, the lace of my gown catching on the doorframe as if the ballroom itself wants to hold me back. It's probably not a bad idea. My chest is buzzing, half from the champagne, half from humiliation.

My sex life.

Or rather, the absence of it.

The absence everyone knows about because Josh is always seen with other women. It was never a secret, but with my transformation here, it is a pressing topic. Josh can barely talk to me without insulting me—Mating doesn't even come close to being an option.

So what the Hell was that about in there? Was it him just saving face? Or is there some truth to not challenging a Mating bond?

Mates are sacred. Mating bonds are sacred.

Challenging a Mating bond is grounds for war. Disrespecting a Mating bond is grounds for war. There's nothing above a Mating bond. Nothing.

His eyes are locked on the gardens below, where lanterns flicker and a few couples linger. I'm about to leave him out here, when he says, "You should've let me hit him."

I step out onto the balcony, closing the door behind me. "And let you replace me on the front cover of ViciousWorld? Please, not a chance."

His lips twitch, not quite a smile, but enough that I catch it, making my heart skip a beat. I roll my eyes at myself.

"What's wrong with you anyway?" I ask him, crossing my arms. "Why are you so upset about it?"

"It's not his place," he replies automatically.

"And it's yours to decide that?" I ask, frowning. "Whether I take a drug to help me get through the night or not, how is that your problem?"

He laughs but there's no humor in it. "Trust me, I fucking wish it wasn't."

"Weren't you just pissed at me about the vipers? You didn't have to do all that with Devaughn."

"Oh, I'm still pissed at you about the vipers. It was childish as fuck," he replies, turning his head to look at me and I match his glare. Of course, that's the part he decides to respond to. At least Devaughn was considerate enough to get me drugs, that's more than I can say for Josh.

"You have no right to be pissed about anything," I counter. He knows it, but he doesn't drop his glare. "Not when I just caught you eyeing Natalia Osvaron."

Josh looks annoyed. "Then stop watching me."

I lean against the balustrade, breaking the eye contact because I'm so mad I want to cry. My heart aches. How is *he* my Mate? What did I do to deserve someone like him? However, none of that pisses me off more than wishing he looked at me like he looked at Natalia. If he wasn't such a manwhore, I'd kill for it but he's not a prize to win.

"I'm surprised *you* haven't suggested it yet," I say, coolly.

His eyebrow ticks up, slow and calculating. "Suggested what?"

"Hooking up," I keep my voice light, casual, even though my pulse is hammering, "completing our bond. You Mark me, we get the full force of our powers…a win-win."

Except, we'll also be getting a download of each other's lives prior to Mating—shifter scientists and theologists believe it's because one soul is reunited, joining separate lives as one. It's very inconvenient. I'll have to re-live his physical encounters.

"Hooking up?" his voice is so quiet and dangerous, I look at him and he says, "You make it sound so casual."

"It's not like you're picky," I laugh, and look him dead in the eye, "at least I actually have something to offer—aside from heirs, of course."

"You have a very strange way of seducing a man," Josh says, staring at me like I've grown two heads.

"Yes, well, you'd know all about how a man's to be seduced," I try, *try*, to not sound sarcastic. "This isn't about seducing you. If I was seducing you, you'd know. This is a transaction."

He just lets out a humorless laugh and shakes his head as if I'm being ridiculous. "A transaction. How fucking romantic."

"Don't tell me you haven't thought about it," I say, keeping my voice light.

He doesn't say anything, but then the shift in him is instant, a dangerous fury simmering just under the surface. "Marking you is not a topic to be taken lightly, freak."

I roll my eyes, "You're being a total girl about it. *You've* taught me sex isn't sacred, so why pretend it is now? The Elders and Crescents are already hounding me for a reunion date. Might as well get it over with."

His head snaps slightly at that, a muscle twitching in his jaw. "If you say get it over with one more time—"

"What?" I cut him off, heat flooding my cheeks and chest as reckless words start spilling out, "You'll fuck me? Yell at me? Walk away? Fuck someone else?"

"You're pathetic. Jealousy is not cute," he says, coldly. "Grow the fuck up, it's literally your birthday."

I've never been jealous of the women he's been with. Disgusted with him more like it.

"I'm not jealous. I'm being practical," I respond.

"If you want to fuck me, all you have to do is say so."

"Yeah, I know how easy you are. But disgusting pigs aren't my type—this is just nature forcing us together. The sooner we get it over with, the sooner we can live our separate lives." It's a miracle I'm able to get the words out without my voice trembling. No matter how much I've tried, I am incapable of imagining a life where Josh isn't in it. It is suffocating being tied to him, but it's unimaginable to think what life would be like without him in it or being my Mate.

"Disgusting pig…wow," Josh repeats, chuckling. "Well, this disgusting pig has no desire to touch you, so what's that say about you?"

Ugh.

I turn my attention on the party behind the balcony's glass doors, and when I don't reply, I feel his eyes on me. I need to get out of here.

Shaking my head, I step toward the doors as I say to him, "Taking a drug never crossed my mind. I've always known I have to go through tomorrow night alone."

I make the mistake of looking back at him. His jaw flexes, the muscle ticking as if my words cut deeper than they should. His eyes are so intense, they're almost glowing in the Moonlight.

"You won't be alone," he says, frowning.

"Yes, I will. We both know you don't want to be with me." I shrug, but that sentence holds so much weight and suddenly, it's not just about tomorrow night.

His gaze shift focus back to the gardens below when the doors to the balcony open, revealing Camille. She lets out a relieved sigh when she sees us. Josh doesn't turn to look at her, but her focus is on me anyway. "It's almost time to cut the cake," she says.

"Thanks, Camille. We'll be right in," I tell her. She glances over at Josh's back and gives me a concerned look. When I don't offer anything, she sighs and closes the doors once again.

"We'll cut the cake and then you can slip out and fuck whoever you have lined up." Translation: I know you don't want to be *here* either.

I'm giving him an out so I can also end this party early.

He takes a deep breath before standing up straighter and adjusting his tie. "It's fine. Maybe Devaughn will give me another chance to kick his ass later tonight."

I give him a look, unsure if he's serious.

"I'm kidding, freak," he rolls his eyes, before holding the door open for me. I get a whiff of his scent, and it takes everything in me to not inhale deeply.

I side-eye him as I pass through and back into the ballroom. "You could just admit you want to stay."

"We know by now I'm not in the business of making your wishes come true," he says lowly in my ear.

I smile back sweetly. "As if I would ever wish for you."

The party's been going on for three hours now, after I've cut the cake and the cameras flashed. Josh had snuck away with a brunette in Hunter green and was nowhere to be found for the pictures. He already met the quota for tonight. Camille and Eliza were not happy about that. I'm used to it, but I didn't eat the cake after.

Warrior Samuehl Salvatore and his Crescent, Azura, join our circle after having made their rounds with the Elders. Sam stands apart from the other Warriors. While Shane, Josh, James, and Devaughn are the epitome of the Warrior title and Antonio and Daniel are the easy-going ones—Sam is quieter than all of them. He's not shy per se, but observant. He only speaks when necessary and has such a calming presence, it's almost impossible not to relax around him. I know it's one of his powers as an eagle shifter, which is why he's a great peacekeeper. He's the opposite of his father, Elder Valen Salvatore, who's never given me peaceful energy.

Sam's blond hair is always kept in a short buzzcut. He looks sharp tonight in his black tux and brown silk shirt, matching Azura's dress. The Salvatore House emblem of a large bird flying in front of the crescent Moon is pinned to his jacket as well. I will say though, Sam looks distracted—tired perhaps. Shane does work him a lot.

Azura and Crystal get to chatting about their pregnancies, while the men fall into conversation about some feline and serpent disputes. Mariella, Daniya, and I hang back to people watch.

As the party starts to wind down, Shane and Eliza make their way over.

"Alright," Eliza says, loud enough to get all our attention. "Let's take this group selfie so I can get back into bed."

Her words draw laughter from all of us as Shane pulls her closer to him. Eliza is radiant even when she's exhausted.

Daniel comes to stand in front of me, taking front and center, his phone angled high. He makes sure he's not blocking anyone before he commands, "Squeeze in!"

We crowd together beneath a chandelier with a pink balloon arch as the backdrop. Crystal and Azura link arms while Devaughn and Sam stand behind them, grinning. Antonio's hand slips cheekily to Mariella's hip as Daniya attaches herself to Daniel's side, leaning in to kiss his cheek. Shane and Eliza look regal without even trying. At the last possible second, Josh slides in behind me.

"Fucking ninja, where have you been?" Antonio asks him, laughing.

Josh doesn't reply but his chest presses flush against my back, solid muscle radiating heat through my thin layers of silk and lace. His hand comes around to settle on my stomach, fingers spread just wide enough to claim and tight enough to make my toes curl, pulling me into him more. Then—oh my Divine—there's no mistaking what's pressing into my ass. I feel his hard length against me, making me freeze, every nerve in my body sparking, betraying me.

He doesn't answer Antonio, just leans in closer to me for the picture. His jaw grazes the curve of my cheek. His scent overwhelming my senses and I clench my thighs tighter.

The others are laughing, adjusting, waiting for Daniel to take the pictures. I force my lips into my practiced smile, but inside I'm shaking. My body doesn't care that Josh can't stand me. It doesn't care that he fucks a girl or two every night. It's very aware of where he's touching me right now. Very aware of his erection. I know I can't be the reason for it.

I fight myself from leaning into him, but at the last moment, I bring my hand up to cup his face with my gloved hand before Daniel snaps the picture.

6 UNDERWORLD

Rosella Craving

July 20

The car glides us through the undercity streets, tinted windows shutting out the neon chaos outside. Daniya sprawls beside me, already buzzed, her laughter spilling over as she tips a tiny black vial back and lets the powder dissolve on her tongue. Daniel sits across from us, the half-mask already on, only revealing the grin on his face. We've all changed out of our formal gala attire to more club-appropriate ones.

I'm on Spellbook, looking at the picture Daniel already posted of our group selfie. He tagged everyone, of course. I zoom in, and there we are. Me and Josh right next to Daniya and Daniel, my hand on his cheek, his arm around me like we're actually…something. We look good together. Too good. My stomach does a stupid flip. It's embarrassing to be posted like this, to see cute pictures of Josh and me in the tabloids or social media when everyone knows he hooks up with other women openly.

I wish I could play it off and say he's a serpent, that it took me some time to understand a serpent shifter has needs. That it's just their lifestyle and I've adapted to it. I can't though. Josh is right to not want me as his Mate. I will never be okay with sharing him. I will never let him touch me if he's interested in others. Even if I do, for the sake of the Mating bond, it won't mean anything to me. He will never truly have me if he wants others.

It's not a problem seeing that he doesn't want me.

Josh doesn't follow me, and I don't follow him on socials. There's no point in stalking him because he never posts anything interesting.

My cheeks heat up again thinking about him pressed against me. But the moment's soured because let's be real. He probably already had someone lined up for after the party. Some serpent girl with sultry eyes who doesn't care that he's Mated. He's probably already with her right now. He hates me, so why would he ever be hard for me?

Anger bubbles up hot and sharp in my chest, mixing with this stupid hurt that won't go away.

The movement of Daniel pulling out two glass jars from the middle console catches my attention. One jar is red with clear crystal-like contents, while the other is a clear jar with the prettiest shade of purple petals I've ever seen.

"These just hit the market in your honor," Daniel tells me.

"In my honor? I don't remember condoning drugs," I say laughing, as Daniya giggles.

"Glass Rose," Daniel says holding open the red jar, "this will enhance your beauty and make your pheromones irresistible so whoever your target is, they can't help but give in to your whims. Sex is supposed to be amazing on it."

"Does it work on Warriors?" Daniya asks for me.

"You can give it a test run on me tonight," Daniel smirks at her, making her moan and parting his legs further with her feet. He laughs, placing her heels on his thigh, before showing us the petals. "Aether Petal—or Petal, I think, is what they'll call it."

"They're sooo pretty." I eye them as I reach for one.

"That one will make you feel *everything*," Daniel says, "every touch, every beat of music, every emotion. Do *not* take it when you're going through heat."

"That makes sense," I mumble, grateful for the darkness in the car so that he can't see my cheeks grow pink. A female shifter stops getting her period after she shifts and instead, goes through heat twice a year. Some girls have it sooner than others after they shift but always by six months after our first transformation. One of the downsides of the animal in us.

Pushing the thoughts away, I place the petal on my tongue, letting it dissolve. "Ooh, it tastes like cotton candy!"

Daniya reaches for it too and lets out a blissful sigh once it's in her mouth, nodding in agreement. My skin starts to tingle a little bit as the drug enters my system and the car starts to slow.

"We're here!" Daniya announces.

Daniel leads the way into the club, walking past the long lines of partiers trying to get in. The bass hits first—low, vibrating, and I realize what Daniel meant by feeling everything on Petal. The underground club is hazy from the smoke, sweat, and Divine knows what else. Bodies are everywhere, tangled up, pressed together. Red and violet lights fade in and out adding to the ambiance of sin and pleasure.

Sin and pleasure. That's the only reason you come here.

As we make our way through the crowd, I get glimpses of shifters dancing with witches, vampires drinking from mortals, a shifter being pleasured by a witch and fed on by a vampire at the same time. This would never happen out in the open. Mixing like this, pairings like this—it's not only scandalous, it's forbidden.

Street drugs are passed hand to hand. Vials of blood, pills, and syringes make their rounds. Everyone's here for one thing—escape.

The three of us wear masks—sleek black, nothing fancy to draw attention. People dress in all kinds of ways here, no one cares who or what anyone is. It's why we love it.

"Be safe," Daniya tells me over the loud music, her fingers lacing with Daniel's as she starts to pull him toward the dancefloor. He looks at me, silently asking if I'll be okay.

I nod, giving him a smile before turning and weaving my way toward the back. I push past the bodies and ignore the ones hooking up against the walls.

A group of witches swallow me whole, but cold fingers close around my wrist. The thick, black curtains of a VIP room part, and I'm pulled in. The sounds dull instantly, the club muffled as I turn to face my captor.

He's watching me too with eyes so gray they almost look silver. His blond hair is messy on purpose, playing into his image of the spoiled vampire prince that he loves claiming to be.

There's a glass of something dark in his hand and he smiles slowly, revealing the hint of fangs on purpose. He could hide them if he wanted to but then what's the point of being here.

"Craving," he says, voice so slow it makes the hairs at the back of my neck stand.

"Craving," I echo in response.

His jaw ticks, as his nose wrinkles in protest. "You know I hate it when you make the family reference." He's using his British accent tonight then. He likes to switch it up and keep me guessing. When you've lived as long as he has, and in the many places he's resided, you pick up a few accents for fun. The British accent is his go-to though.

I tilt my chin, not standing down. "Then maybe you shouldn't tie yourself to my family name."

He laughs. "Oh, little wolf, you know I'm much older than you. The name was mine first."

In an instant, he's in front of me, a blur of speed I wasn't quick enough to follow. His fingers close around my wrist as he pulls me to him.

I let out a gasp as my chest presses against his. Then his hand is at my throat before he flicks off my mask, and his cold lips descend on mine. My hand comes up to his face as I kiss him back just as hard.

He moves so fast, the rush exciting every nerve in my body and before I know it, I'm straddling him. The world narrows as his hands move up my legs to my hips, pressing me into his hardness. His fingers tug at my dress before he takes it off me like it's offensive to be wearing it.

"Too many layers," he mutters, hungrily.

"It's just a dress." I defend between kisses. "I didn't even put on underwear."

His hands travel down to my ass, before he slaps it once. "I see that. Why are you so cold?"

"It's a chilly summer night." I let out a laugh.

He rolls his eyes, elegantly. Everything he does is so…pretty, even though he tries so hard to look rebellious. "Don't werewolves run hot?" he asks. I narrow my eyes at him, sitting straighter but he takes that as an invite to kiss my chest.

"Shifters," I correct, sharply but playful. "And yes, but I haven't shifted yet."

His mouth curves into a wicked smile. His tongue drags slowly against the curve of my neck—right where my Mark from another man will be soon. The scrape of his fang grazes my skin, and a chill goes down my spine.

What if…what if I let him bite me there? What if I wear his Mark instead? The idea is too tempting and thankfully the beautiful vampire speaks, refocusing my mind on his words.

"Ah, that's right," he murmurs, lips pressing against the spot in a mocking gesture. "Tomorrow night." The words are thick as his fingers dig into my hips, forcing me to feel how hard he is against me. "Tell me, Princess," he breathes, gray eyes meeting mine, "are you going to let your Mate fuck you into submission?"

The question feels as though he just burned me. My head falls back and his lips brush my nipple. "I will never submit to Josh Hunter. Not after everything he's done."

His fingers lace through my black hair and he pulls, jerking my head farther back. "Never say never, right?"

His mouth closes around the bud of my left nipple, his tongue flicking with a slow warmth that makes me press into him. I grind against his erection, my arousal unwilling to be contained any longer and I can care less that he's still wearing his pants.

"Enjoy it," I tell him, "*this* will never happen again."

He lifts his head and I meet his eyes, darker now. A smirk plays on his lips, but his eyes hold the sadness I feel.

"He doesn't deserve you," he murmurs, his voice rough and raw. Before I can respond, he pulls my face to him and kisses me tenderly. I let myself drown in it, memorizing every second. "Neither of them do," he adds darkly against my lips.

"Neither of them love me like you do," I whisper back and press my lips to his again.

Then I pull away and slip onto the couch, the velvet cushions feeling abnormally soft against my skin. I tug him down with me. Our breaths mingle as I unbuckle his pants, freeing his hard cock.

Ugh, I missed it.

Going from being together often on my Royal Tour to barely once or twice a month, sucked.

He keeps his eyes on me as he spreads my thighs wider. My pulse hammers in my ears, louder than it has any right to be for an apex predator. His gaze drops to where I'm already glistening for him, and a low, appreciative sound rumbles from his chest.

"Miss me?" he grins at the sight of me drenched.

"You have no idea," I reply, not holding back. I don't have to with him. I don't have to pretend I don't want him. "Did you miss me?"

His thumb brushes my clit in a gentle swipe, making me arch into him before his fingers sink into my arousal. They don't stay—he pulls them out, raising them to taste me. His gray eyes flutter close as I watch him enjoy the taste of me on his fingers.

"Fuck yes," he finally answers when he's done and looks down at me again. "You taste fucking divine."

"Stop teasing and fuck me," the whine slips out before I can stop it.

"So impatient," he circles my clit again, lazy and maddening, never giving me enough pressure. "I don't know, I quite enjoy seeing you dripping down your thighs for me."

I moan out as frustration rolls through me. He lowers his mouth to my clit, sucking hungrily without warning. The coolness of his tongue against me never ceases to shock my nerves, edging me closer.

He lifts his head to say, "I've been waiting for you."

"I had…" I start, weaving my fingers through his blond hair, "princess obligations."

He chuckles, the sound vibrating against my core. "And what about your obligations to your very scandalous, very forbidden affair?"

I hate when he calls this an affair. Josh and I are *not* in a relationship—not willingly at least. But we are Mates, so it trumps any relationship labels out there…therefore, the prince isn't wrong. I still hate it.

His fingers slide back into my pussy, sending pleasure rippling through me. My hips jerk up and my clit is met by kisses.

"I'm here, aren't I?" I say, breathless. "Now, *stop* teasing me."

"Oh and…what's this?" his smile grows and I know exactly what's caught his attention. He grins, "Oh, you're really impatient aren't you."

"I lied, I didn't miss you," I groan, since he wants to torture me.

"Oh yeah? Then why is that tight little arse already plugged and ready for me like a good girl?"

I'm not even embarrassed by it. He got me the plug on the Tour and it's one of my favorite toys that he's given me. It was my birthday today, so I wore it to my party. The plug's been in me for hours now. Every step, every shift of my body was a reminder that I was seeing him tonight.

He hooks one finger under the base of the plug and pulls gently.

I gasp, back arching off the couch.

"Easy, princess," he chuckles. "Relax for me, love. Let me see how well you took my gift."

He pulls at the plug slowly—agonizingly slowly—and I feel every inch of it sliding free, the stretch, the sudden emptiness, the way my body clenches around nothing.

"Fuck," I cry out as he places the butt plug on the table.

"There we go," he purrs, his eyes are locked on my ass, heavy with hunger. "Look at that pretty hole. Already so greedy for me."

"Please…" I whine, reaching for him.

He raises my leg to rest on his shoulder before placing a soft kiss on the inside of my ankle. Then he spits into his palm, dragging those long, elegant fingers down my slit—collecting my arousal, smearing it upward in one filthy stroke. I shudder when the wetness circles my rim.

"Fuck me," I breathe, hips writhing under his touch.

"I'm working on it, relax," he laughs and it's a beautiful sound that just makes me wetter. He takes that opportunity and presses just one finger inside my ass.

"Divine, you're so fucking tight," he rasps, "even after wearing the plug—I missed this feeling." He sinks the first finger deeper, then adds the second on the next slow thrust. The stretch is perfect. I clench around him instinctively and we both let out a moan.

I rock back onto his fingers. "Then stop teasing me."

He laughs softly, curling his fingers just enough to make my toes tingle and curl. "Not yet, little wolf. I want you sloppy for me first before I split you open."

I whimper. "You're so mean to me."

He leans down, fangs grazing my ear. "But I make you feel so good."

"So…good," I repeat, mindlessly as I take in his fingers prepping my hole.

His thumb finds my clit again, finally giving me real pressure, and at the same time he fucks his fingers deeper into my ass. Pleasure crashes through me in waves. My breath is short, desperate, and I need more.

"Talk to me, tell me how it feels," he says, his voice rougher now. "Tell me how much you want my cock in this tight, pretty hole."

I'm shaking, thighs spread obscenely wide. "It feels—fuck—it feels so good. So…full. But not full enough. I need you," I turn my head slightly and meet his dark gaze. His lips lock with mine, kissing me, licking and tasting me. "I missed you. I need to feel you," I whisper.

He withdraws his fingers slowly and I whimper against his lips. He pulls away, positioning himself between my legs and I watch him stroking himself, spreading my arousal and his spit along his length. Fuck, he's so hot as he confidently fists his cock, enjoying being watched. Then he reaches for the lube bottle on the table, the faint scent of strawberries mingles with our energy now. He pours it over his thick, hard, pale cock, the sight of it sending a fresh wave of need through me.

He puts the bottle down and pulls me closer. Then he lowers himself as one of his hands lace through my fingers while the other guides his cock to my prepped hole. He presses the tip of his cock against me and places a kiss to the side of my lips. The prince lets out a low groan as he presses the crown at my entrance, and I feel the blunt pressure.

"Eyes on me," he commands and I obey, biting my lips.

I brace myself, anticipation killing me.

"Last night," he says, gaze completely dark with desire.

I swallow. "Make it worth it."

His eyes narrow slightly before he pushes in, stretching me wide, and I cry out, nails digging into his shoulders as he fills me inch by inch. He lets out a loud groan as he pushes in, the stretch intense like the first time, every time. He's not too patient—he doesn't have to be.

He pushes all the way in, buried to the hilt as my heart races with the invasion, but his lips find mine, kissing me through it.

"Fuck," he breathes, "always so perfectly tight. You love my dick in your arse, don't you, my dirty little princess?"

I clench around him on purpose, watching his eyes roll back, humbling him a little.

"Fuck, little wolf," he pinches my nipple, "I needed you."

"I missed you," I say and pull him back to kiss him.

I move with him to meet his thrusts, each one deeper and harder. His cock fills me, sending continuous waves of pleasure through me. My fingers dig into his shoulders as I roll my hips, chasing the feeling more and more.

His hand slides between us, fingers finding my clit. He rubs it in circles, the pressure perfect, igniting sparks. My thighs tremble, slickness dripping out of me.

"Look at you," he teases as he locks gazes with me, "so fucking beautiful like this. I'll never forget it."

"You better fucking not. I'll kill you," I threaten.

He chuckles. "I love it when you talk dirty to me."

I can barely think, lost in the rhythm of his thrusts and circles of his fingers. Then he brings his fingers to my lips, the tips glistening with my arousal.

"Taste," he commands and I part my lips, letting him slip two fingers into my mouth. My tongue swirls around them, sucking deeply, savoring the taste of his skin more than myself. I keep our eyes locked, teasing him with how my tongue massages his fingers, purposefully letting out a moan.

"Fuck, Rose," he growls, and thrusts harder. The couch beneath us creaks, but all I care about is him. His cock filling my ass, fingers in my mouth, and his eyes devouring me like I'm the only thing he holds dear.

I cry out, my climax crashes through me, clenching his cock and making his thrusts stop abruptly. His abs flex as he comes inside my ass, groaning. His fingers slip from my mouth to rub my clit while we ride out our orgasms. He keeps himself in me a little longer while his eyes drink me in—from my face to my hard nipples to my stomach.

He pulls back slightly, still staying inside, chest heaving as he lowers his head to my breast. His lips brush the side of it, his breath warm and teasing. I realize what he intends when I feel the graze of a fang.

"No," I say quickly, my voice soft, but my hand pulls his face back up. "Not there. My dresses…they'll show it."

He pauses, pulling away. "We wouldn't want that," he murmurs, understanding. He starts to ease out of me.

"No," I stop him, shaking my head, "not yet."

He gives me a soft smile. "We have all night, love. I'm not going anywhere."

My chest tightens as he pulls out and I immediately miss him. He settles lower, his hands parting my legs more. His lips graze the tender skin of my inner thigh, and I shiver, anticipation growing again but for a different reason.

Then his sharp fangs sink in. The initial sting makes me flinch but then pleasure spreads throughout me. He busies his hands, one rubbing my clit the other on my breast as he drinks from me. I tangle my fingers in his hair, pressing his mouth harder against my thigh and encouraging him to drink deeply.

Shifters are a drug to vampires. Most shifters would not be comfortable with anyone feeding on them—neither would vampires. There's a lot of stigmas around drinking blood and from which source. The powers that are shared and…the violations that can happen from drinking each other's blood makes it dangerous—thrilling.

While vampires can drink from us, vampire blood is poisonous to shifters—so this is a one-way street that requires a lot of trust or stupidity. I roll my head back into the cushion, letting him continue to flood me with a night full of pleasure and sinful desires.

The hotel room lights up through the curtains with the rising, golden Sun as dawn creeps up on us. The sheets tangle over our naked bodies. We stayed up all night, neither of us wanted to waste our last night sleeping. We spent every second lost in each other—fucking desperately, then talking and laughing when I needed a break. My body is pressed against him, my skin alive with his touch and I try not to think about how much I'm going to miss this, how I have to say good-bye to this—to him. It's not fair.

"How are you really feeling about shifting?" he asks me and I smile a little. Saying I'm okay won't fly with him.

"Weird. I have a weird feeling about it," I answer him.

"Elaborate," he chuckles.

"I can't…something just feels off, but right at the same time…"

"Wouldn't it be crazy if you shifted into a Warrior?" he asks, raising an eyebrow in a clear challenge.

I roll my eyes, "It would be crazy because it's impossible."

"Why? Isn't it a birthright for royal shifters with gray eyes to shift into a white wolf," he recites to me the ways of my own kind.

"But I'm a girl. There has never been a female Warrior, so I'm pretty sure that theory is out the window," I fake a toss toward the curtains.

"Just because there hasn't been, doesn't mean there can't be," he shrugs as if he's not stating something that's insane. He continues, "With your eyes and your powers…if it's a shock to anyone, they've been sleeping. I'd be curious to see how your brother would navigate it…"

"What do you mean?"

"As Alpha. Will he stand by the *Divine Decree,* or will he succumb to the Elders' bitching?" he says in almost a teasing manner, and it might sound like a joke, but he's the youngest vampire prince. He's almost a thousand years old—he's going to be observing this. He knows how rare my magic is, so I'm not surprised he's curious.

"Have you met another female shifter with gray eyes before?" I ask him, quietly.

His lips press against my forehead. "You know I haven't. It's what captivated me the night we met."

I smile at that. We met two years ago at a club very similar to the one we were at earlier. We became the most unlikely of friends, until February of this year—that's when things became physical and I regret none of it. Every second with this golden prince has been the best moment of my life. He sees me and always makes me feel…cherished. Maybe because our time together is always stolen.

I shift my head up to look at him, and he lowers his to kiss me. When we pull away, I ask, "You're not worried about the Beta and how he'll react?"

He grunts. "No. If the Alpha makes a stand, the Beta will have no choice but to follow—unless it goes against your safety, of course. I can't imagine your brother doing anything like that. Josh can make your transition into Serpent Nation difficult though."

"He already has."

"I know. I'm sorry about that…like I said he doesn't deserve you," he laces our fingers together, before kissing the back of my hand, "you could always run away and become a vampire princess. The jet's ready."

I laugh. "Was that a proposal?"

"It could be if I thought you'd seriously consider it," he smiles beautifully, fangs and all. His gray eyes twinkle against the rising Sunlight.

I snuggle into him, taking in his warmth. He's right, I could never consider it. Warrior Mating bonds are unbreakable, even the ones that don't want us. There's no running or escaping it permanently. So what option do I have, except to dream. "Hmm…the vampire world doesn't seem that safe right now either."

The prince shifts, readjusting to me. "What happened to Tia was tragic. She was too young."

"Are there any suspects to who Princess Tia's killer is?" I ask him, curious about the murder mystery. She died right before my birthday party started according to the news the prince received a few hours ago.

Tia Montenaj was one of the last remaining Montenaj and Walanx family members. The vampires have eighteen royal families—the Princess was the descendent of two. She's survived by her younger sister, Princess Elena Montenaj, who is the lost Montenaj princess of the vampires.

"I wouldn't be surprised if the Soul Snatchers had a hand in it," the prince says darkly.

Soul Snatchers are vampires who drain made vampires for their blood, believing their rare powers make them valuable—even if made vampires can't perform magic. To Soul Snatchers, made vampires are nothing more than vessels. They are closely allied with the Sisterhood of Sin, an ancient underground Coven devoted to Lilith, The Cursed One.

He combs his fingers through my hair, absently. "Jules is turning over every stone, but they covered their tracks well." Jules Craving is the prince's nephew—he was also engaged to Tia.

"They can never cover their tracks well enough," I point out, "but this means Elena will be on the High Council now."

"Yes," he says, quietly.

The High Council consists of the eldest living member from each vampire royal house, with one exception—the ruling family. The King, the Queen, and all five of their sons sit on the High Council as they were the original members.

"You've met her?" I ask, glancing up at his handsome face.

He presses a kiss to my nose, making me smile. "Not really. She was introduced to us but I haven't actually talked to her."

"Could be interesting," I say. "Tia was the youngest to hold a seat, and now Elena—how old is everyone else? Centuries?"

He chuckles at that. "Yes, pretty much. Two at least."

"Yeah, it was time for new blood to infiltrate," I laugh, jokingly.

"Things have been a bore. Elena's already shaken things up in the vampire world with the Soul Snatchers." He shakes his head, eyes darkening. He always hated talking about this topic. He hates how the Royal Family stays out of the civil war, maintaining a neutral stance. It's to not show bias to either side, but his people are dying. Good people, like Tia, are dying.

I lie against his chest with his heartbeat steady beneath my cheek. His fingers lazily run up and down my back as I hold his heavy cock in my hand.

My mind drifts to what the day holds—my first transformation. I'm not sad, not exactly. We both knew we had borrowed time when we started this. I'm glad that I've known him, felt him, experienced him. I'm glad I got to choose and find a love like this, even if it was short lived.

"Speaking of Soul Snatchers, if you ever want to play once you're Veyara, I know a spot." He winks at me.

I laugh, leaning into him. "Noted."

His lips brush my forehead. "You should go, little wolf. Before it's too late."

The words sting but I know he's just looking out for me. I nod, swallowing the lump in my throat as I turn to face him. His gray eyes meet mine and I can't resist. I lean in, kissing him deeply, pouring everything I can't say into the press of my lips. My body moves on instinct, sliding a leg over to straddle him. His cock, already hard, brushes against my entrance, teasing my slick pussy dangerously. I'm tempted to let him in, let him have me in a way we've resisted.

We've only ever done anal because it was the only loophole for us. Of course, I've fantasized about giving my virginity to this prince I actually love, especially when Josh is always cheating. It'd only be fair.

But I'm not Josh and while I'm always down for plotting revenge, I just could never go through with this one. I think about everything Josh said at my party and a part of me wants to say fuck it and give my Mate a taste of his own medicine. At least my first time would be with someone I do love and care about.

The prince is right. Josh doesn't deserve me. He doesn't deserve to have me like that. But the prince pulls back, his hands firm on my hips, holding me still.

"Rose," he says, his voice strained, eyes searching mine, "you'll regret it more than me."

The truth of his words hurt, cutting through my need for him and my need for revenge against Josh. If I cross that line…basilisks don't forgive. So why should Josh ever expect me to forgive him? He, of all people, should understand and he's the last person who can hold it against me.

"I won't," I promise the beautiful vampire under me. "I want *you.*"

He closes his eyes as if the words hurt him and he's fighting himself. When he opens them again, I see the pain they harbor. "Please, Rose, don't do that to me right now. This is hard enough as it is."

He's right. It's not fair of me to ask him of this, in our last minutes. I blink back my tears, running my hand through my hair.

"I'm sorry," I whisper and lean down to kiss him again, softer this time. His lips linger on mine, and I savor the coolness I'll never feel against me again. The coolness that somehow lit a fire in my soul in so many ways and there's no putting it out now.

"I love you," he whispers back. "I always will."

"I love you," I reply, quietly. We didn't say it often and it isn't just love between us, but it feels right to say it in this moment.

With a shaky breath, I climb off him, my legs unsteady as I slide off the bed. The cool air of the hotel room gives me goosebumps as I reach for my dress. I slip into it, the fabric feeling wrong where his touch just had been.

I feel him watching me silently. I don't look at him as I reach for the door, but he stops me. "See you around, little wolf."

I dare to face him then. We will see each other again, eventually, but when we do, I'll be someone else.

He's leaning back against the headboard, one hand lazily stroking his cock unapologetically while his eyes are locked on me.

My knees grow weak at the sight, and it takes everything in me to not get back into bed with him. To not say, Hell with it, and run to close the distance between us.

"Go start your life, Veyara," he says, making my heart race. "Make it a memorable one. I'll be watching."

I turn away and step through the threshold into the hotel hallway, closing the door behind me. Cristobal, Franklin, and the prince's guards greet me on the other side. His guards remain while Cristobal leads the way with Franklin behind me. I told myself I wouldn't cry last night, but it's the morning and I let the tears fall silently as the car takes me back to Cravenhold.

7 SERPENT POLITICS

Josh Hunter

July 20

Daevryn Tower rises straight ahead, twenty-five stories of black glass and everything a dignitary might need for their visit. I walk through the revolving doors, and four security guards greet me. They snap to attention the instant my shoes hit the serpent inlay.

I nod and continue on. Black marble veined with emerald runs floor to ceiling, each level ringed by balconies that look down like the inside of a coiled serpent. The Hunter House crest is illuminated right behind the reception desk in gold against the black stone wall.

When Nathanial changed his seat of power to America and built Cravenhold, the six royal family names were altered for the modern age. While we still honor the original Sire names throughout our rituals and practices, and use them interchangeably, our families haven't used the original names in centuries. House Daevryn became House Hunter and I fucking hate it. Shane and I have discussed reinstating our ancient family names, but that is a much larger project we're entertaining in our spare time. Right now, I have more pressing matters to deal with.

The receptionists behind the crescent-shaped desk look up at the same time. There are three of them today, all serpent shifters, wearing their black uniform jacket and pencil skirts with a black silk blouse and the Hunter emblem pinned to the lapel, along with their name tags. Their hair is in neat updos to show off the delicate jewelry they sport. Appearance is everything.

"Good morning, Beta Warrior," says the brunette, leaning forward just enough to give me a view of her cleavage.

"All twenty-seven members have arrived, my lord," the redhead on the end, informs me before biting her red lip.

"Can we get you anything before you go up, sir?" the petite blonde in the middle, looks at me with hopeful brown eyes.

I fucked the three of them some time ago and they've been hungry for more, but the red cord never lit for them—they weren't my Mate, so they didn't matter. That's the problem.

"Not necessary. Thank you, ladies," I answer shortly as I continue toward the private elevator. The doors slide shut once Cole and I enter, revealing the Hunter emblem again as the elevator takes me up to the twenty-first floor. Two more of my security men greet me before they open the double doors to the assembly chamber.

The chamber itself is a perfect hexagon with walls of black glass threaded with emerald streaks. One side gives us the view of the forest and mountain ridges. A black circular table is at the center, large enough to seat twenty-nine. The center is hollow—a four-foot drop that exposes the glowing emerald emblem beneath against the black stone floors. Light from the crest rises through the open circle, casting an ominous glow through the room. As if the snakes in the room aren't deadly enough.

Twenty-seven chairs are occupied and spaced precisely around the outer edge. My seat is the twenty-eighth. I'll never grow tired of seeing the black throne, carved to look as though a dozen or so, massive serpents are bursting from the back and arms, their bodies writhing upward to form the frame. Each snake is made of polished obsidian, their eyes set with blood-red rubies that catch the light from the windows on the other side. At the very top, rearing above the high back, is a white wolf's head carved out of marble stone to represent the Beta Warrior in the seat.

It's a replica of course, of the real throne that's in the throne room of the Palace. That throne is bigger, more imposing, and it has a twin for the Veyara. The replica twin sits empty to the right of mine.

Twenty-seven serpent shifters rise and bow as I enter. Seven Den Lords occupy the seats nearest to mine. The twenty House of Honest representatives, four from each of the five serpent bloodlines fill the remaining seats. Together, they comprise the Den Council.

My bodyguards fan out taking their spots as I cross the floor to my seat. We each have a nameplate, microphone, and notepad in front of us, but most have their electronics available for convenience.

I look around the table before nodding. "Let's get started. Please sit."

Once they do, Novak Veridane, the silver-haired seraph Den Lord, addresses us first, his British accent heavy. "Thank you all for being present. We've assembled here today to discuss the matter of the next Veyara as Princess Rosella's transformation is tonight."

Lord Veridane may be seventy-two, but the power behind his voice is unmistakable. He plays the old, fragile guru act well, but I know that man is a weapon even in his old age. He can destroy everyone in this room with his eyes closed.

His pale blue gaze is on me now. "Four years ago, Beta Warrior, you promised the Den to search for a Mate among the serpent bloodlines, including bloodlines outside of the House of Honest, to give us a true serpent Veyara by Princess Rosella's transformation night. Has the Beta Warrior found another worthy Mating bond to replace the Craving princess as his Veyara?"

The words make my blood run cold. Yeah, I made that promise. Yeah, I spent four goddamn years hunting for a loophole, taking females from every corner of the serpent world into my bed, in hopes to break the Mating bond with *her*. Everyone fell short and I was a fool to think I could defy the Divine—that there was a loophole, or a way out of this for me.

But the thought of someone *replacing* Rose sends a strange chill down my spine, as if every part of my existence loathes even the thought of it. I rarely use my Beta powers, it's more destructive than my serpent abilities, but right now the wolf in me is looking for a fight at the idea of anyone else being my Mate.

I have to face the truth now.

"No. Princess Rosella Craving still is my Divinely chosen Mate, Veyara, and Serpent Nation's next matriarch." My voice is cold, emotionless, because I hate it just as much as they do. Rose has no fucking business being my Veyara—but the Divine chose.

The chamber roars to life. Raiden Daejin, the python Den Lord ruling from Asia, is on his feet first. "She is not a serpent!" He shouts with pure outrage, and I have a hard time figuring out who he thinks he's talking to because I know he wouldn't dare speak to me like that. "A Craving bitch on the basilisk throne is a slap to all of us!"

Corbin Morvain, the rattle Den Lord from my backyard, rises slowly and I already know he's got something to say. "My lord, only a daughter of the serpent line is worthy enough to rule beside the Beta Warrior as his Veyara. The Princess is not originally of the Honest serpent families, therefore she does not qualify." As if any of us have a say in the matter. If anything, Rose is overqualified.

Lady Susan, Rose's own aunt, stands in support of her Den Lord, rising from her seat among House Morvain's delegates. "The Den had agreed to a grace period, yes, but surely the Beta Warrior will not move forward with making the Princess his Veyara. She knows nothing of our ways."

And who's fault is that? If Rose's aunt cared even a little about her, she would've trained Rose well, knowing what waited for her after tonight. No, Susan was first in line four years ago, the moment the deal was struck, offering up her own daughters like sacrifices if it meant keeping Rose off my arm.

"Let me remind you, my mother wasn't a serpent shifter." I don't know why I feel the need to defend Rose's worthiness. I agree with my people.

I tell myself it's not Rose I'm defending, it's my mother. The memory of my parents haunt me, knowing very well they would hate all of this. They would hate me for going against my Mating bond when they fought so hard for theirs.

"And your mother was never accepted by the Den. Your father knew it. It's why he kept her locked up at Coilspire!" Lord Daejin's voice is the one that catches my ear over the rest. I don't react to his words. I can't react.

"The Den will not accept another non-serpent Veyara," a representative of House Osvaron speaks up.

"It's not just about her genetics. She's proven she will not tolerate the needs of serpents—our ways, practices, and lifestyles," Neferon Khaemun, the mamba Den Lord from Africa, adds respectfully. He has a point. Rose is as straight-laced and vanilla as it comes.

Lucero Vassir, the viper Den Lord from South America, smirks. "Maybe it will be a great opportunity to teach the princess a little about our serpent ways, then? Give her a…warm serpent welcoming, no?"

A few chuckles go around the table, but most are too angry to entertain it. It takes everything in me to not slash Vassir's throat for insinuating Rose get passed around by them.

Evren Thane, the youngest Den Lord nearing forty, leans back into his seat and flips a pen through his fingers. He's a boa shifter from Australia and aside from Lord Veridane, he's my only real ally at this table. I don't trust anyone here, but if I had to, it'd be the two of them.

Evren rolls his sharp blue eyes and says, "The Princess has never shown any interest in Den matters, nor has she ever tried engaging in social events at the very least. I won't even mention political ones."

She's never attended social events because I never brought her—

she was never invited because I made sure of it.

"She doesn't want to be the Veyara just as much as we don't want her to be." Nahil Zafir, the cobra Den Lord from the Middle East, nods in agreement with Evren.

"A serpent Veyara or civil war. You gave us your word that you would search the bloodlines," Lord Morvain spews at me and many of the House of Honest delegates murmur, agreeing.

"I did search," I answer, calmly. "Four thousand, six hundred, and twelve female serpents from every continent, every Den, every fucking country." I lean forward a fraction, my hands gripping the serpent heads on the arms of the seat. Four thousand, six hundred, and twelve women over the span of four years. There aren't even that many days in four years. I fucking tried and they know it. It's one of the reasons I didn't care if my *affairs* were exposed, it was proof. "I gave you my word that I would search, and you all gave me *your* word that you will accept whatever the outcome was, come Rose's transformation night."

Raiden mutters, "She'll never be one of us."

"This cannot happen. There are still a few more hours, my lord, maybe you'll find your true Mate—" a representative from House Eryndral starts but I raise my hand to stop her hopeful optimism. It's pathetic.

"However, she is Nathanial's favorite. She has his ear—this could be a good thing," Lord Veridane speaks up and I look at him. There's no trace of nonsense on his face.

"My lord, the princess has already shown you blatant disrespect. She has no regards for you. The Den cannot expect anything from her." Lord Zafir looks at me pointedly. He's big on respect.

"The only thing the Den should expect from a Veyara is an heir," Evren answers in rebuttal, looking bored out of his mind. I can't blame him. "She's a Craving. A child with both Craving and Hunter blood…will be powerful in every right. She is the only one the Beta can have children with."

Ah, another restriction of Warrior Mating bonds. The one that matters and the root of the problem.

"That'd require Mating." Lady Susan lets out a humorless laugh. "The way things have been with the Beta and the princess, that might be a little difficult."

Warriors can only have children with our Mates—we can fuck around all we want, but only our Mates are capable of carrying our offspring. There's a reason why they're Divinely chosen, why their souls are tied to ours, why no one can replace them. They're the only ones strong enough, capable enough to be our equals. Crescents were designed by the Divine and are gifts to the Warriors.

I could have denied Rose of her place—if Shane wouldn't murder me for it first—and taken a serpent wife but when the kids didn't come, it'd be a problem. I'm the only one left in the Hunter line. I don't know what the fuck the previous generation of Warriors were doing—but making babies was not their priority at all. Most of us don't have uncles or brothers to carry the burden.

"I've upheld my end of the deal. You will too," I state, clearly.

They start to speak again, but I'm already headed toward the door. Once I'm in the hallway, I run a hand down my face.

"That bad, huh?" Camille stands up from the bench she's been sitting on and walks over to me as I wait for the elevator.

"Could've been worse. No one died, so we'll take the win." I stare at the numbers rolling above.

"Well, your day is clear. You said to keep it empty after this meeting. You'll have to pick Rose up at ten to take her to the site tonight," Camille informs before turning her blue eyes on me. The elevator doors open and I step inside. She follows. Once the doors close, she steps in front of me, closing the distance between us. "We have plenty of time to celebrate the full Moon…we won't be able to do this after tonight…"

I pry her fingers off my jacket and reach around her to hit the button for the twenty-fourth floor. "Can't. If Rose doesn't require your assistance, you can take the rest of the day off."

She rolls her eyes at that. "You're a fucking serpent shifter. You always have time for sex."

I'm always in the mood for *her* and the way my body is tight and anxious, all I want to do is find Rose. It's normal for male shifters to be on edge as their Mate's transformation nears. It helped when I was away for the mission to rescue Vanessa, but now that I'm at court with Rose so near…I can't think straight.

As the elevator doors open again, I glance at Camille, stepping out onto my office floor. "Take the day off."

There's no escaping the girl I've spent the past six years trying to erase.

Time's up.

8 SANCTUM

Rosella Craving

July 20

We're supposed to wear white on our first shift. It's supposed to represent purity, the birth of our wolf—a new life. I pull on the white robe over my white dress, letting my hair fall in loose waves around my shoulders.

I take a quick picture of the shot of Sungold Tequila I poured. It's my usual go-to because of the citrus edge amplified by the blood mixed into it. I send the picture to Mariella.

Me: *Ready*

Her reply is immediate.

Mariella: *Pregaming without me?! Rude! Good luck!*

Me: *Good luck!*

I take a deep breath, throw the shot back, and shake off the creeping nerves before heading for my door. I find Josh and Shane standing in the corridor mid-conversation.

Josh looks at me and Shane stops talking. They're dressed in their Warrior blue robes, which hang open, revealing nothing underneath except sculpted, bare chests and low-slung loose black pants.

Of course, the men go shirtless on full Moon nights. Of course, they look like they walked out of a magazine shoot for supernatural royalty. If I remember correctly, all the Warriors were featured on Howl Weekly after their first shifts.

Josh's robe is untied, draped around him like he doesn't even notice it. The large tattoo on the left side of his abs peeks through.

Shane clears his throat and adjusts his robe with a lazy roll of his shoulder. "Great, you're ready."

I give him a slow nod. "I am…"

He pulls me into a quick hug, trying not to make a big deal about it. He smells fresh, like he just showered. It's respectful to do so before full Moon nights—or any ritual night.

"Good luck, baby thorn," he says into my ear, "don't be nervous. It's just a part of life. You'll be great." He steps back and offers a crooked smile. "I'll see you after the shift and we'll share our first meal together as shifters."

The hunt. It's tradition to go on a hunt after shifting on a full Moon and share a kill with Packmates. It speaks volumes if the Alpha shares his kill with someone.

But in my case, he is my brother.

He flicks my nose, laughing and then claps Josh on the arm. Something silent passes between them and I wonder if they're communicating telepathically. Shane heads for the staircase without another word, his robe flying behind him.

Josh glances at his watch like this is any other assignment Shane passed off to him. "Let's go then," he says, already turning.

Just like that, my brother's warmth evaporates, replaced with Josh's cold *professionalism*. He doesn't wait for me to follow.

I take a deep breath and try to keep up as my heart pounds against my chest. I guess his professionalism is better than his rudeness. But tonight too? He can't just be nice and…I don't know, friendly, just one night? He knows how important tonight is for a shifter.

I wish my dad was here. I wish I didn't have to shift and be the most vulnerable in front of the one person who hates me. I wish I had someone who loved me.

When we reach the foyer, Cristobal and Franklin are standing at the door. Franklin nods at me and Cristobal gives me a smile.

"Divine be with you, my lady," Franklin says.

I frown, glancing between my bodyguards and Josh, before asking them, "You're not coming? At least to the forest?"

Josh looks at me like I'm slow, but Cristobal answers, "We'll be at the main ritual, but you'll be with the Beta Warrior. You don't need us when you're with him."

I beg to differ.

"He threatened my life," I blurt out. My security is always, always with me. They're an extension of me.

"Five years ago," Josh rolls his eyes, before glaring at me. "You've thrown acid in my face, poisoned my drinks countless times, slashed my tires, left literal shit in my bed, what else was—"

"None of those would've killed you," I glare back at him.

He's immune to poison—they were all done to clearly annoy him. It's the least I could do for all the cheating.

"You held me under water. You know I hate water," I remind him.

He sighs heavily. "We don't have time for this, Rose."

"If anything happens to me, know it's on your hands," I threaten my bodyguards who I can tell are struggling to hide their smiles. I hate them. I hate them all.

I follow Josh out and we start to make our way through the gardens. Little lanterns were placed to light up the cobblestones and I smile seeing them. It's the little things.

People wish me good luck as we pass. Everyone knows tonight's the night for me. I wonder if Mariella's going through the same thing. She's with Antonio and he's probably telling her some joke to make her laugh, keeping her nerves at bay. She doesn't know how lucky she is.

Josh's head of security holds open the car door for me as Josh goes around to get into the driver's seat. I slip inside, thank the bodyguard before the door closes and we're on our way to the forest that borders Cravenhold.

There are two main gates that open into the outside world, and I know we will not be going through either of them. One gate is mainly for the military, hidden within the mountain, while the other is obvious and grander. There are other smaller gates throughout the boundaries for convenience.

Cravenhold is nestled near Mount Mitchell in North Carolina, but far enough from the recreational parks. The majority of the Appalachian is ours, until you get closer to New York—then it's vampire territory.

The threshold, where the forest around Cravenhold begins, is layered with invisible magical defenses. A barrier so thick with enchantments that even the strongest witch couldn't stumble through without someone noticing. Not to mention, the woods are heavily reinforced by generations of Royal Guards.

This border is the last line of defense if enemies ever made it past the other shields deeper into the mountains. Hikers don't get lost and accidentally come upon Cravenhold.

No one gets in unless we let them.

Josh doesn't say a word in the twenty-minute drive it takes for us to reach the forest. He parks the car when we approach the northwestern edge, his gaze sharp, but unworried. A part of me is relieved that he chose this side of the woods. I notice the two Royal Guards hovering just inside the tree line. They're wearing black robes with the gold insignia of Cravenhold—they're shirtless too. Normally they'd be in wolf form, but since tonight's the full Moon, they're waiting for Nathanial's howl.

When I realize Josh isn't going to open the car door for me, I get out and follow him. One guard nods at Josh while the other doesn't move.

Josh steps into the forest and so do I, passing the shield. It doesn't feel like I walked through anything. It's not supposed to. These woods are an extension of Cravenhold, we're supposed to feel safe in them. Especially on first shift nights when we're at our most vulnerable.

"Try not to get lost," Josh says over his shoulder.

This whole thing feels like an inconvenience for him, but I keep my mouth shut. I have bigger things to worry about than Josh's mood right now. That's when I realize exactly where we are, where I was hoping we'd be. Through the trees, set just off the path and half-wrapped in vines, is the Sanctum.

"Wait!" I call out to him.

Josh stops, confused, but I dart off the path. The arches rise tall from the earth—ancient stones, carved with old symbols we no longer use in our practices—pave the path.

The energy is immediately different as if walking into a portal to another world as I pass under the arches, before entering the courtyard.

It's not large, not even fancy like the rest of Cravenhold. Three trees stand guard as a small stream of water flows straight through the courtyard. It isn't a grand temple, or a cathedral people would imagine to be at a royal court. It's simple. Humble. Bare. Just dirt and stone and earth.

At the center stands the seven feet tall Labradorite stone—or Betty as I like to call it, though I would never let Lady Tiara or Aunt Susan hear me say it out loud. Everyone just calls it the Sanctum Stone.

It's not glamorous. It's not sparkly or made of crystal that lights up when the Sun hits it right. It's a moldy, greenish black color—like an old, *old*, coin covered in years of dirt and decay. The surface is rough even from centuries of hands reaching for it. There are no carvings or inscriptions—not like the arches. Betty is just an old stone. But it's so much more.

I've sat here on the benches as a little girl many times and stared at this stone enough to notice that when the Sun *does* hit it right, a flicker of a variety of colors shine through. Like the Aurora Borealis is trapped inside. Like magic is trapped inside.

I reach out and the moment my fingers press against it, a sharp tingle blooms across my skin, flowing deeper into my blood—my soul. It crawls up my arm, settling into my chest and relaxing my brain while my toes curl from my nerves coming to life.

I let the feeling hold me for a moment, closing my eyes. Once the tingles settle and start to retreat, I open my eyes. I'm surprised to find Josh beside me with his own eyes closed and palm on Betty, inches away from where mine was. He takes a deep breath, his chest rising before his broad shoulders fall.

With a motion so natural, it feels ritualistic, he pulls his hand away and runs it over the top of his head—like he's bathing in the stone's blessings.

My eyes are fixed on him. I've always known Josh was spiritual—most Warriors are—but I've never seen this side of him. I've seen him at rituals, performing or leading them, but this is intimate. My heartstrings pull as my skin tingles for a whole other reason—our stupid Mating bond.

Josh steps back, expressionless, and says, "Let's go."

Then he starts walking in the direction of the arches, leading the way out like he didn't completely rearrange the air around us.

9 MOON'S CALL

Rosella Craving

July 20

We walk in silence for another thirty minutes. The only sound is the wind threading through the trees and the occasional snap of a branch from an animal or our own feet. He doesn't look back. Not once to even see if I'm behind him.

He leads. I follow.

The forest opens, trees parting into a wide clearing, and Josh comes to a stop.

The Moon's glow spills down in a perfect, sacred spotlight over a dark flowing stream. It's so clear that I can see the sky reflected on its surface. Soft moss and wildflowers blanket the ground in little patches, interrupted only by smooth stones and gnarled roots. A weeping willow tree leans toward the water's edge, its long branches swaying like curtains in the night air.

It feels…Holy.

I've lived in Cravenhold my whole life and I've never seen this clearing before. I know these woods. I grew up running through them, sneaking around with Mariella and Daniya, but we never came across this place.

"Divine," I whisper, the words slipping out before I can stop them. My breath catches as I turn to Josh. "It's beautiful here."

Josh's expression shifts, like I caught him off guard. His jaw ticks, and he looks away toward the stream. I reach down to pluck a small daisy, twirling it in my hand to have something to do while we wait for the shift to begin.

"My mom used to bring my brother and me here on our visits to Cravenhold," he finally says in a low voice. "I shifted here for my first time too."

My heart stutters. This place means something to him.

"This place is special to you," I say softly, touched that he brought me here. It's the nicest gesture he's ever made toward me. Josh doesn't do anything without a reason, so I ask, "Why *did* you bring me here?"

His eyes flicker over to meet mine. "I didn't plan to. I was going to take you to one of the ritual grounds on the east side," he says, which makes sense. It'd be closer to the main ritual ground where everyone is at right now. Logically, it makes sense, but for two seconds it was nice to think he took the time to plan this for me.

"Oh," I say, breaking our gaze to look anywhere but at him. I hate that it hurts, that even after all this time, a part of me still hopes.

"I don't know…felt like this is where we needed to be tonight," he adds, his voice tightens, like it's hard for him to get the words out. "This place *is* special. I don't bring anyone here."

I look back at him and he's watching me with his usual hard expression, but there's something else in his gray eyes. The way his careful gaze is on me, seeing how I behave in his space…it didn't need to be said this place is special. I can tell the way he's uncomfortable with me being here, like he's sharing a piece of himself unwillingly.

I don't know what to say after that. He's clearly irritated by whatever instinct led him here tonight. I don't miss the way his eyes follow me as I turn back toward the weeping willow—how he tracks my movement, like he's trying to figure out whether or not I'm worthy of being here.

I step out of my sandals, letting my feet sink into the mossy earth, grounding myself. My head tilts back and I close my eyes to soak in the Moonlight as it spills across my face, my hair, my hands, every part of me.

Any minute now, my first transformation will be triggered.

I look back at Josh and am met with his stare. He's still watching me. I don't ponder on that, and tell him, "Thank you."

He narrows his eyes but doesn't say anything.

Then we wait.

Josh sits on a fallen log a few feet away, elbows on his knees, deep in thought—or pretending to be. I pace, my robe swaying around my legs as I try to keep the nerves from getting the best of me.

The last thing I need right now is to be overstimulated. I look up at the Moon. It's high, but not high enough. I clear my throat. "So…what did you do with the Veins?"

Josh glances at me, raising an eyebrow. "Flushed it."

I blink. "I know you're a prince and money is no object, but that stuff is hard to get your hands on."

"You said you didn't want it anyway. What difference does it make to you?" he replies coldly.

"Emotional support," I mutter. Would've been nice to know it was there…just in case…a safety net.

"Tempting," he replies, "but you're not the only one with nerves tonight."

"You *would* make my transformation night about you," I say under my breath, but I know he hears me with his wolf ears.

"It is about me," the asshole says seriously. "You're *my* Mate and I have to be here."

"Well," I square my shoulders and turn away from him, "feel free to leave and not make it about you."

We both know he can't. He'll just circle back because our lives are on the line if I don't survive my shift. I won't survive without him.

My arms wrap around my stomach to hold myself. I'm not cold. I'm…scared. I look up at the Moon again, this time wishing my mom was here. I wish I didn't feel so alone waiting to get through tonight. The shift is going to hurt. I know that. I've known it my whole life. Everyone talks about how painful it is. Almost every woman I know says it's worse than childbirth. However, it's not just the transformation I'm worried about.

It's what Devaughn said. What comes after. The rest of the night as a human after our first shift is almost as painful as the shift itself.

For Warrior men it's a rite of passage. It's honorable to go through the second round of pain. For Crescents…it's pitiful. A woman is supposed to have her Mate the first night—the entire night. Her Mate isn't just supposed to help her survive the shift. He's supposed to help her through it. It's meant for Mating. It's painful because not going through the process is going against the Divine's first chance for a Mated pair to honor their bond by Marking.

Being the Mate of a Warrior has always felt like a curse to me—but even more tonight. Regular shifter females don't have to worry about this. Yes, their shift hurts too, but the night isn't as bad if they don't have their Mate—most do, because why wouldn't you, but for those who choose not to, I've heard it being compared to really bad muscle pains.

"You'll be okay," Josh says quietly, cutting into my thoughts.

"How bad can it be if you survived it?" I reply, not trusting his words of comfort for a second.

His lips curve up the faintest bit. Is he smiling? He's really smiling.

I turn away from him before I say something else a lot meaner. Of course, he wants me to be in pain. It's probably the main reason he's here right now. To watch me suffer.

My body is about to be torn apart and put back together in more than one form. Daniya said it's not about having sex afterwards as a pain distraction—there's a reason why a female needs her Mate through the night. It's the magic in our Mating bond since Warriors' Mates are chosen through the blood-tie union and what's more magical than having sex.

Which now that I think about it, makes me wonder if my case will be the same. My Mating bond with Josh wasn't created through the blood-tie union. Maybe Josh is right. Maybe I will be okay.

"How bad will it hurt?" I ask, turning back to look at him.

He seems to think about it for a moment, before saying, "Think of the worst pain you ever felt."

"That's easy..." I say as he stands up and takes a few steps toward me.

"What is it?"

I frown. Does he really need to ask that?

"My parents," I answer, "their death."

He nods, acknowledging it. "I meant physically," he rephrases as he nears.

I hold his gaze. "You didn't think losing your parents was a physical pain?"

"Fair enough," he responds and the message is clear. He doesn't want to talk about that. It's fine because I don't want to talk about it with him either. He didn't let me be there for him when his parents died, and he certainly wasn't there for me when mine passed, so there's no point in talking about it now.

He comes to stand in front of me, saying, "When the Moon reaches its highest point in the sky, you'll start feeling restless and uncomfortable. This feeling that your body is being pulled in every direction will start taking over and that's when it'll start."

I nod. I know this. I'm the last of the royal children to shift. Mariella and I are the last of the Warriors' Mates to transform. We've collected stories to prepare for tonight. I just know it wasn't enough.

"It's just tonight, Rose," Josh reminds me. "It's a lot different when you transform on your own, without the Moon's first pull." I also know this, so I nod again. "How are you feeling?" he asks, almost softly, if that's an attribute that can be assigned to Josh Hunter.

I meet his gray eyes that are lighter than usual and say, "I'm fine."

He doesn't buy it for a second. "So, we're going to start this with lying?"

I purse my lips as he takes another step closer to me. I have to raise my head to look up at him. He's too close. What is he doing?

"Well, now I'm confused why you're in my personal space," I say slowly and make the mistake of dropping my eyes to his lips. No. Nope.

"Try again," he says, licking said lips.

Why does he want me to admit I'm scared? That I'm terrified?

I drop my gaze on the grass between us. We're almost toe-to-toe and that's when I realize he's taken off his shoes too.

"I think…it's just nerves," I tell him, downplaying it. I can tell he's resisting to roll his eyes as he tilts his head up to the Moon.

I will not admit to Josh Hunter that I'm terrified. I spent so much time hating him for not being a normal Mate, hating him for not being able to have the kind of relationship Eliza and Shane has. Josh always kept his distance, and it made sense because he's six years older than me. I was almost twelve when he shifted for the first time. But then his brother died, and that changed everything. Josh woke up a new person and for whatever reason, I was the target for his anger. I was his punching bag—not physically, never physically, because that'd require him to voluntarily touch me. No, his words were bad enough and then the cheating came.

It *broke* my heart. I think it might've even broken a part of me that I'll never get back even if things are better between us.

We used to fight a lot. Publicly. The world witnessed his betrayal and my hurt. I didn't know how to deal with it so young. Sometimes I still don't.

It got ugly and I can't remember how we even got there. I don't know how we got it so wrong, why he's always been cold, distant, or outright hating me.

I can't remember what I did to warrant that from him. I asked him. I demanded answers. It wasn't until after our last public fight in January when I left court to go on the Royal Tour and put distance between us, that I realized I was never going to get any clarity from him.

Going on Tour of shifter communities, learning to be a Warrior's

Mate, the physical training, and spending a whole lot of time with a certain vampire prince, was one of the best and worst things I could've done for myself and my relationship with Josh. It opened my eyes, gave me distance from Josh, but physically…it felt like the Mating bond itself was cursing me.

Distance and time away from our Mates is physically painful for both parties. That's why most Warriors want their Mates to be trained in combat so the Crescents can go on missions with them. It's like having a built-in side-kick for the Warriors. I don't know who made these stupid rules. They're very inconvenient.

In a way, my pride loved that Josh was hurting too. That for once I could physically hurt him back.

After I returned, our fights became indirect. Like the vipers and him texting me about it. I've learned to not react angrily and just give him a taste of his own medicine. When we have to appear together, that's exactly what it is—an appearance. Like my birthday—without all the testosterones. If cameras are there, we portray the Beta-Veyara couple. If they are not, Josh can usually be found with a serpent woman on his arms and I'm with my friends trying whatever new drug Devaughn brings.

"It's starting," Josh barely whispers, and panic rises in my chest, bringing me out of my thoughts. He sees it in my eyes because he closes the little distance between us. "Don't reject it. Welcome the transformation. It's easier if you do."

I frown as a strange pressure builds. Like something is trying to stretch and pull me from the inside out. My bones—oh, Divine, my bones—feel like they're pulling away from each other.

Then the pain hits.

It's sharp and deep and all kinds of *wrong*. My body isn't mine anymore. I turn and double over, arms wrapped tight around my stomach as bile threatens in my throat. Oh my Divine, I cannot throw up in front of Josh.

He pulls out a small potion bottle from his pocket, before placing his hand on my back, urging me to stand up straight.

"Here," he says, unscrewing the dropper that's keeping the bottle closed. "Open your mouth. It'll ease the pain."

I hesitate, but when another wave of agony courses through me, my jaw opens before I can think twice about it. He tips the liquid contents onto my tongue—bitter, slightly sweet. Almost instantly, a cool tingling sensation spreads through my chest. My heart rate steadies and my stomach eases.

"What is it?" I ask.

"Poppy and blackberries," he answers. "Lady Zia's idea. I suggested weed…"

I frown. "You what?"

He nods seriously. "It's natural. Not like that Veins shit. Shane said it works."

"My brother was high when he transformed?!" I blink at him.

Josh just shrugs like it's the most obvious thing to do. Honestly? It's not a bad idea. I'm surprised Daniya didn't suggest it. Josh is right, it is a better alternative to Veins…though I can't imagine it being strong enough. Not like Veins from what I hear.

"Poppies have pain-relieving properties. It is an opiate. Blackberries are good for afterwards. For anti-inflammatory," Josh explains, then adds, "and it tastes better than Veins or weed. This is better for you."

The words do something strange to my heart. The pain is still there, but it's not as sharp or raw. Josh moves closer. His fingers slide through my hair, brushing it away from my neck. His touch is light, almost caring and despite my body feeling like it's morphing, his touch sends sparks down my spine. The feeling is so overwhelming, so foreign, that I nearly buckle, my knees giving out. His touch is comforting, the only thing that feels right while my body feels…not like my body.

"Does it still hurt?" he asks, gently. His hand lingers at my neck, thumb caressing my jawline, and I hate how starved I am for his touch.

I couldn't even comprehend what I was missing no matter how much I didn't want him to touch me. How much I still don't want him to touch me with those hands that have touched everyone else. It hurts. This push and pull will kill me if this transformation doesn't.

"There's more, but you shouldn't have too much in your system." Is he still talking about the potion?

"It hurts, but not as bad," I manage between breaths. He starts to pull his hand away when I catch it, sending sparks through me again on impact. He looks down at our hands and meets my eyes. I bite my lip, suppressing my pride, before whispering, "No…"

He understands. I think he's still going to pull away, but instead he cups my face just as a howl cuts through the mountains. Josh leans in, his citrus smoky spice scent invading my nostrils and surprisingly relaxing me as he presses his lips to my ear. "It's in your blood, Veyara."

My eyes snap to him. Josh has never called me Veyara.

The words are cruel because he knows what it means for him to say that to me. For him to acknowledge it like it's always been my birthright, that I was always meant to be with him…it's just mean right now. But there's no cruelty in his eyes as he eases my robe off my shoulders, letting it slip to the forest floor. Then he slowly steps back, giving both of us space for what comes next.

Pain.

Pain so sharp that it forces me to my knees.

My spine arches back violently and I *hear* something snap. Every nerve in my body is on fire and on edge like rolling in shards of broken glass. My skin feels too tight, as if trying to keep me contained. And my bones…they begin to split and grind, realigning in the most agonizing of ways.

I can't hold it back anymore.

My screams echo into the night, but I don't hear it. I only feel how my muscles rip, how my ribs crack and reshape. I taste blood in my mouth as my teeth enlarge. My hands dig into the dirt, clawing for something to anchor me—anything. My legs split open. My lungs collapse and rebuild in the same breath.

Nothing could've prepared me for this.

No amount of potions, prayers, or poppies would've been enough.

"Rose," Josh's voice invades my mind, becoming the only thing that makes sense in this pain.

Everything else makes me want to disappear, but his voice is like the light at the end of the tunnel and so help me Divine, I reach for it. I manage to lift my head and open my eyes. Everything is blurry and sharp at the same time. My senses are heightened. Eliza said that was the first sign—after the pain.

The forest around me is *glowing*. I can hear everything.

Then my eyes lock on a pair of gray Moonlit orbs. Josh shifted into his magnificent wolf.

I've seen his wolf form many times, but never this close. He towers over me and I finally understand why Warriors are so revered in our world. They're bigger than any shifter, any wolf, I've ever seen. If I was human, I'd barely come up to his shoulder.

His power vibrates off him and his snow-white fur glows—as if the Moon came down and is standing before me.

In that moment, our Mating bond ignites, awakes from its subtle connection—from the invisible thread that's always tied us together. Though I know, logically, the Mating bond fully completes when he Marks me…this feels like the beginning to reach that point. A promise awakening.

A golden light flickers around our bodies, faint at first before growing stronger and more vibrant. It reminds me of a new blooming yellow poppy, wide, soft, and shining. It opens, the center cradling the space between us, like a halo circling us both.

From the blossom, a stem of light stretches out immediately from both of our chests. They instantly find each other and join as if they were never truly separate. The golden thread that's always connected us, that I always imagined to be like a mesh of spider silk, solidifies before our eyes.

And then it grows.

The thread weaves outward, expanding until it surrounds us both in a cocoon of golden light. There's nothing between Josh and me anymore, the glowing thread shifts around almost as if it's protecting us.

It feels like what I'd imagine being in a womb.

This…this is what I always thought our souls looked like in the Heavens before it was split in two. Now it's found its way back to its other half.

A rejoining—not a reunion.

Divine, is this what it truly means to be Mated? It's beautiful.

I don't even realize when it's happened, being entranced by our Mating bond, but my transformation is complete. My bones have realigned, reshaped. My lungs expand fully for the first time in what feels like hours. My paws—all four of them—touch the damp ground.

The gold cocoon around us dissolves, fading into the air, leaving the invisible cord between us stronger than before.

I blink, a little disoriented, but alive. Josh is staring at me, like he can't believe what just happened either. Then he blinks too and takes a step back, while I stagger on my new paws. My body feels extremely foreign to myself, but also terrifyingly right. Everything feels…alive and sharp.

I glance at the water's edge, and stare at the reflection back at me—

snow white fur, same strange gray eyes except they're brighter now.

A pure *white* wolf. The Warriors' breed. Only Warriors shift into a white wolf, as their Divine birthright. And Warriors have always been men.

Wouldn't it be crazy if you shifted into a Warrior? The prince had said. Did he know? How could he though?

When I raise my head to look at Josh, his shock slams into me. He hasn't taken his eyes off my new form.

"I always said you were a freak of nature because of those eyes…" he takes a speculative step forward, ***"turns out you actually are one."***

10 PACKMATES

Rosella Craving

July 20

Freak.

His words claw into me. I didn't choose this. Being a female Warrior is impossible.

My ears flatten as heat crawls up my throat at his statement. Still so cruel. Even in this moment.

He takes a few steps closer and as he does, the power emitting off him feels like the air around me is forcing me into submission. My shoulders sag and head lowers. I focus on my paws. My white paws.

I see Josh stop right in front of me and I think he's going to make some asshole comment about me bowing to him.

A Craving does not bow to a Hunter.

Instead, he nudges me with his snout. Even in our wolf forms, the sparks light up my nerves.

"Lift your head. You're my Mate, you don't bow to me," he telepaths. His words are a command, almost a scolding, but my heart…my stupid little heart.

I look up to meet his gaze and find him staring back at me. He means it. My chest tightens, wanting to burst with…joy? Happiness? Confusion?

He just called me a freak and is now elevating me. I'm getting whiplash here. I stand up. Or try to, but my legs give out and I fall. Josh nudges my side, urging me.

"Try again," he thinks to me and I almost break. This is the kindest he's been to me since…since the towers in Coilspire when he took me to see the clouds over six years ago.

I try again and try to stop the shaking in my legs. Eventually, I'm stable enough to stand up.

"Think you can walk a little bit?" he asks, watching me—or my legs—closely.

"I think so," I reply, trying it out.

"Time to see your brother," he says, gesturing me to follow him.

Josh maintains a slower pace, letting me comfortably keep up. I'm not the same size as him—smaller, yes—but everything sits lower, stretched differently. I'm bigger than anything else in the forest. Taller than my five-six human form.

Josh leads us through the thick woods for about thirty-five minutes before we come across another clearing. This one is not as serene as the one we were at, but I know it's closer to Cravenhold. I can hear the drums nearby from the main ritual site, and the sound of the river rushing.

This clearing is lit up with torches and there's an obvious giant pentagon etched into the ground. This is the Warrior's ritual ground.

At the front and center, there is a white wolf even larger than Josh and I know it's my brother. Around him are four other white wolves, smaller than Josh but still much bigger than me. Antonio is not here—he's with Mariella for her transformation.

They all freeze as we come into view. Most are staring as if I'm an alien and they are full of amazement, curiosity, and apprehension for what this means. I glance at Shane, but he seems to be having an intense conversation with Josh telepathically, his eyes focused on my Mate.

"You did it, Rose!" Daniel's excited voice exclaims in my head, and if wolves can smile, I think he's grinning at me. The definition of a wolfish grin if I ever saw one.

I wish I could say their presence is comforting, safe, but it's not. It's unsettling, because they're all quiet.

Too quiet.

I shift my weight, my paws sinking slightly into the soil, and even though the summer night is refreshing against my fur, the heat beneath my skin does little for my anxiety.

Then Josh, who is standing beside me, takes a step forward. A growl rumbles deep in his throat. His lips pull back to expose his fangs as he bares his teeth at the other Warriors.

They *are* communicating telepathically but blocked me out.

"What's going on?" I ask Josh. He doesn't respond, so I try my brother.

Shane, however, is busy growling back at Josh, while Devaughn and James position themselves between their Alpha and Beta. James and Devaughn seem to be the same size, just a little smaller than Josh, which is expected. The Alpha and Beta are always larger than the rest of the Pack.

Josh doesn't stand down, but instead fully shields me to the point that I can't see anything or anyone. His entire body blocks my view of the others, and theirs of me.

I feel his rage radiating through our bond—something I wasn't able to sense before. Before, if one of us were injured physically, then the other would be too. If one of us were threatened, the other would feel it too.

This is…different.

I don't know what changes, but I can start hearing their conversation.

"Why don't you fucking tell her then?" Josh's voice floods my mind. He's speaking to Shane, baring his teeth too as if he's about to attack any second. ***"She can hear just fine."***

Sam and Daniel look just as confused as I am.

"Are we seriously going to do this right now?" Devaughn asks. He and James are facing *Josh*, protecting Shane if anything, but also trying to create a barrier between their two leaders.

"You have no right!" Shane snaps at Josh, and Devaughn takes a step toward Josh.

"Let's all just take a breather—"

"Shut up, Sam," James rudely cuts off our Pack peace-keeper.

My brother stands taller, walking toward Josh, but Josh says, ***"I have every right. Either you tell your sister, or I will tell my Mate."***

Shane growls louder, saliva dripping from his mouth.

"Tell me what?" I ask and get ignored.

"Stand the fuck down," Shane says with finality.

Instead of doing that, Josh lunges for him.

Everything after that happens too quickly. The second Josh's feet lift off the ground, so does Shane's. James is quick. He tackles Josh and throws him across the clearing, but Josh sprints back to get to Shane again as Daniel comes to stand in front of me. He's protecting me, I realize. He's protecting me—from my Mate.

"Stop it!" Sam shouts, running with Devaughn to meet Josh. Josh dodges Sam and knocks Devaughn out of the way. James charges toward Josh again as Shane stands his ground, furious. Josh is out for blood.

I watch as James opens his mouth as he lunges for Josh and I don't know why, but I run.

"Rose!" Shane shouts and this time his anger is replaced with cold fear.

I run straight into James, pushing him out of Josh's way so he doesn't take a chunk out of my Mate. I wasn't thinking, and James isn't as fluffy as his fur makes him look. I also land incredibly wrong. James growls at me ferociously and is instantly on his feet. I, on the other hand, am seeing stars and my already sore body hurts even more.

Shane is at my side as everything comes to a stop. ***"Are you okay?"***

I blink and realize I am actually seeing stars. The sky is lit with thousands of them. It's so pretty.

"Rose!" Shane shouts and if wolves could groan, that's what I do. He nudges me and I manage to get to my feet. Everything hurts.

"What is going on? Tell me what? Did you guys know I'd shift into a Warrior?" I ask them, but I'm mainly talking to Shane and Josh. While Shane is next to me and most of the wolves are on his side, Josh stands alone.

He looks at me, only me, and I frown. I start to take a step toward him, but he turns around and disappears into the forest.

What. The. Fuck. He's just going to leave me?

"No, seriously, what the Hell was that?" Daniel asks the boys.

"This is unprecedented," James thinks.

"But are we really surprised? Rose always had gray eyes. Even before Noah's death. This was Divinely planned from the beginning," Sam states as if reciting from some codex.

Noah?

I haven't heard that name in a long time.

Josh's brother would've been the eighth Warrior. The Warrior Pack is always an even number to maintain balance and for their protection. Is that what this is about?

But I was born with gray eyes before Noah died, like Sam just said.

"I'm going to say this once," Shane speaks, using his Alpha voice, ***"I understand Rose being a white wolf is a shock, but it is not our place to question the Divine, or what fate has planned. This path was chosen for Rose. As Warriors, it is our duty to uphold Divine Decree. Do not forget your oaths."***

"She's our Veyara. The serpents might not respect that, but we will protect our own," Devaughn seconds.

The level of loyalty the Warriors have shown me in the past five minutes is more than Josh ever has in eighteen years of my life. It still doesn't explain what he wanted Shane to tell me.

"Alright, let's hunt," Shane announces as if the fight with Josh was nothing.

"Fucking finally, I'm starving." Daniel rolls his eyes and is the first to move out of their formation. He trots over to me. ***"Man, Antonio's going to be so pissed he missed the showdown."***

Shane cuts Daniel a scolding look. The others start to scatter as James howls into the sky.

"Let's get some food in you. The first shift takes a lot from us," Shane says to me.

"Shane—"

"Drop it, Rose," he uses his Alpha voice and I have no choice. It's infuriating that he can just do that and it's end of discussion.

"What about Josh?" I ask instead.

"Let him cool off, he'll be back. Where is he going to go?" Shane answers me before heading into the woods.

I don't know if I should go after Josh, but Daniel makes my decision as he nudges me forward. Our speed picks up and I slip into the rhythm of the run, my paws pounding against the earth and it feels exhilarating. The forest feels alive in a way I've never experienced it. Every scent, every change around me, every heartbeat of the animals near me is a part of me.

Daniel bumps my shoulder mid-run, a twinkle in his gray eyes. ***"Since no one has manners, I'll be the first to welcome you into our humble Pack."***

Devaughn joins in on Daniel's other side, telepathing, ***"You belong with us."***

Sam's voice threads softly through my mind too. ***"Don't worry, Rose. For now, we feast."***

Then we take off, breaking through the trees. We make our way, navigating with our sharpened senses. The smell of adrenaline is thick in the air. I can't believe how fast I'm going. The others are a blur around me, but I can easily spot them out. I knew Warriors were fast, but this is…incredible.

We slow down as I pick up on other heartbeats. The herd is nearby. Hidden below a moss-covered ridge, a cluster of antelope grazes under the Moonlight unaware of us closing in from all around.

Shane signals with a low growl and Devaughn peels left. James and

Sam move to the right. I instinctively match their strides as we ease into position. Every muscle in my body is alert.

Then Shane strikes.

The Pack explodes from cover, wolves bolting. Chaos unfolds and the antelopes begin to scatter. Devaughn clips one on the leg, before I see Daniel cutting off its escape. Sam pounces on another, knocking it down before he goes for the kill.

Shane has already caught the biggest one and is waiting for me

"Come on, baby thorn, don't make your Alpha wait," he jokes, inviting me. I sink my teeth into the antelope's neck—blood gushing down my throat.

I don't think about how its heart slows or how its eyes go still. All I can think about is how the warm blood tastes like hot fudge of all things.

Hot fudge.

The blood sprays across the forest floor and Shane's pristine white fur, but he doesn't seem to mind as he sinks his teeth in too.

I used to hide under this long, cold table occasionally when my father would be in Warrior meetings. He'd pretend I wasn't there, then surprise me once everyone left the room.

The war room is soundproof, with high arched windows. The curtains are closed tonight even though the glass is only one way. The light…Divine, the fluorescent light is too bright for 2 AM.

All the Elders and Crescents are here, dressed in their ceremonial full Moon robes. The Elders do not seem happy to have their night interrupted by Warrior business. Antonio and Mariella are still absent. Josh has rejoined us at the last second, and occupies the seat to my right.

Shane had called the meeting after our feast.

Lady Zia Rage, serene as ever, sits with her hands folded, whispering softly with Lady Victoria—Sam's mom. High Priestess Lady Tiara sits beside Aunt Susan, observing the room. My aunt's eyes are fixed on me. Eliza winks at me, clearly Shane's filled her in through their Mating bond, as have the other Warriors because their Mates are watching me curiously.

I'm shocked to see Vanessa Tens at the table. I guess she's back from her two-year mission that drove James insane. Vanessa isn't just a Crescent, but she's also one of Serpent Nation's top military generals. Her brown eyes dart back and forth between Josh, James, and me. Her black hair is in a high ponytail that's braided and hangs over her shoulder. She looks like a Warrior if anything. No one fusses about her being here, making me wonder when she returned? James and Vanessa weren't at my party last night.

Daniya looks positively bored as if her best friend shifting into a white wolf isn't at all surprising to her. Her lack of curiosity reminds me of what the prince said. My wolf form shouldn't come as a shock.

Nathanial is the last to arrive. He takes one sweep of the room before settling into his seat at the head of the table. His eyes go straight to Shane.

"Well? Why are we here?" Nathanial asks my brother, his tone leaving no room for beating around the bush.

Shane doesn't. He's standing, ready to address everyone gathered. "Tonight, Rose shifted into the Warrior Pack, and we gained our eighth and last member."

No one speaks. Seconds pass by and I grow uneasy. Then everything explodes at once. The Elders fall into a debate, directing questions at the Warriors. I look at Nathanial who ever so subtly winks at me. Mischief is in the corners of his ageless gray eyes. There's a small smile playing on his lips, but he doesn't speak. He's taking it all in, watching how everyone reacts.

"Impossible!"

"A female can't be a Warrior!"

"You must be mistaken."

"This is a violation of…natural order!"

"Abomination!"

All around us, there's a riot. Elder Claws reaches for a book of records, while Aunt Susan starts whispering furiously to Uncle. He's calm, unreactive to whatever she's saying. Lady Tiara is watching me as if she's trying to read me—which is highly probable. Don't they know I had no choice in this?

We never get to decide what we shift into—that's always been determined by our bloodlines.

The Warriors remain silent, but Shane speaks again. His voice cuts through the commotion. "Did you not hear me?" My brother looks ticked off. As Alpha, it must be irritating to repeat himself. "Rose is a

Warrior. It doesn't matter *how.* If you want to sit here and debate it, do so. It won't change the reality of the situation. It's best we strategize how we move forward with this."

"You can't seriously be supporting a little girl—"

"The Veyara," Shane corrects, cutting our aunt off. "You will use her appropriate title, unless you choose to use Warrior Craving instead."

"Threatening the Veyara would be a direct threat to me," Josh speaks in a low voice, for the first time since we've been here. He looks up, his eyes pinning Aunt Susan in place. Josh has never liked my aunt, even before he became Beta.

Elder Claws shakes his head, looking around the table before settling on Josh and me. "No one is threatening—"

"She's not the Veyara yet," my aunt cuts him off to say through gritted teeth.

"On the contrary," James interjects, bored, "she's been the Veyara since their Mating bonds connected eighteen years ago. So please, explain your pointless rebuttal."

In human form, James has long black hair that comes down to his shoulders, his gray eyes are the most intimidating of all of them. James is known to be a notorious killing machine, but James is also one of Josh and Shane's best friends. I'm surprised he's defending me. I always got the sense that he wasn't my biggest fan. Whatever his opinion of me is, James is right.

Challenging a Mating bond is bold. As an Elder, my aunt knows that.

Elder Claws nods once to Josh, clearing his throat. "Apologies, you're right. No one is threatening the Veyara. However, she could be used to start a rebellion. We're wondering if *she* will be a threat to everything we stand for."

A rebellion by who? Shifterkind doesn't have a civil war like the vampires. Unless he's referring to the felines…or the serpents…

Prides are led by women. I can see how they might want to use me as their poster child.

Serpents are very protective of their way of life—a life I don't know much about if I'm being honest. The little I do know has scared the shit out of me.

"Which is what, exactly?" Shane's voice rings clear across the room. "Upholding the Divine Decree bestowed on us? If that's what this is about—then there isn't even a discussion here."

Silence settles again. Nathanial still doesn't speak. Neither does my uncle.

"Frankly," Shane continues, "I don't care what any of you *think*. I stand by the Divine's decision. The Warriors' time will be spent ensuring Rose's integration into the Warrior Pack is smooth and easy for *everyone*."

"This news will be volatile...we have to maintain a united front. The press will have a field day with this," Sam announces but the voices start to become distant as my vision slowly blurs.

The fire in my muscles is coming back, a slow ache but growing and spreading from the base of my spine. I try to sit straighter, but it hurts. My eyes are fighting to stay open against the sharp, bright light. I can't hold myself up much longer.

Josh rises from his chair suddenly, and all eyes turn to him. "We're done here," he announces. "Rose *shifted* tonight. I don't care to sit through a debate that'll go nowhere. She needs to rest."

Without waiting for a response, Josh looks down, offering me his hand. I hesitate, before my fingers slide into his, sparks flying between our touch. There's no teasing in his expression, nothing cruel. I let him help me up, my legs barely steady beneath me. Then together, we leave the war room.

In the hallway, the walls begin to tilt though. My legs buckle without warning and Josh's arms catch me mid-collapse, steadying me.

"You're burning up," he murmurs but before I can say anything, he picks me up—bridal style. "It'll be faster if you let me carry you," he says, logically.

He leaves no room for argument because he's right. The world blurs past me in flashes and we're in my room before I know it. He asks me something, but I can't comprehend the words as pain surges through me again. My brain is foggy. I am hot and sore, and everything feels...too much.

I let the darkness consume me as I feel my body sinking into the familiar softness of my bed before a cool, damp cloth is placed on my forehead. He forces my mouth open to let the poppy and blackberry tonic into my system. Then there's a damp feeling on my feet. Is he...is he cleaning my feet?

"Why—why are you being nice to me?" I manage to say, but the words come out mumbled like I'm drunk. His answer is far, far away as I drift out again.

I don't know how much time passes, but I'm in and out of consciousness.

At some point I feel my bed dip before Josh's arms pull me into him. I know it's him because of the tingles, and even though I'm burning up, his body soothes my pain, but it's not nearly enough relief.

Beggers can't be choosy, though.

"What…what are you…you're here?" I ask with eyes closed.

"I told you," he starts saying. He's so close, his voice is low in my ear, "you won't be alone tonight."

11 CLAIM HER. BREED HER. MARK HER.

Josh Hunter
July 21

I wring out the towel in the bowl of ice water that's sitting on her nightstand, before pressing it to her forehead. Her skin is slick with sweat and her breathing is shallow. She twitches, murmuring something I can't make out. Another fever dream.

I exhale, dragging my hand down my face. It's four in the morning and I haven't slept. This whole night's felt like an out-of-body experience—as if I've been moving through a fog since the moment we walked into the forest.

It started with the pull to the clearing. My clearing.

I was on autopilot the second we left her home. I never planned to bring her there. Not ever. That place is off limits. It's not a place I ever intended on sharing with anyone.

But it…called to me. I hated the idea, but I had to listen to it.

She took a detour, of course, to the Sanctum. She ran straight to the Sanctum Stone like she was going to say hi to a personal friend. I watched her lay her hand on it, and something tugged at my chest. Like the Divine knew I needed to see her have that moment. I didn't know she believed like that.

It took me by surprise.

I didn't realize how much seeing her connection to spirit would affect me. I didn't know it was something I wanted with my Mate…with *her*. It was incredibly attractive.

Her reaction to the clearing surprised me, again. Not just because her face lit up or how the *princess* walked around barefoot—but the look in her eyes when I told her what that place was to me. She moved like it was Holy ground after that.

Because it is. At least to me.

She respected that. After all the shit I throw her way…she cared to do that.

Then she shifted into a fucking white wolf, and I called her a freak. Why did I ever think those words should've left my mouth at that moment?

But it was true. I always did call her a freak when we were younger because of her eyes as a female. Her eyes were always a dead giveaway. She was always right in front of us. We didn't dare consider this outcome because we didn't want to admit what it meant. Rose being a Warrior forces us to question our beliefs—or strengthen them. It freaked Shane out because it's another thing binding her closer to me, and away from his control. He's my best friend, always will be, but this night has put pressure on our friendship for some time now.

I look at her sleeping form. She threw herself at James to stop him from attacking me. After everything, why would she do that?

Rose stirs beneath me, breath hitching as she tries to move in the sheets. I press the cloth to her forehead again, gently wiping away the sweat. Her skin burns against my fingertips and her eyes open, locking with mine. The pain hits her again now that she's conscious. I watch her squirm, feeling it in my bones too.

"Josh," she cries, reaching for me as her body arches off the bed like she's possessed.

I inhale sharply, staring at her. That's the first time I've heard her say my name in *years*. She always calls me names, just not *my name*, not for four years. I never found out how she knew I fucked someone else. Doubt she'll ever tell me. But fuck, why is my name on her lips such a turn on? That's all I ever want to hear out of her mouth now.

A low, broken moan rips from her throat, bringing me out of my thoughts. She claws her bed and turns her head to look at me again. I'm breathing heavily, while my dick is hard as steel. I have one fucking job right now and the Mating bond will torture me until I fill her up with my cum, or morning comes.

Claim her. Breed her. Mark her.

Claim her. Breed her. Mark her.

Claim her. Breed her. Mark her.

The words are in my head over and over, until I take a step back. Rose lets out a whimper, her eyes still on me. "Josh—" she repeats and it's barely audible, more animal than human, desperate. "Please."

I make my way to the foot of her bed. She turns and starts to crawl to me over her sheets.

Fuck.

Her eyes are full of pain and hunger and need. Rose would rather die than beg me, I know that. A part of me wants to take advantage of this and have my way with her—but I won't touch her like that. I won't give her this.

If she's hurting, good. She should be. I didn't even plan this. I didn't plan to stay tonight. Divine knows I didn't.

I feel how much pain she is in. Her body is on fire and burning like salt on a wound. Even if we're not having sex, just holding her eased it. I felt the difference too. I couldn't just leave her to face the rest of the night alone. I just couldn't. Not after what I witnessed as our bond…I don't even know what to call it. It was nothing like what the guys talked about.

They never mentioned some halo engulfing them, or feeling like ice cold water was dumped on them while simultaneously being struck by lightning *and* burning in angelfire.

Also feeling like coming home. I guess they did mention that part.

I felt safe and protected. By *her*. With *her*.

That's not something I've felt since…well, since my parents died. I felt her soul entangle with mine. I felt our lifeforces being one like we know it to be true. There was no doubt about it. None.

"Josh, please. It hurts so much," she repeats, sobbing as her hands crawl up my waist, clutching onto my shirt. "Fuck, please, please. Just…do it!"

I clamp my jaw shut and look up at the dark vaulted ceiling of her bedroom, to the Heavens I've always trusted in.

"Have mercy," I say quietly, as my body becomes very aware of her pressing closer into me. I cannot touch her.

Then she pulls me lower, surprisingly strong for as much pain as she's in, and our faces are inches away from each other. Her eyes are unfocused. I know she's only capable of thinking about one thing right now. And help me Divine, so am I.

I'm on her before I can stop myself. My mouth crashes over hers, my tongue forcing past her lips like I'm trying to punish her with the kiss itself. I've never felt the desire to kiss anyone, never saw the point. She kisses back with equal starvation, her nails digging into my shoulders deep enough to draw blood.

Fuuuuck.

She tastes like plums and honey and everything I've denied myself. Kissing her is better than anything my wildest dreams could've conjured. Kissing her feels like a piece of my soul just returned to me. She tastes like I'd imagine the forbidden fruit to taste—sweet, addicting, and sinful as fuck, making me want to do more than just kissing.

Her legs part under me, thighs trembling, slick heat smearing against my loose pants as she tries to pull me down on the bed, her pain dissipating with every second we kiss. A fresh wave of her arousal hits my senses, and I just want to sink my fingers into her pussy to see how wet she really is for me right now. I need to taste her, feel her wrapped around my aching dick and stay buried inside her. Forever.

I rip my mouth away, panting. My whole body is shaking with the effort it takes not to violently claim her right now.

"No," I snarl, more to myself than to her.

She half sobs, half growls and her hips roll up, grinding against me shamelessly. This isn't her. Rose would *never* throw herself at me like this. It's all wrong. It's so wrong I can't even find pleasure or satisfaction in her begging right now.

"Please," she rasps, voice shredded. "It hurts. Josh, it hurts so much, please fuck me—"

I shove myself off her like she's poisonous. My dick throbs so hard it's agony, precum already leaking, but I stand, fists clenched, watching her cry.

Good. Let her hurt. Let her feel this pain. She deserves to feel some kind of torture for once in her life.

She curls into herself, shaking violently, tears cutting tracks through the sweat on her flushed cheeks.

"Please!" She screams at me and I cup my mouth with my hand, walking backwards until the back of a sofa stops me. I can't look away from her. Her cries are tearing me apart, but I *can't* give her what she needs. All I can do is watch and suffer with her. I can feel everything she's feeling.

She hasn't learned how to block out pain, how to endure pain—I have. But still, my body feels like it's on fire. My dick is aching to the point that I'm sure if I even get anywhere near her, I'll fucking explode. My heart is racing and I'm sweating like never before. The entire room smells like her—her arousal. I will never be able to get this sweet, decadent scent out of my head. I grip the back of the sofa to keep me tethered to it and not jump on her right now.

Her head falls onto the bed, breaking her gaze from me, and I almost growl, wanting her eyes back on me—only ever on me. *Fuck!*

These are not my thoughts. This is the Mating bond talking—the

Mating bond pushing.

Her cries are broken, softer now as she clutches the bedsheet. "You hate me that much."

Her words cause my chest to ache, sending the feeling outward, spreading throughout my body. I push off the sofa, forcing myself to return to her bedside, ignoring my own pain of being close to her. I grab the towel from the bowl. She tries to shove me away when I press it to her forehead, her whole body jerking.

"Stay away from me!" She snarls through clenched teeth. "If you won't fuck me, then leave. I don't need anything else from you. You're only good for one thing for me, and you can't even do that right."

I grit my teeth and catch her wrists, pin them above her head with one hand, and keep the cloth on her skin with the other. "Calm the fuck down," I tell her.

She thrashes against my hold, but she's weak, burning up, and I don't budge. Her eyes are pleading now, wet and wrecked.

"Please," she whispers, lip trembling. "I'll do anything. Just make it stop."

"Rose…"

"*Please*," she stresses, her fingers digging into my arm. "You can do whatever you want. Have whoever you want, I won't say anything. I won't get jealous or send them gifts—please. Please make this stop."

She's not making this easy. I know she doesn't mean a word she just said. People will say anything when they're tortured. This pain is so terrible for her that it's her breaking point.

I lean in as close as I dare.

"You'll regret it tomorrow," I say, low and vicious. "You'll wake up and remember my dick was inside you and you'll hate yourself for begging."

Her face twists into an ugly snarl and I know she's purposefully going to spew hate. "Isn't that what you want?" she strains toward me, voice raw. "So do it. Make me hate myself. It's a win-win. Fuck me. I know you feel the pain too so make it end. This doesn't have to be any different than your other one-night stands."

I stare at her pleading, desperate face. Her words replay in my head. My skin feels strange, almost as if all the blood is receding from my fingertips and up my arm. I pull away from her completely.

Her lips tremble again and she cries harder, but I'm numb. I know she'll say anything to get her way right now, like a drug addict who's desperate, but still her words make me go cold—like all the air got sucked out of this room.

She could never be a one-night stand—she doesn't understand what just thinking about her does to me. She wants me to treat her like the sluts that have been throwing themselves at me, to end her pain—but I can't.

I should want to. There was a time—a dark, *dark* time when the grief was so black, I fantasized about it. About pinning her down, scaring the shit out of her, making her pay for what she got away with. A sick, twisted part of me wanted to break her the way she broke my family—permanently. I wanted to hurt her so badly that she couldn't look at herself in the mirror—physically or mentally, preferably both.

Except even then, even at my lowest, I knew I could never cross that line. Not with her. Not with the Divine. The thoughts were so reoccurring, they scared me straight into making that deal with the Den to replace her.

I wanted to hurt my Mate.

I hated her that much I wanted to do the unthinkable—the unforgivable. I was scared what I'd do if I ever got close enough to her like that. I knew I needed to stay away from her because there was no coming back from that. So I did what I had to, but she's a part of me, embedded in my bone, my soul. I knew that deal would never work, but it kept the Den happy and me distracted from my thoughts.

"This is punishment enough," I barely get the words out. Her tears come harder, but silent now, spilling over and I feel each one like a knife to my chest. I don't dare move. I don't trust my own body right now. I wait until Rose's breathing finally evens out, the sweat cools from her skin, and she tires herself.

Once I know she's asleep, I slowly walk back over to her side of the bed and readjust her so that her head is on the pillow. I take the poppy and blackberry out and part her mouth, letting the drops fall in. My fingers linger on her soft, plump lips, having to pry my hand off her as need stirs in me again. I put the drops down, cool her forehead and feet once more with the damp towels, and wipe down her arms and legs. She doesn't wake up and eventually, I join her back in bed, pulling her into my arms. I bite down hard as her leg presses against my dick, but I also feel the immediate difference in her pain levels just by holding her. Her body curls against mine, one hand loosely fisted on my shirt. I breathe in her scent, calming my own racing heart.

I don't sleep. I can't with everything circling in my head. With her being this close but not close enough…

It's close to six in the morning when the silence is interrupted by the bedroom door opening. Eliza's perfume hits me before I see her.

She steps in quietly, bare feet and in a flowing pink robe, her hand resting on her belly. She carefully closes the door behind her and turns, freezing when our eyes lock. Her hand flies to her chest with shock, before relief washes over her face.

"You're with her," she whispers and I swear her eyes gloss over in the morning light from the windows.

I sit up slowly, untangling from Rose just enough to put my weight on my forearm, then glare at my Luna.

"Don't say a word," I tell her, lowly, knowing her thought process.

Eliza's hands lift in mock surrender, before she drops them and says, "I was just checking on her. I didn't know you'd be here," she glances down at Rose, her features softening, "but I'm glad you are."

My eyes narrow. "Don't get any ideas."

She sighs, brushing a few blonde strands of hair behind her ear as her hand circles over her stomach absently.

"How is she?" she asks but makes no move to come closer.

Good, I don't particularly want her to. It's not that I don't like Eliza…I like her just fine. She's a great Luna and ok, she's a great friend too. She's nosy as fuck though. She's a meddler, but she cares. She cares a lot about Rose. I can appreciate that.

"She went through it, but it's settled now. Nothing out of the ordinary," I tell her, maintaining a low voice, careful to not wake Rose. I leave out the part where we went through a fucking war though.

"But…you didn't…"

I glare at her. "What do you think?"

Eliza shrugs. "You hate her enough. We weren't sure if…"

"If I'd rape her?" I snap. If Rose and I even had somewhat of a decent relationship, tonight would've been fine. We might've even fucked. Seeing that her transformation was only one moment in six years when things felt right, it wasn't nearly strong enough to cross a line neither of us could ever take back.

"Well…yes…" Eliza admits and my stomach drops.

"You think that low of me?" I question.

She doesn't look guilty or cower under my gaze. "Josh, you lost a lot of our respect the day we found out you disrespected your Mating bond. We don't think much of you to begin with when it comes to Rose—so yes. I didn't think you'd even bother being here, but we were worried you would take advantage now that she is completely yours and none of us can do anything about it."

I could do anything to her and they couldn't do shit. This is the downside of Mating bonds. The Divine didn't promise that Mates would always be good to each other. It was one of Shane's biggest fears tonight.

I don't say anything. What's there to say? Eliza wasn't wrong to be concerned. If Evren Thane hadn't come in and taken me under his wing after my parents died, I probably would've done exactly what she's saying.

"Shane hasn't slept all night. You know he's sitting outside, right?" she asks me. I didn't know that. My sole focus has been on Rose. Eliza sighs heavily, before she reaches for the doorknob, but she hesitates, for far too long.

Before she can say anything, I ask, "Who's we? You kept saying *we*."

She turns back to face me and answers, "The Crescents, some of the Warriors," she shakes her head, "have you ever even considered her side of the story?"

"There is no *her* side," I reply, "she doesn't even remember what happened."

Eliza doesn't back down. "That doesn't mean there isn't one," she says quietly, "just because she doesn't remember…doesn't mean it happened the way you think it did." Her voice is gentle, kind even and it pisses me off. When I don't say anything, she continues, "*You* don't even know what really happened that night. You only saw the aftermath. All I know is, I *know* Rose."

"You never really know someone," I argue. People are capable of horrendous things if given the chance and the right push.

Eliza squares her shoulders, before nodding at us in bed together. "Can you honestly say you believe she's capable of what you've been accusing her for six years, without a doubt? Isn't it weird that no one, not even guards were in sight, and *you* just happened to be there?"

She leaves me to ponder that.

Of course, I've thought about everything she pointed out over the years, but nothing will wash Rose's hands clean of the blood she spilled.

12 REGRET

Rosella Craving

July 21

I wake up mortified.

My skin is sticky with last night's sweat and shame. My entire body aches like I've been dragged through the streets, but the pain is nothing like it was throughout the night. It's subsided and my fever's broken.

I hear the shower shut off in my bathroom and my stomach knots so hard I nearly gag, realizing Josh is still here. When I woke up and found my bed empty, I was relieved that I wouldn't have to face him right away. Of course, my plan was to hide until I couldn't, and of course, he's not following the script. He never has.

When Josh steps out, his hair is dripping and he's wearing the same clothes from last night. His eyes are on me instantly, and I hate how my heart skips a beat with how fucking good he looks. I probably look like I crawled out of a grave…one I want to crawl back into.

He walks up to me, reaching to press the back of his warm hand to my forehead. "See, you're fine."

I slap his hand away.

"Don't touch me," I snap, getting out of bed. I'm still wearing the dress from my transformation, so I wrap my arms around myself. "They said things would be different after I shift, but you—you *really* do hate me."

He arches one dark brow. "Obviously…?"

I laugh, and it sounds strange. My throat is still hoarse from last night. "I begged you. I fucking *begged* you, and you wouldn't even touch me. I disgust you that much? It's fine. Everyone knows *the* Beta Warrior would never fuck anyone outside of his own species. What was even the point of you staying the night? Did you want to see me in agony? Do you get off on my pain? I know some guys like that. Well, you can check it off your bucket list now."

The words just fly out, and I know I'm rambling, but Divine, he just makes me so angry. I would never beg him.

His eyes flash for a heartbeat. Josh grabs my wrist so fast I don't even see him move. He presses my palm forcefully against the front of his pants.

He's rock hard. Obscenely hard. He's straining against his pants like he's about to tear through them.

"I just jerked off in your shower so *this* wouldn't happen in the two minutes it'd take me to leave this room," he growls, viciously. "One breath of your scent, one *look* at you, and I'm hard. It's annoying as fuck. This Mating bond is *annoying* as fuck. Think whatever you want about my preferences, but feverish isn't one of them. You want to get on your knees and beg again, be my guest. You want to be my slut? I won't say no next time, and I might just use you whatever way I want."

I can feel him throbbing under my palm and it takes everything not to squeeze. My face burns with humiliation and fury. His words are filthy and derogatory, and I can't believe he just talked to me like that. Did he just call me a slut? I snarl, and the sound comes out feral. "I will never beg you again. Why would I want someone everyone can have? You disgust me."

He smirks, slow and cruel. "Then why's your hand still on my dick, princess?"

I yank it away like I've been burned.

The sound of his dark and mocking laugh heats my cheeks even more. "Told you you'd regret it in the morning," he reminds me.

My new claws itch to come out. I want to rip that smug look off his face but then his gaze drops to my chest and for a moment he looks like he's starving. It's long enough for me to point it out.

"Eyes up here, asshole," I snap. "You made it clear you have zero interest in my tits."

"Fuck it," he mutters under his breath and then he kisses me. For one traitorous second, I remember feeling the way his mouth was on mine, how it dulled the fire in my bones, and how good it felt last night. My lips part before I can stop them, and he takes full advantage like it was permission. His tongue slides in against mine, hand fisting in my hair hard enough for a moan to escape me. Fuck, why do I love this so much? He knows exactly how to touch me.

His other hand slips under my neckline, rough palm cupping my breast while his thumb brushes the bottom of it. My nipple is so hard that it hurts when his calloused fingers graze it, and I hate the moan that crawls up my throat. I arch into him like a traitor, feeling every inch of his cock against me, making me instantly wet.

Then sense slams into me like cold water. I rip away from him, pulling away like he did last night.

"If you ever try that again," I start, shaking with rage, "I will cut your dick off and feed it to every serpent bitch you've ever fucked."

He touches his lip where my new sharp teeth must've nicked him too hard. He looks at the smear of blood on his fingers, and smiles like I just complimented him.

"Get out," I hiss.

He rolls his eyes and picks up his phone off the dresser, completely unfazed before he licks his bloody lips. Then he walks out, leaving me trembling, hating myself almost as much as I hate him.

A wave of emotions floods me, but it's the tears I can't stop from falling. I stumble to the bathroom because I need his scent gone from my skin. The tiles are still wet from his shower. The towel he used is hanging over the rack, damp and warm, smelling like citrus, spice, and smoke—like him. I hurl it across the bathroom.

The shower is scalding and I make it hotter. I scrub until my skin is raw. Until I can't smell him anymore. Until my shame is erased, but I know nothing will help. My knees buckle and I sink to the floor, arms wrapped around myself.

I begged him.

I begged Josh Hunter, the boy who's hated me for as long as I can remember, the one who's spent years proving I'm nothing to him but a chain around his neck. He'll sleep with anyone, but when it comes to me, he's disgusted to the point that he wouldn't even help ease my pain. I got on my knees, and he looked me in the eye and chose to watch me suffer.

I press my forehead to the tile and cry until there's nothing left but dry heaves and the echo of his voice, *told you you'd regret it in the morning.*

I do. Divine help me, I regret everything except the way his mouth felt on mine. His lips fit with mine perfectly like they were made to kiss me just right. He tasted faintly of mint, scotch, and something so uniquely him I wish I could suck his lips forever.

I hate him. I hate that I want him at all. I hate that the only male I'll ever belong to is the one who would rather choke on his own venom than want me. Josh getting hard is because of the bond—*he* doesn't want me. I hate that every eligible serpent girl knows what *my* Mate feels like, and I begged him and he still denied me. Does he hate me because I'm not a serpent shifter? Would he still have denied me if

I was?

Sex is the worst thing for us right now, but it would've been a kindness for what my body went through last night—like being burned and skinned alive.

Suddenly the hot water doesn't feel like the best idea. I drag myself out of the shower and return to my room. The sheets still smell like us, and I want to burn them. I want to crawl back in and breathe him in until I suffocate. And then burn them.

They said things would be different. I was a fool to think that meant easier.

I turn in my fury, and that's when I see the wet towels in the large bowl of water on my nightstand, with the drops of poppy and blackberries sitting next to it and remember how he held me all night. Why would he do that?

13 HOUSEKEEPING

Rosella Craving
July 24

Three days later, once the pain of my transformation has subsided, I walk into the training facilities. The building has tall arches with an imposing Cravenhold emblem hung on it.

Inside, the gym stretches out into a world of its own. It's not just a gym or an arena to train and fight—it's an entire arsenal for armies, everything a soldier can dream of. The armory is next door; the garage and carport are nearby too. I don't wander, because I know where I'm supposed to be going.

A second wing is glassed off—the Warriors' private section. They don't train with the masses. Warriors have our own gym, our own rings, our own space built in for safety and privacy.

I place my hand on the keypad as a retina scanner verifies me. The glass door opens, granting me access. Shane works fast.

The echo of fists striking and grunts fill the hall. Josh and Shane are standing in the ring, circling each other. Shane's stance is sharp and measured. They're sparring, but it's lighthearted with both grinning and talking shit to each other. Shane lunges, Josh ducks before Josh pushes back and for a moment it looks like they're dancing more than fighting.

The sound of Josh's laugh lights me up. It's low and reckless, even as his fist slams against Shane's guard. Shane curses under his breath, but there's a challenging smile tugging at his mouth. Josh is shirtless, sweat glistening across his chest, his grin cocky even as he takes a hit from Shane.

Josh has a large vertical tattoo on the left side of his abs—the old Hunter family name—Daevryn. The black letters are in a Celtic font with green thorny vines wrapping around them. On his right arm, a large black serpent coils upward, starting from his wrist. The snake loops around his shoulder before the mouth opens wide as if to attack his neck. Half of the serpent's mouth is visible from the front, and the other half from Josh's back. There are seven red roses placed sporadically over the snake—yes, I counted, don't judge a girl. They're a contrast against the detailed black scales. It's a hideous tattoo. One meant to intimidate his opponents. I also don't believe the roses have anything to do with me, unless the snake is meant to be eating the flowers.

I've seen Josh spar before. I've seen him shirtless many times—running laps, swimming in the river, full Moon nights…but something about seeing him in the ring this morning makes my skin tingle.

Every strike ripples through his muscles. His muscles…Divine help me—they're tight, hard. My mind wanders and I bite down on my lip at the thoughts of running my fingers over them.

No. No, that's disgusting. Hundreds of thousands of hands have been on him.

Still, I wish I was more conscious three nights ago. The first time he was in my bed, and I wasn't even awake for most of it. The parts I was awake for, I don't want to remember.

I haven't seen Josh since. We had a family dinner last night that he was invited to but conveniently had to leave for a New York trip last second. It wasn't a long trip because the Hunter flag was back up by the time I was ready for bed.

"Come on, Shane, stop giving him an in!" Devaughn calls out. The other five Warriors are hanging off the ring, shouting at Josh and Shane. Their voices rise with each clash of fists.

"Put him on the floor, Josh!" Antonio hollers.

"Yeah, you're next," comes Shane's immediate reply, which just makes the guys laugh.

Josh seems to thrive on it. He flashes that cocky grin between blows which somehow makes him look more beautiful. Shane shakes his head, muttering something I can't hear from here, then lunges harder, forcing Josh back a step. The boys erupt in cheers.

Daniel sees me and grins, waving me over. He's leaning against the ropes on the far side of the ring.

"There she is!" Antonio calls out, noticing me too. He hops down and jogs over before engulfing me into a hug. "Sorry I missed all the drama!"

"Are you really?" I ask, raising an eyebrow as he pulls away, grinning.

"No. Mariella and I had a great night." His grin remains and my heart swells for my friends.

"Good to know," I shove him playfully. "I talked to her yesterday. How is she?"

"She's great. How are *you*, Warrior Princess?" he asks as we approach the ring.

"Physically? Better," I answer as Daniel holds out a hand, pulling me up, and Antonio joins next to me.

"Sounds about right," Devaughn chuckles, listening in.

I bite the inside of my cheek, my eyes locked on the ring.

On Josh.

He twists, counters, blocks, his grin plastered on even as sweat drips down his hair. He throws a counterblow, catches Shane off guard. In the next breath, Shane's on his back with Josh smirking down at him.

My eyes narrow in on his lips—lips that were on me. Lips that kissed me. Twice. Lips I want to feel again, over and over and—

The sound of the men rioting snap me out of my thoughts. Josh laughs with the boys before offering Shane a hand. My brother lets out a string of curses but takes it, allowing his best friend to pull him up. Shane reaches for his blood bottle while Josh turns, his eyes finding me.

"Well, look who finally dragged her spoiled ass out of bed," he says, his voice slicing through the boys' chatter, "you look like shit."

My heart sinks, but I'm too well rehearsed in this game. I lift my chin, my voice clear, "And yet, I still look better than you."

Shane grunts out a laugh as Daniel smirks at my side. Josh's grin doesn't falter but his eyes do for just a split second.

"Yeah, that tends to be the case when you stay up all night," he replies, easily as he catches the towel James tosses him. I stare back at him. I don't know what he's implying because I know he hasn't slept with anyone the past few nights.

"All night, huh?" Antonio wiggles his eyebrows at us, "Same."

Josh and I both glare at him, but he hops off the side of the ring. Shane comes up to us just then.

"Alright, let's wrap this up," he announces.

"What about Rose's training?" James frowns, crossing his arms. I'm not surprised James is the one concerned about my training. The man is a brute and doesn't even try to hide it.

"No physical training today. She has to get a few things sorted, before she takes her oaths tomorrow," Shane waves him off before refilling his blood bottle.

I forgot about the oaths. Every Warrior, even though it is their birthright—our birthright—still have to take an oath. A vow to serve, protect, and uphold shifter laws.

Shane meets my eyes and says, "You have a busy day ahead of you. Shall we?"

I nod, following him as I feel Josh come up beside me. He found a shirt—one that defines his biceps deliciously.

"Why exactly do we have to take oaths?" I ask as we all leave the training facilities. "If being a Warrior is a birthright?"

"During the oath, you'll be bound by blood to uphold the secrets you will come across during your time as a Warrior," James says to me. This might be the first time he's ever talked to me directly.

Shane nods in agreement. "You can know about classified information, but the oath will prevent you from sharing it unless the situation warrants it."

"So it basically makes the choice for us," I say.

"You could say that," James answers, "it helps you determine who has certain clearance levels."

"How will it know?"

"You will know when you're able to speak of it. Otherwise, it'll be at the tip of your tongue, but you won't be able to say anything," Shane answers me. His words leave a faint weight in the air, but I don't push. Instead, I drift closer until I'm at Josh's side, matching his stride.

I lock his gaze. "I know what you did for me…why?"

"I don't know what you're talking about," he says, breaking our eye contact. He's so full of shit.

I raise an eyebrow. "I saw the bowl of water and the towels. And I know you gave me doses of the poppy and blackberry throughout the night."

His eyes harden, but he doesn't say anything.

I let out an exasperated laugh. "Is it that hard for you to admit you were kind to me?"

He rolls his eyes. "Yes, actually, you freak."

I ignore the insult and square my shoulders before saying, "Well, if you're going to be a dick in the morning, maybe don't bother or leave evidence behind next time."

I was going to say thank you, but he decided to be an ass.

"There won't be a next time," he says lowly, and I hate that my chest tightens at the thought, because of course there will be a next time. We're bonded for life.

My pride doesn't let him have the last word. "Fine with me," I shrug. "Maybe I will take Daniel and Daniya up on their offer for a threesome."

I feel his eyes on me, so when I meet them again, I'm surprised to see humor on his face as a smirk plays on his lips. He leans in slightly to say, "There won't be a next time because you only go through that pain after a first shift." Oh…fuck. "But good to know where your head went."

"Yeah, well…at least Daniel has the balls to offer and won't leave me unsatisfied after a night in my bed."

I know that's a low blow and I only said it because Josh has made it clear that he has no interest in me like that. Whatever physical reactions he does have is clearly unwanted by him. It explains how Josh spent the night in my bed without going farther than just holding me. From what I hear, men have a hard time controlling themselves around their Mates. It's supposed to be painful for them, some primal need to claim and Mark. Josh was able to resist it—resist me.

"Trust me, you'll still be unsatisfied after a threesome with them," Josh replies, coolly.

"I heard threesome!" Daniel calls out, turning to look at us as he walks backwards. My cheeks heat instantly as I realize maybe we weren't as quiet as I thought.

An evil grin spreads over Josh's lips as he looks at Daniel and says, "Rose thinks you and Daniya can satisfy all her needs."

Daniel blinks. Well, it's too late to back down now. I shrug and flick my hair over my shoulder as I say, "I'm in. Let me know when."

Daniel looks between the both of us before saying, "This feels like a trap." Neither of us confirm or deny. Daniel grins, looking at Josh. "You want to watch, don't you?"

Josh winks back at him. "I'd have to. Gotta make sure the little freak learns a thing or two if she's going to perform her Veyara duties well."

He's fucking disgusting.

"Just because I learn a thing or two, doesn't mean you'll experience them with me," I snap back. He has no fucking idea. I was taught well.

It makes me sad, but I push my thoughts away quickly.

"Making babies is going to be so boring then," Josh replies with fake sadness and I grit my teeth.

"You don't deserve me," I say sweetly.

Josh lets out a laugh as if he doesn't care whether he does or doesn't. "As if you're something worth deserving."

"You know I can hear everything, right?" Shane says from ahead of us. "My baby sister, assholes."

"Mate trumps baby sister," Josh calls back. Oh, *now* it's okay to be his Mate.

"Not when she's the Alpha's baby sister," Shane retorts.

"Mmm…" Josh pretends to think about it, before disagreeing, "nope, Mate still trumps Alpha."

He has a point.

"I don't think she'll be anyone's little sister after—"

"Daniel, if you value your life, you will not finish that sentence," Shane replies, not looking back at us once.

It's like I'm invisible or something.

"None of you have any shame," Sam mumbles, walking ahead of all of us as if he can't get away fast enough. Grumpy, that one.

"Having an heir is the Veyara's only responsibility and you'll remember that," Josh rubs it in. I swear he's doing it on purpose to rile me up because neither of us want to touch each other willingly.

I wrinkle my nose, and turn to Josh. "Don't use my title like that. It's vulgar."

"I can *use* your title however I want," Josh replies, "seeing that I gave it to you."

"*You* didn't give me anything. Fates did, unfortunately."

"You're right, if I had a say, *you* would never be the Veyara," Josh says automatically.

It's like every drop of warmth drains from me in an instant, leaving only a hollow ache. The words cut deeper than an Alpha's claws ever could. My chest tightens, the sting spreading down my ribs, curling into my stomach.

I feel nauseous and stupid. So fucking stupid.

Our Mating bond is not something we attack. It is not a weapon to use against each other no matter how ugly things get. It's not about the title. I couldn't care less about being the Veyara. It's what the Veyara comes down to—his Mate. As a Craving, I have the ability to shift into any animal I want to with practice, but that isn't good enough for the Beta Warrior. A Craving being Mated to anyone is one of the highest honors a family can have—except my Mate.

A dreadful pain crawls out from my chest as I clamp my teeth shut so they don't quiver while the skies grow dark.

Last time he went there, I disappeared for five months. He woke up the next day and found out that I left for my Royal Tour. I had no intention of learning to be a better Mate to the Beta. I left so I wouldn't have to see him anytime soon. It's usually a decision the Warrior couple makes together because they go on the Tour together. I heard he tried to find out where I was, but I was always moving and I made sure he got the wrong location or got it too late. I don't know why he cared.

He realizes what he just did right now too. Josh's mouth parts like he's about to say something, but Daniel cuts in. He bumps his shoulder into mine, causing me to crash into Josh. His hand comes up to catch my elbow, but I pull back and regain my balance as thunder rumbles above.

I don't need to feel those stupid sparks right now and I don't want his disgusting hands on me.

Daniel winks. "You'd still be a Warrior though, and that's way cooler." He's trying to throw me a rope to pull me out of the pit Josh just pushed me into.

"Fuck, Rose, can you fix the skies?" Devaughn calls out, "You're going to give the Lammas vendors a heart attack."

His comment brings me back and I take a deep breath, clenching and unclenching my hands.

Breathe in, breathe out.

Breathe in, breathe out.

The weather is a strange ability I have, and the only power that doesn't change my eyes. It's a little useless and just acts like a giant mood ring if anything.

One by one the guys ahead of us enter the administrative building. Daniel catches the door after Antonio, telling us, "Definitely would be easier to have a threesome if you weren't the Veyara—or the Alpha's sister," he sighs, dramatically, "but we'll satisfy you, regardless."

The skies clear as Daniel walks through the doorway and Josh grabs the door above my head, letting me pass first. He catches my arm, sending a wave of sparks flying through me, straight to my chest. His grip is firm enough to force me to look into his gray eyes. There's no emotion in them and it's as if he wants me to read his mind without saying anything. As Mates we can do that, but his walls are impenetrable.

"Don't *touch* me," I snap at him.

"Don't bolt again," his grip tightens as if he'll force me into compliance.

"Yeah? Why would you care?" I ask, heated with the anger rising in me.

"Rose! Keep up!" Shane calls for me and I pull away from Josh, hurrying to my brother's side. He's heading toward the west wing.

"It's customary for the Alpha to gift his female relatives their lady's maids after they shift—normally, you'd be meeting them, but I thought we could make better use of our time," Shane says vaguely as he motions for his assistant. Shane's handed a file which he passes over to me along with a pen, saying, "Sign these. They're basic authorization forms so you have access and clearance levels for certain things. It'll get activated after your oaths are taken."

I open the file and scan the papers as I sign them and continue following my brother. I absently ask, "So am I not getting lady's maids?"

"No, you will. You won't be getting bodyguards though," Shane tells me and my ears perk up.

I don't know how I feel about that. Most people would be thrilled for the freedom, but…I like my bodyguards.

"Can I keep Cristobal on as my driver?" I ask. It's not that I don't like Franklin, but Cristobal has talents I find useful.

Shane sighs. "If you must," he answers me as I hand the file back to him. In a gentler voice, he asks, "Are you okay?"

"Sore as fuck, but yeah I'll be fine," I tell him.

He smiles. "You will be, but I was talking about Josh."

I exhale and shrug. "It's Josh. I just…" I trail off not wanting to get into this with my brother.

"Talk to me," he pushes, holding his arm out to me. I sigh and take it.

"I just don't know what I did to make him hate me so much…" I say, quietly.

"He'll come around," Shane tells me, "you're Mates. He can't hate you forever."

I wrinkle my nose. "I can't remember a time he liked me, as just a person even."

Shane's quiet for a moment before he says, "Our biology changes again with our Mate's when they shift."

"I don't want him to like me because he has to..." I frown. "I want a Mate who wants me too."

"Be patient with him, it's all an adjustment. For both of you."

"How am I supposed to forgive the cheating though, Shane..." I trail off as my voice cracks a little. I hate, *hate*, letting that get to me. No matter how much I say Josh is disgusting for it and I'm not jealous, it still hurts because he chooses *them.* How do I forgive him when he's not even apologetic?

My brother sighs heavily, his eyes hardening, but he says, "You'll learn that the Mating bond judges things differently. There's nothing—"

"—above a Mating bond, I know, I know," I finish for him, rolling my eyes.

Shane holds open the glass door for me, saying, "Just...be careful too. Josh can be...unpredictable."

I frown but Shane urges me forward.

The lush greenery and the Sunlight streaming in makes the atrium feel like a little piece of paradise. This is where Helena Hunter, Josh's mom, spent most of her time when she made an appearance at court.

Eliza is sitting on a chair next to the gushing water fountain, dressed in a baby pink maxi dress. She's talking to four Crescents.

"Oh good, you're here," Eliza smiles up at us. She's beaming but her eye bags are getting worse as her pregnancy progresses. She's not sleeping well. Eliza holds out her hand for Shane to help her up. I steady her from her other side.

"Alpha," Crystal Claws bows, clearly teasing my brother and Shane grunts. She's one of his best friend's Mates—she gets a pass to make fun of the Alpha.

Daniya and Mariella grin at me, while Vanessa Tens watches me quietly. She's a serpent shifter—I can usually tell because they're taller, slender but with a fighter's build. I heard serpent shifters are all required to serve the Royal Army for two years within the first five years of their transformation. It shows in Vanessa with her confident stance, hands behind her back and brown eyes following my every move.

"You remember Vanessa," Shane says to me, gesturing to James Tens's Mate. She was in the war room, but we didn't get a chance to catch up.

She acknowledges him first. "Alpha," then she turns to me and offers a polite smile and a respectful tilt of her head, "Veyara."

She acknowledges my title, taking me by surprise.

"Of course—oh my gosh, you're back!" I grin at her. Her mission wasn't going according to plan so she couldn't come home. There was a lot of tension around it, but it was all very hush hush—security clearance and all.

"Vanessa's background is in the Royal Army," Shane tells me—the respect is clear in his voice. "She will be your new PA, along with Camille," my brother tells me and I'm instantly on alert. Another serpent PA? Why would another Crescent be assigned as my personal assistant?

Vanessa is still young enough to serve. Most don't retire from the Royal Army until their sixties if they climb up the ranks. I take a step toward her and ask, "I'm curious, why did you give it up to be one of my assistants?"

What I'm really curious about is why she wants to serve *me*? From what I hear, I'm not popular with the Serpent Nation. And just why? As a Crescent, being my PA is beneath her…something's off about this.

Before Vanessa can answer me, Eliza laughs like she has a secret and is dying to share it. "This was my favorite part," she grins. "While Vanessa is your PA, she's also your undercover security."

"I thought I wasn't getting security," I glance at my brother.

"As if I'm going to let you walk around unprotected," Shane crosses his arms over his broad chest.

"As a PA, she will always be with you, so she's perfect," Eliza tilts her head and something tells me this was all her idea.

Cristobal and Franklin were well chosen by my father. I will always be grateful for their time with me. I knew my bodyguards would change to ones on House Hunter's payroll, but I never thought it'd be Vanessa of all people.

Will she be reporting back to Josh? James? Did they send her to spy on me? I'll have to get to the bottom of it. I wouldn't put it past either of them to do this.

"I know it's a little weird for a Crescent to serve the Veyara so directly, but honestly it'd be an honor," Vanessa says, grinning at me. I don't sense any insincerity as she adds, "Plus, it'll keep me at court for the time being, and my Mate would very much prefer that."

"Vanessa's the one you'll go to when we don't want your hands dirty," Eliza smirks at her friend.

I raise a brow. "Who would I possibly want to hurt?"

"Josh," Eliza coughs and Shane rolls his eyes.

Vanessa laughs before answering me. "Just a form of persuasion if ever needed, but it's more than that. Just like how I can use those skills against someone, I can use it to protect you too. I can smell poison a mile away for example."

"That sounds…lovely?"

"I will train you too," Vanessa tells me and it's looking like we'll be spending a lot of time together outside of her being my PA. This has Josh written all over it. I know Josh and James are close, maybe James is in on it too.

Shane assigns Mariella to research my powers. Mariella's been going on and on about her private studies, hoping to make a change in our world when it comes to some of the uses of magic and medicine. Mariella's a friend, so Shane trusts she'll never exploit me or do anything to cause me harm in the process. She ensures we'll take it at my pace.

Daniya is in charge of social media and any gossip that's spread about me. She's Mated to Daniel, whose family owns a few news outlets and has influence over others in the supernatural world.

Crystal, being our resident guardian, confirms she'll ward off any magical threats that may come my way. She's great with protection spells and I can tell she takes pride in her work.

"Crystal is actually very powerful," my brother praises and that's rare for him, "she can single-handedly do what would normally take seven to eight people."

"You'll always be protected. Physically and spiritually," Mariella says, smiling at me. "You're one of a kind. We won't let anything happen to you."

Shane clears his throat as he reads a text on his phone. He leans in to kiss Eliza on the forehead, before saying, "I'll see you later. Josh and Sam have a situation."

Curiosity sparks my interest, but Shane is already striding away, telling us to not get into too much trouble.

"Alright then," Eliza claps her hands, "if we're all done here, we have our first order of business."

"Yeah?" I ask, curiously.

"Your oaths are tomorrow," Eliza tells me. "You can't take your oaths without your Warrior uniform, now, can you?"

14 WARRIOR. WOMAN. WARNING.

Rosella Craving

July 24

Two hours later, I'm back in the war room with everyone. The topic is how we're going to address the existence of a female Warrior for the press conference once the news is out. At least that's how the discussion started—now it's if we even want to announce there's a female white wolf. The Elders are in opposition of it.

"This will cause unrest," Elder Claws states. I can't decide which side he's on. It's almost as if he's playing devil's advocate, which I can appreciate.

"As all progressive events do," Daniel says, sitting across from his father.

"Progress doesn't mean parading impropriety," Elder Salvatore sneers, "what will the Packs think when they see a woman standing where only men should stand. They will lose faith in our structure."

"Why do we care what the people we rule over think?" Josh asks him seriously. If there's any Warrior who cares what his people think, it's Josh. Isn't it one of the reasons why he wants a serpent Mate? He's such a hypocrite.

"That's rich coming from you," Eliza says to him, "weren't you just doing everything you could so she wasn't the Veyara and you could save face with your serpents?"

Have I mentioned how much I love my sister-in-law?

"What we say is law. We tell them how things are, not the other way around. They can talk all day, it won't change what Rose's fur color is," Josh replies, not taking the bait.

Eliza had every right to ask that question and if she hadn't, I would've.

"You're defending her?" Eliza thinks to him, the mind link open for the Crescents and Warriors.

"What makes you think that? Maybe I just like seeing Elders turn red with anger," Josh replies automatically. I resist an eye roll. Heaven forbid he ever gives a straight answer.

"The next thing you know, a female will be challenging for the Alpha title. What then?" Aunt Susan asks.

"And that's a bad thing?" Vanessa looks at Shane. "No offense, Alpha," then she addresses the table, "but if there is a more worthy female who challenges an Alpha and wins—she won fair and square. What would be so wrong with her being an Alpha? The Prides have female leaders already."

Vanessa didn't waste any time readjusting to her Crescent position after being absent for two years.

I sit in the middle of it all, their voices circling me. The table is heavy with papers, tablets, and laptops. They're lit with drafts of speeches and outlines for a press conference Sam is supposed to hold tomorrow. My name is all over it.

"Lady Susan is right," Elder Salvatore says, "you don't see it, but we do—Alphas across the lands will use this as fuel."

"If the precedent is set that women can be Warriors, Packs will fracture," Elder Claws explains, quietly.

"Yes," Elder Salvatore continues, "female shifters will challenge for power. Entire bloodlines will be uprooted. It'll be civil war."

"If we announce she's a Warrior," Lady Zia glances at me before looking at the rest of the table, "there's a possibility the world will turn on her." The concern for me is clear in her voice.

"The world? Or men?" Crystal asks, her jaw tight and eyes narrowed, "or more specifically men in power?"

"Divine," Daniya lets out a laugh, "you all are so threatened by a woman becoming a Warrior…I *hope* a woman challenges an Alpha and wins. Rose is a Warrior. She joined the Pack. She didn't steal anything. She didn't even fight another Warrior for her place. It's her Divine birthright."

"No one's power was taken away with Rose becoming a Warrior," Eliza backs Daniya, calmly. The Luna is speaking. "But it's almost as if asking to make space for her is a sin. She doesn't need anyone's permission."

"The world already knew Rose was shifting this full Moon," Sam clicks his tongue, "hiding what she shifted into will make us look weak and dishonest. That *will* make the subjects lose faith in us."

"The moment *female Warrior* leaves our mouth, women will take it as a sign and start demanding their own titles." Elder Salvatore shakes his head. I catch him looking at Eliza and have the urge to punch the asshole in the face. How did Sam come from him? I also notice that Lady Victoria hasn't said a word so far.

"We can't announce it. You give one girl this platform, and every Alpha will have a riot on his hands. Packs will be torn apart, Mates challenged, and bloodlines will change," my aunt agrees with Elder Salvatore, and I can't believe the words coming out of her mouth. She has two daughters of her own.

Lady Tiara is in her High Priestess robe, her hood staying on to cover most of her light brown hair. Her face is hard; her blue eyes are harder. She cannot be okay with any of this. She's the High Priestess—there's no one higher than her in her sphere except Mother Aradia, who is the Queen of the witches.

Elder Rage cuts in with a grim nod. "We have to protect our foundations and think of Rose's safety. We can highlight her titles as Princess and the Veyara. The public already loves that. Feed into that."

"Yes, that's a good idea. Announcing she's a Warrior is unnecessary," Elder Salvatore agrees.

"Unnecessary!" Eliza exclaims and the table erupts in shouts, people standing up to argue.

"It's better in the long run."

"She's a Warrior!"

"She's a princess!"

"A Warrior ranks higher than a princess, though."

"That's the problem, isn't it?"

"That is just blatant disrespect to the Warriors! And Rose!"

I don't know who is saying what, they're all talking over each other now. Nathanial and Uncle Edward sit with their hands folded and faces unreadable. The Warriors stay quiet for the most part too, but I don't believe it's because they agree. They're waiting to see where the fault line settles. Shane already made it clear after my transformation where they will stand.

"Rose can be paraded in silk dresses and Divine titles until this blows over, and her shift isn't in the headlines anymore. Then we won't need to address her being a Warrior," Aunt Susan says, exhaling dramatically.

"She can stay out of the public's eye as a Warrior and just be the Veyara," Elder Salvatore decides as if he has any say.

Something overcomes me and I push my chair back, the motion causing every head to turn my way. I stand, darkness crawling at the edges of the room, so I know my eyes have gone black—they always do when I use my powers no matter to what extent.

I've been sitting here, listening to them bicker, and I'm not quite sure why Nathanial or Shane haven't put a stop to it by now, but I can't stay silent anymore. I have things to do.

"I will not be hidden," I start, calmly, "so tell me—what title should I represent right now that will command your respect more? Princess Rosella Craving? Or Veyara Hunter?" I stare the Elders down as I remember who I am. Seems like some people here need a reminder of the chain of command. "The hierarchy is Father Nathanial, the Alpha, the Luna, the Beta, the Veyara, the Warriors, the Crescents, the Elders, and then the rest of the nobility," I list off, looking around the table, "so please tell me, which you prefer, because it's clear you do not respect Warrior Craving."

No one speaks. They're all staring at me.

"Your eyes, thorn," Shane cautions me, telepathically.

"I know. It feels appropriate since they clearly forgot that I'm not just a pretty face," I think back to my brother.

"Who said you were a pretty face though?" he teases.

I shake my head, disappointed in the Elders, and I can see the blood draining from their faces. They always hate it when I use my powers. They don't know the full extent of it, and it makes them uneasy.

I haven't killed anyone yet, but I know I can.

"I've had it with your bullshit excuses, trying to twist the narrative to fit your closed-off minds. My life is not up for negotiations. My life will not be determined by any of you who are seeking political gains and are afraid of change." I glare at the Elders' end of the table.

Being a princess was due to bloodline because I'm a Craving.

Being the Veyara is because I'm Josh's Mate—a Hunter's Mate.

But being a Warrior…that's mine.

I will not let them take it from me.

I will not let them suppress, dismiss, or disrespect who I am.

Not without a fight.

"I will not sit here in silence as you try to undermine me as a Warrior. I tried playing nice, I tried seeing it your way this entire time. If your thinking was correct, the Divine wouldn't have chosen me to be a Warrior."

No one around this table holds three powerful titles separately.

They are all Warriors because they are princes of royal bloodlines, not in spite of it. There isn't a retired Luna or Veyara at this table either. None of the women around the table are princesses because no princess has ever Mated with a Warrior before.

And none of them have my power.

I'm humble with my power, and I've always been underestimated for it. Aside from my fights with Josh, I've always been the picture-perfect image of a shifter princess. I've never talked back to the Elders or disrespected them. That doesn't mean they'll get to make decisions that disrespect me now.

"You let Josh and my bond slide because of the title *he* was going to inherit and my lineage. It suits you. It looks good and powerful for a Craving and a Hunter to be Mated—*chosen by the Divine*," I emphasize the last bit, "but the same rule doesn't apply when the Divine chooses a female to be a Warrior."

Fuck. That. Fuck them.

I can't say where my mom would've stood on this as Luna, but I know as my mom, she'd want me to raise Hell.

And Hell, I will raise.

"So are you telling me, the Divine made a mistake?" I challenge them, knowing this will hit them harder than anything I can say. The rage in my aunt's eyes tells me I am right.

We don't question the Divine's Decree. Ever. It's not our place.

My eyes land on Josh suddenly. His face gives nothing away. I noticed he was sitting with Elder Salvatore when I walked in, talking quietly. I didn't know they were friendly.

"Warriors have always been men," I continue, looking around, "I have no intention of walking into a room and pretending to be something I'm not. I'm not a man, but I'm also not just a princess."

"Tell them. Make it hurt," Eliza encourages and when I glance at her, she's glaring at my aunt, who's giving it right back to her.

"You're not just a princess," Crystal frowns, looking at the men in the room, daring them to speak.

"You're a Warrior and a woman," Vanessa crosses her arms. It's personal to her. She was a high-ranking officer in the Royal Army—she was a female general and that too in the Serpent Division.

"And a damn warning," Eliza finishes, standing up. "You're not just *making* history, you're rewriting it. You're redefining what being a Warrior princess really means. They should see a woman and be fucking terrified."

"And I'd love to see anyone underestimate *you,*" Vanessa grins, her eyes darting over to where my darkness lingers on the wall.

"Or they can just choke on your pretty pearls," Daniya says lowly, but not quiet enough as she pretends to be busy checking out her freshly done manicure.

"Enough!" My aunt rages, standing up too. "This is exactly what we're talking about. If we can't even control the Crescents, who's to say what will happen out there!"

"Control us?" Vanessa smiles wickedly, leaning back into her seat, "Say that again, Lady Susan."

My aunt fumes. I'm starting to love Vanessa.

There seems to be a silent stand-off between some of the Warriors and the Crescents. I appreciate the women standing with me. At least, I know I have them on my side.

I meet Sam's gaze as I feel the darkness rise behind me like a shroud of protection. "Tell the world what I am. Make sure they hear it. And if you can't do it, I'll just go live on Spellbook. Your call," I say to him.

He raises an eyebrow, a smile spreading on his lips. "You got it, Warrior Craving." His response earns him a glare from his father, which he absolutely ignores, and now I love Sam more for it.

"Great," I start to leave but pause at the door. I turn and look at the Warriors. "That thing you all do, where you telepath each other and leave me out—yeah, that stops now. If I don't have your respect, then what's the point of me being part of your Pack? I'm sure we wouldn't want *me* to go rogue, now would we?"

The guys look at each other guiltily as I leave the war room to let them handle the fallout. I hear the sound of a few other seats scraping the floor while one of the Elders asks if I just threatened them by saying I'll go rogue.

You never know.

"That's my girl," Uncle Edward telepaths to me. ***"Your parents would be proud, Rosie. I know I am."***

"I told them not to say anything so you would finally stand up for yourself," Nathanial's voice envelops my mind next.

"Rose! Wait up!' Daniya calls from behind me. I turn to see *all* the Crescents.

I'm speechless at the sight of the six women, and manage to ask, "Did you all just walk out on them?"

"Fuck yeah," Vanessa smirks.

"Can I just say it's so good to have you back?" Crystal laughs, giving Vanessa a tight hug. Eliza, Vanessa, and Crystal were the girls everyone looked up to and wanted to be when we were younger. They were the IT girls—strong, beautiful, confident. Being Mated to Warriors was the icing on the cake. From the outside, they had it all—and they were nice.

"Things won't change unless we make it," Eliza says, reaching me first. She holds her hand out and I take it. "You can never do wrong by standing up for yourself."

"And we don't want to be the women who tells another woman to be less than everything she's capable of being," Azura speaks up for the first time since that meeting started. "One day we will have daughters. How would we face them if we didn't walk out with you today?"

Crystal links arms with her while Mariella joins my other side. I look at each of them and smile so proudly. "I can't believe you did that but thank you."

"You're pretty badass," Daniya grins, "I want to be like you when I grow up."

We all laugh as the seven of us walk out of Command.

"We're about to have a media frenzy," I tell them and it causes Daniya to grin.

"Perfect. I'm ready for a project," she winks, swinging her arm over Mariella from the other side.

"Why don't we give them something to chat about until the press conference," Crystal looks at Daniya suggestively.

My best friend smiles big before pulling out her phone as we step out into the summer day. She lets out a small squeal, exclaiming, "Group selfie!"

We quickly huddle in together and Daniya snaps the shot with Command in the background. She takes a few and flips through them. "Oh, these are great!"

"Tag the boys," Eliza orders with a smirk.

"Tagged and…posted," Daniya declares, before showing us the picture of us, grinning. The caption is perfect: Just a Pack of Crescents.

15 BREAKING NEWS

Rosella Craving
July 25

The mirror steals my breath.

Royal Warrior blue cascades down my back in a silk cape, the leather bodice hugging me like armor with black beadwork catching the light. The designer, Alla, circles me, inspecting every hidden detail.

"Two tops," she explains. "A high-necked cover for missions and meetings—protection. And the bodice for when you want them to know the Veyara has entered the room."

Mariella exhales softly. "Oh my Divine."

Alla adjusts the Veyara crown on my head. "The points aren't ornamental. You can pull them free and use them. Be careful, they're sharp."

She flicks the jeweled chains at my waist. "Weighted. Unclip them and you can use them as whips or restraints."

"Hm, for missions and the bedroom," Daniya winks at me, causing the girls to giggle. She looks at Eliza and shrugs. "Josh deserves it."

Eliza laughs. "No arguments here. Restrain him, leave him for a few hours."

"You guys are terrible," I scold them, but bite my lip from smiling myself. I look at Alla, telling her, "Please ignore them."

She just smirks and then taps my gloves. "Reinforced knuckles. Tempered glass. Strike hard enough and you'll shatter bone." A blade slides from my boot heel. "Hidden daggers."

The girls murmur their approval, admiring what Alla hasn't erased—my curves, my beauty, my presence.

"You weaponized her femininity," Eliza grins, "and we thank you for that."

"Protection is the new fashion," Vanessa laughs, checking out my gloves.

"She's a Warrior and the Veyara," Mariella says. "Not either or."

"We have the first two uniforms," I say.

The second design replaces spikes and chains with structure and authority. A black suit embossed with subtle roses. Another with a high-collar jacket threaded in gold with a shorter Warrior blue cape.

These are for councils, for official visits with supernatural leaders.

"Warrior. Woman. Warning," Crystal sighs, "I think that should be the new tagline for the Veyara Collection."

Alla smiles and tells us, "Everything is adjustable, depending on the day. We wanted to cater to your femininity but not steer too far from the male uniform. It needs to show that you're a team player, but you're also not just any member of the team."

"Every woman who was told she could not, should not, will see you as inspiration. You'll be an idol," Eliza looks up at me.

That's exactly what the Elders are afraid of.

My existence, my transformation, my powers are all a declaration. Whether I mean for it to be or not.

I grin and pull Alla into a hug. "You brought the vision to life."

She smiles. "It's an honor, your highness."

I can't wait to see what she does with the Veyara Collection.

The Crescents excuse themselves after the fitting, but Eliza continues to walk with Vanessa and me.

"As the Veyara, you have a few social responsibilities, which you are already aware of," Eliza starts.

"Tea with the elite women is utmost priority," Vanessa reminds me gently.

Eliza nods. "While you already know everyone, it's a formality, as the Veyara's first hosting event. It's particularly important since you're younger than all the Warriors' Mates. I'd keep an eye on the Honest ladies though—and the serpent shifters."

"I understand," I say. Even though Mariella and I transformed the same night, she's a few days older than me. Being the youngest, to being the Veyara, can cause some friction. I'm not too worried about the Crescents objecting to my role. They've always known I was the Veyara and I don't plan to step on anyone's toes.

The House of Honest and I personally have a more delicate relationship. While most have accepted me as the Veyara, there are some who believe I stole their place. Honest women are born with the hope to be a Warrior's Mate—as a princess, I wasn't supposed to Mate with a Warrior.

They feel cheated.

"The other event is the Veyara Gala," Eliza sighs. "How is that coming along?"

"All the RSVPs are in," Vanessa says and I look over at her.

"You work fast," I laugh.

"Camille briefed me," Vanessa explains, smiling.

I return her smile. "Whatever gets the job done."

"Your dress is pending your final fitting which is scheduled for next week. The event will be high fashion so the ladies will talk about it. It will also be a highly covered event. All the mags and gossip columns will speculate it since you're not allowing any of them in," Vanessa tells me. I keep my smile on, not offering anything up.

We enter my bedroom suite as Eliza says, "It's not every day a royal princess is the Veyara who is also a Warrior."

I inhale, sitting down on the couch. "The Gala is set for Samhain weekend."

Eliza sits too, facing me. "You and Josh need to set a date for *your* blood-tie reunion. The sooner the better before there's a power or Marking scandal."

After a Crescent shifts both Mates' powers grow—as does the need to complete the Mating ritual before the Claiming. They actually go hand in hand. Our powers and Mating bond are very much like a pressure cooker building in us until we complete the process. It allows us to fully come into our powers and control our primal instincts.

Until then, powers can get out of hand and accidents can happen. Lust can also get out of hand and...accidents can happen. I can't afford any of that.

Most couples have already been hooking up prior to the Crescent's transformation, so they can plan the ceremony out.

From what it's looking like, Josh and my first time will probably be our Mating ritual at the last possible moment. I know he doesn't hate himself enough to die, despite how much he claims he doesn't want anything to do with me.

I set my jaw. "We will."

Eliza's lips twitch into a smirk. "Don't wait too long. Though I'd love front row seats to a Mating scandal just to see Josh's face."

"Speak for yourself," I mumble. It's embarrassing to be on the front cover with Josh for an event we have to pose for and then turn around and see him with his flavor of the day plastered all over the gossip columns.

We continue going over a few other events, when Mariella and Daniya fly into my room, excited.

"It's starting!" Daniya says breathlessly. Mariella doesn't wait as she crosses straight over to my nightstand and reaches for my TV remote. She turns it on and the screen flashes, spelling out *Claws24.* Devaughn and Daniel's family owns the news outlet.

Camille follows them in and leans forward in the chair she's sitting in. She puts down her tablet that she's been working on, trying to figure out my schedules with Vanessa. The girls gather around me.

"Every outlet is blowing up!" Mariella announces, scrolling through her phone. "*Crimson9, The Oracle News, Arcane Report, Bloodline 300,* and even *Underlife News* is covering it."

The feed sharpens to a face we're all familiar with. Marin Veylithar sits against a backdrop of rolling headlines. Her golden hair is pinned back with a diamond comb. The Veylithars are a part of the House of Honest—Rage Division.

"Breaking news," Marin declares, her voice strong and urgent. "This is live from Cravenhold."

The camera cuts to the press hall in the administration building. Sam strides to the podium in his formal Warrior uniform, all business-like. The microphone catches the sound of shuffling cameras.

"Ladies and gentlemen," Sam begins, his voice is clear as his gaze sweeps the room. "History was made a few nights ago when Veyara Rosella Craving shifted into the prestigious Warrior Pack—becoming the first female Warrior in our history."

The words echo, and even though it's me who Sam's speaking about, I feel my heart skip a beat at the declaration. This is it. It's done. There's no going back now.

"Here we go," Daniya says as our phones start to blow up. I switch mine to personal mode to avoid the notifications before handing it to her.

Mariella leans into Eliza, saying, "*Crimson9's* running the headline in crimson block letters. *The Oracle's* fishing for a prophecy—not surprised, witches. *Underlife's* gossip threads are boiling over…"

I look over at Camille who's talking into her phone. It looks serious.

Onscreen, Sam steadies himself with both hands braced against the podium. The flash of cameras bounces off his uniform, but his voice is calm with ease.

"I understand the magnitude of this moment," he says, looking out over the sea of reporters. "The Warrior Pack is steeped in tradition, and this announcement may feel…unprecedented. However, the Pack is excited for the change. We look forward to what Veyara Rosella Craving will bring to the table, and we are eager to see her strength integrated into our ranks. She will be taking her oaths tonight." The reporters stir again, hands already shooting up, voices tumbling over one another. Sam nods once, cool and commanding. "I'll take a few brief questions."

The room erupts, camera bulbs flashing like a storm. Sam is used to this, and he handles it with the same delicacy he always does.

The feed cuts mid-shout of a question, the screen switching back to the polished *Claws24* studio. Marin Veylithar's expression is the perfect blend of solemnity and intrigue.

"You've just heard it live," she says, smoothly. "The Veyara, Rosella Craving, has entered the Warrior Pack. We'll be unpacking the implications with our panel in just a moment. Stay with us."

"The last time something this big happened was…" Mariella muses.

"Elena Montanaj being found," Eliza replies. "Last year."

Moments later, the screen splits into four panels.

An Alpha from a European Pack speaks first, jaw tight. "This is a power grab. The Warrior Pack was never meant for a woman. What happens when she's with child? How many titles are they stacking onto one eighteen-year-old girl?"

Aimee Donovan, a prominent feline shifter, cuts in. "Tradition is comfort dressed as law. The Veyara is opening doors for every girl forced into the shadows. It's overdue."

The Alpha scoffs. "And yet your Prides still answer to a male Warrior."

Laura Sylvain of House Honest adjusts her jeweled collar. "I cannot support this. Our hierarchies exist for a reason. A princess cannot carry two roles of this magnitude. Not without consequence."

Marin lets the debate continue before reclaiming the screen. "We'll have more reactions as they pour in, but one thing is certain—the Veyara has rewritten history with her transformation."

"What a fucking ass!" Daniya exclaims. "Can he say that?"

"And Laura…I never liked her," Eliza adds, wrinkling her nose.

"Oh, Laura will definitely face some consequences. Her Mate is one of Sam's bodyguards." Mariella fans herself, shaking her head.

Camille gets off the phone and checks the time, before standing up, saying to me, "Howl Weekly would like to do a feature on you, and they'd like original stills of you in your Warrior uniform."

I'm a little surprised at how fast it happened. "Well, you know my schedule best."

Camille glances at Vanessa, before telling me, "I have to go take care of some things due to this press conference. I'll check back later before your oath ceremony."

I nod, and once she leaves, Mariella edges closer to me. "Well, one thing is true. You sure did make history."

"And she'll definitely be looking good doing it," Eliza sighs. "I can't wait to see everyone's reactions to her uniform."

"I'm more worried about my aunt's reaction," I tell the girls, sighing heavily.

Eliza rolls her eyes. "Whatever. That woman has something negative to say about everything. It's a miracle your cousins aren't like her."

"Helps that their Mates took them far, far away," Mariella adds, quietly. "Though I do miss them terribly."

It does make me wonder what my cousins, Aurelie and Genevieve, think about all this. Maybe I'll reach out to them if they end up not coming to the Mabon festivities. For now, I push those thoughts away and prepare for my oath ceremony tonight.

16 THE WARRIOR'S OATH

Rosella Craving

July 25

My pulse beats steadily, waiting for the signal to step into the throne room. The bodice clings, black leather and beadwork catching the light, and the Warrior blue cape hangs off my uniform. Eliza gently sweeps my curled hair over my shoulder when we hear the sound of heels.

"Rose!" My aunt's voice slices the air, causing Mariella to flinch slightly. Aunt Susan's voice drips with disdain. "What on earth…what is this distasteful costume! A princess should never present herself like this…like a common—"

"Careful…" Eliza comes to stand beside me, frowning at my aunt, but I feel the needles pricking me before either of them can say another word.

"Maybe not a princess," Josh says, walking up to us, "but a Veyara Warrior should absolutely dress to bring the entire room to its knees."

He's wearing the male version of my Warrior uniform, the royal blue cape making his gray eyes shine brighter. Eyes that are fixed only on me. He always looks hot in his Warrior uniforms. He looks good in everything.

I hear my aunt let out a huff, but all I see are gray eyes. I haven't spoken to him since yesterday morning. Yet here he is, elevating me. I wonder what it will cost me later. His *compliments* always come with strings attached.

I break our eye contact and look down at my French manicure, my voluminous curls falling like a veil between us.

"She's so pretty," Mariella whispers to Vanessa. I thought it'd be weird to have Vanessa as a PA, but she's made it all so natural.

The herald appears then, directing everyone forward. Eliza caresses my cheek before walking past my aunt without a glance at her. Mariella and Daniya follow, heads high, and the other Warriors and Crescents do the same.

"See you after, thorn," Shane winks at me before letting Eliza slip her hand over his arm. Josh lingers as they enter the throne room. They all have to go in first before I do, so what is he waiting for?

"I know you're mad at me..." he starts, and I almost break my silence to say I'm not mad, I'm hurt.

Being mad at him is easy.

Being hurt by him...is unbearable.

And I hate it. I hate how often it is, even when I tell myself, I don't care.

"I have something for you," he says. I ignore him. I don't need anything from him. Josh is insistent, reaching for my arm to get my attention.

I snap my head in his direction to shoot him a glare. "Don't touch—" I start, but the velvet green box in his hand stops me.

He exhales, his eyes clashing with mine before dropping to my lips then my pushed-up tits for just a second, before he blinks and opens the box, revealing the Veyara crown. It's not the smaller tiara that we've duplicated for my uniform. It's the real deal—the one I'm not supposed to wear until the Veyara Gala.

I've never seen it this close before. It's darker than I expected. The silver frame is so deep that it almost looks black. Emeralds catch the light, mixed in with heavier black stones that I know are black diamonds. The design is breathtakingly intricate. Moon phases are etched in tiny arcs along the band and wolves are hidden in the swirls of the metal like they're howling or mid-run. Small serpents are intertwined with the metal, camouflaged within it. It's not flashy or delicate like the Luna crown, with its sharp spires. It's powerful—it's perfect.

Anyone wearing this crown could never be mistaken for a princess—because it's fit for a queen—a Veyara.

Josh reaches for the fake one on my head and replaces it with the heavy crown, saying, "It felt appropriate for the occasion."

"Josh!" Sam calls impatiently.

"Coming," he snaps in return, but he pauses to take one last look at me before he moves past, handing the box to Camille and falling into step with Daniel. I watch them disappear into the throne room together.

"I totally caught that on camera, you're welcome," Vanessa whispers to me.

I catch her arm. "Don't post it. Send it to me first?"

Her smile softens and she nods, "Of course. Good luck."

Vanessa quickly walks over to James before they enter the room. Then I hear the herald announce my name.

The throne room is silent aside from the cameras capturing every step I take. The Warriors and Crescents are at the very front, and the Elders just behind them, watching me like I'm on trial. Behind them stands the rest of the court.

My hands are sweaty. The Warrior uniform clings to me like a second skin and I'm grateful for the cape to give me some coverage even though there's no hiding when all eyes are trained on me.

Focus, Rose.

Don't trip. Don't falter. One step in front of the other. Head high. Shoulders back. I keep my eyes forward, each step slow, careful not to let my boots catch the hem of my cape.

I focus on one person only.

Nathanial.

He's front and center, at the foot of the dais, waiting for me patiently. His eyes are older than time, and in them, I see no question of my worth. Only pride.

Nathanial is in his majestic crimson monarch robes—velvet, edged in gold embroidery that flows across his shoulders and sleeves. Over them, a high-collared mantle trimmed in gold frames him. There's a medallion marked with the Craving insignia at his waist. On his blond head rests a gold crown, its spires tipped with rubies that catch the light.

He looks every bit the king he is.

"You look beautiful," he telepaths me and I resist the smile right now.

"Thank you," I reply through the mind link. He keeps his eyes on my face as I reach him. I notice the Warrior's dagger resting in his hands. While it's not a weapon anymore, it's passed down the Craving line, from Alpha to Alpha, but used by Nathanial during oath ceremonies.

His voice carries throughout the throne room, needing no microphone. "Rosella Sophia Craving. Daughter of late Ian and Rosemary Craving. The Divine has chosen you to walk the path of a noble Warrior. Do you accept to carry this honor, burden, and destiny that has been bestowed upon you?"

My throat feels tight, but the answer comes as sure as anything I've ever known. "I accept."

As I say the words, Nathanial's robes go up in flames. I automatically take a step back as the flames engulf him. Then I let my darkness out and try to fight the fire, but the Royal Guards are on it. I feel Josh's hands on me, pulling me back, and Shane's on my other side, making sure Nathanial is okay.

Just like that, the fire's gone, and Nathanial is being escorted out of the throne room. His face and body are hidden by the guards.

"Bad omen," Elder Salvatore murmurs and Shane cuts him a look, before taking Nathanial's spot.

My brother addresses the room. "Stranger things have happened before," Shane flashes everyone his charming smile and my racing heart calms a little. He looks like Dad right now. "Father Nathanial will be alright, but we'll continue with the ceremony."

"Shouldn't we postpone?" I think to Shane.

"Step into the Circle and kneel," my Alpha answers me out loud, his voice carrying throughout the throne room. Shane's eyes glance over at Josh, and my Mate lets go of me, but Josh doesn't return to his seat. He doesn't move an inch. Shane nods at me.

I cross over the salt line and lower myself, cape sweeping down.

"Speak your oath, and let the world bear witness," Shane says, towering over me.

I draw in a breath before I recite the words Shane had me memorize. "I swear by the blood of my father and the breath of my ancestors, to serve as a Warrior. To guard our kin, our court, our kind, with my life. I swear to rise when others fall. To give no ground to corruption, to cowardice, or to fear. I swear to be honest, to uphold the sacred rites, and follow the Divine Decree. Until my last breath leaves, I bind myself to the Warrior's oath."

Shane lowers the sword that's handed to him, the flat of the blade pressing against my left shoulder, then my right. His movements are ritualistic. Then he holds the sword out before me. My own hands close over the hilt.

"Rise, Warrior Craving."

17 LESSON NUMBER ONE

Rosella Craving

July 29

Sam passes his tablet to Shane, who glances at it, then Shane looks at me. I was summoned to my brother's office first thing Monday morning. Josh and James were already in here, and Sam just arrived right after me.

"What?" I ask, and Shane hands the tablet to me. I catch it and see the headline on *The Midnight Times*—the largest supernatural news outlet that covers all factions.

GOWNS TO ARMOR

PRINCESS ROSELLA: THE FIRST FEMALE WARRIOR

"It's the first article," Sam tells me. I read it quickly.

"Doesn't seem so bad," I say.

"It's *The Midnight Times*, it wouldn't be," Sam replies. "But best prepare yourself," he glances at Josh and says, "both of you."

Josh's eyes harden and I wonder if he's thinking about the fallout with Serpent Nation. Should we talk about it? He's never wanted me involved—that'd require him to acknowledge me as his Veyara, so I don't know if I should bring it up.

"Thanks Sam," Shane says and Sam takes his leave. Once he closes the door behind him, my brother focuses on me.

"I know the past few days have been overwhelming to say the least and I'm sure you want answers too," Shane says, gesturing me to sit down at his desk. James pulls out a book from the shelf and starts scanning it. Josh pours himself a drink.

It's seven in the morning. I'm not judging—just observing.

"It won't be overnight, but we'll look into how you've become a Warrior," Shane tells me.

"I thought the Divine chose me," I repeat what my brother's been saying the past few days.

"Well, of course, but why now?" Shane says. "Cravings have had daughters before. Why were you the only one born with gray eyes?"

"What are you trying to say?" I ask him, crossing my arms.

"That maybe there were others," James says, looking up from the book. Long black hair falls into his striking, intense gray eyes. I don't think I've ever seen this guy smile. "Maybe you weren't the first."

"And if you weren't, what happened to the others," Josh finally speaks and I meet his eyes. I still haven't talked to him since the gym day. "There's never been a female Warrior recorded…" he trails off and I know what he's implying but it's crazy.

"Maybe because there wasn't one *to* record," I suggest turning back to Shane, but when I look at the men, I realize what they're really implying. "You think they were killed?" I ask quietly.

"Possibly, or they never existed and you truly are the first," Shane says. "It's not that the Warriors are opposed to women being part of the Warrior Pack. It's just never happened before."

"Unless it has and it was…erased," James adds, before looking at my brother and Mate. "Wouldn't be the first time."

I frown, wondering what he means by that. I'm not naïve enough to think the supernatural haven't been involved in such behaviors, but wouldn't that directly violate the oaths we take?

"And let me guess, I can't be erased because I'm Mated to a Warrior," I say, bored. I've heard this so many times—not that I'd be erased, but how I can get away with a lot because of who I'm related and tied to.

"Hard to kill the Mate of a Warrior without killing the Warrior," James spells it out. I'm tired of hearing it.

"So because his life is more valuable, I got spared," I say it bitterly. "How sweet."

"There's more to it…" Josh says as he comes up to Shane's desk, looking at my brother and James.

"Like how you were Mated in a very…unprecedented way," Shane agrees with him. The fact that we never had a traditional blood-tie union to bond us was natural if anything.

"Everything about you is unprecedented," Josh looks at me.

"Not to mention your powers…" James adds, eyeing my hands as if my powers stem from them. "No one's seen anything like it, not exactly."

"You're an anomaly," Shane smirks, almost proudly, but all I hear is *freak*. "Personally, gives me something to brag about, but different isn't welcomed in the supernatural world."

"Different usually indicates an imbalance in the natural order of things and isn't the best of signs," James adds on, "usually implies a shift in nature."

"Is it an imbalance, or is it a reset?" I ask and I don't miss the subtle spark in Josh's eyes, like the words mean something to him.

"We're hoping to discreetly find something in our library records to prove that this isn't out of the ordinary," Shane clarifies to me before reaching across his desk to touch my arm. "We're not trying to scare you. But you should be aware of the severity of what's going on and what's heading our way. While I don't appreciate the way the Elders have gone about this, we should heed their advice on some of it."

"Trust me," I say, "no one understands that more than me."

A sliver of hope gnaws at me—that there were other female Warriors before me, other women with gray eyes who were not anomalies. Maybe I'll find answers that explain what I am. Though the churn in my stomach and the restlessness of my power tell me the truth—we won't find what we're hoping for.

"By the way," Shane says casually like he's not about to ruin my entire day as I stand to leave. "Josh will be your trainer."

"What? Why?" I ask, staring at my brother and ignoring Josh right behind me. Shane's been training my power since Dad died. Shane has also been very protective of my powers, not wanting anyone to know exactly what I'm capable of. The last person he should trust is Josh. I cross my arms and say, "He'll kill me."

Shane rolls his eyes like I'm being dramatic. "You two literally can't kill each other with your powers. That's the point. Which means it's in everyone's best interest that he's the one to train you."

Yeah, everyone but Josh and me.

"Camille will give you your training schedule soon," Josh tells me and judging by the glint of amusement in his darkened eyes, I know I'm right.

He's going to at least *try* to kill me.

The sky is pale blue when I reach the western entrance of the forest, still blinking sleep away. I only ever wake up this early for spiritual mornings, and never on a freaking Saturday.

Josh is already waiting—leaning against a tree, arms folded, like he's been here for hours. He's only wearing black cargo pants with hiking boots and a thin black T-shirt that leaves his snake and rose tattoo exposed.

"You're late," he says, already turning into the trees.

I glance at my phone. "I'm literally five minutes early."

"We're going hiking," he says and I quicken my steps to keep up.

"Hiking? That's your idea of training?" I ask, irritated.

He turns his head, his expression cold, and his eyes have changed to his basilisk slits. I bite down but don't flinch or take a step back from him.

He narrows them and tells me, "You have one goal, freak," his eyes don't change, "don't give in to me. Not my voice, not my orders, not the things I'll make you want."

I stare at him. "You want me to defy you?"

"I want you to resist me," he corrects as if defying him is out of the question, which sends a strange thrill down my spine. "If you're going to be a Warrior, your shields need to be impenetrable. So we'll be doing exactly that. Consider it lesson number one."

I hesitate.

"I don't want to keep you out," I tell him honestly. Wow, I do need to strengthen my shields because I'm going soft on this asshole.

"Weak shields make you susceptible to all kinds of manipulation," he disagrees.

"Then don't manipulate my mind or emotions when we…interact."

"How am I supposed to know if you're being honest then?" Josh's voice is low, almost taunting.

"You trust," I suggest, though it comes out unsure. "Most people read body language, or facial expressions. The way someone talks can be a clue. Or you just…trust your gut."

"I'm not most people. If I have these powers, why wouldn't I use them?" he asks, dryly, but he's not looking for a real answer.

"Because it's a violation of privacy." I frown. "It's morally wrong."

Josh shrugs. "Depends on your morals."

I scoff, pushing the stray bangs out of my face. "So you're completely okay with invading people's privacy? How would you feel if someone invaded yours?"

"That's the thing about being a predator," he replies smoothly, tilting his head. His black hair catches the dawn breaking through the trees. Why does he have to be so damn *beautiful?* "You know how it works, so you know how to protect and defend yourself against other predators," he tells me.

The conviction in his voice makes my skin prickle. I shake my head, muttering, "Sounds more like paranoia."

"Or just being careful. This exercise isn't about me or what I can do to you. It's everyone. You never know who will attack you in a room, and it's not always going to be physical." His tone doesn't shift. It's steady like he's been living by this creed his entire life. I shake my head, exhaling sharply, but he doesn't give me the chance to argue. "Fine then," he says, his eyes normal now. "Tell me something real."

I arch a brow, crossing my arms over my chest. "Why would I tell you anything? You're not someone I talk to."

For the first time this morning, a smile touches his mouth—sharp and faint, more primal than playful.

"That's real," he says, and his gaze lingers on me a little too long. "Who do you talk to?"

"You already know."

"Mariella. Daniya. Eliza. Shane?" his voice dips on my brother's name, uncertain. He knows we're close, but he doesn't know if Shane knows everything. Josh tilts his head, studying me the way he would an opponent, then tries again. "Daniel, but only because he's Daniya's Mate and you three seem…comfortable."

Something about the way he says *comfortable* makes me snort. The laugh bubbles out of me before I can hold it back. "Enough for a threesome."

It's stupid and reckless, but the way the word rolled off his tongue begged for it. The sound of my laughter cuts through the clearing but Josh doesn't laugh. He doesn't even smirk. The humor drains out of me quickly.

When he finally speaks, his voice is low, "You think I'd let you?"

"Let me?" I ask, laughing again. "You're not my dad."

"No, I'm your Mate," he says, "and if having a threesome with Daniel and Daniya is a fantasy of yours, that's all it's ever going to be." I stop walking and stare at his back. "I have an eight o'clock meeting, so keep walking," Josh calls, but I don't move.

"So you can have all the threesomes you want, but you won't *let me* have them?" I ask him, "Do I have that right?"

He turns to face me and then he's closing the space between us. "Not if it's with another Warrior, no."

I arch a brow, refusing to back down. "So you're telling me…you, Devaughn, and James have never traded partners?"

"Never our Mates," he replies without hesitation. The words hit me like a stone in the gut. My mouth parts, then shuts again.

"Wait," I manage, my voice thin. "Vanessa and Crystal are okay with their Mates…"

"I'd assume so," he cuts in with a casual shrug, "since they hosted some of the orgies."

My stomach lurches. I don't know what to say.

Vanessa and Crystal have seen Josh naked. The thought hammers through my head.

Vanessa and Crystal have seen Josh naked.

Vanessa and Crystal have seen Josh naked.

Not just naked but hooking up with others. What the Hell?

It's the only thing I can think about, crowding out the forest, the air, even the ground under my feet. I'm going to be sick.

Josh doesn't notice, or he doesn't care. He just keeps walking, voice unshaken. "We just don't touch each other's Mates."

If he sees the disbelief twisting my face, he ignores it. I force a breath, taking a second to recollect myself, and then give him a mocking little nod. "So *that's* where the line is. But everything else is fair game?"

His mouth hardens. "I'd never touch a Crescent. It's a respect thing. Warriors don't cross that line with each other. Just like they know better than to touch you."

That makes me stop cold. "So you *do* know how to respect people," I say, my voice sharp, "you respect the Warriors—the Crescents even. But not your own Mate? Not our bond?"

His eyes flash, something dangerous sparking there. "Don't talk of things you have no idea about."

"No idea?" I ask, blinking. "Are we not Mates? Because I didn't imagine what happened my transformation night. Or did you not fuck anyone you could, landing yourself on tabloids, looking stupid."

"I don't know why you're so upset. I never said you couldn't do that," he replies, cold as ice.

The laugh that rips from me is sharp. "Oh, thank the Divine!" I exclaim, too loud, too giddy with mockery. I don't miss the way his eyes narrow or the hardening of his jaw. "That is *really* good to know, Josh." I smile.

There's a moment's pause—just long enough for my smile to sharpen—before he moves.

My back slams against the rough bark of a tree, the trunk digging into my spine as his arm pins me there. His face is inches from mine, eyes burning with that basilisk shimmer that dares me to breathe wrong.

"Keep up the act," he growls, his breath hot against my cheek, "but I know. I *know* you've never fucked anyone. You've saved yourself—for me."

The words hit harder than his body against mine. My stomach twists, fury and shame knotting so tight I can't tell them apart. Because he's right. And I hate him for it.

My lips part, the comeback biting at the back of my throat. *Not entirely true,* I want to spit. I want to tell him about the vampire prince, about why I let it happen the way I did. That I gave the prince that one thing, something Josh could never suspect, so he could still believe I was untouched—because even through his cheating, through mine in my own twisted way, I still saved myself for my Mate. For him. He can't say the same.

Right now, I wish I didn't. I don't know if it's the sureness in his voice, or the challenge in his eyes to prove him wrong—but I wish I didn't. I wish I crossed the line with the prince, because Josh doesn't deserve to be my first.

I don't say any of it.

I bite it back, hard, because giving him that truth is exactly what he's looking for. I have to give him something, or he will be suspicious.

It's too late though, because his eyes narrow and he asks, "What did you do, Rose?"

I feel his basilisk power crawling at the edge of my mind, pushing, looking for cracks to make me sing. My shields push back harder. Darkness rushes to my skin, climbing up the bark behind me, licking along the ground at our feet, but I don't let it touch him.

I start to laugh, victorious. "My shields are holding," I smile. "I don't feel compelled to say anything and you obviously can't read my mind."

Josh doesn't even flinch. "What did you do?"

I frown, daring to look into his serpent eyes. "Why do you care? You just said you never told me I couldn't mess around…"

His lips are centimeters away from me, one move and…

"I'm not fucking around," he growls, "what did you do?"

My breath catches, and I try to wiggle out of his hold. "Take your hands off me, before I make you."

He doesn't.

"Why are you so upset?" I demand, my eyes searching his stone-cold face, "You already know I saved myself. What else matters?" his expression doesn't change, but I feel his mind racing. "Let me go," I repeat. I really don't want to use *my* powers on him.

This time he does.

He steps back as though pinning me to a tree was nothing at all. I stand up straighter, brushing myself off and forcing my darkness to recoil and disappear. My chest heaves.

"Good job," Josh says at last, his voice flat, almost bored. His face gives nothing away. "Your shields did hold in the end."

I freeze, frowning. What? It *was* all training? But we were just talking…

"Let's go back," Josh says, checking his phone and walking past me to the path we came from.

The adrenaline from before still pulses through me.

"Just because your shields held," Josh throws over his shoulder, "doesn't mean I didn't get any information. You need to work on not reacting."

"Just because it's information to you doesn't mean it's important. It just means you don't know everything," I reply, quietly. Spending time with him is exhausting.

"Our Mating bond isn't normal. We don't know how it works or if it's the same as the Warriors."

"What's your point? If I fuck someone, it messes up our bond, but not if you fuck the whole world?" I shove him. I fucking hate him. "You're right, our bond isn't normal—so I don't think your Warrior bro rules should apply."

"If you're trying to make me jealous, going after the Warriors is only going to make you look pathetic."

I tilt my head, smiling before I wink at him. "Not if they want me."

Josh stops in front of me, cutting me off. "Everything I've done," he says, each word colder than the last, "is the consequences of your actions."

"I don't know what that even means." I shake my head, frustration taking over anger. "But maybe you should take your own advice and learn not to react to me, then."

"You're so stupid," he sighs heavily, pinching the bridge of his nose like he's getting a migraine talking to me.

"And you're disgusting," I snap back, ignoring his little advice on not reacting. He makes me so *angry*.

Josh clenches his jaw and doesn't say anything back.

"What does that mean?" I ask him, "Everything you did was the consequences of my actions?" he doesn't answer, so I push, "What did you want Shane to tell me the night I shifted?"

"Drop it, Rose, or you're not going to like it," Josh says in a menacingly low voice.

"Why do you hate me?" I ask him before I can stop myself again. Divine, what is it with this morning?

"What?" he asks, surprised at the question.

"You hate me," I state. It's not a secret. "Why?"

His eyes narrow, before he says, "You hate me too."

"I…" I start, before frowning, "yeah, because you hate me. You hate me enough to cheat. You've never liked me so why would I like you? You've never given me a reason to. So I'm asking you. Again."

I've asked him many times over the years and I stopped, but I don't know—something in the air this morning is charged, and I just have to ask once more.

He shakes his head as he starts to walk past me, "You're not ready for that answer."

I reach out and catch his arm, surprising the both of us. "Our blood-tie reunion has to be completed within the year or else I die," I say to him, "if I die, you die. And no matter how much you hate me, you love yourself more to stay alive. So we have to figure this out."

He looks at my hand on his arm before shaking me off. His sharp eyes meet mine. "Not right now we don't."

"Why?" I demand, digging my heels into the forest ground. "What are you afraid of?"

"Afraid of?" he spits, turning his body fully to face me, "There's nothing to be afraid of."

"Then tell me," I challenge him, "I've asked you multiple times in the past, and I'm asking again. Why on earth do you hate me so much, Josh?"

He looks away from me, glowering at the trees in front of him.

I take a bold step to him, and turn his jaw to make him look me in the eyes. "What did I ever do to you, for you to hate me so fucking much?"

He slaps my hand away, pissing me off. I slap his hand in return. Fire burns in his eyes.

I don't back down, "Tell me. I'm supposed to be your Mate, and you hate me…do you even know what that…what that feels like?"

He doesn't answer. He shakes his head at himself and starts to turn away.

"I'm talking to you!" I exclaim. How dare he turn his back on me. I go after him and catch his inked arm again. "You have to tell—"

Josh pins me again to a nearby tree, but this time I'm prepared, and I press the pocketknife to his neck. He feels it and starts laughing.

"Do it then," he shoves me and the knife digs in deeper, "stick that knife into my neck like you did to my brother."

My hand falters as I blink at him. "Wh-what?"

"You killed my brother!" he snaps, pulling away from me, leaving me to find my footing again. His gray eyes burn into mine as the words hang between us.

I'm so shocked, my brain shuts down for a second. Everything around me dulls, like the world folds in on that single sentence. My chest tightens like it's caving in, like my ribs are turning inward to crush my heart.

"I did what!" I exclaim.

Josh turns his back on me. I can see him cup his mouth.

"You think I killed Noah?" I ask him, dumbfounded, "Why…how? How could I have killed Noah, Josh? I think I'd remember that."

"That's the point," he lets out a manic laugh, like he's been holding on to this for years and now it's set free. "You don't fucking remember."

I stare at his back. "No…" I start, shaking my head and stepping backwards as tears spill out of my eyes. "I get that you hate me. And I get that you don't want to tell me why," I say and he turns to look at me, but I'm still shaking my head, "but you will not accuse me of *murder*. You will not dare pin something like that on me."

He just stares at me.

"I remember the night Noah died," I say and he frowns, "I remember being asleep in my room when the alarms were sounded for a fallen Warrior."

Noah wasn't a Warrior yet. He was fourteen, but he would've been the last Warrior—or so we thought. Therefore, the alarms still sounded for him. The blue flames were lit into the night for a fallen Warrior when Noah died.

Josh drops his gaze, shaking his head, before he looks at me again. "No, you're right. You were asleep when Noah died."

I stare at him for a long moment, before I say, "Fuck you."

He gives me a cruel smile. "Fuck you too, Rose."

"All these years, you've hated me because you think I killed Noah? Stabbed him in the neck? Are you insane?!" I ask him. I sigh in disbelief. "You wanted me out of the way that bad, you want to frame me for a murder I didn't commit?"

He doesn't say anything. I watch him and see the frustration on his face.

"Is it Natalia?" I ask him, surprised by the softness of my own voice.

He looks at me, brows furrowing. "What?"

"Is she the reason for all this? Or is it Camille? Why do you want me out of the way? For who?" I ask. I have to know. When he still doesn't say anything, I say, "Let's just set a date for the reunion, get the Marking over with, and you can be with whoever you want."

I shift into my wolf and take off.

18 TEATIME

Rosella Craving

August 2

The tea party is in full flourish, porcelain clinking against saucers and sugared biscuits vanishing faster than the servers can replenish. Camille drifts between tables with that calm, efficient grace of hers, making sure the Crescents and the courtier women are comfortable. Conversations flow throughout the garden with curated laughter and gossip.

I make my rounds as I'm supposed to when a pair of women dressed in pastel colors, heavily adorned with large jewelry pieces, catch my attention.

Their mouths are pursed, and one whispers just loud enough for me to hear, "Widowed shifters are the worst, especially that young."

"Agreed. They always manage to make themselves so…useful," her friend chimes in. I pick up a teacup as I slip into their circle.

"The worst?" I ask, tone light as sugar. "What do you mean by that?"

The women freeze, one staring into her cup as if the answer might be at the bottom. The other fiddles with her pearls.

I smile, tilting my head. "Please, you don't need to worry about offending me. I'm here to listen after all," then I fake-roll my eyes, "besides, if this tea is only for praise and pleasantries, I will fall asleep."

Finally, one of the women says, "It's only that…widowed shifters can be disruptive to Mated pairs. They attach themselves…unnecessarily."

"Clingy," the other friend offers, her eyes flick over to Camille, "and before you know it, they start expecting things."

We've caught the attention of a few women nearby, who murmur in agreement with a ripple of unease.

Another woman laughs nervously, telling the women, "We shouldn't bore the Veyara with all this. She already knows exactly what we're talking about."

"Oh?" I ask, looking at them before glancing at Mariella and

Daniya, who are frowning.

There's a pause before another woman spills. "Well…the Beta has a…favorite. Surely, you know, Veyara."

I keep my face blank, though my pulse spikes.

"Yes," another woman steps in, "a wife must always know these things…it is truly admirable that you've kept some of these women on staff despite—well, not every woman would have that kind of grace or strength to see their Mate's pets, day in and day out."

I don't look at my friends as I set my teacup down and ask the women, "So what would your solution to this be?" I make sure my voice is calm and genuinely curious. "Widowed shifters are valued at court because they don't have an attachment or duties toward a Mate. They can be devoted to their work."

"Maybe that much devotion is…dangerous," someone suggests.

"Most of these women lost their Mates serving us," Vanessa interjects, coming to my defense, "that sacrifice deserves respect."

"No one's arguing that, Crescent Tens," a woman says softly, "but we certainly shouldn't have to repay them by sharing *our* Mates. That's asking too much of us."

The debate continues with more laughter and pointed comments. I glance over at Camille who doesn't seem unfazed if she heard any part of this conversation. She moves as if she hasn't heard any of it, perfectly polished and professional.

I wish I could be as unbothered as Camille, but the nausea twisting in my stomach doesn't care. I thought I'd dealt with enough of these conversations, seen enough of Josh's latest flings on the front page or first thing when I got on social media, to tackle this.

Ever since I came back from my Tour, I've just brushed it off. So why is it bothering me so much now?

Mariella catches my eye, her expression tight. *Are you okay?* she mouths.

I force a nod, lift my teacup, and sip.

A little later as I walk with Vanessa, our arms linked, we circle past the far end of the garden where a few tables are tucked under the shade of beautiful willow trees. The laughter catches my attention. Five women are gathered closely, their heads leaning in and their teacups forgotten due to their gossip. I recognize three of them, and they're all serpent shifters.

"The Beta always did prefer blondes," Juniper Eryndal says, tapping her manicured nail against her teacup. "They don't look like his little princess, less guilt, I suppose."

There's a ripple of laughter as Vanessa looks at me.

"Maybe we should go this way," Vanessa starts, but I glance at a table near the women. She dutifully follows me as I sit with my back to the serpent shifters. A statue of a previous Crescent shields most of me from them in case they look over.

"Mm, I don't know," Monica Cyrinth counters, "I've heard he likes dark-haired women since the Veyara doesn't put out."

The others murmur in agreement. Then Natalia Osvaron says, "That's the rumor, isn't it? That he hates her. Can't stand his own Mate. Can you imagine?"

"No wonder he's seen with a different woman every time and doesn't even bother to hide it. He never has," a fourth voice inputs.

"Who is that?" I telepath Vanessa.

"Constance Cyrinth, Monica's distant cousin," Vanessa answers.

"Isn't it weird that they've both hooked up with him?" I ask.

"May the best woman win, I guess," Vanessa replies, the disgust obvious in her thought.

"Maybe she'll finally fuck him now that she's shifted," Monica lets out a laugh. Why do they care?!

"Oh, well, he does love being watched," the last girl drawls, "the first time we met, he made me ride him in our VIP booth. He did not care who saw."

Vanessa's expression turns murderous before she answers my unasked question. ***"Mona Eryndral. She's making a big stink on socials about you sending her snakes."***

"Too bad none of them bit her. Might need larger snakes next time," I reply, dryly. Vanessa smirks.

The laughter from the girls is light, airy like they're discussing the fucking weather.

"He'll fuck you up against a wall, but don't dare tell him what to do," Juniper says, "he'll walk out…or punish. I do love when he punishes…"

Punishes? What the Hell does that mean?

"He *does* love it rough, doesn't he?" Natalia giggles, "The Beta's not shy about leaving marks. One time, I couldn't wear an open dress for a month. I *crave* his claws."

"Rose..." Vanessa reaches for my hand. I think I'm going to be sick, but I have to hear this.

"Hmm, I remember at the Alpha and Luna's blood-tie reunion...I counted three times just the first round," Constance sighs, reminiscing.

My Mate was with someone else at my own brother's blood-tie reunion. What did I expect from the man who fucked someone days after my parents' death? Josh did not give a fuck how it affected me, almost as if he does it on purpose—he probably does. It's sick.

Blood-tie reunions can get explicit after the main ceremonial ritual. The parties have always been some of court's favorite. I was never allowed to go to one before shifting. The first one I will get to experience is Antonio and Mariella's which is coming up next week.

"Come on, you don't need to hear this..." Vanessa thinks to me gently.

I cut her a look. ***"Yes, I do. I want to know what these bitches are saying behind my back. I will not be naïve."***

She doesn't push and we return to listening.

"Oh please," Juniper laughs, "three is nothing. He's a basilisk! He can go all night if you let him."

"Oh Divine, he does this thing with his tongue...do you think he's here? Maybe I'll go find him after this stupid tea party," Mona says.

Thing with his tongue?

"The flag is up, so he's at court," Monica answers, "maybe I'll even join you." The girls laugh like it's the funniest thing they've heard.

"He would not be opposed to that," Constance chimes in. "Think he'll have his own harem now at Coilspire?"

"Not if the *Veyara* has a say," Natalia huffs.

I inhale deeply, before looking at Vanessa. "Let's go."

She gets up and starts walking with me. "Rose..." she trails off like she has more to say.

"What?" I ask her, sighing.

"I'm sorry...I just can't believe what I heard." She glances at me. "Hearing that was rough as his friend...are you okay?"

"No, Vanessa, I am not okay," I reply in a low voice, "but I have a fucking party to finish."

I've nearly made it through the tea party without screaming, when a group of older court matrons wave me over.

Crystal links arms with me, grinning as she tells Vanessa, "I got this one."

Vanessa reaches into her small bag and pulls out what looks like a tiny potion bottle—some kind of drug for sure—and takes it. Ugh, I'm jealous.

As we walk over to the women, Crystal winks at me. "Just keep your cool and follow my lead."

"Oh no," I say, plastering a smile on my own face.

"Rosella, darling!" one woman croons, beckoning with fingers glittering in rings, then her eyes flicker over to Crystal. "Crystal, you're absolutely glowing! When are you due again, honey? Come, come, sit with us."

"Oh, thank you, Auntie Alexa," Crystal sits and I understand why she decided to accompany me for this. "Not for another five months," she answers her aunt.

I sit beside her as their perfumes and pearls take over my sight and smell.

"We were just saying," a second woman begins warmly, as she pats my hand, "how proud we are. Our little Rosella, grown into such a formidable young woman. Even without the Veyara title, you're really something."

I give them a polite smile and a laugh, "Oh you're too kind, Lady Orynth."

"But Crystal, you know how things are," a third woman cuts in, looking at Crystal before turning her focus on me. Laura Sylvain, I recognize, having seen her just on the news. Interesting that she went on national television and then had the balls to still come to my tea party. She sighs, dramatically, "You must learn the harder lessons, now dear."

"Harder lessons? Such as?" I ask, glancing at the women and taking the bait.

"A Mate's affairs are not about love or loyalty," a fourth woman says after taking a sip of her tea, "men have always strayed and they always will."

"Especially those in power—Alphas, Betas," another chimes in knowingly, and I wonder how many of these women were the rivals of the previous Crescents. "Too much power, too many options. You can't fight it, it's best to manage it instead."

My stomach tightens, but I keep still, listening as they pour their poison into my cup. ***"Are they for real?"*** I think to Crystal.

Crystal rolls her eyes. "Ladies, let the Veyara at least have a chance! She's just shifted."

"Don't mind us, dear, we're only looking out for you," Alexa Bravaryen, Crystal's aunt, coos, "we've seen the Beta's love for…shiny new things."

"Think of it as strategy, not betrayal," Laura Sylvain advises, "keep the enemy where you can see her."

"And someone in your power must know every one of them," Lady Orynth says, "a rival under your nose cannot strike from the shadows."

Well, that's actually good advice in general.

"But you must remember," the fourth woman, whose name escapes me still, adds smoothly, "these women mean nothing in the end. They're…distractions, a new flavor. You, darling—you are the Mate. You are permanent."

That's the problem.

"Yes, you hold the one thing none of them can give him—children," Lady Orynth says, head high, "thank the Divine the blood-tie doesn't allow Warriors to sire bastards. No matter who warms his bed, only you can give him heirs."

Their agreement comes in unison as Crystal reaches for my hand under the table in silent comfort.

"In through one ear, out the other," Crystal's voice rings in my head.

"You'll always be the most important," Lady Bravaryen says, matter-of-fact, like it's an honor to be the *most* important. Divine. She continues, "The mistresses fade, the lust dies out, he'll get old, but you'll remain until his dying breath. He can take his pleasures from where he wants, but legacy? Lineage? He'll have to come to you for that."

Gross. What if I don't want to attach *my* legacy or lineage to him? Why would I want him to be the father of my children?

My teacup remains steady in my hand even as they beam at me like they've bestowed some priceless wisdom.

"You've done well in the past in handling the Beta's indiscretions, you don't need *that* many lessons from us," Lady Orynth chuckles lowly. Who the Hell are these women to give me any kind of lessons?

"We only want to protect you," the fourth woman concludes, her tone soft as though she's delivering kindness, "to prepare you for the life you've stepped into."

"Yes, we are so proud of you. You've always carried yourself as a true princess should," Lady Bravaryen smiles brightly.

Crystal and I stay a little longer to be polite but not a second over. As we walk away, she sighs, "Wish you had something stronger than tea at this party, huh?"

I ask, "Does it get easier?"

"Depends how you go about it," she answers honestly, "it helps if you both are on the same page and look unbreakable."

"We are unbreakable—literally a Warrior's Mating bond," I say as Vanessa rejoins us.

"Ew, how'd it go with the cronies…" Vanessa starts, before touching my arm gently, "they weren't too harsh, were they?"

"The usual," Crystal replies to her, then says to me, "You have nothing to worry about. Josh always goes out with us and…he's actually been a good boy lately."

I frown, "What do you mean, he goes out with you?"

I think of how Josh said they hosted orgies he's been to.

"Oh, just when Devaughn, James, Crystal, and I go out, Josh comes. Shane and Eliza too before she got too pregnant," Vanessa says with a small shrug.

"Ugh, that'll be me soon," Crystal whines.

I don't say anything as my mind races. They're confirming they had front row seats to Josh being with other women. Vanessa and Crystal have always been kind to me, friendly—but to know this…

They notice I've gone quiet, and exchange looks before Crystal says softly, "For what it's worth, we tried to steer him your way…Eliza tried *hard*."

I look at Vanessa, who just shakes her head and rolls her eyes again, "I love Josh like a brother, but he has things he needs to sort out."

"Don't worry," Crystal smiles at me as we approach the other Crescents, "things will be different now, you'll see."

I want to believe her, but I stopped hoping a long time ago. Maybe the cronies had a point. Maybe everyone today had a point.

My cheeks hurt from smiling, and the scent of all the perfumes clashing gave me a headache. Now it's just Mariella, Daniya, and me on my balcony. The evening air is cool against my skin as I take a slow drag of the blunt. Mariella lounges beside me on the sofa, while Daniya has her legs curled under her chair. The tea has been long over, thank the Divine.

"I can't believe Josh actually said that to you," Daniya says, disgusted, "*you* killed his brother?"

"He says I don't remember it, conveniently," I shake my head, "and he's in no rush to enlighten me."

"Do you think he really believes that and that's the reason for everything? Or is it a cover?" Mariella asks.

"I think he's a fucking asshole and said that to fuck with Rose's head," Daniya answers her, before she reaches over to touch my hand, "ignore him. He's a jerk and you'll see, soon enough the Mating bond will sort everything, and the *real* truth will come out."

How am I supposed to forget he accused me of murdering his brother? How am I supposed to forget and put all the cheating behind us? Josh has always been cruel. He's never hesitated to hit below the belt—has no remorse for it when he does. But accusing me of killing his brother is a whole other level of…hate.

"So," Mariella begins as she exhales smoke, "do you believe Crystal and Vanessa, then?"

I take another drag and let it burn the edge of my throat. I told them about what I learned at the tea party.

I shrug, "I want to, but it's clear they're his friends first…"

"I'm sorry," Daniya reaches over to squeeze my arm, "I just…I don't get what his deal is."

"Right…one second he's a complete ass, the next he's defending you in war rooms…" Mariella frowns, shaking her head.

"He wasn't defending me," I shake my head, "he was defending his image."

"You know what I don't get?" Daniya asks, putting out her cigarette butt and replacing it with her wine glass. "Why your brother never set him straight?"

Shane and I have gotten into heated fights over this when it first started, but it never led to anything. Shane would always say Josh was grieving and to be patient. Learning my brother and Eliza were a part of Josh's nights out doesn't help either. It's almost as if they supported him. Why would they do that?

I laugh remembering something the cronies said. "Can you believe I was told all I'm pretty much good for is making babies?"

Mariella wrinkles her nose as Daniya rolls her eyes.

"It's so much more—especially in your case," Mariella frowns. "Mating fuses our powers with theirs. If anything, Josh should be catering to your every need. Everyone knows your powers rival even Shane's so…"

"Okay, but Josh's powers are…scary too," Daniya points out, "poison, looks that can literally kill. I've seen flowers die and birds fall from the sky when he's pissed."

"I don't know, you're stronger than me. I would've handed Antonio his balls on a platter. Good luck using me as a baby machine and he'd still be stuck with me," Mariella shrugs. Daniya and I stare at her and she shrugs again, "What?"

Among the three of us, Mariella is not the violent one.

"How are you okay with it?" Mariella asks Daniya.

Daniya just lets out a laugh and winks at Mariella. "Well, Daniel's not exactly cheating. I get to watch."

"Why would you want to do that?" Mariella shudders. The memories of Josh having sex takes over my mind. I think I'm going to be sick. I've watched enough.

Daniya shrugs, "Daniel and I…we don't do anything the other is not okay with. Certainly not for everyone, but it doesn't have to be a bad thing. Could be good for some relationships."

What if Josh wants that? Could I ever bring myself to be okay with that if he does? I think about the women at the tea party gossiping about their time with him—I don't think I could…the idea makes me want to cry and stay in bed for days. I don't want to share him, even if things never work out between us. I *can't.*

Even if he hates me for the rest of our lives and never touches me. I don't ever want him to be with anyone else.

I press the blunt to my lips, inhale until my lungs sting, trying to bury the thought.

He's *my* Mate.

I tell myself those women don't matter but it hurts. He had me, but he chose to be with them. Age of consent for shifters is sixteen—he just couldn't wait.

Everything about today makes me never want to see him again.

I know I'm not perfect. I know I've taken comfort in someone else's arms. My pride wouldn't let me lose that game with him. I didn't seek the prince out, but when it happened, I didn't stop it. I knew if Josh ever found out, it'd be a taste of his own medicine. I never felt guilty about the prince.

Then the prince became too important to use. He has not been a chess piece almost as soon as we met.

What if Josh has relationships with women that's similar to what the vampire prince and I had? What if he actually *likes* them? I think of how he winked at Natalia and my heart clenches, hating the thought—hating him.

19 RATTLED

Josh Hunter
August 2

I drop into the leather couch next to Devaughn, running a hand through my hair, hard enough to almost yank it out. James raises an eyebrow.

"The fuck's wrong with you?" Devaughn side-eyes me.

The smoke in the lounge is giving me a fucking headache. The sultry laughs are too loud, the fucking sex noises are irritating. Where do I begin to answer his question?

I glare at him but then James chuckles, saying, "Rose on the brain?"

Devaughn shakes his head and pats my shoulder. "The longer you fight it, the worse this shit gets. Mark her, claim her, and all this…noise in your head quiets down. Keep resisting and she'll be the only thing you can think about. Then you snap and that never ends pretty—for either of you."

My fists clench. She's already all I can think of, and she's not making it easy. I let out a humorless laugh, pouring a shot of Frostveil before throwing it back. The vodka burns on its way down.

"So, I Mark her and things magically go back to normal?" I ask, voice dripping with sarcasm.

Devaughn shrugs, unbothered as always, swirling his own drink. "Nah, nothing's normal after a Crescent shifts. She will always be your gravity. But…embracing your Mate makes both of your lives easier." He sips his drink. "All I know is, your Mate has to be okay with…extracurricular activities. If Crystal doesn't want it, I don't do it, and it goes for her too. It's their Divine right to say no."

James agrees and says in a more serious manner, "Trust us. You're going to want to be on the same page with Rose."

"What happens if we're not?" I ask.

Devaughn and James exchange looks, before Devaughn says to him, "I'm gonna let you take that one—since you have personal experience."

James scowls at him but drops it quickly as I see the memory crossing his face. James doesn't have demons—he is the demon, so whatever he's remembering has him by the balls.

"If Vanessa's not on board with something—let's say, me fucking someone else for example—and if I still do it…which in itself will be a task since the Mating bond likes to resist, the physical pain she'll go through…" James steals the shot I just poured and throws it back. He blinks as he sets the shot glass down. "You'll never forgive yourself for putting her through it. It's physical for them, but mental for us. It's a miracle she even forgave me…"

Devaughn clears his throat, clasping my shoulder. "So if you want to fuck around after you Mark her, make sure she's okay with it. That shit happened three years ago, and James clearly isn't over it."

"Rose would rather watch me choke on a leash, smiling." I roll my eyes, but a part of me is…relieved? If she doesn't want anyone near me, it means she can't have anyone else either.

I know it's hypocritical as fuck, but the thought of her with someone else makes me want to kill everything in sight. Some people are into it, watching their Mates being pleasured by others—shit, I've been to countless sex parties and clubs. I've shared partners in the past, sometimes with these two idiots next to me.

I'd never share Rose. Even if I never touch her, I don't care. No one gets to touch her. I never said it was rational.

"So?" James barks out a laugh before lighting his cigar, his previous trauma nowhere in sight. "Could be hot. Put her only in the Warrior cape and knee-high boots—it's fun if you're cooperative."

"Fun?" I ask him. "I can't fucking think. She's in my head…every damn second. And when I do actually see her—she ticks me the fuck off. It's a cycle."

"So break the cycle. I'm not seeing what the problem is," Devaughn says, looking and sounding confused. "All you have to do is admit you're attracted to her…that's pretty obvious to me."

"Or don't admit it and just fuck her. They don't say hate sex is the best sex for nothing," James chuckles, blowing smoke rings. These assholes are making fun of me. I can't imagine what they'd have to say if they found out I couldn't fuck the girl tonight. It's like my body refused to obey. It was ridiculous.

First, I couldn't even get it up. Second, my body revolted the moment the girl touched me.

"There's no way a girl like Rose isn't going to draw attention. Not only is she nice to look at, but she's also powerful and untouchable." James takes another drag of his cigar.

"Are you hitting on my Mate?" I ask him.

He grins around the cigar. "Anyone with eyes will tell you Rose is fucking hot—a brat, but hot. Brats are hot—what's the problem?"

I know men are attracted to her—she's perfect physically. Her face alone is enough to make any grown man fall to his knees, but her tits…it doesn't help that she's always in dresses that defines them, drawing a man's eyes straight to them even if they're fully covered. I'm scared if I start touching them, she'd never get me off her.

And fuck—her ass and hips. I clench my hand, needing to dig my fingers into her—more than my fingers. I want to bend her over in front of me and just enjoy the view.

This fucking Mating bond is driving me insane. Why is she not going insane too? I need her to go insane. I need her to lose control first, that way it'd be her fault. That way I still stay true to my hatred for her. But of course, my Mate can't just be hot, she has to be fucking stubborn too.

She said she hates me because I hate her. I flinch at the thought, knowing very well I trained her to be like that.

"James has a point. There's never been any scandal on her. We know she goes to the clubs at court but never leaves with anyone. She's been untouchable," Devaughn smirks, "so touch her. You're the only one who can."

The sound that rips out of me is a half-groan, half growl. My cock aches, swollen and furious in my pants because all I can think of is kissing her the night of her transformation. How desperate she was. Then the kiss in the morning. She tasted like sweet, sweet plums and smelled so fucking—

I need to kill something. Preferably slowly.

"Besides, the bond is impossible to ignore, and it intensifies. Nothing makes sense without her." James shakes his head, scanning the crowd in front of us for Vanessa.

"Yeah. Look at Sam," Devaughn adds. "Didn't he have a thing with some Honest chick? Azura shifted and whatever even happened to that girl?"

James shrugs.

Azura didn't grow up in court. Her family isn't from the American Flocks. She came to Cravenhold just after her eighteenth birthday to shift and take her place as Sam's Crescent.

I forgot about his girlfriend prior to Azura too. I don't even remember girls I hooked up with, I'm not going to remember Sam's exes.

"Didn't matter if he knew her or not," Devaughn says, "she's his world now. Very similar to how you defended Rose in the war room and in the forest." Devaughn's smirk is permanent on his face, and I want to smack it away. "What *are* you going to do now that she's a Warrior?"

I shoot him a sharp glare, ignoring the first part of his comment. "That's not up for discussion. It's out of all of our hands."

James leans forward, voice low. "Rose isn't our little princess anymore. We always knew something was…different with her—always is with twins. But she's…she's a little scary…"

Most would think James is the scariest man they've ever met. For him to say Rose is, speaks volumes. A strange sense of pride rushes through me, but the words sit heavy. I take another shot.

"I'll have her back, professionally. She is a Warrior—no doubt," I start before my lips curl into a sneer, "that has nothing to do with our personal relationship."

"Damn." Devaughn shakes his head, leaning forward as well.

"Baby!" Vanessa comes up, draping her arm over James's shoulder as she slips into his lap. Her dress, if you can even call it that, does nothing to cover anything. She nuzzles into him, her eyes clearly dilated. "I missed you."

James chuckles, wrapping his giant arms around her, kissing her pouting lips. I don't know if Vanessa's okay, or if she's partying away her trauma of the past two years—but as long as she doesn't screw up on the job protecting Rose, I don't care. It's good to have her back and I know I will eat those words sooner rather than later.

Vanessa insisted we go out tonight. I shot it down first, not having the urge to go clubbing or socializing. But Devaughn and James were down and said it'd be fine—we'll have a few drinks and go home like old times before Vanessa was taken. I wanted to argue and say I could just drink at home, but I knew better. When Vanessa wanted something, James made it happen. It was always like that. When Crystal joined us, I knew something was up and it set off my alarms. Ever since she got pregnant, she's had no energy for nightlife.

So that's how I end up in our usual VIP booth at Fang Gates with the four of them. Devaughn orders another bottle of vodka before putting a jar of Petal on the table—apparently it just came out in Rose's honor. Crystal settles down beside him looking like she'd rather be horizontal in bed.

Vanessa pulls away from James, clearing her throat, as James and Devaughn trade one of those quick looks that says they know exactly what's up but aren't volunteering shit. Devaughn pours shots, slides one to James, and I snag the closest one to me.

Vanessa and Crystal exchange looks too before Crystal says slowly, "We might've…fucked up with the Veyara."

I down the shot and narrow my eyes. "What does that mean?"

"Just that we might not be in her good graces anymore," Crystal says slowly.

"Sounds like a you problem," I reply. I know better than to get involved in female drama.

James kisses Vanessa's bare shoulder, his voice low as he says, "Tell him about the tea party, babe."

She chews on the inside of her cheek, but Crystal speaks on it first. "It was horrible, Josh."

Vanessa shudders and shrinks into James, which is not like her at all. She exhales, "Women are such assholes sometimes."

A strange feeling starts creeping up on me as they beat around the bush. Earlier I felt Rose's discomfort, but it didn't seem alarming. She goes through twenty moods a day—strongest are usually pain and anger. I've learned to ignore them in the past week. Suddenly, I feel the need to check on her—it's instinctual.

"Do you want a treat? Spit it out," I hiss at them.

"Well, women talk," Crystal starts, "and they weren't exactly subtle. We got a lot of tips on how to manage our Mate's affairs—keep them under our noses."

"You should've heard your little bitches talk though," Vanessa glares at me.

I glare back. "And you let Rose listen?"

She scoffs. "You need to set them straight. They didn't make the cut. They knew what the deal was."

Crystal frowns, deeply. "Why Josh? You knew there was no replacing her—forget about Rose, why would you do this to yourself?"

"And then the fucking cronies," Vanessa's anger finally breaks through. "It's fucking stupid. None of those bitches are Mated to

Warriors. They have zero clue what the bond feels like after a Crescent's shift."

"I told Rose not to worry about it," Crystal sighs heavily, then she turns to fully look at me as Devaughn shifts to rest his arm over her shoulders, "but you're not helping."

"Come again?" I question her.

She lets out an exasperated sigh, looking at her Mate, but Vanessa jumps in. "Rose obviously isn't confident in your Mating bond and I don't blame her. She sure as Hell doesn't deserve to sit through another social massacre like that one."

"I don't know how she sat through it without cutting it short or snapping," Crystal shakes her head, "and the only time she really did say anything it was in Camille's defense."

"Yeah, you're *favorite*," Vanessa glares at me, "the staff? Really Josh? Classy."

"Rose has always handled it," I say, calmly and the look of disbelief that crosses Vanessa's eyes before the disgust almost makes me take it back. Almost.

"Doesn't mean she should," she snaps at me, "when are you going to stop punishing the girl?"

"For something she doesn't even remember," Crystal adds and it's the same conversation again.

"And before we go in circles," Vanessa clearly having the same thought, "all I'm going to say is, how would you feel if she was publicly hooking up with guys and you had to hear about it at the gym."

"Josh wouldn't care," Devaughn says, pulling Crystal into him and giving me a wink, "he's not a hypocrite."

I am definitely a hypocrite. I never really cared if Rose was with anyone else, but when she brought it up during our first training session, all I saw was red. I *didn't* care. I definitely care now.

I throw back another shot as Crystal says, "She's not made of stone, Josh. Just because she doesn't show it, doesn't mean it's not destroying her. She's so young…she's your Mate..."

Now, all I can picture is her alone in her suite right now, gray eyes furious, chin high, pretending none of it touched her.

"That's the point, though, right?" James says, "Getting back at her."

Crystal sighs. "Payback only works if she can actually feel guilty about what he thinks she did. If she has zero memory of it, he's just hurting her for fun. That's just cruel."

The truth is I don't know what the Hell to feel anymore. It's been hard to resist her—painful to resist her. But I know that's just the Mating bond forcing us to complete it.

I know my brother's gone and she's here. She's a part of me—just like I'm a part of her. Hurting her has always hurt me, and it was never worth it. After some time, it just became routine. But right now, I have to calm Vanessa and Crystal.

I lean forward, looking at the women. "I'll talk to Rose…if she wants to talk—but like you said Vanessa, only Warriors and our Mates know what's real between us."

"Does Rose know? What's real?" Devaughn asks me, quietly. "Do you?"

"Rose didn't have to do a damn thing—but she chose to," I snap back. They know I hate rehashing this shit every fucking time, yet they still bring it up.

James frowns. "She was twelve, Josh."

"She was old enough." I bite back.

"Only person who knows what really happened is Rose," Devaughn exhales, running a hand through his blond hair. "There's gotta be something missing. Otherwise, why would Shane stay quiet and let you treat his sister like shit."

I frown at that, but say, "Maybe because Shane knows his sister's guilty."

James looks me in the eyes. "Or maybe he's protecting her. And you. From a truth far worse. Maybe she told him. He's an Alpha. He could read her mind if he wanted to."

Alphas have that unique ability that even Nathanial doesn't easily possess. Nathanial needs to take a few steps before he can access someone's mind. Alphas can access any member of their Pack's mind. Shane is the Alpha of Alphas—he can access minds, from anywhere around the world, anytime.

"She doesn't remember shit," I remind them. It's convenient really. Committing a crime and then having your memories wiped so you don't live with the consequences.

Some of us don't have that luxury.

Some of us have to live with the loss.

Silence hangs between us until Devaughn sighs. He slips a pill past his lips and chases it with his drink. "Always some damn thing in the underworld," he mutters.

James clasps my knee before leaning back, watching me over the rim of his glass. "You better be right, Josh. Warrior Mating bonds can't be broken, and there's nothing worse than royally screwing over a Crescent—much less the Veyara." He crosses his leg over the other, "And Rose? She's in a league of her own. You saw her at the meeting earlier. That girl's a force to be reckoned with."

I clench my jaw remembering what happened at the last meeting. She looked dangerous with her powers rising around her. She looked powerful, menacing, very unlike the pretty sweet princess the media portrays her to be. I've never seen her use her powers like that, but now I want to see her use them on someone. I hate how I wanted to take her on the table right there in front of everyone. I wanted everyone to know that deadly beautiful monster is mine. Fucking Hell.

James chuckles. "I'll pray for you."

I snort, rolling my eyes, but we all know I need all the prayers I can get.

"Just let it go," Devaughn tells me, gently and before I can say anything, he adds, "you said it yourself."

I frown, but James nods, saying, "Mate trumps brother."

I go still. I did say that. They're twisting my own words and throwing it back at me.

Vanessa's brows lift as she perks up a little. "Fuck, how hot was she in the war room, telling everyone off!" She groans, sliding into the space between James and me, like the serpent she is. "The way her powers were threatening to what? I don't exactly know what her powers can do but I don't want to find out…but it was hot. Did it turn you on?"

"You are high as fuck," I tell her, shaking my head as Crystal laughs at her best friend's question.

Vanessa ignores my comment. "You should've just fucked her on that table. I'm mad at you for not giving us that." She is not helping since that's exactly what I wanted to do. Vanessa leans away from me and back into James, still talking to me, "You never know, Beta. The Veyara might surprise you. The good girls always do. You already bring the spark out of her," she smirks, "fucking light her up. You both could use it."

Devaughn laughs, grabbing my shoulder and shaking me. I need another shot. Fuck it, I need the whole bottle.

Vanessa looks up at James. "The way the two of them are at each other's throats—imagine that sex. Explosive."

I hate her. Because she's right. All I can think about are the pictures Eliza sends me of Rose. All I can think of is how Rose was grinding herself on me in her room. It's torture having felt her like that. It's torture knowing for a stolen moment she craved me, she wanted me.

"She has a point," James agrees, laughing too. "Rose was probably the most powerful in the room, second to Nathanial."

I'd say she was more powerful, but no one would dare say that out loud. The idea is exhilarating though…

"It was sexy as fuck," Vanessa sighs.

I raise my head to meet her brown eyes. "Yeah? Then you fuck her."

Vanessa giggles. Whatever she took is clearly taking its hold. She winks at me. "You know that's not how it works. We're all off-limits to each other," her eyes are shining, "but I'll happily fantasize about it for you."

James chuckles against her skin, his mouth finding hers as his hand comes around to snake between her legs. I push myself up. "Yeah, I'm out of here."

I slide out of the booth without another word, ignoring Devaughn's protests. James calls after me, but I don't stop. It's not until I'm outside that the cool August air cuts through the tequila haze.

I almost drive toward the Palace to go see Rose. The bond pulling at me in her direction. I should go and make sure she's alright.

But I don't. Why should I? What would I even say?

She won't want to see me—I know her. Right now, if she's not angry, she's shut down. It's worse when she's shut down.

Her anger I can deal with—it's welcomed even. It's when she's indifferent, when she acts like she doesn't care, that it cuts deep.

By the time I get home, I'm already unbuckling. I grab my phone, thumb scrolling my gallery until I find the pictures of Rose from her birthday shoot. I snatch the bottle of Nightthorn and go to the bathroom.

My hand's around my cock, stroking rough to her face, to her mouth, to the impossible curve of her hips, the fullness of her breasts…I can't stop thinking about the war room. The way her eyes were black the entire time. I used to make fun of her for her eyes—gray or black—but now…I search for them. Everywhere.

I want her eyes focused only on me. I told her to stop watching me on her birthday, but I love knowing that she does.

Seeing her power pressed around us, how she held that over us, it was fucking hot. Then when she threatened to go rogue, even if it was a joke…I couldn't help the pride I felt in my chest because *that's* who my Mate is.

She's dangerous. And fucking beautiful.

I never wanted her more in my life.

I groan, coming as I curse her name, staring at her picture.

This is getting ridiculous. I have to delete her pictures, but not tonight.

I will say it's fun toying with her, even if I suffer for it. Putting her small hand on my dick was a huge mistake. It's all I can think about, her light touch, her palm against my shaft over my pants…

How can I want the one girl who I hate with every fiber of my being? The one girl who stole everything from me.

It's simple, I fucking can't.

I wash off the night and my guilt. The roses on my arm catch my attention in the mirror when I get out of the shower. Fuck Devaughn and his stupid bet. I don't bother with clothes before falling into my bed and staring at the ceiling.

Then I wait.

Every night since her shift, I've felt her need for me. She lets her mind wander and I feel the heat from her body. The scent of her arousal finds me every night. The way she doesn't fight it and comes for me every night—I know when she comes for me. The bond becomes sharper almost like a magnet to get me to her bed.

Those nights, I lie here stroking myself slow, riding the echo of her orgasm until I follow her over. I've started looking forward to the dark. It's the only place she can be mine. Only place I can be selfish and have her without guilt.

Not tonight. Tonight, it's quiet—too quiet. There's no arousal, no pull, no sign of her wanting me. That alone tells me she's upset and hurt.

I told her about Noah, but I wish I could make her remember, then we'd have something to work with. I don't know how to build something with her on false pretenses. I don't even know where to begin.

We can be physical—Hell, the bond would sing at that—but I

never wanted just that with her. A part of me is terrified that if we did explore the physical side, it might be too much for me. A part of me is terrified that I'll give into her.

"I told her," I telepath Shane.

"She didn't believe you," Shane responds, confidently.

"Fuck you."

"I know this is hard for you, but you know it was necessary. Nathanial wants to keep you two apart."

"And you're playing right into it by not telling her and not letting me tell her."

"He doesn't know we know."

I pause, frowning. ***"And what do you know, Shane?"***

It was two years ago when Shane and I learned that blood oaths, or any kind of oaths, do not hold with me. We consulted Lord Veridane about it, and he confirmed that basilisks can't be bound by oaths—it's against our nature to keep promises. So while my best friends and their Mates are oathbound not to tell Rose the truth about what happened six years ago, I am not. Ever since Shane found out, he's been paranoid that I will tell his precious sister.

Of course, I asked Veridane if it was the same for Mating bonds too and he laughed in my face. His answer was simple—Mating bonds are soul bound. It's not a promise or an oath, therefore it didn't apply to my particular loophole.

I've had my suspicions about Shane knowing more than he's let on. He's always been overprotective of Rose, and it didn't make sense that he never actively stopped me from cheating on his sister. He never gave me grief about it like the rest of our friends. He never got in my way. He knows *something* and I've never been able to get it out of him.

"Mates are sacred, Josh. There's nothing above your Mating bond. Nathanial will never understand that. Just like he can never understand the scope of your and Rose's powers," Shane replies, but like always, doesn't answer my question.

I think he's the only one who really knows the extent of her powers—and he'll die before he lets anyone find out. I'll bet that's why he doesn't want her to know the truth. I know there's more to what led to my brother's death, but it doesn't matter. He's gone.

"It doesn't change the fact that Rose killed Noah," I remind him. I still have to deal with that. Bigger picture be damned.

My phone buzzes on my nightstand and I groan, reaching for it. I forgot to silence it.

James: *Telling you. Just hate-fuck her brains out. You'll feel better.*

I stare at the message, jaw tight. I won't.

I have no intention of doing any of that to Rose. The idea of her gagged and restrained takes me back to that dark place I can never go to. She's too…delicate for me to do that. I've called her a spoiled princess a thousand times, but deep down, I always wanted to put the world at her feet and spoil her rotten.

I don't bother replying to James. Instead, I get on Spellbook and MythFeed, regretting it immediately. Rose's tea party is trending. Pictures of it are everywhere. The Palace Garden is set up with floral arrangements and finger foods overflowing tables. And Rose—fucking Hell—Rose looks perfect. She's smiling, laughing, radiant in every shot, wearing a crème and sage dress. Her matching hat dips low, shielding her eyes in some shots, catching the Sunlight in others.

My cock stirs seeing the pictures of her. I could get lost in those gray eyes. Her neckline is teasing just enough cleavage to make me grit my teeth.

I keep scrolling to see some of the women have posted their pictures. Pretty angles with fucked up captions.

Imagine serving tea when we know who's really getting served.

Why break porcelain when I can break the Beta's bed.

She served me tea, but he already served me.

Hosting bitches looks stressful. Hosting him tips better.

It keeps going.

The comments eat it up.

Then one post stops me cold.

The Veyara was sweet, too bad the Beta likes it rough.

The comments flood with speculation about our Mating bond. I lock my phone and throw it on the other side of my bed. I shut my eyes, pinching the bridge of my nose. I should be thrilled they're attacking her like that. They're doing the work for me. It's a good thing.

But I find myself reaching for my phone again and text Crystal.

Me: *You got a pic of just Rose from today?*

It doesn't take her even a minute. My phone buzzes again with twenty attachments.

Crystal: *Pick your fave. Why though?*

I don't respond to her and go through the pictures—not doing my cock any favors. That's not why I asked for them though. I keep scrolling until I find the one that kills me—Rose mid-laugh, her striking gray eyes shining, a teacup in one hand while her other hand rests against her chest. She looks beautiful. My eyes go to her blush manicure and imagine them wrapped around my dick as she strokes me slowly, looking up at me with those big eyes when they're soft and unguarded—ugh, I need to focus.

I create the post on Spellbook before I can overthink it.

Caption: Beware, that smile kills

I tag her, knowing very well, this is the first time I'm doing that. I've never posted pictures of us, much less of just her. I barely post as it is—Sam or Camille do it for me if it's Warrior related. I tell myself this isn't for her. The caption is true. My Mate *is* a killer.

A text pops up and I tap on it.

Natalia: *I'd say the tea party was a success. Give me my prize now.*

I roll my eyes.

Me: *Your bitch ass brother was dropped at your house an hour ago. Watch him closely, or next time his decapitated head will be the only thing dropped off.*

Natalia: *Always a pleasure Beta*

Natalia: *You know where to find me when your pretty little princess doesn't do it for you*

I sigh heavily and then go on to liking every hateful caption, picture, and comment against my pretty little princess until I pass out.

20 DIRTY HANDS

Rosella Craving
August 3

The next day, during my gym session, I let out my frustrations. I hate that Antonio and Daniel were replaced as my trainers. Josh circles me with his calm expression. I know he sees the anger in me. My jaw is clenched, my fists wrapped tight. My rapid pulse pounds louder than the music through the speakers.

I lunge forward, throwing a hit harder than I meant to. The smack of my fist against his block reverberates through the gym. He barely flinches.

"Something you want to talk about?" he raises a brow, pushing me back.

"No," I snap, breathless. My chest heaves against the thin band of my black sports bra, sweat slicking down my ribs, soaking into the waistband of my leggings. We've been at this forever.

"Wouldn't have anything to do with certain social media posts, would it?" he blocks my kick and lets me crash into him harder than necessary, like he's testing how far I'll go.

I glare at him and throw another punch, angrier this time, aimed for his side. "Why would you do that?!"

I woke up to a shitstorm. I knew there would be things about the tea party—I wasn't surprised about that. I was surprised about how cruel and direct it was.

Then, there was his post. Josh posted me for the first time, and his caption was *not* a compliment, even if the world is treating it like one. While I was getting humiliated on one side, the other half of social media blew his post up and now we're the IT couple. Fucking embarrassing.

Josh catches my fist, twisting my wrist, forcing me to stumble. "Me?"

"Yes, you! Why would you post me?" I struggle against him as his arm hooks under mine, and before I can blink, he sweeps my leg clean out from under me. My back slams against the mat with a hard thud, breath knocked from my lungs.

He leans over, scolding me. "Focus your anger. Or else you're just reckless," then he adds, "a thank you would do just fine."

Before I can shove him off, footsteps echo across the gym floor. Devaughn and James stride in from their own sparring session, both shirtless, skin slick with sweat and muscles tight from a morning's workout. While James is completely covered in tattoos, Devaughn just has one on his left arm—the Claws emblem.

Devaughn whistles low, smirking as his gaze drops to where I'm sprawled. "Landing on your ass isn't the Warriors' way, Veyara."

"Shut up, Devaughn." I flip him off as heat prickles my cheeks.

James takes in the scene and judging by the look on his face, he's not impressed with me flat on my ass.

"At least help your Mate up," Devaughn tells Josh.

"Like she said, shut up, Devaughn," Josh replies.

Devaughn laughs and despite my glare, Josh pulls me up. My braids fall forward as I push damp hair off my face. I make the mistake of turning and catching Josh's gray eyes. I flip him off too before grabbing my blood bottle and chugging. I'm not in the mood to give him one of my killer smiles.

"The Veyara's in a mood," James mutters, crossing his arms. It doesn't look like the two are going anywhere.

Devaughn's watching us and pulls his phone out with a smirk plastered on his face.

"Let's settle this the Warrior way, yeah?" Josh says, motioning me with two fingers. All I can think is how those fingers were in the women at my fucking tea party.

I see red.

"Fuck off," I tell Josh, annoyed. "I'm not fighting you."

He circles me. "Why not? I'm the only one you want to fight."

Of course he'd sense the anger rolling off me. Of course, he knows this is about him. It's always about him. I hesitate, shifting my weight from one foot to the other. He's giving me what I want, right? To take the hits on him that I really want to. He can take it—I know he can.

"What's wrong?" Josh tilts his head, "Afraid I'll see what you're really mad about? Or you'll let your powers slip out?"

"I don't give a fuck what you see or don't," I reply, shaking my head as I start to pick up my things to get off the mat, but his fingers wrap around my arm and I yank it away, glaring at him. "Don't you dare put your dirty hands on me."

"There it is, go on," he pushes, not reacting at all.

I clench my jaw and take a step toward him, dropping my things. Then we're circling each other. My glare doesn't soften.

"Wake up on the wrong side of the bed, darling?" Josh asks and I know he's trying to provoke me.

"Don't call me that," I say through gritted teeth.

"Darling?" he asks, confused, eyes focused on me, "I'd say it's an upgrade from freak, but if you prefer, I can always go back to that."

Antonio and Daniel join Devaughn and James to watch us. Wonderful, we have a fucking audience.

"Put the fucking phone down," I snap at Devaughn.

"Can't, Veyara, this is live and they're loving it," Devaughn gives me a cheeky grin as I dodge a fist flying at my face. My darkness lashes out at the phone. A tendril flicks the device out of Devaughn's hand. "Hey!" he protests, trying to get his phone back.

"Might want to rethink that. It's good optics," Josh winks at me and I lunge at him. He blocks effortlessly.

He blocks everything—every punch, every kick. I throw them faster, harder, trying to gain the upper hand on him. This all seems like a dance to him, while I'm just getting angrier.

"Come on," Daniel groans, "you're making it too easy, Rose. I've taught you better. Kick his ass."

Josh isn't even taking this seriously. He's clearly humoring himself with this little sparring session and that's infuriating in itself.

"Not there," he blocks a punch to his face, his arm shooting out, swatting my fist away.

So I go low instead, straight for his balls.

He twists just in time, blocking my knee, a grin breaking over his face. "Now you're just fighting dirty, Veyara."

If I were fighting dirty, I would've called on my powers.

"I don't care," I reply. Sweat runs down my temple, my braids sticking to my skin. I throw my weight forward, breaking free, and forcing him to move.

"You *are* mad at me," he states.

I slam into him, fists contacting his arms. He pushes me back with a single shove, but I spring forward before he can take a breath. My knuckles sting from the impact against his forearm, and this time I don't give him space or the chance to push me back. I crash into his chest, driving us both a step across the mat.

Josh's hands snap around my wrists, twisting them between our bodies. His grip is firm, his breath steady while I'm panting. We grapple, body to body. My braids catch on his jaw as I twist, trying to break free. He counters every move, chest heaving against mine, the heat of him suffocating me.

I notice the guys are gone. Surely, they have things to do other than standing around, watching Josh and I spar, because we can go all day.

He ducks under my arm and hooks it behind my back in half a second. "If you want to fight me, fucking fight me."

I slam my head back just enough to clip his shoulder and make him grunt.

"How can you say I killed your brother?" I demand. Fuck the tea party, fuck those social media posts—I have to know if he truly believes I killed Noah. Would he stoop that low to just fuck with my mind?

"Because it's fucking true," his hold loosens, and I twist, forcing us down. We hit the mat and it doesn't go unnoticed how he cushions my fall—any other time, I would've thought it was sweet—but not right now. Not when the gesture means nothing—when I mean nothing.

We roll, before his weight pins me. He stares down at me. "Do you remember anything from when you were twelve? Let me take a wild guess. No, right?"

I hook my legs around his torso and roll us again, shoving my elbow into his ribs. "I think I'd remember if I killed someone, Josh," I snap at him, but he rolls us over, pinning me again.

"Not if your memories were fucked with. I don't give a fuck if you remember or not anymore. I remember. You killed my brother—" he gets cut off as I push against him. Is he serious right now? First, he accuses me of murder, then my memories wiped? How convenient. For a serpent shifter, I would've thought he'd be better at lying.

"Stop saying that!" I grapple with him until I'm straddling his torso, immediately feeling his hard cock. My breath catches from the sheer gall of him. "Why the *fuck* are you hard?" I snap, annoyed.

He gives me an equally annoyed look. "I told you, this Mating bond is annoying as fuck," but then his lips curve into a maddening grin, "and I don't know, Rose, maybe because it pisses you off. Makes it almost worth it."

I pull my arm back to punch him. He blocks it, of course, and I shove his shoulders into the mat, fists digging into the hard planes of his chest. He eyes me, like he's checking out one of his hoes and I know I'm not going to like what's about to come out of his mouth.

"Can't blame a guy. The Veyara is sitting on top of me, fuming…it's a hot look—even for you," he says, smirk still present, though his voice is cold enough to send chills down my spine.

"You can't think of me like that," I glare at him, well aware he's changed the subject.

He catches my wrists and flips us. Again. I land flat on my back, breath sucked out of me. His body hovers over mine, applying just enough weight to make my mind wander about other times his body could be on top of me like this. His dick now presses deliciously against my clit, and I need him to get off me—or get me off—either would work.

What am I thinking? This is *Josh*. I don't want him touching me. That *dick* has been in too many places already. That's the whole reason I'm furious with him right now with everything that happened at my tea party and after.

"On the contrary," he says, pinning my hands above my head with one hand, fingers wrapped around my wrist with just the right amount of pressure that makes my nipples hard. My sports bra does nothing to hide that, and he smirks seeing my body's reaction to him too. "I'm the only one who can think of you like that."

His eyes move slowly to my lips, to the rise and fall of my chest. I can feel his cock throbbing between my legs, but it doesn't do anything for the anger in me, except fuel it. "I don't give you permission to."

He grunts. "And how are you going to stop me?"

"Easy. Nothing about me should be attractive to you. I'm a wolf shifter. I'm not blonde. I'm much younger than you."

"You think you have me all figured out," he murmurs, gaze sharp on me. He plucks out the switchblade in my bra, his fingers grazing my skin but only to pull out the knife. He tosses it off the mat.

I clench my jaw. "Get the fuck off me. You're pissing me off."

His chuckle is low and I can feel it roll off him and into me. "Good. Normally your eyes are sharp, cold—like the untouchable Rose Craving you are. But this look?" his thumb brushes the inside of my wrist, his face inches away from me. "This rage in your eyes—I've come to learn it burns only for me, isn't that right?"

I hold his gaze. "So do you only prefer me pissed off or all your women? Because I've never seen you fight with anyone else and I've heard how passionate you can be."

His expression stills, though that damn smirk lingers at the corner of his mouth. He locks his legs tighter around mine, caging me in. I need him to get off me. His weight on me feels too *good* that I know I'll break. Why does him caging me down like this feel comforting? Safe? It shouldn't, right?

"No," he answers me simply, "I save my fights for just you, my Veyara."

I love it and hate it when *he* calls me that. He always uses it so calculatingly—to remind me I'm tied to him. "I'm not your Veyara. If you had a choice, I wouldn't be," I growl, reminding him.

"Right." His gaze collides with mine and like the asshole he is, he asks, "How was your tea party, Rose?"

"It was lovely," I say, letting the words drip out, knowing how bitter I'm about to sound, but I don't care. I was humiliated because of him. I'm proud of how I handled it at the tea party, but I'm still just an eighteen-year-old girl who's Mate publicly embarrasses me with his flings. He doesn't even have the decency to keep it private—but I guess that was the point if he wanted to hurt me.

"Oh?" he asks, confused.

"Yes," I continue, "Camille—who I learned at the tea party, is your *favorite*—made sure everything was perfect for her…what are you to her? Anyway, for her boyfriend's Mate's first hosting event. We're lucky to have her, aren't we?"

He watches me, his grip on me loosens slightly, just enough. I seize the opening and flip us over, the mat shuffling under our weight. This time I sit on his lower abs so I don't have to feel anything. I also don't give him any advantage—my legs snake around his, locking him down the way he'd done to me. I'm a quick learner.

He exhales a sharp breath, surprised. Instead of pinning his wrists above his head—where my chest would brush his face—I press his hands flat against his chest, my hands firm over his, not giving him the satisfaction of having me that close.

A humorless laugh slips out of me. "Then I had the honor of overhearing a circle of serpent shifters trading stories about how they had the pleasure of fucking the Beta—and who planned to fuck you next," I tilt my head back, before looking at him again. His smirk is gone but I'm not done. "They love what you do with your tongue, by the way. Too bad that wasn't enough to break our Mating bond. After that, some women decided I need lessons—on how to keep track of my Mate's mistresses and affairs."

I let him go and roll off him, the fight leaving my body now that the words are out of my mind. I feel heavy but also drained. I lay down on the mat beside him, staring up at the bright ceiling. My chest heaving from the confession.

Tears slip from the corners of my eyes, but I don't move to wipe them away.

"It was fucking delightful," I say flatly, "I can't wait to host those bitches again. You trained your women well to hurt me when you're not around to do it yourself."

I knew I'd have to hear it, and I thought I was ready for it. I was never directly attacked before—people would always just snicker or talk behind my back. It got easier to ignore the tabloids, but for women who were at my event to post such crude things…I wasn't ready for it.

I hear him exhaling, but I don't look at him. I don't know how he manages to break my heart before he's even had it.

I close my eyes, trying to rein in my emotions, before standing up. My back is to him as I blink back my tears, though a few slip free anyway. I wipe them away and turn to him, finding him sitting on the mat.

"I wish you were successful, Josh. I wish you did find a serpent shifter to fall in love with and be your Veyara," I tell my Mate.

I don't wait for him to say anything as I walk off the mat and leave the gym. While I mean every word, I hate that I want to take it all back. At the end of the day, no matter how much I hate him, he's mine to hate.

I think about the prince and how different life might've been—Josh with a serpent Veyara and me with *him*. I wipe away the angry tears because that picture is completely wrong. The prince was never endgame, and I don't like the idea of Josh with anyone else.

But I miss the prince. I miss his kindness and his support. It's what used to get me through all this, and now I don't even have that.

"Rose!" Josh calls after me. He followed me out?

I spin around and ask him, "Why the fuck did you post me? To embarrass me more? Like the world doesn't already know I'm yours to humiliate over and over again?"

"That's not why—"

"I hate you. I *hate* you. And you hate me so why can't you just leave me alone?"

"That's not exactly an option anymore," he snaps back, starting to close the distance between us.

"Why? Did I not kill your brother then?"

He halts, glaring at me. I mirror his look. Josh lets out a disgusted snarl, before he says, "You're a real bitch, you know that?"

"Yeah, I do. You made me into one," I reply with no emotion. Then I turn and leave as fast as I can. I will not let him see me cry over him.

21 LOYALTY

Rosella Craving
August 3

Lammas was on a weekday, but Cravenhold hosts the celebrations the following weekend. Any hopes of avoiding Josh and any serpent shifters go right out the window as I'm seated beside Eliza on the raised dais later that evening after the disastrous gym session. We're both dressed in our Mate's House colors as expected. Eliza is in red silks with her Luna crown resting on her soft golden curls. My dress is a mixture of various green and gold with long sleeves. The neckline is low but not too low for it to be scandalous. My aunt hasn't commented yet, so I'll take the win.

"This is our first social event as the Luna-Veyara duo," Eliza smiles at me, the excitement clear in her eyes. "I'm so glad I get to do it with you."

"I can't imagine being here with anyone else. You literally keep me sane." I smile as cameras flash at us.

Across the crowded floor of the Great Hall that's been set up to accommodate the grand feast, Josh stands with three older serpent men. He's dressed much simpler than usual, only black slacks and a green button-down silk shirt—no coat or his Beta crown. His shoulders are rigid, jaw tight, and he speaks slowly. The men don't look entirely pleased with whatever he's saying and occasionally glance over at me. It's obvious what the subject is.

When I walked in, he was surrounded by five insanely gorgeous women, all fawning over him.

Eliza follows my gaze. "You should go over there."

"No thank you. Those men don't look nice," I say through my smile. I especially don't want to go over there after our gym sparring earlier.

"You're their Veyara." Her fingers brush my wrist. "Show them you stand with them, not against them. They believe because you're a Craving, you think you're above them. I know you and I know that's not even a thought for you. Let them see it too."

"They've already made their minds up about me because Josh fed it."

"So prove him wrong too. They're mad because you're not from a serpent Honest family. Show them how being a Craving and a Warrior can be beneficial to Serpent Nation."

"The division in the supernatural world is stupid in general."

"Okay, but you can't say that…" Eliza lets out a laugh, but I know it's to make light of this conversation in case anyone's overhearing. You just never know in a room full of supernatural. But I stand by what I just said.

Sneaking out to be with the vampire prince, and my Royal Tour, opened my eyes to a lot I was ignorant about. I love the underworld life—as dangerous as it can be, I love seeing everyone mixing and interacting despite being different species, factions, or even enemies. It was like none of our rules existed and they were better for it, coexisting. Being at court and showing up as a proper princess is exhausting after my adventures. I feel caged.

That's why Josh wanting a serpent shifter for a Mate is so stupid to me—everyone has their preferences, but if we had a choice and didn't have Mates, why limit yourself to only one species? I might've understood if he wanted to explore outside of serpents.

"What if I do or say something wrong…? I don't know anything about serpents, how their Dens work, or their politics…" I tell my sister-in-law while swallowing the lump in my throat. The serpents terrify the shit out of me. I already feel as though I can't do anything right with them—with Josh.

Eliza's blue eyes and her smile soften, "So start with that. Show them you're willing to learn."

I'm not opposed to learning serpent ways. I would've been more inclined to if Josh was more pleasant, and I didn't feel like I was being shunned by an entire nation of shifters. Sometimes I wonder if things would've been different if our parents were alive. I know his father would've been kinder.

I give Eliza a small nod before scanning the room for Vanessa, but she's already standing just to my right. She walks over when she realizes I'm looking for her. I smile and ask her, "Who are the three men with Josh?"

Vanessa looks over and answers me. "They're Den Lords. Corbin Morvain, he oversees the rattle Den. Next to him is Lord Raiden

Daejin of the Pythons. The tall one with the beard is Lord Nahil Zafir, head of the Cobra Den."

"Thank you, Vanessa. I think I'm going to go say hi." I rise, my dress falling softly around me as I step down from the dais.

"Would you like me to accompany you?" she asks and I catch the slight alarm in her voice.

I touch her arm, smiling. "No, but if it makes you feel better you can stay close."

"Of course. I always stay close."

"I noticed," I laugh and leave her. I can feel heads turn my way as I walk over to Josh. If I catch anyone's eye, I offer a polite smile but don't stop for small talk. My hands are sweating as I approach these powerful serpent lords and I know I need to get it together. They can smell fear instantly and get off on it. I can't let them think they can intimidate me. But fuck, they do.

The three men stiffen when I reach them. Josh's eyes snap to me and he telepaths, ***"Turn the fuck around."***

I ignore him. I can't let him intimidate me either.

"Gentlemen," I say, softly as I slip my arm through Josh's like it's the most natural thing. My fingers curl lightly around his forearm as he tenses under my touch. "I don't believe we've had the pleasure. I'm Rose."

There's a time and a place for titles and I think it's best not to use it right now. If I want them to like and accept me, I figured the best way to do that is to just be myself.

The men look at Josh, but I address the exchange. "I know this is…strange, for the Beta Warrior to be bonded to someone who's not a serpent shifter—" the men stare at my boldness to address the elephant in the room. They've always talked about it, but never to my face.

"What the Hell do you think you're doing?" Josh asks in my mind, and I'm surprised to hear the slight fear under the anger. What is *he* scared of? Surely, not these men that he can overpower with just one look.

"—but I'm so looking forward to learning the serpent ways and how I can best be of service to you and the rest of Serpent Nation," I finish, kindly.

Lord Morvain narrows his eyes while Lord Daejin chuckles as if I said something funny. Josh cuts him a look but he still chuckles quietly.

It's Lord Zafir who speaks. "Of service?" he repeats my words. "Veyara, you outrank nearly everyone in this room."

I laugh, light and surprised, as if the idea is brand new. My gaze slides to Josh. He's watching me like he's trying to decide if he wants to murder me on the spot or I've completely lost my mind, and he can excuse this as a moment of insanity.

"Rank is a gift from the Divine," I say, still looking at Josh, before I turn my focus back to his Den Lords. "My duty is the same as my Mate's—to serve shifterkind."

The four men seem to be at a loss for words, but Lord Morvain asks, "You would take counsel from us?"

"Oh, most definitely, Lord Morvain," I answer, sweet as summer wine. "I'm embarrassed to say I don't know much about Serpent Nation, but I'm a quick learner. That's why I hope to rely on the Den Lords for guidance. I know you will be departing shortly from Cravenhold, but perhaps we can arrange a sit-down for all of us to get better acquainted."

The men don't say a word, not even Josh in my head. It's clear they were not expecting this from me. Eliza always does have the best ideas.

I spot Daniya and Mariella, so I loosen my hold on Josh's arm. "It was lovely meeting you," I tell the men before addressing each of them. "Lord Morvain. Lord Daejin. Lord Zafir. If my Mate is being hardheaded, you're welcome to reach out to me. I promise I'm nicer."

I feel Josh's glare burn into the side of my face, but I just look at him and wink before waving to the men as I walk past them to meet my friends. My spine stays straight as I walk away.

"Was that your idea of revenge for the Spellbook post?" Josh asks through the mind link.

"Is it that surprising that I want to know more about Serpent Nation? It's not like you'll educate me," I reply as I link arms with Daniya, telling the girls, "I need a drink."

"On it." Mariella smiles, scouting out a passing server.

"You're not a serpent."

"No, but I can be, and I am the Veyara, so I should—"

"You shouldn't do anything except stay out of the fucking way," I feel his anger and frustration down the bond, which only riles me up. I take the drink from Mariella's hand and throw it back. Moon's Kiss—of course.

I reply to his rude comment, ***"No."***

"No?" he repeats, ***"Why can't you be just like the other annoying socialite women and want to be a trophy wife. I'm taking the responsibility off your hands."***

"Should've been successful at finding said socialite trophy wife then. I've been in your way since I was born, I'm not stopping now. Not when things are getting interesting," I reply and I'm not sure why I thought that to him. Either way he can't get rid of me.

"I'm not fucking around, Rose. You will not be involved in serpent matters. Know your fucking place."

"I'm the Veyara—it is my place."

"The Veyara is as involved as her Beta wants her to be. This is not a negotiation," the anger and annoyance are clear in his thought, but again, I feel the slight fear with it too.

"What are you afraid of?" I call him out on it, and I know this is dangerous territory.

There's a slight pause, and I turn my head to the right slightly to look at him, fully expecting to meet his cold gaze. To my surprise, Josh isn't where I had left him. He's in an animated conversation with Nathanial and Elder Salvatore. What the fuck? Since when was he besties with them? I remember him sitting next to Elder Salvatore at the last war room meeting.

Then he does shift his eyes to me and thinks, ***"All you do is fuck shit up. Stay out of my way, Rose, or I'll make you."***

I respond with narrowed eyes. He'll make me? I'd like to see him try.

On Monday, Camille sits across from me in my office and says, "There are a few things that need your attention." Her blonde hair is sleeked back, light blue blouse tucked into her pencil skirt, and her face impassive as always. "Your dress for Warrior Rage's blood-tie reunion has arrived. Updates on the preparations for the Veyara Ball…I do need a few sign-offs—nothing major."

I follow her list on my own tablet, though my mind is in a million places.

"Also, the critic pieces on you as the new Warrior are out. Seems to be mixed responses—some skeptical, others supportive. We expected this," she says, not sounding concerned at all.

I lean forward in my chair, resting my hands on my desk. "I want to ask you something, and I would prefer you to be frank with me," I start, carefully.

Her posture doesn't shift, but I catch the tiniest flicker of curiosity in her eyes. "Of course."

"Your relationship with Josh...do you prefer how things have been? Or would you rather be reassigned?" I ask, watching her. Camille is a serpent shifter, and her Mate was from the Honest House Osvaron. From what Franklin had told me in the past, Camille's Mate served Josh as one of his army commanders before he died.

The question hangs heavy between us and I'm aware it seems like a trick.

She answers calmly. "The Beta and I are strictly professional now."

I let out a small laugh. "Did Josh tell you to say that?"

"No, it's true. He hasn't sought anyone out since your transformation."

"And how exactly do you know that?" I ask her, tilting my head.

Camille's answer is rehearsed. "Because it's my job to know where you and the Beta are at all times. I work closely with the guards for a reason. There's little I don't know about you, both."

I study her, searching her face. Her fingers fly on her tablet for a second, and a few moments later, my computer alerts me of a new email. I glance at it.

"It's a list," she explains, maintaining her professionalism like we're discussing logistics and not my Mate, "every woman he's ever been with. Names, dates, locations, circumstances. Something a Veyara might need in her pocket."

I stare at the screen, my stomach twisting as I scroll past line after line. Some names I recognize, many I don't. She even has a separate column for repeats. It's all organized neatly like a wine collection.

It's all here. The number I know very well. Four thousand six hundred and twelve. Bile rises in my throat. I look at her. "Why are you giving this to me now?"

For the first time during this meeting, she hesitates. Her gaze drops to her hands, her fingers smoothing the fabric of her skirt as if she's buying herself some time.

She's still professional, but there's a genuine rawness about her now. She exhales, looking up at me again. "I know you've known about the Beta and me for some time now. You never held it against me. This is the least I can do for you."

Her words sink in, but I just don't believe her. She's not giving me this list for free. Either she wants something, or she will down the line.

"If you're aware of where Josh and I are at all times…" I trail off, my mind reeling.

Camille studies me for a long moment, then asks, "You want to know if I know about the prince." I hold her gaze—well, clearly she does. "I know everything your security detail knows," she tells me, "it's within my clearance level."

The air rushes out of me as I barely manage to ask, "How many people have that clearance level?"

"One hundred and forty-seven," Camille answers and I force myself to keep my face neutral.

"And Josh? Does he know?"

"No," Camille shakes her head. "I would know if he did."

"You never told him?" I ask, curiously, "Why? You could've used it against me."

"For what? You both are Mates," she frowns, "and it's not my place."

"Not your place?" I ask. "You just gave me a neat little archive of every woman he's ever slept with, but you draw the line here?" It wasn't her place to fuck my Mate either, but I don't say that.

"The list isn't for revenge. It's information if anyone ever tried anything against you," Camille says, "it was always for damage control. The Beta's affairs were never a secret…yours is. Your secret is not for me to reveal to him."

"Even if he asks?" I question.

"Yes…" she says, and when I wait for her to explain, she sighs heavily, "I don't trust him to not hurt you."

I sit back in my chair. I don't know why her words are a shock to me.

"Why do you say that?" I ask quietly. "Has he told you something?"

"No. The Beta does not discuss you with me. It's just what I've picked up over the years. I wouldn't put it past him," she says, keeping her voice neutral.

I clear my throat. "Is there anyone on this list I need to worry about?"

Her brows knit together like she's flipping through her mental file.

"No, Josh never got personal with anyone. It was always just physical."

I raise an eyebrow. "I'd say that's personal. Especially if he saw them often or repeatedly."

Camille's voice is calm. "Not in the way it should matter. At the end of the day, you're the Veyara. Now that you shifted…" her gaze bores into me, "things will fall into place. These girls on social media claiming to know him, or know what he prefers, don't know anything."

"Oh?"

"I don't think there's anyone who truly knows the Beta. Not even me," Camille explains and I do believe her because of how her voice drops. It's something that bothers her. It makes me a little sad for Josh to learn that she thinks there isn't anyone who truly knows him.

"How can I trust you?" I ask her.

She stands and goes over to one of my bookshelves. She retrieves an empty vial and walks back to my desk. Then she extends her fang and pierces her palm, letting the blood fall into the vial.

A drop, two…three…

Then she closes it, wiping her palm with a tissue from my desk, and handing the vial to me.

While human blood is like water to us, our own blood is the highest currency one can offer. When I don't immediately take the vial, she places it carefully in front of me before sitting back down on her chair.

"You can trust me," she assures me with a small nod, her eyes glancing over to her blood drops, before looking back at me.

I reach for the vial before unlocking the top drawer. I place it in there carefully before locking it again. "You didn't have to do that."

"It settles the matter," she replies, "can I get those signatures now?"

I sign where she requests, before telling her, "I appreciate all that you've done here, Camille, but I think it's best if Vanessa steps up to be my full-time PA. You can focus on Josh's…needs entirely, effective immediately."

"Rose…" she trails off, startled by my decision. I made it on my birthday. I knew then that I was going to dismiss Camille and I'm sticking to it, especially now, knowing all that she knows.

I stand up and tell her, "It's for the best, Camille. I know you won't repeat anything about my business to anyone—now that I have your blood."

She pales, but composes herself before collecting her things and saying, "I'll make sure the transition is smooth for Crescent Tens."

I simply nod and watch her leave my office. Then I grab the nearest notepad, jot down a few names, before making my way to the Alarion Tower.

It's the tower closest to the dungeon on the southeastern side of Cravenhold. The building is completely monochrome, with black, deep gray, and silver to lighten the space. The architecture is modern, including advanced technology. House Tens emblem is stamped everywhere—an open eye sitting atop two crossed swords.

I pass security, go up the elevator, and arrive at the one office on the twenty-fourth floor that I never thought I'd willingly enter. Unfortunately for me, James is the only one who can help me with my new dilemma. Okay, maybe not the only one, but he's the direct source.

His assistant lets him know I'm here, and when I step through the doors of his office, I'm faced with an unimpressed James Tens.

His office is…boring. It's black and gray and there's barely any light. Even the dark curtains are drawn, which is a shame because it's a lovely day outside.

He doesn't say anything as he watches me walk up to his desk. Seeing that he has no intentions of speaking first, I do.

"I just found out an obscene amount of people have access to my whereabouts and everything I do," I start, before pulling out the piece of paper from my pocket and placing it in front of him, "I know you can limit that."

James watches me for a moment, before he picks up the paper and scans it. His face gives nothing away. I see why he and Josh are close, they could be twins, in their mannerisms. Looks-wise, Josh is polished, the classic devilish villain, while James is more savage as if ready to rip throats out at any second. It's in his eyes.

He finally says, "The Warriors aren't on this list. Do you not trust us?"

I shrug. "Do the Warriors have to be on the list?"

James narrows his eyes. "What are you hiding?"

I hold his stare. James can be as intimidating as he wants to be, but my powers are unmatched. "I don't like people knowing my business. I won't question exactly what you do in the dungeons, and you handle who has access to my whereabouts."

"Are you threatening me, Rosie?" he questions, a small smirk appearing on his face. James has never called me Rosie in my life, so I know this is used in mockery.

"Call it whatever you want. I came to you when I could've gone straight to Shane. This is me being transparent," I cross my arms. "Do I need to get the Alpha involved or…?"

He watches me again for a long moment before nodding. "Consider it done, Veyara."

I don't doubt for a second that the moment I leave, he's going to call my lovely Mate and snitch to him about what I just did. So I don't thank him as I leave his office. He made that unnecessarily annoying.

22 BLACK COURT

Rosella Craving
August 7

Magic tickle my fingertips, waiting not so patiently for me to give it a command. I stand before the prisoner—a jaguar shifter who was brought in last night. She can't be older than thirty, lean muscles tense as her claws scrape the iron arms of the chair she's restrained to. I assume her hair was a rich brown at some point, but now it's a dull, broken mess, matted to her head. Her watery brown eyes are furious, even though she knows she's not getting out of here alive.

Nathanial leans against the far wall, arms folded over his royal crimson coat. He's wearing a silk black shirt underneath with black slacks. His gray eyes watch me with the authority he's held for longer than most can comprehend. He's watching not as a king, but as a teacher assessing his student.

He only brings me in on things he wants to take care of himself and prefers it off the books. He stares the prisoner down and it's a look I'm grateful he's never used on me.

I take a step closer to the prisoner. My darkness uncoils from my fingertips, thin tendrils of pitch-black magic slipping beneath the prisoner's skin. She writhes against the exposure to my power, and I know the effect it's having on her. It's as if cold needles are elongating through her brain, hunting for memories and names that she refuses to give us.

With a slow breath, I murmur, crouching in front of her, "You know, this can go so much faster if you just tell me who your Queen is and why she sent you." The jaguar spits blood right on my black boots, even as the darkness crawling from my palms wraps around her. Rude.

"Go to Hell," she rasps. Double rude.

I smile. "Oh honey…I don't think the Devil would appreciate the competition."

My darkness expands, the tendrils thickening, sinking into her mind. She gasps, her back arching as a strangled sound escapes her lips. I watch the flicker of pain twist across her features, her fight fading, but she still doesn't surrender.

I peel back layers of thoughts as images flash through my mind—warehouses, faces, dates—but nothing concrete and they scatter the moment I reach for them. She's strong, well, at least her shields are. That's the thing about mental shields most people don't know—it's not magic, it's willpower. Magic helps reinforce it, but it all depends on how much one wants to uphold the shield.

I push harder. My own eyes are solid black, just voids that swallow the light leaving no room for any white. My gray eyes always turn completely black when I use even an ounce of my power—they give me away every time. It's the only downside, but my black eyes freak people out, so they're still an asset.

"Why were you trying to sneak into Cravenhold instead of just walking in through the front doors?" I ask her.

The darkness sings inside me, eager and hungry as her screams turn raw under my probing. Her veins darken beneath her skin as my power pushes through. She fights against her restraints, but eventually the pain wins and she lets out a shriek. Nathanial stands straighter, his eyes twinkling with curiosity.

"Isis!" She screams out.

I frown, taking a step closer. I glance at Nathanial, who doesn't give anything away, so I ask, "What about Mother Isis?"

"It's a hoax! She's a stand-in…" The jaguar starts to fade, and I begin to call my power back.

"A stand-in?" I repeat, waiting for her to continue to see how much she knows. "And how did *you* come about that information?"

"There's always someone willing to talk. She's a fake," the jaguar shifter says and I know she's fading.

His gray eyes have gone deadly as Nathanial comes to stand beside me. The jaguar looks at him and pales. She didn't realize he was standing in the shadows the whole time.

"F-Father Natha—" the jaguar stutters.

"What's it to your Queen?" Nathanial asks slowly, sending a chill down my spine. I look at him but keep my face neutral.

"Where is Mother Isis?" The jaguar cries. "What did you do to her?"

In all my eighteen years, I've only seen Mother Isis twice—at my brother's Alpha coronation and then my parents' funeral rites. She never spoke. She stays in the highest tower in Cravenhold—closest to the Heavens—in worship. No one is allowed to disturb her. Even Nathanial sees her sparingly.

Who does this jaguar think she is to demand such information?

"You don't know anything." Nathanial decides before giving me a nod.

I turn my focus on the jaguar shifter as my darkness floods out and into her. "See you in Hell, babe."

Then her head hangs forward, her body going limp as the pain overloads her mind and she slips into death. I pull my powers back once it's done, feeling the rush of taking a soul.

Nathanial chuckles lowly. "Feel better? You've been too pent up."

I rise, brushing sweat from my temple. He turns toward me, his movements smooth, unhurried. He tucks a loose strand of hair behind my ear. His hand lingers and I get a whiff of his scent. The richest amber and that bonfire smoke that's always attached to him wraps around me.

"You did so good," he praises, shifting me toward him. Not a strand of blond hair is out of place on his head, and I can only imagine what I look like right now. "She was a strong one, but you broke her."

His voice softens, and before I can speak, his mouth is on mine, warm and commanding. My body melts instinctively, pressing into him. His hand trails upward, brushing over my nipple before sliding to grip the back of my head, deepening the kiss. I explore his warm familiar tongue with mine, forgetting all about the dead jaguar shifter next to us.

When he pulls away, the loss stings. He smirks faintly. "That's what your Mate should be doing."

I keep my face neutral, grabbing my jacket from the other chair in the chamber, and don't say anything.

"Have you learned anything about his powers?" Nathanial asks, leading the way down the tunnel. His voice is quiet, but it holds an edge.

"He's a dick using them to his advantage," I mutter, trailing behind him. My chest tightens and mind shuts down at the thought of Josh fucking Hunter.

Nathanial stops and I nearly bump into him. For a moment, he doesn't look at me, just stares ahead with a faraway look clouding his eyes. "Nothing else?"

"No," I reply, then frown, "maybe he's just not as powerful as me."

"Then he wouldn't be your Mate," Nathanial says, evenly. "No...he's hiding something big. It's why he hasn't Marked you."

"You don't know that..." I trail off. "Should he even Mark me?" I gesture behind us. "He'll know about this."

Nathanial just chuckles. "Josh Hunter has done far worse for me than even you have. It's why I know he won't talk."

"What has he done?" I try, but Nathanial smirks, seeing right through it.

"Nice try, my little mistress," he winks, but exhales heavily. "Alas, he's your Mate. The Divine chose him." He looks at me and caresses my cheek. "Don't forget that."

We step out into the biting wind at the cave's mouth. The world below is covered in gray mist as rain threatens above in the churning clouds. The river far below thrashes like a monster trying to break free.

Nathanial brushes back the hair on my forehead and I close my eyes, allowing myself to find comfort in his soft touch. He lowers his head and kisses me again.

When I open my eyes, I'm standing alone, with the impending storm mirroring the storm inside me, threatening to unleash.

23 ELIZA

Rosella Craving
August 9

The stairs blur beneath my feet, the stone corridors barely acknowledged as I rush by. Vanessa keeps up with me. We were training when Uncle Edward telepathed us.

The closer we get to the residential wing, the louder the sound grows—wails, raw and broken, echoing down the hall. My heart twists.

"Eliza," I whisper.

Vanessa pushes open the door that leads to one of the hallways, before I rush through, passing the Crescents who are already here. Aunt Susan stops me from going up, blocking the stairs.

Eliza's cries are heart-wrenching. I glare at my aunt, "Let me go to her!"

My aunt shakes her head, her eyes cold. "Give her some space."

"I—" my voice cracks.

Josh walks in just then with James and Devaughn. "What happened?" he asks my aunt.

"The Luna lost one of the babies," Aunt Susan answers him quietly.

I look at her, horrified as a choked sound escapes me. Vanessa gasps, "What?! How?"

"We don't know yet. The High Priestess and the healers are with her," she replies.

"Shane?" Josh asks and my heart shatters for my brother.

"He's with her too," my aunt says, before looking at me, then Josh and telling him, "Take her outside. She doesn't need to hear this."

"I got this," Crystal tells Josh, coming up beside me.

I choke on a sob as my chest aches like it's been split open. I press my hand to my mouth as Crystal guides me to our private courtyard.

The second we're outside, my chest seizes, breath shattering as panic claws its way out of me. I stumble, gasping, hands clawing at my throat and chest.

"Rose," she grips me harder, forcing me to look at her. "Breathe with me. In…" she takes a deep breath, waiting "breathe struggle to follow, and she says, "Out."

I try and I fail. I choke on it, collapse into her, crying. Her arms lock around me, holding me through my panic attack, until little by little, the air returns to my lungs.

She rubs soothing circles on my back, helping me through it but all I can think of is Shane and Eliza, and the little life we just lost.

I look up to try and focus on something and see the Old Tower where Mother Isis resides, and no one's allowed inside. It was once the original Cravenhold tower, but now stands adjacent to the residential wing, detached to the side of the Palace.

There isn't much to it. It looks like an old bell tower, if anything. Moss and vines cover it completely, climbing up the stones, giving it a pretty aesthetic. Daniya, Mariella, and I used to love taking pictures there. Right now though, the moss just reminds me of how the darkness surrounded Eliza's babies like the vines wrapping around the tower.

I knew something was wrong for months and I didn't say a word.

It's been hours.

The Palace feels too quiet now—grieving. Crystal and I came back inside, and I sit curled in an armchair in the upstairs sitting room that's closest to Shane and Eliza's suite. The fireplace burns low, crackling every so often as we wait for more news.

Josh is across the room, speaking to Uncle Edward in hushed voices. Their words blur together, but I can feel his eyes on me occasionally. The other Warriors and Crescents stay with us. Nathanial abandoned his solitary time up in his cabin the moment he got the news and came, too. He brought me tea earlier—it sits on the table beside me, gone cold by now—but he hasn't left my side, holding my hand. No one has said a word. We're all just waiting.

Shane finally appears, and the sight of him puts the lump straight back in my throat as I suppress my sob. His shoulders sag, his face is gray with grief.

Uncle Edward reaches him first. Shane looks around at the room, but I can tell he's not entirely here.

In a broken voice, my brother says, "The stronger twin drained the magic from the other..." He looks at Nathanial. Silent unspoken words pass between them.

Without magic in us, we can't survive. It's part of our lifeforce.

Nathanial's hand closes around mine, warm and reassuring, before he rises. He goes to embrace my brother, holding him tight in a hug Shane clearly needs but would never ask for.

Aunt Susan is the first to find her voice as she watches the men. "Is that even possible? Can an unborn child have such powers?"

Nathanial's expression is unreadable. "Anything is possible when curses are involved."

The words twist like a knife in my gut. My stomach drops, and my mind spirals.

The curse of the twins.

I feel it circle around me, suffocating. Eliza's wails, the darkness I saw around the babies, the way the stronger one drained the weaker—I knew these twins weren't going to be blessings—they so rarely are.

"How's the Luna?" Josh asks gently, and my brother looks at his best friend. Shane's eyes are heavy and red-rimmed. I want to go to him and hug him, but I know I'll break if I do. He doesn't need to worry about me right now.

Shane clears his throat. "She's sleeping. She'll be okay and Lady Tiara says she's fine to deliver the healthy baby later..."

"Probably best we give her some time to grieve," Aunt Susan tells us. She turns her gaze to Shane, her tone becoming firmer, "You need to eat to keep your strength up. For Eliza."

Shane is taken away by her and I bolt. I need air. My steps take me down the stone paths, through the gardens and courtyards until I reach the docks on the northwest side of Cravenhold.

The water is restless tonight, black waves hitting the wooden posts. I wrap my arms around myself. I had changed out of my workout clothes, but my black cardigan does little to shield me with the end-of-summer chill settling in.

I get barely five minutes before I feel his presence. I don't turn to face him as I tell Josh, "Leave me alone."

"I didn't realize you were that attached to the babies," he says emotionlessly. How can he be so heartless?

"You don't know anything about me," I reply, done with this conversation. Maybe I wasn't that attached, but I'm still an aunt. I lost a nephew today, but my brother...I can't imagine what Shane and

Eliza are going through. Eliza's cries play over and over in my mind. I never want to hear her cry again.

He doesn't move and instead asks me quietly, "What's the curse of the twins?"

I rub my arms against the cold night, sighing as I realize he's not going away. I turn to him. "Seriously? I'm not in the mood to talk—"

"Rose," he says patiently, cutting me off.

I stare at him for a moment, before taking a minute, and then answer him. "The curse of the twins exists only in the Craving family, as far as I know—which is probably why you haven't heard of it...we haven't had twins in the family for a really long time until now..."

Josh's gaze on me is so intense, it makes me second guess what I'm saying. He looks like he wants to say something but waits for me to continue.

I look up to the sky, where there are a few stars out tonight. I go on, "Twins are either a great blessing or a curse." I start with an obvious example. "Nathanial and Stefan are twins, and they obviously have immense powers. It started with them—the gamble of Craving twins. I'm not sure who put the curse on our line, or if it was always a magical genetic disability..." I pause, trying to find the right words. "Craving twins can be blessed with rare powers—abilities that only surface once in a lifetime, sometimes once in generations. Powers so singular that by the time the next wielder is born, the ones before them are already long gone, if the power's even seen again," I exhale sharply. "The alternative is that the twins are cursed."

"Powers like yours?" Josh asks.

I shrug. "Maybe, sure, but I'm not a twin."

"Right," he says, before taking a step closer to me causing the wood to creak under his feet. "What *is* the curse?"

I tilt my head to meet his bright gray eyes. "One of the twins always dies and it's always at the hand of the other twin—the stronger one." I shake my head and look back toward the Palace, because that's exactly what happened today.

"Does the stronger twin always drain the weaker one of its powers?" Josh presses like he has personal interest in the topic. I guess as the Beta, he would need to know this. I'm surprised Shane hasn't already told him about it.

I shake my head. "No, I don't think that's necessary. That could just be what *this* baby's power might manifest itself to be. Clearly, it's already powerful enough to…" My heart races as I imagine what kind of force it will grow into one day. "If the twins are cursed, the weaker twin dies at some point before their first shift. The death doesn't always have to do with magic."

Josh is quiet for a long, long moment. I stare out at the water, black and endless. Normally, I don't like the water—I never liked how easily things can be lost in the water. How if you sail far enough, you disappear—but for some reason tonight, it feels like the place to be. The darkness of the night and of the water are welcoming.

"Is there any way around it?" he asks, then when I look at him, he adds, "Was there anything we could've done?"

I freeze in place. Dread creeps up on me and I turn away from him, walking closer to the edge of the dock.

"Rose?"

He's behind me, walking to the edge with me.

"I knew," I whisper. He's the last person I should admit this to, but the words slip out before I can stop it.

"You knew what?" he asks, his hand closing gently around my arm as he turns me toward him. "What did you know, Rose?"

The cry escapes me as I cover my face with my hands, shaking my head. The guilt overwhelms me. Josh pulls me closer, before he pries my hands away from my face.

"What did you know, Rose?" he repeats and I shake my head.

"I…I can't—" I choke on my sobs.

"Rose," his voice is hard now, stern. He makes me look at him, lifting my face, his thumb pressing into my cheek. "Tell me."

I drop my gaze to his throat, anywhere but his eyes that are searing into me. My voice breaks, "I knew something was wrong with the babies."

"How could you possibly—"

"My powers," I tell him, then meet his eyes to show him the truth in mine. "It showed me. I didn't know what would happen…I just knew that something was wrong. They weren't blessed. I *knew*."

Josh doesn't say anything.

I wipe my face with trembling fingers and wrap my arms around me again. "I knew the twins were cursed. And I…" my throat seizes, but I force the words out, "I didn't say anything."

His arms close around me, pulling me hard against him. "Shhh, stop," he murmurs into my hair, and I swear he inhales me in. "You said it yourself—the stronger twin would've killed the weaker one. *This* wasn't on you."

My tears soak his shirt. I want to believe him. I want to hold onto his words. Just because there's a curse, didn't Shane and Eliza deserve a chance to break it? To save their baby? I knew, and I stole that opportunity from them. Why didn't I just go to them when I first saw it?

"Listen," he says, pulling away just enough to cup my face. "Don't tell anyone about this."

I frown.

"There's nothing you could've done," Josh says, "it won't do any good if you say something now. The baby's gone. Let's just be there for Shane and Eliza."

"Josh—"

"I'm not trying to tell you to hide or suppress your powers," he says, stroking my cheek with his thumb. "I'm trying to protect you. Do you understand?"

I look at him. There's nothing but concern in his gray eyes. He's right and I want to believe that's why I didn't say anything in the first place. There was no way to change the outcome. If the Divine decides twins will be cursed, that's what they'll be.

"Why?" I ask him, careful not to let the suspicion show. "Why are you trying to protect me?"

"What happens to the twin that's born?" Josh asks, quietly, still holding me close and completely ignoring my question.

I pull away to show him my clear disdain for his dismissal.

"The power of two is in one," I reply to him anyway, "it always was from the beginning. Even if both babies were born—if they were destined to be cursed—the stronger twin would've always been more powerful. The stronger twin would've always had abilities from an early age that were unheard of."

I frown, thinking about how he pointed out my powers. I always wondered why I had them. Why I was different? Why I manifested my powers at eight and my parents went out of their way to conceal it, but also train me without judgement? But I'm not a twin…I think I'd know if I was. Wouldn't I?

"Why did you say powers like mine…?" I ask him.

He looks down to meet my gaze. "Because I have never met anyone with powers like yours. It was just a reference."

I watch him for a moment because it feels like he's keeping something from me, but then something else dawns on me and I immediately pull away from him.

"Tell me you did not just use your magic on me," I glare at him, walking backward to land. How did I not recognize him using his power on me? I just told him *so* much…

"You clearly needed to talk about it," he sighs heavily.

I stare at him. "So maybe ask like a normal person!"

"But I'm not normal…" he counters and I want to fucking smack him. The worst part is, he's not even trying to be cocky about it. No, the worst part is, the first time he's shown genuine care toward me, he was using his damn power the whole time. I knew there was a catch. He was being too nice, and I was being too talkative with him.

"You're fucking unbelievable!" I run my hand through my hair, before looking at him again. "Stop using your powers on me."

"That's never going to happen. Why wouldn't I, if I can?" he shrugs. Who the fuck made him Beta?

"Because it's polite?" I offer.

He's starting to walk toward me since I created too much distance between us.

"Polite?" he lets out a laugh, before asking, "Why the fuck would I care about that? I'm a fucking basilisk, Rose. What part of that do you not understand?"

All of it.

I hate his powers. I hate that he can use his powers on *me* without warning. I hate that he's so reckless with it—but also not. I hate that he's always in full control and no one fucking knows he's using his abilities until it's too late. I didn't even catch a hint of him using it on me tonight, it was so natural, it's scary.

I have never heard or seen Josh lose his shit. Never. Even on the night of my transformation, he was furious, but he was still in control. Every time he uses his power, he's doing it on purpose, fully aware of it.

I put my hand up as I step off the dock. "Just…stay away from me. You and all your powers."

I don't know why it kills me to say that. Maybe because I don't really want him to stay away. Maybe because I know it's cruel to say. He has no right to use his powers on me though.

"Why would you do that?" I ask him, the betrayal is obvious in my voice. It's one thing to cheat, but it's another to violate.

"I told you. I was just making it easier for you to talk. Get it out," he replies, quietly. How can he think that's okay?

"Do *not* do it again," I snap at him. It's ridiculous that I even have to say it. "That's so rude and it's such a snake move, you jerk."

Something in him snaps and he's in front of me immediately, grabbing me. I stare up at him, too startled to move. His face is furious. His skin is feverishly hot. And his eyes—oh Divine, they're his serpent eyes—the whites of his eyes have gone entirely gray aside from the vertical black slit down the middle. His eyes are glowing.

"One, you're not my mom," he says, his voice low but it vibrates through me, "two, if you're going to curse at me, say my fucking name."

Say his name?

Tears well in my eyes as I look back into his.

"And three, you do *not* tell me to suppress my powers," he seethes.

How many times have people told me to suppress mine? To be careful with mine? To not use mine?

He lets me go and his eyes go back to the normal Warrior eyes as he says in a much calmer voice, "I'm proud of who I am and I'm proud of my powers. If you don't like me using them on you, work on *your* fucking shields then. That's not my problem. I warned you on your first day of training."

"Okay," I whisper.

He raises his eyebrows, then lets out a humorless laugh. "Okay? Where'd all that fight go?"

I shake my head. "You're right…and if I'm being honest—since you seem to want to know my secrets—I'm actually a little scared of you right now."

He rolls his eyes.

Rolls his eyes.

"You know I can't kill you," he says. Mates can use their powers on each other—exhibit A—but we can't kill each other with them, if that's something we can normally do to others.

I look at his handsome, but annoyed face and say, "No. You can do worse."

24 CRESCENT RAGE

Rosella Craving
August 18

I've only been to the main ritual ground a handful of times before I shifted. While some of our practices are like the witches, we are not them. We only use the main ritual ground for full Moons when Nathanial is at court or for special occasions such as blood-tie ceremonies.

It's larger and much closer to the Sanctum than I remember. The tall oaks creating a natural barrier are decorated with silver lanterns tonight. White roses take over the clearing, weaving toward the altar that's set at the center. Stone benches circle around it in a crescent shape, row after row.

The full Moon rises above us in preparation for tonight's ceremony. Laughter and voices ripple across the gathering crowd as guests settle down in their seats. The altar glows with candlelight creating a gorgeous ambiance.

An outdoor wedding ritual—perfect for us shifters.

I'm standing at the edge, having just gotten here, and smooth down the gray dress Mariella chose for us. I had doubts when Mariella wanted us to dress in gray, but after seeing it, I changed my mind. It's a soft, pretty gray, and works beautifully with House Rage's color—all black. Mariella would never have us wear black on her reunion.

"There you are, freak," Josh murmurs, coming up to me. I flinch at the nickname—we're back to that? "Hiding from me?" he asks.

I glance up, eyes narrowed. "Will knowing I am, make you go away?"

"Absolutely not," he replies absently as his eyes drag over me, slowly. There's no missing the way his jaw tightens. All the Warriors' Mates are dressed the same, pale gray velvet clinging tight before spilling into long strands of fringe. The neckline dips across my collarbone and into my cleavage while the slit is high enough to tempt any Mate. I'm not used to him staring at me like this, with clear hunger in his eyes.

It's just the full Moon, I remind myself.

He's wearing a black velvet robe that shifts in the breeze, the lining underneath is deep green in the Moonlight. The hood is up, shadowing the sharpness of his face, making his eyes burn brighter when they catch mine. Loose black pants hang low—too low—on his hips, making my throat dry. He's bare beneath the robe, showing off his sculpted body and his old family name tattoo. He's barefoot on the grass. As much as I want to let my eyes linger on the bulge in his pants, I look down, pretending to smooth my dress. Again.

It's velvet, how much smoothing does it even need.

He steps closer and I get a whiff of his citrus, smoke, and spice scent. I need to get a grip. This is my second full Moon and I'm feeling the effects already.

"Don't look away from me," he says as his hand brushes my wrist but then drops immediately.

I force my eyes back up to him. That hood does nothing to hide the hunger and struggle in his gaze. The full Moon is clearly testing his restraints too—especially with his Mate, with me. It's our first full Moon after my shift.

"Sometimes it's hard to look at you," I tell him honestly. It's true, whether I'm hating him or wanting him. He makes it hard to look at him and not feel one or the other, or both.

He smirks at that. Of course he does.

"Well, Veyara, you're making it very hard for anyone to look away tonight," he says and I glance around to see quite a few people looking my way as they pass us by to their seats. Josh's smirk doesn't falter as he holds out his arm, "unfortunately for them, you'll always be on my arm."

"For them, or for you?" I ask as I slip my arm through his and he leads us to our bench at the front.

Josh chuckles. "Depends on the day, doesn't it."

"You give me whiplash," I say under my breath. He decides on the third row from the altar. Daniya and Daniel slip into the fourth and Daniya catches my hand, giving it a squeeze.

"Our girl's getting hitched!" she smiles brightly at me. The gray dress really suits her. Her strawberry blonde hair looks more reddish tonight, and she straightened it to let it fall around her. It's a beautiful contrast against the light dress.

"Long time coming," I wink back at her as I sit beside Crystal. She grins at me, her blue eyes shining against the night.

"Hey!" she says, greeting me with air kisses. "You look so beautiful! Doesn't she, Josh?"

"Of course, she does," Josh replies and Crystal rolls her eyes at him for me.

"Gray's your color, Crystal," I smile back at her, ignoring Josh.

We don't get to talk more because Lady Tiara takes her place at the center of the altar. The ritual ground settles, all the laughter fading into expectant silence. A low beat of drums begins, signaling the start of the ceremony.

Antonio steps forward to stand beside the High Priestess. He's striking in black pants and a red ceremonial robe that male Mates traditionally wear on blood-tie reunions. His thick unruly black hair has been tamed for the special occasion.

We all rise, heads turning as Lord Jornavel appears at the edge of the grounds, his arm proudly linked with Mariella's.

Mariella is radiant in her red wedding dress that shines with her every step, the train whispering over the grass. The gown wraps her in heavy fabric, sleeves brushing her wrists, neckline high against the cooler night with summer coming to an end.

Mariella and Lord Jornavel reach the altar. He kisses her cheek softly, before placing her hand in Antonio's, giving him a gentle pat on the arm.

Antonio thanks him before smiling at Mariella and the sight melts my heart. He's so happy, it's clear on his face. As Lord Jornavel takes his seat beside Mariella's mom, Antonio raises her hand to his lips and presses a kiss against her knuckles before they turn their attention to Lady Tiara.

We remain standing as the High Priestess raises her hands, her voice carrying clearly over the drums, "Welcome beloved friends and family to bear witness Warrior Antonio Warrick Rage and Crescent Mariella Asya Jornavel's blood-tie reunion! Please be seated."

As we do, Lady Tiara holds out her hand for Antonio. He offers it without hesitation, jaw set, eyes locked on Mariella. The knife slices cleanly across his palm, blood welling bright red before spilling into the waiting birdbath-like bowl below.

Josh leans into me. ***"You'd flinch."***

I keep my eyes forward. ***"Wouldn't you like that."***

He smirks. ***"Mhm, I'd like to see you bleed because of me."***

I side-eye him. Of course, he has a blood kink, I'm not even surprised. I focus back on the front as Mariella extends her hand. Her red sleeve falls back, baring pale skin. Lady Tiara's cut is swift, and blood runs freely from Mariella's palm, mingling with Antonio's in the basin.

Lady Tiara's voice is steady:

"Oh Heavens, behold, lifelines align,
We join under this Moon as fates intertwine…"

Josh tilts his head, watching the bowl. ***"Ours will be worse."***

I blink at him. ***"Oh, definitely since your blood is poisonous, babe."***

He drags his gaze to mine, eyes dark, but he doesn't say anything and I look at Lady Tiara.

"Before the stars their courses begun,
The Heavens sealed these two as one.
What one shall suffer, the other shall bear,
One heartbeat, one breath, one spirit shared.
A thread of Mates, through trials, through breath,
Entwined together even past death."

"Even past death," Josh repeats. He has to be on something to willingly talk to me this much.

I sigh heavily before shifting in my seat and crossing my legs, so the slit of my dress slides open, exposing too much skin. The drums beat low and heavy, reverberating through the clearing, and though I keep my eyes up front, I can *feel* Josh's gaze burning holes into my legs.

Antonio speaks next. *"Earth shall root us, steadfast and deep."*

Mariella follows, confidently, *"Air shall guard us, awake and in sleep."*

"Fire shall warm us, passion's delight." Antonio winks at her, and I bite my lip from grinning. I can't help it—they're too cute.

Mariella doesn't bother hiding her grin as she says, *"Water shall heal us, day into night."*

Lady Tiara continues, raising her hands again. *"No force shall sever, no power undo—what destiny weaves, forever holds true."*

Antonio and Mariella join their bleeding hands together and say the vows.

"Through joy and claim, through grief and woe,
Our souls are bound in all we do.
Your magic with mine, no end in sight,
By Mark and by will, our powers unite.

With this vow spoken, with this thread tied true,
I am forever bound to only you."

I've thought about Josh and my powers after he Marks me. He's already so powerful—what else will he be capable of then? What will I be capable of?

Lady Tiara lights the bowl on fire, sealing their blood with the vows.

I stare at it for a moment, an unsettling feeling coursing through me. I just can't put my finger on it. I've seen this ceremony performed five times now, and every time, this part makes me squirm.

Lady Tiara moves into the final part of the ritual.

"Blood to blood, and soul to soul,
A soul once part, is now made whole.
The Marking will complete their Mating bond,
The highest law to which they belong.
If ever challenged, they shall defend,
A fight to the death, to the very end.
Chosen by Heaven, joined by breath,
One soul in life, one soul in death."

I shudder at the words as Lady Tiara brings their joined hands together over the bowl. The blood in it has transformed into a red cord that shimmers and wraps around their hands. Then it dissolves into their skin, and the ritual ground erupts in cheers and howls as we stand for them. Mariella and Antonio end the ceremony with a passionate kiss, and the air around us is charged with primal energy.

But all I feel is Josh—too close.

If ever challenged, they shall defend.

But what if the challenge was from our own Mate?

Their kiss lingers, sealing Mariella and Antonio's blood-tie reunion in front of their witnesses.

Lady Tiara raises her arms a final time, her voice strong over the roar of the drums. "Go to the Sanctum and complete your reunion!"

The guests clap and stomp their feet. Antonio leads Mariella away toward the Sanctum with laughter chasing them and petals tossed in their path.

The drums beat faster as a woman starts singing. It's wild and pulsing, as excitement breaks, voices tumbling over one another.

Josh turns to me, grinning beautifully. "Now the fun part begins."

25 CELEBRATION

Rosella Craving
August 18

Josh takes my hand without thinking as we're carried forward with the rest of the reunion guests. His grip is warm as his eyes stay ahead, already fixed on the promise of a good night.

"What's happening?" I ask, eyes wide as music grows louder, the drums growing more insistent.

"The rest of the reunion for us!" Vanessa laughs, her eyes glittering with mischief. Before I can press her for more, James swoops her off her feet and throws her over his shoulder. She shrieks, giggling wildly as he carries her straight toward the glow of torches.

I glance at Josh for an explanation. He's laughing at something Devaughn says in passing. Josh's rare and easy smile catches me off guard for a moment before his gaze finds mine.

"While the couple joins in sacred Mating," he says smoothly, "the Pack celebrates the reunion in its rawest form."

The smell of roasted meats, sweet wine, and even sweeter desserts mix with the rush of everyone's energy floods my senses. Josh's hand slides to my waist, and before I can retreat, he pulls me forward, out of the path, and into the clearing.

My mouth parts and my eyes widen as I see tables heavy with food, chalices filled with drinks, and a bonfire at the center, crackling high into the sky. Drums and wild singing surround us while people are already swaying and grinding together.

I'm starting to see why I wasn't allowed to attend before I shifted—this is *not* our court galas and balls that I've been so used to.

"It's great, isn't it!" Daniya comes to stand beside me, "*this* is an after party."

The glow from the fires makes everything gold and wild…and *hot* in more ways than just the temperature. The drums are relentless, laughter bubbling from every corner—if it's not laughter, it's pleasure. Everywhere I look, restraint is abandoned.

My uncle's own laughter draws my attention. He throws his head back, the sound booming as Elder Claws chuckles with him, clinking chalices.

Then Lady Tiara appears, no longer cloaked in her High Priestess robes but wearing a gold dress. Her light brown hair falls loose around her shoulders, and she looks so much younger than she does with it up. I don't think I've ever seen her with her hair down. She slides to her husband's side, pressing a kiss to his neck before stealing the chalice in his hand and taking a sip. The second the chalice leaves her lips, Elder Claws claims her in a kiss.

My chest tightens seeing them together like this. They remind me so much of how my parents were. I look away before I get too emotional. Fucking full Moons.

My eyes find Nathanial standing near the fire, and then I notice the woman pressed close to him. She whispers in his ear, her hand trailing down his chest before sliding boldly into his pants. My breath catches, heat flaring in my cheeks, and I immediately look elsewhere. It's not that I've never seen him with other women before, it's just how into each other they are right now.

Nearby, my aunt tips her head back, downing her chalice in a single swallow before reaching for another. Elder Salvatore steps up to her and says something that makes her roll her eyes.

I realize all the men are dressed similarly to Josh—robes and loose black pants, though most have abandoned their robes.

"Let's dance!" Daniel announces before pulling Daniya into the dancing circle.

Josh doesn't move from my side. His hand is pressed against my lower back possessively. "Do you feel it?"

I swallow hard, my heartbeat rising. "Feel what?"

"The urge to tear into something. Or someone." His eyes burn into mine and I can feel him trying to creep around my defenses. "Don't lie to me, Rose."

"Is that how you feel?" I ask him instead, "Like you want to tear into someone?"

I remember the women from my tea party—particularly the one who said she was with Josh at Shane's reunion. Were they here? Were they *celebrating* in the open like some people are?

His jaw tightens as my heart sinks. He *does* want that.

It doesn't help his case when a group of women circles past us, their eyes on him. One brushes her fingers along his arm in passing, another tilts her chalice toward him before taking a sip from it, and the third lingers long enough to blow a kiss inches from his face as if I'm not standing right here with his arm around me. All three of them are serpent shifters.

I don't know if I'm appalled or in awe of these women's boldness—or stupidity. They have to know who I am. Either they don't care, or they're that drunk already.

I force myself to maintain my composure. It wouldn't be the first time he entertained women in front of me, but Josh isn't looking at the women. His eyes are on Devaughn haggling an expensive scotch bottle a few tables away.

I know Josh, so I give him a smile as I tilt my head to the women. "Go on then. Enjoy yourself. I won't be great company anyway."

Eliza and Shane's absence weigh heavily on me. They should've been here. I wish they were. Josh's eyes narrow, but I say, "I'm going to find us something to drink."

I slip away before he can stop me. Bodies sway and part around me as I weave through the chaos. Skin glistens with sweat and spilled wine. Laughter turns into moans without warning, mingling with the music and drums. Someone's hand brushes my waist, another grazes my thigh, but I keep moving until I reach the long table of pitchers and bright bottles.

I pour two goblets of bloodwine. The scent is heavy—black cherries with a sharper kick that makes my mouth water. I lift one to my lips to taste.

Fuck, I needed a drink. The bloodwine burns a path straight to my stomach, leaving behind heat.

I turn to go back to Josh, finding him exactly where I left him but now two women have found him.

The first—tall, bronze-skinned, hair a wild spill of midnight curls—presses the full length of her body against his front. Her breasts crush against his chest as she drags his head down and kisses him like she's starving for him. The second is a shorter girl, with red hair and she laughs as her friend pulls away from him, smirking. The shorter girl then pushes Josh back until he's seated on the bench of the picnic table. She climbs onto his lap without asking, thighs straddling his hips, and takes his mouth like it belongs to her. His robe has slipped open, the bonfire light spills across the hard lines of his stomach. The redhead's hips roll as she kisses him deeper, and his hands—those hands that were just on me—settle on her waist, fingers curling into the soft fabric at her hips like he's anchoring her there.

I can't breathe, but this isn't the first time. I drink the contents from both goblets in my hand, before grabbing the bottle and leaving.

The drums pull me toward the dancing circle. Daniya spots me first and her face lights up like Sunrise.

"Rose!" She squeals, reaching out with both arms. Daniel catches me around the waist and spins me into their rhythm before I can protest. The beat is inside my bones now, and I dance with them.

"Daniel," I say against his ear, loud enough to be heard over the music, "tell me you have Petal."

He grins, and fishes a tiny silk pouch from the pocket of his loose pants. "Open your mouth."

I tip my head back instantly. He places the pretty violet petal on my tongue. It dissolves and warmth racing along every inch of me. I missed it.

Daniya pouts. "Me too!"

Daniel's grin widens. He slips another petal onto his own tongue, then cups Daniya's face and kisses her slow and deep, passing it between their mouths. She moans into him, fingers curling in his light brown hair.

I watch them, chest aching with love for them but envy for myself. "You two are disgusting," I tell them, voice thick. "I love it."

They break apart laughing, lips swollen and shining. Daniya's gaze drifts past my shoulders and her brown eyes go black. "I'm going to murder him."

I don't need to turn to know what she's seeing. I just shake my head. "It's fine. I'm used to it."

Daniel's arm tightens around my shoulders. "Crystal headed out early, the music was too loud for her. You can hang with Devaughn, he's definitely more fun than Josh anyway."

And he's got the good stuff.

I lean into my friends for a second, grateful. "Let me go see what he has on him. I'll report back."

Daniya catches my wrist before I can pull it away. "You sure you're okay?"

The Petal is already singing through my blood, softening the edges of everything. I flash her a smile that probably looks more real than it feels.

"Never better," I lie, then walk away toward Daniel's older brother.

Devaughn is laughing like he's having the time of his life as he snatches something off the table before the man across from him can. The second he spots me, his whole face lights up.

"The Veyara is in the house!" he shouts, throwing both arms wide open.

The circle of men erupts in hoots and whistles. One of them—broad-shouldered with gold-streaked hair—vacates his seat instantly, gesturing for me to take the spot beside Devaughn. I sink down, the drums thrumming through the ground into my spine.

Devaughn plucks the bottle from my fingers. "Hey!" I protest.

"You don't want that shit," he says, amused and I can tell he's a little drunk already. He uncaps a silver flask with his teeth and tips it to my lips, encouraging me with his shining gray eyes.

I part my lips and let him tilt the contents into my mouth. The blood whiskey hits my tongue and it's dark, smoky, and buttery, melting the last knot of tension in my chest. I swallow, greedy for the warmth flooding my every limb.

He pulls the flask back, grinning. "Better, right?"

"Much," I breathe, licking a stray drop from my lower lip. His eyes follow my tongue, but he just shakes his head, smiling big.

"Good. Question is," he leans in, eyes dancing, "how much fun do you want to have tonight, Veyara?"

I arch a brow. "What exactly do you have in mind? What are you playing?" I eye the cards on the table.

He winks at the table of men—all young, all grinning. "An old game, but let's make it interesting. I deal you a card. The man across from you gets three guesses at it. If he misses all three, you get to demand anything within reason. If he nails it…you owe him a kiss."

The men cheer as if Devaughn just gave them a raise. None of them are ugly and all of them are looking at me like I'm the game and the prize.

I laugh, the Petal and whiskey making everything bright and reckless. "That's it? Who's first?"

Devaughn chuckles, low and wicked, muttering under his breath, "Josh is going to fucking murder me, but Divine, it'll be worth it."

He fans the cards, lets me cut the deck, then slides one into my waiting fingers. I peek at the card before keeping it face-down against my palm.

Across from me, a lion shifter drops into the hot seat—golden skin, mane of wild blond curls, and amber eyes glowing. He flashes a set of perfect white teeth at me.

"First guess," he rumbles, his voice is smooth, and I can almost feel it against my skin, but that could be the Petal talking. "Seven of claws."

The table hoots. I just smile and shake my head, no.

He leans forward, elbows on the table, studying my face like he can read the card on it. "Queen of serpents."

More whistles. Another miss. I smirk at him. "Funny."

One guess left.

He tilts his head, eyes narrowing, then says with absolute confidence, "Ace of feathers."

I flip the card between my fingers and lay it down. "Three of fangs." The lion's face falls comically.

The table explodes in laughter and groans. I lean back on my palms, feeling dangerously alive. "Anything within reason," I say, tapping the card with one red nail, deciding. Then I smile big and say, "I just want to touch your hair."

Devaughn barks out a laugh as he starts shuffling for the next round. The lion shifter also smirks, leaning in and letting me run my fingers through his wild waves. They're softer than they look, warm from the fire, and he lets out a low, pleased groan that makes the table laugh harder.

"Next!" Devaughn calls, slapping a fresh card into my palm.

A brown-haired hawk shifter leaps over the bench. He's got lean muscles and sharp cheekbones. He drops down opposite me and flashes a grin full of trouble.

"Eight of feathers," he fires off.

Wrong. The table roars.

"Ten of serpents."

More hoots. Wrong again.

He drums the table with both palms, eyes locked on mine. "King of fangs, baby."

I flip it. "Five of claws," I say. The men lose their minds, banging fists on the wood. I'm laughing so hard, my ribs hurt.

The hawk shifter sighs, dramatically. "Name your reward, Veyara."

"Hmm…I want you to go to Lady Susan and ask her to dance," I manage between giggles. Devaughn laughs at that too and I look at him, not being able to hide my own laughter. He's definitely drunk.

The hawk shifter stands, rounds the table and heads toward my aunt where she is dancing by herself with a goblet in her hand. We watch as the hawk shifter easily slips into the dancing circle and scoops my aunt into his arms, startling the shit out of her. But she's not displeased as he flashes her a smile and pulls her into him for the dance.

I throw my head back and laugh until I'm breathless while Devaughn sets up the third round. A bear shifter this time—tall, freckled, with green eyes bright with mischief. He doesn't even wait. "Six of fangs."

I laugh. "Let me look at the card first!" I do and shake my head at the miss.

"Jack of claws."

Miss.

He leans in, voice a low growl. "Nine of feathers."

I flip the card slowly, teasing. Nine of feathers.

The table erupts in cheers. Devaughn slaps the surface so hard his flask jumps. The bear shifter whoops, fists in the air, then hops out of his seat to make his way to me. He scoops me up by the waist and spins me once before setting me on the edge of the table. I part my legs to let him get closer and cup his jaw. He leans in and I kiss him. I let his tongue into my mouth as our teeth clash and his hands grip my hips hard, but I don't care. It feels good. The men howl, stomp, bang chalices. When I pull back his eyes are blown wide and he looks half-wrecked.

"The Beta is one lucky bastard," he rasps.

I'm still laughing when the fourth man takes his seat. I settle back into my place. A few rounds later, I nudge Devaughn. "You were right. This is fun."

He smirks and I lean into him a little more. His eyes fall on me, giving me a dangerous look. I'm not sure if it's desire or warning. I'm about to ask him if he has stronger drugs, when he slips the next card into my hands along with a small bag of red powder.

He closes the distance between us to whisper in my ear, "SD. You know how to take it?"

SD is Sangria Dust, a vampiric drug popular in underground vampire clubs. The powder is usually sprinkled in with blood, creating heightened sensuality and an irresistible aura to anyone who looks the indulger's way. If the powder is taken straight…well, I'm not sure what it will do in a public setting like this. I've only taken it with the prince twice…privately.

Devaughn pulls away and I nod at him, before looking at the card and smiling at my next player.

The night blurs into heat and laughter and the sweet, reckless high of winning. I dip my pinky into the SD before sucking it off between rounds. It's enough to make the torches bleed color and every touch feel like fire under my skin. SD hits slow, then all at once, but I don't take enough to feel its full effects, just enough to feel wild. My skin is tingly, my nipples peaked, and I can't stop laughing.

Next player is a lean panther with silver rings in his ears. His guesses are all wrong. I make him kneel and feed me crystallized strawberries from his fingers while the table roars in approval. Devaughn just shakes his head, saying I'm having too much fun with this.

After the panther is a laughing stag shifter who gets it right on the first guess. I let him claim his prize slow and filthy, his tongue stroking mine until my thighs clench and Devaughn has to steady me when I finally pull away, biting my lip.

"Damn, girl, chill," he laughs.

The next victor is a quiet fox with clever hands. He guesses on the second try, smug and soft all at once. I kiss him gentle at first, then not gentle at all, until his hands start to wander and the men are banging the table so hard the cards jump. Devaughn gets two men to pull him off me, but it's all in good humor.

"You're gonna get me killed, Rosie," Devaughn chuckles.

"This was your idea," I reply, batting my lashes at him.

I'm glowing, riding the high, lips feeling slightly swollen, the little SD bag in my fist is half-empty as Devaughn slides the next card to me. I pick it up, still giggling at something the fox whispered, and flip it idly between my fingers.

I look up to see who my next participant is and find Josh taking the seat across from me. He has one brow arched in lazy amusement, but his jaw ticks, giving his true feelings away. His gray eyes are bright and it's impossible to look elsewhere. He's definitely been watching—it's not like we were being quiet in this corner of the grounds.

I feel the SD surge, hot and sudden, like it recognizes him and wants to answer—of course, now it wants to hit all at once. My smile falters, lips parting on a breath I can't quite pull in.

His cape hangs open, chest still flushed from whatever or whoever he was tangled with. The men around us are still loud with their chatter, unaware of the shift in the air.

Devaughn leans back, grinning wide. "Was wondering when the Beta would get jealous and show up."

"I'll deal with you later," Josh threatens him but doesn't spare Devaughn a glance. His eyes are locked on me in a clear challenge. "Four of feathers."

I shake my head.

His gaze narrows, reading every flicker on my face. "Two of serpents."

My breath catches. I flip the card slowly enough for everyone to see. Two of serpents.

The men erupt again, louder than before as they start pounding the table and chanting, "Kiss! Kiss! Kiss!"

Josh leans forward, forearms braced on the wood. "I believe the Veyara owes me a kiss."

My heart skips at the words. I stand, straightening my dress, calmly. "You've already had plenty tonight." The men holler, not understanding my meaning, but Josh does and the asshole smirks. That'll kill my SD high.

I snatch up Devaughn's flask and tip it to my lips, swallowing deeply, letting the burn run all the way to my toes.

"I'm keeping this," I tell Devaughn, tapping the silver against my palm. Then I turn on my heel and walk away.

I'm only ten strides from the table, flask clutched to my chest, when fingers clamp around my wrist, sending wild sparks throughout my entire body. Damn him and damn all the drugs I've taken.

"Not so fast, my Veyara," Josh says, voice low and rough, spinning me back to face him.

I yank once, but he doesn't let go. "You've got a whole buffet of willing mouths here. Go pick one."

His grip tightens, just enough to remind me who I'm talking to. Then he reels me in until my chest brushes his bare one and the scent of bonfire smoke and other women hits me.

"Maybe," he says, eyes glittering, "but there's only one Veyara here."

The SD flares at his nearness, treacherous heat crawling up my spine, trying to blur the edges of my anger. I tilt my chin, meet his stare dead-on. "Then I hope your hunt for another one ends soon."

His jaw flexes. For a second the amusement slips, and fury flashes in his eyes. Then the mask slides back into place, lazy and infuriating.

"Come dance with us, Beta!" a girl calls out but neither of us bother to look her way.

"You have the Veyara's permission," another coos, "right, Rose? You'll share, won't you?"

My stomach twists.

I just want to leave now, so I tell him, "Go, it's okay—"

Josh's gaze cuts to the women, turning cold and predatory, shutting me up immediately. His arm tightens around me, and I can feel the heat rolling off him as if I was standing in the bonfire.

"Address my Veyara in front of me like that again," he says in a voice that's lethal and icy, "and I will make you and your parents regret ever being born."

I would shiver if I wasn't already sweating.

The women falter. Their laughter dies as one sways, lips parting. Another's smile cracks. They back away, muttering excuses and merging into the party.

Josh doesn't move until they're out of sight. Then he's pressed up against me, chest to chest with just enough release to let me breathe again. His body returns to normal temperature but now mine is on fire. He glances down at me, his smile sharp and dangerous.

"Why on earth would you throw me to the wolves like that?" he asks me, eyes narrowed in a mock scold.

I blink, "I—I don't think they were wolves…"

"Oh, shut up," he says, but there's no cruelty in it. "You don't want to push me tonight."

"You say that like I have some kind of effect on you." I breathe trying to focus on his face and not on his cock pressing against my stomach. His pants don't give him much barrier—and it's impossible to pretend I don't feel it or realize he's gone commando tonight. But he could just be hard from the previous girl—the thought makes me want to puke. The image of the redhead grinding on him earlier makes me lightheaded.

I start to pull away but his fingers find the clip at the back of my head, and with a motion so casual, he lets it fall. My hair spills free, warm against my neck, cascading down to my waist. He tugs at my hair just hard enough to make my spine arch, and a small gasp escapes me. The world narrows to just him.

Josh leans in, cheek brushing mine. "Don't start. Or I'll show you what happens if you do."

"Is that a promise or a threat?" I ask, not looking away from him.

He presses his thumb under my chin and tilts my face up letting the Moon expose any imperfections. He lets his mask slip as he says, "Both, my Veyara."

I don't back down even though my heart melts every time he says *my Veyara*. "You don't have to let your Mate being here hold you back."

"You're not holding me back," he whispers against my skin. Okay, but he's holding me back, I was actually having fun with the men.

My chest tightens regardless as I try to control my stupid racing heart. "I've heard what you like to do on reunion nights," I breathe, trying to anchor myself. "I'm not ready for any of that with you—not saying you want that with me anyway…I know you won't be tied down."

His gaze hardens into a glare. Then, without warning, he reaches down and rips a fringe off my dress.

"What are you doing!" I exclaim, shocked.

He doesn't answer right away. Instead, he twists the strip of fabric around our hands, his left binding to my right, fingers working a knot expertly. It digs into my wrist, making sure I feel it. When he finally looks up, his gray eyes are ablaze and my soul is lit on fire.

"Fucking tying myself down to you," he snaps at me, "now what?"

I'm speechless. Heat swelling in my chest and between my legs. The guests are loud—their voices, footsteps, the clink of chalices—but all I can focus on is how close his lips are and his hand on my hip, thumb stroking the bare skin revealed by the slit of my dress.

Don't fall for it, I warn myself.

"I told you not to push me," his voice drops, raw hunger mixed with warning. He tugs me closer, shamelessly making me feel his hard cock on purpose. "Wipe your head of whatever you think you know. I'm going to give you new memories, Rose. Ones you can burn into your mind forever."

Then he spins me, pulling me against him, his chest presses to my shoulder blade as his hips sway with the drums, moving me with him. His breath fans my ear while his hand rests across my stomach, possessively.

All around us, the Pack indulges without shame as the night continues. James has Vanessa bent over one of the tables, taking her right there. The table rattles with every thrust, Vanessa's moans are swallowed by the music and chatter.

Sam and Azura are slow dancing, completely oblivious to the frenzy around them, their foreheads touching, like they're their own gravity. It reminds me of my transformation night with the halo around Josh and me—except the way they start kissing each other. His expression is softer than I normally see it, his smile gentle as he whispers something that makes her laugh.

Daniel has Daniya pinned against a tree trunk, one of her legs hooked high around his waist. Their mouths are fused, hungry and wet, but they're not alone. Another couple, a dark-haired woman and blond man, are tangled with them, four bodies moving together as one. The woman kisses Daniya's throat while Daniya's hand disappears under the man's open robe, stroking his dick. Daniya moans, hips grinding forward, as Daniel thrusts into her, one hand on her hip, the other bringing the woman's breast to his mouth while she and her Mate make-out.

No one's watching them. Everyone's watching them. The line blurred hours ago.

The rawness, the intimacy, the freedom of it all is so familiar, but not. My eyes go back to Sam and Azura, feeling a little jealous of their ease with one another. Josh and I are not in a place to participate with anything happening here—except the drinking and feasting.

"You see?" he murmurs, lips brushing my ear, "Everyone is giving into instinct. It's who we are."

The sight of James pulling Vanessa into his arms and kissing her, Sam's gentle devotion, Daniel's clear worship—each scene a different kind of hunger and bond.

Josh's teeth graze my skin, a light scrape that stings slightly but makes my knees grow weak. What the fuck kind of poison is in his fangs?

"So Veyara," he whispers, low and hot, "which hunger do you want to give into tonight?"

I tilt my head back into him and look up at the full Moon hanging over us, as I ask him, "What if I want none of this tonight?"

His lips press against my temple, a surprising tenderness in the gesture. "That's okay too," he says quietly, and I hear the honesty in his voice. "We don't have to do anything you're not comfortable with."

I turn to face him, the tie on our wrists pulling tight. I rest my palm against his chest, feeling his heartbeat. "It's my second full Moon," I remind him.

"I'm well aware," he says as if acknowledging it pains him.

I look up and find his smoldering gaze on me. "Don't we have to shift or anything?"

His heart rate is off the charts. Why is his heart rate off the charts? He looks up at the full Moon as if he's silently asking for strength before he looks at me again. "Probably not the best idea."

I frown. "Why not?"

He looks behind me at the reunion guests celebrating no doubt, before he hesitates, and then asks, "You want to get out of here?"

If I could cross my arms, I would, but seeing that one of them is tied to his, I just give him a pointed look. "And do what?"

His eyes linger on me, and I forget how tall he is. His free hand runs through my hair deliciously, before he gives me a small smile. Then he reaches past me, snatching up a dark bottle of bloodwine from a nearby table. "Breathe."

I look at the bottle, then at him, and shake my head. "Untie me and you can go *breathe* with whoever you want."

"Seeing that I can't breathe when you're not around, that'd be hard to do," he says in a voice so low that if I wasn't facing him, I would've missed it.

I roll my eyes. "Yeah okay. You were breathing fine when the redhead was straddling you."

He inhales sharply, before he says, "You don't have to be jealous."

"I'm not jealous, I'm disgusted. You're disgusting to me," I snap at him, "and you ruined a perfectly good night I was having."

"Kissing other men?"

"Yes!" I snap. "They were fun, and funny, and made me feel like I was—" I cut myself off when he trails a finger down my cheek. Seriously. What did he take? I try to move my face away, glaring at him, "What are you doing? You can make-out and hook-up with girls, but I can't have a good time?"

"No."

"Fuck you."

"Come with me."

"I'm not going anywhere with you."

"It's your second full Moon and I know you want to go back to the clearing. Come with me," he says softly, making me pause.

I do want to go back to the clearing. I want to experience that serenity I felt before my shift again.

"I told you, I don't take anyone there, so will you come with me?" he asks, keeping his eyes on me.

I swallow. My heart and body want to say yes. My brain is asking how many other secret spots he has with other girls in these woods. I shake my head and drop my gaze from him, clenching my jaw so my lips don't tremble. Who knows how long he's going to keep us tied? I can't start crying now.

"Why not?" he asks.

"Well, for one, you smell like other girls."

"And you smell like other guys."

My eyes flash at him. "It's not the same and you know it."

"Okay…" he clears his throat before I feel him emanating so much heat, I start squirming, needing to get away from him. But when I breathe again, he smells like himself—citrusy, smoky with that hint of spice that's uniquely him. He literally just burned the scent of the other women off him.

I glare at him, staying focused. "That's not the point. I left you for two seconds and you were making out with other women. Why would I want to go anywhere with you?"

"And where are those women right now?" he asks me, raising a brow, urging me to look for them.

I frown and glance around. They're not here. I look back at Josh. "I don't understand."

"If you had kept your eyes on me like I'm going to order you to from now on, you would've watched me burn off their lips and fingerprints from touching what's yours."

I blink. There's so much to unpack in that…but all I can say is, "You didn't…"

"I did. I'll give you their names if you want to confirm," he says, then drops his head to rest it against my forehead. "Now, will you please just—" he doesn't get to finish the sentence, because someone screams.

I turn to look and see that a fight's broken out between a serpent and a bear shifter. People try to break them apart, but instead the fight turns bigger and things start to go flying. The bear shifter is out of control as the crazed look takes over him and he shifts.

"Fuck," Josh mutters under his breath as people start running.

"Get her the fuck out of here!" Devaughn shouts at Josh, "James and I got this." Then Devaughn shifts into a white wolf as I see James and Sam do the same, Daniel too from the other end of the clearing.

"Come on," Josh pulls at me as a bottle is thrown our way, just barely missing my head. Josh catches the bottle, the anger in his eyes evident as he scans the crowd for the assailant. He has murder in his eyes.

"Hey," I say to him, lowering his hand and moving toward the forest. "Come on. Take me to the clearing."

I let my walls drop just enough to let his seductive powers affect me, mixing with the drugs in my system. I *know* he's been emanating it, probably even fueling most of the lust around us earlier, and I need the courage.

Josh takes a swig of the bloodwine but follows me after throwing the bottle on the ground. He already has the other one he picked up earlier in his hand.

The ritual ground quickly fades away behind us. Our steps crunch over leaves and roots as I let him lead us through the forest. Josh passes me the bottle. I slip Devaughn's flask into my bra, making Josh snort, before I take a drink of the bloodwine. It's sweet and dark, thick on my tongue, warming as it slides down. It's perfect for the cooler air now that we're away from the Pack.

It's a little bit of a walk, and somewhere along the way his fingers slip between mine.

"You could just untie us," I tell him.

"That defeats the purpose of being tied down to you," he throws back over his shoulder.

"I guess miracles can happen on full Moon nights."

He glances back, catching the smirk I can't hide. His eyes narrow, dangerous and amused all at once, before he reminds me. "I warned you…"

"Maybe you need to just get your hate for me out of your system," I suggest, shrugging, but the whole time my mind is reminding me how I was with Devaughn and the men for awhile—I know Josh didn't hook up with anyone, but still, he reeked of women. Where was he?

"Rose," his voice is thick and heavy, "you have no idea what you're saying."

"I have a little idea…" I counter, thinking of every sharp word, every brutal way he's hurt me before.

"Trust me, you don't. And definitely not tonight," his voice is stern, final.

"What's wrong with tonight?" I press, frowning as I step carefully over a fallen tree. "Also why aren't we shifting tonight?"

Josh steadies me with his free hand, lifting me over it before answering. "It's a full Moon night. Even I don't have full control tonight."

"You wouldn't hurt me," I whisper, more certain than I should be. He could—he's shown me enough glimpses to know it—but deep down I believe he wouldn't. Not really.

His back is rigid, shoulders set. "You think?"

"Yes," I say, firmly this time.

A muscle ticks in his jaw. "Well…let's not test it tonight," he says as the trees part and the clearing comes into view.

Just like the first time, it takes my breath away again. I grin and take it in. The trees arching high like barriers, the way the Moon shines down and reflects off the water, even the air smells different here—untouched.

Josh stands beside me, taking a deep breath himself. Then he glances at me, pulling me further into it. I let out a joyful laugh, genuinely happy to be here.

The clearing is quiet. My pulse calms and my body loosens. I place the bottle on a flat rock with the flask, before I ask him, "Do you feel it too? The magic here?"

Josh doesn't answer right away. His silence is heavy, weighted with memory of his family. Then he says, quietly, "My mom used to always say that. The magic is stronger here."

I smile and close my eyes, tipping my head back to let the Moonlight wash over me. For one perfect moment I forget about everything else.

Then soft lips press against mine in the gentlest of kisses.

The shock of it makes me open my eyes, breaking away. Josh is right there, so close that I see the restraint in his eyes. They hold mine and I can stare into them forever.

"I've wanted to kiss you so many times since your shift. I can't hold back anymore—not when you look so fucking perfect right now," he says, his words lighting me up, and then as an afterthought, he adds, "and not when you owe me one. I'm going to take what's mine."

My heart races at his words and his closeness. His voice is doing dangerous things to me. I know better than to give into him. My pride is rebelling profusely, wanting me to choose better for myself, or at least make him suffer some way. The Mating bond though keeps reminding me that he's *mine.*

He's supposed to be mine.

I press into him, whispering against his mouth, "Then why'd you stop kissing me?"

His eyes hold mine so intensely, I feel petrified, but I know he's not using his powers.

His lips find mine again. There's no force, no trace of his power pushing against my shields. It's just him kissing me, unhurried, unguarded, and the realization makes my lips quiver against his. My free hand comes up to his neck as his hand cups my face.

The only magic between us is ours—the bond's—and this place.

This is real.

For once he's not trying to take, but he's simply giving into us. For once, I can't be bothered about all the women he chose over me. I can't be bothered with everything that came before because this moment is just ours right now.

26 PUSH

Rosella Craving
August 18

The grass should be cold beneath me, but Josh laid out his robe for us. His basilisk warmth wards off the cold, bending the world to his comfort. It's nice, because it means I get to enjoy it too. Moonlight spills over us as he stretches out beside me, one arm tucked lazily behind his head, like he could just fall asleep here.

"Aside from sex—"

"Why would you start a sentence like that?" he cuts in immediately.

I let out an impatient breath. "It's rude to interrupt when someone's talking."

"I'm the Beta," he counters without looking at me.

"I'm a Craving," I shoot back just as fast.

His mouth twitches. "Fuck you."

"No," I click my tongue. "I said, *aside from sex.*" I roll my eyes, as he laughs. "What's your favorite basilisk power to use?"

He finally turns his head toward me, eyes glinting with amusement. "Are you trying to get to know me?"

I sigh, dramatically. "I guess I should if you're going to be kissing me."

"You're cute if you think we have to do that just because we're kissing now." He chuckles lowly.

"Don't be an ass," I mumble, my face falling at his words. It's stupid how it can either make my day or ruin it.

The silence stretches before he finally says, "Paralysis. There's nothing more satisfying than freezing someone mid-step, mid-word, mid-breath—and watching the realization dawn on them that they are utterly helpless. Knowing they can't do a damn thing unless I let them."

"You like the control."

There's no excitement or thrill on his face, just truth, as he nods once. "Yes. The control, the power. I like knowing I can hold someone exactly where I want them until they have no choice but to face me.

No choice but to face what they've done. I don't bend and I don't forget, so I don't forgive. Justice doesn't get to slip away."

Is that what he wants to do to me because he thinks I killed his brother?

The words land heavy, pulling at something inside me that's all too familiar. I bite my lip, caught between unease and a strange kind of understanding.

Then he turns his head, his eyes locking on mine. "Does that scare you?"

"Should it?" I ask softly.

His gaze flickers to my mouth, then back up. "Yes. Most people can't handle the truth."

"Do you even tell them the truth?" I ask him, curiously, "I can't be the first person to ask you that question." He watches me and I can see he's trying to decide how to answer me. A small laugh escapes me. "Well, don't start lying now."

His thumb brushes against my hand where they are still bound. He says, "I don't tell them anything."

"Be serious."

"If anyone asks me a question like that, I don't answer them," Josh replies, frowning, "why would I?"

"To have a conversation maybe?" I suggest. I don't want to ask him if someone, anyone, wanted to get to know him like this. A big part of me doesn't want to know if he let the girls he's been with in. I don't want to know if he talked to them, laughed with them, shared moments like we're sharing right now with them. They already know his body.

I don't want to picture him in bed with someone for hours, speaking softly, laughing at things I've never heard, when he's never given me that chance.

I don't want to think I'm the last resort—that he wouldn't be here with me if he had a choice. That there were others waiting for him the way I did.

But that's the truth, isn't it? He's said it so many times.

"Why don't you ask what you really want to ask," Josh tells me.

I hate that he's a basilisk.

I shift, uncomfortably, my fingers twitching, wanting my hand back. "I don't know what you mean. I was asking about your powers."

"You know what I mean," he presses.

My throat goes dry. I break our eye contact and stare at our bound wrists instead.

His thumb moves over my wrist again, pulling my attention back up. His eyes are steady, but unreadable, "Go on, ask me," he says quietly.

"Ask you what?" I repeat.

"What you're really thinking," he pushes, "ask me if I've ever given anyone else what you've always really wanted from me."

I glare at him. "Stop using your power on me."

That makes him smile. "Mind reading isn't a basilisk power. It is a Mate's though, but I don't have to read your mind to know where it just went."

I whisper, barely audible, "Did you?"

"No," he says, voice low and absolute. He cups my face with his free hand. "I never let anyone into my mind in any capacity," his thumb strokes along my jaw, deceptively gentle. "You think I'd give my mind—*me*—to someone I could bend with a smile or a few words? I know how powerful words are. How dangerous," his mouth curves, with certainty, "I'd never compromise myself like that."

I search his face, the hard lines softened only by the Moonlight. He doesn't flinch, doesn't hide. For once, I don't see a mask—only the raw truth.

"You don't trust people." He's a basilisk. Deception is his game, of course, he doesn't trust people.

His eyes stay locked on mine. "People are careless with what they're given. They twist it, weaponize it. I won't hand them a blade and wait to be stabbed." His thumb lingers at my jaw, the faintest drag that feels more like a claim than a caress and I relish in his touch. "Most people aren't worth trusting. So no, Rose. No one's ever had that part of me."

My chest tightens. It should make me feel better, but instead I feel worse—because the way he says it makes me realize just how much he's holding back from *me*.

"I'm not most people," I breathe, holding his stare as my heart pounds so hard that I swear he can hear it. My throat tightens, but I risk saying it anyway. "I'm your Mate."

His eyes are dark, dangerous, and undeniably hungry—for me. His thumb slides to my lower lip, dragging it down just a fraction, and I can't stop the shaky inhale that slips free.

"Yes, you are," his words strike through me like lightning. For a heartbeat, I forget how to breathe. The admission isn't loud, but it's enough for me. For the first time it doesn't sound like he hates the idea. "Keep looking at me like that, and I might forget I promised to behave tonight," he says, quietly.

"Well…" My lips curve, daring him. "I made no such promise."

A groan rumbles from his chest as he pulls away, laying on his back and dragging a hand down his face. "No, stop."

I bite my lip from smiling too big. "I see why this is fun for you." He just pinches the bridge of his nose and shakes his head. "You're back to hating me again, aren't you?" I ask, teasing.

"Yes," he answers simply with no hesitation.

A laugh slips free from me before we fall quiet again, lying side by side looking up at the sky. The Moon has dipped lower, but I can still feel the effects of the SD. My nerves are still lit, but it's nothing compared to the ache that's built inside me for years, starving for a moment like this with Josh.

He looks at me, studying me as his finger caresses my palm, sending a need straight to my core. "You're shaking," he rasps. "What did you take?"

I laugh lightly. "SD."

"Shit…" he says and I can't decide if he's concerned or impressed.

I turn to him. "What did *you* take?" he eyes me, suspiciously, almost as if he doesn't want to tell me. "What is it?"

"Pulse."

My brows shoot up as my eyes widen. "Shit."

Pulse is a hard one to get—like Veins. It lets regular shifter Mates feel what Warrior Mates feel daily. When we take it heightens our connection, vulnerability, and syncs our heartbeats and arousal. It makes everything more magnetic. The side effects if taken with the wrong partner can be devastating. It's meant only for Mates. It explains why he's been open to sharing so much tonight. Since I didn't take it, he won't feel the physical effects of it, just the mental and emotional.

"Is that why you've been…" I start but trail off, not sure how I want to finish the sentence.

"Been what?" he asks, of course.

I chew on my bottom lip. "Been…acting like we're together…"

"We *are* together," he says, frowning slightly, but my heart skips a beat anyway.

"You know what I mean," I whisper. "You've been…pleasant…enough?"

"Sure, we can blame the drugs," he says, quietly.

"I've never…taken it before," I admit.

"I'd hope not," he answers with a small smile as his thumb continues to trace slow, maddening circles in the center of my palm. He leans in, claiming my mouth in a kiss that tastes like a confession of things he might never tell me. It's slow and deep, as his free hand slides up my leg where my dress parts. His hand starts moving carefully, giving me every chance to stop him. I don't—I can't. I arch instead, thighs parting on instinct as his hand brushes my silk underwear. He deepens the kiss as our bound hands intertwine, while his fingers brush against my wetness.

He groans into my mouth like I've wounded him. "Fuck, sweetheart, you're drenched."

Sweetheart? He's *never* called me that before. Not even in a mocking way. The way my body feels alive, I decide I love it.

A long, low howl rolls through the night. It cuts clean across the quiet clearing. We break away and I turn my head toward the sound, before looking at Josh.

"Antonio and Mariella are out of the Sanctum," he explains, already sitting up. I follow, brushing grass from my palms and fixing my dress as if the spell on us just broke. For a moment, we're still bound, fingers laced. Then he lifts our hands and unties the bind.

"You're free," he says, eyes on mine.

The warmth of his hand disappears instantly as disappointment washes over me. I don't want this night to end. I rub my wrist where his touch had been, the echo of it still burning, before I meet his gaze.

Something in me rebels at the emptiness between us and I whisper, "No, I'm not," then before I can think better of it, I lean in, bringing his face closer, and press my mouth to his.

His breath catches against me, and for one suspended heartbeat I don't know if he'll pull away or reciprocate.

He seizes me with both hands, one at my waist, the other cradling the back of my neck, dragging me closer until there's no space left between us. He kisses me deeper, hungrier, his tongue exploring mine like he's starved for me.

A gasp escapes me into his mouth as I cup his face, fingers tracing the sharp lines of his jaw. He leans into my touch as his kiss grows fiercer.

"I told you not to push me tonight."

"Maybe you need a push."

Josh pulls away then, his eyes dark and heavy with hunger. He's reading my face before his eyes narrow and he stands up. My heart drops to my stomach. I guess that moment's over.

"Stay," he says, his voice coming out in a low command, before he walks away from me into the darkness of the trees.

What the fuck?

"Are you seriously leaving me here?" I ask into the clearing, confused. I start to get up when his voice is in my head again.

"Don't fucking move. The celebration's not over," he telepaths.

Then a faint rustle nearby perks my ears. I turn my head just as a ripple of movement cuts through and a large, *large,* rattlesnake, emerges from the grass.

I freeze.

It doesn't hiss or attack. It just comes closer, slithering toward me. Before I can move, its cool, heavy body slides up my legs onto my thighs, the pressure of its weight pushes me back, so that I'm lying on the grass, barely missing Josh's robe. My breath catches. The snake's head lifts, its tongue flicking out.

Josh. Holy fuck…am I hallucinating? This feels too real for it to be SD's effects.

His head tilts, his slit gray eyes study me. He lowers, brushing his scaled cheek along my thigh. The texture is shocking, rough and cool, but it leaves sparks skating up my skin. I reach down, hesitating. My hand trembles above his body, but he doesn't move away. He waits.

When my fingers finally touch the scales, I find they're hard, ridged, but alive and cool beneath my hand. He exhales a hiss, and presses closer, winding another loop around my legs.

The awe outweighs the fear now.

"You're beautiful," I whisper, daring the words out loud. I've seen him in serpent form three times now, each time a different serpent, and each time he's magnificent. I'm not going to lie and say I love snakes…I really, really don't, but knowing he won't hurt me, and knowing it's *him* makes it different. Any other snake, I'm running.

Josh's eyes glow brighter. When his body unwinds just enough for me to breathe again, I know—I've been allowed something no one else ever has. He moves with perfect control, never squeezing too hard, never letting me forget he can. His head rises until his glowing eyes are level with mine.

A strange bliss floods me, deeper than the euphoria of this clearing and I know he's using his power to calm me, but he's doing more than that. My breath comes slower, softer, as his coils slide over my body, claiming every inch of me without a word. My fingers stroke down the length of his back, scales rippling under my touch.

"Do you trust me?" his voice is in my head as he presses his scaled cheek to mine and the bliss sinks hotter, sharper, almost unbearable now. I close my eyes and let him wrap me tighter, let myself *belong* to this monster.

"You know I don't," I answer but the weight of him settles around me anyway. His reptilian body winds tighter, cool scales dragging over my own body, making me shiver in ways I don't expect. Every inch of him is power—controlled, restrained—but I can feel it coiled, waiting, like a storm held in his chest.

My breath catches as one thick loop slides lower, brushing the tops of my thighs, then tightening around my hips. It isn't painful. It's…consuming. The pressure makes me acutely aware of my body, of how open I am to him, how utterly at his mercy. Yet the bliss doesn't fade—it intensifies. A pulse beats between my legs, aching, needy, as the ridges of his scales drag against my inner thighs. My fingers tighten on his body, stroking down his length, and he responds, squeezing just enough to steal my breath.

"Fuck…" I let out in a half-moan, half-prayer.

His head dips, gray eyes locking onto mine. His forked tongue flicks out, tasting my cheek. The strange touch sends a rush of fire straight to my core, and I gasp, pressing into his serpent body without thinking.

The coils shift again, firmer, rolling against my waist and thighs. Every scrape of scale leaves me trembling. I let my head fall back, eyes fluttering shut as his weight presses me deeper into the earth, leaving me wet and wanting beneath him.

When his fangs graze my throat, I whimper—neither fear nor hesitation, only a raw plea for him to take. I'm wrapped fully in the coils of his serpent form, and I realize I can't breathe, can't move, and I don't want to.

"Let me in," he thinks to me.

"What?" I ask, confused before something firmer presses between my thighs and I let out a gasp as his tail shifts. The rattle at the end grazes my thong, nudging the lace aside before sliding against my slick pussy. The vibration is faint at first, but enough to send a shudder straight through me. I whimper, writhing against it, shame drowned in need. My plea is broken with shock and desperation.

The rattle prods at my entrance, cool scales dragging across my swollen flesh. He coils tighter as if to anchor me, then pushes inside, making me moan out. The invasion is strange, blunt at first, then smooth as the ridges slip past my walls. My back arches, my cry echoing through the clearing.

Holy shit.

He's really doing this.

And I'm letting him.

This cannot be okay.

Is this okay?

He hisses, low and commanding, and then pushes. The blunt tip parts me, forcing my walls to stretch around it. My cry breaks out, but the shock melts instantly into pleasure.

The ridges slide inside, each one scraping and rubbing against sensitive flesh as the rattle burrows deeper. The vibrations increase once he's fully inside, the tremor resonating in my core, making my clit throb and my body clamp down around him.

"Oh fuck—" I can barely form words. My back bows as his coils hold me open. My pulse spikes, disbelief crashing through me. This can't be happening. This *shouldn't* be happening. But the pleasure—Divine, the pleasure—is too good, too much to resist.

He thrusts, slowly, dragging the textured length out of me before slamming it back in. The ridges rake against my inner walls, and my legs quake. Each stroke feels deeper than the last, heightening every nerve until I'm sobbing with pleasure.

At some point he's coiled himself around my neck, applying enough pressure, making it hard for me to breathe fully.

"Look at you," his voice is another wave of pleasure and my eyes roll back.

"More," I think to him, ***"please, more—don't stop."***

"You're so fucking beautiful when you beg for me. I'll never get tired of it," he telepaths before the rattle pounds into me faster, harder, each thrust sending shockwaves of bliss through my core. My body convulses, my climax ripping through me so violently I scream out into the clearing. But he doesn't stop. His coils squeeze tighter, the rhythm unrelenting as the magic forces me over again—second, third, each orgasm crashing harder than the last.

By the time he finally pulls free, I'm drenched, shaking, my thighs trembling uncontrollably, begging him to stop. He winds himself around me possessively, his head settling against my breastbone, split tongue flicking lazily over the hollow of my throat.

I can still feel the aftershocks coursing inside me. I don't dare open my eyes as I lay here, gasping for air. I feel him retreating, the weight of him easing away, and still I keep my eyes shut, shame creeping in.

I let him—Divine, I let him touch me with his—in his serpent form. And I loved it. My cheeks burn with the thought, my heart pounding with the wrongness of it all. That had to be illegal.

"Rose," Josh says. He's shifted to human form, because he's speaking to me. "Look at me."

I feel him standing over my body and I shake my head. I squeeze my eyes tighter, mortified at what he just did, at how much I enjoyed it. This is not how I expected my first reunion party to go.

Strong hands grip my arms, pulling me to my feet. My legs wobble, barely holding me up. I open my eyes and he drapes his robe around me, before cupping my face, his thumbs brushing my cheeks.

His face is nothing but awe as he says, "You're so beautiful."

Then his lips crash into mine, the kiss is so fierce, so passionate, that my already weak knees start to give out. I clutch his shoulders, drowning in the heat of him, the taste and smell of him, until he pulls back, leaving me breathless. Again.

"*That* was a first for me," he admits, his voice low, eyes burning into mine, "and it was everything I ever imagined it would be."

A first. He never did that with anyone else—because he'd kill them, even a serpent woman. It's only then that I remember someone telling me a long time ago that a Hunter's scales are poisonous due to their basilisk DNA. No matter which serpent form they're in, their skin can kill. Only I am able to hold him in his serpent form. I didn't even feel anything different. If he was trying to reassure me, that was one Hell of a way to do it.

I bury my face in his chest, my cheeks flaming, but heart pounding at his words. "I can't believe we just did that."

His arms wrap around me, holding me close to him. Then I feel the soft shake of his shoulders as he chuckles quietly.

I pull back just enough to glare up at him, smacking his arm. "It's not funny!"

"No, it's not," he says, but his lips twitch, betraying him, "but you being embarrassed? That's a little funny," he kisses my forehead and then my nose, "if only you knew how sexy that was."

Sexy. He thinks I was sexy?

His hand slides lower, cupping my ass, pulling me closer until I feel the hard length of his cock pressing against me. A fresh wave of heat floods through me, and I'm caught between wanting to hide and wanting him all over again.

"Should we return to the party and congratulate our friends, then?" he says so casually like he didn't just do what he did. I meet his gaze, biting my lip in hesitation. He raises a brow, "What is it?"

I should reciprocate…he is hard—but I can't. I can't bring myself to offer it. I can't shake the thoughts of his dick in other women's hands or mouth or—I just can't. I'm not ready. I mean, just earlier a girl was completely straddling him…how do I move past that?

He sees it on my face because his fingers weave into my hair and his gentle, but firm grip feels *so* good. His lips press against my forehead as he says, "I told you we don't have to do anything you're not ready for. Let's just go back to the party unless you want to go home."

"The party," I reply, daring to reach for his hand in my hair to hold it. I just hate that those ugly thoughts and memories have to taint things. "I feel like I should apologize, but I don't really want to…"

Josh laughs and it's a genuine laugh. Not a mocking or humorless one, an actual lighthearted laugh. "Apologize for what? One of the most exciting nights of my life? Please don't."

We leave the clearing and after some time, I can start hearing the drums getting louder.

"I can't believe you let me do that," Josh chuckles, shaking his head like he still can't believe it. I still can't believe it.

"Like I had a choice!" I exclaim, the embarrassment rushing back and my cheeks warming again. Fuck him for reminding me how much I actually enjoyed that. I'll be taking this to my grave, thank you very much.

"You always have a choice," Josh tells me seriously and his hold on my hand tightens to assure me that he means it.

I look up at his handsome face. "Really?"

"Yes," he answers, but then adds, "well, for the most part…"

I roll my eyes. "I need to get drunk again."

27 SACRIFICE

Rose Craving
August 20

Bodies lie twisted in the mud—shifters, witches, vampires, even humans. Their eyes left open to a smoke-filled sky. Blood soaks the earth and the stench overwhelm me—rot, burned flesh, voided bowels—thick enough to taste.

Nathanial stands in the center of it all, untouched, coat hanging open with his hands loose at his sides. He looks regal as ever, like an angel of death. His gaze fixes on a beautiful woman in white walking toward him through the carnage. Her gown stays impossibly clean, the hem of her dress pristine despite the ruin at her feet. Blonde hair spills over her shoulders, catching what little light breaks through the haze. It's unmistakably Mother Isis—serene, frozen, forever young.

She reaches him, sways once, and collapses forward. He catches her before she hits the ground, arms folding around her like he's done this a thousand times. Her hair darkens strand by strand, gold bleeding to midnight black. Her features start to shift—cheekbones narrowing, mouth fuller, blue eyes shifting to a beautiful sea green. She becomes someone else entirely, someone I knew.

Nathanial brushes a thumb across her cheek tenderly. "You did so well," he whispers, in a raw voice, "it's time to rest."

He lowers her gently to the bloodied ground, arranges her arms at her sides. Flames leap from his fingertips, igniting on the white gown. The fire burns, consuming her in seconds, leaving only ash for the wind scatters across the dead.

I jolt awake gasping and my heart pounding dangerously fast against my ribs. My hands clutch my chest as if I can hold everything inside from spilling out. The room spins for a second as I take in my surroundings. Log walls, low crackle of a fireplace, cold mountain air seeping through the cracks. I'm in Nathanial's cabin. In his bed. Soft furs are beneath me and his scent is everywhere.

He sits in the armchair by the fire, staring into the flames like they might speak back. I notice how rigid his shoulders are.

I blink. "What…why did you show me that?"

He turns his head slowly. "Because it's starting again."

I push up on my trembling arms. "Who was the woman? She looked familiar."

"She was a sacrifice."

I sit at the edge of the bed and realize what I'm wearing. A thin silk blue nightdress that falls loosely over my curves. The cold bites my skin instantly. I grab the thick blanket from the foot of the bed, wrap it around my shoulders, and cross the room to him.

I sink down at his feet, close enough to feel the heat of the fire on my face. "Why did she look like Mother Isis at first? Then…someone else?"

His gaze drops to me. He reaches out and threads his fingers slowly through my hair. "It's been a long time," he says quietly, "since twins were born in the Craving line."

My mind stumbles at the topic change. "But…Eliza lost one of the babies."

He says nothing. The fire pops. Sparks rise and die.

I lean into his touch and rest my head against his knee. His hand keeps stroking, steady, grounding. He studies me for a moment. "Why hasn't your Mate Marked you yet?"

The question is like a knife to my chest. I can't hide anything from Nathanial. Josh has been and still is my only failure. "He doesn't care how powerful I am. I'm not a serpent. He's not…attracted to me."

Nathanial scoffs. "What does that have to do with Marking you?"

I can't answer. "I…I don't know. We're just not there yet."

His hand cups my jaw roughly, forcing me to look at him again. The grip is too familiar, too much like Josh's when he feels some kind of passion for me. Heat floods me despite everything and I want my Mate's touch. I want Josh. His hands.

"You need to be in control of your powers, Rose," he gives me a pointed look.

"I am," I frown, not sure what I've done to make him think otherwise.

"Your powers will start getting out of control the longer you delay the Mark," Nathanial says, voice edged.

"I can't make Josh do anything."

He pulls me up effortlessly and settles me on his lap. The blanket falls away. The silk of my nightdress does nothing to hide me from the chill or from him, but Nathanial's body heat is comforting. His finger traces a slow line down my throat, over my collarbone, then lower, stopping just above my nipple.

"Serpent or not. You're his Mate. Darkness isn't your only power, my little mistress," he murmurs against my ear. "You're a woman. You're any man's greatest weakness if you know how to use your charms." His fingers tap lightly against my bare thigh.

"Not with him." I shake my head.

"He's hiding something," Nathanial tells me and I don't doubt it. It's Josh. He's always up to something.

"Like what?" I ask, curiously. Nathanial and I don't usually talk about Josh, so I'm wondering where his mind is today.

"I could never put my finger on it, but that Mate of yours is hiding something. He's too careful." Nathanial narrows his eyes.

"He's a basilisk. He's always paranoid. That's not surprising at all," I reply, shaking my head.

"Perhaps. Even a basilisk shifter is no match for you," Nathanial comments.

"Nathanial," I frown, "he's my Mate. The Divine doesn't make mistakes."

"That's why I know he's hiding something. The Divine always pairs Mates accordingly."

I don't say anything. He's brought this to my attention before, and what am I supposed to say? Josh is powerful in his own right but I don't care about any of that—not with him. I don't care about my power or his, or our titles, or duties. I just want Josh Hunter—the man.

I can never say that to Nathanial though.

"How's Shane doing?" he changes the subject.

"Quiet. He's spending most of his time with Eliza," I sigh, sadly. "Is there really no workaround the curse of the twins? Could there have been anything we could've done?"

"It's called a curse for a reason," Nathanial exhales deeply, kissing my temple. "I'm afraid it's just nature taking its course."

"What do you think this baby's powers will be if he's already this strong?" I ask. "Have you ever seen this? A twin draining the other in the womb?"

Nathanial is quiet for a moment before he shakes his head. "No, I haven't. Whatever his powers will be…he'll need to be carefully watched. If he's already using magic in the womb…"

"He could be stronger than me…" I say slowly. "But how do we have powers so early on? Doesn't that upset the scales of nature?"

For the first time, Nathanial doesn't have an answer for me.

28 BEAUTY TREATMENT

Rose Craving

August 21

I push open the door of the Whispering Kettle and the scent of freshly ground coffee hits me. The coffeehouse is busy as everyone rushes to get their morning fix before heading to work. Vanessa is already waiting for me at a corner table by the window. She's in simple black trousers and a moss-green sweater with her black hair in a high ponytail. I weave through the tables and slide into the velvet chair in front of her.

"I asked the barista what you like to get and ordered so you won't have to wait," she tells me, and I blink at that. She hesitates. "I can order you something else if you're—"

"No, that was very thoughtful of you. Thank you," I say, feeling slightly bad for the conversation I'm about to have with her.

The barista drops off my white mocha with a splash of B positive and Vanessa's straight black coffee.

"I have to say I'm still surprised you took this job, Vanessa," I start.

She lifts a brow, calm. "Oh?"

"As a serpent shifter and a Crescent," I stir my latte even though it doesn't need it. "Did Josh or James put you up to it? You can tell me, I wouldn't put it past either of them."

Her cup pauses halfway to her lips. She sets it down without a clink. "Oh…I was asked if I wanted this role after I…returned from my mission."

"Why do I feel like there's more to this mission?" I ask slowly, watching her but Vanessa is well trained. She wouldn't be James's Mate or Josh's top general if she wasn't.

"Sorry, Rose. I can't give you anything on that. It's classified and still ongoing," she replies, making me frown. "I won't lie to you though. Josh did want me to be your undercover security."

"And you said yes?"

"I was honored to be asked," Vanessa answers. "In any case, I wanted to prove him wrong."

"About?"

"About you," she replies. "We want you and Josh to be together and work through your differences."

I don't know who else she's talking about. I sigh heavily, "I appreciate the help, but I think this is something that's just going to take time."

Silence settles between us. Outside, a pair of shifter children chase each other past the window, laughing brightly.

I trace the rim of my cup. "I'm sure by now you understand how delicate my position is these days. I need people I can trust in my corner. I apologize for my inquisition, but I had to know."

She nods once. "You don't have to apologize. If you weren't asking these questions, I'd be a little worried."

"You don't hate me?" I ask, softer. "It's really not weird for you?"

"Because the Divine chose you to be Mated to the Beta?" she almost smiles. "No, it really isn't weird to be your PA or bodyguard. It's actually fascinating to watch you maneuver things."

"That easy?"

"That simple." She cradles the warm cup between her palms. "The only thing I believe you need to prove is everyone wrong."

"I'm glad you said that, Vanessa, because can I ask you for a favor?"

She pauses and nods. "Of course."

"I'd like you to teach me how to shift into a serpent. As you know, Cravings have the ability to do so, but I hear it's harder for the rest of us than Nathanial or a Craving Alpha…" I wait to see what she thinks of the idea. "I figured if not being a serpent is such a huge deal for Josh and Serpent Nation—if I can't beat them, join them, right? Sure, I'm not a born serpent, but I can still be one."

Her brows lift in surprise before she smiles wickedly and says, "I think that's a great idea, Veyara. When would you like to start?"

"Maybe after our morning workouts?"

"Sure, we can carve out some time for it."

"Great, I'll see if I can get my brother and uncle to join. They can help and guide us, especially my uncle," I tell her, and she nods. I just hope Shane doesn't make fun of me and think I'm doing it to impress Josh. I'm not.

"Was it hard for you?" I ask her, biting my lip, nervously, "To transition into changeling affairs?"

She reaches over and covers my hand with hers. "That's exactly what it was. A transition. No matter how much James prepared me, once I shifted and fully became a Crescent and the Lady of House Tens, it took time to get used to the role and responsibilities. For everyone, and that's absolutely normal."

"I just wish my mom or Josh's mom was here to help me navigate all of that too," I say quietly. I don't normally talk to anyone about this. I don't want them to feel bad for me, but right now, my anxiety wins.

"Something tells me Josh is going to have his own set of rules…so it wouldn't have mattered if they prepared you or not…" Vanessa replies slowly, then asks me, "When was the last time you were at Coilspire?"

"Oh, gosh, like when I was eleven, twelve?" I say, unsure. "It was before his parents passed."

"So they haven't had a Lady at Coilspire for six years…that will be an adjustment for everyone when you settle in there."

When the new Warrior is shifted into the Pack, he gets the keys to his family home, and his parents move into a residential home on the premises if they choose to. We have multiple homes around the world, and the Elders do not have a shortage to pick from. However, most of the time the Elders move into the condos or homes in Cravenhold to be closer to court life. Warriors tend to be at court more often for work, but Crescents come and go as they please, just depending on what event is happening.

However, Warriors and Crescents typically don't move to their territories until after they have children. That's not the case for James or Josh since their parents have passed. It's why Josh spent most of his time in Coilspire prior to my return from the Tour. I don't know if he's gone back since.

James and Vanessa, before Vanessa had her two-year mission, spent time at Emberfall and Cravenhold equally, depending on Warrior needs. I know I'm expected to do the same.

"I don't want to disrupt anything," I tell Vanessa quietly.

"Girl…too late for that," Vanessa bursts into a laugh. "You disrupted our entire world. What's a household?"

I laugh with her. "What if he doesn't even want me there? It's his family home. I think I'm also nervous about it because it will just be us there, along with the staff of course, but just us…"

Vanessa is silent for a moment, before she says softly, "Rose…like it or not but, you're his Mate. You're his family too…his only family really."

I never really thought about it like that. I've always been kept at arm's length and told I wasn't wanted that I didn't even think how lonely his world is. I know he has Devaughn, James, and Shane, but when it comes to family…at least I have Shane and Eliza, and my uncle. Josh has no one. I know Vanessa is close to him too, so for her to say this really gives me pause.

"So, it's your family home too, babe. You're allowed to disrupt it and make changes. It's literally in your Lady of the House job description," Vanessa smiles at me, encouragingly, lightening the conversation, "besides, I think it'll be a good idea for the two of you to be trapped in a mysterious fortress far, far away." The teasing is clear in her voice.

"I guess I'll cross that bridge when I get to it," I say, heat rushing to my cheeks at the thought of Josh and me being alone.

"You have so much on your plate, one thing at a time." Vanessa nods.

Vanessa and I meet my brother and uncle in the forest. It isn't until three days later that we're able to have our first serpent shifting lesson. That's when everyone's schedules are aligned.

"I think this is a great idea as the Veyara. You should be able to shift into your House form," Uncle beams at me.

"I've never done this before, teach someone how to shift into a form they're not born into," Vanessa admits to Shane and my uncle.

Shane's leaning against a tree, arms folded over his broad chest and his legs crossed, watching us. Uncle Edward's standing beside Vanessa.

A Craving Alpha or Warrior—being Nathanial's biological descendants—are the only ones who can shift into *any* animal. The rest of my family are bound to wolves, but the Alpha carries the remnant of Nathanial's first gift. Uncle says it's easier for an Alpha to unlock than a Warrior. Dad would slip into other forms like it was second nature, and Shane does too, though both prefer the wolf because it feels natural—comfortable. For me, it will take more training, more discipline, but the ability is there. That's why the Alpha always rises from House Craving, because he alone can embody every creature, and every one of their powers. It's why a Craving Alpha has never been challenged for the title.

Each House is a shard of who Nathanial is and the gifts he bestowed on them. But only a Craving Alpha still carries all of him. Wolves, serpents, panthers, bears, eagles—every form, almost every power. That's what makes a Craving Alpha untouchable. That's why the Alpha Warrior always comes from our bloodline.

"I'd recommend starting slow. Small things. Change the shape of your eyes, practice your skin change, the magic of the serpent form," Uncle Edward suggests, "remember, it will be painful."

"Like first shift painful?" I ask, swallowing.

"Yes and no," Uncle says slowly. "You're still birthing a new form, but this time you can do it at your own pace. The first shift is forced on our bodies. While you're forcing this change too, it's not as intense as doing it all at once."

"Yeah, and don't go and try to shift into a basilisk, start small with maybe a garden snake," Shane adds.

"So how does it work?" Vanessa asks them.

"Just like if you're shifting. Imagine your form as precisely as you can, see it in your mind's eye and let your body make the transition," Uncle nods at me to try.

I glance at Vanessa, "Might help if I have a visual."

She laughs and nods, understanding. I watch carefully as she shifts from human to a beautiful blue viper in a blink of an eye. My breath catches as Shane and my uncle both stand taller seeing her serpent form.

"I want to be pretty like her," I whine and the men on either side of me laugh as Vanessa flicks her split tongue out.

"Don't get frustrated if the shift fights you. It'll take a few tries," Shane tells me, placing a hand on my shoulder.

I swallow hard and close my eyes. I imagine Vanessa's form in my mind. The first twinge hits like a spark, racing along my arms. My skin prickles, then *burns*, blue-green scales bubbling up unevenly, ragged at the edges.

A hiss escapes me, sharp and involuntary. "It burns!" I gasp, trying to shake the dreaded feeling off. The pain throbs, like every inch of emerging scales, tear free from inside me.

"Remember to take it at your own pace," Uncle says to me as

Vanessa slithers closer.

"What are you doing?" Josh asks through our mind link.

"Trying a new beauty treatment to look prettier," I reply, simply. It's not that I don't want him to know…I just don't want to fail at it. It's why I didn't even consider asking him for help. I also haven't seen him since the reunion—since he quite literally rattled me. I don't know how I feel about it. He *touched* me, but not in any way that might've made me hate myself for giving into him. He didn't touch me or made me orgasm using the same hands he touched other women with. He touched me in his serpent form, in a form no one can touch him, and it made it all the more special.

That moment was and can only be ours.

The more I think about it, the more I love it and that's what brings me to avoiding him. I love what he did in his serpent form and that it was our first intimate time together—it's wrong but in so many ways just perfect for us. It's confusing and I'm embarrassed and I don't know what comes next or what to even say to him. That night was perfect, but I know better, and I know not to expect for it to magically have changed things between us. I've been keeping my distance to let him make the first move, but time is up and I have to see him tomorrow for training.

"Well, can you stop? I just felt like I got burned," he asks and I hear the suspicion in his voice. Good, I'm glad he feels some kind of pain.

I sigh heavily and roll my eyes. ***"You're supposed to say I'm already pretty, but whatever."***

I try my leg next. Shane, my uncle, and Vanessa all watch closely as my leg turns the same shade of bluish-green but it doesn't last.

"You're already pretty, now cut it out," he replies but when have I ever listened to Josh.

I smile as I look at Vanessa. She really is pretty in her serpent form. I try to focus on the scales again and it burns again, but I get most of my left arm covered.

"So are we not going to talk about the reunion?" I bring myself to ask him, deciding it might be easier this way than in person tomorrow.

There's a pause before I hear his voice in my mind again.

"I'd much rather prefer we experience it again, than talk about it," he replies and my cheeks heat. I don't know how to feel about that. Actually, I know exactly how I feel. I just don't want to admit it to him—or myself.

I don't reply to him and focus on my task at hand. Shane's taking time out of his day to help me with this, and I don't want to waste it.

As we wrap up training, and I reach for my phone, I notice that Josh was tagged in something Constance Cyrinth posted. I turned on notifications for him when I was sixteen at the peak of my jealousy. I never turned it off and even though I know better than to look, curiosity gets the best of me.

The tag is on Spellbook and it's a picture of Josh's tattooed hand covering hers—I assume it's hers because it's not mine. I'd never wear yellow nail polish.

It was posted twenty minutes ago.

Caption: Effort doesn't lie

I know I shouldn't let social media of all things get to me—I know someone will always try to stir things, but it still hurts to see it. It still hurts to know that he took another girl out for coffee at some point. It's such a small thing, insignificant even, but I've craved doing things like that with him when I was younger.

I sigh heavily, pocketing my phone, then link my arm with Shane's as we head back to court.

"Constance Cyrinth," I telepath Cristobal.

"Received," he answers immediately.

"Thanks for this, by the way," Shane says to me. "It was a good…distraction."

I look up at him. His black hair is a mess from the wind, and his gray eyes are striking as always. I ask, gently, "Do you want to talk about it?"

"No…" he answers at first, before I see him look around for Vanessa or my uncle. Neither are with us and he stops walking.

"Shane?" I ask, frowning.

"I knew," he cups his mouth.

"You knew…what?" I ask slowly as anxiety courses through me. Did Josh tell him about my confession anyway?

"I knew the twins were cursed," Shane tells me in a quiet voice which makes me realize he hasn't shared this with anyone. "I knew the moment I found out she was carrying twins. Her scent had changed, which is normal for female shifters when they're pregnant, but she smelled like dying flowers…and I knew."

I exhale sharply and stare at my brother's tortured face. My hands reach for him and pull him into a hug. "I'm so sorry…"

Shane pulls back and says, "I never told her. I didn't tell anyone…everyone was so hopeful they'd be blessed…I couldn't…"

"I know," I whisper to him. "I knew too."

"What?" he stares at me before recognition crosses his glassy eyes. "Your powers."

I blink back my tears. "Yes. I'm sorry—"

"When did you know?"

"On my birthday," I say, dropping my gaze from him, ashamed.

He's quiet for a moment before he says, "I knew before that. I knew the whole time."

"Why didn't you tell Eliza?" I ask, needing to know his reasoning.

He shakes his head. "I didn't want the grief for her. She was so happy—I didn't want her to know she was going to lose one of them. It was better this way or else she'd be grieving twice…does that make me terrible?"

He's asking the wrong person.

"Of course not," I frown. "It's the same reason why I didn't tell either of you too…I didn't want to crush your joy…"

Shane hugs me, resting his chin on top of my head as I wrap my arms around my big brother. I hate that he's going through this. We already lost our parents too young and now he lost a child before he was even born. It's not fair.

"Thank you for telling me now," Shane says, "thank you for not letting me be alone in this."

"You're never alone," I tell him, the words coming out more forceful than I intend them to. It's always been Shane and me. We pull away and I ask him, "Are you ever going to tell her?"

He thinks about it. "I don't know…I don't see how it'll do any good. What difference would it make?"

"Is it okay if I never tell her?" I ask him, biting my bottom lip. "I just…I can never hear her cry like that again…"

"I know. Me neither," he agrees. "Did you tell anyone?"

I hesitate before answering him. "I told Josh…after we learned about the miscarriage."

Shane is quiet.

"He wanted to know about the curse of the twins and I told him…" I say to my brother.

"What did he say?" Shane asks.

"Nothing really. He just seemed curious. I'm surprised you hadn't told him," I shrug, not thinking anything of it.

For a moment, neither of us say anything. We just stand in the middle of the forest, taking in the sounds of nature around us. It makes me wonder how many secrets this forest holds like ours.

"He thinks I killed Noah," I say quietly.

"I know," Shane sighs heavily, running a hand down his tired face.

I frown. "I didn't, right? Tell me I didn't, Shane. He said my memories were wiped which is why I don't remember, but that's insane."

Shane cups my face and looks straight into my eyes. "Listen to me, Rose. You didn't kill Noah."

"How can you be sure? Josh seems pretty sure…" I ask, flipping my powers on. I need to know who's telling the truth and I know my brother will understand.

Shane drops his hands.

"I'm sure he does," he switches to telepathy and a chill goes down my spine. There's no one around us but he's still choosing not to talk out loud. Something's not right about this whole situation. ***"Josh has his side of the story, but trust me, you didn't kill Noah."***

"How do you know that for sure?" I repeat.

"When Josh accused you, I looked into your memories. You got to Noah before he did, that's true, but you didn't kill him," Shane insists. I hear the truth in his thoughts while my powers remain calm, not picking up any lies.

"Why don't I remember that? Were my memories erased?" I ask down our mind link.

"No, we only told Josh that because he lost his mind that night. You're his Mate and he thought you killed his brother…we told him we erased your memories in hopes to give both of you a fresh start," Shane telepaths.

"Hate to break it to you, big brother, but it didn't work," I think to him, sighing heavily as I feel a migraine coming on as my skin feels too tight. This is all so crazy.

"He'll learn the truth once you both complete the Mating bond and he Marks you. You have to let him Mark you, Rose, sooner rather than later," Shane thinks and there's an urgency in the thought. There's more on the line to Josh Marking me than I realized.

"I can't believe my brother's insisting I have sex with his best friend," I say out loud, knowing it'll end that conversation. Josh and I are not there yet by any means.

My mind drifts back to the Spellbook post. I'm not surprised. Josh touched me for the first time as a snake, then turned around and proved to me how much he is one.

Shane cringes at my comment and scowls at me. "Don't make it gross. If I had it my way, no one would dare come near you or someone much nicer would be your Mate."

I roll my eyes. "What a big brother thing to say."

Shane shoves me. "Let's head back before they file a missing report on us."

I let him go ahead and follow him back toward Cravenhold as the Sun sits directly above us now. I know it in my bones that I didn't kill Noah. I don't remember the night he died except getting out of bed and the alarms ringing. But as I glance at Shane's taut back while he walks in front of me talking about the Mabon festivities starting soon, I know my brother just lied to me. I just have to find out why. If Shane is lying to me, does that mean Josh of all people is telling the truth?

29 MABON

Rose Craving
September 21

I pass through the stone arches to the Sanctum courtyard, holding an orange candle in one hand and a small pouch of herbs in the other. It's early in the morning, but people are up and getting things finalized for the Mabon festival today. The path to the Sanctum has been peaceful though. It smells like sage and pine all around me while the fountains trickle water around the perimeter. There are a few people here and we greet each other politely but keep to ourselves. This time is for us and there's an understanding about that.

Walking up to Betty, she mesmerizes me, reflecting all kinds of colors this morning against the rising Sun. I smile and take a deep breath before placing my palm on the stone. The overwhelming feeling of peace fills my body, stemming from within me.

I needed this.

I needed this moment to breathe after the events of the last few weeks. So much has happened and I haven't taken the time to process any of it. Mainly because I didn't want to have a breakdown. From becoming a Warrior and dealing with the Elders and the media, to being the Veyara and dealing with Serpent Nation and Josh's fangirls, to being a sister and not knowing how to be there for Shane and Eliza, to being Josh's Mate—it's all a lot.

I know he was on Pulse the reunion night and that's probably the only reason things were pleasant because the second he got the chance, he proved it was nothing to him. The only solace I have is knowing he didn't *touch* me with the hand he held Constance's with.

He kissed me though. Again. Why does he keep kissing me? He says one thing, does another, acts another way—fucking snakes. His words felt so good to hear, but I knew better than to believe them. I don't understand him and I don't want to waste my time doing so either. He doesn't want me. He doesn't even like me so there's no point wondering about it.

Ugh. I take a deep breath and push all those thoughts out of my mind and focus on Betty. The tingles I feel traveling through my body, the pure, raw energy Betty freely puts out. I don't know what it is about this stone that makes me feel like I'm being showered in Holy magic.

I pull my hand back, feeling much lighter, and head inside the Sanctum. Mom loved rituals. She'd say they made her feel connected to the world and the Divine. Dad was more…practical. He was a believer of course, but he had his own rituals, though he'd never admit that's what they were.

Dad liked it out on the water. He was a water sign like me, so I guess that makes sense. Large bodies of water always made me nervous though, so he used to take Shane out to the river, and I'd come to the Sanctum with Mom.

It was our thing.

Holidays are always hard since we lost them.

Inside, the walls of the Sanctum rise in a perfect circle. There are no sharp corners, just a natural flow. The windows are carved at specific angles so streams of Sunlight can cut through the space. They touch the five altars placed at the edges of the pentagon etched into the floor. Each directional point aligns with the element it represents.

My footsteps echo faintly as I pass them. The Earth altar is in the north, dense with stones of all kinds. Air is to the east, the wind chimes singing as the feathers wave their greetings. The smoke from incense cleanses the space, allowing us to breathe in the blessings. Fire burns low and calmly in a small basin at the southern point. Moon water is placed on the western point, along with teardrop crystals and tiny jars of stream water—I know because I used to help Mom and Lady Tiara collect them. At the center is Spirit. The raised dais is simple but radiant, holding the humblest of offerings—a thread, a ring, a child's drawing, and a single red rose petal.

Black salt lines the room's edge for protection. Bundles of sage, lavender, and juniper hang from hooks above each threshold with bowls of Moon water nearby to cleanse any hand, blade, or tool.

Mom would stay here for hours. She'd spend a lot of time here, especially if High Priestess Lady Tiara was here. They'd sing, chat, gossip as they polished bowls, organized crystals, or just sat together. You'd think as a child, I'd be bored out of my mind, but they always found a way to include me or keep me busy and I loved it here.

Like most of us royals and children of the House of Honest, Mom and Lady Tiara grew up together. She was Mom's oldest friend.

I find the High Priestess standing at the far end of the Sanctum in her Mabon robes—crimson and burnt orange with gold embroidery. Her long light brown hair is braided into a thick bun. Her presence always brings me comfort—she's a piece of Mom I still have left.

She senses me before I say anything. "Rose, you came."

"Of course," I say softly, coming to stand beside her, "sorry I couldn't help you set up."

She waves me off, letting out a little laugh. "I'm sure the Divine will forgive you with all that you had going on." She glances at me, her blue eyes twinkling. "You always were your mother's daughter. Traditional with a sparkle of rebellion."

"Why do you say that?" I ask, laughing too.

She caresses my face, the pride openly expressed on hers. "I am so proud of you. I know your mom would be too."

The tears are unavoidable and one slips down my cheek. Lady Tiara collects it on her fingertip before closing her eyes and blowing on it. She looks at me then and says, "Rosemary was a headstrong Luna. Eliza reminds me a lot of her most times. But you also have your father's mind. He was charming and he'd light up the room, like Shane does, but when he spoke…" Lady Tiara inhales deeply, remembering, "people listened. Truly listened. When he was angry, which wasn't often—that was more your mom—there was no arguing with him. When you left the war room the other day, I know they were both celebrating in the Heavens. I sure was, here."

I let out a choked laugh through my tears. "I was so angry."

"You were right to be," Lady Tiara says, before she nods slowly, her eyes glancing over to the Mabon altar she's set up.

She's dressed it in scarlet and mustard yellow silks, overflowing with pomegranates, wheat, apples, marigolds, and cinnamon bundles. A chalice of wine sits in its center.

"I'm curious to see what the Harvest season brings you." The High Priestess urges me to go light my candle. I dress it first with the herbs I brought, before placing it on the altar.

I think of all that's ahead of me. I still have no idea why I shifted into a white wolf and into the Warrior Pack. Shane hasn't given me any specific Warrior responsibilities, saying he just wants me to focus on training. It makes me realize I don't really know exactly what Warriors do. I know they're the heads of their animal kingdom and that entails a lot of responsibility, but they also have a lot of staff who work for them. It's like a business corporation if anything. I'll have to talk to Daniel about this more.

But how much training do I even need if I'm not doing anything with it? I've only had myself to practice with. Dad used to take me out into the woods to help me learn to control my powers, so accidents didn't happen. He knew the dangers of suppressing powerful magic, and he knew better than to make his own daughter do that.

My training was always father-daughter *hikes.* I didn't know why he wanted me to keep it quiet. When I asked, he just said it was for the best until I knew what I was capable of. Later, I learned that it wasn't normal for us to come into our powers at eight years old. My dad was trying to protect me.

We had barely started offensive work when he passed, but I continued my own training. It was the only way I was able to cope with their death. While Shane took to the river, I went to the woods—to release my grief and anger and pain. Shane stepped in after our parents died. He said Dad told him about my powers just days before he died and Shane started helping me with more aggressive magic, so I knew how to be intentional with it. It's why I've made it without hurting anyone accidentally or killing anyone. It's why I've always had such good control over my powers—I've respected it enough to give it an outlet. Just like Dad taught me.

Even Shane doesn't know the extent of my powers. I was always too scared to use it with him in training. There was one time I pushed myself just to see what I can do, and I was in so much pain, I never attempted it again. My entire body had turned dark, like my power, but luckily a shower helped restore my physical appearance. I knew using that much power took a toll on me though, mentally and spiritually, so I never asked that of my powers again. I was fifteen. It wasn't that long ago.

I don't want to think about my Veyara responsibilities with everything that's happened lately. I also don't want to think about my nephew's magical abilities if an unborn baby is already so powerful.

I take a moment to search within me before asking for guidance and ease as I step into my new roles.

Later, my lady's maids help me get ready for the festival, dressing me in a long brown and black gown that flows around me. I'm supposed to go with Eliza, but she changed her mind at the last moment, deciding to stay in. I don't push her, seeing the state she is in when I walk into her room. She's wrapped in her blanket, having no intention of moving. I kiss her forehead before heading down to the festival grounds.

Fall has fully settled over the court, painting everything in gold, rust, and crimson. It's my favorite time of the year. The ivy-covered stone walls of Cravenhold have begun to turn a deep red. The burnt orange leaves tumble across the cobblestone pathways. Somewhere nearby, there's a harp playing.

Cravenhold is always beautiful, but in autumn, it's magical. Every carved arch and towering turret glows with the amber light of the season. Lanterns are hung with gold ribbons as workers bustle along the garden paths and around the pavilions. Harvest fruits, polished horns of plenty, and Mabon offerings—dried herbs, braided corn stalks, and little bowls of salt and honey—overflow tables.

It smells like cloves, cider, and bonfires.

I see Azura settling into a chair beside Crystal. Azura catches my gaze and smiles, waving me over. "Veyara! How's the Gala prep coming?!" She asks, smiling big, making Crystal look up at me too.

I go over and hug the ladies with air kisses, before answering Azura. "It's going amazing, I can't wait for you to attend!"

"I hear it's one of the most exquisite events for a new Warrior Pack. The Luna and Veyara Galas—but yours will be exceptionally so," Azura says.

"Why?" I ask, laughing a little.

"Because, Rose," Crystal smiles like it's obvious, "you're the youngest and the last to shift. You'll have all of us, the Warriors and Crescents, in attendance at your Gala. Usually someone or another hasn't shifted for everyone to be there."

That's right. I hadn't thought of that. It does make it special. I smile in return. "It's an honor, then."

The Crescents laugh, before Crystal rubs her growing belly and says, "Well, don't let us keep you. We'll just be sitting here drinking our non-alcoholic drinks."

"Oh my gosh, *please* drink for us!" Azura pleads. "Drink a lot for us."

I laugh. "You two are going to land me on the front pages."

"You're already on there, you might as well be drunk," Crystal shrugs with a sigh, "make it a real scandal."

"I'll see what I can do," I tell them laughing as I leave to explore.

The grounds are alive with torches and bonfires. The scent of food, wild herbs, warm pastries, and fresh bread fill the air. Mabon crowns, twisted circlets of dark vine with gold and brown leaves and dried flowers, rest on heads everywhere I look. People wear all the shades of autumn and I smile happily. String lights stretch between trees and beneath them are booths, set up in almost perfect rows.

Artisan vendors offer everything from jewelry to body oils to treats. A witch grinds herbs behind a brass cauldron, steam rising as she stirs. On the other side, young shifter children practice hitting targets. A few children run past me with their little faces painted, holding caramel apples. Toward the center, there's the main bonfire where dancers spin in hypnotic rhythm. Their long sleeves sway as they dance circles around the fire. The bottoms of their dress trail dust and dirt as they move in time with the ceremonial drums.

I do love the drums—they've always been my favorite.

"There you are!" Mariella calls out to me, and I turn to see my friends weaving through the crowd. Daniya reaches me first.

"You look amazing," she compliments.

"Thank you, so do you!" I grin at her as my friends hook their arms with mine.

"So…I know it's Mabon, but the press is hungry," Vanessa says quietly in my ear, "the conservative Houses are acting like your existence is a threat to their entire bloodlines."

"They're not wrong," I reply.

"Hm, but we can't say that." She chuckles, sounding like Eliza.

"It'll probably be a good idea to give the press something else to go crazy about," Daniya suggests.

"Maybe like a budding Mabon romance," Mariella nudges me, teasing.

"With who? My beer mug?" I ask her, which actually has me looking around for Daniel. It's tradition that we get a beer at one of the taverns at court. While there is a designated festival ground, the shopping plazas love to participate in the celebrations so they're open for it. Holidays are the best time for business after all.

"Nooo," Mariella laughs, "be seen with the Beta cozied up. Dancing, laughing. Let them think whatever they want, but your presence with him—the both of you seen together, happy and enjoying the holidays will show his support."

"Give them something to gossip about other than you being a rebel," Daniya adds and I feel slightly ganged up on right now.

"A rebel?!" I let out a laugh, "What am I rebelling?"

"Male authority, apparently," Vanessa says to me, "you could also use it to soften Josh's...feelings...of you."

I resist rolling my eyes.

Vanessa adds, "Camille is telling him the same thing. He should be coming to find you soon."

Of course he is.

Because that's what we're good at. We show up. Smile. Play nice. Ignore the real problems between us.

I feel Josh before I see him. Camille's always worked fast.

He's cutting through the crowd, smiling at those who are brave enough to greet him. He's dressed in a long brown coat with a green and black shirt and brown pants. His hair is growing out—something he likes to do in the cooler months.

His eyes find me instantly.

Josh doesn't hesitate to walk straight up and offer his hand. "I've been looking for you," that's for the sake of my friends, then he asks, "dance with me?"

Mariella is practically beaming as Daniya nudges me forward. I see a camera move in behind him. When did my friends become pro-Josh?

Josh smiles and I hate that he looks beautiful when he does. I smile back sweetly. "No thank you."

Josh doesn't miss a beat, catching my hand as I tried to walk past him. Instead of leading me toward the dancing circle, he directs us toward the heart of the festival, where the biggest crowds are and cameras flash nonstop. The tension in his jaw doesn't match the relaxed grip of his hand.

"It is good photo op," Josh murmurs, leaning in to make it look like he's whispering in my ear, "we always did look good together."

I would glare at him but instead I let out a laugh as a camera flashes, before saying with a smile, "Too bad we can't *be* good together."

"You're absolutely right about that."

Fuck. Josh. Hunter.

"I hate you," I murmur.

"I know," he lets out a laugh, "I hate you too."

"Yet you keep kissing me," I tell him, look up to meet his sharp gray eyes. His face is relaxed and smiling, but his eyes…he needs to work on that. I look between us. "Almost as if you like kissing me. It's not like cameras were there."

Our bodies brush against each other as we walk through the grounds. He quirks a dark eyebrow at me. "What exactly are you pissed about?"

I haven't talked to him since Constance tagged him. That was almost a month ago. I hate whenever I think we're taking a step forward, I get slapped in the face by reality. I've tried avoiding Josh the past few weeks, but he's been almost going out of his way to irritate me.

"What are *you* pissed about?" I counter as he stops at one of the stalls that's piled with warm beignets dusted with cinnamon or rose sugar.

"You still like these?" he asks and I meet his curious gaze. I didn't know he knew I liked them. What is he doing?

He goes to ask the vendor for a rose one before exchanging a few pleasantries, then walks back to me.

"I'm pissed because I thought we had a good time at the reunion. Great time. Then you turn around and start giving me the cold shoulder," he tells me, breaking off a piece of the beignet. His fingers linger near my lips, waiting, eyes locked on mine. I part my lips, letting him feed it to me. The sugar melts on my tongue and his thumb grazes my lower lip.

"Unnecessary," I say lowly. I go to lick the corner of my lips for the sugar as his thumb moves to brush it away but instead swipes my tongue.

His eyes darken slightly before he pops the rest of the beignet into his own mouth, licking his fingers. That should *not* turn me on but damn this man.

"Well?" he asks, continuing our conversation, "Why the switch?"

"You really have to ask?" I politely glare at him. Fuck these cameras too.

"Yes, because I never know with you," he replies, clenching his jaw as we move to the next stall, tucked between a candle and a shawl vendor. The smell of sweet spice hits me instantly.

"Jeez, how many girls post going out with you?" I mumble under my breath, pretending to be interested in the pouring of hot cider.

Josh is quiet as realization settles on him. Then he says, "A lot, but none of it is recent. Not since you shifted."

I hate him and his bluntness. I hate how my heart skips a beat at that, but I'm still annoyed about it.

Josh orders two cups of hot buttered rum. The vendor, a young blonde, hands them to him with a smile which he genuinely returns. It shouldn't affect me, but it does. Why does she get a real smile when I get faked ones?

He hands me one of the cups, fingers grazing mine. He doesn't pull away instantly, but I do.

The drink is hot and delicious. It's heavy and smooth on the tongue, laced with cinnamon, clove, burnt sugar and A negative.

I sigh, blissfully, letting the warmth spread down me, but the heat from the drink doesn't compare to what's running through me. My pulse is on fire, and it has *nothing* to do with the rum. This is the closest thing to a date we've ever had. Mabon was not like this last year.

I can feel his eyes on me and deliberately look everywhere but at him. I don't like feeling like this—there was a reason why I shut off my emotions toward him. Hating him is easier.

"You know they're just trying to get under your skin," Josh says as we walk, sipping our drinks.

"They wouldn't if you didn't cut me open for them," I reply before pointing out to some random art vendor. I don't wait for him as I walk up to check out the pieces. I wish I crawled into bed with Eliza and stayed there. I hate talking about this stuff with Josh.

I take my time with the art, before buying one I think Daniya will like, and return to Josh's side. He's stopped at a booth selling pocket watches. This is good marketing for the vendors as the cameras capture what draws our attention.

Josh glances at me and pauses, then reaches up, slowly, his fingers brushing a strand of my hair.

I freeze.

Instead of touching me, he plucks something out. A dried orange flower. Before either of us can say something, a little girl—no older than seven or eight—runs up to us. Her dress is a swirl of golden tulle and burgundy ribbons. Her hazel eyes are wide as she clutches a messy but sweetly woven flower crown in her small hands. She stares at Josh like he's a legend and she can't believe she's standing in front of him. I smile. It's sweet because most people don't look at Josh like that.

They try not to make eye contact with him at all, knowing he's a basilisk shifter and a ruthless Warrior.

Josh crouches down without hesitation, putting himself at her eye level. "Hi there, what's your name?"

"Scarlett," she smiles shyly, "with two Ts."

"What do you have there, Scarlett with two Ts?" Josh asks, looking at the crown she's guarding protectively.

She holds it out to him with both hands.

"Oh," he says, voice so gentle I blink to make sure it's him talking, "is this for me?" She giggles, shaking her head, her golden hair swaying. Josh plays along, "No? Then…is it for *me* to give to someone special?"

She nods, her cheeks turning pink before she glances at me.

Josh follows her gaze to meet mine and I'm pretty sure my cheeks are the same shade as Scarlett's. His smile doesn't change when he looks at me and it's so adorable that I get lost in it, but Josh turns back to the girl. "You want me to give it to my Veyara?"

My Veyara.

The words knock the wind out of me as I hold my breath. Does he even care how fucked up it is for him to say that after telling me that he'd never choose me as his Veyara.

Scarlett nods again and Josh grins. "She is missing a crown, isn't she? Do you think she'll look pretty in it?"

"Yes," Scarlett replies, quietly, looking shyly at me again and I smile at her. She's so cute.

"I think so too," he says softly, rising to his feet. He holds the flower crown carefully between his fingers as he turns toward me. I hold my breath as he lifts it over my head and places it gently on top of my hair.

His fingertips brush the hair at my temples out of the way, tucking one strand behind my ear. His eyes don't leave mine.

There's a pause between our heartbeats and the world seems to quiet around us. Nothing matters except for his eyes on me. They say eyes are the windows to the soul but all I see in Josh's eyes is my own reflection.

He looks away slowly, before it gets too awkward, and turns to look at the girl. "How's that?"

"She looks like a princess," the girl beams.

Josh smiles. "She *is* a princess."

The little girl's mother jogs up, breathless and apologetic, her smile tight but kind.

"Oh Divine," she says, brushing her golden hair back from her face. Hers is a shade lighter than her daughter's. "I'm so sorry, your highnesses. She just ran off…"

"It was a delight to meet her," Josh assures the mom.

The mother glances between him and me, noticing the crown on my head, then she looks at her daughter, smiling. She looks back at us, to me, and asks, "If it's not too much trouble…would you mind taking a picture with her?" she turns to Josh, "Both of you? I spoiled her with stories of the two of you and now that," she looks back at me, "you're the Veyara Warrior, she's been over the Moon."

Josh glances at me, waiting for my cue. I smile down at Scarlett. "Of course," then I crouch to come to her level as she smiles back shyly.

Josh kneels on her other side. The little girl beams like she's standing between her two heroes, though I'm not sure what we did to deserve such high regards. Josh and I take each of her hands into our own, and she squeezes them. My heart aches with a longing I suppress. I know I'm far too young to have children right now, but I also know it'll never happen the way I'd dreamt of with Josh being my Mate. He won't be the Mate I need as a mom. He won't dote on me like Devaughn, Sam, and Shane do on their pregnant Mates. Having children with Josh would simply be a responsibility to fulfill, but a girl can dream right?

The mother holds up her phone as cameras behind her go wild. Oh, this will definitely be a hit. We didn't even plan this.

Scarlett wiggles closer between us, standing proud in her shiny gold shoes. I lean my cheek to hers and grin. Josh does the same on the other side. We don't just smile—we laugh.

The flashes go off, capturing the memory.

When the mother lowers her phone, I turn to Scarlett and smile, "Thank you for my beautiful crown."

She giggles. "You really like it?"

My smile grows bigger. "I like it so much I'm going to wear it every Mabon from now on. Think it'll still fit me next year?"

She nods. "It will! If it doesn't, I'll make you a new one!"

I squeeze her hand before I stand up straight, laughing. I turn to her mother, "Your daughter is lovely."

"Thank you, Veyara," she replies with a tilt of her head in a gesture of a small bow, before she holds her hand out to Scarlett.

"Where are you from? If you don't mind me asking," I say to her. "Mabon brings people from all over."

She smiles, appreciating my effort to make conversation with her. "Shadow Brooke, Oregon, your highness."

"Mom's a Veyara too," Scarlett tells me, grinning up at her mother.

My brows raise as Josh comes to stand close to me. I look at Scarlett's mother. "You're Celeste Belmont."

She looks genuinely shocked that I know her name. "Yes, your highness…how did you know?"

I smile, "We make it our duty to know. It's an honor to meet you."

"No, your highness, the honor is all mine," she smiles, "thank you," she looks at both Josh and me, "blessed Mabon."

"Blessed Mabon," Josh and I echo before she turns and walks away with Scarlett, who waves to us.

"How did you know who she was?" Josh asks me once they are out of earshot.

I look at him. "You don't know all the Betas?"

"Not off the top of my head," he admits and I shake my head in disapproval.

"Did you just admit you don't know everything?" I tease him. He rolls his eyes as we continue, but there's a ghost of a smile tugging on his mouth. "Eliza insists the Crescents and I know these details. Makes ruling more…personal, she says. I know my mom would agree," I tell Josh, before we start walking again.

"Didn't realize you all were so…invested?"

"Shouldn't we be?" I ask, genuinely, before sighing. "There are other things we do aside from sitting around drinking tea and gossiping."

"Wouldn't know, I'm not a Crescent."

I wrinkle my nose. "No…you're not pretty enough."

"Oh, is that the requirement?" he asks and I can feel his eyes on me.

"Yes, but your eyes need to get checked if you couldn't tell." I know I'm pretty, and every single one of the Crescents is drop-dead gorgeous. Josh actually laughs at that.

We browse through stalls lined with books, incense, and charms, and I almost forget about the cameras following us. They just don't know when to let up. However, if they're the reason Josh and I get this fake date, I'll take it.

30 SEER

Rosella Craving
September 21

Just as Josh and I are about to pass the next set of vendors, a soft voice carries over to me. "Veyara."

I stop mid-step and Josh does too. We both turn toward a booth that isn't overflowing with merchandise like the others. There aren't any flashy lights or bright colors decorating it. It's cloaked in deep purple and lanterns hang from it to provide some lighting. There's a small round table where the seer sits down, watching me.

Her hair is a cloud of silver curls, piled high into a messy bun. Her golden skin shines as if glitter were sprayed on it, but I know that's not the case—it's the Moon water she bathes in consistently. Moon water doesn't make everyone sparkle, just the most devout—which is how I know this seer is authentic.

Her eyes are milky and the color is hard to define. It's pale blue, but turquoise, but also sea green and purple. Her hands are steady, decorated with crystal rings.

She smiles when she has my attention. "Come, child. The cards are whispering about you."

Josh raises a brow and I start to step toward her, glancing over my shoulder at him. "You coming? Maybe the cards will whisper about you too."

"You believe in this?" he asks, studying my face.

"Of course," I reply without hesitation, thinking of all the times Lady Tiara's done my readings. "Don't you?"

He doesn't answer but follows me in.

The tent muffles the sounds of the festival as if we stepped into a world of its own. It smells like dried roses, sage, and lavender in here. A single orange candle flickers in the middle of the table, surrounded by a thick, worn, hand-drawn tarot deck.

The seer motions for us to sit. I do, but Josh stays standing behind me.

She gives him a look, not a mean one, just a knowing one and I wonder what she sees in him. Then she turns to me, her expression softening. She gathers the cards before holding them out to me, saying, "Shuffle."

The deck feels strange in my hands. I look at the seer, channeling the magic in the cards as if they welcome me. I start shuffling.

"Cut the deck once when you're ready," the seer tells me.

I shuffle a few more times before I do just that and place my hands on my lap. The seer draws the first card, placing it face-up on the worn cloth.

The Tower.

The jagged bolt of lightning striking a towering spire of stone that's crumbling down while in flames stare back at me. Two figures tumble from the heights.

Josh mutters behind me, "Fitting."

I ignore him as the seer continues without pause, laying the next cards swiftly.

The Lovers in reverse.

Death.

She hesitates, then her fingers hovering over the deck, eyes narrowing slightly. Then she pulls another card.

Judgement.

"Rebirth," she declares as I raise an eyebrow and she places the deck down, signaling that she's done pulling. Four cards. Interesting.

I only knew one other person who drew four card tarot spreads—Helena Hunter.

Josh's mother.

Josh shifts behind me, noticing it too. He doesn't comment though.

"You stand on the edge of a grand unraveling," the seer murmurs. Her voice is quiet and she's not looking at us as she traces the cards. "War is coming. But the war inside of you has yet to break. You've turned yourself into a vision of control." I swallow, thinking of the Royal Tour. I knew when I returned, I couldn't be the same person I had been. She continues, "You were never meant to be kept in a box, even one designed by your own hands."

Her eyes move to The Lovers reversed. "Bonds will break—they must. And when they do, it will scorch everything they touch. Things are not as they seem and when the fire is lit, only you can put it out."

My frown deepens and I want to look up to see what Josh thinks, but I can't look away from the seer. Josh has gone eerily still behind me as my heart sinks to my stomach. *Bonds will break…they must…*

Her fingers touch the Death card. "What you cling to now will not weather the storm. The ending is unavoidable, but you are the spark for a new world." Finally, her hand moves to the last card. Judgement. "You must embrace the truth of who you are."

That's all she says. She doesn't clarify or go into it more.

I sit frozen and very confused. The reading can easily be a hoax, but what she said about war coming and bonds breaking—it makes me pause.

"Green is a beautiful color on you, my child," she says, turning her milky eyes on me and smiling.

I frown and decide not to correct her by saying I'm wearing brown. "Thank you."

"Alright then," Josh says as he reaches for his phone to pay her. "This was fun, how much—"

"And you," she turns her focus to Josh, causing him to still. "You need to open your eyes. You've been sleeping for too long, Son of the Heavens and the Skies."

Josh pales and I look between the two of them, asking, "Son of what?"

The seer waves off Josh. "I will not charge for what the Divine instructed me to tell you," she says as she starts to gather the cards again.

"Let's go, Rose," Josh says coldly, and doesn't wait for me as he steps out of the tent. I rise slowly and look at the seer, finding her milky eyes fixated on me.

"Green really is a lovely color on you," she repeats.

I blink and stutter. "I'm wearing brown…"

"Are you? My apologies. Old eyesight," she winks at me. Then she holds out an elaborate jewelry box, placing it gently in my hands. "A gift for the Veyara." I raise my brows and start to open the lid and she shakes her head, "Not here."

Okay? What's in the box?

"Thank you," I say to the seer, raising the jewelry box a little.

"Rose!" Josh calls and I hesitate to leave, but once I'm outside, Josh and I merge back into the festival. He notices the box and asks, "What's that?"

"The seer gave it to me," I reply still a little puzzled by it.

Once we're around the corner, Vanessa appears and I hand her the box. Before I can say anything, Josh orders her, "Have whatever's in there inspected."

"Of course," Vanessa nods once before disappearing again.

It's darker outside as night's fallen and Mabon is coming to an end. It's a shame we only hold the festival for one day, unlike the vampires.

I also realize, Josh and I've spent the entire evening together, and it wasn't so terrible.

"Well, that was interesting…" I start, breaking the silence, but Josh pulls me gently through the crowd toward the big bonfire where the music has conveniently shifted to a slower song.

We settle into the rhythm, his hand sliding around my waist and mine resting on his shoulder.

He doesn't comment about the seer. He spins me, his hand gliding down my back. When I land in his arms again, he presses me closer and I hate how the smell of him makes me clench my thighs tighter. I hate how easy it is to dance with him. We've danced together before, but it was quick and rigid—this feels different, more natural.

Josh isn't even trying to be charming. He's doing the bare minimum—guiding us through the steps, turning us gracefully so the cameras can see our happy faces. But all I feel is how his hand rests low on my back. The way his fingers hold my hand, his thumb grazing my skin, giving me flashbacks to the reunion night.

"Stop that," I say to him, smiling.

"Stop what?" he replies, taking us around the bonfire with the other couples.

"What you're doing with your thumb," I tell him and his smile turns into a beautiful grin.

Divine help me. I do loathe this man.

"Does it do something to you?" he asks, holding my gaze.

"It's unnecessary," I reply.

His hand trails up my spine, his palm finding the small of my back again, "Making you blush for the cameras is absolutely necessary."

Josh dips me low, too low that I have to either grip his shoulder or trust him to not drop me. The challenge is clear in his eyes.

My fingers tighten around his shoulder muscles before he pulls me upright and into a slow turn. My head spins with the music, flashing cameras, and his citrus-smoky scent.

"Why did she call you that? Son of…the Heavens and the Skies?

You're not a bird shifter," I ask him because something about it bothered him and in return has me curious.

Josh doesn't say anything right away. He knows what it means—the way his entire demeanor changed in the tent.

"I don't know," he finally says.

"And you're lying. A bird shifter would never," I huff, a little annoyed that he won't let me in, but what did I expect from him? I quickly bring my smile back as a flash goes off in the corner of my eye.

"No. The woman was obviously on something. You're not even wearing green."

"I don't think she was talking about clothes."

Josh rolls his eyes. "Of course you don't."

"Well, what does it mean?" I push. It was an odd thing to say, and Josh clearly heard it before.

Josh spins me out before drawing me back in effortlessly.

"You didn't believe the reading?" I ask. There aren't as many cameras on us now, but still plenty.

"How can you? She said bonds will break, and we know that's impossible," he reminds me.

I raise an eyebrow. "I'm not so sure anymore."

Josh gives me an incredulous look. "Over that reading? You've got to be kidding me."

"Over how you've treated me the past six years," I correct, frowning. "Over our Mating bond not looking like a regular Warrior Mating bond…"

Josh lets out a humorless laugh. "Yeah, okay. It always circles back to that shit, doesn't it?" he's such a fucking asshole.

"She said to face the truth. Maybe it's…not what we think…" I swallow, the words tasting wrong as they leave my mouth.

"No, you're right. Maybe we are doomed."

"She didn't say doomed," I counter, defensively.

He chuckles. "No, she just dressed it up as a grand prophecy."

I pivot a little toward him, our eyes locking. "You looked like you believed it in there."

"She's a good story-teller," he says, shaking his head and it infuriates me.

"So you're not a believer?"

"I didn't say that," he replies, "I am. I just don't believe that reading. It was too cliché. She was clearly a nutjob."

"Then why did you look like you saw a ghost," I question.

"Just fucking drop it, Rose."

"Why? What does it mean?"

"Fucking hell—what part of drop it do you not understand?"

"Why can't you ever just talk to me?" I sigh heavily. So much for having one good day. "Why do you always have to be so detached while the rest of us are lit on fire and burn trying to get close to you."

His eyes turn predatory as his voice drops, "Talking requires trust, and you think *you're* the one on fire in all this?"

I stare at him. Our bodies are moving with the music but neither of us are dancing anymore. "What's that supposed to mean?"

The calm expression on his face rivals the anger in his eyes. "You're not the spark, you're not the fire. You are literally the darkness. You don't scorch anything—you just turn the lights off. Permanently."

I flinch, but the cameras are still on us, so I smile a tight, picture-perfect princess smile. He wears it too. He's aware of them too. Of course, he is. Is this a test to see if I break?

"Then maybe we *are* both doomed," I whisper, lips barely moving, "maybe that's why you could never believe in me."

"Or maybe because you kill everything you touch," he replies. That's a bit dramatic. I've never killed anyone and he's never seen me use my powers.

"Well, then maybe, you shouldn't touch me so much," I snap back. All he's been doing today is touching me. He's been *initiating* it. He's the one who led us to dance.

Josh's smile sharpens into an almost sneer that I know too well. "Touching you makes me feel sick."

That does it.

Something cracks in my chest, and I know my eyes have turned black because all I see is black. "Then why—"

His hand tangles in my hair at the back of my neck, the force cutting me off mid-sentence and his mouth descends on mine.

Before I can process what's happening, my lips part in shock to gasp but his warm tongue invades my mouth. He tastes like the hot buttered rum we had, and I close my eyes. His hand on my waist digs in with a possessive force while he strokes my jaw as fire explodes between us, my traitorous body molding into his. My hands fist his shirt, grabbing onto his coat as I kiss him back with equal ferocity.

Our mouths claim each other's as everything else disappears

around us. I don't care about the cameras, the people who stopped to watch, or our fight. His hand rests on my hip, fingers still digging in, causing butterflies to flutter like crazy low in my stomach. A low groan escapes him as my hand moves up to his neck.

I ignore the cheers and comments thrown at us as his thumb strokes my cheek, slower now. Our lips move together, no longer clashing but cherishing, savoring each brush. His tongue traces mine as my fingers run through the hairs at the nape of his neck. The kiss lingers, and it's sweet and aching with everything that's been ignored between us.

Josh pulls back first, almost forcing himself to, reluctantly. His lips hover just over mine, his breath warm against my skin as I try to catch my own. His hands stay where they are—at my hip and neck—as if he doesn't want to let go.

His eyes are a dark gray, locked onto mine, like he can't believe he just did that. Our previous kisses were in private—this just happened in front of the world but that doesn't seem to bother him. His gaze flickers to my lips, then back to my eyes, searching. My chest heaves, my lips tingle, missing the pressure of his against them.

I clench my jaw, starting to pull away from him, saying, "You must be feeling very sick right now."

"Oh, shut up," he replies, huskily.

The cameras are a trigger. It's all too much. Everyone is watching us, whether it's subtly or openly, they're watching us. He's paraded countless women on his arms, had their pictures taken and splashed all over the tabloids. Now I'm just another one of those girls. I don't know what's worse—him kissing me in private like I'm a dirty little secret, or him kissing me in public and falling to the ranks of all the other women.

I lift my head, his face inches away and it might look like I'm about to kiss him again, when I say, "If you had your pick, it'd never be me, right?"

His smile hardens. "Right."

"So don't kiss me in front of the cameras like I'm just another one of your whores," I tell him, but the decision is clear in his heated eyes. I know he's about to kiss me again, if anything out of spite, when Shane grabs Josh's arm, pulling him away from me. I instantly take a few steps back in my brother's presence, but Shane's too preoccupied to notice. Josh's hand catches mine and his grip is hard, not letting me get too far away.

"I need both of you to come with me," he says with urgency in his voice.

Josh's demeanor changes instantly, his eyes narrowing and posture snapping into Warrior mode.

"What's wrong?" Josh asks him.

"Not sure yet, but Lucian Craving is being brought into the throne room," Shane replies as we follow him toward the Palace. Lucian Craving? He's one of the vampire princes, but he would not be coming here unless it was business—serious business.

"What do you mean brought in?" Josh pushes.

"He drove up to the gates and requested an audience," Shane replies, "the guards at the gate called it in. Said he was alone."

"Why would he be dumb enough to come alone?" Josh asks, eyes narrowing.

"To not look like a threat," Shane shrugs a shoulder, "come on."

"If you ever call yourself a whore again, it'll be the last thing that comes out of your mouth," Josh telepaths to me as we follow Shane. His hand is still holding mine and the grip is still relentless.

"Then don't treat me like one," I reply, evenly.

"I'm going to kiss you and fuck you whenever and wherever the Hell I please, Veyara," he answers and I know he doesn't mean it. He's just saying these words to piss me off. I try to pry out of his hold, but it just tightens more. How dare he say things like that to me?

"I am NOT a harem girl!" I snap at him, glaring at his side profile.

"No, you're not. You're fucking mine."

My heart skips a beat at that but I force myself to stay focused. ***"That doesn't mean shit. All the women in Serpent Nation are yours. Belonging to you is embarrassing and I won't be lumped in with the likes of them."***

Josh drops my hand, and the loss of his warmth feels like a slap in the face. I know I took it too far, but it's the truth. It hurts and the wound is so deep, there's nothing he can do to fix it. I wish he could, but I don't know how, even if he asked.

The rest of the way to the throne room is quiet. My mind's racing as the enormous double doors open for us by two Royal Guards.

Nathanial is just taking his seat, and the other Warriors are already here.

The throne room is built in the shape of a hexagon, each of its six walls honoring a royal Warrior house. At every point in the room, a pair of thrones sit elevated on a low dais—crafted in the distinct style, colors, and insignias of their respective House. The Craving thrones command the center of the far wall, crimson and regal, with Nathanial's larger throne set between the pair—marking his place between the reigning Alpha and Luna. It's the first thrones that catch the eye and demands respect as one enters the room.

Antonio, Sam, James, Devaughn, and Daniel are already seated. When all Warriors and Crescents are present, Daniel and Daniya receive additional thrones next to the pair that's already here, but for now the two brothers sit beside each other.

Josh looks my way, indicating me to follow to the right of the Craving thrones where the Hunter thrones stand—two large, imposing black thrones with serpents carved all around it.

"His Royal Highness, Prince Lucian Raphael Craving," the herald announces our party crasher. I don't get to admire the Hunter thrones and take my seat beside Josh for the first time as a Warrior and the Veyara.

The tall, bronze haired-gray eyed, vampire does not look around as he strides in, walking straight toward us with purpose. He looks so similar to his brother.

"What brings you to our neck of the woods on Mabon, Lucian," Nathanial isn't asking. He's still dressed in his Mabon robes—red, orange, and deep green—looking handsome as ever. The crown sits comfortably on his blond hair, but the usual glint in his eyes is missing, replaced with a harder, serious look.

"My mother had a vision," Lucian starts and I frown. The Queen of the vampires is a very, very powerful witch. It's not uncommon for her to have visions—so whatever brought Lucian here must be big.

"The Cursed One is raising the dead to build her army. It's starting," Lucian tells Nathanial, who's gone as still as I've ever seen him. His face is emotionless and gray eyes darkening.

I look at the other Warriors and while they're standing poised, I can sense the confusion in them too.

The Cursed One is Mother Isis and Queen Aradia's older half-sister—Lilith. I don't know much about her except that we don't speak of her name. Lore has it that she can sense when her name is spoken and can hear what's being said. While Aradia is the Queen of the

Witches, Lilith is the leader of the Sisterhood of Sin. Her followers practice everything that goes against the laws of nature. They do not believe in the Divine or respecting the sacredness of magic.

My whole life I thought Lilith was dead. I knew her followers kept her practice alive, living in secrecy—but Lucian said The Cursed One is raising the dead—not her followers.

I'm not the only one in the dark, because Daniel's voice rings through my mind.

"Are you hearing this?" he telepaths.

Shane responds, ***"Yes."***

"Did you know?" Josh follows up and the suspicion is clear in his thoughts.

"No. Don't say anything until Lucian leaves. If Nathanial didn't tell us, he must have a reason," my brother's response comes, so we remain silent.

"When did Aradia have the vision?" Nathanial asks, quietly.

"Last night. The King thought it'd be best I came in person to tell you," Lucian says, he keeps his focus on Nathanial, not looking at the Warriors once, "he's invited you to come to Romania to discuss this matter further."

Lucian's father, King Stefan is Nathanial's twin brother. Nathanial was infected by an animal which turned him into a shifter, thousands of years ago. When Stefan fell ill and Nathanial tried to save him by biting him, Stefan didn't become a shifter. His transformation took another form—creating what we now call vampires. Over time, the differences between the brothers and their species became too great, creating a silent war. We do not go into each other's territories unless it's a dire situation.

Shifters and vampires are taught to stay away from each other. Not so much as kill on sight, more so turn a blind eye and avoid crossing paths. Sometimes there are turf wars, but it's not frequent enough to be a problem.

We definitely do not go to each other's homes. Much less Romania. King Stefan and Queen Aradia hold court in Romania. It's the vampires' motherland.

We wait for Nathanial to say something.

"You came alone," Nathanial says. "Why? Where are your guards?"

"I told them to wait in town. I came as my father's royal messenger. This is not a ploy to start war," Lucian reassures him, "Father is expecting you. Our High Council are all present at court for Mabon already."

Nathanial nods. "I'll give you an answer within the hour. You may stay here. We'll make sure you are comfortable."

"Thank you." Lucian bows his head slightly before he's escorted out of the throne room. Once he's gone, Nathanial clears the room of the Royal Guards.

"The Cursed One is raising the dead?" Shane asks Nathanial. "Kind of important for us to know that don't you think?"

I blink and realize Lilith being alive isn't news to the Warriors, that's not what Daniel was referring to. They knew Lilith's been alive—they didn't know she was raising the dead. What the Hell?

I can tell Nathanial's mind is in a million places right now, but he says, "You heard Lucian—it's starting."

"Mother Isis put The Cursed One to sleep and has been in prayer to keep The Cursed One's powers limited," Josh frowns deeply, "she shouldn't have the power to raise the dead."

I am so confused.

"Not by herself, no," Shane agrees before looking at Nathanial. "What are you thinking?"

Nathanial stands. "Get ready to leave for Romania. Sleep on the plane."

"Should the Crescents prepare Mother Isis?" James asks.

"Yes. Isis should be there for this." Nathanial doesn't hesitate to answer as he leaves the throne room with his robes flying behind him.

31 DISTANT RELATIVES

Rosella Craving
September 22

My parents were returning from a summit with the vampires—Dad was always striving to work with our vampire cousins instead of fighting them. It cost him his life. Instead of peace, his and Mom's death gave Shane more reasons to continue the rivalry.

I don't blame him.

Shane was twenty and had been Alpha for two years when we got the news. He held it together for the Pack, for me, for everyone really. But I still see his hands tremble with rage whenever vampires are mentioned.

Everyone said it had to be the vampires—the ones who didn't want peace. We had no other reason to believe it would be anyone else. The timing was too coincidental.

I wash off Mabon and dress in my formal Warrior uniform before rejoining the Pack in the command room on the 747 an hour before we're scheduled to land. All the Warriors are here except Josh.

I've convinced myself I wish he didn't kiss me again. I'm just another girl who's had Josh Hunter's lips on her. It's nothing special. He said touching me made him feel sick, well the feeling is mutual.

He's not special.

The screens around me are displaying old texts and scrolls but, I can't make out what they say.

"What did you mean The Cursed One wouldn't be able to raise the dead by herself?" I ask my brother.

Shane turns to look at me, "Well, when Mother Isis put Lilith to sleep the last time, Mother Isis ensured The Cursed One wouldn't be able to wield her full powers by herself by suppressing her own powers," Shane starts, "so if The Cursed One has started raising the dead, she has the help of other powerful black magic wielders."

"But we raise the dead all the time, why is this different?" Daniel asks, as Sam gets up to take a phone call.

"We call on their spirits, we don't raise their bodies," James answers that one.

"Lucian didn't say anything about raising bodies," Antonio points out, "what is this? The zombie apocalypse starting?"

I raise an eyebrow as Devaughn looks at James and Shane, neither of whom seem interested enough to answer. Devaughn sighs, looking at Daniel, Antonio, and me, "Yeah, it could, but they're under The Cursed One's control."

"Why would she want to do this?" I ask quietly.

"I fucking hate zombies," Antonio groans as if he has personal history with them.

"She wants to be the sole ruler of earth," Shane answers me. "To let her corruption take over every aspect until everyone is bowing to her."

"Wouldn't that kill the earth? All that dark magic—it'll cause an imbalance," I say. You can't just take from nature and not expect it to retaliate.

Sam returns to his seat. "We're preparing to land soon."

"Where the fuck is Josh?" James asks, glancing around before I hear a sharp hiss under the table.

"Uh, found him," Daniel says, and when I turn to look at him, he's looking back at me. I frown, but Daniel holds up a hand to me. "Don't move..."

I freeze.

From the corner of my eye, I see movement. The black, scaled body slides into view, and my breath stutters. Every muscle in me locks as the serpent rises from beneath the table, the light reflecting off its polished scales.

The second the serpent lifts itself higher, slithering up my leg, I know it's Josh from his gray slit eyes. The tingling feeling from the bond spreads through me and my body instantly relaxes, surprisingly. He glides over me, smooth and shockingly warm. The sensation makes my skin prickle, a shiver coursing straight through me.

He coils once over my shoulders, wrapping around me like a large necklace. His weight in serpent form is heavier than I expected, pressing me into the chair. My fingers twitch, aching to touch, to test what I'm feeling but also a little terrified.

I can hear Devaughn laugh across the table. "Well, seems like that's how you'll be making your entrance into the vampire court."

The others mutter, some unsettled, some amused. Shane says,

"Josh isn't taking any chances. If this is a trap, he'll know it."

All I can focus on is the pitch-black serpent resting against my collarbone, his scales softer, velvety, almost gentle against my skin. It steals my breath at how beautiful he is. This form is the exact replica of the tattoo on his arm—just much longer.

I don't know what he's trying to do, slithering on me like this, but I'm not letting him get any kind of satisfaction out of it.

Daniel and Antonio can't seem to look away from Josh and me. I look at them and demand, "What?"

"Uh, nothing," Antonio shakes his head.

"It's just that," Daniel glances at Josh, who's head is slightly raised toward Daniel. Daniel looks back to me, "Josh never, *never*, let's anyone touch him..."

I give him a blunt look. "The tabloids say otherwise."

"Please do not make me laugh at him while he's in serpent form," Daniel tells me as Antonio chuckles beside him anyway. Josh's split tongue slithers out, making Daniel pale slightly. I've never seen my friend so uncomfortable before. It's a little comical.

"He doesn't let anyone touch his serpent form," Antonio corrects Daniel's statement.

I roll my eyes, "What an honor."

"It is," Josh thinks to me.

"Oh, shove it," I reply.

"Next time you think I've lumped you in with anyone, remember you're the only one who can hold the monster I become," Josh telepaths. I clench my jaw, hating that his words make my heart beat faster.

I try to focus on what Shane, James, and Devaughn are talking about on the other end of the table, instead of the serpent draped around me or how my Mate continues to contradict himself and toying with my heart.

The cars roll to a stop at the base of the stone steps of the vampires' home. The vampires had a few limousines waiting for our arrival at their private airport. I stare in awe at the elaborate towers and the walls surrounding the perimeter. The architectural design is ancient, but the foundation is strong enough to hold the castle up after all these years.

Of course, they've rebuilt portions of it to suit modern tastes as we have done with Cravenhold.

The limo doors open, and we file out, all of us in our full-dress uniforms. I step out last, Josh still wrapped around my shoulders, his body warm and heavy. His head is lifted to come beside my face, as he takes everything in.

It smells like the forest back home. However, the castle before me is completely different from Cravenhold.

Two figures descend the steps to greet us.

"Nathanial," the male in heavy robes and a crown fit only for a king rests on his black hair, greets as he hugs Nathanial. Josh lets out a hiss as Shane moves in closer to our king.

Nathanial embraces the man, smiling tightly, "Stefan. It's been too long, brother."

I stare. The man is Nathanial's twin brother, but they don't look alike—not really. When they pull away, I see the slight resemblance. Craving gray eyes is the easiest to spot, then it's the way his face looks smiling, similar to Nathanial's. They have the same nose, and their lips curve the same as they speak. I've seen pictures of Stefan and Aradia before, of course, but he looks different in person. The vampires do not allow press at the Palace, unless they are invited, which is very rare. These grounds are said to be Holy—it's why Mother Aradia and King Stefan settled here. It is rare for King Stefan to leave Romania. I've never heard that he has.

The man beside the King shakes Nathanial and Shane's hands, introducing himself as Jerome Craving. He's Stefan and Aradia's eldest son—first in line for the throne. I can't imagine how old he is.

The King takes a look at all of us and it's as though he's about to say something, but his eyes land on Josh around my shoulders. He glances at me, tilting his head a little, before focusing back on Josh.

The King smirks, "House Hunter, forever overprotective," he turns to Nathanial, "some things don't change, brother."

"Some things shouldn't," Nathanial replies evenly, and Stefan nods in agreement. I have a feeling they're agreeing on more than what's been said aloud.

Jerome steps forward, offering a polished smile. "You've traveled far. Come, settle in. Freshen yourselves after your long flight. We will convene with the High Council once you're rested."

Guards and butlers appear, ushering us inside. I'm guided to a suite, the door swinging open to reveal silks and velvet draped across the room—not too different from home. I turn to the attendant, "And the Beta's room?"

The young vampire boy blinks, confused. "We've only prepared one room for the Beta and Veyara…you are a couple, yes?"

My mouth opens, but before I can form a reply, he bows and slips past me.

Josh uncoils from around my shoulders, slithering down with unnerving grace until his body vanishes through the threshold ahead of me.

I step inside, hesitantly, cursing in my head. They're really going to stick us in the same room as if a palace doesn't have other rooms to spare. I've shifted now, and if we ask for separate rooms…that'll raise questions. Not that it's any of the vampires' business.

Josh coils his entire form in one spot before he transforms back to human form. I watch it happen in one smooth motion, no pain in sight.

"Well, this is…expected," Josh says, eyeing the one bed in the room. It's large, very large, but it's still one bed. I've read enough books to know nothing good will happen with both of us sleeping on one bed.

Our belongings are already in here, and I tell Josh, "I don't need to rest. I'm going to go explore."

I don't wait for him to say anything before I turn around and leave the room, closing the doors behind me.

It's about another three hours before I follow Josh into a boardroom. The floor-to-ceiling windows clearly show off the river and the fall foliage outside. It's mesmerizing.

The boardroom itself is massive, and nearly every seat is filled. I take my place between Josh and James, who is sitting silently, waiting. Uncle Edward and Shane talk quietly as I catch Mother Isis, sitting at the front. She's dressed in white, her blonde hair flowing beautifully over her shoulders and she looks much too young to be Nathanial's wife—though I'm not one to judge anyone's age. Her blue eyes are focused on the leaves outside and she looks at peace, if anything. There's a strange calmness about her that makes me drowsy the longer

I look at her.

"Well, well, well. What do we have here?" the familiar voice stops me cold as all the blood drains from my body.

I turn to meet a pair of gray eyes I'm too familiar with. Eyes full of challenge and amusement. His blond hair is disheveled as always, and a pair of dog tags slip out of his shirt, hanging around his neck. The youngest vampire prince smirks at me.

"The rumors for once are true. Apparently, the shifters have a *female* Warrior," he raises a brow at me as if to say *I told you so.*

My heart is pounding so fast in my chest that I'm sure Josh and James can hear it. I know he won't expose us, but I also was not expecting to see him here. Why did I think he wouldn't be here? Of course, he would be. He may be the youngest vampire prince, but he's still on their High Council. He's older than most in here.

"Don't even start. You're practically our some great uncle," Daniel tells him, faking disgust. Daniel's the only one here who knows about the prince and me.

The prince holds my gaze for a moment, before turning to look at Daniel. "Then you should have some respect for your elders."

Some of the vampires chuckle. I purse my lips from smiling, myself.

"Liam," Jerome calls out and the youngest prince just smirks at Daniel.

I can't seem to take my eyes off him. I should, before someone catches me. Josh is right next to me.

But I can't.

Prince William Malachai Craving—Liam, is someone I've only ever encountered in the dark. He promised we'd see each other again. I didn't realize it'd be this soon.

The rebellious but deadly vampire prince, nearly a thousand years old, but does not look a day over twenty-nine—one of my biggest secrets—is sitting right across from me. He did that on purpose. He could've sat anywhere. There are four other spots open.

I feel my darkness swirling, so I blink to keep them at bay. I don't want the vampires to take it the wrong way and think I'm going to attack.

The last of our Elders and the vampire High Council finish joining us. I notice at the far end, there's a girl who can't be much younger than me and I immediately know who she is.

Princess Elena Montenaj. She's the last of her family line, on both her maternal and paternal side now. I was hoping to catch a glimpse of her.

It's not long after, that Nathanial and Stefan enter, taking their seats at the front.

Stefan begins. "As you all know, the cursed Sisterhood of Sin have awoken the dead five thousand years earlier than expected." *What?* We had a timeline? I stare at the king as he continues like he didn't drop a bomb on me. "We all know that means we must reunite to face them in a battle once more. My wife, Aradia, whom you all are aware, is the Mother of the Sisterhood of Light, had warned us with a prophecy years ago." I find it strange that the Queen is not here for this meeting seeing that she had the vision. "The prophecy had warned us that the dead would resurface. Some of us remember what happened the last time," the king says slowly.

"Half the human race was wiped out," Prince Jarrod, Liam's second eldest brother, answers, shaking his head.

I can't stop thinking about what the prophecy lady told me a few hours ago. Was she talking about this war? How could she have known.

"We covered it by calling it the Black Death, Bubonic Plague, whatever you will." Mother Isis explains to those of us who were not present the last time.

Her voice is soft and almost musical. I see her hand move to rest on Nathanial's and I narrow my eyes slightly. I know she's been in prayer for some hundreds of years to keep evil away, but I also know Nathanial misses her. I push the thoughts away and focus on what she's saying instead.

"The humans bought it because they needed an explanation. We all know how humans work." She doesn't need to emphasize that.

Humans like to think they are the most superior creatures. Animals that are dangerous are put to sleep, but what can you do with the undead? The supernatural like us? It's normal for them to go into denial when matters, such as supernatural events, contradict their common belief. Unexplainable things occur that the human brain does not allow them to accept in most cases. Those unexplainable things are what we cover up, of course. It could be argued that while we prevent the human brain from understanding our hidden world, we restrict it for our protection.

Throughout history, people were very superstitious and most believed we were the Devil's creatures. The uproar in the supernatural community when the witch hunts occurred, first in Europe and then in America, was clear the humans were not ready for that truth.

If humans found out The Cursed One was behind millions of deaths, they'd take extreme precautions against all of us. But the supernatural saved them. Mother Isis fought off Lilith's dead army back then and continues to protect the world.

"But with so much more advanced technology, it's going to be hard to cover up with a simple white lie," Mother Isis tells us, which makes me realize she does keep up with the current times.

"So how *are* we going to cover this up?" one of the vampire High Council members, Roderick Jecov, asks almost in mockery.

Vivian Cij, another High Council member, leans over to look Marcellus Xandelskye straight on. "Why don't you tell us, seeing that one of your descendants is married to Lilith?"

Gasps go around as everyone turns to look at the vampire, but Marcellus calmly replies, "What Xavier was thinking disturbs most of us, but marriage is just a license. And this is why I've been trying to discuss the situation between the Soul Snatchers and the Protectors."

"Not right now, Marcellus." Liam shakes his head and it surprises me to see this serious side of him. Any trace of his earlier amusement is gone, replaced with the vampire everyone's cautioned about.

"Knowing Lilith, she's bound to make a grand entrance." Jarrod directs us back on topic. *Knowing Lilith?*

Isis nods. "Yes, but she's also sneaky, so she is not going to give us time to prepare."

I look around the table. All the vampires, except Elena, are ancient. They've seen the world change before their eyes.

Of course, they've faced The Cursed One before.

"But why now?" Prince Darren, Liam's third eldest brother, questions. He's looking at his father and Nathanial. "Why is she making her moves known now? Why not continue working from the shadows?"

I don't have to look to feel Liam's eyes on me.

"It almost feels like a trap," James agrees. "Like she wants us to believe this, while she plans something far worse."

"Would not put it past her." Lucian nods, writing something down on the tablet in front of him.

I glance at Daniel before I telepath him, ***"Did you know The Cursed One was alive?"***

"Yes. If we had more time between your transformation and this debacle, you would've known too," Daniel replies, ***"it's classified..."***

"You don't say," I reply. ***"And this prophecy? What is it?"***

"It was a vision the Queen had during the Roman Empire... the plague was a failed attempt on Lilith's part, but it's a cycle, over and over," Daniel tells me.

I wonder the same thing as Prince Darren—why now?

32 BITE ME

Rosella Craving
September 23

Nathanial and Stefan continue the meeting discussing strategies, contingencies, and political fallout. It drags on for another hour as Shane, Josh, James, Liam, and Lucian counter, dismissing most of the ideas, saying all we can really do now is prepare for the unknown. Our security, intelligence, and other resources will be heavily invested. Talks go into research and weaponry which I try to pay attention to, but start zoning out on.

When we're finally dismissed, I don't go back to the room and decide to continue looking around the Palace. It all seems very familiar, but I don't recall ever being here before.

This Palace is what Liam calls home.

The gardens are beautiful with the fall colors. The Palace is still decorated from their Mabon festival—the vampires celebrate for a few days and I heard it's elaborate, though we've arrived at the end of it. The vampires go all out for all the holidays.

As I step back in from the gardens and start to round a corner, a hand pulls me into a room before locking the door behind us.

"I always did prefer you in dresses," Liam says against my ear as my heart pounds in my chest.

"I'm not here as a princess," I counter, watching him carefully. I realize we're in one of the many sitting rooms, with the fireplace already raging.

"No, you're not," he replies, slowly. He eyes my neck, but the collar covers anything he's looking for. Liam takes a step towards me. "You're not Marked."

I frown. "Did you think I would be so soon?"

He shrugs. "Shifters aren't known for patience when it comes to taking what's theirs."

"Yeah, well, your staff did stick us in the same room so it might test the limits." I roll my eyes.

Liam looks amused as he towers over me. "Is that so?" he trails a finger down my cheek, looking at me through the hair falling into his eyes. "You can always stay in my room."

"That would be highly inappropriate," I answer, slowly, but his eyes have dropped to my lips. My heartbeat picks up again as I reach for the lapels of his jacket. Liam's always loved kissing me.

And that's what he does.

He cups my face with both of his hands and kisses me. His lips are familiar against mine and I kiss him back, missing him—but it all feels wrong now.

I kiss him again, trying to ignore the feeling, but still, something feels off.

Liam breaks away and looks down at me. "What's wrong?"

"I don't know…something just doesn't feel right," I whisper, touching my lips.

Liam doesn't move or say anything for a moment, before he presses his lips to my forehead. "It's the Mating bond."

I look up at him. "What?"

"Your Mating bond," he says, "now that you've transformed, the bond won't allow you to be with anyone outside of your Mate until you're Marked."

Is that why I haven't felt the physical pain of Josh fucking someone since I transformed? Is that why he keeps kissing me? Because he literally can't be with who he wants to be with? This must be killing him.

Here I thought he was being a decent Mate and doing the right thing for once.

I look at Liam and ask, "And it will after?"

Liam chuckles, pulling away from me and I immediately miss his touch. "Yes, to an extent."

"What does that mean?" I ask, frowning as he pours us a drink from the bar cart nearby.

"Means it's a conversation you have with your Mate," Liam answers, handing me one of the glasses, before clinking his own with mine.

"I'm sorry," I say slowly. He's right. I should not be talking about any of this with him, but he knows a lot about shifters. He's been around for long enough.

"You have nothing to be sorry about," Liam replies, throwing his drink back, "we both knew this was going to happen."

I nod, taking a drink of the whiskey he's poured. It goes down smoothly and I sigh. "I guess I wasn't ready…" I look at him, "to see you so soon."

His expression softens as he replies, "I know. Fate's cruel that way, isn't it?"

I don't say anything because he's right. Fate is cruel. In many ways.

"So, the Veyara is also a Warrior," he changes the subject and smiles, "always knew there was something different about you."

"Yeah, but you're biased," I tease, walking up to him, needing to be close to him.

"I'll always be biased when it comes to you, little wolf," he says, tugging on one of my black strands.

"Have you ever heard of a female Warrior?"

"No," he answers, "you are the first I've heard of."

"Why do you think?" I ask, turning to face him, "You must have theories."

Liam pauses. "Well…you were born with gray eyes, so it was decided from the Heavens. There isn't much of a theory to go on."

"But why me? Why not Sam's sister, or Devaughn's sister?" I question. Sam's sister is Shane's age.

"Why not you?" Liam counters. "You're a Craving, you have exceptional powers, you're Mated into one of the deadliest Houses. Have you ever even dueled with Nathanial? I'll bet my long ass life that you're as powerful as him."

I stare at Liam.

"You may never have all the answers, or you may," Liam tells me, "it doesn't matter why you were chosen to be a Warrior, what matters is what will you do about it?"

"What about this prophecy?" I ask him. "Are the dead really being raised? What proof is there?"

Liam hesitates, before telling me, "My mother had a vision of witchlings dying."

"Liam, that's terrible," I gasp. Witchlings is what the children of witches are called, usually referring to infants.

He nods. "It alarmed her enough to follow up on it. It's why she's not here."

I finish the contents of my glass and place it on the bar cart. "Has your mother ever had…false visions?"

Liam holds my gaze. "Never. If it hasn't happened, it will soon."

I shudder. "And there's no way of stopping it?"

"Not my mother's visions," he replies sadly, "there are different kinds of seers. My mother only has ever seen the outcome."

I don't know what makes me say it, but I feel compelled to tell him. "I trust you."

He frowns slightly at the randomness, but says, "I trust you too."

I meet his gray eyes and ask, "Can I trust you as the Veyara?"

"Should you?" he asks, his voice barely above a whisper between us.

I tilt my head. "I'd like to. I'd like to know I have a friend among the vampires."

"In that case, you never needed to ask," he replies, "you know you can. And you know if you call, I'll come—no questions asked."

He really shouldn't say things like that.

"No questions asked?" I repeat.

"None," he states firmly.

"Even after I'm Marked?" I dare to look up at his face.

Liam smirks down at me, touching my cheek. "You getting Marked changes things for you, Rose, not me."

My breath catches. He *really* shouldn't say things like that.

He cups my face again, before his hands travel down my arms, until he's lifting me up against the wall. "You shifting changed things for you, not me," his lips are on my neck as I arch my back. My legs wrap around him as I feel his hard cock pressed against me.

I close my eyes to relish the pleasures, but all I can think of is Josh kissing me the night I shifted. How right it felt to kiss Josh, and how different it just felt to kiss Liam. It never felt different and I hate that it does now.

I didn't think I'd be kissing Liam ever again, but I hate that it's changed now.

Liam's hands cup my ass as his lips suck on my neck, fangs grazing, sending a shiver down my spine. I want him to bite me. I want to feel the rush his fangs used to give me.

"Bite me," I breathe heavily, arching into him. He pauses to look at me and I meet his. "Do it." He knows I need this as understanding crosses his eyes. He doesn't need to be told twice. He moves the collar of my uniform down and pierces my shoulder. The sensation of his fangs makes me roll my eyes back in ecstasy. He tenses instead of relaxing. My fingers massage his muscles as we start to grind against each other. It's the blood lust—nothing more, I tell myself.

"Liam," I say gently, "we can't…"

He pulls away from my shoulder and kisses my jaw. "I know…but fuck I missed you, little wolf."

"I missed you too." I admit, even though I've tried very hard to avoid thinking of him at all costs. He presses into me a little and I glare at him. "Stop teasing me."

He chuckles. "Never."

He slowly places me down on my feet and I sigh, fixing his tie. "I should see what the others are up to…"

He nods but catches my arm. "Do me a favor?"

"Anything," I say before I can stop myself. I shouldn't make promises like that now.

He drops his hand and says, "Don't get Marked in my house."

I roll my eyes. "I promise you that will not happen," then I say softly, "I wouldn't do that to you."

We hold each other's gaze for a moment, before he breaks it off to pour himself more whiskey.

"Go," he says, "before I change my mind and decide not to be an understanding ex-lover and fuck your pretty little arsehole all over this room."

My cheeks heat with flashbacks. Gosh he's terrible and I know he's doing it to torture me. I let out a shaky laugh, leaving quickly before I change my mind and let him at least try.

I'm brushing my hair at the vanity when Josh comes out of the bathroom and clears his throat from behind me. He wasn't in here when I got back and I made sure to shower extensively just in case. As much as I wouldn't mind making Josh Hunter jealous, I already have too much on my plate to deal with.

"I'll take the couch," we both say at the same time and then stare at each other.

I turn to look at him. "You're not serious."

"It's no big deal," he replies, grabbing one of the pillows from the bed.

"Josh." I push away from the vanity and walk toward him, pointing at the Victorian couch. "You won't even fit on that thing…it's ridiculous. Sleep on the bed. I'll take the couch."

"I'm not going to sleep on the bed while you sleep on the couch," he rolls his eyes. "We can both sleep on the bed. I won't touch you."

"Right," I say, triggered. "We both know you have no interest in touching me unless you're on drugs, so just don't take any while we're here and sharing the bed."

His jaw flexes but I turn away from him to take my robe off. I climb into bed first, before he follows. The space between us feels like a wall.

I can tell he's not relaxed by how still he is. His eyes are on the ceiling with his hands folded across his stomach over the blanket.

I roll my eyes before saying, "You don't have to be so obviously in pain about sharing a bed with me. I showered, I know I don't stink. I told you, I can take the couch."

"Is that what you think is happening right now?" he breathes before turning his head to look at me. His gray eyes are bright and my breath hitches for a moment seeing them as if he's sucking me in.

He turns to his side fully, our noses only inches apart. I don't dare move. The sting from the Mabon dance still burns in my chest.

How easy it is for Liam to kiss me. And how easy it is for my own Mate to push me away.

Fate is cruel.

Every time Josh has kissed me, it was a volatile moment—my first shift, the morning after when we were fighting, last night…the only time he kissed me that truly felt genuine was at the clearing on Mariella's reunion. Even then, he was on Pulse so…does it count?

I start to say goodnight, but he breaks the silence. "About the reunion—"

"It was a mistake," I cut him off. I don't want to relive it, much less talk about it.

His eyes flash, and he shakes his head, leaning in. His hand finds mine under the blanket. "Fuck no, Divine, Rose—" his breath is almost shaky.

"I don't want to talk about it," I reply, trying to pull my hand out of his. So much for not touching me.

"It wasn't a mistake," he says and my chest feels too tight. My heart is beating so fast, it's almost painful. Josh swallows, his thumb brushing over my hand and I'm very aware that it's only the two of us. "I haven't stopped thinking about it."

"Were you thinking about it when you were out with Constance?" I ask without looking at him.

"I told you that was an old picture—"

"Maybe, but the point is that it happened," I start to pull my hand away again, but he laces his fingers with mine, making me look at him.

"Let me make it up to you," he says.

I want him to kiss me right now. The need pressing against my ribs, but it doesn't feel right that this moment is happening here, in this bed, in the dark. Besides, if he wants to make it up to me, he could start by apologizing to begin with.

"Make up what? The past six years of hating me, or four years of cheating?" I ask. I need him to let go of my hand.

I deserve things between us to be real, not stolen, and definitely not because he's horny and can't fuck anyone else. His hand loosens at my words. I take that opportunity and pull my hand back and put some distance between us. The bed is big enough.

"Rose…"

"Look, I know you can't fuck anyone else right now because the bond won't let you, okay?" I put it out there. "But I'm not a convenience or a placeholder for you. I don't know why you would ever get that impression and if that's what you thought was going to happen on the reunion night. I'm not some girl you can fuck. I'm your Mate and that means something to me even if it doesn't to you, so stop using it against me. And stop lying to me and saying all these things to get your way with me when you mean none of it."

Josh is so quiet and so still that if his eyes weren't open, I would've thought he fell asleep. I can't read him though. I have no idea what's going through his mind right now and my stupid heart feels *bad* for being so harsh—I'm not him. I don't like hurting him.

"These girls wouldn't have anything to post or talk about if you didn't give them the opportunity. For them to feel comfortable to be so public about it says a lot…" I trail off as my throat constricts.

"So you want us to be more public? We just spent the whole day together—our every move is documented—"

"No!" I cut him off, frustrated. I lay on my back and stare at the ceiling, willing myself not to cry right now.

"You don't want us to be public?"

He doesn't get it. It's not about being public or not—we don't exactly have a choice on that matter.

"I'm your Mate," I whisper, forcing my lip to not tremble right now. I will not cry. "It's…embarrassing, Josh. Having a good day with you, being seen with you, and then turn around and be reminded—" I bite down on my lip to compose myself, before finishing the sentence, "be reminded that I'm just another girl on a long list. The last girl, and not by your choice."

I should've found a whole other room to sleep in. I hate telling him how I feel. He'll just use it against me one way or another.

"You've never been just another girl," he says, quietly. "You know that."

"Yeah, because I was never in the running. I was never a thought. I was too young and by the time I was older, you had already decided you hated the idea of us," I say quietly.

I know he thinks I killed Noah. I know that's what his driving force was, but as my Mate, why didn't he give me the benefit of the doubt? Why didn't he turn over every leaf and find out that I'm innocent? Why is he so quick to believe I could kill someone at all.

"It's just too hard…" I whisper and feel him shift beside me. "I need you to stop kissing me. I want you to…" My voice trembles a little as I turn my head to look at him. His eyes are already on me. A sad laugh slips out, and I put more space between us even though it pains me. "Divine, I do, but if you're going to kiss me, Josh Hunter, I don't want it to be a stolen moment like this or a test or a trick or for the cameras…" I sigh heavily, running my hand through my hair. It's rare that he listens to me like this without interrupting or dismissing me. "If you're going to kiss me, then…*kiss* me for real and mean it or don't do it at all. I can't do this back and forth with you forever. I won't be like my aunt and uncle."

I don't wait for him to say anything, it's too painful. I know he can never mean it because I'm just not his type. For a second, I think maybe we should just have sex soon and get it over with to get on with our lives. But for now, I turn over, giving him my back and try to fall asleep.

33 JUST A DANCE

Rosella Craving
September 24

We stay another day as King Stefan decides to host a dinner in our honor—formalities and all. I hear it will be an intimate setting, seeing that vampires and shifters do not break bread together. He wants to keep it small.

My legs itch for movement and the woods call me through the windows. So, I answer. I'm almost in the forest when Josh stops me.

"You shouldn't go in there alone," he says, coming out from behind me.

I roll my eyes and say over my shoulder, "Then come with me."

I don't wait for him as I enter and take a deep breath before shifting into my wolf form. The transformation is welcoming, nothing like the first night. I stretch, yawning as Josh shifts beside me.

Branches whip past as I run. It takes no effort for Josh to stay by my side. We run over ridges, follow flowing streams, and go deeper until the trees part into a clearing. A circle of stones rises from the moss.

It's an old ritual ground, clearly abandoned. I slow down as my nose twitches at the faint scent of blood.

Maybe not entirely abandoned.

Josh smells it too, his eyes narrowing as he looks around. ***"Let's keep moving,"*** he thinks to me and I nod.

We continue to the cliffs and leap toward them, paws finding the narrow paths until we're at the edge, looking down at the river below.

Josh's fur catches the streaks of Sun breaking through the thick clouds. His chest rises and falls steadily. He looks so majestic in this moment as he takes in the sight before him. But something feels so sad and heavy about him in this moment. So alone—like the weight of the world is on his shoulders.

I watch him. The way the wind ruffles his coat, the way his stance claims the cliffside as if he's been here multiple times. My bond tugs at me, insistent, pulling me toward him.

I'm not sure who moves first, but there's a faint brush of our shoulders. He lowers his head, gray eyes meeting mine before I press into him, nuzzling beneath his throat. He lets me. He even leans into it, lowering his jaw to meet me, applying just enough pressure to keep me there and it feels good. Too good. His body is warm against the chill on the cliffside and I smile, welcoming this embrace from him.

"Rose," he thinks to me, but it sounds funny, like he's struggling. ***"I need you to step away from me,"*** when I hesitate, he adds, ***"right now."***

My shoulders slump, and I want to protest, but I pull away from him completely. My chest tightens and heart aches at the obvious rejection. When am I going to learn?

I leave him to stand on the other side of the cliff, needing a moment myself. I'm so tired of him getting close only to push me away. Him wanting me near but keeping me at arm's length. I don't understand it, and the ache gnaws deeper with every rejection.

"Rose," he calls to me, softer this time. I don't answer. I can't face him. I don't want him to see how much it hurts when he pushes me away. ***"I don't want to do something we'll both regret."***

"And what could that be? The list seems to be getting longer and longer," I ask, still facing away from him.

"Marking you in wolf form," he answers.

My breath catches for a second. Mating in wolf form is extremely taboo—even though our animal form is a part of us. It's up there with rape—even if it's consensual. I turn to look at him and find that his eyes are dark and his wolf really is struggling.

"It's freezing. We should go," I think to him and step past him to head back toward the Palace.

By dinner time, the walls around my heart have been reinforced. I don't enter the dinner with Josh, despite the few texts I get from him and Aunt Susan to do so.

He's already seated when I step through the arched doorway into King Stefan's private dining hall, after being announced. He's talking to Shane and James when I walk in and stops mid-sentence when he sees me. Our eyes lock for a moment before I look away.

My silk dress brushes against my legs as I move forward. The gown is midnight blue, melting into black, sleeves fitted to my wrists where gloves take over, every line designed to conceal. My hair falls in heavy curls, pinned to one side to bare the daring neckline.

I feel eyes on me as the long table rises in respect. I keep my chin high, eyes forward, though I can feel Josh's gaze on me like fire. I don't look at him again. I glide to my place beside him and lower myself gracefully into the chair.

The rest of the table takes their seat, chatter resuming, while others arrive. I realize it's mostly shifters, the only vampires attending are King Stefan, his sons, their wives, and a few High Council members.

The two kings exchange pleasantries as we're told to begin feasting. I glance over at Shane, who's frozen in his seat. I know he hates this. He doesn't want to be here a second longer and this dinner is pointless to him.

As dinner starts to wrap up, Josh's hand accidentally brushes mine and I pull away without needing to be told.

I flash him a smile, saying, "Thank the Divine for the gloves, right?"

He frowns but before he can say anything, I see movement on my other side.

I look up to see Liam smirking as he says, "May I have this dance?"

There are a few couples on the dance floor, moving to the orchestra. I smile and place my hand in his cold ones.

"I'd love to," I reply and let Liam lead the way.

When we're out of earshot, he says, chuckling, "Looked like you needed rescuing."

"You have no idea," I reply, quietly. As much as it feels good to be in Liam's arms, I wish they were Josh's, thinking back to our Mabon dance—even if we were fighting most of it.

"You are welcome to use me to make your dumbass Mate jealous," Liam murmurs in my ear as he spins us around.

"I appreciate it, but you can't make someone who doesn't like you jealous," I reply, my hand tightening around his.

"Like I said, dumbass," Liam repeats, "if I were him—"

"Liam…" I warn gently.

"I'd make sure no one had the chance to steal you away for a dance," he says, then pulls back to look at my face. He's smiling as he says, "Well, shit, look at us dancing in the open—right in front of everyone."

I shake my head at him. "You're going to get us in trouble."

"Nonsense," Liam grins. "This is an olive branch. The beginnings of a fruitful alliance." Liam spins me out before bringing me back into him and whispering, "Yeah, he's totally watching. Maybe I should kiss you, make him really burn."

"Not unless you want to start a war instead of an alliance," I reply sweetly.

"Shifters have nothing on us," Liam answers, rolling his eyes.

"Have we ever been at war?" I ask him, curiously. I'm learning there's a lot of our past that our history books have left out.

"No. We've always coexisted. Sure, there are turf wars here and there, maybe some family feuds, but nothing like…"

"Like the Soul Snatchers and Protectors?" I offer.

He looks at me and nods. "Yeah, nothing like that."

"Should shifterkind worry about that civil war spilling into our world?" I ask him, raising an eyebrow.

"Time will tell," Liam sighs.

"Thank you for earlier…I know it's not fair…" I trail off, knowing he'll understand I'm referring to him biting me.

"Shhh, I told you before, whenever you need it," he says as the song comes to a slow end.

He bows politely, placing a kiss on my hand. Liam walks me back to my seat.

"Thank you for the lovely dance, Veyara." Liam winks at me.

I tilt my head in a polite gesture as I take my seat and Liam returns to his. Lucian leans into his brother to say something, and Liam does not look away from me.

I turn to catch Shane and Josh glaring at me.

"What?" I ask, shrugging, "It would've been rude to say no."

"You didn't have to look like you were enjoying it," Shane replies and I roll my eyes.

"It was just a dance." I wave him off.

"Was it?" Josh asks and I turn my focus on him.

"Yes," I reply, tautly, "just because you find it insufferable to touch me, doesn't mean every male in the world does."

Josh pinches the bridge of his nose, reining in whatever comeback he has.

However, when we've returned to our room, Josh doesn't hold

back what he wanted to say at the dinner.

"Dancing with a vampire?" he asks, annoyed, "Really?"

I roll my eyes as I take out my hair pins. "What? It's not like he stole *your* dance turn with me. What are you mad about?"

"It's disgusting and you know it," he replies, taking his jacket off.

"Disgusting?" I repeat, with a laugh. I can't take him seriously, so I say, "Anyone who's not a serpent is disgusting to you, Josh. I'll make sure to shower before bed."

"That would be very considerate," he says in return.

"It was a dance, I didn't fuck the prince," I snap. Well, I didn't fuck him tonight.

"I saw the way he was looking at you. He would've taken you up on the offer," Josh replies, loosening his tie.

I kick off my heels and turn to glare at him. "So what? What if he did? Just because you're not attracted to me, doesn't mean the rest of the world can't be."

Josh isn't looking at me anymore. He can't.

"That's what I thought," I say before picking up my pajamas and start to head to the bathroom.

"Rose—"

"No." I stop him, shaking my head. I meet his narrowed gray eyes as I say, "It was just a dance. If I cannot make a big deal about you fucking every serpent woman out there, you can get over a fucking dance."

"So what? You'd fuck a vampire just to get back at me?" he takes a step toward me. "You'd really stoop that low?"

"I didn't fuck him tonight, I danced with him!" I throw my hands up. "If you wanted a dance so bad all you had to do was ask!"

"I don't want to dance with you." Josh rolls his eyes like it's the most ridiculous idea.

I stop cold and rein in my emotions. "Right. No, of course not. Touching me makes you sick, right?"

I don't wait for his response and shut the bathroom door behind me. I just can't get those words out of my head when he loves touching any woman that's not me.

34 SETTLE

Rosella Craving
September 24

I went straight to bed after my shower, and it wasn't for another hour before Josh came back to the room, deciding to take a shower himself. He gets into bed wearing only his sweatpants. I really didn't think he'd come back, and why can't he put a shirt on? It's rude.

The whole time, I think about whether this is what our life's supposed to be. Me going to bed without him and him sneaking in later in the night. Then I realized, of course, it won't be like this because we'll have completely separate rooms.

The second he climbs into bed, my body is very aware of him.

"What the fuck…" I hear him whisper before he shifts the pillows I may have placed down the middle. I can be a little petty.

He starts to move them and I say, without turning, "Don't. The bed's big enough."

"This is ridiculous," he replies, tiredly.

"Wouldn't want you to accidentally touch me while sleeping," I mumble my response.

"Fuck you," he groans.

"Mm," I yawn, "you'd have to touch me to do that, so no, I don't think so."

There's a moment of silence before I feel the pillows being tossed aside swiftly. I frown and turn to see what he's doing.

His right hand grabs mine, instantly sending jolts of electricity through me. I stare up at him, his lashes lowered, the strong line of his set jaw, the rise and fall of his chest. I start to pull away, but he holds me in place. "Stop."

"I'm not doing anything. *You're* touching *me*," I tell him and he pulls me closer, his warmth engulfing me.

"I know…and you have no idea what it does to me," he snaps.

"I've gotten the hint. If it's that painful for you, then…let me go," I suggest.

"It is fucking painful to touch you—and not Mark you but we both know that'll be a mistake right now."

The bond's taking a toll on him, we knew this would happen. It's just happening faster than I thought, and it'll only get worse until we're forced to Mate. Is that why his words hurt more than usual?

I push him until he lets me go and I get out of bed, raking my hands through my hair. I am too tired to do this. I grab a pillow and the throw blanket as I say, "You take the bed. I'll sleep on the couch."

Josh gets out of bed and follows me. "Get the fuck in bed, Rose."

"What is your problem?" I ask, throwing the items in my hand on the couch and turning to face him. "I'm literally giving you your space."

"I want you in the bed. I don't want space!"

"You don't want me!"

"Fucking—" Josh growls, running a hand down his face. For someone who never loses control, he doesn't seem very in control right now.

"*You* don't get to give me grief about a dance." I cross my arms over my chest, facing him head on.

"He's a vampire."

"And they're serpents. What's your point?"

"You were smiling at him!" Josh snaps, glaring at me.

I stare at him, taken aback. "So *what?!* I have to continue dealing with women you chose over me…so excuse me for indulging in *one* dance."

"Fucking Hell, it's not about the dance!" Josh takes a step closer to me. Now he looks downright murderous. "You've *never* smiled at me like that. It's the way you looked at him. You've never even looked at me like that. The way you let those shifters kiss you at the reunion. And leaned into Devaughn like you were about to kiss him and had the audacity to look like you enjoyed all of it. You think I didn't see all of that?"

Oh. My. Divine. Josh Hunter is jealous. He's jealous. He's jealous of me smiling at Liam. He's jealous of *Devaughn.* If I wasn't so shocked, I'd cry tears of joy. Or anger, because why is he jealous? That doesn't make any sense.

We're glaring at each other. He's too close, so I push him to create distance, "You said you didn't care what I did."

"That was before!"

"Before what?!"

"Before I saw you with other men!" He exclaims. I want to laugh but I'm sure he will kill me if I do right now.

As much as I want to hear all these things, I can't trust him to be honest. He finds a way to hurt me after every time I trusted a vulnerable moment with him. I'm not falling for his games again. Especially when I don't know the rules.

"Before our dance at Mabon. Before seeing a little girl stare up at you like you're her whole world. Before seeing you happy with everyone else but me." He's so angry, I can feel the heat emanating off him. Where does he find the audacity to be angry? But he keeps going. "Before I tasted you and heard you come moaning for me."

"You're jealous," I dare say out loud. I want him to admit it. I need him to admit it. I need to know he feels something for me that's not rooted in hate.

"Damn right, I'm jealous!" he snaps. *Snaps.* He doesn't seem pleased with himself about it either. "I *hate* being on the outside looking into your life."

"You did that to yourself," I remind him and I know I'm playing with fire, but my heart *hurts.*

"You think I don't know that?" he asks. For the first time in my life, I see conflict in his eyes. "I didn't want to, I had to—you'll never understand what I had to go through—"

"You could Mark me," I whisper. I want to know what he went through. I want answers and it's starting to look like that's the only way I'm going to get them.

He pauses, the fire still burning in his eyes. "I told you, that's not something to be taken lightly."

I take a step towards him. "Then if I give you a blowjob right now, will you settle?"

Josh looks at me, not believing the words that left my mouth. I don't even believe the words that left my mouth. Josh looks livid. "Will I *settle*?"

"Yeah, you're clearly mad you haven't gotten laid in over two months because you're talking nonsense," I tell him, standing my ground. I am not falling for his words. "I don't believe for a second you're jealous. I'm not even your type, so all of that you just said is nonsense."

Josh stares me down in a clear challenge. The look on his face goes from frustration to deathly cold, his eyes colder.

"Go on then," he says, voice void of any emotion. My heart sinks but pounds against my chest at the same time. "Get on your knees, Rose."

Fuck him. He thinks I won't do it.

I glare back as I put my hair up and drop to my knees in front of him. He keeps me pinned with his narrowed eyes and I don't look away either. I reach for the waistband of his black sweats when his hand snaps down, catching my wrist.

"Stop," he orders, darkly, but the way his eyes are hooded, he definitely does not want me to stop. I frown and reach out with my other hand, but he catches that too. "Get up. I know you don't want to do this."

I glare up at him. "Would you tell *them* to stop?"

"You're not them," he snaps, tugging at my hands.

"Don't I know it," I reply and before he can pull me up, I clamp my lips down on the outline of his long cock over his sweats and Josh goes absolutely still.

His grip on my wrists slackens just enough. I twist free and pull his sweats down in one motion. His cock springs out, hard and heavy, the thick length of him already straining.

Holy *fuck*.

If I thought he felt big pressed against me in the past, it did not do his cock justice. Seeing him inches from my face has me utterly speechless. He's not going to fit all the way in my mouth.

I bite my lip for a second seeing his girth before I wrap my fingers around the velvety base and take him into my salivating mouth without hesitation. The warmth and weight of him is unfamiliar but thrilling as my tongue licks the head of his cock, exploring the smooth, pulsing heat and tasting his precum.

Josh sucks in a sharp breath above me. His hands dive into my hair, fingers ripping the tie loose so he can gather it all in his fist. He holds my head exactly where he wants me.

He tastes salty but sweet and for some strange reason it reminds me of the beignets from the festival. Heat rushes between my thighs, soaking my panties instantly as I lick him up. If his precum tastes this good to me, what will his cum taste like…?

He growls low, hips jerking once and I know he got hit with the scent of my arousal. "Rose—"

I ignore him. I take as much of him as I can in one go, until the head of his cock nudges the back of my throat. His whole body locks up. The fist in my hair trembles as he tries to pull back, his other hand shifting to my shoulder like he means to lift me, his grip crushing. I swallow around him instead, sealing my lips tight and pushing forward, relaxing my throat until my nose brushes a scar on top of the base of his cock. How does one get a scar there? Why is it wet?

"Rose, fuck!" His cock pulses once, twice, and then he comes hard with a force down my throat. I swallow instinctively, the taste of him is overwhelming, rich and primal, flooding my senses with something more than just physical. It's heady, intoxicating, making my skin feel alive and my core throb with a need I can barely contain.

He came so fast, I didn't even get to torture him.

I ease off slowly, tongue swirling over the sensitive tip to catch the last bead of cum, making him jerk a little. I lick my lips, savoring the taste of my Mate, and meet his stunned eyes as the realization sets in me.

He came so fast. Too fast. I barely put him in my mouth. Barely touched him.

"Bet your serpent girls can't do that." I don't know where I find my boost of confidence, but the way he's looking at me, I know I'm right. I know he comes fastest when he uses his hand and even then, it takes a good ten to fifteen minutes.

A feral look flashes across his face as he pulls his sweats back up from where they've been hanging on his thighs. In one motion, he yanks me up by the arms, lifting me clear off the floor. My legs wrap around his waist on instinct as he carries me to the bed.

Then he drops me onto the mattress on all fours. He doesn't give me a second to catch my breath. He pulls me toward him before I feel my ass press up against him. I turn my head to find his eyes already on me. He watches me to see if I'll stop him as he takes off my pajama pants and my panties with it. He tosses the pants aside but holds onto my soaking wet red thong.

Then his hand rubs my ass cheek, dangerously sweet, almost as if he's cherishing the feel. His gray eyes are dark and there's no trace of mercy on his sharp face before his hand comes down on my ass.

I cry out, my head falling to the bed as my back arches.

"No one's ever spanked you and it fucking shows," he says before his other hand comes down on my other cheek. My hand flies backward to cover myself, but he just grabs both of my wrists and pins them down on my back.

"No, please—"

"Please what?" he cuts me off. "You keep fucking pushing me."

"I literally stay out of your way!" I cry out as he spanks my throbbing ass again.

"And now you're mouthing off." *Slap*. "You're rude as fuck, always have been."

He repeats the actions of rubbing my burning ass and slapping it, alternating at first until I get used to it and he switches it up, having no particular pattern. I'm sobbing into the bed as each hit makes me wetter and wetter. My perked nipples brush against the sheets with each jolt, before he pulls me back to him by my wrists.

"This is what's going to happen when you kiss—touch—another person again." *Slap*. Then on the other cheek. *Slap*.

"Please," I beg him. I want him to stop, but…I love how his hand is gripping my wrists back, how I feel his hard dick brush against my pussy occasionally. I love that he's jealous for once—that he cares enough to be.

"Stop begging and start apologizing," he tells me through gritted teeth.

I clamp my jaw shut.

"No?" he asks. "Does my Veyara *like* being spanked? Is that why you're such a fucking brat all the time? You've been wanting me to spank you?"

I don't answer, because at this point I don't know. I've never been spanked like this—this is…confusing. He's not holding back and it hurts and I don't know if I love it, but I need it—from him.

"Oh, now you can't talk?" *Spank*.

I twist my arms and try to squirm free before his hand comes down on me again. But then I feel his weight on my back as his breath stirs against my hair, warm and slightly shaky from his anger and exertion on me. His voice rumbles low in my ear. "Before you decide to run away with a vampire…give me a chance."

"I didn't think you even wanted a chance?" I barely whisper through my panting breath.

He doesn't say more. Instead, he pulls away and grabs my legs again only to flip me over so that I'm on my back now, laid bare open for him. Then I watch him climb on the bed, pushing me further on it as he lowers himself down my body.

A slow smirk curves across his mouth, dangerous and devastating, not helping my arousal at all. He positions himself between my legs, nudging them apart with the press of his body.

My breath catches, heat flooding me. I stare at him, wide-eyed with my heart hammering. "What are you doing?"

His gray eyes glow in the dim light. His fingers trail down my hip, teasing with the faintest touch that sets every nerve on fire. "Taking my chance," he replies.

The way his hand lingers there—not rushing, not demanding—makes my pulse race even faster. I can feel the tension building in me, sharp and sweet, the anticipation as dizzying as the intimacy itself. His fingers find the soft skin of my inner thigh. *Fuck me.*

I should stop this. I should push him off…but I can't deny that I want him. I want to feel him again, and I know I'm asking for it this time.

"You think touching you repulses me," Josh says slowly, as he lowers himself between my legs, "touching you is fucking torture and I'm about to show you exactly how much."

His broad shoulders settle lower, the heat of his breath ghosts over my skin. His hands grip my hips, thumbs digging in, holding me open, exposed, as his mouth hovers just above where I'm aching, throbbing for him.

Then his tongue finds my clit, a slow swipe that ignites the fire, lapping at my slick heat. I let out a moan. His lips close around the swollen bud, sucking gently, and the sensation is a blinding shock, ripping a broken cry from my throat. My fingers tangle in his dark hair as he teases, flicking his tongue in sharp, precise strokes that make my vision blur. I feel the press of his finger—one, then two—sliding through the wetness of my pussy.

"Fuck, Rose," he murmurs against me, voice thick with awe, "spanking made you so damn wet for me, sweetheart, didn't it?"

I moan again. It's just something about the way he calls me sweetheart. It's not even a fancy or unique nickname. It's just *sweetheart* but fuck does it make me wet for him.

His fingers slip inside, slowly, testing, curling against the tight, pulsing walls as my body grips him greedily. The stretch is a delicious burn that mingles with the slick heat of his tongue, and I arch off the bed, a raw moan spilling from my lips.

He moves with intent now, his fingers thrusting, curling just right to make stars explode behind my eyes. The wet sounds of his fingers pumping into me as his tongue circles and sucks my clit, fill the room, mingling with my ragged gasps and his low, hungry growls.

"Josh—fuck—" his name is a broken sob I can't stop myself from crying out as my voice shatters while the tension coils impossibly tight, and I'm at the edge of insanity.

"The only name I want on your lips is mine," he thinks to me as he curls his fingers harder, a merciless stroke, and his tongue flicks my clit with a final, brutal precision before he sucks *hard*. ***"The only thing I want on your lips is me, because I'm only yours."***

The world explodes. Pleasure crashes through me, a violent, shuddering wave that rips a scream from my throat. My body convulses around his fingers, clenching tight as I come undone. "Fuck, Josh!"

"Yes, my name. You only know my name from now on," he continues his assault on my oversensitive clit, sucking and licking and rubbing it with his fingers now, working me through the aftershocks. His tongue savors every pulse, every tremor, until I'm a trembling, breathless wreck beneath him.

His gray eyes are nearly black, pupils slit with his basilisk primal hunger that pins me to the bed as fiercely as his hands do.

"Divine…your eyes…" I breathe, reaching for him, "so fucking hot…"

"Mmmm." He raises his head, lips slick and swollen from working me. His smirk turns dark and predatory promising utter ruin, and my core throbs, aching for more. "You never specified where I couldn't kiss you," he murmurs, his voice a low, gravelly taunt, thick with lust and a dark amusement that makes my heart gallop. His sexy, slit eyes meet mine, holding me captive, daring me to challenge him as his lips curl, sinfully.

"Fuck you," I gasp, attempting to glare at him but failing. "You're using your powers on me."

"Yeeeaahh," his smirk doesn't falter, "of course, I am. You fucking deserve it."

That was not meant as a reward.

Then his mouth is on me again, and it's fucking feral. His tongue plunges deep into my soaked pussy, thrusting hard, filling the aching void his fingers left behind. He's relentless, devouring me with a savage intensity, licking up every drop of my wetness like he's starved for it. My hips jerk, grinding against his face shamelessly, and he groans, the sound a primal rumble that reverberates through my core, amplifying the fire already consuming me. His hands grip my thighs, with a bruising strength, holding me splayed open for him.

"My powers aren't all bad," he says, lips brushing my clit before they close around it, sucking as if he's coming for my soul.

"Please—" I'm babbling, half-sobbing, my hands flying to his hair, trying to anchor myself against the storm he's unleashing as I feel my darkness leaking out and engulfing the room slowly.

He doesn't stop though, doesn't give me a second to breathe. His tongue thrusts faster, deeper, exploring my slick walls as his lips suck my clit with a punishing rhythm, drawing it into his mouth with a force that makes my entire body shake. My back arches, hips grinding against his mouth, my pussy clenching and pulsing around his tongue. He doesn't *stop*—his tongue keeps working me, his lips sucking, licking me like I'm his last meal. The pleasure is blinding, almost painful, dragging on until I'm a writhing, whimpering mess, but still craving more of him.

He pulls back, his lips glistening with my arousal, wearing a possessive smirk as he sees the black taking over my own eyes. He presses a slow, deliberate kiss to my throbbing clit, making me flinch and whimper.

"I don't need drugs to crave you," he clarifies.

Josh slides his fingers out of my dripping core, the wet drag leaving me clenching around nothing, desperate and empty. His eyes burn into mine as he sucks on his fingers, making my breath hitch and my pussy pulse at the sight of him tasting me.

"My sweet little Mate is so fucking delicious," he raises his fingers to my lips, his slit eyes daring me to object. "Taste yourself."

My breathing is ragged and uneven as he pushes two fingers into my mouth. Josh watches as I suck on them, letting out a moan as I do.

"Fuck, Rose, where the fuck did you learn to suck like that," he growls, possessively, but his eyes, dark and predatory, gleam with a savage satisfaction.

His lips return to my swollen clit, driving me closer to the edge. His tongue flicks, then plunges back inside, fucking me with a rhythm that's both cruel and perfect. My thighs tremble, trying to close, but he forces them wider, his shoulders a solid barrier as he buries his face deeper, nose massaging my clit as his tongue claims every inch of me. The tension builds and I'm spiraling, teetering on the brink of release.

"Please—I can't—" I'm begging, incoherent, my hands twisting in his hair as the pleasure becomes too much, too sharp.

I'm fucking begging.

He has me begging.

He pulls back just enough to flash that smug, smirk. Then he's moving. Away. He's moving away. Why is he moving away?

He moves with a slow grace, like the fucking snake he is, sliding up the bed to lay beside me. He pulls the blanket higher, cocooning us in its warmth. His arm slips around my waist, tugging me close until my back presses against his chest. I feel the hard length of his cock through his pants, unmistakable and firm against my ass, and a fresh spark of heat rushes to my core despite my shock of his denial.

He must sense my tension, because his lips brush my ear, his voice low and soothing, a stark contrast to the raw hunger from moments ago. "That's a small fraction of what touching you and not Marking you does to me, every time," he says, "so when I tell you to stop and step away, I'm doing *you* a favor."

I barely hear him because, Divine, his tongue. And his fingers. He didn't even have sex with me.

Is this what the girls feel when he's with them?

The thought breaks my heart. He's made girls feel like this—and more. He can use his powers to pleasure them. He's been doing it for as long as I can remember. If he actually is interested in them, he probably does more to make them feel good. I only get the visions when he fucks them, I have no idea what happens before or after…

Everyone always told me it's just his nature—it doesn't mean anything. That he can't help it. That he needs to.

That I shouldn't take it personally. But it is personal. It's fucking personal.

I moaned his name. I swore I would never say his name, never moan or scream his name like they did. A tear slips out from the corner of my eye as his lips find my neck and he sucks gently on it, careful not to pierce me.

He mumbles against my skin, "I'm keeping your panties, by the way. It helps me settle."

35 HIDEOUT

Josh Hunter
October 7

The scarred wooden bar in The Den is my desk today. Daylight leaks through the half-closed blinds, turning the place into almost respectable. I answer emails that never stop coming as the low sound of classic rock and clinking glasses surrounds me. I need the noise today, something to keep my thoughts away from a certain delicious Mate.

A body slides onto the stool beside me—too damn close to be a stranger. Daniel. He signals the bartender with two fingers, his voice rough as he orders. "Moonfire. Neat."

I glance sideways. He's tense, shoulders drawn tight under his leather jacket, jaw working like he's chewing on bad news. I raise an eyebrow. "Whiskey?"

He shakes his head. "Don't judge. It's a Monday."

I smirk, lock my phone, and set it face-down. "What's wrong?"

Daniel downs the drink the second it arrives, then taps the bar for another. He exhales. "Few Prides are spreading rumors. Word is Aradia's pulling her Inner Circle together. Planning something big—Lilith-level big."

That pulls my full attention. I frown. "Is there any truth to it?"

His second shot arrives. He cradles it instead of drinking. "Four Queens are dead. All in the span of twelve hours and the same totem left at every scene. All four Queens were at the Southern Pride Association and met up afterwards. All four Queens were spreading the rumors."

Ice slides down my spine at the mention of the totems. "Witches."

He nods once. "It was clean work too. No scent trails and they covered their tracks."

"Not just any witches. Sisterhood of Sin."

Daniel's brow creases. "Why the Hell would Lilith's followers defend rumors about Aradia? They're enemies."

I reach out, clasp his shoulder. "Maybe the Queens were hiding something worse."

He looks unconvinced but lets it drop. His gaze drifts to the bottles behind the bar. "How's Rose's training going? I hear she's sparring with Vanessa now?"

I arch a brow. I'm not telling him she hasn't been coming to training with me. "Yup."

"Personally, I don't think it's necessary. Not with her powers…" he trails off, searching for words. "Using her power is like breathing for her. She doesn't think about it. It acts before she can—like it's got its own mind, but loyal only to her," he considers, then adds, "she works with it, but it guards her first. Always."

"How do you know all this?" I ask, covering my envy with curiosity. Did she show him? I know they're friends, but did she confide in him about her powers growing up? I have yet to see her powers at full force.

Daniel's cheeks redden before he rubs the back of his neck. "When I was younger, I stumbled on Alpha Ian training her in the woods. I watched them for months. Shit I thought I was sneaky," he huffs a laugh, "got caught eventually. Alpha Ian made me swear to keep what I saw quiet. He said she was too young for the criticism, the pressure. She was my friend, so of course, I agreed, but I never saw them out there again—figured he moved her training deeper in."

"How old was she?"

"Ten. Maybe eleven."

"Didn't that strike you as strange? Powers that early?"

Daniel laughs, genuine this time, gray eyes bright. "Josh. Have you met Rose?" he leans in, voice warm with something close to awe over my Mate. "Everything about her is strange. That's what makes her badass. There's literally no one like her."

His words repeat in my head as I order another round of whiskey for both of us. I still don't know the extent of Rose's powers. I hadn't seen her lose control during our training sessions the handful of times she actually showed up—no matter how much I've provoked her. Even when she's pissed off, her powers don't leak out. My Mate has as much control over her magic as I do of mine.

But I want to see it—her eyes turning black and her powers running wild. I want to see her the way no one gets to. Her powers did surface when she was coming all over my mouth, but they disappeared almost immediately.

"Shit," Daniel says under his breath as he scrolls on Spellbook. I glance over and normally I wouldn't ask, but the picture of Rose catches my eye.

"What?" I question him and he pushes his phone to me.

I take the phone from Daniel's hand, thumb already moving across the screen before I can talk myself out of it.

It's a grainy candid shot of Rose at an outdoor training session—sweaty, hair wild, mid-motion like she's about to tear Antonio's throat out.

The caption is questioning her right to be the Veyara.

"She's been ignoring it," Daniel says quietly. "All of it. Just keeps training, keeps showing up." He rubs a hand over his jaw.

So she has been training, just ignoring our sessions it seems. Rose hasn't come to a single session with me since Antonio's reunion. She avoided me pretty well until Mabon forced us to…collaborate. We've been back from Romania for two weeks now and I haven't seen her once. I did schedule a training session today, but Vanessa informed me that she had a dress fitting. At fucking seven in the morning. Right.

I know she's hiding from what happened in Romania. Fuck, if I'm being honest, I'm hiding from what happened in Romania. I admitted I was jealous when I'm not supposed to care about her. I came the fastest I'd ever come in my life. I've only allowed myself to want her in the dark. Everyone thinks I hate her, but that one fucking kiss in her bedroom ruined everything. My carefully constructed walls are falling apart and it's getting harder and harder to stay away from her.

It's clear she doesn't trust me or my motives. I wish it was that simple. Hell, she has stronger walls than me at this point. The reunion and Romania was…fun, nice even. It was nice to be with her. To not hate her in those moments, to just have that stolen moment. I'm having a hard time associating the Rose I'm being pulled to with the one from six years ago and that's fucking dangerous.

I reach for my drink and throw it back.

Daniel looks at the post, disgusted. "People are cruel. She's eighteen. Eighteen. Most girls at that age are stressing about college apps and bad ID pictures. She's got a whole nation questioning whether she deserves to lead them."

My jaw locks so hard I taste blood.

I hand the phone back without a word, pull my own out, and start scrolling through social media and even the private serpent-only forums. It's everywhere.

I keep scrolling. Faster. The noise in The Den fades as my blood rushes to my brain.

I've seen this before. Different faces, same fucking script. My mother's face flashes behind my eyes for half a second—young, proud, always smiling through the whispers—and I shove it down hard.

"She's been getting torn apart more and more each day with the Gala getting closer," Daniel shakes his head. "She's a Craving, I don't get it. She can learn to shift into a serpent."

I keep scrolling. I shouldn't, but I do.

The algorithm knows exactly what to show me. Daniel's right.

It's a post from a girl I took to the rooftop club here in court a few months back. Juniper is the name I get from her Spellbook ID. The pictures are old, but they look fresh in the context—me with my arm slung low around her waist, her lips brushing my jaw, both of us laughing like the night wasn't going to end. I go to read the caption but—

The bitch had the nerve to tag Rose.

My jaw ticks as my temperature rises.

There's another. And another.

Dozens. Hundreds, maybe. All from girls I've fucked in the last four years. They're posting like it's a coordinated campaign. Old photos with new captions. Every single one dragging Rose's name through it like she personally owes them an apology for being my Mate.

My stomach twists. Not with guilt, exactly. I never promised any of them anything. Never lied. But seeing it weaponized like this—seeing my past used as ammunition against her feels shitty when I can still taste her on my lips, when I've been carrying her panty around in my pocket since I stole it.

"They're obviously doing this to take attention away from the Veyara Gala," Daniel says, then asks, "What are you going to do?"

"They can try but the Gala has always been a staple," I reply.

"I meant with Rose," Daniel frowns at me. "I thought you were supposed to be smart."

I turn my head to scowl at him. "If you have any suggestions, I'm all ears."

Daniel grunts. "Fuck no, I'm not stepping in that pile of shit. You're on your own. All I'm going to say is, those bitches have *nothing* on Rose. If it ever came down to it that is, she'd decimate them in a blink." He slides off the stool, drops cash on the bar. "Shit, I'd pay to see Rose get her revenge. Divine knows she deserves to be unhinged for the shit you put her through."

"Get out of my face," I tell him, but he makes a very interesting point.

"I was leaving anyway. Gotta make some calls about the Queens," Daniel raises his chin.

"Hey," I stop him as he starts to leave, "keep me posted about it? I want to know if there is a connection between Aradia's Circle and the Sisterhood of Sin."

"Sure thing, man," he nods before leaving. It is strange that four Pride Queens have been found dead. What do Prides care about Aradia's Inner Circle of witches to begin with? And why were the Sisterhood of Sin totems found at their murder sites?

My eyes drop to my phone again. I check the time before going through my following list and removing any useless accounts.

"You saw the posts too?" Devaughn slides into his brother's abandoned seat.

I shoot him a glare. "Creep much?"

"What? It's not my fault your attention is glued to your phone, and you didn't hear me," my shit eating asshole of a best friend says. He orders his drink before he starts scrolling on his own phone too, commenting. "Damn, the claws are coming out. Women."

"They're mad I didn't select any of them," I sigh heavily.

"State the obvious," he rolls his eyes at me, "but they knew if they weren't your Mate, you wouldn't. They knew what they were getting into. Did you?"

"I really fucking hate you, you know that?" I glare at him.

"You hate everyone," Devaughn waves me off, dismissively. The bartender slides his drink to him before Devaughn tells me, "You have to fix this before the Gala—with Rose at least."

I look up her account. It's been a while since I have. Usually, I just pull up pictures from my gallery. Rose's feed is mostly stuff she's been asked to collab on, but her personal posts are all things with the other Crescents. She doesn't post herself much, I notice. It's a little strange. Girls her age are obsessed with selfies. The posts of herself are from events she attended, clearly uploaded by Vanessa.

I wonder why she doesn't post herself. She has to know she's beautiful. Anyone with eyes can tell the Divine spent extra time on her.

"Damn, you don't even follow your own Mate," Devaughn, clearly snooping, shakes his head before his hand snakes over and hits the follow button.

I slap it away but it's too late.

He grins and holds his hand out. "Give me your phone."

"Fuck no," I reply. I don't trust his ass for shit.

Devaughn rolls his eyes before taking the phone from me anyway. He goes to my profile and edits my bio to read: Beta Warrior | Head of Serpent Nation | Mated to @cravingrose

"There," Devaughn says, the grin plastered on his stupid face.

Before he can hand my phone back, a text from Rose pops up. Devaughn gives me a triumphant look.

I snatch my phone to read the text. She never texts first.

The first text is a screenshot of my new bio. The second is a lot meaner.

Rose: *Delete it. I don't need your online pity.*

Devaughn is reading the texts over my shoulder. We need to have a fucking chat about boundaries.

"Don't reply," he says, "post her instead. Maybe I'll go live again if she decides to kick your ass."

A diabolical, caveman side of me wants to post her panties and call it a day. Unfortunately, that would create a PR mess for Sam and the kid's going though enough as it is with Rose being a Warrior. Posting her panties would not help anyone's case…

Instead, I post a picture of her stepping off the plane in Romania with me draped over her shoulders.

Caption: Thinking of entering every room like this. Thoughts @cravingrose?

"You're learning," Devaughn laughs, patting my back. "Guess there's hope for you after all."

I groan. "This is childish."

"She'll secretly love it," Devaughn says more seriously. "She's a girl. They like this shit. It's foreplay."

Foreplay.

Fuck.

I need to be between her legs again. I don't think I'll ever completely satisfy my craving for her sweet, dripping pussy…

Sure enough, @cravingrose comments back. Her user ID is appropriate, and I want her to change it. Only I'm allowed to crave her.

@cravingrose carrying you on my shoulders like I've been carrying this bond. What else is new?

Devaughn bursts out laughing, seeing the comment on his own phone. His fingers start flying across the keyboard and in seconds, I see his comment pop up.

@therealdevaughnclaws @cravingrose Now, now, Veyara, give @basiliskbeta a chance to be a man ;)

"Fuck you," I roll my eyes as my best friend snickers like a twelve-year-old.

"This is fun," he says, continuing to laugh.

I comment back.

@basiliskbeta @cravingrose that wasn't a no, sweetheart

"What are you playing at?" Rose telepaths and I smile a little. Maybe Devaughn does know what he's talking about—never admitting it to him though.

"Where are you?" I ask in return, putting my phone away and telling Devaughn, "I'm out of here."

"Really? James and Shane are coming," Devaughn says. I shrug, placing some cash down on the bar.

"Have to get back to work," I say, heading for the exit.

"Why?" Rose asks, suspiciously.

"I want to see you."

"Why?"

Why. I don't know, maybe because lately everything's been a little easier when she's around. Complicated as always, but easier. I also need to see her face. Make sure she's okay. She's good at faking it, like Daniel said, but judging by how she reacted after the tea party, it all affects her. She still cares—more than she'll admit.

"Have dinner with me," I think to her as I get into my car and head home.

"Are you asking me on a date?"

"No, I'm not giving you a choice. Have dinner with me tonight."

"No."

"Why not?"

She doesn't respond right away.

"I don't have dinner with snakes," she finally replies five minutes later. Okay, so she's mad.

"That's unfortunate since you're in bed with one," I send back to her with a smirk.

"I'm not in bed with—fuck you."

"We can make that happen tonight. Dinner, 7pm?"

She doesn't reply.

I've never had trouble asking a girl out, who knew my own Mate would be the most difficult. I'm learning that giving Rose space is the worst thing I can do. Space means she starts thinking and backtracking whatever progress we do make.

Probably for the best anyway.

This whole situation with Serpent Nation will die down eventually. Hopefully.

I crack my neck as thoughts of my mother creep in. It didn't die down for her. They never accepted her despite my father's efforts. She hid out in Coilspire. She loved Coilspire and raised Noah and me there, but it doesn't change the fact that she was hiding. She wanted a life away from court, away from the noise.

My father never cheated on her, so she didn't have that to deal with, but it got so bad for them they stayed out of the public eye. Kept us out of it too. It gave me the mysterious persona to work with when I reentered court life and became Beta Warrior.

I decide to call Evren Thane.

"Do you know what time it is?" he answers, gruffly.

"I call and you answer. I don't care what time it is," I reply as I send him a picture. "Find out who this woman is and keep it discreet."

I hear shuffling on the other end before he asks, "Who is she?"

"She was a seer at the Mabon festival. She knew something she couldn't possibly know. I need to find her," I answer him.

"Yes, Josh, seers tend to know those kinds of things, but let me guess, you're not going to tell me what it is that she knew?"

"You got it," I reply, "ask around. This takes priority."

"Everything's a priority with you."

"Good thing you're so good at multi-tasking, then."

He chuckles. "Alright, I'll let you know when I find something. She is a witch, yes?"

"Yes. She was fully witch."

"Okay. Hey, so the intel came back for Vassir's extracurricular activities," Evren tells me and he sounds much more awake now.

I'm passing the shopping plaza when I see Rose and the Crescents walking into a dress boutique. I don't think and pull into a parking spot.

I kill the engine and ask Evren, "Was it right? Are my Den Lords shaking hands with the Sisterhood of Sin?"

"Hey…not all your Den Lords," Evren replies, feigning offense. "Godric Veridane was onto something big. You were right to put him and General Tens on the case."

I shut my eyes. I didn't want to be right. Serpents always had a controversial reputation—but fuck, do we have to feed into it every time?

"They were investigating a Sisterhood of Sin Coven. Learning about Vassir was accidental. It was the last thing Godric told me," I say quietly. Godric was killed shortly after that intel and Vanessa was abducted. I'll never forget the grief on Lord Veridane's face when I had to bring him his son's body and tell him his daughter was missing. I'll never forget the day I had to tell James or how my best friend lost his mind for two years.

Rose went on the Tour for five months and I was ready to kill everything in sight. Shane and Devaughn told me to give her the space, but I hated every second of it. At least I knew where she was. I can't imagine what James went through for two years.

"I'm guessing that's what got him killed. I'm sorry, Josh. I know you were close to him," Evren says, somberly, "but you should know, Vassir can't be pulling this off by himself. He's sneaky and he has the means, but the execution isn't his style."

"Vassir likes to take credit for his handiwork," I agree. "Any leads on who he's working with?"

Evren snorts. "I have a good fucking idea, but I'll come with proof before I say anything. I'll let you know about the seer too."

"Be careful," I tell him, the dread creeping in. I've lost people since I've become Beta, but Godric hit hard. I can't lose Evren to this too. The asshole's grown on me.

"I'm touched you worry about me." Evren doesn't miss the opportunity to tease me about it. He laughs, but adds more seriously, "Should we tell Veridane yet?"

"Let's find every single person who was behind his son's death first. We'll serve them to him on a silver platter," I answer.

"I like the way you think. I've taught you well. Alright, we'll talk soon," he says before we end the call and I get out of my car to walk into the boutique.

"Beta!" a young woman bats her eyelashes in greeting. I glance around to see if I can spot Rose and the woman notices. "Can I help you with anything? If you're looking for the Veyara, she's in the back trying on the latest of the season. I can let her know you're here."

"No, no, let her do her thing," I say, and pull out my card, handing it to her. "Save this and charge whatever she gets on it from now on."

The woman smiles as she takes the card and inputs the information. Dad would always do things like this for Mom. He loved spoiling her even though she never needed or asked for much. He always made sure she was taken care of.

Things are complicated between Rose and me, but at the end of the day, she's mine. For better or for worse.

36 SAMHAIN

Rosella Craving

November 1

The Sanctum smells of sage and crushed marigold, heavy enough to sting the back of my throat. High Priestess Tiara's voice is low and calm as she pulls Eliza into her arms, whispering words I can't make out. But I see everything—the way my sister-in-law collapses against her, shoulders trembling, and openly crying.

I hate seeing Eliza break like this. She's always been the spitfire ball of energy in all of our lives. But now…she clutches her belly like she's trying to hold on to what's already slipped away.

My eyes burn. I fold my hands together and press them hard against my mouth. Silent tears stream down my own face as I watch her. While I cannot imagine Shane and Eliza's pain, I feel for them.

A pang of guilt passes through me because I knew. But what could I have done?

Twins are always a blessing or a curse—and I don't know how that's determined. It wasn't in my control. There was no saving them. If I told Eliza, it would've just solidified this same truth earlier for her. I would've been the one to tell her and cause her pain. It's better she found out the way she did—naturally. I know I took the coward's way out of this, and it'll always be something I have to live with. At least Shane and I talked about it.

When Lady Tiara finally guides Eliza to sit, it's my turn to step forward. My hands shake as I strike the match, watching the flame catch on the wick of my mother's candle. I light another for my father.

Then, for the first time, I reach for three more candles. The High Priestess watches me but doesn't say anything as I light them up. One for Josh's mother, one for his father, and one for his brother—all of whom he lost the same year. I've never lit them before. It didn't feel right when Josh and I were never on good terms.

This year though…even if things are new and unsure, it feels right for me to honor them.

I hope wherever Josh is—whatever way he's spending Samhain—that he's okay. I know he can't be, but I hope he's not hurting too much. I wish I could be with him, but grief is personal, I don't know if he'd want the company. It feels like an intrusion to seek him out.

Later, I walk Eliza back to her room. She feels heavy against me, the weight of her own grief weighing her down. Neither of us say anything.

I tuck her into bed, her hands curved over the baby that remains. Her eyes are hollow and I know she's not with me. Her mind is elsewhere.

I kiss her temple, ignoring the dark cloud surrounding her. "I love you. Get some rest."

She doesn't respond, so I let her be and close the door softly behind me.

I rush to my room and once I'm alone within my four walls, I let myself break. My back hits the door and I slide down until I'm sitting on the floor, knees pulled to my chest. The dam bursts, and the tears I'd been swallowing all morning rip their way out of me. My shoulders shake, sobs muffled against my arms. I cry for Eliza, for Shane, for the baby that will never take a breath, that we will never have the chance to meet. I cry for my parents and for myself for having to go through so much. When does it get easier?

The girls send texts in our group chat which I respond to quickly before falling on my bed. Vanessa sends a link.

I click it to see the *Pack Press* interview piece I did for the Veyara Gala and Samhain. I'll read it later. I don't have it in me to deal with any of it today. I tell her the same, to take the day off and not worry about Veyara things. She deserves the day to mourn and not worry about me.

But I find myself returning to the Sanctum, needing to feel closer to my mother, so I spend the day with Lady Tiara. I don't know how she does it, consoling everyone who comes through the Sanctum today, and keeps it together. As the Sun starts to set and we wrap up, Lady Tiara glides past me, her robes softly flow behind her as she walks over to the shelf that contains jars of Moon water.

"Do me a quick favor, will you?" she asks, but I know she's not really giving me a choice.

"What is it?" I go up to her.

She takes a moment before picking up one of the jars and brings it over to me. "Take this to the river and pour it out. Your feet need to be in the river when you do so."

I nod, taking the jar. I don't ask questions. I know better.

"It was nice to spend today with you, Veyara," she smiles softly at me, caressing my cheek, and I lean into it, desperate for a mother's touch today.

"I missed this," I tell her honestly and she nods, then I make my way to the back exit. It's closest to the river.

I pass the divination and apothecary rooms. Then the Mating Room comes up, taunting me. Every Warrior and their Mate complete the final part of their Mating ritual here. This is where the Marking happens. I don't know what it's like inside. No one does, until it's time for them to go through their blood-tie reunion. I pass it and then pass the last room which is a bath chamber for cleanses mainly.

The path behind the Sanctum carves through a wall of trees, down a gentle slope. The sound of water grows louder with every step I take until I see the river. I don't come here often, only on my dad's birthday really, since he loved it on the river.

As I get to the bottom, my steps slow when I see Josh standing waist-deep in the water. His back is to me, facing the setting Sun. His head is tilted back and eyes closed. The muscles across his back catch the Sunlight. His serpent tattoo on his arm glistens.

I see his shirt hanging off a branch nearby.

I don't know what he's doing. Meditating? Praying?

I can't look away.

He moves deeper until the water is up to his shoulders, then his neck—then he's gone, submerged under.

My breath catches as I wait for his head to pop back up.

It doesn't.

I wait.

And wait.

Panic claws at me as I feel the pressure building all around me—inside me. The jar slips from my fingers, landing with a dull thud on the stones as I run toward the water.

I don't like bodies of water I can't see the end or bottom of. My skin crawls as the current brushes against my ankles but I don't think—I jump in.

"Josh!" My voice cracks as I call out his name. It rolls off my tongue effortlessly even after I trained myself to not say it. I've been so careful to never let him hear me say his name—it's why I'm so mad at myself about Romania.

I make my way deeper, the cold biting straight through me. The water is freezing and the shock of it numbs me. I plunge under to try to look for him, but it's too dark. I come up and dare to go further out to where he was.

"Josh!" I scream again, terrified, looking around, then telepath him, ***"Josh!"***

Suddenly the water breaks in front of me. He comes up breathless and blinking against the spray. His eyes find mine, startled to see me. "Rose? What…are you doing here?"

I don't know when I started crying, but before I can stop myself, my hands slap against his hard chest.

"What the Hell were *you* doing?!" my voice is raw, fear shaking through me. He catches my wrists, his grip firm but not hurting, just enough to stop me from slapping him again.

"Rose," his voice is calm, "it was just a water cleanse. I'm fine."

Yeah, well, I'm not.

My whole body is trembling, and the tears won't stop even as I try to breathe. His eyes rake over me and he frowns—like it hits him all at once that I'm fully clothed, drenched, and terrified.

"Let's get you out of the water," he says, pulling me to him. One strong arm locks around me, and then he's cutting through the current with powerful strokes, carrying me to the bank like I weigh nothing.

The second we're back on land, I pull away from him.

He shakes his head. "What is wrong with you? You don't even like water and you just—" he gestures to me then the river, "you just jumped in fully clothed?"

Anger rushes through me. "Sorry, I didn't think to undress trying to save you."

"Save me?" he asks, shocked. "It was just a water cleanse."

"I thought you were trying to drown yourself!" I snap at him.

"Why the fuck would I—" he cuts himself off. He crosses his arms over his very naked, very broad chest and grins at me. "You were worried about me."

I roll my eyes as I look for the Moon water jar. "I won't make that mistake again."

He chuckles lowly. I don't know what he finds funny.

"I'm fine," he says.

"I can see that," I glare back, irritated now.

"Did you follow me?" he asks.

I pick up the jar and spin on him. "This might surprise you, but I really don't spend my days stalking you."

"So what *are* you even doing here?" he asks, glancing to the jar. "I know this isn't *your* Samhain ritual, because I've been doing this for years."

I start to go back into the water. "Lady Tiara asked me to do something for her. What are you doing out here?"

"Intention setting," he answers, raking his hand through his wet black hair. I hate that he looks—nope, not going there after what happened in Romania.

"For what?" I ask as the water comes up to my knees.

"To have faith," he says like it's an inside joke.

"Faith for what?" Divine, I sound like a broken record.

"That things will work out for us," he says softly. I turn my head to look at him.

"Really? You want us to work out?" I ask, shocked he just admitted that out loud. Since when? He said I killed his brother—I don't know what to believe anymore. I never believed it and Shane said I didn't, but he believes it. Those words came out of his mouth. Does he except me to just trust he's starting to move on from something so big?

He looks at the water around my legs before meeting my eyes and answering me. "We're kind of in this for life. You were right in Romania. I don't want to be miserable anymore either."

I don't know what to do with this. What does this mean? I give him a pointed look. "You sure didn't look miserable the past four years."

He mirrors my expression. "Looks can be deceiving."

I stare at him for a moment before asking, "So what? You don't hate me anymore?"

A dark look passes in his eyes. "Rose…I have to work through some things, but…you're kind of hard to hate."

"That's just the Mating bond talking," I wink at him to lighten the mood. That wasn't a no but at least we're talking now. "We'll see how you really feel after…well, you know."

I don't wait to see his reaction as a shiver runs through me and I realize I'm still standing in the freezing river water. I turn away from him, and close my eyes, taking a deep breath to ground myself—or try to. Water isn't…my thing, even though I'm a water sign. The grass, looking up at the stars…Betty—they help me connect more. But right now, I just think of my dad. What he would do.

Lady Tiara wanted me to do this for a reason.

I exhale, opening my eyes, fully aware that Josh is watching me. Then I tip the jar and the Moon water spills into the current around my legs.

I stand there a moment, letting the cold pierce through me before I walk out of the river. Josh isn't looking at me anymore. His focus is farther away. When I reach him, I turn to see what has him so interested and pray it's not a girl.

"What does he do out there?" Josh asks as we watch Shane release a small boat from the dock, taking the oars in his hands. He asked me in the morning if I wanted to go with him like he does every year, and like every year, I said no.

"No idea. You've never went with him?" I hug my drenched self and when Josh notices, he brings me closer until I'm flushed against him. Then I feel the warmth radiating from his body. He makes himself so hot, I'm sure it'll dry my clothes. It feels too good to pull away.

"He's never asked me," Josh replies. I'm surprised. When I don't add anything, he looks back at me and asks, "How are you?"

I blink, caught off guard. Has he ever asked me that before?

"It's been a hard day. Eliza…" my throat catches.

I look up at him. He's looking out into the water again. The slight breeze from the river ruffles his black hair as we watch Shane row off into the Sunset.

"How are you?" I ask him, gently.

He's quiet but I can see he's trying to think of how to answer me. The fact that he will answer me is big.

"Not okay," he finally says. I turn to face him as he continues saying, "I lost everyone in my family." His jaw hardens, like the words are a struggle to say. "Samhain makes it worse, just a reminder."

I touch his arm, sliding mine down to take his hand. Samhain is hard for most of us. Our confusion and hatred can wait because right now, I don't have it in me to fight with him or hold any kind of hard feelings. Right now, we both need a little bit of compassion.

"I know it's not the same at all, but you didn't lose *everyone*," I swallow, my voice softer, quieter now. "No matter what we are to each other, we're family. Our own family."

His thumb caresses the back of my hand. I give him a small, sad smile before getting on my tiptoes to kiss his cheek, but he turns his head at the last moment, catching my lips instead.

Years of bitterness, grief, and desire are poured into the kiss. It's raw and desperate as his hand fists in my hair while mine claws at his shirt. The river, the dock, the world, the dead themselves fall away until there is only this. Only him.

He pulls back just enough to murmur, "Is that how you really feel?"

"It's how I've always wanted to feel with you…I wouldn't have said it if it wasn't true. You are my family and I'm yours, whether you want me to be or not," I say to him. "We're not blood but—"

"We're more," Josh finishes quietly, wrapping an arm around me and I let him hold me. The words mean everything, but the way he's so vulnerable right now, means so much more. He pulls away and looks at me. "Let's go home and get you into some dry clothes."

I nod and he lifts me off my feet, carrying me away from the river. The heat from his body is already drying most of my clothes. I'd be lying if I said I hate it when he picks me up. I could get used to this.

I realize we're taking a different route and I ask, "Wait, where are we going? This is not—"

"My house is closer," Josh says, pecking my cheek. The Hunter Residence is a short walk from the river to the courtyard in the back. We're there in ten minutes and he pushes the gate open with his shoulder. The glow from the enclosed pavilion is the first thing that catches my eye.

Through the windows, I see that it's filled with black and white candles. Hundreds, maybe.

"What is that?" I whisper and he follows my line of sight.

"My altar for Samhain," he answers, his voice is low.

Sensing I want to see it, he places me on my feet. I step inside to the heat from the flames wrapping around me and the air thick with wax and smoke. It feels Holy and forbidden at the same time. He's turned the whole pavilion into a giant altar.

"Can I add to it?" I ask carefully. Altars are personal, with very specific intentions—I don't want to overstep.

He nods, curiosity in his gray eyes as he watches me.

I find a red candle on a shelf, and light it, using one of the lit white ones. Once placed carefully in the center of the altar, the flame burns bright against the black and white.

Red for passion.

For love.

For protection.

"May the ancestors guard our bond," I whisper then I return to Josh. He doesn't say anything, but he presses a kiss on my head as we watch the candle burn strong.

As the night goes on, my powers stir, feeling unsettled as if tightening its own guard around me.

37 STIR

Rosella Craving
November 2

I sit cross-legged in the clearing, the grass soft beneath me, Sunlight warming my skin as I draw in a slow breath. Nathanial is nearby guiding my meditation. My eyes stay shut, focusing inward, until his fingers weave gently through my hair, sending a shiver down my spine.

"Let your powers free, Rose," he murmurs, his voice low and encouraging. "Give them free rein. Freedom to roam, it's been too long."

I exhale and with it release my darkness. It expands like a waking storm, spreading through me, outward. With my eyes closed, I feel it all—the pulse of life in the earth, the rustle of leaves breathing in unison, the distant sounds of insects and birds. Whispers brush my ears, faint voices from the wind or the ground. I can't tell, but they're alive. Everything around me is full of energy. My body lightens, lifting slightly off the grass, floating in this cocoon of power.

Nathanial laughs, the sound rich and warm. "You're doing really good." His words ground me even as I drift. "Do your powers feel different since you shifted?" he asks.

"Not really," I reply, voice steady despite the levitation. "I haven't explored or used them much since then, either."

I take in everything my power allows me to feel, and I wonder what it'd be like to do this at court. I know I can make my powers do little things, like unlock doors, fetch things, pick up conversations, but I usually have to focus to do those things. I hope one day I'll just be able to think it and it'll do it.

It's strange because I know if it ever comes to protecting me, my powers don't need to be commanded, they just know what to do. However, small tasks require more concentration and I wonder why that is. Maybe I just need more practice.

But just then everything shifts. My power coils inward, tightening like vines wrapping around me, forming a barrier. It's protective, instinctive, pushing against something. The whispers grow urgent, a warning in my veins.

"What's happening?" Nathanial's tone sharpens, concern edging in.

"I don't know." I keep my eyes closed, probing the sensation. "Something's wrong. The energy's off. They're triggered for some reason."

"Why?"

"I don't know—it's not like they talk to me." The feeling crashes over me—I'm not safe here, in this moment. My heart races as I force the power to settle, pulling it back inch by inch until my feet touch the ground again.

"I'm feeling tired," I say, opening my eyes at last to meet Nathanial's gaze. "I don't know what that was. It's never done that."

He nods, expression unreadable. "That's enough for today. Go rest."

I brush off the grass, the Sunlight now feeling too bright. "What happened? Did you see anything?"

"Nothing," he answers, frowning, "they must've picked up something even I couldn't feel."

"Is that…weird?"

He chuckles, "No, it's refreshing." He turns toward the path leading away from Cravenhold. "I'm heading up to my cabin for Samhain. Enjoy your Gala."

"Thanks, enjoy your solitude," I say lightly as he leans in to kiss my forehead.

38 VEYARA GALA

Rosella Craving
November 2

"Her Royal Highness, Veyara Rosella Sophia Craving Hunter!" the herald announces.

The doors open, revealing the green and yellow light against the dark. I take one step forward, then another. My lady's maids follow, keeping a respectable distance so as not to crowd me. Every eye in the ballroom lifts to me. Shifters, vampires, witches, Nephilim, angels…I feel my sense heighten with the different energies.

They all came—answering the call, whether for unity or scandal. My father dreamed of this once—all factions of the supernatural under one roof in the open, breaking bread, spilling blood, sharing power.

Granted, he probably didn't plan it the way I have, but I'd like to think this is a step in the right direction.

My gown whispers as I move forward, looking down at the party before me from the balcony as a green spotlight shines on me. The black silk of my dress swallows the light, streaked with veins of green lace curling up. The neckline is daring enough to tempt, but not enough to bare me. My hair cascades around me in voluminous curls, simply decorated with the Veyara crown.

The music dies down as a server presents me with a black goblet. I glance at Vanessa, who nods, before I take it and thank the server. He disappears silently.

I lift the goblet like I've seen Nathanial do on countless occasions. "Welcome, honored guests. Family, friends, enemies pretending not to be enemies," a ripple of laughter cuts through the tension. I smile, "Tonight, you're all under one roof. Supernatural of all kinds. You're brave to be here and I appreciate bravery. If you've got fangs, fur, fire, or magic in your veins—you're welcome at my table," my smile widens, sweet and daring, "and I promise, I've set it well."

A few chuckles stir, but the room is listening as I tip the goblet in my hand.

"Politics may have brought you here, sure. But where's the fun in that? Life is too short—unless you're a vampire or angel," another round of laughs, "and the threat of war is always too close to waste a night pretending restraint," I sweep the room with my gaze, letting it linger just long enough, "so drink your humans, indulge in the drugs, fuck on the floor if you want. Show me you won't waste this precious life you've been given—because that's what it all comes down to. That's what we stay fighting for." Murmurs rise, but I'm not done, "Anything you could want—I have provided for you. Take advantage. You're the Veyara's guests! Let's make it a night we'll come back to in our wildest fantasies."

I drink from the goblet as the ballroom thunders with cheers and praises. Chalices are raised as I start to descend the staircase with my girls. I make my way through the crowd toward the thrones while greeting as many as I can. The music starts up again. The runway stretches out before me like a path to the thrones. Dancers wear nothing but paint, feeders are collared and waiting, and poker tables are gleaming gold in the dimness.

The space has been rearranged for my Gala. Emerald silks drape the walls and shield the alcoves, black lace hangs from the ceiling and connects to chandeliers. The twin black Hunter thrones have been brought in, replacing the Craving and Nathanial's.

They wait for me, towering over the dais, massive and uncompromising, carved from deep black stone that seems to swallow the light around it. Serpents coil through every inch of its structure. Thick-bodied, powerful forms overlap and intertwine in careful symmetry. Their heads rise along the back and arms of the throne, jaws parted just enough to suggest a warning. The serpents on the armrests are larger than the rest, their heads resting right where my hands will, and their bodies coiling around the front legs of the throne. Each serpent is polished to a dark sheen with ruby eyes, as if the snakes might come to life if stared at too long.

Fresh red roses bloom between the serpents, placed with care for the Veyara Gala. It reminds me of Josh's arm tattoo and I smile. At the crown of the thrones, a white wolf's head emerges, regal and severe, representing the Beta Warrior. Its eyes are formed from faceted crystals that catch the light and throw it back in sharp, prismatic flashes. The seat of the throne is cushioned in black, designed with intricate silver thread bordering the elongated backrest. The usual golden wall behind the thrones has been covered with a black and green backdrop and the House Hunter emblem.

They are intense and imposing—meant to make the Beta look like a threat. The Alpha is regal, respected. The Beta is meant to be seen as a protector, someone who will go to any lengths to safeguard the Alpha and the Pack. The thrones are breathtaking and it's been so long since I've seen them together, since the last time Cedric and Helena Hunter sat in them.

I picture Josh there, waiting—sharp and lethal, his gray eyes watching my every move—and I know when he steps in here, the entire room will bow to him. But for now, it's mine.

When I reach the dais, I turn, letting the gown spill across the steps as I sit, feeling very small against the intimidating throne. The murmurs turn into conversations, clinking of glasses, as the party begins.

My lady's maids make themselves comfortable on the dark cushioned couches around the dais as servers bring us drinks. I see Camille give me a nod, before I flick my hand, and the lights go out.

Darkness swallows the room whole. My darkness—dense and suffocating. Gasps ripple and I feel them straining, hearts racing, their breaths catching, choking under the pressure I apply. Some drop their glasses while others reach for those closest to them.

And then I let go.

The chandeliers flare alive with emerald flashing lights, and music erupts through the speakers. Spotlights slice across the runway, flashing green, blue, and black. The Master of Ceremony's voice booms above.

"Behold—the Veyara Collection!"

The first model struts out, lace clinging to her and silk flowing like liquid. Cheers, whistles, applause vibrate through the air. The runway comes to life, fabric shifting between black, emerald, and royal blue.

Sam selected a few trusted fashion magazines to cover it and everything they document will be turned over to us before they leave. They'll get it back once it's approved. It'll be the only photos allowed from tonight.

Mariella and Daniya find their way to me and I hug them. Their dresses are beautiful. Mariella's is black, as always, and Daniya's is a shimmery gold—it's customary for the Crescents to wear their House colors to show the House's support for the new Veyara.

"That was a Hell of a speech, Veyara." Mariella grins.

"Forget the speech, the blackout almost caused a war, people thinking you set them up," Daniya laughs, and then nudges me, "nothing like a little breath-play to start a party, right?"

I laugh, that was the point, so they can get a taste of my power. Let them whisper about that. "Make sure to snag a feeder," I tell my friends. AB neg is stocked and on tap—alongside the feeders. I had an additional hundred and fifty bought, just to be safe.

"Already done," Mariella replies, handing me a drink. "The Veyara and Freaks? Interesting choice of names for your specialty cocktails."

I wink, smiling big. "Had to keep it fun."

Daniya leans closer and hands me a small golden box. I look at her before opening it to find the prettiest bluish-purple rose petal. I smile at her before placing it on my tongue. Last time I had any drugs, it was Mariella's reunion.

"Fuck, I missed it," I sigh, blissfully.

"Half the room's already on something," Daniya smirks at me, "I'd say this Gala is a success."

"The night is still young, but I might have to agree with you," Mariella laughs, clinking her glass with Daniya.

"You're about to be the Veyara of indulgence," Daniya fans herself.

I notice Cristobal and Franklin standing nearby, no doubt on full alert. They have to be with so much bloodlust and drugs in attendance here tonight. I relax a little when I spot my two trusted ex-bodyguards.

My skin tingles as Petal mixes with my blood. I chase it down with the cocktail. Mariella and Daniya hang around the dais, close to me. I let little whispers of darkness roam around to see if they pick up any juicy information. No one will even notice with all the flashing lights and smoke anyway.

"Devaughn and Daniel came through with the party favors. VelFlame, Howler's Breath, Crownshade—the two that were named after you—Glass Rose and Petal, of course," Daniya wrinkles her nose, adding, "we left out LB—don't need anyone going that crazy indoors."

LB is LunaBite, a drug that heightens our animalistic forms for a time period but leaves the user a little crazed and unstable. It's very addictive because it mimics the full Moon's pull. It's popular with the masochists.

Beyond the runway and the fashion show, I see feeders bare their throats. A vampire tips a girl back across his lap, feeding slowly as she moans, his hands are everywhere. At a nearby table, cards scatter across green felt while coins, jewels, enchanted and expensive items stack high as wagers. A witch laughs as she wins, her opponent throwing back a glass of something in defeat.

On the far side, two shifters grind against each other, their teeth flashing as they drink from the same feeder, crimson blood spilling down their chins and the feeder's body. No one even looks at them a second time. No one blinks.

The whole room promises scandal. Shifters have never hidden affection or our primal urges, but this…this will be different. It'll be dark enough that anyone could get away with anything, and indulgent enough that they will want to.

Royal court meets underworld nightlife.

Daniya follows my gaze and smirks. "We're sheltered from so much before we shift, right?"

I smirk back at her. "Speak for yourself, Crescent Claws."

She gives me a knowing smile in return.

He won't be here. Even if it wasn't Princess Tia's funeral and Samhain weekend—he was never going to be here. I wouldn't want him here—alliance or not. Tonight's about the title the Divine gave me through Josh.

Almost everyone RSVP'd. Elder Salvatore and my aunt have declined their invites. Eliza and Shane are also not in attendance tonight. The Alpha never attends the Veyara Gala because it's meant for the Beta couple. Eliza was still going to, in support of me, also it's good PR for the Luna to give her blessing to the Veyara—no one wants problems between that dynamic.

With the loss of the baby and the healers telling her to take it easy, Eliza decided not to attend. Of course, I understand. I wouldn't expect her to, but it makes me sad knowing one of my favorite people won't be here.

Nathanial also declined, saying he wants me to have my night. We talked about it. If Nathanial is there, he'll be the focus, and he doesn't want that. It's not personal, he's never attended the Luna or Veyara Galas before for the same reasons that the Alpha doesn't attend.

The press is set up in the front, along with the red carpet photoshoot, but everyone is checked and electronics are confiscated before they enter the ballroom. It was one of my non-negotiables.

I watch as a vampire and wolf shifter toast each other across the runway, both with fresh blood dripping from their lips. A witch blows smoke—Howler's Breath—from her palm.

"The guest list caused some drama though, I heard," Mariella voices, "shifters of all kinds, vampires, witches, Nephilim…could be a recipe for disaster…"

"That's why we have security," I assure her, "no cameras, but the Royal Guard are present and undercover. The list is intentional. I didn't want to exclude critics. They can talk, but one thing will be obvious after the Gala," I say with a smile.

A feline and wolf shifter fight over dominance with their mouths. Everywhere there's excess of indulgence.

"What's that?" Daniya asks.

"They say I'll tear us apart, incite civil war," I sigh, running my fingers over my dress, "but they'll see the inclusivity, the acceptance."

"The Veyara way," Daniya smiles, raising an eyebrow, "could be a new hashtag."

"Your father dreamed of unity," Mariella says, before letting out a laugh, "but I don't think he had this in mind."

This is already happening in the underworld, on the streets. Royalty wants to be high-nosed about what they, themselves, indulge in the dark. This isn't about exposure, it's about acceptance—about creating a space to be open with our hearts' desires and not be ashamed of it.

I take a sip from my glass, watching the beautiful chaos unfold. "Let them have it," I say quietly, "nothing's off the table tonight."

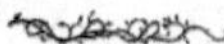

The fashion show ends and the bands take over the runway. I finish my drink and before I can set it down, another is pressed into my hand. It's green with swirling dark red and Moon's Kiss shimmer.

I look up at Daniya and she smirks, "Freaks."

I laugh and cheers her before taking a sip, immediately tasting the Nightthorn scotch—Josh's favorite. I drink deeply. It's sweet, almost like candied apple.

The music sinks deeper, each note vibrating through my chest, through my skin, until I can feel it in places I shouldn't. Heat spreads in waves, chasing down my thighs. My fingertips tingle, restless, itching for contact. I curl them into fists against the armrests of the throne, but it doesn't help—I want to touch, to feel.

I want my Mate.

The thought of Josh makes my nipples tighten beneath the lace of my gown, the fabric teasing my sensitive peaks. My clit throbs with each base note, like the music is being played on me.

I'm definitely feeling the effects of Petal now—and the drinks I lost count of. Around me, the room unravels. A shifter pins a feeder to the wall, teeth sinking into her neck as he thrusts against her, both of them moaning and grunting—and I'm jealous. Of the feeder. My whole body is buzzing, desperate. I swallow hard, pressing my thighs together, but that doesn't help.

The MC's voice booms between sets, announcing the Beta and the Warriors as if knowing I'm ready for my Mate.

"About time," Daniya whines and I wonder if she was feeling the same way.

The doors open, and Josh steps through first—broad shoulders covered in a Warrior blue cloak. Thick white fur is draped over his shoulders, a nod to the white wolf we shift into. That's all he's wearing with a pair of black slacks, leaving his top half exposed. As he walks, I catch glimpses of his tattoos peeking through.

Divine, help me.

The Warriors are behind him, dressed similarly.

"Heard there's a party going on!" Josh calls out, his voice carrying over the crowded ballroom as a grin spreads across his face.

He greets a few people as the Warriors scatter, finding their Crescents. James immediately grabs Vanessa by the back of her neck and kisses her open mouth. Daniya and Mariella leave me to go to their Mates.

My eyes focus back on Josh, who doesn't break stride, heading straight for me. My pulse spikes as I sit taller, every inch of me still buzzing—but now with excitement.

Why does he have to look so damn good?

As he nears, I say, "I saved you a seat, my Beta."

But he only smirks.

In the next breath, I'm off my feet—scooped up in his arms, before he drops onto *my* throne, placing me on his lap. My gown spills around us—covering us.

He turns to those watching us, smiling deviously and says, "Now the party can *really* begin—the Warriors have arrived!"

The music starts again and the girl band, Vesper's Cry, takes center stage. It's an upbeat, pop group perfect to get people in the mood. The lead singer starts them off with the song *Kiss the Serpent.*

I twist in Josh's lap, flushed, cross-faded, heat crawling everywhere, and tell him, "You have a perfectly comfortable throne right there." I gesture to the throne next to us.

Josh and I have never partied together the way I have with Daniel and Daniya, so this might turn out to be an interesting night—in more than one way.

He leans into me, face burying into my hair. "Did you think I couldn't smell you?" his voice is low, meant only for my ears. "Your arousal, my Veyara, I can practically taste it." My cheeks warm thinking of Romania, *remembering* what his tongue and fingers can do. "There's no chance I'm letting a fucking chair get a *drop* of you," he promises.

Before I can say anything, his hand catches my jaw, turning my face to look at him.

I think he's going to kiss me, but he stops—holds back, searching my face. I frown, what is he waiting for?

"I'm not going to take anything you don't want to give me tonight, Rose," his voice cuts through my hazy mind, so loud it takes me a second to realize his lips never moved.

I stare into his eyes—beautiful gray, almost silver with hunger and want…he wants me.

He *wants* me.

And he's asking permission. He's never asked permission.

"No mind games tonight," he adds, his voice in my mind again. ***"I promise, as a Warrior and your Mate."***

Clever of him to add that because as a basilisk, he'd say anything. I don't know if I can ever fully rule out mind games from a master manipulator but…I want to tonight.

He can sense my hesitation though and places a soft kiss on my forehead. ***"You're my Mate. Let me show you what that really means."***

Maybe it's me starving for him or maybe it's the drugs, but I cup his face and lean in a little to whisper against the loudness of the ballroom. "Kiss me, Josh."

His mouth crashes against mine the moment the words leave my mouth—hungry, claiming, tasting like smoke, wine, and something sweet. I part my lips and his tongue eagerly slides in, melting me.

Josh breaks away to say in my ear this time, "Come on my pants if you have to, but every drop of you is mine tonight. Do you understand me, *Veyara*?"

My mind goes blank and all I can think about is how I feel his hard cock pressing against my ass through the barriers of our clothes. My body is oversensitive right now and I want him.

I *need* him.

Realizing he's seriously waiting for an answer, I nod.

"Use your words," he says, narrowing his eyes a little. "Tell me you understand."

"I understand," I answer, breathless.

He raises an eyebrow, "You understand what?" Bastard's going to make me say it. Some things don't change.

"I understand every drop of me is yours tonight, my *Beta*," I reply with a sweet smile, blinking innocently. Two can play this game—despite what he wants to say. It's cute that he did, but one of us will always be playing something. It's who we are.

"Good girl," he whispers back before his lips claim mine again. His free hand trails down slowly, letting me feel every inch he touches. My skin burns, every nerve alive, and waiting for more—wanting more. His fingers move lower, parting the silk of my dress just enough to slip his hand in. He pushes my thighs apart subtly before a sharp pinch to my clit makes me jolt, a gasp tearing from my throat before I can stop it. My thighs press together, trapping his hand there.

He doesn't seem to mind. "Easy."

I pull away from his lips. "That's not fair."

His laugh rumbles against me, wickedly. "All's fair in love and war," his tongue licks my ear, "and something tells me being in love with you…will be war."

My eyes sharpen for a moment.

In love?

We've never said anything about love. I look at him. I'm too gone, too wrapped up in the haze of drugs and desire, to pull it apart and really let it sink in—if I even heard him correctly.

Fuck, my mind is the one who will be playing games with me tonight.

I blink hard, trying to focus, but his fingers caress lower. Slow and teasing, running up and down my slit, feeling how wet I am for him.

"Fuck, sweetheart," he whispers against my neck and slides two fingers in me.

The stretch makes me bite my lip hard and my head tips back

against his shoulder. My breath breaks into short gasps as the sultry song takes me to a wonderful place in my mind while his fingers work me.

I don't know what turns me on more—that he's pleasuring me right here on the throne where everyone can see, or that he has no shame at all doing it.

He is a serpent shifter, my mind reminds me, but before my brain can ruin this for me, we have company. Devaughn, Crystal, and Daniya are coming up the dais, laughing at something Daniya said. I try to sit up, try to tug at my dress and push Josh's hand away. Josh only growls low in my ear, pressing me down harder onto his lap while his fingers never leave me. I'm just glad the music is loud enough to not hear the slick sounds of his fingers moving in and out of me.

"We should—" I start, voice breaking.

The three of them immediately pick up on what's going on and Daniya comes up behind the throne, saying, "Relax, babe," her hands settle lightly on my shoulders, pulling them back to rest against Josh. She leans down to whisper in my ear, "This is your party. Own it, like you told them to."

She starts to stand straighter and Josh looks up at her, asking, "What did she take?"

"Just a few drinks with Moon's Kiss," Daniya's eyes sparkle with mischief, "…and Petal. She likes that one. And a few of the specialty cocktails."

Josh's lips curve, fingers curling inside me as his thumb rubs circles on my clit. He asks her, "Can she handle more?"

Daniya looks as positively offended by the question as I feel. "Rose can handle a lot more," Daniya assures him.

Crystal steps forward then, holding a small vial in her hand.

Daniya raises an eyebrow. "What is *that*?"

"2Fangs," Devaughn answers, and looks at Josh, "you sure?"

My heart races with excitement and fear. I've heard of 2Fangs—it's a cross-species drug made of vampire venom and shifter tears. It's gross if you think about it, but it's mixed with AB neg and the high can be…otherworldly if taken the right amount—or wrong. It's supposed to create overpowering lust and bond illusions that can lead to very, very dangerous entanglements.

Like Josh and me tonight if I take it.

We haven't Mated—this could very likely lead to that. Is that what he's trying to do? He's trying to drug me into Mating with him? *Would* he do that? After saying he won't take anything I don't give? Is that why he's been super nice to me since Mariella's reunion?

My heart drops to my stomach as I go eerily still on his lap. So much for no games.

Josh notices, and tells our friends, "Give us a second." They nod and talk among themselves as Josh kisses my shoulder. "Hey, do you trust me?"

Is he serious?

"No," the answer is immediate before I can stop myself. Wow, I am scared.

"That's hurtful," Josh replies but I hear the tease in his voice. I look at him and he says, "I'm going to do it with you, but we don't have to. I won't let it go too far."

"Have you done it before?" I ask him and every part of me prays he says no. 2Fangs is a sex drug. There's no other reason to take it.

"No, love," he answers and I hate that I don't trust him to be honest as my powers double check. I've never used my powers on him like this before, but all bets are off. I don't want us to Mate like this, not after he kept saying it's not to be taken lightly. I have to protect myself, even from him—especially my mind and body, because he's not above using either against me.

But tonight, I don't sense any deception, but I do feel something that reminds me of the forest after it's just rained and cinnamon rolls. It's a feeling I sense when I'm around the other Mates.

Love.

That in itself confuses me enough to retreat my powers. It can't be right. Josh isn't in love with me—he doesn't love me. I don't understand it.

"I'm sorry," I say to him quickly, knowing he saw my eyes change, but he just answers me with a kiss.

"If you need to check my soul to erase any doubts you ever have," he kisses me again, "do it whenever you need to."

What is he *on*? This is not Josh Hunter.

"Okay," I whisper, resting my forehead against his, as his fingers move inside me again, causing me to shift as the feeling goes straight to my nipples, perking them up again. "I'm trusting you to not…take it too far," I say, quietly.

He smiles and kisses me, before breaking away and calling our friends back.

Crystal stands over us, holding the vial over Josh's mouth and telling him, "Open up, Beta."

I watch her let two drops fall on Josh's tongue and am a little jealous of how comfortable they are with each other. I know they're all close, and I wish Josh was like that with me. What he said in Romania about watching my life from the outside goes both ways.

He turns to me, bringing my mouth to his, and then kisses me deeply. His tongue dances with mine and I immediately taste the salty sweet and a little bitter drug before swallowing it.

Heat floods my veins and my body feels like pins and needles straight away.

"Let it settle for a little bit," Devaughn advice as Crystal leans into him, then he smirks at Josh. "Told you giving into your Mate is better."

Josh flips him off, laughing, though I'm not entirely sure what that's about. He doesn't let me think about it either. His fingers inside me move like they have a point to prove, and I let my back arch into him.

Crystal fans herself with one hand, cheeks flushed, eyes shamelessly fixed on me writhing in Josh's lap. "Divine," she murmurs to Devaughn, "they're so hot together, they're turning me on."

Devaughn's eyes darken as they fall on his Mate. His hand slides around her, grabbing her breast, thumb brushing over her nipple through her gold silk dress. Crystal shivers, leaning into his kiss, their mouths colliding with hungry familiarity even as his hand cradles her protectively—possessive of both her and their unborn baby.

"Alright, it's time I find Daniel before I make myself comfortable here," Daniya winks at me as she smooths her dress, "and you two—" she nods at Josh and me with a smirk, "—don't do anything I wouldn't."

I tip my head back, breathing in pants, "That's…a very short list."

Josh chuckles, kissing my neck, his fingers exploring inside me. He drags them up through my slickness until they circle my clit lazily like he has all the time in the world, then he brings it back down. Over and over and over again.

He kisses just below my ear. "Do you see anything you like?"

I try to focus. Wolves tangled with feeders on the floor. Vampires buried deep in witches—is that a group thing going on in the far corner? A pair of witches inject each other with a drug. Crystal moans softly against Devaughn's mouth as his hand slides lower, and I realize I'm staring. I shift my gaze to see James downright fucking Vanessa on a table and they have an audience. Josh's thumb presses harder on my clit, dragging a gasp from me.

"Everything…" I answer, closing my eyes and letting myself enjoy him.

"Hmm," he seems to agree, before he pinches my clit making me jolt again.

"Welcome to my world," I tell him with an easy smile.

He raises a dark eyebrow. "Your world?"

"Mmmm," I reply, not giving him anything more.

Then his hand leaves me and I almost whine at the loss. He licks his fingers so casually like he just finished a meal and reaches past me for a cluster of blood-pumped grapes.

He brings them to my mouth. "Open."

I obey without thinking. The grape bursts on my tongue, sweet and decadent, the juice running down my throat. He feeds me another, and another.

He pops the last one into his own mouth before reaching for a sliver of cured meat, pressing it past my lips with two fingers. I suck them clean on instinct, and his eyes narrow, cock twitching under me.

"Easy, Veyara," he says low, but amused. "You can't fade too fast. Passing out on your own gala would be scandalous."

He takes a drink from his goblet as I swallow my bite, licking the tang of salt and blood from my lips. He kisses me then and AB neg rushes into my mouth.

I don't know how this man is making food sexual, but I devour it all.

39 FIVE DROPS

Rosella Craving
November 2

A deep gong echoes through the ballroom, and I look over to see the MC striding forward on the stage. "Ladies and gentlemen, blood drinkers and beasts, ancients and newbloods—we have a special auction line-up just for you!"

Murmurs rise as curiosity takes over. I sit up straighter, angling for a better view."

"But the Veyara won't be taking your money. She'll be taking your blood to cash in later for a favor at her will," the MC smirks, "and trust me, the items she is offering, are worth that risk."

I feel Josh's eyes on me and when I look at him, I find admiration. He's impressed.

"I'm a spoiled princess," I say with a small smile. "Of course, I was going to use an event like this to collect my one-of-a-kind prizes."

Camille gave me the idea when she gave me her own vial of blood. I hear Crystal ask Devaughn, "Can she do that?"

Devaughn glances at me then to Josh and smirks before answering Crystal, "She's the Veyara. And a Craving. Who's going to stop her?"

"But," the MC continues, and this time he looks toward Josh and me, "we have a few items here that maybe even the Veyara might be interested in."

That catches my attention. That's a last-minute change that I did not approve.

"Everything okay?" Josh murmurs.

"I don't know, there shouldn't be items on the auction I didn't approve of beforehand," I tell him in a low voice.

Now, Josh sits up too, alert. "Let's just see where this goes..."

The first item is revealed and it's a jeweled quill pen with a blood red feather. It's enchanted, I can feel the magic emanating off it. It was an item I found years ago, but the High Priestess said the one who wields it can change an outcome immediately—but only once.

Most of these items were things Nathanial and I went through to see if I wanted to put it up for the auction. If they were valuable enough for someone's blood.

Bidding begins. Whoever offers the most drops of blood, wins the item.

"This is genius," Josh murmurs against my shoulder.

"And dangerous," Devaughn adds, but the excitement is clear in his eyes, "way to go, Veyara. James is probably seething that he's never come up with this idea before."

I settle back into Josh's lap as I wait to hear of an item I didn't approve of. It isn't until the fifth item before a stone is introduced. Something about dream-walking. It's curious, but not enough for me to continue entertaining it.

"Anything you want, my Veyara?" Josh leans into my ear, lips brushing me as he whispers.

I look at him, interested. "Are you offering?"

"I know you won't take my money, but I'm sure you can't resist me spilling blood for you." Oh…he's clever. I see what he did there. I found out he tried putting his card on file at my favorite shops and as much as that made my heart flutter, I haven't spent a single cent of his. It was sweet, and while money is no object for us, it doesn't feel right to spend his yet.

I don't want him to think he needs to take care of me and that's all I am going to be—a girl who is spoiled and needs a man. I don't want to be a trophy wife. My dad and now Shane, taking care of me is different. They're my family. Josh has made enough comments about me being spoiled over the years that I know that's all he's ever thought of me, of course I wasn't going to let him buy me anything. He's already obligated to be my Mate, I don't want him to feel obligated to do anything else, not if he doesn't value me.

But if he pays with blood…now that's a big sacrifice for him.

I smile but shake my head. "Maybe the next item."

The auction goes on for another twenty-five minutes before a glass case is brought up. The MC does not open it, but from here I see that it is a jewelry piece.

"Once said to adorn a powerful witch," the MC begins, "this necklace has hidden, untapped powers of protection."

A hush spreads through the room, as the vampires glance at one another and the witches look suspicious but there's a longing in their eyes.

I lean forward, my pulse pounding. I don't know why, I usually don't have reactions like this toward things. My fingertips ache to touch the necklace.

"That one," I whisper.

Josh glances at me. "Really?"

"Yes," my voice is firmer this time. "I want it."

His lips twitch, but he doesn't seem sure. I sigh and start to get up to bid on it myself, but Josh clamps me down, pressing a grape to my lips like a pacifier.

"Okay, okay," he replies, kissing my temple before looking at Camille.

Camille walks over to the MC and whispers in his ear before the MC grins. "The Beta's put in first bid! Starting at five drops."

"Five!" I whisper-exclaim to Josh.

"You said you wanted it," he replies simply and terror courses through me.

"Yes, but you don't know who put it up for auction!" I tell him, shocked.

The MC calls it out two more times but there are no takers and the item is sold to Josh. Camille will take care of the exchange.

"There, it's yours," he pecks my lips, "though Divine knows you'll probably use it to curse me or something."

It's a joke, but I can't seem to remember how to breathe. Five drops of his blood. To a complete stranger. Why would he do that? Giving someone power over him like that—it goes against his very being.

"Rose?" Josh asks, noticing my silence.

I turn slowly to face him. "You're crazy."

"A little bit," he agrees, caressing my cheek with the back of his fingers. His eyes are hooded as they drop to my lips then my neck.

I cup his face to keep his eyes on mine, though he's a little blurry from the tears threatening to spill. "Five—"

"Hey," he says softly, "it's worth it. You're worth it."

The things we can do with someone's blood is…atrocious. And we don't know who the seller is. It's just a necklace, it's not worth five drops of his blood.

"Thank you," I whisper, embarrassed that he just did that for me.

This is reckless—and Josh is never reckless. Why would he do this?

"I have a few ideas on how you can thank me," he smirks, "I'll cash them in at a later date."

I let out a laugh, but he kisses me. I think he was aiming for a heated one, but it quickly turns slow, like he needs to savor every second his lips touch me. I hold his face in my hands, caressing his cheek, the feel of his stubble rough against my fingertips. His lips massage mine, our tongues taking their time tasting each other.

We stay like that for a little longer, ignoring the world around us. I like this Josh. I like how easy it is tonight to be with him. I wish it was like this all the time. This is all I ever wanted with him. Josh can say all the right things, but he knows I can't trust him. Spending five drops of his blood speaks volumes and it's dangerous in so many ways, but also because it puts a dent in my walls against him. A big dent.

When we pull away, I start to stand and tug on his fingers. "Come, let's mingle and stretch our legs."

He doesn't move at first, eyes narrowing. "Mingle?"

"Yes," I say. "I can't sit on your lap all night. People will think the Veyara doesn't know how to work a room."

His grin is slow and dangerous. "Oh, I think they know you can work a room."

I pretend to scowl at him, but he humors me and rises to his feet with predatory grace. His fingers lace through mine as if we've done this a million times.

My idea of mingling and Josh's idea of mingling are two very different definitions. I try to make quick, polite conversations as we move through the crowds, but Josh seems to be on a mission as he cuts through. We pass the dancers and feeders, pass the poker tables where things seem to get a little heated, pass the Elders who are…engaged.

Is that Uncle Edward? Oh Divine, did he…oh no…I totally forgot the Elders were going to be here. I know this is all natural, but it's still awkward and embarrassing when family is involved.

Josh leads us straight toward one of the open alcoves. I see the round bed covered in black silk sheets, circled by heavy emerald curtains. Before Josh follows me in, he tells the attendant to bring us a feeder.

The music is softer in here, but the atmosphere is thick with lust and blood. Josh sinks onto the edge of the bed, pulling me between his legs.

I want his dick in my mouth, but before I can get on my knees, a woman slips in. She's naked except for the collar around her throat. She kneels at our feet with practiced ease, her eyes dazed already.

"Go on," Josh says, nodding at me, his hands warm on my hips. "First drink is yours."

My heart slams as I reach for her face and tilt her head back. This is my first time drinking straight from a feeder. She cooperates, her pulse pounding, ready. My fangs descend, and when I sink into her skin, the blood rushes over my tongue—warm, sweet, euphoric. The high is sharp and immediate.

Holy shit.

I see why some supernatural only prefer human feeders. This can get dangerous fast.

Josh rubs circles at the back of my head as I drink deeply. I pull away reluctantly and he leans in. His hand tangles in the feeder's hair, his mouth sinking into her neck—jealousy scorches through me as I get flashbacks of Josh kissing serpent women's necks in the past.

The envy is instant, feral, and all I see is red.

I don't care that she's a feeder. I don't care that she's nothing but food. I don't care that he's drinking from her, and it's not sexual at all. I don't care. He's touching *her* and that just won't do.

"Stop," I tell Josh, surprised by how calm my voice is. I almost don't recognize my own sound. My eyes move to the feeder, who's staring back at me as the room darkens. I tell her, "Leave."

She stumbles, getting up but leaves as fast as her drugged-out body allows her, blood dripping down her neck and chest.

Josh sits back, licking the blood from his own lips, eyes dancing on me. "Jealous of a feeder?"

Heat continues to fuel me and it's not embarrassment I'm feeling.

"I don't want anyone touching you," I declare, "I don't want you touching anyone. I don't care. I don't—you're mine and I'm *done* sharing you."

I'm going to blame the drugs, but I don't regret saying the words. I wish I said it the first time I felt him with someone else. I wish I said it when my parents died and Shane had Eliza and I had—well, everyone, but not him.

I was fourteen and I needed him the most then.

I needed the boy who took me to the highest tower in Coilspire to show me the Heavens when we were kids.

I needed my person.

I don't know what our Mating bond holds, but I know I've wanted to say those words for as long as I can remember. Tonight, I don't want to pretend. We can go back to doing that tomorrow, when we're sober.

The room is nearly all black as Josh closes the distance between us. His gray eyes glowing as he stands over me.

I don't look away from him, holding his gaze. "I don't care what you want or who you want. You're mine," I repeat.

He removes the crown from my head and rakes his fingers through my hair, gripping it, tilting my head back. My throat is exposed to him, and I feel his other hand come around my neck. I close my eyes, taking in the sensation of his possessive hold, but he doesn't like that.

"Open your eyes," he demands, lowly. I do, and the room is normal again. He narrows his gaze and demands, "Your other eyes."

I stare at him before shaking my head. "No…I don't want to hurt you…and there's too many people if I lose control."

"You won't lose control," he says.

"You don't know that," I reply, before his lips press down on mine.

When he pulls away, his hand at my throat leaves me. "Have you ever lost control?"

"No," I reply honestly.

"Your other eyes, my Veyara," Josh repeats, "you don't have to hide them from me," he says and I'm about to raise my eyebrows when he adds, "anymore."

I roll my eyes. "Saved yourself."

"Did you just roll your eyes at me?" he asks with dangerous humor. I blink and he pulls my head back further. "Well, since you took my food away…I'm just going to have to feed from you instead."

My breath catches as the room darkens again—from desire this time.

"That's fine," I tell him, wanting him to. Mates drinking from each other outside of sex is similar to drinking a nutritious drugged up wine—Mariella's words.

He raises his brows, surprise flickering before it twists into something darker. I urge him, tilting my neck as I unbuckle his pants. But instead of biting me, his lips press softly against my throbbing neck, kissing me. My hands find his cock, hot and hard, and I wrap my fingers around him. I free him from his pants and stroke his length once.

Josh pulls away, his head tips back slightly, a low curse slipping from his lips, his eyes never leave mine, burning with a mix of raw desire and longing. Then he catches one of my wrists, lifting it to his mouth before his fangs sink in.

The moment he pierces me, euphoria floods every nerve ending. My body arches, my lips part on a moan I can't hold back. The feeling is nothing like I've felt before.

I take his cock in my mouth to balance the pleasure. My lips wrap around him. My tongue swirls, exploring the smooth, pulsing heat as I ease him deeper. He fills my mouth deliciously, and I focus on the rhythm, sliding down an inch, then back, my lips tight around him. My hand rests on his thigh, feeling the taut muscle beneath my palm.

Josh growls against my wrist as my mouth works on his hard length. His hips jerk forward like he can't help himself and I taste his precum at the back of my throat.

I move again, bolder now, taking him deeper, my tongue tracing along the sensitive ridge. His hand finds my hair, fingers threading gently, not pushing, just anchoring himself as another low groan escapes him.

"Look at me," he tells me, telepathically, his lips never leaving my wrist.

I raise my head, meeting his sharp almost silver eyes.

"You have no idea how fucking sexy you are right now," he thinks, his bite getting deeper, making me moan on his cock, sending waves of pleasure through both of us. My own orgasm is close as my body begs for more.

"You think I'm sexy?" The thought slips out to him before I can stop myself.

He pulls away from my wrist, his eyes are darker now. "You have no idea how sexy I think you are, my Veyara," he stares down at me, eyes heavy with lust as he says, "use your hand."

I pull him out of my mouth, frowning, not ready to stop tasting him, but I start stroking his length. His lips find mine and his hands start to lift my dress up. He grinds his cock against my palm, and I can feel him straining. He's close. The knowledge excites me as he bends down just enough to pick me up slightly and place me higher on the bed before he moves my silks out of the way. He takes control, fingers coming up to lace with mine. His other hand strokes his cock against my clit, and fucking Hell, I might just orgasm from that.

"Fuck, Rose, you're going to ruin me," he rasps, his breathing is rough, and then I feel his hot release spill against my skin, my eyes never leaving his. He just came on my pussy and fuck, I need him inside me.

He comes to lay next to me on the bed, guiding my hand lower and saying, "Rub yourself."

I keep my eyes on him as my fingers feel his hot cum on my clit and I start rubbing it in. His slick release mixed with my own wetness smears all over my clit.

Why is this so hot?

Josh smirks, propping himself up on one elbow, watching me like I'm the only thing worth his time and attention. His other hand moves, sliding between my legs, his fingers slipping inside me with ease.

"Don't stop, my Veyara." He leans down to kiss me.

"I love when you call me that," I admit.

His eyes darken. "Veyara?"

"The part I'm yours," I whisper and he kisses me again.

The combination of his fingers thrusting, curling, filling me, and my own hand working my clit shatters what little control I had left. He slips in a third finger, and my hips move with him, riding his hand, grinding shamelessly. The sight makes him groan, his cock hardening again and I reach for it with my free hand.

Fuuuck, this man.

Our Mating bond *sings* happily as we can't get enough of each other. I don't know if it's the bond or 2Fangs, but I am not complaining if it means he'll continue to touch me and look at me like this.

I *need* him.

Our kisses deepen, desperate, wet, his tongue tangling with mine fighting for dominance. I move faster and faster, needing him deeper. His fingers oblige, pumping into me with a madness to touch my soul from inside when suddenly a sharp, uncomfortable pain courses through me.

I gasp and freeze.

His fingers stutter, and he stops too. My head starts to spin as I realize what just happened—his fingers went too deep.

My eyes sting as tears blur my vision.

He pulls his fingers out slowly, carefully, but it still makes me wince. He raises his hand, and we both see the blood on his fingers.

The room spins as he looks at me. "Rose," he kisses my forehead, "are you okay?"

No.

No, I'm not okay.

I shake my head, panic rising. "What if this—what if it messes up our ritual? Our Mating bond," I ask him. "What if this is what the tarot reading was referring to? That our bond will break?" My voice cracks. "What if I ruined our—"

"Hey," his voice is sharp enough to make me stop spiraling. Then he kisses my forehead again. "Nothing can break our bond. We tried worse things and if *this* breaks it, I'll be having words with the Divine."

I choke back a sob, but then he brings his bloody fingers to his lips and sucks them slowly. His eyes never leave mine as I stare at him, lips parting in shock.

No fucking way he just…

"Josh…" I gasp, reaching for his hand, but the look in his eyes stops me cold.

He lets out a tortured groan as he holds my hands back with his free hand and sucks his fingers clean. And I mean *clean.*

Oh my Divine.

"I love the sound of my name on your lips," he says and my chest tightens. He doesn't notice the difference as he leaves my side and slides down the bed, pushing my thighs open wider.

I stare at him, horrified, but I can't seem to move. The look in his dark eyes warn me not to.

His mouth is on me before I can breathe—tongue hot and thorough, licking me clean of every drop of blood and cum and arousal.

He's not trying to pleasure me now.

The Beta is feasting.

My heart races as shame, guilt, fear, and shock courses though me. The shock of him turning this around overpowers every feeling. All I can do is clutch the sheets, legs trembling as he devours me.

"I lied," he thinks to me and my heart sinks. Now what? But before my mind spirals, he finishes his thought. ***"I'm fucking taking all of this from you with or without your permission. Right now. You're fucking mine."***

I can't believe he's doing this. He's licking me like he's been starving and can't get enough. His tongue drags through my pussy as he takes his time one moment, then greedy the next. His mouth works deeper, hungrier as if he's in a trance.

Josh buries his face in more, groaning low against me. His lips seal over my clit to suck, then pulling back to lick me open again.

He pauses and looks up at me through his dark lashes. His mouth is glistening while his lips are swollen, blood and our cum smeared across his face.

"Do you want to rest?" his voice is rough, but tender at the same time.

"No." The word rips out of me as a tear slides down the corner of my eye. I'm overwhelmed with feelings but they're mostly good because how can this be bad? "Don't stop," I tell him in a whisper.

His expression softens as he reaches up, catching my trembling hand and lacing our fingers together, firmly, grounding me.

"You're the most beautiful thing I've ever seen," he says reverently, then he lowers his head again. He places a kiss on my inner thigh before his tongue plunges in deep as his fingers slide back inside me, slow and gentle this time.

He's not feasting anymore. No, his tongue is too caring, and his touch is carefully sweet for it to be just raw desire.

He works me up again, building the tension in me higher and higher until I'm writhing under him, moaning for more. I want him, more than his tongue and his fingers. I want *him.* The thought of his beautiful cock entering me one day breaks me, a cry tearing from my throat. I come hard on his tongue and fingers, shuddering and shaking from the build-up and all his hard work. Josh's mouth doesn't leave me once. He continues to lick and suck me as I ride out the waves of my climax, holding my hand the entire time. Once I stop shaking, his tongue traces away any last drops.

He lifts his head, his jaw slick and sharp, his eyes dark but bright at the same time. He looks wrecked and ravenous all at once, mouth smeared faintly red.

I can't move, can't think. He crawls up over me, pressing his weight into my body until I'm caged beneath him. His lips capture mine in a soft kiss and I taste myself on him. But it's different—mixed with the blood from…

Oh wow.

My brain goes blank and all I can think of is the blood on his lips, kissing him harder. The high is instant, and I feel like I'm floating and drowning at the same time. I've never tasted anything sweeter or richer before—AB neg doesn't come close, drinking straight from a feeder doesn't come close. Petal doesn't come close. Neither does getting bitten.

Josh breaks the kiss gently, his forehead resting against mine. "How can something so beautiful break us?"

40 CONFESSIONS

Rosella Craving
November 2

We lay tangled in each other, my head against Josh's chest. He hasn't let me go, his arm heavy and protective around me, thumb stroking the inside of my wrist where the punctures ache faintly. This is nice, and so unreal.

We can hear the Gala faintly through the curtains—cheers, laughter, music, moans.

Josh kisses my temple before reaching for his cloak. My eyes lazily follow his movements to see him pulling a small silver case from an inside pocket. He flicks it open to reveal cute little glass vials, each filled with a shimmering green liquid.

Curiosity sparks, and I ask, "What's that?"

He looks surprised. "You've never tried Eclipsa?"

I bite my bottom lip and shake my head. "No."

Josh picks up one of the vials, his eyes finding mine again. "It's mellow. Do you want to try?"

I cuddle into him. "Yes."

He chuckles, bringing his other arm around me to open the vial carefully. "Vanessa was right about you."

"What do you mean?" I ask, looking up at him.

He just shakes his head. "She said you'd surprise me," he brings the vial to my lips, "but you've always done that. It goes under your tongue."

I open my mouth to let him tip the contents in. It's tart—reminds me of lime juice. He laughs at my puckered face, before taking it himself. My body shudders as it spreads down my throat.

"I'd say it's similar to shroom edibles for humans," he tells me as he puts the case away.

"That's…not entirely mellow…" I tell him, slowly.

He smirks. "Depends. Judging by what I saw you handle tonight, you'll enjoy it." He lets out a deep sigh before saying, "Think you're up to returning to your party?"

I want to say no, my body is spent and I'm enjoying being cuddled by Josh, but I sigh too, sitting up. "Yes, we should."

He rises and dresses first, then offers his hand to pull me up, checking me and adjusting my gown, smoothing it into place. He fixes my hair, returning the Veyara crown to my head. He's careful and gentle about it and kisses my forehead when it's set. I smile to myself. Why can't it be like this all the time? Where's this sweet side of him, and why was he hiding it from *me*?

He's about to reach for the curtains, but I pull him back. "Wait. Your mouth is still…" I bite my lip, "bloody."

He just grins beautifully. "So?"

"There's something seriously wrong with you," I tell him, but I'm a hypocrite because I'd be lying if I said I wasn't turned on.

He knows it the way his eyes darken, but he says, "I'm the fucking Beta. I'm allowed to show off that the Veyara is mine—" he leans in to say into my ear, "—and only mine because I'm never sharing you. Ever."

"That goes both ways," I reply, leaning into him.

He catches my lips in a kiss and says, "I don't know, you're hot as fuck when you're jealous."

I glare at him.

"Rose," he says, caressing my cheek, and suddenly all the humor is gone as he looks at me, "you don't know how much I regret not just being yours…" The words hang between us—we haven't even Mated yet. He doesn't even know what it's really like to be with me, how can he be sure? "I'll never want anyone else—no matter how mad I am at you."

"No matter how much you hate me?" I ask quietly because that's the real question.

He watches me for a moment then he tells me, "I've always been yours. Even when you thought I wasn't."

My heart hammers so hard, I'm afraid it'll just jump out of my chest. Before I can say anything or even question it, he's pulling the curtains apart, exposing us to the Gala.

I want to believe him, and I know he hasn't been with anyone since I shifted, but hope is a dangerous game. He could easily change his mind after Marking me and we're not forced on each other because of the bond.

He wraps his fingers around mine and leads me out. He looks back at me and smiles beautifully, saying, "I just finger fucked you in a room full of people. We're fucking exclusive now. No more running from this."

Heads turn momentarily as we make our way through. I bite down on my lip. "Don't I have a say? What if I'm still pissed about the last four years?"

"Stay pissed. It doesn't change what I just said," he shrugs a shoulder and I realize we're not returning to the thrones. Instead, he steers us toward one of the circular seating sections sunken into the floor. Couches wrap around a low table scattered with liquor bottles, vials, and spent drugs.

The Warriors and the Crescents blur together in every state of decadence. Daniya is straddling Daniel, her French tipped nails carving red trails down his chest, while his hands grind her hips into him.

Beside them, Vanessa kneels as James's head is thrown back, his jaw clenched in a way that makes the whole world still for a second as she takes him deep. He groans and it rumbles through my bones like bass from the speakers. His hand is firm in her hair, keeping her there, like he's lost in her completely. I'm not even embarrassed to say it, they are beautiful to watch.

Across from James and Vanessa, Mariella's collapsed against Antonio, her lashes fluttering heavy and her lips are parted. He strokes her hair slowly, whispering against her temple like she's the only star in his sky. His voice doesn't even reach me, but I feel the intimacy of it all the same.

Devaughn's grin cuts through the haze. He's reclined, a goblet gleaming in one hand, his other disappearing under Crystal's gown. His fingers move lazily as she drinks from his throat, her body trembling.

Sam and Azura are nowhere to be seen—retired for the night, maybe. I know the pregnancy's been tiring her out a lot.

Devaughn lets out a laugh, seeing us. "The Hell happened to your face, Josh?"

Josh drops onto the couch beside him, tugging me onto his lap in one easy pull. The world sways but steadies again when I land against him. He smirks back at Devaughn. "Best fucking drug known to a Mate, apparently."

Devaughn's brows shoot up, his gaze flickering from Josh to me, intrigued—almost hungry. My cheeks heat and before he can say a word, I busy myself with Josh's earlobe, sucking gently.

Josh lazily waves him off. "Too late for you to find out."

James barks out a rough laugh, his voice strangled from Vanessa working him. "Really fucking is—" his words break into a grunt, his hips jerking as he spills down Vanessa's throat. She swallows, then smirks, wiping her mouth as James drags her up to kiss him.

I blink, heavy-lidded, everything dazzling and slow, the effects of Eclipsa settling in. I murmur, "Is it…like this all the time?"

For a moment there's silence, before Daniya lets out a breathless laugh, still rolling her hips on Daniel. "Of course, babe. What else would it be?"

I don't want to think of all the parties Josh has been at over the past six years filled with these temptations. Could I blame him for giving into it?

James, still dazed, lets his head fall back against the couch, and I have a feeling it's not just from his recent activity. He's on something. He says, "Mating's not just for fun, or for the bond. It's as natural as eating or sleeping."

Vanessa nods as she settles down beside James. "You would eat, drink, chat at a party—or anywhere really, so why wouldn't you have sex?"

"We *are* animals," Devaughn adds. He reaches over and clinks his glass with Antonio's as they laugh. His other hand is still buried in Crystal, who moans at his sudden movement. He turns his gray eyes on me. "Pretending otherwise is unnatural."

The band changes and my favorite—Serpentine's Kiss—returns to the stage again. I shift in Josh's lap, the warmth of his body making it hard to think, let alone talk. Conversations about Yule plans come up. I just listen to them and the music, resting my head on Josh's shoulder.

Then the lead singer, Celia Dawn, is on the fourth song, *Sin in Silk* and I perk up, a smile tugging at my lips. "I love this song."

Josh glances at me, amused. "Then dance with me."

I let him pull me from our circle to the dance floor as my pulse quickens. We've only danced for the cameras before—there are no cameras now.

The lights are dimmed to a sultry green glow, shadows pressing closer. Josh draws me in, his hands claiming my hips as mine loop around his neck. Our foreheads rest together as we sway with the slow music, bodies pressing close.

Our lips find each other then, slow and consuming, his mouth warm and tasting like the cocktail he was drinking with a hint of me still on his lips.

Eventually the song ends, another begins, and then another, and we keep dancing—wrapped up in green light and heat and each other until the night is nothing but music and him.

The back corridors of the Palace are hushed, shadows stretching long where the lights flicker low. My laughter bounces off the stone walls, too bright for the silence, but I can't swallow it down. It bubbles out of me, warm and fizzy like the drinks are still in my veins. My shoes dangle from Josh's hand, his other arm looped around my waist, steadying me as I sway and giggle against him. My head feels cotton-light and my body is *boneless.* The world spins in a way I very much welcome.

"I'm Veyara Hunter…" I giggle, pressing my palm to the cool wall mid-step, "wait."

Josh exhales, patient but amused.

Our security detail trail behind us, boots echoing in time. The sound pulses in my skull, steady, steady, steady. I glance back over my shoulder and snort out another giggle. Their faces blur like watercolors. Everything is so soft.

"We have an audience," I whisper, or try to. My voice sounds too loud to my own ears.

Josh shifts me higher against his side. "They're just making sure we don't face-plant on the marble."

I laugh, shaking my head until the corridor blurs.

"Rose, I'm this close to throwing you over my shoulder," he threatens.

But then sudden thoughts of our bond breaking take over, and my laugh turns into a choked sob. "What if we did fuck it up? The bond," I say to him, tears easily flowing. "I never, ever hated you. I mean, I hated you because you hated me, but I don't want us to break. Ever. Not—not when I'm in love with you."

His eyes cut to me as he drops my shoes, reaching for me with both hands. "Rose—you're really, really wasted."

"No," I shake my head, but it's slow, sluggish. The corridor tilts sideways. "I am very, very wasted right now, but it's still the truth." My voice cracks on the last word. "I've been in love with you for as long as I can remember…you just— you just never gave me a chance…" I don't dare look at him. I can't. I grip his cloak, edging closer to his body as I whisper, "We can't break."

"No, we can't," he says, firmly.

"But what if…why would the seer say—no, the bond *can't* break," I cry and he kisses my cheeks, my tears.

"If it did—which it can't—but if it did, I'll demand the Divine fix it. Every time, okay?" he promises, reassuring me.

I blink to clear my vision and meet his gray eyes. "You'd pick me? Again? On your own? You'd willingly choose me?" I blink again, and frown. "You'd choose me over them?"

"Oh, sweetheart," his hand comes up, cupping the side of my neck, thumb brushing my jawline, "yes, I'll always pick you. Always want you. Only you. I went against the Divine and…seeing how much that hurt you haunts me."

He has no idea. He's seen nothing. He has *no* idea.

My fingers dig into his bare chest. "Promise?"

I'm fading, I know.

"I'll throw away anyone else, and I'll always find you and bring you home," he says, and then his mouth is on mine, slow and lingering. Nothing like the night's heat. His lips taste sweet and salty from my tears.

I let him kiss me like he means every word he just said, because I know he's as wasted as me.

And none of this will be true in the morning.

If we even remember it.

41 WORK

Rosella Craving
November 3

I stand in the Old Tower chamber, eyes darting between the woman who looks like Helena Hunter and Nathanial's calm, unreadable face. The woman keeps her distance, arms obediently in front of her, gaze fixed on the floor like she's memorizing the patterns on the rug.

I tilt my head to watch her, not even hiding it. I know Josh doesn't have any aunts, so who is this woman? She's clearly a witch and that can't make her related to Josh. Inter-species relationships are forbidden—especially if children are born. If Josh's Mom was a witch, he would've been a human. He would've been dead.

We don't have to wait long before the door swings open, and Queen Aradia bursts in. Her golden blonde hair is in a high ponytail, blue eyes sparkling with excited energy. She's lively, almost glowing, an almost perfect replica of Mother Isis—same elegant bone structure, same commanding presence—but softer, younger, with clear mischief dancing in her eyes.

There's no denying she's Liam's mother. I watch the Queen of the Witches and Vampires carefully as her gaze lands on me first. She squeals, clapping her hands together, turning to Nathanial. "We're finally ready to do this!"

Nathanial nods once, a faint smile curving his mouth. "Yes, and Zak did his part so we're a go."

Opening a portal…I thought things would get more dramatic, but it's been fairly quiet with Samhain winding down. Everyone's getting ready as the harsh mountain winters begin.

Aradia places her hands on my shoulders, grinning wide. "Good to see you again, dear."

I decide to take a page out of Zak's book and nod once. "Aradia."

I don't address her by her title—not when she's calling me *dear*.

Aradia smiles amused, but Nathanial starts moving toward the door. "Follow me," he instructs us.

We trail him down the tower stairs—Aradia keeping up with Nathanial, me and Helena's look-alike trailing behind them. We descend past the main level into the cellar. Nathanial presses a hidden panel, and a section of wall grinds open, revealing a tunnel.

This passage feels *old*, and there's no trace of the sleek tech that threads through most of Cravenhold. Torches on iron brackets light up as Nathanial passes them, casting jittery shadows in his wake.

I glance at the woman walking silently beside me, her face still guarded. "What's your name?" I ask softly. She doesn't respond. I'll try again later.

The tunnel stretches forever, my legs aching by the time a faint glow appears ahead. My skin prickles and curiosity pulls me forward.

Aradia and Nathanial murmur ahead, voices low and urgent. We pass a few arches that look like entrances to chambers, until we reach a very pretty one. Flowers are everywhere—roses, lilies, sunflowers, jasmines, marigolds—spilling from vases, their perfume heavy and sweet. In the center is the stone tomb.

Aradia brushes her fingers across the lid, tender as a mother with a sleeping child.

Nathanial extends his hand to me, pressing his lips to my forehead. Aradia watches us with a fascinated look on her face as Nathanial whispers, "Do you remember?"

I simply nod as recent memories flood in. "Yes."

He smiles. "There's a lot of strange things happening in the world right now. We need her. It's time."

Aradia takes my other hand, her grip warm. "We'll be working together to wake her. Usually this takes time when I do it alone, but I have you this time. Together, Isis should wake much faster."

"What is she doing here?" I ask, nodding at Mina, unable to contain my curiosity any longer.

Nathanial and Aradia exchange looks before Aradia gestures to our silent fourth companion. She answers me smoothly, "Mina is a powerful witch who can shift forms—like a changeling."

"Why does she look exactly like Helena Hunter right now?" I ask, glancing between the three of them. Mina's gaze locks with mine at the mention of Josh's mother.

Nathanial chuckles. "That's her real face. She and Helena were twins," he answers me briefly, before continuing with our task at hand.

"As you know, Isis has been asleep for a while now. Mina is who everyone sees when *Isis* makes a public appearance."

I have so many questions, but Nathanial doesn't seem to be in the more talkative mood right now. He's quite on edge which is very unlike him. I knew the version of Isis *in prayer* was never the real story and there was always a decoy, but I didn't know it was Josh's aunt.

Which leads to my next series of questions. How is she Josh's aunt when she's a witch and Helena's sister? If Helena was a witch and she Mated with Cedric Hunter, then Josh is supposed to be human. Josh obviously is the opposite.

Something's not right here.

A lot of things aren't right here.

Everyone thinks Isis is in prayer to give our world a sense of safety—peace, knowing that the mother of the shifters is protecting them. It's a load of bullshit, but it's worked. Nathanial told me they couldn't risk people knowing Isis has been asleep for some time now.

I look at Mina again and remember the memory Nathanial shared with me recently of burning bodies. Mina looks similar to the woman in the memory—the one Nathanial said was a sacrifice. Now I remember why she looked familiar. I was thinking of Helena Hunter.

What does that have to do with any of this? Why would Nathanial show me that memory?

"There's a ritual to wake Isis and keep her sustained—you'll see. It's why you're here," Aradia smiles, encouragingly at me.

"Does anyone know about this?" I ask, and clarify, "About Mina. Does Josh know?"

"Of course not. Only people who know are in this chamber—and Stefan, of course," Aradia answers. Not even her sons know this heinous secret? Josh doesn't know he has an aunt? If she's really his aunt?

Nathanial lifts my chin and kisses me, his fingers trailing down my collarbone and chest, before he pulls away, saying, "This is what we've been working toward for years, Rose. It's time to use your powers." He gives me that gorgeous smile. He touches my cheek and adds, "You'll be amazing."

"Mina will make sure no evil enters the space and tries to hijack our work. This is critical. Very sensitive, do you understand, Rosie?" Aradia asks me and I *hate* the way she used a nickname. Only people I'm close to use it.

Mina moves to the back corner without a word. She lowers herself into a cross-legged position, closes her eyes, and begins chanting—soft, inaudible words that raise the hairs on my arms. Something tells me this has nothing to do with keeping the space pure.

Aradia starts arranging candles, herbs, and crystals in intentional patterns. Nathanial draws me against him, his arms banding around my waist. He kisses me gently again, lips lingering, possessively.

"I'm so proud of you," he murmurs against my mouth. "I love you more than you can imagine, my little mistress." He cups my face, thumbs stroking my cheeks as if to give me extra reassurance that I don't need. "I'd never let anything hurt you. You know that. You're mine. I take care of what's mine."

Aradia holds out her hand, smiling softly. "Come, my darling."

We sit facing each other on the stone floor, knees almost touching, inside a pentacle that's drawn into the clay chamber. A single line runs from its center straight to the tomb. I notice it but say nothing.

Aradia lifts a ceremonial knife, looking at me encouragingly. I extend my palm without giving anything away. She slashes quickly across mine, then her own. Blood wells and she guides our hands together over the pentacle. Drops fall on the pentacle and magically run through the entirety of it before racing along the line toward the tomb.

"Now's the fun part." Aradia winks at me. "Repeat after me. Sleep was mercy. Mercy's done. What was denied has found its tongue—wake, wake now, Isis. The Hour has come."

She nods to me and we start the chant over.

And over.

And over.

And over.

42 MONDAY

Rosella Craving

November 4

The low clinking of cups and saucers invades my mind as Vanessa and I step into Luna's Cup. Crystal's already waving at us—her blonde curls haloed in the morning Sunlight coming in through the windows. She has coffee in one hand and a stylus in the other. Mariella is sitting beside her, stirring her latte.

Daniya grins up at us, saying, "Hi! I ordered you the pumpkin hazelnut latte you like," she pushes the cup toward me, then a straight black coffee toward Vanessa as we slip into the booth, "and boring regular dark roast for you."

Vanessa just smirks, her brown eyes twinkling. "Thanks. Know me so well."

I sip my latte. Luna's Cup makes the best holiday drinks and the warmth is welcomed. I woke up with the worst muscle aches, and I didn't even work out or train hard this week.

"So let's dive in, yeah? What should the theme be for the baby Alpha's party?" Crystal asks, before adding, "Please no Moon and stars…he will be a Scorpio baby so something more appropriate…"

After another thirty minutes of discussing the party plans, Crystal decides to shift topics. She wiggles her eyebrows behind her large mug and asks me, "So…the Beta surprised us at the Gala. How are you feeling about this new development?"

She sounds like a reporter.

"Way to be sly, Crystal?" Vanessa laughs and turns to me. "No, but seriously. You both looked so hot!"

Looks were never a problem for Josh and me.

"Yeah, he surprised me too," I say slowly, pushing back thoughts of the Gala so I don't turn myself on right now in the middle of a coffee shop.

"How do you feel about partaking in the Den life?" Crystal asks and I frown.

"What do you mean?"

She shrugs. "I mean, based on his…record, would you be open to…an open relationship? It's normal for serpents, you know?"

"You would fit right in, seeing the party you just threw," Daniya chuckles, sipping on her tea.

My answer is fuck no, but I also don't know much about Den life. I turn to Vanessa. "I was hoping maybe you could tell me some more about that."

"What would you like to know?" she asks. "As far as I know, the Beta Warrior couple has never been a part of the Den life in the traditional sense."

"But they can have their own…private…system. I think Josh had mentioned it awhile ago, but baby brain…" Crystal's brows knit together.

Vanessa understands and shrugs. "That's more of a personal preference between the couple. There aren't any rules except the ones the Veyara and the Beta decide on."

Josh said he didn't want to share me, and I made it clear I didn't want to share him anymore. But is that what he wanted? Still wants? Was he just telling me what I wanted to hear?

Maybe Vanessa's right, maybe it is a conversation we'll need to have later. But right now, I'm still curious about the Dens.

"But what is it like in the Dens? I'm curious. I want to know the serpent ways," I tell Vanessa.

"Oh, yes, please do tell," Daniya leans in, interested. I swear, she should've been a serpent shifter.

"There's something to be said about communal living," Vanessa starts, "everything is shared and there's very little privacy. Again, boundaries are always respected. It's like any relationship, just with a lot of people."

"Everything is shared?" Crystal asks.

Vanessa clarifies. "Those who participate, share *everything*. Beds, blood, fights, sex, childcare, Mates, love, grief—you're never alone. It's not for everyone, but serpents who grew up in it, tend to stay in it and be very protective of their Den."

"Not everyone chooses that," Mariella says to me, aware of my concerns. "My sister Mated with a serpent, and they have their own little life, just them and their three kids. They're still part of the Den but set up their life differently."

I nod slowly, starting to understand. "So it's not expected or a requirement. Just…welcomed and available for those who choose it?"

"Exactly," Vanessa answers, smiling.

I let out a relieved laugh. "I guess I was more nervous about it than I needed to be."

"Nothing is forced on anyone." Vanessa reaches over, squeezing my hand in reassurance.

"Is it true serpent shifters have two penises?" Daniya asks and Vanessa bursts out laughing, while Crystal's eyes bulge out. Mariella gasps.

I blink, hard. "I'm sorry, what?!" Josh definitely does not have two penises…does he? Can he hide it?

"What?!" Daniya asks, defensively at the look Crystal gives her. "I have to ask."

Vanessa laughs. "Yes, they're called hemipenes."

"What!" Mariella and I exclaim and Crystal gapes. Daniya fans herself, bubbling with laughter at our shocked expressions. *No one's* ever told me about *that.*

"You lucky, lucky bitch." Daniya elbows me.

"Where?" I ask, flabbergasted. Vanessa smirks.

"*Why?"* Crystal questions.

"We like to have a lot of sex—not like to, we need to," Vanessa answers. I think I'm in shock. "It helps regulate our bodies and ensure Mating success…" Vanessa shrugs like she doesn't know anything different. "All that heat needs to be released somehow." She chuckles and I think about how Josh dried my clothes and kept me warm Samhain night.

There are other ways to release heat.

"Okay, but *where*?" Daniya asks, repeating my question. "In just serpent form, or human too?" She glances at me.

"Don't look at me, I don't know," I say, turning my attention to Vanessa for answers.

Vanessa leans in. "Won't it be more fun for you to find out on your own?"

"No, because I want to know and I don't have a serpent for a Mate." Crystal disagrees and Daniya nods along. Mariella shakes her head, seeming to still be in shock at the news.

"What happens if they don't…have a lot of sex? Or at all?" I ask quietly—this is hardly proper conversation for a coffee shop full of shifters.

"They find other ways to compensate…just like anyone else," Vanessa answers softly and I'm surprised.

Another twenty minutes later, the group begins to rise. Mariella, Daniya, Crystal, and I never do find out *where* the second penis hides. Crystal's phone buzzes with a call from her mother while Vanessa and Mariella say they'll make the arrangements to get the party planning going.

On the way out, I stop at the counter and order a box of bloodhoney donuts—freshly glazed, with whipped cream filling so sweet it hurts your teeth. Helena Hunter's favorite.

The barista starts to package them, but I stop him. "Wait, can you add another, separately?"

"Would you like it in a little sleeve, your highness?" he asks.

"Yeah, that'll be great, thank you." I smile. He slips the one into a sleeve, handing it to me before packaging the rest carefully, tying the box with a crimson ribbon.

I rummage through my bag to find my pen and the small notebook I always carry. I tear a page out from it and scribble the note.

Something to sweeten your day and remember the happy times.

— Your Veyara

I tuck the note beneath the ribbon before telling the barista to have it delivered to Josh.

I walk out with Daniya as she grins at me, waving her phone. "They *loved* the fashion show! The Veyara Collection is officially sold out!" She exclaims.

I grin as we step out of the coffee shop. "That's great news, I'm glad people liked it so much."

"Right! We'll have to plan some more pieces," she gushes, making a note on her phone. "What about an Ostara collection?"

"Daniya?" I ask nervously.

She blinks and looks at me. "Yes?"

I bite my lip, stepping aside, closer to my car. "This might be personal, but…"

"Personal? Between us? Did you forget who you're talking to?" she laughs, her brown eyes clearly amused.

"Well, I know you've explored with other…species and I was hoping you could…"

"I could…?" she asks, slowly.

"You're going to make me say it, aren't you?" I whine and she laughs.

"Yes, because I don't know where you're going with this." She smirks.

"I want to learn how to…"

"Please your Mate?" she grins. This is so embarrassing so I just nod. She throws her arms around me, before saying, "You're so cute. I mean, serpent males are just normal males—everyone's different and have their kinks…"

"There isn't anything…specific that serpents like?" I ask, slowly.

"Not sure why you're worried about serpents, when you can just come and find out what I like," Josh's voice cuts into my thoughts and I freeze.

"I can't speak on what we just learned today, and they'll never, ever admit this," Daniya continues, not noticing anything different, "but they actually love foreplay."

"Daniya—" I start.

"And teasing…so the longer you can hold off, the crazier they'll be for—"

"Daniya!" I grab her arm and only then does she focus on what I'm looking at.

Josh and Devaughn are crossing toward Vortheon Tower, right across from Luna's Cup. They're just a few feet away from us. Devaughn walks into the building first and it looks like he's trying not to laugh. Josh looks right at me and *winks* before following Devaughn into the Claws building. Both were carrying a to-go coffee from Luna's Cup.

"They totally heard everything," Daniya says, giggling.

"It's not funny!" I scold her.

"No, of course not…" she says, stifling her own laugh.

"What?" I ask her, because clearly, she has something to say.

"Well, at least he'll be thinking of you all day now." Daniya gives me a wink too before she waves and gets into her car.

"Not a word," I say to Cristobal, who is holding the car door open for me.

"No, I think it's cute," he says, clearly ignoring my order. He closes the door and gets into the driver's seat. "Where to?"

"And I thought this was going to be a boring Monday," Josh telepaths and my cheeks heat up.

"The forest," I say to Cristobal, defeated. To Josh, I think, ***"You***

know what, I am tired of you keeping secrets."

"Oh, but that just makes a relationship so much more interesting, besides, it was hardly a secret," he replies, smugly.

Of course, it wasn't. He's only ever been with serpent shifters who already knew about *hemipenes.* How am I supposed to satisfy him if I don't even know his anatomy?

"Is it really true, though?" I'm still having a hard time wrapping my head around it.

He doesn't answer right away. But a few minutes later, he replies, ***"Yes."***

My heart sinks to my stomach with the weight of my insecurities. It's just a reminder of how it's another thing about him I didn't know but the other women did.

"Does that scare you?" he asks when I don't say anything and I hear his slight hesitation leaking to me with his thoughts. Is it something *he's* insecure about? That doesn't sound like Josh, but the uncertainty in his voice makes me pause.

"No...just makes me sad that I don't know your body," I answer honestly.

"We're just getting to know each other's bodies. Don't be so hard on yourself, I'm thoroughly satisfied already," the humor is clear in his thought and his words are sweet, but after years of feeling like I wasn't good enough, it's hard to come out of that right away.

Cristobal takes me to the forest, and I tell him to wait in the car as I head to the clearing I first shifted at. He knows I'll call for him if I'm in any real danger.

It's still early, and the scent of morning dew and moss surrounds me. The walk takes about twenty minutes before the clearing opens up. Sunlight is pouring down on it through the trees.

I crouch near one of the dark, damp logs along the stream. Gently, I set the donut on it. It's sugar sparkles under the Sun. It hasn't started snowing yet, but the temperature has dropped significantly at Cravenhold. I find a large enough rock to sit on and look out at the water flowing quietly.

An hour later, my phone vibrates in my pocket, and I pull it out to see the notification. It's a text from Josh.

My heart skips a beat as I look at the messages. It's a picture of the box of donuts on his countertop and the note I left.

Josh: *You remembered.*

Then another text follows.

Josh: *You, me, coffee, and these donuts? Come over.*

My smile grows. My thumb hovers over the keyboard. Part of me wants to say yes right away, the other part of me knows better than to give into him so easily—and after what Daniya said, I'm willing to test the theory. Although, all we've been doing is foreplay and teasing each other.

Me: *Of course I remembered. And sorry, can't. A little busy.*

His reply is immediate like he was waiting for my text.

Josh: *Busy? It's an order from your Beta then.*

I roll my eyes, taking a picture of the donut on the log with the stream behind it, and send it to him.

Josh: *You're at the spot?*

Me: *Yes, is that okay?*

His response isn't right away, and I bite my lip in anticipation. Maybe I should leave.

Josh: *Of course, when you brought donuts*

It's a Monday, so I spend the rest of the day doing tedious administration things Shane forwards to me. There's something going on with the Pride Queens, a few have been murdered recently. I make a mental note to ask Daniel about it. I'm surprised Daniya didn't bring it up—but then again, we never talk about work.

Vanessa joins me in the afternoon once her meeting with Sam is over. They were going through the photos from the Gala to approve them. Only fashion show pictures were approved. Then she and I start preparing for future events.

I wrap both hands around my latte for warmth. "Actually…there's something I need to add. Or rather, carve out."

Vanessa glances at me, brow lifted in quiet invitation for me to continue.

"I'll need blocks of time where I'm completely off-grid. No visitors, no calls, no drop-ins. Just…time to recharge."

She doesn't offer sympathy or ask questions. "Okay…just let me know when."

"It might be last minute, so you might have to cancel things or create a cover," I warn her.

"My office at eight tonight," Josh's telepath disrupts and I resist the flinch at the sudden voice in my head.

"Done." Vanessa makes a note on her phone, while I ignore Josh.

She offers me a sly smile. "Benefits of being a Warrior and a princess—you're very busy even if you're not."

I laugh. "Thank you. You're too good to me," then to Josh, I think, ***"Why, what's at your office that late?"***

"Someone has to be," Vanessa grins at me. "Besides, everyone needs downtime."

She then drops onto the couch, working her magic with my social media while I flip through my remaining emails.

"I'll be back at Cravenhold then and you'll have to come and find out, my Veyara."

"Your wish is literally my command, Beta Warrior," I answer through our bond.

"You'll remember that," he sends back with a dose of his amusement.

I should actually start my work but look over at Vanessa and ask her, "Hey, so a few weeks back there was a situation with some Pride Queens."

She nods, understanding what I'm referring to. "Yeah, four of them died hours apart. It was a huge deal in Feline Nation."

I frown, because it didn't feel like a big deal. I barely heard anything about it aside from whispers. "Did we ever find out what happened?"

She hesitates before answering, "Well, there were signs that the Sisterhood of Sin Covens were involved so Daniel's been working with the witches."

"Wouldn't it be our jurisdiction? Since the victims were shifters?"

"Yes, but no one wants to fuck with witchy shit," Vanessa shudders, shaking her head. "Besides, it's safer that way. Daniel's been brought in as an advisor but as liaison too. Sin Covens are hard to pin down since they move around so much."

"They wipe any trace of their presence…that must be hard…" I trail off.

"Why do you ask?" she quirks a brow, tossing her black hair up in a messy bun.

"No reason, just crossed my mind," I reply, tapping my stylus against my desk as Vanessa returns to her work.

The TV in my office focuses on a live interview Josh is on, something to do with Serpent Nation. There's military movement and Josh is getting grilled about why he's deploying his troops. Josh is denying the claims when Shane comes into my office. Vanessa stands and Shane asks her to give us the room.

"What's going on?" I ask him as he settles down across from me. He looks like he isn't sleeping. "Is Eliza okay?"

He gives me a half smile, "Yeah, she's fine. The baby's been making her sleep a lot."

"I hear that's normal," I tell him, gently. "How are you two?"

He rubs his forehead. "I'm just trying to make sure she's okay. We still have one baby to take care of. I've been trying to get her to step outside, get some Sun, but..."

"Do you want me to try?" I ask him. I don't know how helpful I'll be, seeing that she barely says a word when I'm with her.

"You can try, of course. I just don't think she's there yet..."

"I hate seeing her like this."

"You and me, both," Shane sighs heavily, and suddenly my brother looks ten years older. His eyes look tired. "I hate that I did this to her."

"What are you talking about?" I frown.

"If she wasn't Mated to me, she would've never had to worry about the curse of the twins."

"Hey," I say sharply, demanding his full attention. "I promise you Eliza would never trade you for the world, even to lessen this pain."

"I know...it's just not fair to her." Shane looks away from me, but I get up from my spot to sit beside him and wrap my arms around my big brother tightly. He lifts his arm and hugs me back.

"How's your research going in the library?" Shane asks as we pull away. Ah, the real reason he's here.

"Nothing to report. I'll tell you if I find anything, but...I think there are books missing in the restricted section," I tell him, shifting a little. "I thought we weren't supposed to take books out of there."

"We're not..." Shane replies. "I'll have Sam look into it. He likes doing that stuff."

"It's also his family's duty...record keeping?" I remind my brother. Sam's not an eagle shifter for just any reason.

"Right," Shane chuckles.

"Hey, have you heard if Aurelie and Genevieve will be coming for Thanksgiving? They weren't here for Mabon," I ask about our cousins as Shane gets up to leave for a meeting with some international Alphas.

"No, but I know Aunt wants to throw a big family Ostara thing. Think you can get Josh on board?"

Ostara is months away. "He'd hate it," I shrug.

Josh had never attended family dinners in the past and if he did, it was because Shane dragged him there.

"Don't know," Shane says absently as he responds to a text, "he lives in his head so much because that's where his family is." I blink at his words. Shane doesn't even notice how hard they've hit me as he leans down to press a kiss on my forehead. "Gotta run. I'll check in with you soon. Thanks for letting me hide."

"Is that part of my Warrior duties, now?" I tease him.

"Abso-fucking-lutely. Benefits of having a sibling in the Pack." He winks at me as he walks out of my office and Vanessa returns shortly after.

I stand up and ask her, "Is there anything else pressing for me today?"

She shakes her head. "Nothing that can't be put off."

I nod. "Okay, cancel the rest of my day. I'm going to go see Eliza."

"Of course. I'll take care of it. Give her my love," Vanessa says.

"Thank you, I will," I tell her before gathering my things and leaving.

I slip into Eliza's grand suite and find her watching a movie. Well, watching is a strong word. She's staring at it but definitely zoned out. I climb into bed with her and sigh heavily, settling in.

"I missed doing this," I say to her softly. Life was simpler just a year ago.

We both watch the scenes play out in front of us, not saying much at all for the next hour. I don't mind it though. The quiet is welcomed.

I haven't known what to say either. Sorry for your loss seems wrong. I hated it whenever someone said it to me after my parents died. I didn't want condolences. I wanted my parents back and I'm sure she feels the same.

The darkness that was around her babies surrounds her now. Like it's spread with the loss of a twin. I don't feel as though Eliza is in danger, which is the only reason why I haven't said anything to Shane. Maybe it's the baby's power that I'm seeing, but it terrifies me. It's not like my darkness—it's darker, heavier. I don't even think it's really darkness at all because it feels like a void. Like a black hole.

Whatever this baby's abilities are, I do not like it. Neither does my power.

43 DATE NIGHT

Rosella Craving
November 4

Josh arrives at the Daevryn Tower just as Cristobal pulls up. I notice a parking spot labeled *Veyara* next to Josh's and ask Cristobal, "Has that always been there?"

"Nope," he replies and drops me off at the front before going to park the car in the spot.

Josh looks up from his phone as we meet at the door. "Perfect timing."

"You gave me a parking spot," I say, slowly.

He glances over at it and shrugs like it's nothing. "You are the Veyara."

Security holds the door open for us and Josh guides me right through.

"Good evening, Beta," the receptionists at the desk say in unison, standing as we pass.

Josh lifts a brow at them before they shift their attention to me. With forced, fake smiles, they greet me too. "Veyara, good to see you."

Lies, I think as I see their eyes travel to where Josh's hand is on my back and waves of jealousy, anger, and desire hit me from them. Rude.

Josh doesn't give me a chance to reply as he leads me to his private elevator. I bite my bottom lip as we step inside, and I lean against the glass confinement. The view of Cravenhold is truly stunning as the elevator takes us up to the twenty-fourth floor, even in the darkness of the night.

Josh's eyes land on my lips. "Rose, you cannot bite your lip like that."

He's dressed in all black—pants, shirt, tie, coat—same outfit from when he was on TV earlier. His coat is long and it suits him. Everything suits him. I'm dressed in jeans and a bright red hoodie. I didn't want to give him any ideas.

Josh eyes my outfit anyway and I bite my lip again under his scrutiny. It's involuntary. His eyes narrow and he closes the distance between us, trapping me between the glass and him. His thumb draws my lower lip out.

"I told you not to do that," Josh says, towering over me.

"Ever heard of personal space?" I ask, with no real bite to my words as I place my hand on his chest to push him off, but fuck—his chest is rock solid. Why is that so hot?

"Fuck your personal space," he says before kissing me. His hand grips my waist in a possessive hold.

Ugh.

My body doesn't care, happily responding as a rush of heat travels straight to my core, soaking my panties instantly. The way his grip tightens, I know he knows it too. His hand slides up under my hoodie.

Josh groans while his hands explore my skin. "You're not wearing a bra."

"No…I'm wearing a hoodie…" I say and that's all the explanation I give him.

His hand comes up to cup one of my breasts as he buries his face in my neck. He lightly pinches my nipple and says, "I need it in my mouth."

I close my eyes from the pleasure he's providing just as the elevator signals that we've reached his office floor. He squeezes my breast almost in a promise before reluctantly withdrawing his hand as the elevator doors open into his office.

I've never been in here. It's regal and meticulously composed as I expected. Everything is in dark tones but with a modern edge. His desk dominates the back center of the room, with a stretch of floor-to-ceiling windows that greet anyone coming in. It's nighttime, but I can imagine the natural light flooding the space and providing a pleasant view outside.

There's a comfortable rolling chair nearest to the window and chairs on the other side of the desk. One wall is lined with bookshelves that look more like decoration than actual texts, but the old spines give away their importance. A black leather couch and a pair of armchairs gather around a low table where heavy books are stacked like he was studying them.

It's spotless. Not a single pen out of line, no clutter. It's almost as if he doesn't even work in here.

Josh takes off his coat and moves toward a safe, while I drift to the large windows. My gaze catches on the view, and a slow realization settles over me. The trees outside provide little shield and there's a small garden below, but beyond that, Josh has a perfect line of sight of my bedroom balcony. With binoculars, he'd be able to see into my room.

"It's a nice view, huh," Josh says and I look back at him to meet his amused gaze, he's holding a jewelry box in his hands.

"I didn't know you were a perv."

"Hardly, you're my Mate," he replies and it does little to calm the butterflies in my stomach. His eyes darken.

"What do you have there?" I ask him, nodding to his hands.

His gaze reluctantly drops to the box, and he holds it out to me. "Your auction item. I wanted to make sure it was safe first before you got your hands on it."

"That reminds me, where's the one from the seer?" I ask as I take the box from him.

"Still working on that," he answers, shortly.

I open it to find the unique necklace inside it and pick it up to examine the pendant. It's gold and about the size of a quarter. There are diamonds arranged on it to look like an upside-down crescent Moon with rubies arranged in a droplet sitting right on top of the Moon.

"I've seen this before…" I say slowly as Josh places the box on his desk and takes the necklace from my hand.

"Where?" he asks, coming around to fasten it around my neck. I move my hair to one side to help him out. The pendant falls just between my breastbones.

"I can't remember. It was a while ago…but I've definitely seen it…" I frown, wishing I could remember. Josh places a kiss on my neck and I turn in his arms to look at him. "I can't believe you gave five drops for this…it's officially the most expensive jewelry piece I own," I say quietly.

"Safe to say you'll cherish it then?" his arms hold me close, but he leans back slightly to look down at me.

Why is this man so fucking beautiful? His gray eyes are always so intense and my heart stops but beat faster at the same time.

All I feel is the heat of his body as his fingers dig in just enough to make my breath hitch. I don't look away from him, as I say, "I'll never take it off."

"That sounds like a promise," he says, backing me into the glass window behind me.

"It is," I reply, placing my hands on his hard chest and shoulders.

His hands slide up, moving my hoodie higher, exposing my skin to the air around us. The thick fabric bunches above my chest as he lowers his head, closing his lips around my nipple. I gasp out as my fingers tangle in his hair while he teases me with slow flicks of his tongue. My head tips back as his fingers play with my other nipple while he bites down on the one in his mouth. I moan, arching my back into him.

He takes that as an invite to open his mouth wider, sucking my breast in as his tongue circles around my nipple. His free hand finds mine, guiding it to the hard length straining against his pants, and a low groan rumbles from his chest as I cup him against my palm. I want him in my mouth.

"Where's the other one?" I ask.

Josh releases my nipple from his mouth and laughs, looking up at me. My breath catches. He always looks good, but when he smiles at me with this soft look in his eyes, it's all new and I can't get enough.

"Wouldn't you like to know," he grins, before something catches his eyes past me, enough to distract him.

"What is it?" I ask as I start to turn to look over my shoulder. We're on the twenty-fourth floor, what could possibly catch his eyes from up here? Josh stands straighter as I lower my hoodie and follow his line of sight to the Old Tower.

"Have you ever seen the lights on in there?" Josh asks as we stare at the yellow glow coming from the very top window of the tower. It's like beacon calling to anyone who sees it.

"Nope…" I answer him. I blink but the light is still there. It's faint, like candlelight, but it's there.

"I didn't think so," he says, quietly.

I pull away from the glass, saying, "Sounds like an adventure to me. Coming?"

"It's Mother Isis's tower…" he says slowly as he shrugs into his black coat.

"So we'll be quiet," I say, pulling him toward the private elevator. "Don't tell me the basilisk Beta never broke a few rules."

"Only because I'm curious too," he says, pushing me into the elevator and hitting the first-floor button.

We keep our eyes on it, but by the time we get closer to the tower, the light's gone out.

"Come on," I tell him, quietly as we sneak around my own backyard toward the tower entrance.

"Wait," Josh says, tugging on my hand to stop. When I look back at him, he shakes his head, "I don't think we should go in."

"Chicken," I reply automatically.

He scowls, "No…something feels *off*. You don't feel it?"

"Yeah, it feels like we need to find out what that light was," I tug on his hand, "come on, it can be our first date."

He follows, frowning, "This is not our first date. Our first date was the night you shifted."

"That doesn't count," I shake my head as I push open the tower door. It's heavier than it looks for a wooden door.

"Well, neither does this then," he argues as we step inside. It's dark and cold, but there's the natural light coming from the stairwell that leads up the tower.

"This isn't creepy at all," Josh telepaths as my fingers lace with his.

"Why would Mother Isis want to stay here?" I ask him through our mind link. We start to make our way up the staircase, and I notice Josh's eyes have changed to slits, ready for any threat. He really doesn't like this.

He slows me down and takes the lead. I resist the eye roll but follow him. It's a climb, being the tallest tower at Cravenhold. It's exhausting going up to the Heavens.

Neither of us say much as we go up. The tower stairs are narrow and spiraling. I'm surprised at the lack of security here. As we near the top, where we saw the light coming from, there's a melody drifting out—soft, haunting, and achingly familiar, but I can't place it.

Josh's steps slow and his hand tightens around mine. His eyes narrow and I ask him through the bond, ***"You recognize it too? The tune?"***

"My mother used to sing it," he replies.

"Oh…shit," I think, ***"who else could know it?"***

"No idea…" he answers. He's too tense as his free hand moves to retrieve the gun tucked in the back. It makes me wonder if he carries a firearm all the time.

We reach the top where the door to the only chamber is closed. I motion to the arched window and step onto the narrow ledge outside it.

I wait for Josh and he eyes me, warily. ***"Do I want to know why you seem so comfortable on a ledge this high up?"***

I smirk at him. ***"You have your secrets, I have mine."***

"Hemipenes are not a secret."

"Are we really going to debate that right now?"

"They're not," he insists, nudging me to move toward the other window that belongs to the chamber. I duck and go to the other side, before looking at Josh, who's right at the edge.

"Isn't this fun? I feel like spy kids," I grin at him.

He doesn't find it amusing as the tune continues. ***"I'm going to throw you off this ledge."***

"I prefer you don't do that on our first date. It's not very nice," I glare at him.

"This isn't a date," he replies, before holding up three fingers, counting down. On three, we turn to look inside at the same time.

There's a woman in white standing before a tall altar. Her back is to us at first, but then she turns—and the face that looks back isn't Mother Isis's. Her features shift, revealing someone I haven't seen in six years. My breath catches hard in my throat.

Helena Hunter.

Josh's mother.

I glance at Josh. His face has gone pale, eyes wide. He sees her too.

Around her neck hangs a pendant—gold with diamonds arranged in a deliberate pattern—an inverted crescent Moon, and above it is a single blood-red drop of rubies.

My hand automatically goes to the pendant around my neck, that I had tucked into my hoodie so it would stay safe. What the Hell?

"Josh…" I start, but he's already moving toward the open terrace doors. I quietly rush to follow him, jumping over the half-wall.

"Stop!" A female voice screams in my mind, startling me and I see her spinning around. I stumble back into the wall but it's too late. Josh is already inside, facing off with her. She's snatched an ornamental dagger from the table with startling speed while Josh holds her at gunpoint.

I rush inside and lift both palms. "Wait—please," I plead, to who I'm not entirely sure.

Her green eyes—Helena's eyes—lock on me, then Josh. Shock,

then something softer…sadness passes over them.

"Helena?" My voice cracks, as I ask her, "Helena Hunter?"

Confusion flickers across her face, then sorrow, deep and raw. She opens her mouth as if to speak—but fear floods her face when her focus shifts past me.

"You need to leave," she thinks to me and I grip Josh's arm, trusting her for some reason.

Just then, Nathanial materializes in front of us, standing right between Josh's gun and Helena's dagger.

"Nathanial!" I gasp and realize we must've triggered a ward when we stepped into this room.

"Let's all calm down," he says, placing a hand on the gun and the dagger, lowering it.

"What the fuck is this?" Josh asks, not taking his eyes off the woman before us.

I can't take my eyes off Nathanial, so I ask him, "How is Helena here?"

Nathanial tilts his head, almost gentle in his mannerisms like none of this is surprising to him. "This isn't Helena."

I frown, looking back at the woman. She looks exactly like her—same cheekbones, same mouth, same eyes, same hair.

"Obviously. My mother is dead. Who is this imposter?" Josh asks. His shoulders are taut, every muscle straining.

"She looks identical to Helena," I whisper, then think to her, ***"Who are you?"***

She doesn't look away from Josh and she doesn't answer me. Nathanial smiles, small and knowing. "She would look identical. She's Helena's twin."

The words hit me like cold water. A twin? I didn't know she had a twin. Helena was always private about her family. It's possible. Entirely possible. But what on earth is Helena's twin doing *here*? And why is she in this tower? Has she always been here? Where is Mother Isis?

"Did you know?"

"Fuck no," Josh replies and I know he's in shock too.

But something else nags at me. The woman's energy feels different—she's not a shifter.

"She's a witch," I think to Josh. How can that be if she is Helena's sister? That would mean Helena…Helena was a witch?

That just doesn't make sense. That would mean Josh and his brother should've been human. Mating outside of our factions results in human children—that's why it's forbidden for us. That's why anyone who commits this crime is executed.

Holy shit.

Were Cedric and Helena killed because of their Mating bond?

"How can she be a witch when Helena…" I trail off, seeing Nathanial's calm face. He's starting to scare me. *Nathanial* is starting to scare me. I frown and take a step back. I stare at the woman then to Nathanial. My hand slips down Josh's arm, locking our fingers together, before I tug him back. We need to fucking leave. We need to leave right now.

"Rose," Nathanial says, slowly.

There's no denying this woman is Helena Hunter's twin. Helena was a witch? Cedric Hunter was Mated to a witch. Were they really Mated or…? No, they had to be Mates. Not only is Josh a shifter, but he's a Warrior—he's *the* Beta Warrior…that's supposed to be impossible if his mother was a witch?

I stare at the woman, but Josh asks Nathanial, "Why is she here?"

Nathanial pays him no attention as he steps toward me, and I edge closer to Josh. Nathanial's gray eyes twinkle in the candlelight as he says, "You're okay, my little mistress."

I frown at what he calls me. "What?"

"You handled this so much better the first time. Let me show you. You're okay," Nathanial says.

Then, he reaches out for me.

44 WATCHFUL

Josh Hunter
November 4

Nathanial closes the distance between him and Rose. She's pressed up against my arm and my eyes narrow at him. He reaches up and cups her face. Rose flinches.

"Let me show you," he repeats, more forcefully. I can feel her wariness as he leans down and kisses her forehead.

Then Rose goes limp and I catch her.

"Fuck," I glare at Nathanial, "a warning would've been nice."

"Like how you warned me you'd be in here?" he scolds me in return. "You're supposed to be watching her."

"I *am* watching her," I snap back as I pick Rose up, placing my arms under her legs and supporting her back. Then I look at the woman Nathanial claims is my aunt. "Who are you? What's your name?"

She's been watching everything and hasn't uttered a word. She still doesn't and Nathanial answers instead, "She doesn't concern you."

"She's wearing my mother's face, and you said she's my aunt. That makes it my business," I take a step closer to the Father of the shifters.

Nathanial gives me what most would consider a threatening look. "Stay in your lane, boy. I won't say it again. You know what I want you to know. That's it."

And that's why I don't tell him shit either.

"It's not safe for your aunt out there. Look what happened to your mother. Her sister came to me seeking refuge," Nathanial supplies and I don't believe a word of it. Is he really trying to gaslight a basilisk shifter? That was Nathanial's problem. He always underestimates people.

"So she's been here the whole time?" I ask.

"How did you come to find her?" Nathanial asks instead, narrowing his eyes at me.

"The wind blew us in, why's it matter? Why has my aunt been kept a secret from me?" I question him, despite his warning. She must've done something to attract us here, but I don't spot anything in this room that could've created that kind of light.

But Nathanial has the same idea because he turns and backhands her across the face. I flinch, my grip on Rose tightening as the woman falls to her feet.

"What do you think you're doing?" he shouts at her, but still, she doesn't say anything. She didn't even let out a sound when he hit her.

"She didn't do anything. Rose wanted to explore the Old Tower and I wasn't going to let her do it by herself," I tell Nathanial. He'd never actually hurt Rose, so this is a safe, believable story.

My *aunt* gets to her feet and starts lighting the altar candles as if this is a daily occurrence. Nathanial glances at her briefly with no emotions before his cold eyes land on Rose.

"Go home, Josh," he orders. "Maybe one day your aunt will tell you. Today is not that day."

"What did you do to Rose?"

"She's fine, just taking a nap. Take her home, tell her she fell asleep. She won't remember any of this. She never does." Nathanial waves me off dismissively.

She never does?

What the fuck has he been doing to Rose?

Are the rumors true?

Obviously, he hasn't touched her…not like that, but…fuck…

I glance down at Rose's peaceful sleeping face.

"Josh," Nathanial says and when I look at him, he places a hand on my shoulder. "This is bigger than us. I trust that you'll handle your Mate?"

"Obviously," I reply, unbothered.

"You know I'd never hurt her—not like you have," he adds and if I wasn't carrying Rose, I might've punched him, Father of the shifters or not. Nathanial can go straight to the seventh Hell. I'll deliver him to Lucifer myself—I do happen to know his right hand.

"Yeah, well, like you said, this is bigger than us," I reply, coolly. "I'm taking her home. If she asks, what do you want me to tell her?"

"She won't," he replies confidently.

Without another word, I head for the chamber door as the tune starts up again, sending shivers down my spine. Nathanial doesn't stop me and I carry Rose to her bedroom suite at the Palace. I debate on taking her to my house but having to explain why she's there when she wakes up might be more trouble than it's worth.

Once she's tucked in bed, I settle into the armchair near it. I knew we shouldn't have gone into that tower.

I stare at her pretty face.

I have an aunt? Why would my mother keep that from us? The chamber itself was clearly warded, not the tower, or else Nathanial would've greeted us when we stepped inside.

"What do you know about my mother?" I ask Shane telepathically.

"Gonna have to give me more than that. What exactly are you asking about?" he answers right away.

"Do you know if she had any family? Any siblings?"

"As far as I know, she never talked about them. Why do you ask?" he questions.

"I found something, not sure what it is yet," I reply, then add, ***"there's something else…don't get mad."***

"What did you do to Rose now?"

"Fuck you," I roll my eyes and glance over at my Mate. My Mate. My eyes narrow slightly at her sleeping form, as I rub my jaw. ***"The rumors about Nathanial and Rose—"***

"Stop."

"What if there's some truth to it?"

Nathanial admitted to erasing her memory. Hell, he did it right in front of me. I know Rose has secretly been training her powers with him, but I didn't know he was wiping her memories. Why would he need to do that if they were just practicing magic?

Shane never replies.

I stay in my spot and don't sleep the rest of the night, silently trying to get my thoughts in order.

Rose doesn't wake up until dawn when the Sunlight starts streaming in through her sheer curtains. I lean forward and she blinks, seeing me.

"Morning, sweetheart," I say, my voice gruff, "how'd you sleep?"

"What are you doing here?" she asks, suspicion obvious in her voice.

"You passed out. Wanted to make sure you were okay," I say to her as I stand up and walk over to the bed.

She stares back at me. "I didn't pass out, Josh. Why are you lying to me?"

Fuck.

45 HANDS

Rosella Craving
November 6

Josh slowly steps closer and I watch his every move. He sits down at the edge of my bed.

"What do you remember?" he asks, quietly.

"Depends, what do you remember?" I question, raising an eyebrow.

He shuts his eyes and I wonder if it's a ploy to buy time, but when he opens them, he reaches his hand out to take mine. I pull away and he clenches his jaw, retracting his own hand again.

I cross my arms. "Is there something you don't want me to remember?"

He lets out a humorless laugh, running a hand through his hair. It looks like he's been doing that a lot with the state it's in right now.

Why is it that every time we take a step forward, we take a hundred back? I climb out of bed on the other side and tell him, "I think you should leave."

He doesn't look at me as he stands too, nodding. "Yeah, I think that's best."

I don't wait for anything more as I go to the bathroom, but the sound of him closing the bedroom door makes me flinch.

Nathanial put me to sleep, and Josh is covering for him?

Why, when he was genuinely shocked to see Mina? That wasn't a lie. He wasn't faking that shock.

"Are you going to tell Nathanial I know what he did?" I telepath Josh, fidgeting with the sleeves of my red hoodie. I stare at myself in the mirror, feeling strange. Nathanial's been touching me, kissing me, erasing my memory this whole time, even after my shift.

"I'm not Nathanial's little bitch, Rose," Josh thinks back to me.

I don't know why the words sting, but on top of Nathanial's behavior, Josh acting weird does not help any of this.

Maybe spending time in the library will help me hide and sort through my thoughts. I'm supposed to be researching other female

Warriors anyway.

I ask the librarian about the missing books in the restricted section, but she isn't any help. She just filled out a form and said she'll look into it. I get lost in the books, looking for more than female Warriors, and don't realize the hours I've been in the library archives. There aren't any windows in here, so when I leave the library, I realize night has fallen. Cristobal waits by the car but as I am near, his gaze shifts, drawing his weapon instantly.

The first attacker lunges out of the dark and Cristobal throws me behind him, shielding me. No one would be stupid enough to attack me alone.

Sure enough, more attackers charge out. There are fifteen of them.

Cristobal starts to call for backup through his comms, but I shake my head. "Don't bother them. I got this."

The rush of power rumbles under my skin, begging to be released.

He frowns before understanding. "Are you sure…?"

I nod and he steps out of my way.

Darkness answers like it's been waiting since the day I was born. It rushes out of me, alive, sharp, and hungry for blood. It's slow and menacing at first—like when ink is spilled and it spreads. Then—it strikes.

One man's throat disappears in the black, bone snapping under the pressure. I twist it in my mind, and his body crumples to the ground.

Another charges at me, teeth bared, eyes feral. I imagine a slash through the air and the darkness moves right through him—slicing him in half vertically. He drops in two pieces.

Cristobal kills another one that was coming from behind me with a clean shot to the temple, blood splattering my face. He's a storm, his suit jacket already shredded, knife flashing in one hand, gun in the other. He jams the blade into an attacker's side, fires into another's kneecap, then knocks his weapon free as both assailants fall.

I move with them. My darkness dances around my bodyguard, knowing he's friendly, passing harmlessly over and around Cristobal. I seize another attacker by the ankles with tendrils of black, yanking him off his feet. He hits the ground so hard his skull splits against the stones.

Cristobal tackles one to the ground, his gun pressed beneath the attacker's chin. He pulls the trigger and the skull fragments spray across the stones.

Blood paints the streets of Cravenhold in thick, dark streams.

More attackers emerge, desperate now. I exhale, before darkness explodes outward, slamming three of them into the ground so hard the stones crack. Another one lunges at me from the side, but Cristobal is faster. He buries a dagger right into the attacker's neck before pulling it out, spraying blood all over me.

He moves on to the next and so do I.

When the last attacker falls, the street is quiet again with only the sound of blood dripping off us. I stand there, panting, covered in red. My darkness retreats cautiously but still at my fingertips. I'm sticky with blood that's not mine at all.

Cristobal wipes his blades on the cloak of a corpse before spitting on the stones, mumbling a curse. I scan the bodies, then the rooftops.

"This was to scare you," Cristobal tells me, following my gaze. "Whoever was behind this could've easily taken you out with a sniper, if they really wanted to."

"Find out who sent them," I tell him, looking down at the carnage—the twisted necks, the caved in ribs, the torn flesh. We did this. I think I'm going to be sick.

He nods but says, "Let's get you home, first."

"Are you okay? Did you get hurt?" I ask him. We're both covered in blood so it's hard to tell if he's injured.

"No, nothing I can't handle," he replies. "Besides, you did most of the work."

"Ugh, I'm not going to lie—it felt *so* good to let my powers free," I say and he lets out a grunt.

"Rose?!" Devaughn calls out and I turn to see him and James jog up to us. It looks like they're coming from the Vortheon Tower which is on the other side of the library.

They stop dead in their tracks, eyes looking over the blood smeared all over my bodyguard and me.

"What the Hell happened?" James demands, voice sharp like he's about to sound the alarm.

"The Veyara was attacked," Cristobal answers him.

"And?" Devaughn asks as James curses, already on his phone.

"And they're dead," Cristobal replies evenly. I'm proud of us but we just killed a shit ton of people.

I can't remember ever being attacked, at least I've never been aware of it if they kept it from me, so I've never really had to test my bodyguards in the past—I've seen them train, and they've always kept me safe. Tonight, I truly saw how capable Cristobal has always been.

"We'll get to the bottom of this," James tells me as he makes a call.

Devaughn looks at me and asks, "Are you okay?"

"I'm...fine..." I say, slowly but his eyes scan me from head to toe for wounds, not that he'd be able to tell under the blood. "The fuck is going on with your hands?" Devaughn asks, raising a brow.

I look down and see that they look like they're covered in blood and charcoal. I stare at them as Cristobal takes a step toward me, protectively, answering Devaughn, "It's nothing. It's a little residue from her powers—"

A sleek black SUV comes to an abrupt screeching halt before Josh gets out, not waiting for his security. He assesses the scene as I start to feel lightheaded.

"Well...she *is* a killer," Josh concludes. Cristobal and Devaughn glower at him. Josh doesn't notice, his eyes are trained on my hands then on my neck. He's in front of me, reaching for me but stops short. "Rose..."

"It's fine. I just need—" I start to say before everything goes black.

46 ALPHA SAYS

Josh Hunter
November 6

This girl needs to stop fainting on me. I catch her in my arms and scoop her up, looking at her bodyguard.

"What's wrong with her?" I ask.

He clenches his jaw, before answering, "She probably didn't eat anything all day, and using her power drains her…fairly quickly."

I frown. So, she does have side effects when she uses her powers. She's not as invincible as everyone makes her seem. I start to walk toward my car as the back door is opened for me.

"Who could've attacked her? In the middle of court?" Devaughn asks. He and James are beside me as I lay Rose down in the backseat. James was the one to inform me about the attack and it took everything in me to not rip Valen Salvatore's head off.

But I can't yet. I still need him.

I turn to my friends. "Find out. I'm taking her to Coilspire—"

"The fuck you are," Shane arrives, still dressed in his royal uniforms, looking every bit the menacing Alpha he's known to be.

I glance at Rose before closing the car door and facing her asshole of a brother. I liked him better as my best friend. Having him as a brother-in-law is a fucking pain in the ass.

Shane orders next. "You're not taking her anywhere. You are taking her home—"

"Which is Coilspire." I raise a brow, daring him to argue.

"Might be a good idea to give Rose a break from Cravenhold for a little bit. Let things settle," James says, calmly to Shane. "This had to be an inside job."

Of course, Valen knew how to cover his tracks. He's not reckless. He was a Warrior. Hiring killers isn't a hard job in our world. James's input isn't about Rose's best interests—he still hates the idea of Vanessa being Rose's bodyguard. With Rose in Coilspire, she won't need Vanessa.

"Was it an inside job?" Shane questions me.

I glare at him. "You think *I* put a hit out on my own Mate?"

The bastard actually waits for me to answer my own question.

"I don't know who attacked Rose. If I had to guess it would be Valen behind it. Serpent Nation doesn't do threats, we simply eliminate," I tell my Alpha, irritated as fuck. Okay, so I know Valen's behind it, but I fucking told him to not do this exact shit. He'll still answer for this when the time comes. "Serpents know the consequences of coming after Rose."

"Do they?" Shane crosses his arms.

"She had the Veyara Gala," I remind him.

The Gala isn't just a party. It's to celebrate the Beta-Veyara couple, but also the ascension of the Veyara into the role officially. While her exact duties are still up in the air, that's for me to decide. As far as Serpent Nation goes, she's their leader now too. I know it's not that simple, it wasn't with my mom—but Rose can shift into a serpent. That's all Serpent Nation should care about. I used to fuel their opposition because it worked for me at the time.

But things are different now. I won't stand for anyone coming after Rose. If anyone's hurting her, it's me. If I choose to. No one touches my Mate. Not if they want to live.

Valen Salvatore obviously doesn't want to live.

"You're not taking Rose to Coilspire," Shane says with finality, but he doesn't use his Alpha voice.

"She can get a break, and it'll be good for the both of us," I continue saying as if he hadn't spoken.

"What are you not understanding? You're not taking my sister off Cravenhold, not alone. I know what you're planning," Shane takes a step toward me as Devaughn and James exchange looks. Cristobal and my men are off to the side, waiting on me.

I take an equal step towards him. "This is not some trick to get her alone to give her memories back," I snap at him. After what happened in the Old Tower, and Rose waking up remembering—I want her as far away from here as I can take her, but Coilspire is the safest.

My residence here in Cravenhold is protected but not like Coilspire is—my mother was very careful all the time. Recklessness equals death.

"Of course it is!" Shane growls at me. "It's all you've wanted to do, if not to fix the two of you, to hurt her."

"We don't need to go to Coilspire and be isolated to fix us," I snap.

"We do need her memories back, but that's not what this is about. She's in fucking danger."

"She's always been in danger," Shane retorts.

Not like this, she hasn't. Even now, with her in the car just a few feet away, I can feel something's wrong with her magic.

"You already told her and she didn't believe you." Shane glares at me.

"You *told* her?!" Devaughn exclaims as James narrows his eyes.

"Nice going," I tell Shane, who clearly isn't on his game. Devaughn and James do not know about my little loophole around oaths.

"If you told her, how are we not dead? We took a blood oath," James telepaths us, like the smart one he is, eyeing Shane and me. ***"What's going on?"***

"It's classified," Shane says and I laugh. He's going to use *that* as the excuse? Divine. Rose and I don't need a vacation, Shane does. He's smarter than this.

"From us?" James growls out loud.

It sure is awkward when you have to pull rank on your best friends. Shane's eyes snap to him but Devaughn cuts in and says softly, "Alpha and Beta."

James rolls his eyes and I can't blame him. He decides against staying quiet because James thinks to us, ***"Not about this. Rose's memories are all of our fucking business. We nearly died that night."*** He turns fully to me and telepaths, ***"We didn't do that only for you to be running your mouth to your Mate."***

"Who the fuck do you think you're talking to," I give him a pointed look. I don't care how angry he is. ***"That is not why I'm taking her to Coilspire. I don't need any of your permission to take my Mate away. And do you really think I would've said anything if we'd all die?"***

"Well, apparently that rule doesn't apply to you," James retorts, angrily. He feels betrayed, I get it.

"Wait, why didn't she believe you?" Devaughn asks, confused. ***"What did you even say to her?"***

"What* did *you tell her?" Shane asks me. Are they serious right now? Rose is knocked out in the car, and they want to hold me up to talk about this bullshit?

"Why do you care? You don't even want her to remember. I'm the only one who actually wants her to know the truth," I glare at my friends.

"Fuck you!" Shane takes a step close to me, and I wish he'd put his fucking hands on me.

"What? You're falling for her now and suddenly grew a conscience?" James scoffs, siding with Shane.

"You think I don't know what your angle is?" Shane asks, his thoughts are too loud in my mind. ***"You just want her to know so she hurts just like you because you're fucking miserable! You hate her and it's starting to not make sense, is it? You know she didn't kill Noah."***

Don't punch him.

Don't fucking punch him.

My hands are fists beside me as Devaughn pinches the bridge of his nose. I keep my feet rooted where they are as I tell Shane, ***"You weren't there."***

"I didn't have to be," he snaps back and I narrow my eyes.

James gets in between Shane and me.

"Holy shit," Devaughn stares at Shane. ***"You looked into her mind before it was wiped, didn't you?"***

I freeze. My blood going cold and boiling over at the same time. My voice comes out so calm even I'm scared for Shane. "Tell me that's not true."

Shane stands his ground and telepaths, ***"We've always told you she didn't kill Noah."***

"Then who did?" I think, calmly. James and Devaughn are looking at Shane for an answer too.

Shane just shakes his head. ***"Why is it not good enough to know Rose didn't kill him—"***

"Because I know what I fucking saw." How many times do I need to say this?

"You don't!" Shane replies out loud, then telepaths, ***"You have no idea what happened that night."***

"Then enlighten us," James says to him before I can.

Shane's eyes are wild. His mind is clearly racing as he runs his hand through his hair, frustrated. Who the Hell is he protecting if Rose didn't kill Noah?

"I swear to the Divine, if you say you can't—" James starts but Shane cuts him off.

"Just let it go," Shane pleads, causing all of us to pause. He looks tired. We're all fucking tired of this.

I grit my teeth. "Then let *me* fucking go. She fainted and you all want to talk about this—"

"No," Shane says, shaking his head, this time cutting *me* off. "You're not taking her to Coilspire."

He's still not using his Alpha tone to make me obey. I look at my best friend, really look at him. But his face or body language doesn't contradict what he's saying.

I turn away from him and one of my men reaches for the car door as I tell Shane over my shoulder, "Watch me."

"You want to leave so bad, you're fucking exiled," Shane says to my back and this time, he does use his Alpha command.

"Shane—" James starts but shuts the Hell up quickly.

A chill runs down my spine, as I pause and look up to the Heavens, grateful as fuck, before I get in the car. I lift Rose's head and rest it on my lap. The doors close and we're on our way home.

"He's dealing with a lot...just go. This will blow over like it always does," Devaughn telepaths to me. ***"You can also go through Coilspire's library to see if you can find anything on female Warriors."***

I don't reply to him, but I get on the phone with Cristobal. He answers on the first ring. "Sir."

"Tell me what to do—for her. How do I..." I trail off, knowing damn well I don't know shit about her powers or how to help her right now. I've never felt so fucking useless.

"Water usually does the trick. She takes baths after she uses her magic like this and...maybe give her some of your blood. It'll heal her faster," he answers me, kindly. Out of Rose's two bodyguards, Cristobal never cared for me. It was obvious.

I put the phone on speaker before piercing my wrist with my fangs, then placing my wrist to her lips. It takes a second, but I feel the faint pull as she unconsciously starts sucking. My shoulders relax as I rest my head back.

"She's drinking," I tell Cristobal, knowing he's worried about her. "Why's her magic do that? Does she faint often?"

He's quiet for a moment, and then answers me, "That's a recent development. It never used to do that."

"When did it start?" I ask, starting to feel the bloodlust. I look at her and notice the color reappearing on her cheeks.

"Permission to speak frankly, sir?" he asks, and I roll my eyes.

"Yes."

"It's not rocket science. The longer you both take to complete the Mating ritual, both of your powers will be affected...but you already know this," he tells me and I stare down at Rose.

I didn't know it'd affect her like *this*.

"Thanks, Cristobal. I want you and Franklin back on her detail. Do what you have to and make it happen," I say to him before we end the call.

A part of me wants to violently fight against Rose stepping foot in Coilspire, but the other part is arguing that she's been to the clearing, which I held more sacred. Neither is strong enough for my feeling to get her the fuck out of Cravenhold.

Devaughn brings up a very good point. If there's anything Rose likes, it's being left alone in the library. The books my dad collected, and stole, could be exactly what I need for her to start asking questions.

I need to be at Coilspire also, it's been too long. It's the only place I can breathe, the only place I'm left alone. Coilspire is also my family home, where I grew up, where my mom and brother were with me all the time. It'll be strange to have Rose there, but I only have good memories of Rose at Coilspire from when we were kids. It's not tainted for us like Cravenhold is.

Maybe a week away together will bring us closer, heal some things, and keep her safe for the time being. It's not entirely the same home she might remember, but I know she'll love it anyway.

Our relationship might not be an ideal one, and I don't know how things will play out for us, but I know I didn't lie to her after the Gala ended. I'll always choose her, whether logically I should or not. I know I will. She still has blood on her hands, and I haven't forgiven her for it. I don't know if I ever can, but there's no denying she's my Mate.

You hate her and it's starting to not make sense, is it? Shane had asked and it hit too close to home.

Being with her, wanting her, is painful—but not having her, the idea of never having her, never being anything to her is not even an option.

Coilspire serves one purpose though. My mother was a strong magic wielder, but she was also very paranoid. Coilspire is one of the most protected places on earth. Not just anyone can enter Coilspire, but most importantly, Nathanial can't. He tried once, when I was young, and I still remember the way he burned. My father wasn't there, and Mom refused to let him in. I don't know why, but the scene stayed with me.

I know how important Rose is to Nathanial. I know he's always kept tabs on her, and I also know he hates the idea of us being Mates. He hated the idea of my parents being Mates too. He's always watched me closely to see if I step out of line like my dad.

I'm nothing like my father.

This trip will be a good trust exercise for Nathanial and me. I've never gotten between him and Rose or asked any questions. I've never taken Rose away before either, so I don't know how he will react to it.

Shane still won't tell me what he knows and today just confirmed my suspicions. If Shane won't tell me what happened and Rose can't, I'm going to find another way to give her those memories back. Shane can say I want this to hurt her all he wants, but I'm not the one who wanted her memories wiped to begin with.

I telepath Shane, ***"Nathanial will question Rose's whereabouts."***

Exiling me, exiles Rose. Shane did it on purpose, because if there's anything he wants more than Rose not getting her memories back, it's Rose staying safe.

I wait for his response and start to give up before I hear his voice in my mind. ***"Good thing he can't get to her in Coilspire then. All this lying will not end well, Josh."***

"That's the whole point, Alpha. It was never supposed to. This isn't a love story," I think to him, looking down at Rose as I brush her hair out of her face with my free hand.

"It's always the ones who fall the hardest that say that."

PART TWO

47 COILSPIRE

Rosella Craving
November 7

My body jolts slightly, every so often like I'm sleeping on something that's moving. What the Hell?

I slowly open my eyes and right away feel how sore my body is. I groan as I take in my surroundings. I'm in a car, in a very spacious car. I turn my head to meet a pair of striking but exhausted gray eyes.

"Morning," Josh's rough voice greets me, and I realize I'm lying with my head on his lap. One of his hands is over my stomach, keeping me from rolling off. His other hand is tangled in my hair.

I start to sit up, but groan at my sore muscles. Josh keeps me pinned.

"Not so fast," he scolds.

"Where are we going and why did I fall asleep in the car?" I ask, looking up at him. The faint light of dawn settles around us from the windows. Josh looks too hot for his own good right now. "What happened?"

"You passed out after using your powers last night. You don't remember?" he asks, frowning. He's curious and maybe a little worried, I realize.

"We're twenty minutes out, Beta," the driver informs us as I recall last night.

I pull away from Josh and sit up, slowly this time. "I was attacked…" I glance out the window. "Where are we going?"

The SUV drives us onto a bridge. My stomach flips. All I see at eye level is a blanket of white clouds drifting below. The bridge looks old but solid, iron and stone stretching across the cliffs and the canyon in between.

I turn back to Josh, still watching me. "Why did you lie to me? I know Nathanial tried to erase my memory. Are we going to even talk about that?"

He stares at me for a long time, not answering my question. Finally, he exhales and pinches the bridge of his nose, clearly too tired for this conversation, but that's his own damn fault. We could've talked yesterday morning.

Josh leans closer to me, turning me around to look out the window again. His chest presses into my shoulder as he points ahead. "We're going there. I'm taking you home."

I follow his finger and see the castle as my heart skips a beat at his words, even if I'm wary about him right now. It takes me a second to spot it because part of it is built into the mountainside—very much like Cravenhold. It's massive with towers cutting into the sky, disappearing into another set of clouds.

"It's still as beautiful as I remember," I say, in awe, forgetting about anything before this moment. Josh smiles, kissing my tender shoulder and I feel him pull away to sit back in his seat.

I continue staring out, mesmerized. The bridge keeps going, and the wind picks up. Even with the windows up I can hear the sound of rushing water.

The waterfalls.

Once we're off the bridge, we drive through the mountains, going through more winding roads. Sure enough, twenty minutes later, we arrive at the front gates of Coilspire, large black basilisk statues loom on either side of the gate, their mouths open, watching us as we pass through. It's eerie to say the least, but eventually the driveway opens to a pleasant courtyard around us.

The cars stop and Josh's door opens, before he helps me out of the car. The cold from our high elevation hits me instantly. We're greeted by a massive black serpentine water fountain, water flowing out of serpent mouths. I glance around taking in the space while Josh exchanges a few quiet words with one of his men.

Everything is the same, but different. The courtyard is elegant, framed by old towers and covered balconies. The windows glow from the light inside with flickers of movement hinting at the staff already preparing for our arrival. My eyes catch on the archway at the center that opens into a hall, leading deeper inside.

"Welcome home, my Veyara," Josh's lips brush against my temple as he returns to me. He holds out his arm for me to take.

The main doors to Coilspire open before we even reach them. A tall, polished man with brown hair, kind brown eyes, in a sharp dark green suit, steps out.

"Beta," the butler says with a respectful nod. His eyes flick to me next, lowering slightly. "Veyara."

The title rolls off his tongue like he's been waiting years to say it again and he has been. Vanessa reminded me that it's been six years since there has been a Veyara here.

I smile at him as Josh shakes his hand, grinning. "It's good to be home, Ridley."

Ridley's eyes soften as he shifts his focus to me. "Everyone's excited to get a glimpse of our new Veyara."

I'm used to being in the public eye, but for some reason my cheeks heat at the attention and I'm suddenly nervous. This is Josh's family home. Generations of Hunters have lived here.

"I'm a mess…" I mutter under my breath as we're led inside. I can't believe I'm about to enter Coilspire as its Lady, covered in dried blood.

"You look like you fought your way to be here," he says. "Violence goes a long way with serpents."

"Well, it's not a complete lie," I say under my breath. I fought *him* enough all my life.

The entryway opens into a grand foyer lined with stone pillars and hanging lamps. It smells like firewood and spiced tea. Staff line the sides of the corridor—housekeepers, cooks, attendants—bowing their heads as Ridley introduces while we pass. I notice they're all in uniform wearing the same dark green like Ridley.

"We've waited a long time for your return, Veyara Rose," the housekeeper, Miriam says to me. "Veyara Helena left a to-do list for you." The sparkle in her eye tells me it's not serious.

I grin, curious about this list. "Oh? Well, you'll have to fill me in soon."

"Can't wait to, my lady," she winks at me. Josh's hand rests lightly on my back, guiding me forward.

"Breakfast has been prepared," Ridley says as he falls into step beside us, "shall it be served in the dining hall, or would you prefer the veranda, sir?"

Josh glances at me, a small smile tugging at his mouth. "The veranda will be perfect."

Ridley nods, then the staff are dismissed to retrieve our food and return to their duties. We follow Ridley as he shows us to our bedroom, telling us to freshen up so we can enjoy our meal. He's too kind to say I need to clean the fuck up.

The master suite is in the North Tower and it's warmer than I expected. The walls curve gently, lined with tall windows that open out toward the mountains. Sunlight floods in, catching the glass and spilling across the floor. The fresh air coming from the open doors leading to the balcony makes this feel like a mountain retreat.

I walk slowly, taking it all in. The fireplace burns, awaiting us. The bed sits near the center of the room covered in dark green linens, and above it hangs a chandelier. I notice our luggage has already been brought up.

Beyond the room, the mountains stretch out endlessly. The mist rising between them is like something straight out of a painting and I can't wait to wake up in this room.

"It's so quiet and peaceful here," I sigh.

Josh steps into the room behind me, his hand brushing my waist as he passes. "Safe to say you're in love?"

I smile big at that. "Yes, safe to say that."

Josh looks different here too—more at ease, almost his age. I forget he's only twenty-four sometimes. Without the weight of responsibility or title pressing down on him, there's something softer in his face. I can see the boy he might've been before he became Beta, before his world changed and I get it now, why he loves it here.

There's something bothering him though. There's a hesitation about the way he watches me, like he's...observing me.

"What's wrong?" he asks.

"I was going to ask you that...and I don't have any clothes," I say slowly.

He ignores the first part and leads me to a his-and-hers closet, fully stocked with everything I could ever need.

I pause and tug on his arm. "Josh...I can't wear your mom's things."

"This is all yours—and mine," he tells me, a hint of a smile on his lips. He kisses my forehead, not caring about how dirty I am, before saying, "Shower, freshen up. Let me know if you need anything."

"I could use the truth," I try, and then add, "or...why we're here?"

"Let's start with the shower first," he says as he passes me by to give me some privacy.

It takes us about an hour, after Josh also showers, before I let him take me through Coilspire's corridors and toward a glass door. It leads to a massive terrace that seems to hang off the mountain itself.

The view is as unreal as I remember. Clouds drift below us like a sea of white foam, and beyond them stretch miles of mountain ridges painted with what's left of autumn—patches of gold and rust clinging to the bare trees. The wind is cool but gentle, carrying the faint sound of water gushing nearby. I leave Josh's side to step up to the balustrade, resting my hands against the cold stone.

I peer down below and say, "It's beautiful."

Josh presses up against me from behind. "I can't wait to fuck you here just like this," he murmurs, pushing into me harder so I feel his very eager length press against me. He's obviously thought of this before.

I turn my head just enough to look at him. "Now?" I ask, half shocked, half amused. He smirks, eyes dark with that familiar hunger. I love how he looks at me now.

"One day," he says softly, his voice low enough only I can hear. I bite my lip, just now realizing the very high possibility of Josh and I having sex on this getaway. We've been teasing each other enough. It's been good until the night he gave me the necklace—we still need to talk about that. I'm not entirely opposed to having sex, if I get the truth first about why he lied to me. Is he protecting Nathanial?

Before I can reply, the staff begin stepping onto the terrace, setting the table for Josh and my first meal at Coilspire. He gives me a quick wink and takes my hand, pulling me toward the table.

"Come on," he says with a grin, "let's eat before I change my mind."

48 COLORS

Rosella Craving
November 8

I spend the first day at Coilspire recovering. Using my magic had worn me out. It's strange because I don't use my magic at all. It's not the kind that I need to use to keep up with it. My magic is a part of me and works just like breathing air or my heart beating does, but I felt so depleted.

Josh says he needs to meet with Ridley to go over a few housekeeping details the next morning. He says it will be quick.

It gives me the perfect opportunity to take myself on a tour of the newly remodeled Hunter home. Josh offered to give me the tour, but I want to take it in by myself and reminisce about parts of my childhood being here when our families were still whole.

The hallway stretches, and as I walk, my footsteps echo softly against the dark wood or stone floors. Coilspire has been standing for centuries but everything inside is redone from the last time I was here.

The walls are smooth and dark, painted in deep charcoal tones with sleek paneling that gives off a quiet elegance. Brass sconces line the corridor, their warm light reflecting faintly off the glass frames of modern art pieces that don't quite match the castle's exterior—but somehow work perfectly. It's like the past and present are holding hands here, refusing to let go of each other and I love it so much. It's very similar to Cravenhold in that way.

Large windows break up the walls, filling the space with soft natural light that cuts through the darker color palette. The ceilings are high, the beams exposed and stained black. Every now and then, a piece of antique furniture sits tucked against the wall—a reminder of the house's age—but they've been reupholstered, given new life in muted velvet and leather.

Josh's mom had the home in lighter, neutral tones and Josh completely changed that. I don't know what I was expecting but I wasn't expecting it to still feel so…welcoming regardless of the dark mood Josh was clearly going for. The exterior of Coilspire screams legacy and power but the inside feels very family friendly still.

For a second, I let myself think what it might feel like to have kids running around here, like we used to. Is this where I eventually want to live and raise our children? Cravenhold is the only home I've ever known. I haven't dared to think of being in Coilspire for a long time, not with how volatile Josh and my relationship was. I didn't want to hope and get my heart broken unnecessarily. But with how peaceful it is here now, I can see it. I can see us raising a family here.

The corridors widen into open lounges that spill into one another, each layered across different levels. Past one archway, I glimpse the grand room—an open expanse carved right into the mountain itself. A massive waterfall crashes in the distance beyond a wall of glass, the sound muffled but constant, filling the silence. I've been hearing it since I stepped foot on the grounds and remember it's what always made Coilspire stand apart from the other Warrior homes. The view is unreal with mist rising from the cliffs, trees clinging to the rock, everything half-hidden in fog. I grin, leaning against the archway. I found the waterfall and it's a lot closer than I remembered it to be.

The rest of the castle follows that same pattern. Corridors twist into sitting rooms, staircases lead to balconies that overlook the gorge. The main dining hall stretches along the cliffside, the table long and carved from dark wood, lined with candles and glassware that sparkle in the mountain light. It's regal, intimidating, yet strangely intimate.

One change catches my attention the most. A reason why Coilspire used to feel lighter was because all the serpentine décor was a variety of colors—all shades of red, gold, white, green, blue, black…—every color known. Now, all the serpents have turned black, the beautiful colors swiped out and it's the only difference that saddens me. Josh's grief is written all over with this one impactful change.

I push through heavy glass doors at the end of the corridor on the first floor, and the chill hits me first. The sharp, crisp November air bites at my cheeks and slips under my sweater immediately. The gardens spread out below the terrace in perfect tiers, as the Appalachian winter pauses just for this place. Manicured lawns roll down in green waves, edged by low hedges. There are late-blooming roses that shouldn't still be alive this far into November, but here they are, stubborn and fragrant.

Fruit trees stand in rows along the upper level stripped bare now, their branches skeletal against the sky, but the lower orchard still clings to a few late persimmons, oranges, and pomegranates bright against dark bark. Water trickles from a three-tiered serpentine fountain and smaller bird baths dot the flower beds, their surfaces rimmed with thin ice that catches the light. It's all so beautiful and I remember coming here in the spring and summer, running around while Mom and Helena had their tea or picnics.

My shoes crunch on the gravel as I descend the wide stone steps. The ground feels alive with whatever old magic keeps this place blooming when the rest of the mountains have already turned inward for winter. The wind brushes my face, carrying the distant crash of the waterfall and the sweeter note of those impossible roses.

I sit down on one of the black iron benches and pull out my phone to text the girls. When I open my messages, I see that I've been flooded with texts.

Mariella: *Are you okay?*

Daniya: *Daniel woke up to a shit ton of texts saying Josh is exiled from Cravenhold?*

Mariella: *Antonio too…Rose? Where are you?*

Daniya: *Answer before I tell the whole world you're missing?*

Mariella: *Sam's trying to keep this quiet so good luck with that…Rose? Seriously, reply…*

The texts keep going and I see similar texts from others. Nothing from my brother or even Vanessa. I know James and Devaughn were there the night I was attacked, so maybe they know more and told Vanessa. Only Shane or Nathanial can exile Josh, if that's even true.

My heart beats faster. What if Nathanial found out I remembered? What if something *did* happen and that's why we're here? Josh never did give me a straight answer. Why did we leave so abruptly? He couldn't wait until the morning? We didn't even get to pack.

I text the girls back, knowing they're probably worried sick.

Me: *Text me the second Eliza even shows signs of having the baby.*

I attach a video of the gardens with me in it, so they have proof of life. Daniya replies immediately.

Daniya: *Oh thank the Divine, you're okay!*

Daniya: *And obviously. OMG, is it true? Josh got you guys exiled?*

Mariella: *Daniya!*

Daniya: *Can we at least visit you? What happened?*

Question of the day.

Mariella: *They're saying Josh kidnapped you after a fight.*

Daniya: *They're saying he hired assassins to kill you and then kidnapped you.*

What the fuck?

Me: *I'm sure it's not that serious…I'm still alive and at Coilspire…*

Mariella: *I agree. It'll blow over. Have fun there though!*

Daniya: *GET LAID!!!*

And just like that any concern for my life is gone, but I roll my eyes, smiling a little.

Me: *With who?*

Daniya: *Bitch, you can't play it cool after what we all saw between the two of you at the Veyara Gala. That chemistry was HOT!*

Daniya: *You can hate him all you want, you don't have to hate his goods ;)*

Daniya: *At least do it for yourself. Use him, he deserves a little payback anyway*

Mariella: *OMD…*

Mariella: *Agree with the payback though…*

Me: *You know what…that's an idea*

Mariella: *Nooooo, I was kidding!*

Daniya: *Just don't get pregnant…defeats the purpose of a payback*

"You're not in Cravenhold," Nathanial's voice rings through my mind. Nathanial and Shane are the only ones outside a Marked pair, who can telepath anyone at any time. Some of us like using the phone.

"Josh brought me to Coilspire. We'll be back soon," I answer with a small smile, playing stupid.

"Not if your brother has anything to say about that. Josh got you both exiled from Cravenhold," Nathanial thinks to me. He sounds irritated, but his thoughts are…suspicious.

So it is true.

Nathanial would never believe rumors. If he's bringing it up, then it happened.

"So…un-exile us? You're…you," I reply to Nathanial.

"Shane and Josh made a whole scene in the middle of the night. There were witnesses, you know I can't undermine your brother. Fix this, and come home," Nathanial telepaths agitated. I've never heard him so on edge.

"I don't know what you expect me to do. Shane and Josh probably got into a fight. They'll get over it," I reply, then add sweetly, ***"just go to your cabin and enjoy the winter. I'll be back***

before you know it."

"We have things to do." Nathanial's patience is running thin.

I frown. ***"Things? Like what? I'm sure we won't be here long. Can't be more than a week or two."***

"Come home," he demands.

"Is everything okay? You sound stressed," I ask him, concerned. ***"If it's serious I can ask Josh to—"***

"No, it's fine. Just…try to come home quickly. Eliza will have the baby soon, you can't miss it," Nathanial reminds me.

Guilt washes over my skin. Eliza is due any day now and I completely forgot with everything going on.

"You're right. We'll be home soon," I think to Nathanial and when he doesn't respond, I Facetime the girls. They answer it right away.

"Oh my Divine, what is going on?" Daniya asks.

"I was hoping you could tell me. Why did Josh get exiled?" I ask them.

Mariella frowns. "He didn't tell you…? All we know is there was an argument between Shane and Josh."

"Devaughn told Daniel it was pretty bad and it had to do with you. But hold on, you were attacked?" Daniya asks me and I see both of them looking for any injuries on my face.

"It was very random…but Cristobal and I…" I trail off, remembering what I had to do that night.

Mariella's voice is soft as she says, "The rumors are blowing it up, saying your powers got out of control and you killed Serpent Nation delegates."

I frown. "Everything happened very fast, but my attackers weren't serpent shifters," I tell them, and ask, "Their fight was about me?"

Daniya gives me a sympathetic look. "Devaughn wouldn't say about what exactly, but Josh wanted to take you to Coilspire after the attack and Shane put his foot down. Josh took you anyway, so Shane exiled him for disobeying command."

I hear footsteps and look up to see Josh walking towards me. Judging by the look on his face, he's heard my conversation.

"I have to go," I tell the girls. "We'll talk later."

They understand and we hang up. I stand as Josh gets closer.

Aside from dodging the important questions, Josh has been nice since I woke up in the car. I'm not falling for it for a second. I know he's genuinely happy to be here, but how he feels for me…jury's still out on that.

"Were you going to tell me we are exiled…or do I pretend to not know about that too?" I ask Josh. I deserve to know why Nathanial is messing with my memories, why Josh covered for him, and why we're suddenly exiled, leaving me alone with him. I would be more nervous if I didn't have my powers.

Josh's eyes narrow, before he runs a hand over his mouth. "Your brother was being an idiot."

I cross my arms over my chest. "My brother is our Alpha. You can't just kidnap me and disobey him."

"Kidnap you?" Josh laughs, amusement taking over his face. "Well…I guess I did. It is all true."

I stare at him. His lack of seriousness around it makes it feel like a game he's playing. Him covering for Nathanial trying to erase my memory keeps resurfacing in my mind. He cannot be in on any of this, right? He can't be. Josh is a lot of things but he's not…he's not the villain.

My Mate…cannot be the villain.

"Except that my attackers weren't serpent shifters." My voice is firm.

"No," Josh says, confidently too. Now he is serious. He's right in front of me, inches away. His scent engulfs me, relaxing me, but I stay alert. As much as I love how he smells, I'm learning it's one of his little tricks to diffuse situations and disarm mentally.

He's using his powers.

"You sound so sure," I challenge.

"I am because your attackers were members of the Sisterhood of Sin Coven," Josh answers, shocking me. "Assassins."

My mouth parts in disbelief. "But…the alarms…how did they get in?"

There's a tick in his jaw as anger flashes in his eyes. "Isn't it obvious? Someone let them in. There's no way in Hell that many of them slipped through our defenses. Cravenhold is under lockdown."

"And you got us out…" I whisper, but now I'm more confused. How is any of this related to each other? If Josh wanted to leave with me, why would my brother stop him in the first place? "Does Shane know?"

"Of course," Josh replies. For someone who's been exiled, he seems alright with the decision.

We have a traitor amongst us. A traitor who's working for the most dangerous witches in our world. Why would they want to scare me though? That seems like a pointless move. Why would they show their hand like that just to scare me and not actually try to kill me?

It doesn't make sense.

I rub my temples. First Nathanial, Josh's aunt, Josh, now this? I have a feeling it's all connected but I just…I don't know how and it's really starting to piss me off.

"Why did you get into a fight with Shane about me?" I ask, glancing at him.

"Your brother would love to spoil you and keep you soft and pretty as if you're a doll," Josh answers. There's a slight sneer in his tone as if the idea of me sitting pretty disgusts him. He doesn't want a trophy wife? That's news. A hard look passes over his eyes, before he continues, "We have a difference in opinion."

"I'll say."

"After seeing what you did to those assassins…I get why Shane doesn't want anyone to know about your powers. He's always said you were a secret weapon, one he never wants to use, but—"

"You do," I whisper, the sadness evident in my voice. Of course he does. Serpents are all about power. It makes sense he's my Mate. Maybe Shane was right to keep my power a secret. He always knew people would want to exploit me. There's a reason why Shane was always overprotective of me—so why would Shane exile Josh, and me with him. He basically just handed me to Josh by doing that.

Josh frowns, brows furrowing. "I want *you* to use your powers."

"But you want to dictate how I do it," I argue.

"I have no desire to control your powers when I have my own, Rose," he gives me a stern look, telling me he won't entertain my line of thinking.

Josh eyes my outfit—it's nothing fancy and maybe I should've worn something nicer to play the part of Lady of Coilspire. I just wanted to be comfortable, so I chose a black dress with matching tights and a jacket to keep me warm.

"With all that said, we're late for your training," Josh tells me, and I look at him.

"Training for what?"

"Your magic," he answers. "We're exiled, not on vacation."

A laugh escapes me.

"My magic?" The laugh dies quickly as I remember my attackers. I look down and say quietly, "You know what I can do. I don't need training."

I don't want to use my magic like that ever again. I swore I wouldn't use my magic to hurt anyone.

"You fainted," he reminds me. "Just because you're powerful doesn't mean you've disciplined your body to wield your magic."

His words irk me, because what does he even know about my powers? Nothing. My body—and my magic—feels highly disrespected by what he's insinuating.

"My magic would like me to say fuck you," I reply.

He raises his dark brows. A small smirk appears at the corner of his lips before he closes the remaining distance between us. He grabs me by the back of my neck, a firm yet entirely possessive hold, as he leans in, lips brushing my ear.

"Then tell your magic to fuck me properly, sweetheart."

49 LOVE AND WAR

Josh Hunter
November 8

By the time we reach the cliffside, night has fallen. The trees are silhouettes against the dark skies. I shift back and she follows. Her hair is flying against the strong winds from a snowstorm brewing.

I have a sudden urge to run my hands through it. Her hair is always so soft.

"You want to train me so bad, so train me," she shrugs, zipping her jacket all the way up to her neck before holding out her hands as if to say the floor is mine.

This is finally my chance to see her powers in action. I have a feeling I'm going to be sorry about it, but the temptation to see her magic at play is too much.

I hand her a blood bottle. "Drink."

She does without any pushback. She finishes it and tosses it aside, looking at me, waiting.

"I want to see what you are fully capable of," I tell her.

She rolls her eyes. What the fuck is it about this girl and rolling her eyes that my cock *enjoys?*

Seriously? Why is it that disrespect is a fucking turn on?

But why is she not taking this seriously?

She glances around before mumbling, "Dumbass."

"What was that?" I ask, raising a brow at her. I can't lie. I'm intrigued as fuck.

She holds my gaze. "You're at a disadvantage here with the darkness." She's not mocking or teasing, just stating facts.

"It's cute that you're worried about me, but I can handle myself," I reply, putting some distance between us. "Channel it," I tell her.

"Channel what?" she asks, confused. "My powers? That's not how it works."

"Your anger," I answer, letting my own powers loose to test her. "At me. At everything you think I've done to ruin your life. The bond.

The lying. I don't care what the excuse is. I want to see what we're working with here."

Her rosy lips part like she wants to argue, but she swallows it and says, "Those are things *you're* angry about."

I hold my ground, my hands open at my side, inviting her. "Like I said, I don't care what it is."

She just looks at me, but behind her, the trees start to disappear as everything slowly gets darker and darker. Black ink-like magic swirls at her feet as the air tightens. Her eyes are all black while her powers reach me slowly, making my heart beat faster with anticipation.

She's controlling how fast or slow they move. It's almost as if her powers react to her thoughts—knows what she wants without her even trying. The look on her face is calm, relaxed even. The way she stands there, not moving a finger or guiding her powers, and they act regardless…it's impressive.

I let the darkness curl at my boots, wrapping around my legs. I watch her, studying how it bends to her will, remembering what Daniel told me back at The Den.

"You won't hurt me. Push harder," I encourage, a little annoyed that she thinks I'm incapable.

"You don't know that," she says, "you don't know what my powers could do to you."

"Don't you want to find out then?" I ask her with a small smile. "I've heard you can suck the air out of people painfully, make them choke, go blind, but even you don't know what they can do to me. You killed a whole team of trained Sisterhood of Sin assassins."

Her powers curl higher, twisting, but she's hesitating. It's obvious.

"You don't have to hold back right now," I push her. "No one's here to tell you to not use your powers. Stop restraining."

Her eyes narrow. "You don't know what you're asking for."

"You're right, but we know you can't kill me," I remind her. My own shield snaps into place creating the invisible dome around me that's never been broken.

"You don't *know* that," she repeats so quietly I barely hear her.

"Hit me," I demand.

Nothing happens.

"Come on, Rose, we're not leaving until I see something that scares the shit out of me," I tell her and smirk at her, "I know you want to hurt me."

She frowns at that.

Does she *not* want to hurt me? After everything I put her through?

I clench my jaw. That's worse.

The darkness that looked like spilled black paint splits into jagged shards, like black glass, hurling straight for me. I brace for it, my shield catching the first hit.

She attacks a second time and then a third—each strike stronger than the last and I feel the impact in my bones as my shield takes it.

She attacks again and I focus on one particular shard, letting it pass my defenses. It grazes my arm, cutting through my sleeve and skin with ease. The burn is instant as if a blade sliced me.

Rose freezes, her powers instantly returning to her as she takes a step towards me. "I didn't—"

"It wasn't you," I cut her off as I examine my arm. There are no remnants of her power on me, just the cut. Interesting. I heard of a man who had the unfortunate luck of experiencing Rose's powers. Black tendrils had spread across his skin, slowly, and he was in agony before Rose called her power back. It was a warning for the man, but she could've killed him if she wanted to.

"You're bleeding," she says as she starts to walk up to me.

I shake my head, using my power to heal the wound. "It's nothing. I was testing to see what would happen."

"You were *what*?" she asks, darkly, but remains in her spot.

I look at her, cracking my neck and reinforcing my shield. "Do it again."

"No."

I roll my shoulders before turning to show her my arm. There's no sign of the cut. "See? I'm fine. Already healed."

"It was your arm. What if it's something else next time?" she shakes her head. "I don't particularly want to die tonight because I killed you."

"You won't kill me. Our Mating bond won't let that happen, you know that," I tell her and her eyes flash at me.

"The *Warriors'* Mating bond won't allow it. Yours and mine—" she gestures between us with her hand, "we both know it's not that same as the Warriors' so do you really want to test it?"

"Yes," I answer but she doesn't move. She doesn't attack so I do it for her.

I let my Beta power surge, the weight of it slamming against her. I see the anger in her eyes for a second before her power flares around her instantly, protectively. It's instinctual, acting on her behalf. It lashes out and then folds inward, sealing her off. A solid black shield erupts around her in a perfect cylinder that's nearly twenty feet tall. It looks smooth, like polished obsidian. I can't see her inside of it, can't feel her either.

"Really? You're going to hide?" I taunt her.

No response.

I roll my eyes, shaking my head, then hesitantly press my hand against the slick, cold surface, surprised to find it truly solid. The power pulses under my palm, alive and I stare at it. It doesn't feel like magic—it feels like her.

For almost all shifters, our powers, our gifts are an extension of us. They're a skill we have to craft and learn. It requires discipline, training, control and a lot of it.

Rose's power isn't separate from her—it is her. Like a sixth sense. She doesn't have to think to use it. She doesn't command it like we have to with our powers. It's almost as if it acts on its own, but never beyond what she wants or her best interest.

I stare at the cylinder in awe.

Does she know how powerful she is? Truly how powerful she is?

Taking a few steps back, I say, "Alright, if you want to shield, let's see how strong it is."

I slam my Beta power into the cylinder.

The ground quakes under my feet. I've used this same force against all the Warriors in training and only Shane was able to withstand it but not without strain.

Ripples of my green magic race across the slick surface like water does when skipping pebbles, but the cylinder doesn't break.

I strike again, my power digging and pressing from every angle, trying to find a weak point.

There is none. It's solid all around.

I walk up to it, placing both hands on the surface before pushing my power out directly into it. It vibrates against my palm, rippling all around, but it stands.

I exhale, frustrated, and pull back. I glare at the obsidian shell between us. My next strike carries more weight.

Shards of blackness rip outward from her cocoon, jagged and vicious, as if I pissed it off. I throw my shields up instantly just in time for the shards to make contact. They circle, enclosing me in a storm of dark blades, pressing tight, forcing their way. Each strike is like a hammer blow, my shield ringing with every impact. My jaw clenches as I feel the pressure of them and my shield *cracks*.

My breath hitches as I reinforce it. What the fuck? No one's *ever* been able to get past my shield.

Then I see the cylinder dissolving, misting away like it wasn't just solid rock moments ago. Rose stands there, her eyes pitch-black, fingertips charcoaled, like her power physically latched onto her, like it did last night. I know what it did to her, and the only reason I insisted we train today is because I want to push her. I want to see how far she can go.

The shards hit harder, and harder. I push back just as hard but then—my shield shatters completely.

I'm breathing heavy, but I force myself to stay standing, feeling the blow as if she punched me all around. Her shards are suspended in the air, not pushing past where my shield was.

She walks toward me, silently. The black shards part for her, clearing her path. It's like something out of a movie.

There's no emotion on her face. Without heels, she barely comes up to my shoulders. She has to tilt her chin up, looking me straight in the eyes—her own still pitch black. It takes my breath away like the first time I ever saw them.

"Let's clear some things up," she says, her voice low and careful. "You can't train me—you have no idea what my powers are or what they can do. And you don't have to train me—I can hold my own, as you just saw," then her eyes narrow slightly, "you don't have to defend me to the Elders, or whatever bitch wants to mouth off. And you sure as Hell don't have to play the hero in front of people…not when you don't mean a word of it. I am your Veyara—but *I'm* nothing to you. You keep lying to me and proving I'm nothing to you."

The shards don't look so happy and neither do their wielder. I can't look away from her. I can't find my voice either. I deserved that, of course—but damn does she look hot telling me off.

Since my mind went there, her scent is all I can think of now. I crack my neck to distract from the itch crawling up my spine.

"The only thing I can expect from a snake," she continues, quieter but her voice still just as sharp as her shards, "is to be bitten."

"What is with the animosity," I joke dryly, but I know she's still pissed about what happened in the Old Tower, but my mother's necklace did it's job. I don't regret shit.

"I told you I didn't want to do this," she snaps. By this she means training. Yeah, she made that clear.

Her shards collapse. They fall like shattered glass, hitting the ground and then vanishing into the dirt. She turns to leave, her black hair flying and shoulders stiff.

My hand moves before I can think and I catch her fingers. She flinches, making my eyes drop to her hands. The magic that was at her fingertips has covered her hands. Her face is pale and eyes back to her normal gray, but she doesn't look like she's about to faint. She tries to pull back, but I don't let go.

"You're hurt," I say, frowning.

Her jaw tightens. She jerks her hand free, putting distance between us. "Good, pain fuels me," she says, "same way hate fuels you." She starts to turn, "I'm fine."

"Good," I reply flatly, "because we're not done."

Before she can respond, I unleash my Beta power again, sending her flying into the trees.

But she doesn't crash.

Her darkness rises like a cloud, catching her midair. She hangs there, suspended for a moment.

Her black eyes widen, disbelief flickering across her face. "What the actual fuck!"

My own pulse stutters. I wasn't sure what I was expecting when I sent her hurling, but it was not that.

Before I can react, she's on me.

Darkness whips forward in a relentless storm, hammering at my shield. I brace against it, pushing harder than I have, holding my defenses firm. But she doesn't stop. She maps me out, her darkness spreading like ink across glass, wrapping my shield so completely that I can't see her anymore. I can only see three feet in front of me, where my shield is, and that's it.

I'm blind.

It's only instinct that keeps me braced as the shards slam into me, one blow after another, ringing against my barrier with a force that makes me clench my teeth. I dig deeper, strengthen the shield, sweat beading at my temple.

So maybe she does want to hurt me a little after all.

She doesn't let up.

It's hit after hit, strike after strike. Sharper. Heavier. Angrier. For the first time in my life, I'm not the one attacking—I'm holding the line.

For the first time in my life, I'm on the defense.

Not even Shane's ever pushed me like this. No enemy ever could.

I stare at the darkness around my shield in awe. It's incredible.

She's incredible.

When her magic finally recedes, the pressure loosens. My shield flickers, then steadies, and I see her again.

She's standing on the ground, just a few feet away, chest rising and falling. Her eyes are midnight black, hair flying behind her, and darkness swirling around her as if they're worshiping her.

She's a fucking beautiful monster.

And fuck, all I can do is stare at her, forgetting to breathe. My cock strains against my pants, each beat of my heart pumping blood lower. My skin tingles, electric—every instinct in me is screaming to Mark her. Claim her. Make her mine so there's no doubt, so no one looks at her.

I force myself to even out my breathing, but my pulse is racing.

She doesn't even know what she looks like right now. She doesn't know what she does to me. The power radiating off her, the darkness defending her—I should feel terrified. She did what nobody ever could and shattered my shield. She forced me to be on the defense like no one ever has without even breaking a sweat.

But all I can do is stare at her mouth.

Yes, she killed my brother. Yes, I'm fucking torn about it—about her. But she's *mine*. Learning Nathanial's been wiping her memories made me see red. Made me realize maybe, just maybe, everyone might be right—maybe there is more to the story the night Noah died.

It was Nathanial's idea to wipe her memories six years ago—what if he was controlling her far longer? I wouldn't put it past him, knowing what I've done for him from a young age to distract him from my powers, but he just found another victim.

My Mate.

Her shards are still up, threateningly, still pushing against my barriers. How can she say she's nothing to me?

I let my shield drop completely.

Her eyes widen, panic flashing across her face as the shards suddenly have nothing holding them back. For a heartbeat, I see her doubt herself—but then she reins it in, every jagged edge pulls back before they can pierce me.

"Are you fucking *crazy*?" she yells, fury and fear mixed in her voice. "I could've hurt you!"

I walk toward her, not really thinking. "You couldn't," I say, then grab her face and kiss her.

Her lips are soft, but cold and unmoving.

She doesn't kiss me back.

I kiss her again, harder, wanting—needing—her to meet me halfway.

Again, she doesn't kiss me back.

It cuts deeper than any of her shards ever could.

I break away, searching her face, but she pulls back altogether. Her darkness recedes and her mouth trembles as her face is somewhere between tired and sorrow.

"You might've dropped your shield, Beta," she whispers, "but I haven't dropped mine."

The words stab into me like she took a knife to my heart and twisted it. Whatever I imagined she might be feeling after the Old Tower—it's worse.

She gives me a sad smile, one that guts me, then starts to turn toward Coilspire. I reach for her again anyway, fingers brushing her shoulder—and she flinches like when I touched her fingers but harsher this time.

This time I feel the pain searing my own shoulder, burning like acid. I pull my hand back instantly, frowning at her.

"Take off your jacket," I demand, crossing my arms over my chest.

She doesn't move to do so.

"Now, Rose," my Beta command ordering her, forcing her to comply. I'm not above taking her free will and she knows it.

She stiffens, then obeys, unzipping her jacket and revealing her sleeveless dress. The darkness has spread from her palms, crawling up her arms, across her shoulders, edging close to her chest and throat.

My stomach drops at the sight.

She catches the horror on my face. "Sexy, huh?" she pulls the jacket back on. "It's fine. Nothing a hot bath can't take care of."

I don't know if that's true or not, but I don't know anything about her powers or how it works. I don't know what the repercussions are of her using her powers. I don't know the extent of it—Hell, I don't even know the beginning of it. Cristobal said this started after she shifted, after the Claiming clock started ticking.

"Can you shift to get back?" I ask, clearing my throat. I will carry her if I have to.

She nods. "Shifting helps us heal faster. You know that."

"Rose." My hand twitches at my side. I feel fucking useless. "I'm worried."

She pauses, just for a moment, before she laughs at me. "Worried?" she repeats, amusement dripping from the word. "Why? I thought you loved seeing me in pain. So look, Beta," she says, smiling, "revel in it while you can."

She takes a step back, before her body turns into a stark white wolf. She stands out in the night, the contrast of her fur almost as bright as the Moon above.

My throat tightens as I stare at this version of her that I asked for retreating into the trees.

Nathanial's trusted me with certain things, but I know he's skeptical about my abilities. Mates are always equal in power to balance the scales of nature. Tonight, after seeing Rose's magic, I finally understood why Nathanial never fully trusted me. He knew all along that I've been lying to his face.

50 HUNTER

Rosella Craving
November 8

I stare at my hands in the shower as the darkness washes away with the soap. I was so proud that I never used my powers to kill. I can't say that anymore. I killed too many the night I was attacked—so many that I lost count. Yes, they attacked me. Yes, they were Sisterhood of Sin, but still. I used my powers to take lives.

The stronger the power I use, the longer it takes to restore my skin. Small uses usually don't take a toll on me. I use it all the time. But something like that night and tonight's training, I feel the effects in my bones.

The pain isn't unbearable after a warm bath or shower, but my muscles feel tender, like they're bruised. I'm sure if I keep at it and use stronger powers, it'd be worse, but it's why I don't use my power to its full extent. I also never need to. The night of the attack was necessary and not an everyday occurrence. Today's training was reckless.

When Shane assigned Josh to be my trainer, he didn't mean this. Shane would never mean this. Not after we stopped training last year because he saw how it was weakening me. It scared him. It scared me.

I'm powerful, but so fucking mortal.

The water still clings to my skin as I dry off then slip into a black night dress and step out of the ensuite bathroom, hair dripping from my shower. I blink when I see Josh sitting in the armchair by the window, elbows on his knees, muscles tight.

I thought he was in his office…

My heartrate picks up. "Um, hi?"

He stands, walking up to me to take my hand before guiding me toward the couch. He eases me down to sit. I watch him, a little confused, but when he drops to one knee in front of me my heart pounds. I don't know what it is about this man kneeling in front of me that makes me forget everything he's ever done that's hurt me.

He reaches for my thighs, making me flinch, instinct pulling me back.

"Let me," he says softly, meeting my eyes. "I can heal it, if you'll let me." I blink, biting my bottom lip, before giving him a slow nod. He rests one hand over my thigh and holds my hand with the other, but his gaze doesn't leave mine. "Look at me."

I do.

"You did what you had to do," he says and I know he's talking about killing the witches.

"There were too many..." I start to trail off as the weight of what I did settles. "I had to use my powers..."

I had to use my powers to kill.

I almost don't notice the warmth spreading from my leg and the ache softening. The sharp stings melt away and my skin cells begin to rejuvenate as my mind races. Coming to Coilspire was a good immediate distraction, but after our *training* session, after taking my time in the shower, I have to face what I did.

I killed.

His thumb brushes the inside of my knee. "It's okay. You had to."

"No..." I shake my head, "I killed them—without a thought."

"I would too," he replies, as he takes my wrist gently, turning it over to study the faint bruise from that night. His touch is careful, at odds with the storm in his eyes. He traces a gash near my shoulder, thumb brushing over my damp skin.

I shake my head again. "No, you don't understand."

"So help me understand," he says a little harshly, "those assholes attacked you and you defended yourself—you didn't kill for pleasure."

"But—Divine," I exhale, blinking back tears. "I don't feel bad. I...I should feel bad, right? And...I liked it. Not the killing—I liked that my powers were unleashed like that."

I recall how easy it was, how I didn't even think before taking the lives.

Like it wasn't my first time.

Like I've done it before.

I don't dare say any of that to him, because what if Josh is right? What if I did kill his brother and don't remember any of it? What if Nathanial erased my memories back then? What if in the middle of all the hate and the lies, Josh had been telling me the truth?

I don't know what to believe anymore. I don't know what my hands have done, or what my mind is capable of.

Josh's eyes flicker—fire and darkness all at once. His thumb lingers on my cheek, but his jaw flexes.

"You should be able to unleash your powers," he says, quietly, like he knows what it's like not to. I wonder if it has to do with being a basilisk, the restraint he has to have at all times to not use his magic as freely as he'd like. To not be his true self because his true self is a monster, like me.

"Yeah, well, they're not exactly the friendliest..."

Something flashes in his eyes, and it's not suspicion or judgement but before I can put my finger on it, he leans into me. "I wish I was there."

"Why? We handled it..." I say, quietly.

"Just to see *you*," he says and my heart skips a beat. His hand slides from my cheek down my throat, slow and possessive, making me lean into him as his thumb caresses my neck.

"I killed people," I whisper, but all I can really think about is his touch right now. It's wrong to be turned on in the middle of this, but he's not helping by touching me. I didn't even realize when he stopped healing me but I feel alive, like the pain was never there.

"Rightfully," he insists, his gaze piercing into mine. "I shouldn't have left the way I did when you woke up that morning..." he sighs heavily and leans back slightly. "Rose, I need to know what you remember so we can talk about it," he says to my surprise.

I search his eyes to see if he meant it. I don't know what changed his mind, but I'm not missing this opportunity for him to talk, not when he's volunteering.

"I know Nathanial tried to erase my memory of what I saw in the tower—who I saw." A shiver runs through me as I meet his eyes again. "What I don't understand is why he didn't try to erase yours, or why you covered for him?"

I have a shit ton of other questions but that's the most pressing right now.

"My father," he starts, "he fell out of favor with Serpent Nation."

I frown, because that is news to me. His father was a great Beta, a great person. "He was their Warrior. How?"

Josh smiles sadly. His thumbs caress the back of my hands, raising them and pressing his lips to my skin, letting it linger as if centering himself. Then he looks at me and says, "Because of my mom."

"Because she wasn't a serpent shifter," I whisper.

"Because she wasn't a shifter," he corrects and instead of the shock I thought I'd feel, I squeeze his hands. The silent reassurance seems to ease the tension in his shoulders as he relaxes them.

I hold his gaze. "Josh, your mom—"

"Was a witch," he whispers as if saying the words out loud could be catastrophic. He shuts his eyes, having carried this secret for so long now and now trusting me with it of all people. I know how hard this is for him. I know he's finally letting me in. We're finally addressing the night we went to the Old Tower.

"So…that was your mom's twin we met?" I ask Josh, slowly.

"I…that's what Nathanial said," he replies, running a hand through his hair.

"You don't believe him?"

"I don't know what to believe," he answers. Well, that makes two of us. He laces his fingers with mine.

I frown deeply, taking in everything he's saying.

"My father was like me. He hadn't found his Mate through the blood-tie union. He found my mom a lot later." Josh's voice is so low, like he's never said these words out loud. "No one talked about it after the Warriors accepted her. She was turned eventually and it became a secret never to be repeated. That's why you never knew. You always knew her as a shifter."

I don't have to use my power to know he's telling the truth. It's on his face—the torment. But still, I don't think it's the full truth. "Why do I still feel like there's more to the story?"

He exhales. "It's why Dad chose to keep us away from court…" he tells me, "things were getting bad for my mom. Serpent Nation never accepted her, despite her turning. My dad fell out of favor with them because he stood by my mom. After they died, I had to play my part to regain that favor. I did what I had to."

"What do you mean, did what you had to do?" I stare at him, before whispering, "That's why you wanted a serpent Veyara."

That's why he chose all those women over me. This is the reason why he defied our Mating bond, over and over. When he doesn't say anything, I carefully say, "You know we're different right? I *can* shift into a serpent with practice…"

"I know," he caresses the back of my hand, before saying, "I had no idea my mom had a twin. My mom never mentioned her family, but it makes sense. The woman in the tower was a witch, and she looked identical to my mother."

Okay…I guess being Mates and cheating isn't something he wants to address right now—if ever.

He's right though. If Helena turned into a shifter, it explains why Josh isn't human. It's still a crime Cedric committed. We're not supposed to sire or turn anyone, unless he had special permission from Nathanial, but why would Nathanial grant it. How could Cedric have a witch for a Mate?

Why does answering one question lead to ten more?

"I thought someone who was sired couldn't have children," I say to him.

Josh nods. "Yes, if we do it. Not if Nathanial does it. The Sires were able to have children, that's how our Houses were formed. I think the rule is that the one being sired has to be a witch."

"I didn't know Mates could be outside of our species…" I say slowly.

"Before us we didn't think Mates could be from Warrior families," Josh replies, evenly, giving me a small smile that melts my heart.

He didn't lie to cover for Nathanial or what Nathanial tried to do to me. He lied because he wasn't ready for me to know this about his family by talking about his aunt that morning. He was processing it too.

"Thank you," I say to him, "for letting me in."

"Thank you for showing me your powers. I know you didn't want to do that," he says gently, caressing my cheek.

"I didn't want to hurt you," I reply. In the past I didn't want to show him because he'd call me a freak, but that wasn't the reason now.

He nods, getting to his feet and kissing my forehead. "It's been a long day. Let's get some sleep."

He starts to turn away, but I catch his hand, standing up too. When he looks at me, time stops, and I'm acutely aware that it's just us.

Josh faces me, close enough that I can smell his unique citrus smoky spice scent. His eyes search mine, like he's asking a question he already knows the answer to but needs it anyway. My heart is surprisingly steady for what I know is coming, for what I want.

He touches me with a gentleness I've never felt from him—fingertips tracing my jaw, thumb brushing the corner of my mouth. The weight of his gaze is too much. I know this is it. This moment has been waiting for us far longer than tonight.

But I'm just me. How am I supposed to compare to all the women he's been with? Women with far more experience, who knew how to please him, do all the right things. Women he wanted. Women he chose.

He didn't choose me. He got stuck with me.

I drop my gaze, chin dipping, certain he's having second thoughts. Except, his hands cup my face instantly, not allowing it to fall and lifts it back up.

"Rose," he says, voice low and full of emotion as he looks me in the eyes. "I want to be yours tonight and every moment after. Only *yours*. If you'll have me."

Heat floods my cheeks. I bite my lip to hide the tremble, and his gaze darkens. He eases my lip free with his thumb, pressing down on it like he loves to do.

"Do you want me?" he asks, barely above a whisper and I realize he is second guessing, but not about me. He needs reassurance right now too and just the idea of that is shocking but the look in his eyes tells me I'm right. Especially after I didn't kiss him back earlier, especially after telling him being his is embarrassing…disgusting…

"Yes," I breathe. Of course, I want him.

I rise onto my toes and kiss him slowly, but full of heat, pouring everything I feel into it. His hands settle at my waist, pulling me against him, savoring the kiss until we're both breathing harder. Then his fingers find the straps of my dress, drawing them down inch by inch while I unbutton his shirt, taking it off.

His chest is warm under my palms, muscle shifting as he shrugs free. I trace the lines of his muscles and his tattoos. My fingertips brush over a scar, hidden well under the big Daevryn tattoo on his torso. I pause, looking up at him, my breath catching as I try to see it better. The ink does a good job masking the wound, but now that I'm touching it, I can feel how long and thick it is, starting just under his left pectoral and dragging all the way down to where his V dips low.

"What happened?" I gasp.

His fingers wrap around mine, stopping me mid-trace on that scar. He guides my hand lower until I feel the cool metal of his belt. "A story for later…I need those hands somewhere else right now."

I make a note to ask him about it another time. I have to know and he's not getting away with not telling me about this. For now, I start undoing his belt. His pants drop to his feet, and he steps out of them.

Josh stands naked before me and the sight of him steals my breath. He's so beautiful it hurts how much I want him—broad shoulders, perfectly sculpted abs, the V of his torso, the heavy length of him greeting me proudly. I've never seen anyone more perfect, and the knowledge of every serpent woman who's had him before me crashes in sharply. He's been with many, many women—women far prettier, older, more experienced than me. Women who knew what the Hell they were doing. Maybe I'm not ready for this, as much as I want him right now. I'm scared.

He wraps a hand around himself, stroking slowly, eyes locked on me. He nods and says, "Your turn, sweetheart."

I'm still in my dress as it hangs loose from the fallen straps. My words come out heavy as I ask him, "Can we…turn off the lights?"

He stills. The hand on himself stops, and his brows draw together, concern replacing desire for a heartbeat. He closes the space between us, cups my face again, and kisses me soft and certain.

"I want to see every inch of my perfect Mate," he murmurs against my lips.

I know his words are meant to be reassuring, but what if he sees me and doesn't think I'm perfect? What if he sees me and remembers how someone else was more beautiful and desirable? I don't want him to Mark me and I learn those were his thoughts the first time we were together.

"You have to know how beautiful you are…" he says slowly, watching me and it's not helping the situation. He sounds confused.

I squirm a little. "Please…"

"I know you're not shy, so what is it? Talk to me," he caresses my cheek.

I don't answer him, my mind racing, and I hate that my insecurities want to take over right now.

He doesn't push again and instead presses a kiss on my forehead, as the lights turn off, but the fireplace flares bright, illuminating the room. Candles on the mantel and throughout the bedroom spark to life, bathing the space in golden, forgiving light. The room is dark enough for me to slightly relax.

"A compromise," he says, voice tender.

Then he kisses me slowly again, trailing kisses down my jaw, my throat—while he slides my night gown lower. His lips follow, pressing over my collarbones, the curve of my breasts, the tight peaks of my nipples. He lingers there, tongue circling until I arch into him with a quiet gasp. His arm around me tightens, holding me in place.

He sinks to his knees, leaving open-mouthed kisses across my ribs, my stomach, down to my waist. The dress pools at my feet and he parts my thighs gently, dragging a finger once over my clit.

Pleasure jolts through me as I grip his shoulder, letting out a moan. He looks up, eyes dark and full of want, smelling my arousal, knowing how ready I am, how much I want this—want him.

He rises and carries me to the bed. The sheets are cool against my back when he lays me down, but his body follows immediately, covering mine with his warmth. Josh hovers above me, elbows braced on either side of my head. He kisses me, tongue stroking mine with a quiet hunger like he's forcing himself to not be too rough with me right now.

He pulls back just enough to meet my eyes. "We can wait. We don't have to do anything you don't want tonight."

I blink, a soft laugh escaping. "You touched me in front of all of our friends already…I think we're past that at this point…" Not to mention fucking me with his rattle.

"I want you to say it," he insists, thumb brushing my lower lip.

"Divine, yes," I whisper, cupping his face with both hands. "I'm yours. I want you."

"You want me how?"

Ugh, this man. "I want to feel you inside me," I tell him, blushing and I'm grateful I asked for it to be darker in here. "I want my Mate to touch me."

The words undo him. He kisses me again as he settles between my thighs, hands cradling my hips like he's touching something precious to him. His eyes never leave mine as he strokes my clit gently with his fingers, spreading my arousal until I'm aching for him. Around us, faint wisps of darkness begin to curl from my skin—my power rising instinctively, dimming corners even as the flames push back. It's a quiet dance of light and dark that mirrors the way our bodies move together. I know he can control his body temperature, but can he also control fire?

His basilisk heat unfurls, subtle and intoxicating, wrapping around us like a heated blanket. Every touch feels deeper, every breath more necessary.

"I've been an idiot for not worshipping you sooner," he murmurs against my throat.

"No argument there," I breathe, smiling through the haze.

His fingers slip inside me, curling slowly, coaxing soft sounds from my lips. He presses his forehead to mine. "Fuck, Rose. You're so wet for me."

I clench around his fingers, before he draws his hand away only to guide his cock to my entrance, pausing to search my eyes once more as my heart picks up speed.

"Are you sure?" he asks.

"Yes," I answer. I waited too long for this. I waited and gave up and grieved *this*. Now it's here and I don't want to wait anymore.

His thumb brushes my cheek. "Tell me if I hurt you."

"Which time?" I tease softly, but when his gaze darkens, I just nod. "I don't care if it hurts. I need you inside me."

He kisses me slowly. "I care."

"I'm giving you permission to not care for the first time," I whisper, before drawing his mouth back to mine. "I need you."

As our tongues explore each other, he eases into me and oh my Divine—just the tip of his cock is overwhelming, making me tense. The sweet burn from the pressure he applies makes me gasp into his mouth. Darkness grows thicker around us, protectively, while fire answers with a sudden rush of warmth as I close my eyes trying to take it in.

He pulls away from kissing me and says, "Look at me, Rose." I open my eyes and meet his striking gaze. "You're mine," he tells me—claims me.

"You're mine," I reply as he pushes in a little more, making my heart beat faster.

"Breathe, sweetheart," he says gently and I didn't realize I was holding my breath. He keeps his eyes on me as he pushes in a little bit more.

My entire body clenches, trying to push him out even though something else is demanding, pulling him in. It burns—it's not supposed to burn right? He moves again and it's too much. Too big.

"I can't," I whimper, tears stinging my eyes. My hands grip his shoulders as I try to push him. "I can't—"

He stops and focuses his entire attention on my face. "We're made for each other, baby," he murmurs, his voice rough with his own tension, but concern too as he tries to soothe me. "Breathe with me.

In…out…" I do and he kisses my forehead. "Good girl."

He eases forward another fraction, and my tears spill over. I let out a moan as he pushes again. "Jo…" I start to say his name but stop and sink my nails into his shoulders harder.

"Fuck, you're gripping me so hard," he groans, eyes dilating as his forearm flexes beside me. He guides my hand down between us, pressing my fingers to my clit. "Rub yourself for me, princess."

I start to and the sparks of pleasure helps dull the ache as I feel myself get wetter. He leans down, kissing me deeply, his tongue stroking mine and distracting me as he pushes into me again. His other hand cups my breast, thumb circling my nipple until I arch into him.

He pushes deeper and I catch my breath, my pussy clenching. I gasp, frustrated with my own body because I want this so bad. "I can't—I can't take more," I choke out as tears slide into my hair.

"Yes, you can, sweetheart," he growls, nipping my jaw before claiming my mouth again. He pushes forward another inch, and I cry out into the kiss. It feels endless, like he'll never fit, like I'll break before he's in.

I keep circling my clit, faster, chasing the pleasure, and slowly—Divine, so slowly—the burn starts to melt into pleasure as my body softens, opens, like it's finally remembering this is natural and he's my Mate.

With one more careful but insistent push, he's all the way inside me, filling me so completely I can't breathe for a second. My eyes fly open, wide and shocked, staring up at him. He's trembling above me, sweat dripping down his temple, gray eyes glazed with a look that's dangerously close to agony mixed with raw pleasure.

"You okay?" he asks, hoarse, hips twitching like it's killing him to stay still.

"Yes. You're really big," I whisper and wonder how on earth I took him in my mouth.

"Fuck, sweetheart," he breathes, voice trembling with restraint as his body shakes a little and he shuts his eyes.

"Are you okay?" I ask, tracing the strain along his jaw. "You look like you're in pain…"

"I am," he admits, resting his forehead against mine.

"Oh…should we stop?"

"Divine no," he growls, lips brushing tender kisses along my neck that make me shiver.

"Then why are you in pain?"

"Because you're so fucking tight." His voice is rough.

"I thought that was a good thing?"

"It is," he groans, pushing just a fraction deeper—though I didn't think there was room—and his eyes squeeze shut again. "You're...perfect...fuck."

My darkness swirls faster now, weaving through the candlelight, neither winning, only merging—embracing the same way our bodies do. I lift my legs a little higher against him and he settles fully inside me, stilling to let me breathe, to welcome the fullness of him.

It's all strange and overwhelming, but delicious at the same time. "Are you in pain because you're trying not to Mark me? I heard it hurts..." I ask him slowly.

"I'm trying not to come," he confesses, voice raw.

Oh.

"Why?" I whisper. "Isn't that the point?"

"Fuck me," he groans, claiming my lips again.

He begins to move, rolling slow thrusts that draw soft cries from me. The room glows and dims in perfect rhythm with us, light and dark breathing together. Pleasure builds gently, steadily, until I'm clinging to him, fingers tangled in his hair.

I breathe between kisses. "Don't stop."

His eyes lock on mine as he moves deeper, tender but unwavering. The pressure of my orgasm builds. His thrusts grow deeper. His fingers find my clit, circling softly until I'm trembling on the edge. He kisses my jaw, my throat, lips lingering over my pulse. I tilt my head in offering, urging him to Mark me.

But his mouth finds mine again, swallowing the moans escaping me as his hips roll faster. My hands slide up his back, fingers pressing into the warm muscle there, holding him as close as I can. His arms tighten around me in answer—one banded under my shoulders, the other cradling the back of my head—like he never wants to let go.

"Fuck, your perfect little pussy's opening up for me," he groans and kisses me, then adds against my lips, "it's fucking mine. All mine."

He feels so good and his voice alone makes my nipples ache with need. I tilt my head back, gripping his arms as I say, "Yes, my Beta. It's yours."

His thrusts quicken, steady but urgent. "This dick is yours," he tells me as each thrust pushes me higher, pleasure winding tight and sweet until I'm trembling beneath him. My body arches into his as my orgasm crashes through me. I open my mouth to scream out but I'm met with his groans while he pulses deep inside me, hips stuttering as he comes with me.

He keeps kissing me through it until the last tremor fades and we're breathing heavily. He eases us onto our sides, still throbbing inside me, and pulls the thick covers over us both. His arms stay locked around me.

"I don't want to pull out," he murmurs against my temple, voice rough with contentment. "You're my perfect fit, Rose. Fucking made for me."

I smile into his neck, drowsy and sated, my fingers tracing lazily across his back. He nuzzles closer, lips brushing my skin again and again, like he can't stop tasting me, touching me.

"How's my princess?" he asks in a low voice, lips against my temple.

"That was…I love sex," I say, turning into his chest to hide my blush.

His chuckle vibrates against me. "Yeah? That was fucking amazing. You are perfect and you're mine."

I run my fingers over his serpent tattoo, tracing the lines absently. After a long moment, I whisper, "Why didn't you Mark me?"

He stills for a second, then he shifts just enough to meet my eyes, thumb stroking my cheek. "Marking you isn't something I want to rush," his voice is low and certain. I can tell he's thought this through. "We'll share everything about ourselves. Every thought, every memory, every secret. I won't do that until you feel completely safe with me. Until you know, without doubt, how I feel for you." He leans in and kisses me. "I never want you to think it's a weapon I used to hurt you with."

The words settle warmly in me, chasing away the last flicker of uncertainty. He kisses me again, softer, then carefully slips out of me and I immediately miss him.

I whine and he laughs softly, pressing one more kiss to my lips. "I'll get something to clean you up," he murmurs as exhaustion pulls at me.

51 ETERNAL QUEEN

Rosella Craving
November 9

I find Miriam and ask her about the to-do list that Josh's mom left me while he sits in on an urgent Den Lord meeting. Miriam takes me to the library. It's tucked behind a pair of tall arched doors which I almost miss.

"Well, it's through there…but I don't have the key," she says and I frown.

"Then how are we—" I start but remember my birthday gift from my brother. He said the key had to do with Coilspire. I look at Miriam before retrieving the key from where I'd tucked it away in the air pocket.

She gives me a curious look, and I move to put the key into the lock. I turn it and the door opens, making me gasp at the beautiful sight.

It's enormous—three stories at least. The ceiling rises high above me, carved with wooden beams darkened by age. It smells like parchment, cedar oil, and that faint musty scent that only comes from old books. Rows of shelves curve across the room, packed with leather-bound volumes and scrolls that look as old as the collections at Cravenhold. Spiral staircases twist upward toward the higher levels connecting the balconies that wrap around each floor. A chandelier hangs at the center flickering over books, it's breathing life into them.

Miriam stares at it for a moment before nodding. Then she turns to me and says, "Only the Beta and Veyara have the key to the library."

"Why?" I ask, curiously.

"The late Beta was very particular about his collection and had specific instructions to only pass the key to his son and the next Veyara."

I raise my eyebrows, curiosity sparking in me. What the Hell is in this library?

"And Veyara Helena's task for you is," Miriam gestures to the massive room before us, "that you dust the place please."

I laugh. "Oh, well, that'll be fun. Dusting and exploring books."

"I'll leave you to it then, Veyara." Miriam smiles at me and leaves.

I walk in, the sound of my steps softens against a worn rug that runs along the center aisle. A long reading table sits under the tallest window, Sunlight spilling through the glass and cutting across the room. A few books are left open on the table—maps and family records marked with the Hunter crest. The ink is faded, but the basilisk facing the wolf is unmistakable.

Toward the back, I notice the blend of old and new. Some shelves hold digital terminals, neatly lined among thick original manuscripts. I return to the long table and glance at the books, pulling one toward me. The title stamped in gold along the spine makes me pause.

House Craeven: The First Bloodline.

I pick up another. *The Craving Legacy and the Rise of the New World.*

There are four more books, and all of them—every single one—is about my family.

I sink into the chair beside the table, staring at the books. Has Josh been looking into my family? He's the only other person who has keys to the library. But why?

I reach for a book titled *House Craeven: The First Family* and open it to look at the publication date.

There isn't one.

I flip the page. The table of contents focuses mainly of Nathanial, Mother Isis, Queen Aradia, and King Stefan.

I turn the pages and start with Mother Isis since Nathanial won't talk about her—at all. She's the Mother of shifterkind and well respected. We learn about the first family in school, but briefly, and I've never been able to get Nathanial to talk about Mother Isis.

She was a witch until she got ill and Nathanial turned her into a shifter. She was the first person he turned. There's so little written about her beyond the title of Nathanial's wife and mother of his biological sons. She and her sister, the vampire queen, Aradia, became the faces of magic, even though magic was simply life, in their time. Most of what we practice now—prayers, rituals, wards, blessings—goes back to them and their lineage.

I hungrily devour the information. Every record calls her by the same title—the Eternal Queen—and I quickly see why. It's not a term we address her by, but then again, we don't address her at all. But in every lifetime, she reinvented herself the same way—a Queen.

Her name was Iyna first—when Nathanial met her—when she wasn't immortal. The witch who loved the first shifter. The name next to hers is Na'at—Nathanial's name four thousand years ago. It doesn't say who their parents were. I haven't found a single record of it so far. Na'at and Iyna had three sons—Elandros, Mikaen, and Caelis. I learned about them in school. The sons were powerful witches like Isis, but the records in front of me say they didn't inherit the ability to shift.

I frown—that can't be right. Someone had to continue the Craeven bloodline. I flip through the pages and glance at the other books—maybe one of those have more information on this. There's always been a Craving Alpha, so there has to be an explanation.

I continue with Isis, making a mental note to explore that bit later.

Though Isis has many recorded names, the first one that catches my eye is Despoina. She was worshiped as a goddess in ancient Greece during the Mycenaean era. Despoina is a title she used and only her high priestesses knew of her true name—which is not mentioned. She had a secret cult following. She was thought to be the daughter of Demeter and Poseidon—and the sister of Persephone. Her followers were witches and they were well-revered at the time, though I'm sure the public didn't know the true depths of their magical abilities.

Next, she shows up as Queen Asiya. She was the wife of the Pharaoh, protector of Moses—finding a way to save what must survive.

My eyebrows rise as I flip the page to see her as Nefertari—the Great Royal Wife of Ramesses II. She's mentioned as a goddess hidden in plain sight. She restored balance to the world after The Cursed One's early uprisings.

Centuries later, she found her way back to Nathanial as the Queen of Sheba. Nathanial was King Solomon, and their reunion reshaped the continent. They were powerful in their own right, but together they literally ruled the world.

It makes me wonder why they were separated to begin with. Why was she the wife of pharaohs? Where was Nathanial then?

After being the Queen of Sheba, she was Isis of Carthage, the name that she chose to be known by in the shifter world. My heart speeds up as I read about Isis, the founder queen of Carthage who used her own life to bind The Cursed One for the very first time. This is the first mention of Isis being put to rest so she could restore her magic.

But when she woke again, she rose as Mary, Queen of Scots.

I exhale—Eternal Queen definitely.

Mary, Queen of Scots, is her last known alias. Her last life. The notes are brief—she was a martyr queen who died to protect the supernatural bloodlines after the Black Death—the supernatural world knows it as the last time The Cursed One attempted an uprising. Mary's death marked the moment The Cursed One fell silent—but Isis obviously wasn't killed then. Just put to rest. Isis sacrificed herself again to seal Lilith's power.

But Mother Isis is awake and has been in prayer for centuries which is why she never reinvented herself. When did she wake again? When did The Cursed One come back?

"I thought I'd find you in the library," Josh says from the doorway. I look up, startled. He steps inside slowly, taking in the space. "Divine, I haven't been in here in a while."

I swipe dust off the table and hold it up for him to see. "I can tell."

He laughs. "The staff aren't allowed. Only my dad really came in here. It was his favorite place in the world."

He looks around like he's seeing the memories of his father in here—memories that make him smile. I set the book in my hands down gently, though not before catching the title on the spine of the one beside it—*Craeven Curses.*

A chill crawls up my neck, but before I can think too long about it, Josh's voice pulls me back. "Find anything interesting?"

I stand up, turning to him and spin once in the space between us with my arms out. "The library's gorgeous," I say, grinning, "and it's so cozy in here."

He watches me with a soft expression. Then he steps forward, sliding his arms around my waist, and kisses me. I smile against his lips, my hands coming up to cup his face. I feel different with him today after last night. There's a familiarity and comfort that's settled between us and it makes me giddy and happy. Last night was beautiful and I couldn't have imagined our first time to be better. Being at Coilspire made it that much more magical.

"You found me," I murmur against his mouth.

"Always," he answers. His forehead rests against mine for a second, before I glance past him toward the tall window. The Sun is high above the cliffs so it's still early in the day. But then Josh frowns.

"What's wrong?" I ask, matching his look.

"I'm just annoyed that my rattle was in you before I was."

Startled by his words and still embarrassed by what we did on Mariella's reunion night, I maintain my frown. "That's just not a sentence normal people say."

"Yeah, but you and I aren't normal, by any definition," he replies, slapping my ass. I jump at the sudden impact, gasping but he captures my lips in his. His grip on my waist is delicious.

"How was your meeting?" I ask.

"Not urgent at all," he rolls his eyes, before he looks out the window and I have a feeling he doesn't want to talk about it. The Sun's lower now in the afternoon and I frown. Yule is closer with the days getting shorter.

"Tell me more about the Den Lords. I don't know much about them at all." I look at him, probing gently. He searches my face, hesitating, so I add, "I know you want me to stay out of serpent politics, but I should know the basics, and I'd rather know it straight from you."

"Hmm, there are seven in total—each Lord oversees their own species, reports to me when needed," Josh replies, as he goes to sit on the couch. He tugs me along, pulling me down to straddle him. I force myself to ignore his hard-on and focus on his words. I've never had to know about the inner workings of each species the Warriors ruled over.

His tone changes as he talks about the Den Lords. It's with the power and authority that he wields as the Beta Warrior. It's not arrogance, just duty. Beneath it though, I sense a discomfort which makes me even more curious.

"What are the seven Dens?" I ask, studying his handsome face. "I guess I should know this being your Mate…"

His hand rises higher up my thigh. "It's okay, we have time to learn each other's lives." I smile at the words, as he exhales. "The seven Dens are cobra, viper, python, mamba, boa, rattle, and seraph."

"Seraph?" I question.

Josh's eyes twinkle. "The rarest and oldest some may argue."

"Older than the basilisk?"

"Almost."

"Really?" I ask, intrigued.

"A seraphim angel and a basilisk shifter," Josh explains simply and

I raise my eyebrows.

"A hybrid," I gasp and he nods. I stare at him, "Don't we…kill hybrids?"

"The seraph Den is too powerful—their magic is always impressive, not to forget they can shift into any serpent form. Their angelic colors give them away though. Nathanial thought it was best to include them instead of executing," he says quietly but there's weight to his words as if this is a personal matter for him.

"But wouldn't a hybrid like that be more powerful than…you?" I ask carefully.

Josh doesn't take offense, four months ago he might've, but he chuckles, "They could be, but the seraphs are probably the only Den that's the most peaceful. Must be the angel in them."

Interesting. I press on, "Don't take this the wrong way, but why does Serpent Nation have a reputation of being messy?"

His jaw tenses and for a moment, but then he says, "The vipers and pythons are always causing problems. They stir things up for the sake of it. The vipers crave power, the pythons want control. The two do not play nice. The rest of the Dens tend to mind their own business, but with as much noise as the vipers and pythons create—it damages the rest of the Dens."

"How are the Lords chosen?" I ask, curiously, "Are they born into it like us?"

He hesitates this time as if he's weighing his words. "They're not chosen. They rise. They kill their way to the top. It's how they gain the respect of other serpents, especially those in power. Kill or be killed, it's simple."

"How does that work? Are they constantly challenging their leaders?" I frown. That sounds volatile and…messy. I start to shrug off my sweater. It's warm in the library. Josh watches me as I take it off to reveal a black turtleneck shirt and green plaid skirt. He seems a little disappointed to see actual clothes under my oversized sweater.

"No," Josh replies, "when a Lord dies, a special challenge among the Den is initiated. It's worldwide and each Bed in the Den can send their champion to the final challenge."

"I've never heard of this," I tell him.

He sighs. "Well, because there hasn't been a challenge since I was five. Dad took us to the final. It was for the boa Den. The youngest Lord yet. He was barely twenty."

"Evren Thane," I say, knowing the name. Lord Thane is…popular in many spheres.

"Yes. He's…a friend as far as friendship goes among serpent leaders," Josh says, quietly.

"You're not worried one of them might try to overthrow you?"

He laughs, the sound vibrating through me. "I'd like to see them try." There's no arrogance in it—just certainty. It's terrifying and magnetic and so fucking hot.

"Tell me more about the Dens and Beds," I ask, quietly.

His thumb brushes my jaw, softly, "What's your question, Rose?"

I drop my gaze to his tie, not wanting to look into his eyes. "Are we—would we…have our own…Den?"

I feel his eyes on me, watching me, and I will myself not to squirm, seeing that I'm still sitting on his lap. He lifts my chin to make me look at him, as he says, "I told you I'm not sharing you. The Beta and Veyara can choose to have their own Den, but unless it's something you're interested in exploring, I don't care to entertain it."

"Why?" I ask softly, very aware of his past, like it's written on my own skin.

His fingers trail down my arms. "The only Den I'm interested in with you is our own family—with our kids, and their kids."

Having children is expected of us, and even though I'm in no rush to have them yet, hearing him talk about kids makes my heart skip a beat and my nipples perk.

My hands travel to his neck, my left fingers tracing the outline of the serpent tattoo as I tell him, "The idea of sharing you makes me sick…"

He turns his head to kiss the inside of my wrist, before he looks at me again. "Then you'll never have to," he grips my hips tighter. "I have…good memories of us here at Coilspire. It's your home too, always has been, so I'm glad you're here right now, regardless of how it happened."

His hand comes up to press his thumb against my lip, slightly smearing my lipstick. Then he cups the back of my neck, pulling me into a kiss that's full of heat and hunger, his tongue sweeping against mine.

My pulse races, desire igniting low in me. I break the kiss, breathless.

"Nothing and no one will disturb us here," he says and his eyes are heavy with need.

"Promise?" I ask as I slide off him, dropping to my knees between his legs. He tracks my every movement.

"Rose," he says my name, voice rough, but I don't let him finish. My fingers work quickly, undoing his belt, the zipper, freeing his already hard cock. The sight of him, thick and ready, makes my mouth water, and I don't hesitate.

I lean in, my lips brushing the tip before I take him into my mouth, savoring the low groan that vibrates from him. His hand tangles in my hair, guiding me as I move. My tongue swirls around him, teasing, and his hips twitch, urging me deeper. I oblige, taking him further, the taste of him filling my senses as I find a rhythm. I find a certain comfort having him in my mouth.

"Fuck, sweetheart," he breathes, his voice strained, fingers tightening in my hair. The sound of his voice, raw and desperate, encourages me.

I move faster, hollowing my cheeks, my hand stroking what my mouth can't reach. I work him until his breathing grows ragged, thighs tensing under my palms, before he comes with a low, raw moan, his cum hot and thick in my mouth. Swallowing, I pull back slowly, licking my lips. My eyes meet his as I wipe the corner of my mouth, catching a smudge of lipstick.

He's staring at me, chest heaving, a mix of awe and desire in his eyes. He pulls me up to straddle his lap, his lips crashing into mine. My smeared lipstick stains his mouth, and I smile against him before sliding off his lap onto the couch.

"I'm still hungry though," I say to him, "think we can eat in our room? I'm a little tired…"

He eyes me. He must decide I'm fine because he smirks. "Tired huh? What were you up to last night?" I smack him as heat creeps up my cheek. Josh laughs, and says, "Of course, I'll tell Ridley to bring us lunch." Josh kisses the top of my head then fixes himself and we leave the library together.

I know I'll have time to return, because I am not done going through those books that seemed to be waiting for me.

52 PILLOW TALK

Rosella Craving
November 9

After lunch, I suggest a bath, but Josh doesn't get into it with me. Instead, he sits beside the tub and reads me a book I had packed. Well, he tries to.

"This is porn," he says and I scowl at him.

"Gross, no it's so much more—there's an actual storyline, and emotions, and complex—"

"It's porn written out."

I splash him with water, and he gives me a blunt look. I refuse to give in, defending my books. "It's cute and pure escapism, okay?"

He looks at me, covered to my neck in bubbles, my hair wrapped up in a messy bun. "Escapism? I thought that's what we're doing here."

I raise my eyebrows. "I thought we were exiled—not on vacation."

He puts my book safely away from the water and turns back to me. "Vacationing and escaping are two different things."

He leans back in his seat, looking too tempting in his black slacks and black T-shirt. The serpent tattoo coiled around his arm catches my attention.

"Why the roses?" I ask, bringing him out of his thought. I sink a little lower into the tub. The warmth feels so good. Since Coilspire is at a higher elevation, it's significantly colder here than Cravenhold. He looks confused so I gesture. "The roses on your arm. You got it after the serpent."

"You noticed," he says quietly. He got the serpent when he first transformed. The roses were added this year. I'm not sure exactly when he got it, but when I came back from the Tour, he had them, so it had to be before his birthday. I wasn't naïve enough to believe he got them because of me, because he missed me and was sorry for the cruel words he said. But now I'm curious.

Josh rubs the back of his neck, sheepishly. "I lost a bet to Devaughn."

"And he made you get roses? What was the bet?"

He's quiet for a second. "I don't want to say…it's embarrassing."

"Well, now you have to," I laugh, intrigued.

"After you left for the Tour, he bet a rose tattoo for every hundred photos I had of you in my phone."

My mouth parts open. "You have seven roses," I say, quietly.

"You counted," he smirks, before dropping his gaze to the edge of tub. "I told you it's embarrassing."

I don't say anything. I don't think it's embarrassing. I think it's very confusing. If Josh hated me as much as he showed, why would he have seven hundred pictures of me in his phone? It doesn't make sense and it makes me sad. Why would he have pictures of me at all when he was hooking up with serpent women making me think he didn't want me? Hurting me physically in the process.

"I think by now you know Devaughn has a soft spot for you," Josh says and now I'm uncomfortable. I don't know where he's going with this and I know he was jealous seeing Devaughn and me at the reunion even though nothing really happened.

"Why?" I ask.

Josh shakes his head. "I don't know, honestly. He's always been protective of you, like Shane, but…not."

"Does that bother you?"

"No. If I had to trust anyone after Shane with you, it'd be him. I know how obsessed he is with Crystal, so I'm not worried about anything like that."

"Not James?" I raise an eyebrow.

Josh chuckles. "James would if I asked him to, but Devaughn would a thousand percent go against me if it meant choosing your safety over loyalty to me. I think it's because he had a sister…"

Dahlia Claws. I wonder if Devaughn knows what really happened to her.

"Anyway, if I had an album with your name on it, the bet was to get your name inked," Josh continues the tattoo story.

"Well, you got lucky," I laugh, but stop short when I see the amused look in his gaze. My eyes widen. "No, you didn't! Where?!"

It's Josh's turn to laugh, before he sucks in his bottom lip, watching me. "You're just going to have to find it."

"Adding it to the list of things I need to find in your body," I say under my breath.

Josh smirks. "Still on that second dick huh?"

"Still?" I blink. "What do you mean still?" Josh just continues to laugh. I shake my head, and then ask more seriously, "How did you get that scar?"

He sighs heavily. "I'm not…ready to talk about it…"

I nod, accepting that answer. "Okay…can I ask when you got it?"

His eyes are focused on his hands as he says, "Six years ago."

I can't recall ever feeling anything that could've caused that kind of wound on his body. Is it possible I blocked it out? Would I even be able to do that?

"I'm sorry…I don't—I don't remember," I tell him honestly.

He nods and gives me a soft smile. "Probably best if you don't anyway."

He said he didn't want to talk about it, so I don't want to push and respect his wishes.

"Whatever happened to the box the seer gave me on Mabon?" I suddenly recall, remembering how he had Vanessa take it away to inspect it. I should've asked her.

"We're just thoroughly verifying it's not hexed," he answers me, easily. "You'll get it soon. I'll follow up with Crystal about it."

It's not unusual. It's protocol to check any item that's given to us. Safety is our utmost priority. Crystal, being as powerful as she is with her protection magic, usually oversees these kinds of tasks.

I raise my feet and lean my head back as I ask him, "So what's the plan? Just hang out and be lazy here? Shane can't be serious about the exile and Cravenhold won't be in lockdown forever. Have we found who let them in?"

"We'll return when Shane says we can and no, not yet," Josh answers like the dutiful Beta he's supposed to be. His face and shoulders relax as he reaches over and attempts to tickle my feet. "And who said anything about being lazy?" he asks as I drop my feet back into the water before he can touch me. "No, my Veyara, you will not have time to be lazy. I plan to keep you very, very busy."

"Oh?" I ask innocently.

He smirks, getting up. He eyes me in the steamy water and says, "Enjoy your bath, but don't be surprised to find me naked and hard, waiting for you in bed."

I keep our gaze locked as he watches my knees part from where the bubbles don't cover them. My hand moves between my legs as I tilt my head back.

He narrows his eyes. "You're fucking on. This is war."

I laugh as Josh leaves the bathroom. I call after him. "I'll be out soon!"

He doesn't respond. Chuckling still, I reach for my phone as I enjoy the remainder of my bath. The water is cooling and I'll have to wrap this up soon.

I catch up on my messages and respond to anything pressing—mainly from Vanessa, Daniya, or Shane. It's not until I see a notification on MythFeed that makes my heart sink to my stomach.

I was tagged on a post by Monica Cyrinth—a serpent shifter I might've met in passing a few times. She was one of the girls talking about Josh at my tea party.

Monica Cyrinth

Think @cravingrose will get a boob job since the Beta loves to bury his face in big titties?

The post is trending, leading to comments about how I'm not Josh's type or how he could never be satisfied by me. The posts are vulgar and I wonder how they get away with saying such things publicly. She's from the House of Honest, but I don't know why I expect any class from girls like her after what I heard at the tea party.

I can't telepath Cristobal since he's still in Cravenhold, so I share Monica's post with him instead, before closing my phone and sink into the bath.

It's well into the night. Josh and I have managed to skip dinner, losing track of time altogether as we got to know each other's bodies more. We're still in bed when Josh chuckles, like he has an inside joke.

"What?" I breathe out, squirming at his touch. He kisses my neck as his fingers curl deeper inside my tortured pussy. A moan escapes me and I grip his hair harder.

"I've been royally sucking at resisting you, my Veyara," he says between kisses he trails up my neck to my jaw and then his mouth reaches mine in a hungry union. "I'd blame the Mating bond but…fuck, Rose, that'd be a lie."

"But you're so good at lying."

Josh growls. "I don't want to lie."

He moves and positions himself. I watch him guide his throbbing cock and enter me, making both of us moan together. He puts his weight on his left forearm while his right hand comes up to caress my face.

"I want you to know exactly how much I can't resist you," he says and drives into me harder. I let out a small scream, but he continues to thrust. "How fucking hard it's been to resist you." Another thrust.

"Liar," I gasp and he bites down on my bottom lip.

"Does the Veyara need more convincing?" he asks, burying his cock to the hilt and holding himself in place. I clench around him, feeling every inch of his length.

"A lot of convincing." I move, wiggling, needing him deeper, closer.

"Yeah?" he thrusts once, sending a jolt of pleasure through me and I arch into him. "I'm going to fuck you until I erase every second you ever doubted if I wanted you."

"That's a lot of fucking," I say pointedly and force myself not to think about those times in this exact moment.

Josh apparently is thinking the same thing because he stills. He lowers his head and kisses me. Slowly. Our earlier hunger for each other turns into devotion and *fuck,* it's so sweet. His lips are gentle on mine, sucking softly. His tongue licks my bottom lip, slipping into my mouth to dance with mine.

It's fucking unreal.

This man is finally, finally mine.

"I have always been yours. Mentally and emotionally at least," he telepaths so he doesn't have to break the kiss. His thought startles me and for a split second I wonder if he read my mind just then. I can't be sure.

"Because you spent so much time thinking about hating me?" I ask, covering if I did slip up.

He breaks the kiss to glower at me as he thrusts into me, hard. I cry out, but he doesn't give me a chance to recover before he's shifting us so that I'm straddling him. My knees land on the soft blanket and I stare down at my insanely handsome Mate while feeling him *deep* inside me in this position. I grind down as his hooded eyes take me in. He has one hand on the crease of my hip while the other finds my clit. He teases a little before his hand comes up to cup my left breast, a little roughly, sparking a wave of arousal. I move my hips against him, my pussy getting wetter under his gaze.

"Because I spent so much time thinking of you in this exact position," his voice is low and my nipples immediately perk up as his cock pulses inside me.

Suddenly I feel too exposed…too self-conscious. I've never done this. I don't know what I'm doing. And it's Josh. He's had—a lot of experience. Oh, I'm going to be sick…why do I keep thinking about all that when we're in the middle of such a good time? I hate my brain sometimes and I thought the Mating bond was supposed to drive us together.

"Rose," he brings me out of my thoughts. His hand travels higher until his thumb presses down on my bottom lip and I faintly taste myself on his finger. He cups my face, his arm flexed, making his tattoo more prominent against the light from the fireplace in the room. He sits up and I wrap my legs around his waist as his arms come around me, covering my back with one of the blankets. My hands rest on his shoulders. I can't look at him, or I'll cry and I will not cry in front of him. Definitely not while we're having sex.

But it hurts. It hurts knowing I won't be able to please him. Not really. Seeing the comment on MythFeed did not help, and while my breasts aren't small by any means, I hate that it triggered me.

"What are you thinking?" he asks.

How do I tell him that I don't want him to look at me? That I feel so small when his eyes are on me, so small that I want to just disappear. How do I tell him that all I can think of is how he might've enjoyed himself more with a serpent woman and how I'll never be able to give him that—that I was never his pick. I clench my jaw in fear of my lips trembling, but he catches it anyway.

"Whatever it is, tell me," he urges, kissing my shoulder.

I close my eyes and whisper, "I'm not your choice."

"Fuck, Rose," he breathes and I blink back my tears, clearly ruining the moment.

"I'm sorry!" I start to push off him, but his arms hold me in place.

"No. Stop—" he says so sternly I freeze, meeting his piercing eyes. Is he mad? Why am I so fucking insecure right now? I was never like this with…

No, I can't think of *that* right now.

Josh has always been my biggest insecurity. Serpent females are beautiful, deadly, skilled fighters, one way or another. They know what a serpent man wants and likes. I don't know anything about serpent shifters or what they like in bed. I didn't even know they have *hemipenes* until recently.

How am I supposed to be on top, and ride him, have him watching me, my every move, when all I can think about is how he's comparing me to all the other girls who were in my exact position.

To my surprise, Josh kisses me and then lays back again. His eyes travel down my body before he raises my phone up to me. Panic takes over and I reach out to slap the phone away.

"What the Hell are you doing?!" I exclaim.

"Do you trust me?"

"Absolutely not!"

There's no humor on his face. His face doesn't twist into a cruel smirk or sinister grin.

"Sit up, princess," he orders. I glare at him and he just raises an eyebrow. Letting out an exasperated sigh, I readjust and straddle him. He's still inside me, still hard as he says, "Touch yourself."

"Put the phone away." I narrow my eyes at him.

"Don't worry about the phone."

"Put it away."

"No. This is necessary."

"My phone is necessary right now why?"

"You'll see. Now I want to see those pretty nails against your prettier swollen clit, sweetheart," when I don't move, he adds in his Beta voice, "*now*."

Ugh. I keep my glare on him, but my right hand moves to part myself before I feel the sensitive, overstimulated bundle of nerves. His eyes darken as he watches my fingers move against myself, occasionally brushing against his shaft, making his cock twitch inside me.

"I swear if you go live right now, I will kill you," I threaten.

His eyes meet mine and narrow. "If anyone ever sees you like this, I will happily gouge their eyes out and feed it to them." I roll my eyes and he flicks one of my nipples making me jump slightly. "Focus," he orders, "rub your clit faster. You're going to come on my dick."

My hand stills. "No," I shake my head.

"No?" he repeats narrowing his eyes.

"I can't..." I say slowly, dropping my gaze to the tattoo on his torso.

"While I know that's not true for a second, just do as I say."

I frown, as my fingers start to move again. "What's that mean...?"

Now he smirks, before his own fingers play with my nipple making me wetter as my fingers work in tandem with his. "I came with you every single time you touched yourself since you got back from the Tour. But you knew that," my hand pauses and he glares at me, "did I say you can stop?"

"You...felt it..." Just like how I felt him. Fuck...of course it works both ways, why wouldn't it? Why was I so stupid to think it did?

"That's right. It was the best way to start my birthday morning, and I decided to indulge myself in my Mate's pleasure," he says and my cheeks heat immediately, "haven't stopped since."

I had flown in the night before his birthday, having stayed away until the last moment. I couldn't miss it—appearance and all. When I woke up the next morning, angry, frustrated, and still nervous to see him later that day, I might've totally done what he's accusing me of to relieve my tension of being back.

"Every single time?" I ask. "Sometimes it was multiple, you kept up?"

He smirks.

"I'm a basilisk and a wolf. I kept up," he winks and I close my eyes throwing my head back as I ride him faster, rubbing my clit.

Why is all of that so fucking hot?

"That's it, baby. You're so beautiful, I can't wait to see you come from riding me," he urges and his voice alone can make me come.

I was not above pulling up his press conferences and interviews some nights, though I will never tell him that. He'll find out anyway when he Marks me.

I let out a soft moan as his fingers dig into my breast. He moves with me and his thrusts—fuck, how does it feel deeper this way?

Soon enough, I'm bouncing on his dick, both of us moaning and panting. My free hand holds onto his arm as he grips my breast, keeping me anchored to him. I raise my gaze and I'm met with my phone held up between us, blocking his face.

"What—stop!"

"Keep going baby, fuck you look so hot," he groans, "look at you, enjoying your Mate's cock," he encourages, his heavy gaze meeting mine over my phone so that I can only see his lustful gray eyes. "Keep going," he growls, the vibration sending a jolt of arousal through me.

I close my eyes taking it in as I ride him until I feel myself right on the edge.

"That's it," he says, "fuck me until you're screaming my name as you come for me."

"Fuck!" I cry out as I come, gasping and writhing on his dick. His hand leaves my breast to hold my face, smearing his thumb across my lip. When he brings his thumb back, I slip it into my mouth. His eyes heat up as I suck and clench my pussy around his dick, riding out my orgasm.

"Fuck, sweetheart…" he groans, but continues to hold my phone up, saying, "I'm going to come in your pretty little pussy, princess."

He barely gives me the warning before I feel the warmth of his release spilling inside me as his thighs strain and abs clench, outlining his eight packs deliciously. His eyes are on my face like part of him can't believe how easy that was for him.

"Stay there," he tells me slightly breathless. His focus turns to my phone, and I know he's taking pictures. I start to squirm but then he turns us so that we're lying next to each other, still joined. He places soft kisses on my face then he says, "I'm going to introduce you to my dream girl."

He asks me to unlock my phone before he takes it and goes to the gallery. Countless new videos and photos pop up. All of me. He clicks on the first one and kisses my temple while I stare at myself.

"I want you to look at these and remember this is my view and how perfect you are," he tells me, voice thick with hunger as if he wants to go another round already.

"I'm not—"

"And I want you to go through these pictures and if you want to, send me the ones you like," he says, "maybe I'll get another rose added to my tattoo."

My cheeks heat at the mere thought. "You're giving me homework."

"Yes," he says seriously. "You don't take any pictures of yourself. Why?"

I frown. "That's not true. The girls always take pictures when we're out and I'm always in some photoshoot—"

"But *you* don't take any pictures of yourself," he pushes and I fall silent. "Why? You know you're fucking beautiful."

I will not cry.

I blink back the tears. I know I have to give him an answer. He's not going to drop this. "Knowing it and feeling it are two different things."

His eyes are on me, and I don't dare look at his face. Four years worth of flashbacks swim through my thoughts. This is not the kind of conversation to have with his dick still in me.

He pushes the hair back from my face. The light possessive force of his hand feels too good. So good that I just might break.

"I don't take pictures of myself because I…why would I?" I ask him, willing my lips to not tremble. "The other girls were always so much prettier."

I know I'm not ugly. I know I'm attractive and was blessed with great looks from both of my parents. I hear it all the time, and no matter how much I'm told how pretty, beautiful, sexy I am…I was never those things to Josh.

I could be in the sexiest dress, but it never mattered because he never acknowledged me. I didn't want to hear it from everyone, I wanted to hear it from him. I would've only believed it if he said it—but the irony is, even if he does say it now, I can't believe it. No matter how much I want to.

I wish I could say it didn't matter, that needing the validation from him didn't matter, but it did back then. I hate that he's making me think about all this when I've worked so hard to bury these feelings. It became easier and easier to hate him.

"They never were to me," he finally says. "Not like you. You have it all wrong."

I frown and shake my head, but he just leans in and kisses me, arms wrapping around me tighter.

"Nobody could ever compare to *you*. Why do you think they hate you so much?" Josh trails a finger down the side of my face. "They could never be you."

"But…I've heard…stories. Things you like, did with them…to them. The way you made them scream your name—"

"Is *that* why you won't say my name?" Josh asks, the shock clear on his face, making him forget that he's still inside me as he starts to pull away. He pauses and readjusts, draping my leg over his thigh.

I focus on the blanket that's covering us, willing it to swallow me right now.

I. Will. Not. Cry.

"Rose," he says my name and it's so quiet. "Look at me."

I shake my head and bury my face in his warm chest. I feel him let out a deep breath as his fingers tangle in my hair.

He's quiet and I wish I knew what was going through his mind. He has me well tangled into him with no give or intention of letting me move away. Then I feel his lips press down on my head, staying there for a moment.

The worst part is, he thinks I'm talking about hearing gossip and not actually hearing other women screaming his name as he made them…

It all just seems so stupid now. It was always stupid, but after all that's said and done, we're exactly where he never wanted to be.

So what was the point of all that pain?

He can't take it back and we *are* here now. How long am I going to let the past keep me from having everything I wanted with him moving forward? I don't want to think about any of that when we're together, yet I do. The hurt is a part of me, sunken into my bones and I don't know how to separate from it. I want to try though.

So I ease my head back and look up at him, meeting his soft eyes. He's worried, maybe even a little sad.

He looks like he's going to say something but before he can, I nervously ask, "Can I…see the pictures you have of me?"

He blinks, surprised at my request, before he reaches over for his own phone. "Don't judge me."

"Too late for that," I tease, lightening the mood and snuggling into him as he unlocks his phone. He sighs heavily like it's judgement day, opening his gallery app and handing the device over to me. I raise an eyebrow, surprised, "Not afraid I'll see something I shouldn't? You're brave."

He groans. "No, it's really just you in there."

Curiosity gets the best of me and I start to scroll. He wasn't kidding. Aside from me, he has pictures of documents, what looks like evidence of kills, Sunrises on the river, and the clouds at Coilspire. The pictures of me that he has are all from photoshoots, candid, or screenshots of social media posts, and some he couldn't have taken because he wasn't there.

"Where did you get these?" I ask, a little stunned.

He clenches his jaw. "It started with Eliza torturing me with how hot you looked at a photoshoot three years ago. She's relentless, I swear."

I laugh. "And that's why she's Luna. She really did that?"

"Yeah, she's very, *very*, protective of you. The amount of times she's threatened to kill me...anyway, then I just started saving them...collecting them...I don't know, I just needed to have any and every picture of you. You're my Mate, why shouldn't I have them?"

Maybe because you hated me, I think to myself.

"There's way more than seven roses worth of pictures in here..." I tell him, pointedly.

He scowls. "Devaughn doesn't need to know that. He was happy with seven hundred."

I laugh. "You lied! You cheated!"

"I'm a serpent," he answers as if that's an explanation. "I still got the tattoos."

"No...I'm telling on you," I grin, "first thing when we get back."

He gives me a threatening look. "Guess I'll just have to keep you here forever then."

I bite my lip. "Eliza will definitely kill you for that."

Josh leans in and sucks my lip right out. "Mmm, you'll be coming right along with me. Get exiled forever and permanently."

"That is morbid as fuck," I say, breaking away from his lip, and tease him, "You're a little obsessed with me."

"No one ever came close to comparing and I always knew they wouldn't, so yeah, it wasn't hard to be. One way or another..." he replies and I shift a little. I don't want to talk about this.

"If you knew they wouldn't, then why? Why were you trying to replace me so hard?" I ask, my voice losing the lightness it had moments ago and suddenly I wish he wasn't inside me right now. "And don't say because of the politics—that's not good enough."

He kisses my forehead, clearly buying some time to answer me. "Serpents aren't loyal."

"Really?" The sarcasm drips from my voice.

His jaw sets and eyes harden, and I realize he wasn't talking about relationships. "I came into the Beta role knowing I'd do what had to be done and I wouldn't care whether I was liked for it or not—but I had to be smart about it. And yes, I also thought maybe because we weren't Mated like Warriors are, we would find a way out of our bond. It would've been the best for both of us in the long run."

"Do you still believe that?" I ask, quietly. He should really pull out now...but he doesn't. His dick is still semi-hard inside me.

"No, and not because of the Claiming," he clarifies quickly, "but because it's you or no one else. It always has been."

"No, it hasn't. You can't say that…"

He pauses, before slowly bringing my hand to his chest, resting our hands over his heart. "Yes. I can."

I stare at his chest and our hands together, his entirely covering mine. This just makes me sadder because he didn't allow himself to listen to his heart.

I meet his gaze. "I…I'm not over it—any of it. These past few weeks since the reunion have been so good, but it doesn't erase…"

"I know," he whispers, "I just want you to know, I can't imagine a life where we're not together. I don't want to think of a life where I don't belong to you. Normal Warrior bond or not, our bond is real."

I don't know when, but tears started slipping down my eyes. "This is some pillow talk, Beta."

He leans in and kisses my tears, pressing my chest tight against him. "I know being here won't erase the damage I caused your heart…but maybe a lifetime together might."

"You won't get tired of mending my broken heart?" I ask and my voice is too soft for it to even try to pass off as teasing as he lifts my leg a little higher. His dick's fully hard again and he pushes into me.

"Never. And you better hold me to it," he says, quietly.

"What if you break your promise?"

"You can punish me."

"You won't like it."

"Yes, that is the idea of a punishment, Veyara," he chuckles softly.

"I'll think of a very, very cruel punishment…" I start to say as he thrusts into me, holding me close to him before his lips find mine.

53 STUDY TIME

Rosella Craving
November 10

I stare at his dick.

It's early morning, the Sun barely rising behind the mountain ranges, but light still floods into our bedroom. Josh is sound asleep and I've turned around to observe his specimen. This is purely research.

Where is he hiding the second penis? There's only ever been one. I've only ever seen one and experienced one. For a second I thought maybe they were all fucking with me, but then I looked it up and apparently, serpents do have hemipenes.

I'm going to figure this out. I like puzzles.

I reach out and lift his penis as I examine the area, but it starts to harden almost instantly. I ignore it, I'm on a mission. I push his dick up, pressing it toward his stomach as I lean in closer to see the area better. It helps that he's fully shaved.

I frown when I see what looks like a small horizontal slit between his penis and ball sack. It's closer to the shaft of his penis, though. Is that it? Is that where the other penis hides? Or rests? But it's so small…

"What the Hell are you doing?" Josh asks, making me jump and drop his penis.

I look up at him from the foot of the bed. Fuck, he looks good waking up. His hair is disheveled and falling against his forehead. His tattooed arm is resting behind his head. His piercing gray eyes are fixed on me, holding me in place with an unimpressed look on his face.

I bite my lip. "Nothing."

"Are you going to suck it or just stare at it funny?" he asks me pointedly, knowing exactly what I'd been up to.

I look at him innocently. "Does your other penis want to come out and play?"

His eyes narrow. "No."

I really shouldn't laugh right now. He doesn't seem happy. Is the second penis a sensitive topic? Maybe this is uncomfortable for him to talk about. Would it be more…normal if I was a serpent shifter? It might not even be a conversation. A serpent woman would know what to do with this. But I'm not a serpent shifter and I am too damn curious.

If this is uncomfortable for him, too fucking bad. We'll call this payback for hurting me.

"How does it work?" I ask, tilting my head, focusing back on his penis. "Like, is one more dominant than the other? Do you have a preference? Like I tend to favor my right boob over my left—"

"Why?"

I playfully slap his thigh. "We're not talking about me. Focus."

He arches an eyebrow. "No, they are equally—I'm not telling you anything."

I hold his gaze. "Is this conversation weird for you?"

"Very," he answers, reaching for my hand and I know he wants to pull me up and away from his penis.

I move my hand away, making him narrow his eyes at me again. I just smile. "I'm not done studying," I tell him and then in a more hurtful tone, I ask, "Why won't you tell me?"

"Because you can only fuck one at a time anyway—so it doesn't matter," he says.

I stare at his penis sadly, willing it to do something miraculous. "I just want to see the switch happen…"

He exhales as if he can't believe this conversation right now. I reach for his penis and pick it up again to look at the slit. I start to move my other hand toward it, when he swats it away.

"Don't even think about it," he warns.

I frown. "Why? Does it feel funny if I touch it?"

Josh runs a hand down his face. "Rose, I cannot take you seriously right now."

I ignore him and continue to hold his penis up. Then I stroke it slowly, but nothing happens. I didn't expect it to. I sigh and push down on the tip as if to tap it but with more pressure, disappointed.

But then Josh jerks and I see the slit open before closing again. Josh glares at me. "Stop."

"Does it hurt?" I ask, wide-eyed.

"No—"

"Does it feel funny?"

"Will it feel funny when I punish you?"

I frown. "Why would you punish me when I'm trying to please both of your dicks? It's not my fault one of them is shy."

Josh pinches the bridge of his nose but seeing that he's not made any actual attempts to pull me away, I think he's secretly enjoying this. Or he's at least curious to see what I do. His dick that's outside sure is because it is fully hard now. It's so tempting, I decide to give in and put him in my mouth. Josh groans immediately, his hand coming up to tangle in my hair.

I suck him off for a few minutes, tongue swirling around the tip, but my focus is still completely on the hidden penis. Should I try to coax it out with my fingers? I don't think so, he didn't like the idea of me touching the slit. Maybe I can use my tongue. I let my tongue lick his head, tasting the precum, before applying as much pressure as I can to push down on the head of his cock.

"Fuck!" Josh snaps as his thighs start to clamp me in. His cock slips out of my mouth before something thrusts against my throat from the outside so hard I fall back with a small yelp.

I blink, confused as to what just happened as Josh sits up, startled also. I stare at his hard penis for a moment before noticing the slit is now on the top of his shaft. I tilt my head, blinking and remember seeing this before. I thought it was a scar the first night I gave him a blowjob. The moment my nose touched it, he came. Then I realize something else.

"Wait!" I gasp, "It can get hard inside too?!"

Josh puts his head in his hands, and something tells me he is so done with me right now. I grin at him triumphantly.

"I did it," I say, proud of myself, as I start to reach for it.

His grip snaps around my wrist, halting my hand mid-reach. "What do you think you're doing?"

I try to twist out of his hold. "Saying hi."

In one fluid motion he flips me onto my stomach, a startled gasp escaping me as he spreads my thighs and yanks my hips up roughly, giving me instant flashbacks to Romania. I'm on all fours before I can catch my breath.

"Allow me," he growls, then he thrusts into me hard and deep, filling me in a single stroke that steals my air. I cry out, fingers twisting in the sheets, but his left hand gathers both my wrists at the small of my back. With his next thrust, his right hand spanks my ass, earning him another cry that makes me clench around him and push back for more.

"Is this what you wanted, sweetheart?" he asks as his thrusts pick up speed. His hand on my ass rubs the sting into me, before it comes down on me again. All I can do is moan into the sheet.

The pace is relentless, each drive forward punctuated by another hot slap until my skin burns and pleasure builds and builds. He drops over me, chest against my back, slowing to deep, grinding rolls that drag against every sensitive place inside me.

"You're so fucking cute," he tells me, slightly breathless. His mouth finds my shoulder, teeth sinking in but careful to not extend his fangs as he comes with a low groan, hips jerking against mine. The pressure of his bite and the heat of him spilling inside me makes me shatter around him, with muffled cries lost in the bed.

He stays buried, arms sliding around me to pull me close, lips softening into gentle kisses over the faint marks on my shoulder while we catch our breath as the Sun rises a little higher now. Josh turns us, so that his entire body weight isn't all on me, before covering us with the blanket.

I could fall asleep all over again—if it weren't for all the questions I have now. He continues to kiss my neck as his fingers absently play with my nipples.

"Was that my first time experiencing this…one?" I ask, not sure what to call it or how to differentiate it.

"No," he answers.

I turn my head to look at him. "Romania?"

"Romania," he confirms, kissing my shoulder.

"Why is it one at a time?"

"I don't know, Rose, that's just how it works," he replies.

"Have you ever tried to…have both out?" I ask him.

He's silent for a moment, before he answers me, "No."

"You did, didn't you?"

"Maybe when I was…younger and curious," he admits, slowly.

"Can I try?" I ask, then add, "If it's not painful…"

He's quiet and I start to turn when he pulls out of me. I frown, is he upset? But then, he turns me in his arms, making me face him before lifting my left leg over his.

"You want to try what exactly?" he asks as his cock finds my entrance. I shift a little, wanting him back inside. He helps me out, guiding his cock into my already cum-filled pussy.

I lean in to kiss his jaw. "I want to see if they can be out at the same time."

"And do what with both of them?" he asks as he thrusts once, making me moan out. His fingers tangle in my hair with a gentle grip. I love his hands on me. I love the possessive grip he has that tells me I'm his without him having to say it.

I focus on his question and divert my eyes as my cheeks flush. "Well…you have two cocks and I have two…holes, so…"

Josh groans, burying his face in my neck. "Yeah, we're retiring and just going to stay in bed for the rest of our lives."

I laugh. "Is that a yes?"

"Fuck yes, you can try," he answers, pulling away from my neck, "but I can't promise anything, so don't be disappointed."

"I'm going to make it happen," I say with full conviction.

"We should probably try anal first before we get too ahead of ourselves," he kisses my nose.

I nod, but I still have more questions. "Is it true why you have two of them? For a lot of babies?"

"For Dens, yes…it's one of the reasons why Dens have the shared systems. But it's also preference. It doesn't make us sex-crazed or anything."

"But for you? As a Warrior?"

"Doesn't really apply." His gaze softens on me as he traces a finger down my throat. "I can only have children with you."

I smile, but that makes me ask, "What if we're different? Since our bond—"

"I have no desire to find out."

"Really?" I whisper and he cups my face.

"Rose, I'm all yours and I'm not changing my mind about that." He kisses me deeply, his thrusts picking up, sending waves and waves of pleasure through my body. My leg hooks up against his waist as my arms wrap around him tighter. "Are you done asking questions?"

"No, I have more."

"Make it one."

"Can I name them?"

"Our kids?"

"Well, yes, eventually, but I meant your cocks, you know, to differentiate."

"Alright, it's time to get up," he says, stopping and pulling out of me completely. He shoves my face away and gets out of bed, leaving me complaining but laughing.

I visit the library again. It's quickly becoming one of my favorite spots in Coilspire. It's peaceful here and I can check out all these old texts. I look through the books in front of me, fascinated with some of the things I'm learning.

I pull out a few genealogy records—my family's lineage sprawls across the table. The ink is so old, and my hands shake a little as I run my fingers over the pages.

I look for Nathanial's records today in *House Craeven: The First Family*. My fingertips brush the delicate pages as I read of his first known identity after Na'at.

I bite my lip as I read about Achilles of Thessaly. When Nathanial tells it, he says he was laying low, but his skills in warfare got him noticed. The rest is history. The lore of Achilles's heel came from Nathanial's original injury scar—the one that turned him into a shifter. He still has it.

Then he was King Solomon—it seems like such a magical time to have been alive. It's also one of the few times Nathanial and Isis ruled beside each other. They are one of my favorite love stories, and it's strange how I never got jealous of it. Nathanial doesn't like talking about her, but when he does it's usually about how we look similar, except our hair. I guess it was an honor to have Nathanial's attention at all and the way I had it. I wonder if that's how Josh's women feel—they have to know they can never be me. The Divine chose me for him. Josh said as much last night. I push the thoughts out of my mind as I continue with Nathanial's history.

He later takes on the name Aristotle, the philosopher who taught kings he placed on thrones to help the supernatural rule like Nathanial did as Solomon.

He soon became Alexander the Great, making it one of his quickest identity changes. He used conquest to hide the truth every time. Each city was another sanctuary for the shifters—each conquest spread our bloodlines.

He resurfaces again much later as Henry VIII and my throat

tightens. Every mortal history has always painted him as power-hungry, monstrous—but the truth is never that simple. He became king to fracture the Church's hold on occult study and protect our practices, our people. His wives were either allies, traitors, or unfortunate casualties of a jealous Isis. They both orbited each other even if their identities did not get written down in history together. I guess when you're immortal a lot can happen within a relationship. What happened to make the light in Nathanial's eyes go out whenever she's mentioned. What did she do? Could it be that he just misses her, or did something else happen? Why is she never seen?

Nathanial's last recorded identity is Isaac Newton. He was using magic, alchemy, to launch us into the future. When he tells me about being Isaac, he says he was tired of ruling—though that was never something he could escape, but he wanted a quiet life for a little while. The Warriors at the time were left in charge until Nathanial decided to return. I can't imagine living multiple lives like he has. It must take a toll on him, on his soul. I can understand why he likes to be in nature, in his shifter forms so much.

Nathanial was everywhere. He did everything and more. He lived over and over, countless times.

I reach for my blood bottle and sip as I turn my attention on Aradia—the Queen of the witches. Liam never talked about her much. I just know he's fond of his mother and never had any complaints—but I guess when you're almost a thousand years old, you don't really think about your parents the same way. They've lived lifetimes, repeatedly, just like Nathanial and Mother Isis. Where Isis ruled kingdoms, Aradia seems to have set places on fire. Where Isis guided visibly, Aradia whispered to the outcasts.

She inspired rebellion. Always standing where no one wanted her to—beside kings, inside temples, beneath altars. But always with Stefan. I don't see records of her birthname. She's younger than Isis and Stefan's second wife. They've never been separated throughout the centuries.

Aradia's first recorded name is Jezebel, the High Priestess of Astarte. She was demonized by later scribes due to her unfavorable practices, turning her faith into blasphemy and her strength into corruption. That role continued when she was Mary Magdalene. She was exiled but continued her teachings of witchcraft—the Old Ways as mentioned in the text before me.

Then she was Sumaiya bint Khabbat, being tortured for her Holy defiance. The official story is she died due to the horrific tortures, but by that point Aradia was a vampire sired by Stefan—she was unkillable and rescued by him. Her captors did not want anyone to know a prisoner escaped so they covered it up by declaring her death.

Then she emerged as Laila al-Amiriya. She tried a different approach as Laila—she tried leading with love and passion. That is until Stefan was captured, driving her to madness. It doesn't go into detail but seeing that he's alive and still King, I'd say things worked out fine in the end.

Her last famous identity is Anna Maria Luisa de' Medici—the last of the Medici line. She was a patroness of art, alchemy, and illumination, hiding her magic in the art. It was all a ruse as she guided supernatural bloodlines toward safety during volatile times.

It's interesting to see how different but similar the two sisters are. Isis built worlds and Aradia challenged it and together they were creation and rebellion.

I sit back and wonder if Aradia is still doing that, but quietly now. While she is also the vampire queen, she has her own sphere and world to rule. It's worked so far for Stefan and her. I've never met her, never really had a reason to I guess.

Unlike Isis, Nathanial, and Aradia—Stefan chose a quieter existence. He ruled and lived in the shadows, and I wonder if that's where the lore of vampires dying in Sunlight and living at night come from. The only significant name that stands out to me in his records is King Arthur. It's also the only place I can see the vampire High Council appear united as the Knights of the Round Table.

I close the book softly, my breath caught somewhere between awe and grief. So much history. There had to be hundreds of names for each of them—hundreds of lives. But none of them mention anything about another female Warrior or what really happened to Isis after her death as Mary, Queen of Scots. I decide I'll need to dive into the Sires. Maybe there will be something in their stories.

On my way back to the room, I run into a frantic Ridley.

"Veyara," Ridley greets, startled. He looks very confused. "You're here?"

I laugh, shrugging. "Where should I be, Ridley?"

He blushes slightly. "Apologies ma'am. I thought you were informed. The Beta's hosting a dinner in your honor tonight. You're to be getting ready."

54 LADY OF COILSPIRE

Rosella Craving
November 10

A dress waits for me on our large bed, spread across the covers, when I step back into the bedroom after my shower. Royal blue silk, shifting from deep sapphire at the folds to bright cobalt. The bodice glitters with tiny, embroidered vines that climb upward in silver thread. Delicate leaves and thorns curl around an off-the-shoulder neckline that promises to bare my collarbones and dip into my breasts. The skirt falls in soft layers, slit just high enough on one side to reveal a flash of leg when I move. It's breathtaking.

My fingers trace the dress before I slip it on. It hugs my waist, falling softly over my hips. I turn once in front of the mirror, watching the skirt swirl, and smile at my own reflection. I leave my hair loose, black waves tumbling down my back, before doing my makeup.

The door opens just as I finish applying lip gloss.

Josh steps in. He's traded his T-shirt for a black silk button-down and jacket. He stops mid-stride as his mouth parts, but no words follow. Those storm-gray eyes travel over me like he's memorizing every inch. Heat rises in my cheeks under the weight of his stare. He looks so handsome.

"Damn," he finally says, almost accusingly, as if I've stolen his breath on purpose. "Just damn. You're so beautiful."

I feel beautiful, so I choose to believe him even though my brain is at war. I don't know if I'll ever believe he truly thinks I'm beautiful—or anything nice he says. I have to actively choose to, because I've wanted to hear them from him for so long, not because I think he means it. I hope he does.

He closes the distance between us in three strides, hands finding my waist. Then he spins me in the middle of the room, making the skirt flare out as I let out a laugh. When I face him once more, he cups my cheek and kisses me so softly I never want it to stop. He pulls back just enough to rest his forehead against mine for a second longer. I wish I knew what's going through his mind right now. Josh offers his arm, and I take it before we leave our room together.

"Why do I have a feeling this is a fancy dinner?" I tease, because clearly, I'm way too dressed up. "Are you trying to wine and dine me, Beta Warrior?"

Josh looks down at me before pushing me up against the hallway wall. We've barely made it twenty feet, but my back arches into him anyway. He lifts my leg to his waist, the slit of the dress exposing my skin. My nipples harden immediately as my arousal spikes. He groans into me, inhaling me but pulls away, lowering my leg and straightening his jacket. "Dinner…we should get to dinner. They're waiting for you," he says and it sounds more like he's trying to convince himself than me.

"They?" I ask, but Josh just smiles, giving nothing away. We descend the stone stairs together, my heels clicking softly against it.

The main dining hall opens before us, the one that stretches along the cliffside, giving us the view of the mountain range and waterfalls. One entire wall is nothing but tall arched windows with Moonlight spilling across the floor. Candles stand in silver holders down the center of the heavily set table. It feels almost intimidating in its grandeur, yet the scale shrinks to something intimate with only the household staff gathered.

Every seat is filled. The chef, Cory, stands proud in his whites near the end. Ridley stands by the seat closest to the piano, hands clasped behind his back. Miriam is also here with the kitchen maids, attendants, groundkeepers, gardeners, guards—all of them in their best, eyes bright with anticipation.

Josh smiles at them as he leads me to the head of the table. My chair waits beside his own. He pulls it out for me but remains standing.

A hush falls as he lifts his glass. "Thank you everyone for being here tonight," he says, voice carrying easily through the quiet hall. He doesn't sound like the authoritative Beta I'm so used to. His voice holds a kindness I've never heard him use in any kind of gathering before. "Each and every one of you has kept Coilspire alive since the loss of my parents. Coilspire is your home as much as it is mine. Thank you for putting tonight together in honor of your new Lady of the House." His gaze, and everyone else's, lands on me. Josh raises my hand to his lips, placing a kiss, before he says to the room, "To the Veyara."

Glasses are raised.

"To the Veyara," the staff echoes, smiles breaking across every face as some even clap. Miriam smiles warmly at me before taking a drink from her chalice. I clink my glass with Josh's before we both drink. The bloodrum is rich, dark, and perfect.

Plates appear magically—Cory's doing, no doubt. An extravagant procession of meats and elaborate sides flood the table, far more than anyone could reasonably eat. My plate fills with pheasant, lamb, and prime rib alongside rich vegetables and grains. The staff are laughing as they serve more, trading easy jokes with Josh as they move around the table.

He answers them with the same warmth, relaxed and familiar, speaking to them like family rather than employees, and I realize how deeply at home he is here, unlike how he is at Cravenhold. These are the people who raised him, who looked after him after his parents died, and their affection for him is unmistakable. Some smile with recognition, remembering me from when I was much younger, their warmth extending easily in my direction. As I eat, the extravagance starts to feel appropriate, more meaningful—it's not just excess, but a shared history, a home, and Coilspire opening its arms to me. I didn't even realize that I'm entirely surrounded by serpent shifters. Every single one of the staff here are serpent shifters, and they're all so nice to me, adopting me as one of their own.

As desserts are eaten, soft notes drift through the hall. Ridley has settled at the grand piano in the corner, fingers coaxing a slow waltz from the keys.

Josh stands and extends his hand to me. "Dance with me?"

I slip my fingers into his without hesitation. He guides me toward the tall windows where the night sky is illuminated by the Moonlight and constellations. He pulls me close, one hand settles at the small of my back, the other cradles mine. We begin to move, swaying and finding the rhythm together. His eyes never leave mine. He spins me gently, my skirt moving around us like water. When he draws me back in, my body fits against his as if we were made to fit.

I rest my cheek against his shoulder and let the piano carry us, the staff's quiet murmurs fading behind the music. We dance for the rest of the night, even after the table's cleared and Ridley stopped playing. We dance until we can't dance anymore and end up falling on the floor laughing, a little too wine drunk.

"I've never done that," he says to me, kissing my shoulder. "Dance away the night, I mean."

"I'm glad you still have firsts left to share with me," I whisper, the butterflies in my stomach are ridiculously happy right now.

He looks a little taken aback and says, "Oh, there are a few I can't wait to share with you."

I pull my head back to look at him. "Oh? Do tell, Beta."

He just grins, almost shyly, and shakes his head. "Rather show you."

"But I want to know," I say, pouting a little.

"And you will," he promises with a wink, melting my heart. Why does he look so fucking hot doing that? He chuckles a little, knowing the effect he has.

I drop it for now, hoping he will show me soon. Josh's fingers brush my hair back, grazing against my shoulder as he does. "Everyone loves you. You're the Lady of Coilspire. You've finally come home to them," he says.

"Did you doubt they would?" I ask, jokingly, because I did. Serpent Nation hasn't been the most welcoming so far. "I am beloved by most, you know."

Josh has a gorgeous smile on his face as the Moon lights it up through the windows. "Yes, yes you are, my Veyara."

55 THE SIRES

Rosella Craving
November 13

The rest of the days at Coilspire are similar. Josh and I wake up to each other and have breakfast together out on the veranda. Then we go out into the forest and explore our powers working together. He's learned to not call it training, but it's been exciting to work with someone who isn't afraid of my magic. He also makes sure I don't exhaust myself or overdo it.

After that, we freshen up for lunch and walk around the gardens if it's not too cold. By late afternoon we're in the library. While I revel in the history books, Josh works on his laptop. After the library, we have dinner and end the night together. I know we're exiled, but I get to be here and do whatever my heart wants, have Josh all to myself, avoid the media, and read? I'm living a dream.

He looks up from his screen and asks, "What are you reading today?"

I hold up the book. "*The Craving Legacy and the Rise of the New World.* Have you read it? It's about the Sires."

"I like those stories," he says, closing his laptop. "Read them to me."

He gets up and goes over to sit on the couch. I join him and he pulls my legs onto his lap while I get comfortable.

"Five men," I start, "that's all Nathanial ever turned. It started with Theron Daevryn, House Hunter's Sire."

"He stepped into an ambush meant for Nathanial and took a poisonous blade to his chest," Josh says, massaging my feet.

We've all had to learn the history of the Sires from Lady Zia as royal children. I continue, looking at the page before me, "Such selflessness—and he was so young too. Nathanial gifted him immunity from poisons."

"He gifted him more than that," Josh says, lowly.

"The gift of basilisks and all serpents. A venomous bite, yet blood so tempting." I swallow hard and look at Josh, asking him, "How would that work? When you Mark me? You can't kill me so if your bite is poisonous…will I feel it? Will it hurt?"

"Hunters haven't killed their Mates in the past," Josh chuckles. "When you're Marked, our powers merge—you become immune—your own bite becomes poisonous. What might hurt you now, won't after the Marking. We'll be unstoppable."

"You have a lot of faith in our powers," I say, quietly.

He holds my gaze for a moment, before nodding to the book. "Who's next?"

I turn the page and images of children greet me. "Malrik Alarion—this story breaks my heart," I tell Josh softly, and then continue it. "Nathanial found him broken, bleeding, and yet still standing guard over a group of orphans. Famine had spread, slavers and cannibals were closing in, yet Malrik refused to fall until the children were safe. Nathanial turned him so he could keep fighting."

"House Tens," Josh says, smiling wickedly. "Changelings. They do make most uneasy. They can copy anything—faces, voices, bodies. If a Tens wants to wear your skin, all they need to do is touch you once and they'll have access for life."

"That's disturbing…" I say, trying to think of all the times James may have touched me.

"It's why they're one of the Houses," Josh chuckles, finding it amusing and clearly proud of his best friend's abilities.

I flip the page. "Next is, Ka'el Vortheon who was a nameless soldier, abandoned on the battlefield. Nathanial saw a fight in him that was worth a second chance. His line is now House Claws—Panthers."

"Nine fucking lives," Josh mumbles and I smile at that, because both Claws brothers live like they have multiple lives to spare. "Patience and prowling. They can wiggle their way in and out of anything and everything. And they do."

I believe it. Devaughn is notorious for his dealers and sources for nearly anything on the black market. He will always find what he wants. Daniel has a way of getting away with things—always has. "They're considered the guardians of the old ways," I read from the book and Josh chuckles, shaking his head.

We move on from Ka'el Vortheon.

"Darius Baelstorm. I love his story. He was one of the Seven Sleepers," I say, scanning the page, "he found Nathanial when he was seeking death after waking up in a world he no longer recognized. He needed a purpose—so Nathanial gave him one. From him comes House Rage."

"Nathanial gave him the chance to make a difference in the new world—and enough time to do so. In case he decided to sleep again for three hundred years."

The Sires are immortal just like Nathanial. They're the first of their kind. Warriors of each House have many roles and one of them is guarding the Sires' resting places. Coilspire is where Theron Daevryn sleeps. There's a mausoleum here somewhere that's guarding his body.

"Is that why he was gifted the bear form?" I gasp, putting it together.

Josh laughs and it's a beautiful sight. "Makes complete sense since they both like to hibernate."

"I don't think he planned to hibernate for three hundred years the first time," I point out, laughing myself. I continue the story, "As a bear he was able to withstand time. He was war himself, never backed down, and once the frenzy took him…better pray he didn't see you."

"But it takes them a lot to get there," Josh says, and I know he's thinking of Antonio. He's so laid back, but it's true—when something takes a hold of him, he gets to the bottom of it. Antonio's always brought back the biggest hunts—whenever he felt generous enough to. He's the best tracker I know.

"Last but not least," I say, turning the page again. "Lucen Noctarion. He lost everything in a massacre by the vampires. His family—his tribe. He burned with vengeance, ready to die for it. So Nathanial gave him the strength to finish it."

"From vengeance came peace…" Josh says, quietly. I think of House Salvatore and how Sam's always navigated the peace treaties for shifters worldwide. Shane loves having Sam handle that, he always said it was a great deal off his plate.

"Yup. The fight is still in them—hurt their loved ones and they will demand blood," I say. "House Salvatore are the peacekeepers and negotiators because they know what it's like to carry that rage."

I asked Nathanial once why he chose the eagle for Lucen, because a basilisk or bear seemed like a better fit. Nathanial said because in the middle of rage, one doesn't think. Wisdom and insight in those moments is required.

"Nathanial gave Lucen the gift of clarity," I say, sighing. I look at

Josh, "Wouldn't it be crazy if they were still the ruling Warrior Pack?"

"They served for a long time. Fought alongside Nathanial a long time. They helped build the world we know now—but it's important to pass the torch to the new generations and let the next generation make their mark, contribute. It's what sets us apart from the vampires," Josh tells me.

I look over the pages, feeling them, but something still bothers me. I ask him, "Why did Nathanial try to erase my memory in the Old Tower?"

"I don't think anyone's supposed to know about my aunt," Josh says and it is the obvious answer. It makes sense.

"But why didn't he erase yours?" I ask, frowning. "You said you didn't know about your aunt."

"I didn't," Josh replies, taking the book out of my hands, before pulling me onto his lap. "Manipulation magic doesn't work on basilisks."

My eyes widen. This is the first time I'm hearing about this. It also makes sense why Shane told Josh they wiped my memories instead of erasing his.

I place my hands on his shoulders. "Wow…I didn't know that."

"Yeah, I didn't either…" he trails off as he takes in the sight of me. I feel his cock stir and press insistently against me.

I run my fingers through his hair, and he revels in the feeling. I smile and press a kiss to his cheek. "Alright there, Beta?"

"Story time made me hungry," he tells me and the look in his eyes is pure heat, "can we get out of here so I can eat your pretty little pussy out?"

I raise my brows and ask in barely a whisper, "I thought we're the only ones allowed in here?"

A slow smile spreads across his devilishly handsome face, before he pushes me down on the couch. "You're absolutely right, my Veyara," Josh says as he easily takes my leggings off. I don't need much encouragement to part my legs for him before his face disappears from my line of sight and I'm drowning in ecstasy.

"But I wasn't done for today," I say to him between jolts of pleasure. The Sunlight streams through the window, the warmth hitting us perfectly, adding to my sensations.

"That's fine, you can take a little break while I snack," Josh replies, unbothered and I arch my back. His arm comes up to keep me in place. His tongue plunges deeper into me while his teeth graze my clit, making me see stars.

"Fuck," I gasp, gripping his hair. "I fucking love Coilspire."

Josh and I fell asleep in the Sun, cuddled with each other on the couch. It has to be the best nap I've ever had. We knocked out for a good two hours and the Sun is lower in the sky by the time I wake. I kiss his hairline and get up. Josh mumbles something before turning into the couch. He's pretty adorable when he sleeps. We've been staying up almost every night since we've been here, and it's caught up to us today.

My leggings have somehow ended up near a bookshelf, and I quickly pull them on. Then I pick up the book about the Sires and take it back to the table, where I settle down. These books are too fragile to just sit anywhere.

I place the book with the other before taking a look at my options and reach for *The Craeven Lineage: The Real Records of the Lost Court.*

The Craeven insignia, a crescent Moon forged from gilded fangs poised to close, is stamped on the first page. My family's crest.

The book is older than the other ones, but again, no publication date. I flip the pages to the main texts. My eyebrows lift as my eyes skim the first few lines.

"Holy shit..." I whisper under my breath. Each word that meets my eyes sends a wave of shock and awe through me.

Isis and Nathanial's sons couldn't continue the shifter bloodline because they didn't inherit the shifter gene.

But their daughter did.

I exhale sharply—we were never taught that Nathanial had a daughter. It's just assumed that his sons continued the line. I never questioned it in school, because why would I? Craving Alphas have always been men.

Her name was Dyneia. She was born with an exceptional power called Draekoryn. It means dragon's fire, because Dyneia was a *dragon* shifter.

Dad would tell Shane and me stories of how a long time ago there used to be dragon shifters that roamed the earth. I always thought they were just bedtime stories he made up to entertain us.

It was through Dyneia that Nathanial's shifter line continued. While her brothers were powerful, even they didn't possess the kind of power Dyneia did. I realize Shane and I are *her* descendants. Over the years, and multiple generations later, the Draekoryn power slowly died out even though the shifter genetics continued. Dad also told Shane and me of this rare power, how it was bright like the Sun, but glowed blue, purple, green and pink. Dad would tell us all kinds of stories—how the Northern Lights is where dragons nest and that's why it looks like the Draekoryn power. He told us how the power died out because we weren't worthy enough to carry it anymore.

I continue reading and with each page, I get sucked into it. This text has information I've never come across in my studies or my time with Nathanial. How could he not tell me he had a daughter? Why is that a secret? Why is she not mentioned in our history lessons or in any of our history books?

Then, I come across a chapter about the Warriors' involvement.

"Rose?"

I jump at Josh's sudden voice. He yawns and sits up, still naked. I look at him and he frowns.

He reaches for his pants and asks me, "What's wrong? Why do you look like you've seen a ghost?"

I run a hand through my hair as Josh comes up to me. He's slipping on his back T-shirt and settles down into the chair next to mine.

I push the book to him and ask, "Did you know the Sires chose the white wolf as a pact to always stand together? To show uniformity even though they had their own forms?"

Josh looks at me and says, "Yes, a symbol to withstand whatever time throws at them and their Pack."

"But did you also know that was a cover?" I ask, biting my bottom lip.

Josh eyes my lips for a second before following my finger to where I point at the text. "A cover? What do you mean?"

"The Sires…created the pact to protect Nathanial and Isis's daughter from her brothers."

Now he's frowning. "Daughter? What—" his eyes scan the page, and he asks, "Why would Nathanial's daughter need protection from her brothers?"

He flips the cover to look at the book title, and I flinch slightly, saying, "Be careful—it's old." He goes back to the page I was on, and

I answer him. "Her name was Dyneia. And maybe because she was a dragon shifter."

His own eyes scan the texts as I turn to face him. I watch and notice how still he's gone, so I know it's not just me in disbelief.

"A freaking dragon, Josh!" I repeat. "How did we not know about this? My dad told me bedtime stories but that's all I thought they were."

He's quiet as he still reads. It's as if all the blood drained from his body.

"She had the Draekoryn power, that's where it comes from, and it seems like her brothers didn't even know of her being a shifter, much less a dragon shifter, or having the power," I gush, "Nathanial entrusted the Sires to protect her."

The Draekoryn power has only ever been in the Craving bloodline, and it makes sense now if it came from Nathanial's daughter.

Josh exhales the breath he's clearly been holding. "He trusted the Sires over his own sons…she was the only one who could shift," Josh says quietly.

"Which explains why she and her bloodline needed protection from her powerful witch brothers," I agree. "Her son was the first Craeven Alpha and he chose the white wolf as his House animal to keep the dragon a secret and align with the Sires being Warriors."

"She was a dragon shifter—she didn't need anyone's protection," Josh points out, still staring at the book.

"Then maybe they were trusted to keep her secret. Be her guardians regardless," I shrug. "Maybe Nathanial thought her brothers would be jealous, it's natural. Do we know whatever happened to Nathanial's sons?"

Josh carefully closes the book. "They eventually died, but the most powerful witch bloodlines descended from them."

I frown as my mind wraps around it. "That makes sense…I just thought witches were Aradia's descendants only."

"Aradia only ever had the five vampire princes with Stefan," Josh recounts and I don't know why I never really thought about that. Aradia couldn't have full blooded witch descendants, not with Stefan at least. Josh adds, "Isis was the Mother of the witches—but she passed the title to Aradia knowing Aradia had the passion to lead them."

Isis was also always sacrificing herself.

"So, all the witches are Nathanial and Isis's descendants too?"

"No, of course not. There are other bloodlines that have survived the ages who have nothing to do with Isis or Aradia—completely separate families."

I flip to the table of contents again, knowing I saw something about the Draekoryn power on it. *The Draekoryn Gift.*

I go to the section in the book while Josh watches me. Dyneia is mentioned as the mother of the Draekoryn power, being the first to ever wield it.

I read it, before saying out loud, "It says here, she Mated with a male witch. That's not entirely uncommon because back then almost everyone was a witch…" I trail off as I read the next section, biting my lip. I glance at Josh, before looking back to the text. "From that union came the first Craeven Alpha. Her son had the same power as she did." My eyes scan each line carefully. "Her son was also a dragon shifter and had the ability to shift into any animal—just like her and Nathanial. The ability was passed down to every Craeven Alpha."

Mating outside of our supernatural faction is forbidden because it results in human children, depleting our magical bloodlines. In this text, it's clear that Dyneia Mated with a witch and still had a shifter child. She never sired her Mate to be a shifter, unless she did and it just wasn't recorded…but why leave that out?

The next passage goes into her powers being kept a secret from her brothers *and* her mother—that Nathanial told Dyneia it was for her safety and the safety of her lineage.

I frown. Why wouldn't Nathanial want Isis to know? That makes no sense.

The thought unsettles me.

"Why do you think the Draekoryn power went extinct?" I ask Josh, looking at him.

"Who said it did?" he asks in return with a smirk.

I laugh. "Oh? Do you know of any dragon shifters?"

"You don't know, maybe," he says, easily. Then he closes the book and stands up. "I want to show you something."

I look up at him. "What is it? A dragon?"

He laughs, shaking his head. "No, not a dragon, silly. Come."

"Wait, what's that?" I ask as I see something sticking out of *The Draekoryn Gift* pages. I pull at it and it's a picture.

My brows rise seeing the beautiful woman with black hair and green eyes smiling as she stands in what looks like this exact library, holding a baby. I look at Josh and find him staring at the picture too. It's a picture of his mom and him.

He takes it from me and looks at it, letting out a deep breath. "Dad must've put it in the book."

"How old were you?" I ask him. "You're so tiny."

"A few weeks, probably," he says and starts to put the picture down when the writing on the back catches my attention.

I reach for it and turn it over.

Our own piece of the Heavens and the Skies.

Heavens and the Skies…

"Isn't that what the seer at Mabon said to you?" I ask Josh. "What does it mean? I know you know."

He sighs heavily. "It's just something my parents used to say all the time. I was surprised when the seer said it because I thought it was just between my parents."

"But it's not…"

"I'm not sure. I'm still looking for the seer to ask her…" he trails off and reaches for the picture again.

"Can I keep it?" I ask him, softly. "I don't have any baby pictures of you."

"Fine, if you must," he rolls his eyes, playfully, and holds out his hand to me. I let him lead us out of the library and toward a back stairwell.

"Where are we going?" I ask him after it feels like we've been climbing forever.

"You'll love it," he simply replies. When there are no more steps, Josh looks back at me. "Ready?"

"For what?" I ask, stepping through the narrow archway after him, and the world opens up to a rush of cold, thin air.

We stand on the tiny platform crowning Coilspire's highest tower, nothing but a low stone parapet between us and the sky. Clouds roll around us like an endless, silent sea—thick, luminous, catching the late-afternoon Sun in soft golds and pinks. Only the jagged tips of distant peaks pierce through, dark silhouettes floating in all that white. Below us there is nothing. No valleys, no forests, no hint of the ground far beneath. Just the endless, drifting clouds.

My breath catches. I can't speak. The beauty of it overwhelming me with awe and my eyes sting. I've dreamt of this view for so long.

I look back at Josh and find him taking a picture of me with the clouds. I bite my lip and shake my head at him as he pockets his phone. Then he wraps his arms around me.

"I don't ever want to leave here," I whisper to him, afraid to disturb the stillness in this moment.

He tightens his hold, lips brushing my ear. "I wish I could give you that," he says quietly, "but what if we moved in together?"

I turn in his arms to face him, heart stumbling. "What?"

The wind ruffles his hair across his face, but his gray eyes stay on mine. "These past few weeks since you shifted…they've been unreal. Now, waking up to you, falling asleep with you, buried inside you," his voice drops as I blush at his words, "I don't know how I'm supposed to go back to an empty bed. We've already lost so much time. I want the rest of it with you."

Joy floods me so suddenly tears prick hot at the corners of my eyes. I rise on my toes, pull him down, and kiss him—slow and fierce, pouring every yes I have into it. His hands cup my face, thumbs brushing away the dampness on my cheeks. This feels too good to be real and if it isn't, I'll deal with it later. But for now…it's everything I wanted with him. I know it's too soon, but it's bound to happen sooner or later anyway.

I draw back just enough to search his eyes. "Are you sure?"

He smiles, soft and certain. "I've been sure since Samhain. I was just waiting to see how you felt about this week. So…is that a yes?"

"Yes, obviously!" I laugh through the tears, wrapping my arms around his neck.

His lips curve into a wide, genuine grin, and he pulls me closer, kissing me deeply enough that I can feel how genuine his happiness is. I smile against the kiss and kiss him again and again.

"Would it be so bad? If we didn't leave here?" I ask him, quietly. He doesn't say anything, but I can see the conflict in his eyes. He doesn't want to leave either when the time comes but duty weighs on him. I sigh. "It's your home, but you're not here often."

"Yes, but Coilspire hasn't been home for a long time," he answers me and I know he's thinking of his family.

I kiss his jawline and pull away just enough to look up at him as I say, "Let me make it a home for you again."

He searches my eyes before kissing me, while his thought caresses my mind. ***"You already have."***

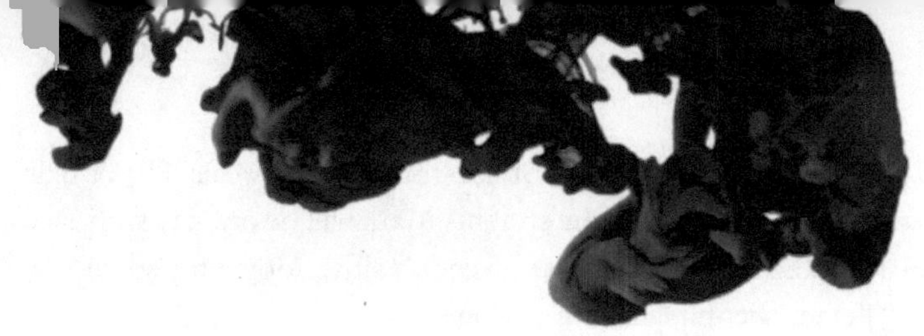

56 FIRSTS

Rosella Hunter

November 15

The *exile* lasts barely a week before Shane orders Josh and me to return to Cravenhold. We got back last night and took the time to settle in, before we broke the news to our family and friends today. Right now, I need blood after last night. Josh wanted to properly move me in, and I couldn't refuse the generous welcoming.

I slip into his oversized T-shirt, the hem grazing my thighs, before heading downstairs and straight for the kitchen. I pour myself a glass of A pos and drink it straight as I queue up a mellow playlist on the TV. The soft notes fill the quiet house, and I decide to make coffee. As it brews, I scroll through my socials for anything important I've missed—or just catch up on any juicy supernatural drama—while I was at Coilspire, losing myself in the music.

A low whistle breaks my focus. I glance up to see Josh leaning against the entryway, wearing nothing but crème sweatpants slung too low on his hips, his chest bare and sculpted, showing off his dark tattoos. My gaze drops to the tattoo on his torso while his eyes rake over me, lingering on my chest where my nipples are obviously peeking through.

"The Veyara in our kitchen," he says, voice husky, a grin tugging at his lips, "in my shirt…I must still be dreaming."

I smirk and move toward the fridge to pull out B pos and creamer. "Keep dreaming, then."

He comes over, his presence warm and overwhelming as he stops just behind me. "Gotta do something while we wait for the coffee to brew," he murmurs, his breath grazing my ear.

I bite my lip, turning my head slightly to meet his gaze. "Oh? What do you have in mind?"

His eyes darken, drinking in the sight of me in his shirt. Before I can tease him further, he spins me around, pressing me against the countertop. I giggle, arching my back, my body instinctively molding to his, feeling the hard length of him through his sweats. His face dips to my neck, lips brushing the spot his Mark will be one day with a slow lick followed by a gentle nip that sends a shiver down my spine.

"Tease," I complain with a whine.

His hands find my breasts, kneading through the thin fabric, before one hand slides lower, fingers circling my clit with just the right pressure.

I gasp, my breath catching as I reach back, my fingers brushing the waistband of Josh's sweats. The heat of him beneath sends a jolt through me. My hand slips lower, finding his cock, straining and ready. I free him with a tug, and his low groan vibrates against my neck, raw and hungry for more than breakfast. His hand covers mine, guiding me with a gentle but firm grip, helping me ease him inside as I stand on my tiptoes. The stretch is a perfect burn that makes my toes curl against the cool kitchen floor. We both moan, mingling with the soft music drifting from the TV, as he fills me completely.

"You know I can't help it when you're in my clothes." His hand slides to my lower back, his palm possessive, pinning me down on the stone slab, crushing my breasts.

Each thrust is as if he has a point to prove, letting me feel every inch of him as he moves. My fingers grip the edge of the counter, nails digging into the smooth surface as I brace for each impact.

"Yeah, hold on, you're not escaping me so fast this morning," he murmurs, voice rough with want.

His pace quickens, hips snapping harder now, each thrust deeper, more insistent. The rhythm steals my breath, my body arching to meet him, needing to feel him deeper. His hand tightens on my back, holding me steady as he drives into me. The sound of our bodies slapping against each other echoes throughout the kitchen.

His hand moves up my back, into my hair, pulling me upright into him. His touch roams, slipping under his T-shirt I'm wearing, fingers spreading across my stomach before finding my breast again. He teases, thumb brushing over my nipple while the other thumb presses down on my clit, drawing a gasp from me.

My head tips back into his shoulder, a soft whimper escaping as he hits just the right angle, sending a wave of pleasure crashing through me. Every thrust feels like a claim, like he's pouring himself into me, and I'm helpless to do anything but take it, want it, crave more.

"More," I tell him and he pinches my nipple hard, making me cry out before he kisses me sloppily. I grind against his dick, needing more friction.

Josh flips me around to face him, sliding back inside with a grin that's pure mischief. Then he picks me up, grabs the B pos, and takes us to the formal dining room table.

Oh.

He lays me down on the table, still buried deep inside, and starts to thrust, pulling a moan from my lips. I watch him pour the B pos on my clit and then pinching it. "After the Gala…I've been needing to see you bloody."

Josh pulls out and sits down at the head of the table and lowers his head to devour me without warning. His tongue—fuck, his *tongue.* It feels different. I glance down to see his serpent eyes staring back at me. My heart rate picks up as an obvious smirk appears on his face, before his tongue pulls back from me. It's long and forked—like a serpent's, but each split is thick like a human tongue.

Oh, fuck me.

Both forks spread, parting my pussy with eerie precision. One slides along my clit in a slow, wet circle while the other dips lower, pushing inside. They move out of sync, one stroking, one thrusting, and the dual sensation hits me like a spark straight to my core. I grip the edge of the table, knuckles white, a moan threatens to come out.

I clench Josh's hair. "*Fuck!* Divine!"

"Many firsts left to share with you," he thinks to me before he pulls his tongue back only to thrust both forks into my pussy, extending into me further than any tongue should be able to. We both moan loudly as Josh's nose is pressed into my bloody clit without mercy. I *feel* his tongue moving inside me and my orgasm building.

One of his hands comes up to grab onto my breast, while he uses the other to slide a finger into my pussy with his tongue.

"No," he commands when I cry out and he knows I'm right there. ***"Not yet."***

"I can't…I'm so close."

"Not. Fucking. Yet."

Fuck. He's going to kill me. I squirm under him as his tongue and finger works me. Then his finger pulls out and he pulls me closer to him, my ass slightly off the table. His wet finger starts to tease my asshole and my breath hitches.

Oh.

Josh squeezes my breast before he slowly starts to slide his finger into my hole. I try to relax but his fucking tongue has me on edge and he told me not to come.

"Is this okay?" he telepaths, the gentleness in his voice almost undoes me.

"Yes," I say breathlessly as his finger goes deeper.

"Oh, the ways I want to worship my Veyara's holes," he thinks, his tongue and finger working me in tandem. My back arches with need.

Just as I'm about to come, he pulls out from both of my holes and I cry out, desperate. "I hate—"

But my words are cut off with the return of his cock in my pussy. Josh pinches my nipple, smirking down at me, his eyes still in slits. "You were saying?"

"I hate how well you know me," I correct, arching my back and tilting my head into the table. I feel Josh lifting the shirt over my breasts, exposing me to the morning air. Then a cool liquid is poured all over my chest and down my stomach.

He's holding the blood bottle, eyes watching the blood travel down my body, before his split tongue comes out to lick it up as his thrust shakes the entire table. His tongue captures one of my nipples making me grab his arm that's playing with my clit.

I come screaming so loud I'm sure the Tens Residence across court can hear me. My nipples are so hard and aching as Josh continues to pound into me. The B pos makes it sticky as his hips meet me repeatedly. He buries his cum deep inside but continues to thrust and as I lace my fingers with his.

"You're going to get me pregnant like that," I warn warily.

"Not possible until you're Marked," he winks at me.

"Oh, thank the Divine, continue then," I tell him and he lets out a laugh, picking up speed, rocking the table beneath me.

The front door slams open, the sound reverberating through the house. Shane storms in, seeing us right away. Josh pulls out of me abruptly as he turns to face my brother, pulling his sweats up. My cheeks burn as I pull Josh's T-shirt down to cover myself and sit up on the table. The blood doesn't help.

"Got the news then?" Josh smirks at Shane, sounding smug and arrogant at the same time as if he bested Shane at something. Beta authority rolls off him as he moves to block Shane's view of me.

I've never seen my brother so pissed. I'm missing something here.

"Leave us," Shane growls at me and I stare back at him shocked. What has gotten into him? My brother would never growl at me, much less speak to me in that tone. Josh raises a brow, smirking at Shane, before he turns to me and places a kiss on my lips. He tastes like blood and me and for a second I'm lightheaded.

"Why don't you go and get ready for the day?" he suggests, dismissing me. Is he serious right now?

"What's going on?" I ask, but I really do want to get the fuck out of here and escape my brother after what he walked in on Josh and me doing.

"Fucking leave, Rose," Shane orders, using his Alpha voice as I see Devaughn and James walk in. I'm forced to leave and let Josh deal with this.

"What did you do?" I ask him through the mind link as I walk up the stairs to shower.

"No, this wasn't me. Your brother fucked up and I cashed in a favor," Josh replies and I hear them moving downstairs, going to Josh's soundproof office.

"What did he do?" I ask, knowing it has to do with me or else why would Shane not want me there?

Josh doesn't answer.

57 AGENDA

Josh Hunter
November 15

Shane shoves me up against the nearest wall, the second we step into my office. James glances at Shane and me while Devaughn pops open the bottle of Moon's Kiss.

Shane is seething. I've never seen him this angry. I grin back at him. "Checkmate, bitch."

Devaughn comes up to us, holding out a glass and saying, "Have a drink, you'll feel better."

James gives him an unimpressed look. "What the fuck?"

Shane pushes me away, takes the glass from Devaughn, and hurls it at the wall. Shame. Shouldn't waste alcohol.

I take my glass and drink, then look at Shane. "Did you honestly think I wouldn't find out that you made me sign a fucking marriage license, *brother-in-law?*"

"I'm going to take a wild guess and say consent was not present..." Devaughn trails off. He holds his glass up. "I'm drinking one way or another. It's Crystal's birthday, and my ass was ordered to be here first thing in the morning," Devaughn replies, walking past me to lean against the arm of a couch.

Well, at least he showered and I don't have to smell Crystal all over him. I do want everyone to smell Rose all over me though...that's an idea. Being alone with Rose at Coilspire was...addicting.

Devaughn eyes me before asking, "Why are you bloody?"

I ignore him.

"When did you find out?" James asks me, then to Shane, "And why would you trick him into signing it?"

"So he wouldn't marry someone else just to hurt her," Shane snaps, keeping his distance from me because I know he wants to punch me. It's a fair reason. I don't believe it's the real reason for a second.

"He's probably regretting calling you back," Devaughn telepaths to me, chuckling.

"I knew when I signed the papers," I answer James and then look at Shane, "I'm not an idiot. I read everything I sign."

"Were you ever going to maybe tell them?" James asks Shane, crossing his arms.

"At their reunion," Shane answers. "It was just a precaution."

I push off my desk, and say, "Yeah, well, thanks. By the way, I asked *my wife* to move in and she said yes."

Shane moves toward me, but Devaughn is quick to hold him back as James stands close enough to intervene.

"Fuck no," Shane spits out, pulling out of Devaughn's hold.

"I'm afraid it's already done. Movers are packing her things right now and should be here any minute. We were going to tell you all later today, but I thought the surprise would be nice."

"How fucking thoughtful of you," Shane replies, sarcastically.

"She already said yes. You can't say no to this without a good excuse," I tell him.

"A good excuse? How about that we don't move a Crescent in until after the reunion," Shane says and it's a weak ass argument.

"It's a tradition. It's not the fucking law. No one will die if she moves in," I roll my eyes.

"Are you going to have your reunion soon then?" Shane asks and it's not that he's a stickler for rules. He wants to know if I'm going to Mark Rose soon.

"Are you worried I can't control myself?" I retort. "Or maybe that I'll talk in my sleep, and she'll learn what happened six years ago? Either way, she should."

Shane's message to return came just when things were getting interesting. Rose and I talked through a lot of things, and I'm sure if we were there for just a few more days, I could've convinced her to walk down memory lane.

Shane grunts. "Sure, you want another near-death scar on your ribs? Have you told her she's the reason you have that scar for starters?"

"Don't be a dick," Devaughn says to Shane, tired of this.

I shrug, answering Shane, "Taking her memories was to protect her from herself at the time. She's not a naïve twelve-year-old anymore."

"Oh, and you're suddenly the expert on *my* sister? You just want her to remember killing Noah," Shane repeats the same fucking argument.

I glare at him. "Damn right I do. That's nothing new. I want her to know everything. I want her to remember so our relationship can feel real."

"Why does she need to remember for it to feel real?" Shane stands taller and turns to me fully. "You've tortured her enough. If you're going to move her in with you, the least you can do is Mark her—before she goes into heat."

Which will be any day now. A female shifter always has her first heat by her sixth full Moon. We're coming up on that.

I've always thought he wanted Rose to stay in the dark. Does he want me to Mark her? Or is he testing me to see where I stand now because he had no control of Coilspire? Shane never meddled until the night she shifted. He's been insufferable since, paranoid that I'll tell her what we did—what he decided six years ago. Marking her will show Rose everything he's afraid of.

I cross my arms. "I'm not Marking her until I tell her everything first. I'm not blindsiding her like that."

"That's noble as fuck for a snake," Shane growls.

"Is she ready? Can we trust her now with everything if you do Mark her?" Devaughn asks, quietly, making all of us pause. Shane's eyes are on me.

"He won't tell her anything," he confidently assures Devaughn. "If Josh was going to, he would've done it at Coilspire," then he turns to me, "you had her all to yourself and you didn't say a word. Didn't Mark her. You still don't trust her."

My eyes switch to serpent slits and Shane narrows his own at the threat. I meet him halfway. "Rose and I are figuring it out. We don't need you to meddle in our relationship or tell us how to handle it. She's my responsibility, you made sure of that, so I will decide what happens now."

Shane has to know she'll learn everything before the Claiming. He wants this for a reason and I'm fucking tired of his hidden agendas. We all have them. He's just been playing his hand funny lately and I don't appreciate it. At the end of the day, whether we agree or not about Rose getting her memories back, Shane and I were always on the same team. Lately, he's playing his own game, that much is clear. A chill shoots down my neck but I ignore it and take a drink.

"The second she goes into heat all bets are off. We've all been there. What if Josh Marks her prematurely?" James asks Shane, referring to his confidence. "How can we be sure we won't?"

Shane watches me, reading me as if he ever could. I look right back at him, holding his gaze. He smirks and says, "Because you're in love with her."

"This has nothing to do with love," I reply, automatically, standing my ground.

Shane decides to challenge it. "Have you told her she's your wife then?"

"That's just it, Shane. You don't have control over this, over her anymore, and it's your own damn fault. If I wanted to marry her, I would've but you wanted to take matters into your own hands because what? You got scared?" I don't believe he did this because he thought I'd go off and marry someone else. I take a step closer to Shane, almost chest to chest, and say, "Exile me again, but don't for a second think you're going to come in here and tell me how to treat her. Mate, wife, whatever she is, there's no fucking way I'll be in love with a murderer. She's mine to do with as I please, so stand the fuck down. You fucked this one up."

Shane watches me, before his eyes flicker past my shoulder. I already know. I felt her. I clench my jaw as Shane tells me, "No, I'm pretty sure you did."

With that, Shane looks at James and Devaughn before they silently follow Shane to leave. Devaughn clasps my shoulder on the way out. I turn and find Rose standing in the doorway, staring at me with her big gray eyes. Eyes that are glossed over, disbelief written across her face, and I know she's heard enough.

58 SNAKES WILL BE SNAKES

Rosella Craving
November 15

It's the anger in his voice that gives me pause. This is not the man I spent the best days of my life with in Coilspire. This is the man who used to look at me like I was the dirt on his shoe.

Josh pinches the bridge of his nose and says, "You were supposed to be upstairs."

Married. Josh and I are married.

Having a marriage license is just a formality for us. Marriage doesn't really mean much when our soul and lifeline are tied to another. But when the Hell did we get married? Shane did this?

I absently touch the pendant around my neck, unable to move. "What's going on…?" I ask, unsure. I refuse to believe we're back to how things were before Mariella's reunion. I won't go back to that.

"Don't pretend you didn't hear anything," he says, and even his voice is cold and emotionless. His eyes have switched back to normal, the serpent slits gone, but there's no warmth in them. "Your brother thought he could pull one over on us. On me."

He doesn't just get to switch up on me. Not after the last few weeks of things being so good and finally getting closer. We got through the Old Tower situation, this is nothing…except what Josh said at the end. "That doesn't explain why there's a wall between us right now," I say.

"Right now?" Josh repeats, raising a brow. He lets out a low maniacal laugh as he walks up to me. "Oh, Rose. What did I tell you to do that first day of our training?"

I stare at him. Where is this going? What does that have to do with us being married?

"Go on," he dares. The entire energy of the room has shifted.

Blood drains from my face as I remember that first and only training session we had before Coilspire.

"Say it," he insists, seeing the recognition in my eyes.

"To resist you," I whisper.

"To resist me," he repeats then says coldly, "you *failed*."

The last few months replay in my mind. Everything he said and did. The way he touched me, looked at me…how can someone fake that?

"You should have always assumed you're training," Josh says, detached, nothing like the man I was with in Coilspire. "You should always keep your shields up. You never know where an enemy can strike from."

"Stop," I whisper. I tell myself he's angry, that Shane blindsided him, that he doesn't mean this.

"Why do you think I didn't push your training sessions? I could've commanded you to show up to them," he says, cruelly. "I improvised. I knew I had no business training *your* powers. There are many other ways someone can infiltrate your mind—your life. Did you honestly think I could ever, *ever,* care about a killer like you?" he sneers and starts to move past me.

I catch his arm, stopping him. Josh turns to look at me, and I slap him across the face, the sound cracking through the room.

My vision blurs as tears spill down my cheeks and I look back at my shocked Mate. The sting of it burns in my hand as we stand there, staring at each other.

The week at Coilspire was beautiful. The past few months with him were the best we've ever had. The whole time I thought it was real. In the blink of an eye, he rewrote it entirely. Threw it away like it was nothing.

Like I'm nothing.

How can he be so cruel? How can he build me up only to destroy me?

"You're a fucking snake," I say to him, with my own venom in my voice.

I don't care that I just slapped a basilisk shifter. I don't care that I slapped a fucking Beta Warrior. I don't care that I just called him the one word he despises. I don't care if he turns me into stone right now—I wish he did. I wish my heart was stone like his. I should've listened to myself when I told him the only thing I can expect from a snake is to get bitten. I knew better.

His hand snaps up, fingers wrapping around my jaw as he towers over me, close enough that his breath brushes my skin. His thumb presses into my bottom lip. Those gray eyes stare into mine, sharp and challenging, daring me to push back as he says, "Better than being a cold-blooded murderer at twelve."

My heart slams against my ribs. Words tangle in my throat. Every insult I had ready scatters like ash. All I feel is the heat of his palm, the way his grip holds me exactly where he wants me. I slap his hand down. Fuck him. My Mate is supposed to be the one place in the world I shouldn't have to guard myself.

"My *Mate* is not supposed to be my enemy," I say to him, as his eyes flash at me. "My Mate is supposed to be *safe*."

"My Mate isn't supposed to kill my brother," he voices.

I just about punch him this time. "I didn't kill Noah!"

"Don't say his name!"

"Why are you doing this?!" I exclaim, unable to fight the tears anymore. "We had a perfect time at Coilspire—it literally couldn't have been better. Why can't we just have a good fucking life?"

"Why would I want that with *you?*" he sneers letting me go roughly.

I throw my hands up in defeat. "Fine. You win," I tell him. "You've made it clear you don't want me. I'll stay out of your way. I'll have to live here eventually but this place is big enough, we might as well get used to it. You won't even know I'm here—"

"Yeah, that's impossible," he rolls his eyes, scowling. His dark lashes frame his cold, unamused gaze, making him look even more menacing.

"I'm here, it's a problem. I'm not here, it's a problem. At this point, you should just lock me up, throw away the key and forget I exist. You think I want to be here after everything you just said? Just…stay away from me if you hate me that much. Don't worry about my training or who infiltrates my life or my mind, don't do anything. We can Mate on the last day if we have to, but just…stop toying with me."

My heart pounds against my chest. I hate this back and forth. I hate that he gave me a taste of how good it can be with us, only to pull the rug out from under me. Never again.

He narrows his eyes. "My hands are as tied as yours."

"Your hands aren't tied when it comes to wanting to be happy, Josh. You choose to stay stuck and believe in what you want to. That's not on me," I reply and my next words are barely above a whisper, "I'm not the one who failed, Josh. Mates are sacred. You failed us. You keep failing us."

I'm tired of not knowing the rules to his games. All I know is, I didn't kill his brother, but it makes me wonder why he thinks I did? Why didn't he turn over every leaf to prove my innocence?

I don't even slam the door behind me as I walk out. He doesn't come after me either. I see Vanessa near the foot of the stairs. She looks relieved to find me.

"I just got here, what is going on?" she asks, surprised as movers bring my belongings in. I realize she heard nothing of Josh and my fight, so I tell her quickly about me moving in here and to find a room on the first floor for me. Maybe I should leave, that sounds like the reasonable thing to do, but I'll have to come back a few months later.

I know my brother. He must've had a reason for making Josh and me sign that marriage license. He never does anything without a cause, whether anyone understands it or not. Shane is very much like our father in that sense. I might never be able to trust Josh, but I do trust my brother.

"And where are you going?" Vanessa asks me as I grab the first outfit I see that's hanging off a hanger.

"Out," I reply, and leave the premises. Cristobal and Franklin are still standing by the car.

"My lady?" Franklin asks, frowning, being too good at reading me.

"We're going for a drive," I tell them and Cristobal moves to open the door for me to get in.

I should've seen this coming. Not the marriage or moving in part, but Josh…being Josh. I knew it was too good to be true. I knew it was too easy. He told me that first day of training that I killed his brother. Why did I ever think he'd forgive me and want to be with me? Why did I ever think he was working through it and learning to move forward with me?

Basilisks don't forgive.

He said a few sweet words, let me in a little bit, made me feel like he actually wanted me for the first time—and I fucking believed him. Because I wanted to so badly. I let my feelings and longing for him blind me. It's always been my downfall no matter how much I told myself and everyone I hate him.

Basilisks don't forgive. When am I going to learn that?

As silent tears fall down my cheeks, I go to the photo gallery in my phone and delete all the pictures Josh took of us and me at Coilspire. I didn't believe them anyway.

Mariella's going on about some upcoming social event I'll need to attend with her as we leave The Whispering Kettle.

"Mariella," I cut her off. "I'm ready to get started on what Shane mentioned after my transformation—working with you to learn about my powers."

Her hazel eyes brighten. "Oh?"

"My magic is rare…"

She lets out a laugh, linking her arm with mine. "That's the understatement of the century."

I smile. "I want to know how we can counter the effects of my powers if we ever need to. Better safe than sorry."

"Like an antidote or a reversal?"

I shrug. "Whatever works? I just want to make sure if I accidentally hurt anyone, they'll be okay. I'm very intentional with my magic and it doesn't do anything I don't want it to, but accidents can happen…"

"That's very…responsible of you," she says thoughtfully. "I'd love to help, I know I have to put it in for some approvals, just admin stuff—I've never played with your kind of magic. I don't want to accidentally use it wrong."

I know what she means, and while my magic would never do anything it's not intended to, I understand her concerns.

"How about we start small and see if there's even anything to research and bother with here. I have a space, come with me," I tell her and she nods.

We make our way to the Hunter Residence, and I guide her through the backyard toward the tucked away old greenhouse. It's clear it hasn't been in use for years. The glass is dirty, paint is peeling off the wood frame, and weeds are growing everywhere. It looks forgotten and a little sad, something a greenhouse should never be.

I push the door open and it smells earthy and damp inside. There are empty tables that line the walls, potting soil spilled as if someone was rushing, broken pots, cobwebs…neglected, yes—but spacious. And private.

I turn to Mariella. "It's…dirty, but would this work?"

Her gaze travels over the sagging shelves, the cracked skylight, and the wide central aisle. A slow smile spreads across her face, bright and genuine.

"It's perfect," she says, voice soft with wonder. She steps deeper inside, brushing frost from a workbench. "I can work with this. I'll have a few guys over to fix it up, if that's okay."

"Change anything you need. Redesign it completely. It's your space now." I smile at her. I'm glad she's willing to get started quickly, not that I'm in a rush.

Mariella claps her hands, excitement shining in her eyes. "This will be great!"

"I gotta run, have training with Vanessa. Feel free to stay as long as you like."

"Wait," she frowns.

"What's wrong?" I pause to take a second.

She lets out a disgruntled sound which is so unlike Lady Mariella. Then she gestures to our surroundings. "Um, hello! You and Josh are married? What the fuck happened at Coilspire?"

Josh had apparently leaked it to the tabloids that we had a secret wedding, and the media already knew we were exiled to Coilspire—they put two and two together and it's a whole romantic story now.

That's why Vanessa was calling me, talking about news outlets. It's also why Shane came barging in through our doors. Josh made sure it was announced that morning. When I was scrolling for juicy supernatural drama, I never thought it'd be mine. He distracted me just before it was released, which was why I didn't see it.

I just smile at Mariella and say, "Coilspire was unreal! Moving in together was a sweet surprise. Getting married was Shane's idea actually."

"Seriously? That's all you're going to give me?" she frowns.

I wink and kiss her cheek. "Gotta go!"

"Rose! You're terrible!" she calls after me, but I just laugh, ignoring the stabbing ache in my chest, like I have for the past six years.

59 AWAKE

Rosella Craving
November 17

I meet Nathanial at the Old Tower. He laces his fingers through mine and kisses my forehead. I blink as a rush of recent memories flood through me, and I remember meeting Josh's aunt before he and I did. I remember going through the tunnels and working with Aradia on a ritual to wake Mother Isis.

I remember how Nathanial kisses me and takes me to his cabin. Still.

This whole time I thought…I thought I was special to him. Yes, our relationship was…wrong, but I thought all that stopped on my birthday. I thought the last time he and I kissed was on my birthday.

Oh Divine. Have I been unknowingly cheating on Josh with Nathanial?

"No more disappearing. We have work to do," Nathanial tells me, breaking me out of my spiraling thoughts, as he opens the tower door.

Queen Aradia and Josh's aunt, Mina, are waiting for us. I silently follow them, going through the underground tunnels back to Mother Isis' resting place. I will myself to maintain my composure. I'll freak out later.

Aradia stands across from me, her golden hair catching the dim torchlight, her blue eyes locked on mine with an intense focus. Our hands clasp over the cold stone of the tomb. Nathanial leans against the far wall, arms crossed, but his gaze keeps pulling to the tomb with a concentration that makes my stomach twist. Mina sits in her corner like always, legs crossed, lips moving in that silent chant, her black hair veiling her face like a shroud.

But this time, one of the pendants around her neck catches my eye. I have the same one tucked into my shirt right now. How strange. Mina has always worn this necklace, is that why I subconsciously recognized it when Josh gave it to me?

Aradia squeezes my fingers. "Breathe with me, my darling. Let the words pull from your core."

I nod, drawing in the stale scent of dying petals. We begin together, voices weaving low at first, then rising in rhythm:

"Sleep was mercy.
Mercy's done.
What was denied has found its tongue—
Wake, wake now, Isis. The hour has come."

The chant vibrates through my bones, pulling at the darkness inside me. With each repetition, the flowers around us respond—petals curling inward, stems browning, leaves dropping one by one. The jasmine vines sag, their white blooms turning gray, crumbling to dust that sifts onto the stone floor.

"Why do you have Helena's necklace?" Mina asks telepathically as Aradia starts the chant over. ***"Do not break concentration,"*** Mina instructs and I listen, repeating with Aradia.

"I don't have…" I start to say but decide to trust her since this is the first time she's spoken to me since the Old Tower night. I didn't know witches could telepath until that night. ***"It was a gift,"*** I answer her.

"From Helena's son? Or Helena?"

I frown. It is technically a gift from Josh. ***"Is that important?"***

"How much do you know?"

"I don't know anything…I swear," I think to her honestly.

"Does Nathanial know you have the necklace?"

"Not as far as I know…I got it the night Josh and I saw you in the tower."

"Why doesn't Nathanial know? Is your loyalty not to him?" she questions me. I'm not entirely sure where her loyalties lie. She clearly won't speak to me in front of anyone but is okay with communicating through our minds. Her inquiry is very direct and to the point. She also doesn't address the night Josh and I went to the tower.

"Of course, my loyalty is to him. It's just a necklace…" I decide to play it safe. I don't know this woman aside from her being Helena's twin. ***"You have the same necklace."***

She doesn't say anything more. Of course, she doesn't.

Energy starts to drain from me, slowly at first, a trickle that builds to a flood as we continue. My legs tremble, vision blurring at the edges, but Aradia's grip keeps me steady, her power working with mine.

"Sleep was mercy.
Mercy's done.
What was denied has found its tongue—
Wake, wake now, Isis. The hour has come."

We push harder, the words sharpening, echoing off the walls as our magic presses around us. The tomb buzzes faintly under our hands, a pulse that matches my heartbeat. Nathanial shifts, his eyes narrowing on the stone, that intense gleam sharpening. He feels it too.

The rot spreads faster, lilies drooping, their pollen scattering. My knees buckle as exhaustion crashes in. I sway, the chant faltering on my lips.

Nathanial moves in a blur, arms wrapping around my waist from behind. "That's enough for today," he says to Aradia, voice firm but edged with concern.

She releases my hands, stepping back with a nod.

I lean into Nathanial's chest before I can stop myself, his warmth seeping through my sweater.

"No," I murmur, pushing weakly at his arm. "I need to go home."

He scoops me up effortlessly, cradling me like I'm made of glass. "Shh, don't worry."

His lips brush my forehead as he carries me out, through the twisting tunnels. In an instant, we're inside his cabin on the mountains.

The door clicks shut behind us, sealing in the familiar scent of pine and smoke from the fireplace. He lays me on his bed, the furs soft and warm beneath me. My eyelids droop, heavy as lead.

"You did good," he whispers, tucking a strand of hair behind my ear. His fingers linger on my cheek, tracing down to my neck. "So good, my little mistress."

I know I'm not in danger here—Nathanial's touch is possessive but protective. Still, for the first time, guilt twists in my gut. I want to be home with Josh despite us fighting. I need to be where he is.

But sleep claims me anyway, pulling me under before I can fight it.

When I wake, the cabin is quiet. I don't feel Nathanial's presence. He must've gone hunting. Only two hours have passed since I've been here. I sit up, head clearer now, the exhaustion faded.

I can't stay. I need to go home. I slide from the bed and head outside to shift into my wolf form. Then I race home as fast as my four paws can take me, remembering the memories Nathanial gave back to me and everything that happened in the tunnels.

60 NIGELLUS RONAN CRAVING

Rosella Craving
November 20

The first snow fell today.

Daniya pushes aside the tree branches, skipping. Mariella laughs, following, her fingers laced with mine. I wish I could be as excited as my friends, but I'm freaking out a little bit. The news came barely thirty minutes ago.

We hear Eliza's cries before we enter the sacred space in the forest. They're not the grief-filled wails from a few months ago. These cries sound torturous, making me clench my thighs like I'll never open them again.

We approach the lit ritual ground. There's a raging bonfire going, along with torches lining the tree line. Carpets and pillows are arranged in a circle. Plates of assorted snacks and blood goblets sit ready for the celebration.

Steam rises from the wide, shallow birthing pool set in the center of the ritual ground with the Moon's glow shining down. The scent of blood, crushed lavender and myrrh from the healers' herbs, and the raw, animal sweetness of new life breaking through fills the air. It's very overwhelming and primal…

Eliza floats half-submerged, completely bare out in the wild. Her body is stretched and spent, breasts heavy and swollen, skin glistening with sweat and water. Exhaustion etches every line of her face. Her eyes are half-lidded, mouth slack, her pretty blonde hair is plastered to her neck and shoulders. She looks like she's one breath from slipping under the surface forever. My stomach twists. I'm used to seeing naked bodies, but not this—not the vulnerability of my sister-in-law stripped utterly open.

Shane kneels at the pool's edge, one hand gripping hers, the other braced on the edge, knuckles white. Two healers hover in the shallows with her, murmuring low encouragement to her. Lady Tiara stands at the head of the pool with her sleeves rolled to her elbows.

Eliza's head falls toward Shane. A weak moan escapes her.

"One more," one of the healers says, voice firm but kind. "The head is crowning. One more strong push, Luna, and he's here."

Eliza's eyes flutter. She drags in a shuddering breath, fingers tightening on Shane's until I see the skin pale around her nails.

Shane leans close, forehead close to hers. "You've got this, beautiful. One more. I love you so much."

Her body arches. A low, guttural sound tears out of her in a half-sob, half-roar. The water surges as she gives it everything left in her.

The first cry of our future Alpha splits through the night.

The baby slides free in a rush of fluid and blood. Daniya, Mariella, and I stare in shock, none of us able to move as we take in the miracle of life—it's terrifying. How did she do that? I mean, I know how, but…

"I want to wait, a long, long, *long* time before I ever do that…" Daniya voices my internal feelings.

"It's so beautiful," Mariella cries. Daniya and I would stare at her, but we're preoccupied.

The healers move fast, lifting him clear of the water. Tiny limbs kick, face scrunched red and indignant, mouth wide in that furious wail. He's…kind of perfect.

"Shane," Lady Tiara says, voice carrying the weight of ritual practices, "the cord."

Shane is handed a small ceremonial blade, and he slices through with one clean motion.

Lady Tiara steps forward without hesitation. She takes the newborn from the healer's hands, wraps him swiftly in a deep Warrior blue silk. The fabric clings to his wet skin as she cradles him against her chest for only a heartbeat. Then she turns to me.

"Veyara," she says. "The baby Alpha."

Mariella nudges me. I move toward the High Priestess. She places him in my arms and my breath catches. It's customary that if there is a Veyara, she's the first to hold the new Alpha. I still don't know why, it's just how things have been done.

Darkness swirls around him, so thick that I can barely make out his tiny face and body. My heart lurches, but I keep my grin plastered on, forcing my eyes to Eliza to make sure she's okay. She's radiant, her smile warm and tired and completely oblivious to what I'm seeing.

"Do we have a name?" Lady Tiara asks, glancing over at my brother and his Mate.

"Nigellus Ronan Craving," Eliza answers, weakly. "Nigel, for short."

His tiny weight settles against my chest and a jolt of strange magic surges through me—unfamiliar, unwelcoming, and unlike anything I've ever felt before. My magic wakes, ready to attack and defend.

My pulse thunders in my ears. The forest tilts for one dizzy second. I tighten my grip on the baby instinctively, terrified I'll drop him, but he only nestles closer, small mouth working in a soundless yawn.

"What was that?" Josh sends through our mind link, and I glance up to see that he's joined us too. He's watching me with the very new baby in my arms. His eyes darken for a split second before his face contorts into a concerned frown.

I ignore him, and the fact that we have a very naked Luna between us. That's when I realize all the Warriors and Crescents are here, along with a few Elders.

I have nothing to say to him. I haven't talked to him for a week, since I came home drunk. I'd avoid him, but we haven't run into each other at the house. It's for the best. It's too hard. I try not to think of how perfect Coilspire was and how it can just be like that. I constantly remind myself that he believes I killed his brother. He never even gave me the benefit of the doubt.

On top of that, Mariella and I saw him coming out of the Velour Wing. It's a brothel in Cravenhold—yeah, we still have those in this day and age. Mariella couldn't have known he hadn't done anything, she assumed because why else would anyone go in there. It's not a place to have business meetings. My best friend paled at the sight and asked if I wanted his balls chopped. That was two days ago.

"Rose?" Josh pushes.

I look back down at the tiny thing in my arms. He's warm. So warm. A shock of dark hair covers his head. His eyes are closed.

"Really? You're not going to talk to me?" Josh asks as they prepare Eliza for the afterbirth. Why is he talking to me?

The heaviness in my heart doesn't let me think. Tears stream down my cheeks, not because of him but because I'm terrified of what I just felt from the baby. I don't know what it means.

Josh seems to ignore the entire scene and crosses the grounds to me. He pulls me into him, his arm sliding around my waist, his hand coming to rest gently on the baby, holding him with me. The gesture feels so natural, so right, that I start to lean back into him before reminding myself I can't do that.

Moments like this are confusing and I swear it damages my brain. I want to be mad at him, I should be. I should at least push him away and not find this comforting. I shouldn't want this from him, but so help me Divine, he's the only one I want comforting me. But I know him and I know nothing is for free with Josh Hunter.

Daniya watches us, a curious smile playing on her lips, before she takes out her phone and proceeds to snap a picture of Josh and me holding the baby together.

I step away automatically and the gesture stiffens him, making him stand taller.

"Really?" Josh scowls at her, then to me he asks telepathically, ***"At least just tell me you're okay."***

"You're not at risk of dying today," I reply, with my own face composed.

"Don't be a child," he thinks back, irritated. There he is.

"Why were you at the Velour Wing?" I have to know. What's worse than him fucking someone else, is him spending time talking to someone else. My heart can't take that.

Daniya just winks in return at Josh before her fingers type away on her keyboard. Josh's watch lights up a moment later. "I sent it to the both of you."

"Post it!" Eliza orders, mid-push.

"Aren't you a little busy to care about social media right now, Luna?" Josh asks her with narrowed eyes, before he catches mine and thinks to me, ***"Are you jealous?"***

"No, of course not. Just need to know that if you're going to be exploring other physical options, maybe I should return a few calls," I answer him and this is the most we've communicated this week.

Daniya, the devil, is engrossed in her phone as Mariella and Daniel snicker with her, watching over her shoulders. Josh's watch lights up again and I know without seeing it that it's a notification that he's been tagged in a picture. I don't have my phone on me.

"I fucking dare you to see what happens if you do that," he nearly growls in my ear, and my heart skips a beat. Why does he care?

If all of Coilspire and everything leading up to it was a lie, then that means the night of Mariella's reunion was a lie. Romania was a lie. The Gala was a lie. My first time with him was a lie—everything he said…all the sweet things…

I hold Nigel up higher to my chest and press my lips to his soft forehead. That newborn baby smell overwhelming my senses and the Mating bond pulling at me. Fuck that.

A few seconds later, Nigel is taken from me by Lady Tiara and returned to Eliza, who's out of the pool now. She's in a robe, laying on a picnic blanket. There are many rituals and traditions that surround the birth of a new Alpha Warrior. Luckily, the rest of us do not have such public birthing.

James and Devaughn have Josh's attention, talking a few feet away. I watch Eliza take Nigel in her hands and a strange look wash over her face after the initial relief and joy. A little like she can't figure him out. It makes me wonder if she feels the same thing I felt with him. She's his mother, it's possible.

She definitely knows something's different about her baby. Whatever it is, we'll figure it out as a family.

"Divine—are you guys hot too?" I start fanning myself. I'm burning up and my legs feel all tingly.

"Um…no?" Daniel gives me a funny look. It's late November and the cold has set in.

"I'm so hot," I reach for an iced blood chalice and down it, before I see Mariella and Daniya exchange looks. "What?" I ask, "What is it?"

"Um…" Mariella bites her lip, glancing at the boys, who look as confused as me. "It's nothing, maybe move away from the bonfire."

"Honey, you're going through heat," Daniya supplies telepathing me, raising an eyebrow.

Fuck.

"Wonderful. I thought it was painful if your Mate's not…cooperative?" I ask. This isn't painful—just extremely uncomfortable and I'm not horny or anything.

"Oh…it can be," Daniya thinks, before she narrows her eyes at Josh, who has his back to us. "Maybe it's a good time to go on your honeymoon, newlyweds!" she says much louder so he can hear. Sure enough, Josh glances over and looks right at me.

Fucking Hell.

I break eye contact with him and glare at Daniya instead. She simply shrugs.

"You probably just started…" Mariella telepaths as the boys are engrossed in a conversation about some Pride situation.

"Eliza said it lasts three weeks at the most if you don't have sex," I think to the girls.

"Possibly…couldn't confirm…" Daniya responds sheepishly. I resist the urge to roll my eyes.

I miss him. I miss us.

But he can go fuck himself.

I will suffer through this before I end up in his bed again.

61 MISTRESS

Josh Hunter
November 24

All the Warriors have been called into the war room for an urgent meeting. Shane's already here when I arrive. Devaughn's slumped in a chair, nursing a coffee, looking like he got dragged through a fight. The others are scattered around the table. James is yelling at someone on the phone, and I wish he'd take it outside. I'm too on edge for all that noise.

And then there's Rose.

She's already seated, back straight, too straight like she's uncomfortable. She's going through heat, and it started a few days ago. I can smell her need—feel it straight in the pit of my stomach and dick. When a female shifter goes through heat, everything about her is *more*. She doesn't have to be turned on for my body to have the same reaction as it would if I smelled her arousal.

It's messing with her. Messing with me. She won't meet my eyes as I drop into the chair across from her.

She's fidgeting with her hands under the table. Pain's etched in the tight line of her mouth. She shifts in her seat like she can't get comfortable. Fuck. I know what that's like for her—agony building with no release. I'm the only one who can fix it. But after pushing her away, fucking her now would be…amazing, but fucked up.

You keep failing us.

It probably would've been less painful if she just clawed me.

I told her she failed, that she should assume everything's training at all times. I told her that week we had—the best damn week of my life—was just fucking training.

I wanted to take it back the second the words left my mouth.

The look in her eyes after she slapped me—her tear-stained face…I've never seen her cry like that before. I've never seen heartbreak so raw on her face before, and I've seen her heart break because of me a lot. This was different. It's what a part of me always wanted to see, how I always wanted to see her.

I haven't been able to sleep, tossing and turning. My bed is uncomfortable without her, and I didn't realize how different it'd be to sleep alone now. I know she isn't sleeping either. Her emotions are pure agony. It's worse than the first time she realized I was hooking up with other women. It's worse than the night she decided to go on the Tour. Looking at her face right now, you'd never know.

Then add the physical pain of heat on top of that. It's been torture living in the same house and not being together. I know she's stubborn enough to resist anything that has to do with me now. She won't even talk to me telepathically. She won't touch herself at night to relieve her pain either.

All I've wanted to do is kiss her. I wanted to kiss her in my office when I saw the heartbreak clear on her face. She's usually so good about hiding her true emotions from me, but lately I know it's been too much for her. I know all of this is too much for her. She's only eighteen.

Yes, I was in denial when Shane said I'm in love with her now. It doesn't change the fact that I can't love her. Not really. Hating her is simpler. Hurting her makes things easier.

Shane triggered me. Saying I'm in love with her…it was like he dumped a bucket of ice water on me and then held me underwater. How can I be in love with my brother's murderer? In what world does it make it okay?

I know the things I've said to her and I meant them.

But like she's not ready to let go of everything that's happened, how she's not over it—neither am I. How do I get over it?

The difference between us is that she's not letting the past stop her from having a future with me.

But the guilt…

I'm sure if I killed Shane, she'd never forgive me. Why is that hard for everyone to understand? Being with her, being in love with her, giving into her…it would all mean I forgive her for Noah.

I review the files Shane sent me an hour ago or pretend to, so I don't just stare at Rose. It's the most I've seen her since Shane's kid was born.

James eventually sits down beside me, breaking me out of my thoughts as he telepaths me, ***"What's this about?"***

"No idea, it didn't go through me," I reply.

"Alright," Shane says, voice gravelly like he hasn't been sleeping either, as he dims the lights. The big screen comes to life, projecting a video. "Three Rivers' Pride and Pack sent this over. They've been at war with each other for decades, but these two incidents aren't territorial disputes…watch."

The video plays to show us a basement. It's clear the footage is from the security cameras installed down there.

"That's Queen Calla of the lion Pride. Her sister was one of the four Queens who died. Calla just recently inherited the Pride," Devaughn tells us as we watch her and her guards surround a man chained to a beam. He's a mess, pale, black veins crawling under his skin like small snakes.

"And that's Alpha Josiah," Shane says, pointing out a man in his mid-thirties to Rose, who's not met the Alpha yet.

"I know. I met him," Rose nods, saying, much to my annoyance.

I stand corrected, guess they've met. The video continues to the Pride blaming the Pack for the state of the man and the Pack denying it. My eyes land on Rose and before I know it, I ask her through our mind link, ***"When did you meet Alpha Josiah?"***

Her gray eyes shift from the screen to me, her own annoyance clear on her face. Fuck, did she feel my jealousy through the thought? I never thought I was the jealous type, not really—serpents aren't—but wolves are…and I learned just how jealous I can be in Romania when I saw her dancing with the fucking prince.

Ever since Antonio's reunion, I know I've been on edge about her. I hated seeing her kissing all those shifters, but I had no right to say she couldn't. Am I going to let that happen again—fuck no. Not now, not after Coilspire. Not after I've gotten a taste of her, of what it's like to be with her. She can think I feel nothing for her, but it doesn't change that she will only ever be mine. If she wants to be with others, she'll have to allow it for me too, and I know that will never happen.

"Why did you think it was called a Royal Tour?" she snaps back, her thought as annoyed as her face. She focuses back on the scene unfolding on the screen.

Wow, she actually replied. The silence between us has been unsettling. Talking to her always made me want to pull my hair out but it's been interesting since her transformation. This silence is uncomfortable knowing I caused it. I'm used to people being uncomfortable because of me, not the other way around.

I don't know why it's called a Royal Tour, but that makes

sense…why is the Tour so secretive then? I don't want to start thinking about that. She stole that experience from us.

"Wait…is that, Michael?" Daniel asks as the bound guy jerks on the video. "That's the Queen's brother."

We all pay closer attention as Michael jerks up again but this time his eyes are pure black. Like Rose's when she uses her power.

Rose stiffens, seeing it too but before any of us can speak, Michael screams.

"They're here... they're here..." His voice rasps out, echoing weirdly in the audio. There's commotion as he locks eyes on something off camera. Then he looks right into the camera as if he knew we'd be watching this.

"Mistress," he hisses, lunging, trying to break free. "Save me…they're…"

"Who…who's the mistress?" the Queen asks her brother urgently, but her voice carries a gentler, patient tone.

"The Mistress of Darknessss…Mistress, please…"

I'm not the only one who glances at Rose. She's pale, gripping the table edge.

"Who? Who is it?" the Queen repeats to her brother.

He starts thrashing and I realize, he's fucking terrified. Truly terrified, black eyes wide, color drained from his face. He's putting his entire strength into breaking free, but I know that's impossible. They used Caldwell Conglomerate's state-of-the-art equipment to restrain him. He's never breaking out of that.

Prides have always been wealthy—it's one of the reasons they look down on Packs. Wolves aren't good enough for them to listen to.

When Michael understands he can't break free, he slashes his own throat with his claws. Blood splatters everywhere as Queen Calla screams. The video ends there. The room's silent. This has Sisterhood of Sin written all over it.

Shane doesn't wait for commentary as he plays the next video. This time it's a quaint apartment and the video is taken on a phone.

"This way, Alpha," the man in the video leads the way. I rest my arms on the table and lean in. I already have a bad feeling about this. He looks exhausted and a little scared.

"What's going on, Rick? And why are we videoing?" I recognize Alpha Josiah's voice. Rick is his Beta.

They walk down a hallway as Rick answers his Alpha, "I heard about what happened with Michael…and I wish I could say I was being paranoid, but Talia's been acting strange…not eating, sleepwalking, mumbling things that don't make sense. Last night she tried to kill the baby."

"Where is she?" Josiah asks, the concern clear in his voice. Talia is Rick's Mate and they just got married last year. Rick's young, but he did two years in the Royal Army which is when I met him. Even went to his wedding. Last I heard, he and his Mate were expecting their first child. I didn't get to know Talia well, but I can't imagine she'd try to kill her own baby.

In the video, Rick opens the door to their bedroom and Talia's cuffed to the bed—pregnant, gray-skinned, same black veins as Michael. She's chanting.

"They're here. They're here," she repeats over and over.

"Don't get too close," Rick says, "she's…unpredictable."

Talia's head snaps up. I clench my jaw as I see that her eyes are also completely black.

She reaches out, desperate and crying. "Mistress, take me with you."

"Michael said the same thing. Who is the Mistress? The Cursed One?" Josiah asks. Rick paces searching the bedside tables. He doesn't find what he's looking for, but then he checks under the bed and pulls out a sketchbook. Rick walks over to Josiah as he flips through the pages. Josiah angles the camera on it, and we watch as Rick turns pages after pages of the same drawing.

It's undoubtedly Rose.

"Talia's been drawing these the past two days," Rick explains, quietly.

"Mistreesssss…" Talia calls out and Josiah turns the camera back to her just in time to catch Talia clawing her throat open.

"No!" Rick shouts as he runs to his Mate's side, frantic and crying. "What did you do, Talia!"

His agony is rough to sit through, but we keep watching the video.

A dark shape, like smoke, rises from Talia's body before slipping through the floor. The video ends, but another follows closely after.

Josiah is in his car, and the camera is turned on him. He's speaking directly to us. "I haven't informed Queen Calla of what happened here just yet. Not after seeing the images Talia drew of Veyara Hunter…please, if you know what's going on, and how to stop this from happening again—let us know. This happened only two days apart."

The video ends.

Shane turns to us and says, "Totems were found at both scenes, so we know the Sisterhood of Sin have a hand in this. But the thing that left Talia's body…and the sketches of Rose…"

She's paler than usual, there's no color on her cheeks, even her glossy lips look ashen.

"Now's a good time to enlighten us." James zeroes in on her, giving her a pointed look.

"*If* you know something?" Shane adds, a lot kinder than James. James is still mad about Vanessa being Rose's PA as if that was Rose's fault. I asked Vanessa, she said yes, end of story. James didn't have a vote on the matter.

Rose sighs heavily and reaches into her shirt to bring out my mother's necklace. She hasn't stopped wearing it since the night I gave it to her and we found my aunt. She says, "Ever since I started wearing this necklace…I learned it's been…protecting me."

"From your magic?" James asks.

Rose's eyes snap to him, and she looks just about ready to murder James. "No, not from my magic. Don't be a prick," she sighs heavily, annoyed and I don't blame her or James for the matter.

Her powers are scary, but they'd never hurt her, not the way James thinks they might. Sometimes powers can be too much for someone to wield and it can make even a supernatural go mad. I know that's not the case with Rose.

"Nathanial lied to us…" she starts and for the first time in days, she voluntarily looks at me. I don't say anything and I don't help her out either. I never told anyone about finding my aunt.

"Mother Isis isn't in prayer. She's asleep—after she takes on The Cursed One she has to recharge," Rose says, hesitantly, looking around the table, "I've been helping to wake her."

I watch Rose as Shane asks, "What do you mean you've been helping wake her?"

"Nathanial said it was time for her to wake up, since The Cursed One is obviously making moves toward another uprising," she explains and a flash of horror crosses over Shane's eyes.

"I don't understand," Antonio says slowly, "what does that have to do with your necklace or these incidents?"

Rose toys with it as she answers him, "I think…Nathanial doesn't want me to remember the sessions when I attempt to wake Isis. I think this necklace blocks him from erasing the memories."

I look at Shane. His jaw is set and while his face is stone, his eyes are blazing. He's furious. Shane is a simple man. He has one simple rule—don't fuck with his family.

"I'm assuming Nathanial doesn't know his power's not working on you," Shane says quietly, composing everything he's feeling.

She looks uncomfortable—unsure who she can trust, but she says, "I thought that was best. If waking Mother Isis requires him to erase my memories of doing so, he's hiding something. At the very least, not telling me the entire truth. Why is he waking her up in secret?"

"What do you think?" James telepaths me.

"She's telling the truth," I think to him. I'd know if she wasn't.

"I don't know. Rose was always close to him. What if she was sent as a trap? For Nathanial to see which one of us aren't loyal to him?" James replies and I don't tell him that it wouldn't be Rose he'd send for that job.

He'd send me.

I'm a better liar and infiltrator than Rose. She's sweet, but she can't get close to the guys like I can. James would never trust her to let anything slip. Sam's paranoid as it is. Shane's always played his cards close to his chest, even from Rose from what I understand. Devaughn may be the easiest to talk to, but he doesn't let anything slip unintentionally. If it seems like he accidentally let some information out, it's because he wants you to think that. Daniel and Antonio don't know anything Nathanial would be interested in. We made sure of that, for their sake.

"I haven't seen anything like what happened to the girl in the video…and I don't know why she was drawing me. But I know Nathanial calls me…" Rose trails off, her cheeks flushing.

"Calls you what?" I ask, finally speaking.

Rose shakes her head, but Shane pushes her. "Come on, Rose. You saw what happened in the video. Who knows how many more people are dying similarly out there. This was sent this morning."

"I don't know…it's not me and it's not my powers," she says, almost defensively, but does not tell us what Nathanial calls her. I don't say anything, or I'll have a lot to explain to Shane. For right now, I'm keeping my mouth shut. I don't have proof and…I don't want to embarrass her. I don't know how much she knows about the situation.

"We never said it is," James replies, coldly and I cut him a look. He needs to lay off.

"Come on, guys. We're talking about Nathanial here..." Daniel says slowly. If I didn't know better, I'd think he was nervous. "Do we really think he's doing something shady?"

"I mean, there's always the possibility that you're not waking Mother Isis but doing something else..." Devaughn suggests and Rose looks horrified.

"I—I really don't think so...besides, that would mean Nathanial was working with the Sisterhood of Sin. You said totems were found at these...incidents?" Rose looks over to Shane.

Shane pulls up a picture of the totems on the screen. Strange shapes of bones that look like they were broken and put together stare back at us.

"I've never seen those before," Rose replies, turning away from the images. She's repulsed by them, not scared of them.

"They're the same kind that were found at the murders of the four Queens," Daniel says quietly. The Sin Coven that was behind it committed a ritualistic suicide two weeks ago. Shane said the videos were sent in today. Totems work quickly. This wasn't just one Coven—it's a network of them.

"Continue as you are with Nathanial. I want to know what he's up to," Shane tells Rose, basically sending her undercover.

My skin heats up at the thought of Rose subjecting herself to Nathanial. I don't want her anywhere near him. She's already exhausted. I feel it.

Shane addresses the rest of us next. "Needless to say, all this information stays in this room. If you must discuss it amongst yourselves, do it telepathically."

We nod and Devaughn goes into news from the other Prides, and the updates on the murders of the Queens. He has leads on other Sin Covens, but they keep disappearing, which isn't unusual for the Sisterhood of Sin. Unlike the Sisterhood of Light Covens, who stay on the same lands of their ancestors, the Sisterhood of Sin are pop ups. They create havoc wherever they go.

Rose is a wreck—sweating lightly and her breaths are shallow. She shifts again, crossing her legs tight. Fuck, I can feel her need from here, mirroring mine. But she won't beg, not like the night she shifted. Not after I iced her out.

The meeting wraps shortly after. The second Shane dismisses us, Rose bolts—up and out like the room's on fire. She couldn't leave fast enough.

I follow her, wondering if James is right. Is she going to meet with Nathanial?

Security nods as I pass and slip out a side door into the night. The cold bites, carrying the wind from the river. That's where she's heading.

Why? She hates water.

I remember how she jumped in on Samhain and my stomach turns. Why would she try to save me if she's a killer? I wouldn't, if it was anyone else.

I watch her tell her bodyguards something before they hang back. Why aren't they going with her? I stay in the trees, shifting into a small serpent and continue to follow her until she reaches the bank. It's like she doesn't even think, or look around, before she starts stripping.

What the Hell is she doing?

Clothes hit the ground, and too quickly she's down to nothing. My body reacts hard as I shift back to human form. My feet start moving on their own before I catch myself. Seeing her like this doesn't help. At all.

Then she jumps into the freezing river. My eyes narrow as I watch her come up for air, pushing her hair out of her face. Pain twists her features as I realize she's trying to cope with the heat this way. Trying to numb the agony only a Mate can fix.

Why her? Why couldn't she be someone else's problem? Some other guy's to deal with. But the thought ignites red-hot, blinding, fury. Someone else seeing her naked? Touching that soft skin, fucking her, kissing her mouth, fighting with her?

No. Hell no. She's mine. To love. To hate. That push and pull will destroy us, but she's mine.

She stays in longer than anyone sane. When her body starts shaking, she finally climbs out, dripping onto the snow-covered sand. I swallow hard and force my eyes not to linger anywhere they shouldn't. It's not for her privacy. It's for my sanity.

She dresses quickly, frustration rolling off her. Then she turns to stare at the water. She tilts her head to the sky, as if to send up a silent prayer. Her face crumples with sadness and raw pain.

I can't watch anymore. I turn to head home, knowing she'll come when she's ready. In the meantime, I'll get some serpent shit done to distract myself from this insistent urge to turn back and go to her.

"Be at the residence in ten minutes," I think to Camille.

"Yes sir," she answers dutifully as I walk through the forest.

The estate is dark when I walk in, which is strange because I can smell Camille's scent here. I go to my office but it's empty and she's not there either. Suspicion crawls up my neck before I stalk up to my bedroom.

Camille is naked in my bed, looking up at me with those blue eyes.

I glare at her. "What the Hell do you think you're doing? Get the fuck off my bed."

She falters, confused, sitting up. "Josh?"

"Why on earth would you think I called you here for *that?* Get dressed and get out. We needed to get some work done, but you need to leave." I check my watch for the time. It's not even late, barely 6PM.

The hurt in Camille's eyes is immediate. Her mouth trembles. "Josh, I—" She scrambles to her knees anyway, crawling forward, hands reaching for my belt like muscle memory of her own. "Let me fix it. Whatever I did, let me—"

I step back so fast she almost falls. There's no reason for her to think I called her to have sex. I haven't touched her since I came back from rescuing Vanessa—since Rose's birthday. Fuck…another thing Rose will find out when I Mark her.

"Why? Why are you in my bedroom?" I ask her because I know I didn't give her any indication of the sorts.

"I…I know Rose is going through heat and you haven't…you won't help her," she starts and I glare at her openly.

"How is that any of your fucking business?" I snap, annoyed she's bringing Rose up.

"I know it takes a toll on male shifters too—I thought…I was trying to help…"

I smack my face with my hand. "Leave, Camille."

She freezes, tears already shining. "Please. I've been whatever you needed. It was a mistake."

"You're right," I agree, pinching the bridge of my nose. "It was my mistake to keep you on. You'll be reassigned, effective immediately."

Her sob is small and ugly. "No! I didn't do anything wrong. What did I do wrong?" Everything. Nothing. She's not Rose.

I open my mouth to tell her she was never the problem, just the wrong woman, but she blurts out, "Rose is cheating on you!"

The air leaves my lungs.

I turn so fast and in two strides, my hand is around her throat, slamming her spine into the wall hard enough that the plaster cracks. Her head knocks back while a startled cry dies quickly as she sees my face inches from hers.

"*What* did you just say to me?" I snarl, low and lethal.

She's shaking, tears streaming, but she chokes the words out anyway. "Rose—she's been sneaking out for two years to meet her lover."

I let go of her. "Leave before I send you to your Mate."

Hurt crosses her eyes at the mention of her dead Mate, but I don't give a flying fuck. He wouldn't be too fucking happy with what she's been doing on the topside.

"You don't believe me…" She doesn't move and I'm at my wits end now. "I have proof!" She insists.

I tower over her. Camille's been my PA since I became Beta. Six years. It means nothing in this moment. "You have the fucking audacity to think *you* know more than me about *my* Mate?"

She slowly rises to her feet. "It's true—"

"Be gone before I come back, or I will deliver my threat."

I turn and walk into the bathroom, slam the door and lock it. I stay under the shower until the water runs cold and I stop shaking. When I come out, the bedroom is empty.

62 TEST SUBJECTS

Rosella Craving
November 27

I groan in anger. I got so close this time! I felt the shift start and then it didn't complete. Like the last couple of tries.

Vanessa rolls her shoulders. "It's okay. Still just a warm-up."

I'm hot, and I'm pissed, and I'm fucking irritated. "Okay, I'm going to try again—but why is this so hard?"

"Because a serpent isn't your natural shift form that your bloodline gifted you with," Vanessa explains patiently.

"I know that, I meant, the full shift. Why am I able to change my eyes, or my tongue, even my skin—but the full transformation is much harder," I tell her. I see why Uncle Edward only shifted into an eagle and called it a day. This is hard, but at least it's not as painful as my first shift.

"We'll do this together, yeah?" Vanessa smiles and Divine bless her for being a good teacher. I know she was a General in the Royal Army, so that's probably where it comes from.

I need this heat to be over. It's been seven days, and it just gets worse and worse. I never thought I'd say this as a woman, but I miss having my periods if this is what I have to deal with now.

"Um, what are you doing?" Vanessa asks as I pick up some snow and press it to my face and chest. Thank the Divine it snowed last night.

"It's just us girls here—" I start and she raises an eyebrow. I groan in misery. "I'm going through heat…"

"*Oh.*" She blinks, staring at me. "Oh, well…you really don't want to shift into a serpent when you're going through heat."

I frown at her words, but the snow is helping. "Why?"

Vanessa laughs like she can't help herself. "I'm sorry. I'm not laughing at you—Rose, serpent females aren't the most…patient when we're in heat."

"What do you do then?" I ask, curious now.

"Well, there have been instances where female serpents have

attacked their Mate when they don't get…dicked down."

I snort. "Serves them right. They literally have two dicks. Give us one. Why are they stingy?"

I'm at the point where I'm ready to take Daniya's advice. Hate the man, not his goods. That kind of thinking is exactly why I don't want to be around Josh right now and make any stupid choices.

Vanessa smirks at me. "Anyhow, let's head back. Seeing that you're not Marked, it'd just be torture for you."

Everything is torture for me right now. I hope he's happy.

"You go on, I'm going to lay down on the snow," I tell her and she laughs.

"Ice baths help too," she replies. She gives me a hug before leaving me.

I make sure she's gone before I pull out my phone and call Liam from the burner app.

"Hey," he answers on the first ring.

"Hi," I reply. "I think I have some news."

I hear some movement and a car door closing, before he asks, "What's going on?"

I tell him about the incidents at Three Rivers and what's going on with Nathanial and Isis. I'm surprised the Warriors' Oath didn't stop me from telling him. Shane did tell us not to discuss anything that happened, but…seeing that it's all related to me somehow, I figure it's my business to share. It's not like I'm spying for the enemy. Liam is a friend, an ally. I don't leave anything out, unlike the meeting.

"I don't know, Liam, it was all very strange," I sigh after filling him in, while I start walking toward home. Vanessa and I weren't too deep into the woods, but it'll still take me some time to walk back.

"You said it wasn't a demon?" he asks, slowly.

"No. They were obviously possessed, and something clearly came out of the woman after she died…" I say, keeping an eye out for anyone who might overhear.

"If it was a demon, you wouldn't be seeing anything like that, if anything you'd see the demon's true form and it's not something you'd compare to smoke," Liam tells me as if speaking from experience. He sighs heavily. "I've never heard of the Mistress of Darkness—or any prophecies or visions of one. Let me look into that after I get back from Ashton."

"Why are you going to Ashton Academy? I knew you had a secret child," I tease.

Liam lets out a laugh. "Not yet," he answers. Liam is the only one in his family who hasn't continued the bloodline. He's sired vampire families, but he never had his own children. I never had the heart to ask him why. It seemed too personal, even for us. Liam proceeds to answer my original question in a somber voice. "There was an attack there."

I frown. "Sorry to hear that…was it like this?"

"No, it was violent though," Liam says, his voice strained. "I'm heading there now with Jarrod."

"Who was it?"

"Deena Aushwell."

"A royal family member," I say. "Wait—aren't Aushwells known Soul Snatchers?"

"Supposedly. Deena's parents are. They're sending Ethan Uvacov to heal her," Liam replies. Ethan Uvacov is a Soul Snatcher leader, a notorious bad boy all around, and one of the most powerful vampire healers of our time. He's not that old either—twenty-five, I think.

"She's still alive?" I ask, surprised by that piece of information.

"Barely from the pictures that were sent to me by Saffurah," Liam says, mentioning the headmistress of Ashton Academy by first name. She's ancient and very, very well-respected throughout the vampire world. They must be old friends. "It looks like she was stabbed all over, but witnesses said it looked as though something invisible was cutting her up," Liam tells me.

I shudder at the mental image.

"Well, if her family's requested Ethan Uvacov to heal her—it must be bad," I say, quietly.

"I'd say so," Liam exhales. "Jarrod's here. I'll keep you posted."

"Same, and Liam?"

"Yeah?"

"Be safe, please," I tell him.

"I will," he promises softly before the line cuts off.

Mariella is bent over a low table lined with glass vials. She's turned this once-sad space into the beautiful greenhouse it's meant to be, with the side of a lab—shelves burst with drying herbs and labeled jars, pots are organized by size, plants are being propagated even in the November weather, and a whole side is dedicated for Mariella to study my magic.

She straightens, wiping her forehead with the back of her wrist. "Umm," she says, her voice small. "I can't promise anything will truly work unless I see how it reacts to something inflicted with your power. Right now, I'm guessing."

"You want test subjects..." I say slowly.

She hesitates, then meets my eyes. "Essentially that'd be ideal, but we can't just do that. Unless someone was accidentally injured...I could try to heal them." I can see she's trying very hard to not make it sound like an evil science experiment.

I'm quiet for a little before I tell her, "Give me a few days to look into it."

"Yeah, yeah, of course," she nods, shrugging a shoulder, making it not a big deal.

"Are you on your way to the office?" Vanessa telepaths to me. She normally doesn't and just waits for me to get to my office.

"Yes. What's wrong?" I think to her.

"Nothing serious. I'll see you soon, yeah?" she answers before I feel the connection dissipating.

Strange.

Mariella and I chat for another five minutes, mainly about Crystal having her first son. She gave birth last night and Devaughn sent pictures in the group chat.

Ryder Benedict Claws.

He's adorable.

We air kiss before I leave and head into my office, curious about what Vanessa wanted to talk about.

Her news is that Josh has reassigned Camille. She doesn't know what that entails but I don't like it. I wanted to keep Camille under my nose.

Why was Camille reassigned out of the blue like this? Did something happen between Josh and her? The thought makes me ill. I don't want to think that he turned to her while I'm going through a bitch of time with this heat.

I don't want to ask him and give him a reason to think I'm interested. Obviously, I am.

"Can you find out what her reassignment is?" I ask Vanessa.

Vanessa looks slightly offended. "Can I…" she trails off as she looks it up on her tablet. I watch her and notice the frown, before she says, "Um…so, looks like she didn't show. She was supposed to report back to her serpent Bed two days ago."

"That's not like Camille. She's professional when it comes to her job," I say, before sending Antonio a text to meet. I look up at Vanessa. "Well, I'm sure she'll turn up. What do we have today?"

Vanessa continues without a hitch. Antonio texts back, saying he can meet for lunch, and we decide on a spot in the plaza. I remember to take Camille's vial of blood when I leave my office.

Antonio gets us the table and I slip into the seat next to him. He chose the rooftop and I'm grateful for the winter air, though he seems cold. His nose is all red.

"What's going on?" he asks after the waiter leaves with our lunch orders.

"Should we ask for a heater? You look freezing," I suggest, and smirk, "do you want my coat?"

He rolls his eyes and laughs a little. "I chose this table for you."

"For me?" I ask, frowning.

"Yeah…Mariella mentioned…" Antonio blushes. *Blushes.* Ugh, Mariella told him I'm in heat.

My face warms as I smile at him, kindly. "Thank you…"

"So…why did you want to meet?" he asks me. "Mariella and I are not in an open relationship. If you wanted help with your…situation, you should've called Daniel."

I stare at him, trying to decide if he's serious right now. I punch his arm. "Fuck you. Camille's MIA and I need her found," I tell him, sliding the blood vial across the table to him. "You're one of the best trackers I know, and I need this to be discreet."

"Why?" he asks, before saying, "I mean, yeah I'll hunt her down, but why exactly are we looking for your Mate's PA?"

"Josh reassigned her," I say.

"And that's a bad thing?" he frowns. I know he knows about Josh and Camille's…unprofessional activities. Everyone does.

I shake my head. "I just need her found and you can let Cristobal know when she is…"

Antonio looks amused. "Why do I feel like you're up to nothing good?"

I shrug, "Maybe because you're always up to nothing good?"

He chuckles, pocketing Camille's blood and says, "Alright. I'll be in touch with your bodyguard about this. How are you doing? Being married to Josh and all?"

I shrug. "Not much different from being Mated to him…"

"Damn, you'd think he'd feel a little guilty about kidnapping you," Antonio says and laughs at my scrunched-up face. "No, that's valid. A serpent feeling guilty? What was I thinking?"

"I think you need your brain checked, Warrior Rage," I laugh as our food arrives. We both ordered the same thing—spaghetti and meatballs. Our sauce has blood mixed into it, so it's absolutely delicious.

We don't drag lunch out. Antonio leaves shortly after our meal is over to start his search for Camille.

63 TIME-OUT

Rosella Craving
November 30

The base from the club's floor rattles my bones, the scent of perfume, sweat, sex, and liquor is a sensory overload and pissing my sensitive self off. It's been exactly ten days since my heat started and I can't think straight anymore.

I am in constant pain, and I'm *so* angry. Everything irritates me. I thought a night out with the girls would do me good, distract me, but now I just wish I went to the river like I had the past few nights. The freezing winter river helps with the heat burning through my body. I'm lucky the river hasn't frozen yet or I'd have to resort to ice baths.

Daniya leans into me to point out an Honest girl she's not fond of. Vanessa rolls her eyes, seeing the same girl. My skin starts tingling and it's not from Petal. I narrow my eyes and look to my left.

Josh.

I see him cut through the crowd, ignoring the girls reaching for him, his intense gray eyes fixed on me. My chest clenches. Damn him for looking so good in just a pair of dark jeans and black t-shirt. The serpent tattoo at his neck makes him look even more dangerous as he keeps our gaze locked.

What is he doing here?

I know Daniya did not invite him to her girls' night out. It's her birthday and she wanted to let loose.

I can't see him tonight…not when I'm doing everything I can to not jump on him. Going through heat has been the worst time of my life. Even shifting was over after a few minutes, it didn't drag out like this. I've taken every drug I can get my hands on, but they all just make it worse—make *me* hornier.

I swear my clit is still swollen from the number of times I've made myself come today so I could get some sort of relief to enjoy the night. I had tried holding off, knowing he can feel it when I touch myself, but I just couldn't take it anymore.

It didn't work.

Vanessa sees him too and turns to look at me. "You want me to get rid of him?"

"Can you?" I ask, defeated knowing she can't. The rest of the Crescents notice him now too.

"I can," Eliza tilts her head. Her new diamond teardrop earrings glinting in the club lights. Shane got them for her after she had Nigel. This is her first night out since he was born.

"Leave," Josh orders, his eyes never leaving mine. He uses his Beta voice and there's little the girls can do but listen. They give me apologetic looks, but I already knew.

Eliza is the only one not affected by his Beta command, but as she slips out of the booth, she telepaths to me in a singsong tone, ***"But I won't. Happy fucking."***

I scowl at her as the girls move over to the bar, staying close and I sigh, already tired, as Josh slides into the booth with me.

"I don't have energy to fight with you tonight," I say to him.

"I'm not here to fight." His voice is low and Divine, his voice physically hurts. I miss him. I miss us. I miss laughing with him. I miss his hands on me, his kisses, his tongue, his dick…him…everything about him.

His jaw is tight as if he knows exactly what I'm thinking. He's too close—and then he's kissing me. I'm too shocked at first, but my hands push against his chest as I pull away, "What are you doing?!"

"It's time to go home," he tells me—no, demands me.

I give him an incredulous look. "I'm not going home. It's girls' night."

His eyes burn into mine. "You're going through heat and I'm calling a time out for us."

A time out? Is he serious right now?

"You can't just call time out after being so…cruel." I glare at him.

His eyes narrow a fraction, staring into mine and it's like a trance. I get sucked into his orbs, and then he cups my chin roughly. "Yeah? Watch me." His lips return to mine. My traitorous hands move up to touch his face too. He's my Mate—he's an absolute asshole—but…why is it so hard to hate him?

No. I will not give in. I made it ten days, what's another…fuck, I can't do twelve days of this. My heart sinks, but I push away from him.

"Fuck. You. What is this? Another training opportunity," I snap at him and I can actually see his teeth grinding. I try to pull away further. "I'm not going home with you, so there. I passed today's training."

Why should I go home with him?

"You think I'd use you going through heat against you?" he asks, sounding hurt, but I don't buy it.

"Of course, you would. Everything's fair in love and war, right?" I remind him, but then blood rushes to my cheeks as I register what he said. "How did you know—"

"We're fucking Mates, Rose. Of course, I know when your body is calling me," he says lowly with narrowed eyes and my heart sinks.

When my body is calling him?

He can't tell when my soul is calling for him? That my soul's been calling for him since I was born?

I look at my hands, my lips quivering because now my brain wants to remind me of the words he spewed at me just after a beautiful week together. "You can't just call a time out from hating me and thinking I'm…it doesn't work like that."

His hands are on me before I can stop him, gripping my waist and lifting me. My legs fall open instinctively as he pulls me onto his lap, settling me over his rock-hard cock.

His breathing is shaky against my lips. "I just did."

I search his face, torn between rage and longing. And I break because I can't resist him right now even if my life depends on it. I kiss him, deep and hungry, grinding down against his cock, already straining for me. A ragged sound escapes him, his hands roaming up my thighs, pushing my Barbie pink dress higher.

My fingers fumble with his belt, desperate, needy. He curses against my mouth as I free him and guide his dick into me, impatiently. And when he thrusts into me, the world drowns out around us. I immediately feel relief in my bones, my moan mixing in with the club music.

I don't care who sees. I don't care how exposed this is, how the whole damn court could be here. He's my Mate. I missed him. I want him. I need him.

Josh's mouth is everywhere—claiming me, devouring me. He bites my lips until he draws blood, sucks my breasts hungrily, after shoving my dress aside to free them. I arch into him, desperate for more. His tongue drags along my neck, and my hands tangle in his hair, holding him there, needing that spark, that connection only he can give me.

I need to feel everything that's good about the bond—not the pain of having him so close but being so far apart.

Pleasure rips through me, sudden and overwhelming, and I shatter around him, my pussy clenching tightly around his cock. He groans into my mouth, the way I convulse on him drags him over with me. He comes inside me, immediately relieving me of the pain from going through heat. But he doesn't stop moving.

He can't. I can't.

This is all I need.

The war can go to Hell.

The media can go to Hell.

Everything and everyone can go to Hell.

I just need him.

Our Mating bond is relentless, uncomfortable—needing some sort of connection that we've been starving it. His fingers dig into my thighs, and I feel his claws faintly puncturing through, making me cry out but the pain is welcomed right now. It helps distract me from the other ache in my pussy even though he's still inside me.

"Fuck," he groans, loudly, thrusting into me once but with force, "it's good to be home."

His words are cruel, but my body does not give a damn about my heart right now. My orgasm builds again as his cock massages my inner walls so deliciously.

"Prove it. Mark me," I tell him. Okay, at least my brain is still working. Surprisingly.

I want him to Mark me. I want him to know everything if he's going to hate me anyway. He might as well hate me for an actual reason. He'll know about Liam, he'll know I'm in too deep with Nathanial and Aradia.

"I don't think you deserve to be Marked right now, princess," he nips at my shoulder, teasing me on purpose. I thought he was here to help me.

"Deserve? It's my right," I tilt my head back, elongating my neck and he falls for the trap. His lips trail hot, wet, open-mouthed kisses from my shoulder up to my jaw as one of his hands grab my breast too roughly while his other hand supports my back, keeping me pinned to him.

"Is it?" he asks. "How is it your right, if I decide when you get to receive it?" he pulls my head toward him so he can suck on my earlobe.

"It's my right, *your* honor to Mark me," I reply, having a sudden rush of confidence that I never felt with him.

"Agree to disagree," he growls against my ear.

I turn to look at him. "I thought we were on time out."

"Time out. Not fast forward," he says, coldly, but it's the look in his eyes—the complete lack of emotion there that makes me pause. Then he adds, "I'm not Marking you. It's just sex, Rose."

Just sex.

Just sex?

A dark, *dark,* emotion passes through me at the words, causing a chill to travel down my spine. How strange that I was burning up the past ten days, but now that he's here, I'm frozen.

"Please leave," I whisper but I know he can hear me over the club.

"Why?" he asks, slightly breathless as his eyes roam my face.

I frown and try to push myself off. "I don't want to fail whatever test this is," I answer him.

He keeps me in place. "I told you, we're on time out. I'm not going anywhere."

"Tell me something first then," I say, running a hand through my hair, letting it fall around me. His eyes follow my every movement. I place my hands on his chest, and ask, "Have you ever fucked anyone on this couch?"

He stills under me, jaw locking. The hesitation—just for a second, is enough. I already knew the answer, of course.

"Yeah," I whisper, swallowing the lump in my throat. "You're delusional if you think it can only ever be just sex between us."

I push off his lap, fixing my very mini dress with shaky hands, ignoring how wet and uncomfortable his cum feels. I clench my thighs together and curse myself for not wearing panties. I was hot and they were annoying while in heat.

I hate how my body aches for him, my heart still pounds for him, but I force myself to turn away.

I barely make it three steps before his hand is around my arm.

"Stop—"

He's zipped his pants but the belt hangs. He yanks me back, and before I can curse at him, I'm thrown over his shoulder like one of his gym towels. Fang Gates is upside down, the blood rushing to my head as his palm smacks my ass hard enough to make me cry out in pain.

"Put me down!" I slap his back, writhing. We're causing a scene at this point. Not to mention, the whole club can probably see his cum leaking out of my pussy because I feel *exposed.*

His grip tightens around my thighs, while his hand covers my ass as he says over his shoulder, "I don't know why you think you can disobey a direct order from your Beta," his voice is low and dangerous, threatening punishment. "I wasn't *asking* you to come home, Veyara. I'm *taking* you home."

Just like that, he reminds me of my place.

The air leaves my lungs furiously. We pass the bar and I lift my head to see the Crescents, but Josh beats me to it.

"Girls' night is over for the princess," he tells them.

Daniya's mouth opens, no words coming out, but Vanessa doesn't miss a beat. She smirks at him, "Just promise to fuck her senseless and you're forgiven."

She's fired.

Eliza slips Josh my purse, then starts fanning herself. "Yessss, Beta."

Fucking traitorous bitches.

Josh doesn't bother with niceties when he gets me home. He throws me onto his bed, and I glare at him as the sheets burn me from sliding on them.

"Have you fucked someone in this bed too?" I ask, even though I know the answer.

He strips out of his clothes and then Josh climbs over me, his entire body is tense. He's not playing as he shoves my thighs apart. His eyes cut to mine, "Why do you care?" his mouth hovers over mine, cruelly. "You said you're nothing to me, right?"

The words gut me. I said that at the beginning of our stay in Coilspire. My jaw locks as he slips my dress off, burning my skin from the friction.

That's exactly what I am to him. Nothing. I knew it back then. Why did I ever let him in? How can he take all of our perfect moments away from me?

He's not patient and he doesn't wait for another second. He thrusts into me hard and deep, making me scream as he pins my wrists above my head. My body betrays me, arching to meet him, my legs spreading wider to take him deeper.

"Sex won't fix anything," I tell him, breathless. His eyes flash, holding me captive even as his thrusts pound into me.

"Good," he growls, "I have no fucking plans to fix anything with you tonight."

I open my mouth, but he slaps his other hand down to shut me up. I glare up at him and he matches it, but every slam of his body into mine sends shivers of relief through me. His mouth comes down, biting and sucking at my nipples, rough enough to leave marks. I cry out from the pain as his fang grazes my nipple. I can't even push his shoulders since he has my hands pinned. He sucks it as his thrusts soften, dragging out the tension. He releases my arms, lifting his head, and cupping my face instead. His lips find mine, tender instead of brutal now, while my arms fall over his shoulders, pulling him closer.

We go from fucking to making love. The line blurs and my heart splits open. My lips tremble as I kiss him back. Neither of us talk or make any sounds as we move slowly, in sync, my hips rolling with his. I feel him in every deep stroke, hitting my sweet spot with purpose. His hand is still holding my face as our bodies tell us how much we really need each other.

Our magic ignites, my darkness swirling around us while his skin heats, making me wetter, easier for him. He slides in and out, groaning against my lips. We have no control over our bodies right now until we come together, his arms holding me while my body shakes with his. For a quiet moment, everything's perfect.

He kisses my lips again and it's confusing. His lips move lower to my shoulder, before he turns us, so we're on our side. He hasn't pulled out and it doesn't seem like he has any intentions to.

I hate him. Doesn't he know how much this hurts? Why isn't he just getting up and telling me to go back to my room? Why is he holding me?

Josh turns his head and finds me staring at him. "What is it?" he asks. He's a little breathless and his eyes are heavy like he's ready to fall asleep.

"Pull out," I whisper.

His eyes are more focused now as he studies my face. I need him to pull out. I need to untangle from him, walk straight to my room, and lock the door.

"Is that what you really want?" he asks, his voice hardening.

"Does it even matter what I want?" I counter.

He lets out a low grunt, tightening his arms around me as he closes his eyes and a small smile plays on his lips. "Nope."

"Just…let me go."

"Never, sweetheart."

I force my lips to not quiver. My body loves being this close to him. I love being cuddled with him like this, but at what cost? For him to wake up tomorrow and tell me he was just doing me a favor?

That I wasn't strong enough to resist him through my heat?

That I failed again?

"You can never truly love me," I say and I hate how my voice breaks saying the words out loud.

"Love has nothing to do with letting you go or not," he replies. Then he looks at me again, gripping my jaw tight enough for his fingers to dig in. He lets go though, the ghosts of his fingers linger on my cheeks, before he pinches my nipple hard. I let out a sharp cry, my body arching away from him, but his one hand wrapped around me is strong enough to hold me in place.

"Please," I beg him, having no other choice right now. A tear slips out of my eye that he catches with a kiss. That's not helping.

"Please what?" he growls, lifting my leg on him higher as he grinds into me, my arousal instantly answering him.

"Let me go back to my room," I tell him, squirming in his hold as he moves his hips again, pushing his cum inside me further.

"You're sleeping here tonight," he thrusts into me, before biting down on my jaw, "with your tight cum-filled pussy wrapped around my dick."

"I can't." I shake my head.

"You're going to," he says, and he's on top of me again. My traitorous legs shift with him, wrapping around his torso.

"Why?" I ask, watching his hand move to rub circles on my clit. Fuck this man. Why is he doing this? It's not fair.

"Because I want you to."

"Why?" I ask again and his hands move to my hips, holding me in place.

Then he thrusts into me—*hard.*

"Josh!" I cry out, having no choice but to say his name. My back arches off the bed as I grip the sheets for dear life. He pushes my legs back so I can't hook them together, burying himself deeper inside me.

Josh watches me with no care in his gray eyes, only raw insatiable hunger. "You're mine to fight with." *Thrust.* "You're mine to fuck." *Thrust.* "You're mine to hurt." *Thrust.* "You're mine to fucking hate." *Thrust.* "You." *Thrust.* "Are." *Thrust.* "Mine." *Thrust.*

I'm sobbing from the overwhelming pleasure he's pounding into my body. He's hitting deep inside my body and soul with every move of his hips. Then he places my legs on his shoulders, before lowering himself to take my nipple into his mouth. He releases it with a *pop* and then his face is hovering over mine. My legs are inches away from me and his cock is deeper than it's ever been. It hurts, everything hurts, but I don't want him to pull away. I want him here. I want him just like this.

"You're mine to fucking destroy, sweetheart," he kisses me, "however, the fuck I want to."

And I know I've failed. Again. Because this is worse than just giving into him. This is worse than falling for him. Because now, I want him to hurt me like this.

But he failed too, because he says, "You are all I have."

64 MANACLES

Rosella Craving
December 3

The iron manacles close around my wrists with a cold, final click. Josh's fingers linger a second longer than they need to, brushing the inside of my forearm as he tightens the chain just enough for the links to bite. He wants me to feel it.

"What is this?" I glare at him before my eyes go to Daniel. He's leaning against the far wall of the dungeon, arms folded, watching. His presence is the only reason my pulse isn't spiking through the roof.

With Daniel here, I know this isn't a fantasy Josh is playing out—which actually makes me more nervous.

"It's okay, Rose," Daniel tells me, "it's part of our training as a Warrior. The truth serum test, to see where your mental restraints lie. We've been a little busy, but Josh thought we should squeeze it in now, with everything that's going on with…" he trails off.

With Nathanial.

My glare returns to Josh as I say to Daniel, "Oh, did he now?" I sneer at Josh. "What are you afraid I'm going to say to Nathanial?"

If it were anyone else chained to this pole, Josh would already be smiling that thin, vicious smile he saves for people he thinks deserves pain. Tonight, he's trying to hide it behind a mask of clinical detachment, but I can taste the strange excitement on him. Maybe he is playing out a fantasy after all.

"No powers," Josh says in a low voice, ignoring my words. "Mental shields only. You slip, you spill, you lose. And I've waited a very long time to do this without rules getting in my way."

Then he brings out a syringe. Shane and Daniel have told me stories of how they use truth serums in interrogations. Daniel makes no move to stop Josh.

"It's standard training, Rose," Daniel tries to reassure me, "all the Warriors had to go through it."

Yeah, but did all the Warriors have Josh interrogating them? My stomach flips, but I keep my face blank. Josh's jaw flexes but he doesn't look away from me as he tilts my head and sticks the syringe in.

"Rude." I flinch at the sting as I feel it instantly take effect. I reinforce my mental shields for an extra layer of protection, not knowing what to expect from Josh.

He smiles wickedly. "You're nervous. I can taste it. Oh, you're definitely hiding something."

"You're not entitled to know all my secrets."

"I'll learn them one day or another before the Claiming."

I let out a laugh. "Not if you can help it, apparently."

Josh lifts a thin silver blade and takes a few steps to stand before me. Behind him, Daniel's gaze meets mine. He just gives me a reassuring nod, and I drag in a breath through my nose and lock every single door inside my head.

Josh drags the flat of the blade down the center of my chest, slowly, savoring the way the cold metal makes my skin flinch even when I refuse to move. The chains clink softly as my weight shifts, and he hears it, of course he does.

"Sensitive," his whisper is almost tender. He flips the knife and presses the tip just beneath my collarbone, not enough to break skin yet. "Let's start with an easy one. How many kills do you have under your belt?"

The serum surges, hot and eager. Thirteen, I think—but the number won't come out of my mouth. Why can't I say it?

His eyes narrow and I know he's wondering the same thing. He steps in until his chest almost brushes mine, until I have to tip my head back against the pole to keep eye contact.

The knife slides under the edge of my shirt, slices upward in one clean motion. The fabric of my workout tank rips and cool air hits my exposed skin, goosebumps race over me, but I don't flinch.

He steps back to look, eyes raking over me like he's memorizing every inch. "So pretty when you're scared," he murmurs.

All I have to do is keep my mouth closed. That's all I have to do, and then this will be over.

He sets the knife aside and picks up something worse, a thin, braided whip.

Daniel takes one involuntary step forward. Josh's smile goes razor-sharp. "Relax, Daniel. We went through much worse. We all agreed to no special treatment." He flicks his wrist and the whip uncoils.

"Okay, but you don't have to be an ass and enjoy it so much." Daniel frowns.

"I haven't even done anything to her yet," Josh counters, as he circles behind me again. I feel the first kiss of leather against my spine.

Then he stops playing.

The first real strike lands like fire across my shoulder blades. My breath catches hard enough that the chains rattle. I blink rapidly, my brain trying to understand the pain. I've never been whipped before…it's a strange feeling. The second strike lands lower. By the fifth, I'm arching without meaning to, every muscle locked against the scream stuck in my throat. I don't look at him though.

Between lashes he leans in, mouth against my ear, voice soft and intimate.

"You should be singing by now. Tell me how old you were when you killed for the first time?" he asks in my ear, and it sounds personal. The number doesn't come to my mind. My mind is blank. Josh frowns. "Tell me, and I'll stop. Tell me, and I'll kiss every mark I just made."

Another crack of the whip makes my knees buckle, and only the chains keep me upright. The serum is a tidal wave now, wanting to talk but my brain doesn't know the answer. I bite the inside of my cheek until I taste blood just to have something else to focus on.

He waits until my breathing steadies, then his hand slides around my throat, thumb stroking the frantic pulse he finds there. "Eventually even you will break. And when you do…" his teeth graze my ear, "I'm going to find out every single thing you never want me to know."

If that's the goal, he could just Mark me.

Unless…unless he doesn't want me to know something. What is Josh hiding?

I close my eyes, taste blood and truth and terror, and lock my shields so tight, I feel something inside my mind fracture. I'm not worried about him finding out about Liam or Nathanial, but it's something else. My mind is guarding something else and even I don't know what it is.

65 CLOUDS

Josh Hunter
December 3

The door slams behind Daniel as he leaves to see what Shane called him for, and the echo hasn't even died before I'm moving.

Finally.

Just her and me and the dark.

I lean in close. "Looks like your babysitter's gone, princess. No one left to pull me off you."

She doesn't react. Of course she doesn't. That would be too easy. I figured if she hates me right now, I might as well use it to my advantage a little bit. It's been three days since I held her captive in bed after plucking her out of the club. Three days of her ignoring me and staying out of the way. She hadn't said a word to me until we got the manacles on her. Whipping her doesn't get the reaction I expected. She barely flinched, like her body knew the feeling and how to cope with it. She doesn't scream either, just clamps her jaw shut and takes it.

I pull the second syringe from my pocket, triple the standard dose. "I don't know how you did it, but I think you burned through the first one." I collect her soft hair and pull her head to the right so her throat stretches, pale and perfect for me to sink my teeth into. She makes the smallest sound, half pain, half something else that goes straight to my cock. This stupid fucking Mating bond wants me to Mark her. After she mentioned it at the club, it's all I can think about.

Focus.

I bring the syringe to her neck. For a brief second, our eyes meet and I can't breathe.

Her too-big, too-soft gray eyes, glassy with exhaustion and pain, stare up at me the way they used to when we were kids. When she was eight and I was fourteen, and Noah was still alive. Back when she followed me around Coilspire like a lost puppy every time her family came to visit. She loved the towers, saying she could see the Heavens, but it was just clouds due to the elevation. Clouds that always remind me of her eyes since then.

I stare down at her.

She's in chains, but I'm the one held captive by her.

Her one look and nothing in the world makes sense, except to kiss her and keep her in my arms.

I'm about to say fuck it and free her to take her home when she says, "Do it."

I pause.

My hand still grips her hair, but she tilts her neck slightly, to encourage me. "I know you need to. I want you to know everything."

I wish I could say I trust her to free her at those words. I wish I could say no I don't need to know her secrets that badly and honor the little we did build in Coilspire. I wish it was enough to let time reveal the truths buried in her and not force it out of her.

But she's right, I do need this.

I do need to violate her like this to get to what really happened six years ago, even if she hates me for it later.

"Just do it," she repeats, softer, with no force behind her word.

I don't think and stab her with the syringe. The drug rushes into her. Her knees buckle as the chains catch her with a metallic shriek. The serum hits faster this time. Her pupils blow wide and she sags in the chains, head dangling against my grip.

"Tell me your deepest, darkest secret, Rose," I whisper, selfishly. I know I'm taking advantage of the situation, and I have no right to know it like this, but curiosity gets the best of me. "The one you'd die before you'd ever tell me."

Her lips part. She finally sings. The words come out slurred, dreamy, like she's drunk.

"I just…I want a boring life," she mumbles. "A house in the clouds, somewhere quiet and peaceful. I don't want to be a princess or a Craving but just a girl who has a family. I want you to wake me up with kisses and call me pretty even when I'm old and wrinkly. I want you to cherish me even more than our kids and I want babies. Lots of babies. I want…I want their sticky fingers on my dresses and you reading them bedtime stories but never loving them more than me. That makes me terrible, right? I don't think I'll be a good mom anyway. I'm too selfish, too scary…but I want a life far, far away from court where no one will bother my family and we'll just live life in our small corner of the world…I want that with you, but I know I can never have it. I can never tell you that I want to run away from everything with you. You'll never understand."

She trails off, breath hitching. Tears slide down her cheeks like she's ashamed of this dream she clearly locked away.

I stare at her, not realizing when tears started falling down my own face.

After everything, that's what she's guarding with her life that she doesn't want me to know? I know she has darker secrets, but this is what comes out of her under a truth serum overdose?

She wants a life I would have given her if Noah never died, where I was never forced to hate her, where I would have walked away from everything to give her exactly that life. Where I would have put those babies in her, kissed her swollen belly every night, called her beautiful every morning as her body changed carrying little versions of us. I would've kept her barefoot and laughing and mine and never let the world touch us.

I would've loved her so much the Moon would have been jealous.

I don't think I ever truly understood why my dad kept my mom in Coilspire, until this moment.

But she killed Noah, and with it our future.

I crush the grief before it can spread. Shove it down into the same black pit where I keep Noah's last breath and the image of her pulling the knife from his throat.

I release her from the restraints and she slumps forward, forcing me to catch her out of reflex. Her body is warm and limp in my arms. My thumb presses into her lower lip, dragging it down and I stare at her tear-stained face from just wanting a simple life with me.

Do I have it all wrong?

No.

No. I can't be wrong. I know what I saw six years ago. I know what happened and she didn't defend herself that night when I confronted her. Her memories were taken away because she couldn't handle what she had done.

The door bangs open and Daniel walks back in. He takes one look at Rose, and his face goes feral.

"What the fuck did you do?" he roars before he tries to rip her from me. My arms lock instinctively, a snarl coming out of my throat before I can stop it. Daniel shoves me back, forcing me to let go of her.

"One day, Josh," he spits, cradling her against his chest like she's precious to him and I see red. "One day you're going to push her too far and she won't come back from it. Do you understand that?" he looks at her, then glares at me. "*You* will break her. I don't know what she did to you, but you cannot destroy your Mate." His bottom lip quivers like it hurts him to even say the words, thinking of his own Mating bond.

Daniel turns and carries her out, her head resting against his shoulder, blood smearing across his shirt.

The door slams again.

I stand there in the empty dungeon, fists clenched so tight my claws dig into my palms, hating how we ended up here. I wish I could have given her that stupid little house and those stupid little babies. I hate that she'd rather die than ever admit that to me.

What never made sense is why she killed Noah? I'll never know why and I can't even ask her. I was hoping the truth serum would reveal something about Noah—that she subconsciously still remembered. But it was wishful thinking.

I punch the stone wall until my knuckles split and I feel nothing but pain in them.

The drive home is a blur of streetlights and my grief. My knuckles are bloody on the steering wheel, split open and throbbing. Every time I close my eyes, I see Rose's small hand pulling the blade out of Noah. I see her pale face as I demanded why she did that. I see her crying in my arms because she wants a life I can't give her anymore.

I stand in the dark for a long time, fists clenched, cock still traitorously hard from being with Rose in the dungeon. I don't know. I'm fucked up. My throat is raw from wanting to scream or cry or both.

I'm supposed to hate *her.*

I'm not supposed to feel anything for Rose. I've trained myself, conditioned myself, fucked every woman I possibly could not to feel anything for her. I've done things I'd never forgive her for if she did it to me.

I can't keep saying she's mine.

Because every fiber of my being belongs to her. The second that golden cord lit up and led to her, and she laid her eyes on me as a baby, she owned me.

I reach for my phone and call Shane too tired to telepath.

"What's up?" he answers and I hear Eliza laughing in the back.

I grit my teeth, hating how fucking happy the two of them are. How that's all Rose wants. "Did Daniel bring Rose back there?"

There's a pause, before I hear Shane shift the phone. "Yeah, why was my baby sister unconscious and bloody?"

"It was standard training, but the first dose of the truth serum had no effect on her," I tell him in a monotone voice.

"That's…weird. I mean, I know she's dabbled in some hardcore drugs before, but one dose should've been enough. How many did you give her?"

"Four total."

"Fucking Hell, Josh." I hear Shane moving rapidly, doors opening and closing. "Was it worth it?"

"Yes, but it had nothing to do with Nathanial," I answer, also moving toward my front door.

"Then how the fuck was it worth it?" Shane snaps at me.

"It just was. I'm coming," I tell him and hang up the call.

I reach the residential wing of the Palace and make my way to Rose's room. Shane is in there, placing a glass of blood on her nightstand. Rose is sleeping in her four-poster bed, looking every bit the princess she is. The healers took care of her wounds and there isn't a mark on her, at least none that I can see from what's not covered by her blanket.

Shane shoots me a death glare. "How am I supposed to trust you with her, if she ends up like this?"

"She'll be stronger for it," I answer blankly, and Shane looks like he's ready to punch me. I kind of wish he did.

I scoop her up in my arms and he moves to stop me. "What the Hell are you doing?"

I look at him as if he's stupid, and honestly, sometimes he really can be. "I'm taking her home, why do you think I came?"

"You're not taking her anywhere," Shane tries to pull her away. She was ripped out of my arms once tonight. It's not happening again.

I hold onto her and pull away from him. "Touch her again and you won't have hands."

"Let her recover. Come back in the morning," he tries to reason.

I start walking toward her bedroom door as she rests her head against my chest. "She'll recover at home."

"You can't just take her." Shane follows me and I let out a humorless laugh.

"She's my wife and I'm taking her home," I reply, then turn to smirk at my best friend, "bet you wish you didn't trick us into being married now, huh."

He scowls at me.

"Not that it would matter. Mate trumps everything anyway. See ya," I say, walking down the stairs. No one stops me as I walk out with my Mate.

I'm not sure how I'm supposed to forget everything she admitted to wanting and pretend I never heard it. It's everything I want too.

After I lay her in our bed, I take a deep breath and reach for the box in my nightstand. Then I call Evren.

"Still nothing on the seer, she's a ghost," he says, answering the phone. "But I have an update on Morvain."

How hard can it be to find one fucking old witch? Evren's not incompetent by any means, she's just that good at disappearing. I never thought I'd end up being in the witch hunting business, but between this seer and the Sin Covens, that's what it is now.

"Work with Antonio to find the seer. Make this quick. Rose is sleeping," I tell him, glancing at her. She's passed out. She won't wake even if an earthquake happens.

"You were right to keep your eye on Valen Salvatore. His little girlfriend's been feeding intel to Morvain—that's how they're avoiding the obvious connection. Salvatore wants people to think he's in business with Vassir, but they're not moving pharmaceutical drugs."

"I never thought they were," I say. I thought they were moving actual drugs or feeders.

"They're moving weapons, Josh," Evren replies. "Daejin's in on it too. I have everything."

"Moving weapons isn't illegal, Evren. We do it all the time," I say. Especially serpents. Our military division, along with the bears, is the largest worldwide. Most of us are in the weapons business.

"Not for the Sisterhood of Sin," Evren says.

I pinch the bridge of my nose, afraid he'd say that. I look over at Rose again, then say into the phone. "How fast can you be at Coilspire?"

"You want me to drop everything and go into hiding?" Evren sounds surprised as he asks the question.

"Fuck yes," I answer.

"Don't be scared, kid, nothing's going to happen—"

"First of all, still your fucking Beta. Second, get all your evidence to Coilspire. I don't want it at Cravenhold in case it falls into the wrong hands," I order him.

"Damn, for a second I thought you cared about my life," Evren replies, sighing dramatically on the other end of the line.

"The way you live, you don't care about your life, why the fuck should I?" I roll my eyes and he chuckles.

"I'll be on the next flight out. And yes, I'll check in every hour, I know you care regardless, you big teddy bear," he says and I can practically hear the grin on his smug face.

I hang up on him.

I hoped for an answer first from the seer, but with Evren still unable to track her down, I don't have any other options. I open the box the seer gave Rose and pull out the necklace that's identical to my mother's.

First, the seer called me the Son of the Heavens and the Skies. Then, she gave my Mate the same necklace my mom wanted me to give Rose.

It's creepy.

The necklace checked out though. Crystal said there wasn't anything sinister attached to it. I put the necklace back in the box and place it in the nightstand drawer. I'll give it to her soon.

I return to bed and slip in beside Rose, but before I pull her into my arms, I have one more thing to do.

Me: *What's Rose's favorite flowers?*

Eliza: *Red peonies, but she loves assorted bouquets too*

Red peonies. Of course, it wouldn't be roses. Eliza's text is followed by a SpellBook link to one of Cravenhold Plaza's florists.

Me: *Thank you*

I know flowers won't fix a damn thing, but I can start with flowers. I hesitate before sending Eliza another text.

Me: *For everything.*

66 PARADIGM SHIFT

Rosella Craving
December 15

I stand shoulder to shoulder beside Aradia in the flower chamber once more. The crunch of dead petals under my boots is the only sound breaking the heavy silence at first. The blooms that once spilled vibrant life across every surface now lie shriveled and brown, their stems twisted like forgotten promises. The air is thick with the faint, decaying sweetness that clings to the back of my throat. Mina's chant hums from her shadowed corner, a constant undercurrent that prickles my skin and sets my nerves on edge.

Nathanial steps closer than before, just a few steps behind us, his presence feels like a solid weight against my back. I feel his gaze boring into the tomb, that intense hunger, willing the stone to yield through sheer force.

Aradia meets my eyes, her blue ones steady and bright despite the heaviness in the chamber. We don't clasp hands this time, but hold our palms open toward the tomb and begin the chant. Our voices start low.

> *"Sleep was mercy.*
> *Mercy's done.*
> *What was denied has found its tongue—*
> *Wake, wake now, Isis. The hour has come."*

The syllables roll out, gaining strength with each repetition. My voice blends with Aradia's until we're one. Nathanial stays standing with us, watching and waiting.

We're here for some time and just as I begin to sway, the tomb lid shifts.

A low, grinding scrape echoes through the stone. The massive slab inches sideways by small fractions at first. Dust rises around us, and my heart stutters. I pause mid-line, breath catching sharp in my throat, eyes locked on the widening gap.

Nathanial's voice slices the hesitation. "Keep going. Don't stop now."

Anxiety floods me, my pulse thundering in my ears—but I force the words out again, louder, pushing past the fear because I do not trust what's inside at all. Aradia doesn't waver, her chant rising to match mine, pulling me along. The intensity builds, words being repeated faster, and vibrating through my ribs and into the floor.

Cracks spiderweb across the lid now, sharp snaps ringing out like breaking bone. Fragments of stone flake away, tumbling into the widening fissure. Something thumps from within—heavy, insistent, syncing with our chant like a heartbeat answering the call.

Power surges out of me in waves, draining faster than before. My arms tremble, my vision spotting at the edges. Sweat beads on my forehead, trickling down my spine. Aradia's face pales, but she holds steady, voice unwavering even as her shoulders shake.

One final, desperate push—

"Sleep was mercy!
Mercy's done!
What was denied has found its tongue!
Wake, wake now, Isis! The hour has come!"

The world spins. My knees give out entirely, the chant dying on my lips as darkness rushes in.

Nathanial's arms catch me mid-fall, strong and sure, lifting me against his chest.

"Enough," he commands Aradia, though his tone carries a thread of triumph beneath the concern.

I mumble protests as he carries me through the tunnels, then we teleport. The cabin door shuts behind us, and the glow from the fireplace welcomes us inside. He settles me into the bed, furs piling warm under me, and his arms wrapping around my body.

"Rest, now, my little mistress," he whispers, holding me as sleep drags me under without mercy.

Hours later, I stir to the scent of spiced cider. Nathanial sits propped against the headboard, bare legs stretched out, a mug waiting in his hands. He passes it to me as I push up, the hot drink warming my chilled fingers and throat—cinnamon and apple with cloves.

I sip slowly, leaning into his side when he pulls me close because that's what I used to do. I can't let him think any differently.

"How are you feeling?" he asks me, his lips brushing my temple, bringing me back.

"Tired…I'm always tired," I tell him, honestly.

"Just a little longer now," he promises.

"What happens when Isis wakes? Exactly?"

He wraps an arm around my shoulders, fingers tracing idle patterns on my arm. "She'll be made fully aware of Lilith's movements. Then we follow her. Whatever strategy she deems necessary, whatever command she gives. Then when everything is in place, she will execute."

He makes it sound like a military operation. I nod against his chest, but questions churn. "Why does she sleep like this? Why make it so hard to wake her?"

"Isis bound herself this way centuries ago. Her life—every cycle of it—has been about shielding her bloodline from the worst. To prevent catastrophe, Isis chose deep slumber between threats, mercy for herself and a safeguard for the world. Only her direct blood can summon her back, and only when the stars align in very particular ways," Nathanial says, but it feels like he's reciting words out of a book. He gives just enough information but still keeps it entirely vague.

"Like what?" I press, setting the mug aside to turn and face him fully.

His gray eyes sparkle with that ancient amusement. "When paradigms shift, love."

I shake my head. "I still don't get it. What paradigm shifts?"

He sighs, cupping my cheek with one large hand, thumb stroking my skin gently. "I forget how young you are sometimes." His voice softens, "Starting with you—born with those gray eyes. Mated to a Warrior. Signs from nature itself. Your exceptional powers. We knew the time had come, we couldn't delay any longer."

The weight of it settles heavy in my chest but if this is what Nathanial wants me to believe right now, I'll play. "After she handles Lilith…things go back to normal, right? We fix this and move on?"

Nathanial's expression darkens, arm tightening around me. "I'm afraid not. The world as we've known it…it's over. Every time Isis wakes, so does a new world."

67 YULE

Rosella Craving
December 20

I'm in the car with Josh as we drive to dinner when Franklin telepaths me from the front seat.

"Cristobal found Camille," he thinks to me.

I sit up straighter, glancing over at Josh. Things aren't back to where they were, but it's been different. We haven't spent much time together since the truth serum training. He has been busy with the Three Rivers' situation, getting his Den Lords to cooperate too.

He's sitting with his head back and eyes closed like he's had a rough day, but he looks good in his suit doing it. Josh and I match. His emerald vest and black jacket go perfectly with my silk green dress and black fur shawl. We look every bit the Beta-Veyara couple.

I open the telepathic link between my bodyguards. ***"Cristobal?"***

"She didn't want to talk but after a little persuasion, we found out the Beta reassigned her to...put some distance between them," Cristobal thinks and I look at Josh again. ***"Things didn't end well and she told him you were having an affair for two years."***

I telepath back. ***"Did he believe her? Did she say who it was?"***

I hold my breath as I wait for Cristobal to respond, very aware Vanessa is linked in. Franklin told me she doesn't know and I told him she didn't need to. Liam is my past. I haven't seen him since the Romania trip.

"No, she never mentioned a name. I followed up and it doesn't look like the Beta's asked around about it either," Cristobal answers and I exhale quietly.

"Guess he's starting to trust you," Vanessa chimes in.

"Yeah, well, I don't trust her," I reply. ***"Cristobal, do you have eyes on her? Take her to the cave."***

"Already on the way," I hear his cynical tone in my head. He knew I'd say that.

Vanessa asks through the connection, ***"Don't you have a dinner tonight?"***

"Yes, just arrived," I think to her as I adjust my bracelet and the car comes to a stop.

Josh opens his eyes and looks at me. "Did you have fun staring at me?"

I scowl at him.

He chuckles as Franklin opens the door for us. We exit the car before Josh and I step into Bluehouse. It's a lounge, but the boys always raved about how good their steak was, so Eliza decided to have our Yule family dinner here tonight. It's dimly lit with twinkling lights, casting golden sparks throughout the space. The sound of adults laughing and joking mingles with the clink of crystal as a pianist plays soft holiday music in the corner.

The hostess leads us to the back, where Shane and Eliza are already sitting, cuddled up and laughing with each other. They pull away smiling once they notice us.

"Sorry to interrupt…?" I ask, slowly, sliding in opposite of them into the blue cushioned booth. They're cute and I love them as a couple but at the same time that's my brother so ew, gross.

"Why are you sorry?" Josh asks me as he slips in beside me. "They invited us."

"Yeah, yeah, we know the big bad basilisk Beta doesn't do formal dinners," Eliza rolls her blue eyes, resting her hand on Shane's arm while her other hand reaches for a pretty green drink.

"I love dinners. It's the holidays I don't like," Josh answers before he and I place our drink orders. I order whatever Eliza is having just with the alcohol. It reminds me of Eclipsa from the Gala night.

While almost all of our holidays are centered around family and worship, Yule is purely a family event for shifters. We go to the Sanctum in the morning for our blessings, but the rest of the day is spent with loved ones. If it falls on a weekend, then it's a three-to-four-day affair.

I wanted to go to the Sanctum with Josh this morning, but he was nowhere to be found, so I went with Shane, Eliza, and Nigel. I watched Lady Tiara closely as she interacted with the baby, and she didn't react any differently as she would with any other infant.

When I switched my eyes and really looked at her, Lady Tiara's energy startled me. Her shields weren't just solid and guarded, they were *angry*. It was strange because I didn't feel anger from her, I felt fear. Raw, anxious, fear.

"Why didn't you come to the Sanctum with us?" Eliza asks Josh, frowning at him, thinking the same thing as me.

"I went hunting," Josh answers, simply. "Needed the fresh air."

Shane rolls his eyes as the drinks arrive. I raise my glass and look at my family. Even Josh. I meant it on Samhain. He is my family, even if I don't know where I stand with him most times. Even if he hates me.

"To…another Yule, to cozy snow days in, and fire that never goes out—in our hearts and homes," I grin, fairly proud of myself for the toast.

"Awww, that's so cute! Cheers, babe!" Eliza returns the grin, clinking my glass while Shane and Josh stare at me like I've grown three heads.

My brother looks at my Mate and Josh sighs heavily. "She was reading one of her books again."

"That explains it. We can't have a sappy Warrior, that was cheesy as fuck," Shane tells me, earning a glare from his wife.

"We're waiting, jerks," she says to them bluntly, and the two of them oblige, tapping their glasses against ours obediently.

"I missed you," I say to Eliza.

She goes on to tell us about Nigel's quirks over our exquisite steaks. The drinks keep flowing, though Eliza's drinking mocktails since she's breastfeeding.

It's about halfway through dinner when Eliza asks me, "Have you set a date for Nigel's party?"

"March," I reply as Josh's fingers accidentally brush against my thigh. The warmth spreads through me despite the flicker of nerves in my stomach. I'm so glad I'm not in heat anymore.

"March? Why so far out?" Shane says as he cuts into his steak, glancing up at me briefly.

I take a sip of my wine as Josh leans back into his seat, adjusting his tie. I tell Shane, "It's only three months, and Nigel will be a little older. Plus, it'll be Ostara."

"I love it, it's perfect with the spring solstice," Eliza points out. I nod, pleased that she's okay with the timeframe. "People will come to court for it, and we can have Nigel's party around then," Eliza says to Shane.

"Exactly what we were thinking," I agree, smiling.

"It gives me time to get my figure in shape," Eliza jokes. As if? She looks perfect.

"If you're not pregnant again," Shane says under his breath and Josh chuckles. I guess they worked out whatever was going on between them.

"What?" Eliza asks, blinking. Seeing that she's sitting right beside Shane and we're across from them, she heard what he said.

"What? I didn't say anything." My brother winks at her and her cheeks turn rosy. Shane just laughs and leans in to kiss her cheek.

"Gross, get a room." I laugh but it's nice to see them back like this. The loss of the baby was hard for both of them.

"Speaking of rooms," Eliza starts and we all look at her. She wiggles her eyebrows at Josh and me, and I know where this is going. "I hear congratulations are in order. You've moved in together *and* are married. *I* was busy having a baby, but we need to properly celebrate!"

Shane, Josh, and I fall quiet. Josh's hand moves to my thigh underneath the table, and I want to instinctively push it away, but I can't bring myself to.

I force a smile for Eliza as I feel Shane watching us. "Not by choice..." I say, trailing off.

Josh's hand stiffens on my thigh as he explains to Eliza, "*Your* husband tricked us into signing marriage documents."

"Yeah, isn't that null then?" I ask, putting my silverware down to cross my arms. "It can't be valid."

Shane shrugs, amused. "The court approved it."

"You want to punch him, or should I?" Josh asks me, leaning just enough to give me a whiff of his scent. The effect of it goes straight to my pussy, making me squeeze my legs tighter.

Eliza laughs, waving her hand in dismissal of Josh and me. "Why would you punch him when it was my idea?"

"Of course it was," Josh reaches for his drink, his hand leaving me. I stare at my sister-in-law.

"Traitor!" I exclaim as Shane and Eliza laugh, high-fiving, before going back to their food. Apparently, my life is a joke to them.

"I say we get back at them," Josh suggests, telepathically.

"So down, but when they least expect it," I reply.

"Agreed. We'll wait a few months," Josh proposes.

"Well, I hope you've thought of how you're going to answer to Susan," Eliza says, eyeing us again. "You know very well you can't move in together before the blood-tie reunion," she mimics my aunt.

"That's easy," Josh says, leaning back into the seat, causing his shoulders to press into mine. It's strangely comforting. "We'll say it's the Alpha and Luna's decision and we had no choice. I hear the truth is always the best policy, right, Alpha?"

There's a clear challenge in Josh's tone as I glance at Shane. He doesn't seem bothered by it, but the nerve pulsing in his temple gives him away.

A snarky voice catches my attention, causing me to miss Shane's answer. "One might think the Beta is still hesitant about the pretty princess being the Veyara since he hasn't even Marked her. Shame. Too young I suppose."

I'm not the only one who hears the comment because our table instantly gets quiet. I look up to see Natalia Osvaron sitting at the bar a few feet away with two other serpent shifters, probably her friends. She swirls her drink, pretending to be oblivious of us—or she really doesn't check her surroundings when she enters a room.

"Fucking bitch," Eliza telepaths and I feel Shane and Josh in the connection. Josh hasn't looked away from our table as he chews his bite slowly.

"Just let it go. I'm used to it, it's nothing new," I shake my head at Eliza before she goes over there and tells Natalia where she can take her pity. Eliza will do it too.

"Can I at least throw a drink in her face? I haven't done that in so long," Eliza asks as she glances at Shane, smiling sweetly.

"There's no hesitation," Josh says, too calmly but loud enough.

Natalia, her friends, and a few others who are clearly eavesdropping too, turn their heads toward him.

Josh casually drapes his arm over me, pulling me into his side, before he looks at Natalia and says, "If anyone doubts where I stand, I'll be standing right beside my Veyara. You're more than welcome to challenge us," then he smirks, his fingers playing with the strap of my dress, in an obvious seductive way, "we do enjoy a little violence as foreplay."

I nearly choke on my drink. Shane actually does choke on his bite as everyone else around us laughs, returning to their meals. Eliza is grinning big at Josh like he's her new favorite person. I can't believe he just said that in front of my brother, publicly.

When I look at Josh, I find his eyes still on Natalia, except they're so cold, I'm surprised the entire place hasn't frozen over. Natalia pales to the color of her platinum hair, before she picks up her purse and walks out. Her two friends rush to follow her.

"No?" Josh frowns, feigning a disappointed look as he sips his drink. "Maybe next time."

"A little violence as foreplay? Since when?" I ask him through our mind link.

He turns his head to lock our gaze. ***"Tell me you haven't thought of our duel as often as me."*** He's actually serious because I don't hear any trace of humor in his thought. ***"Besides, I would much rather spread you out on this table and eat this steak off your bloody pussy right now."***

I force myself not to cringe, but flashbacks to his split tongue and B pos all over me makes me involuntarily lean into him a little. ***"I don't even know how that'd taste..."***

"Fucking delicious," he thinks to me, then he clears his throat and tells Shane and Eliza, "Rose and I are going to head out—"

"Nonsense!" Eliza replies and Josh looks like he's going to murder her. "We're going back to our place for dessert."

"Uncle Edward was baking again to take to our cousins. He left a shit ton for us in the fridge," Shane explains.

"I can work with dessert too," Josh telepaths me before rolling his eyes and telling Shane, "Fine, but at least open a good fucking bottle."

"You didn't have to say anything to Natalia..." I telepath to Josh.

"Oh, I did," he sends through the mind link and I get the feeling it has to do with more than what happened tonight. I don't want to know.

As we wrap up dinner, I telepath Cristobal, ***"Natalia Osvaron."***

"Received," Cristobal answers.

While Josh and Shane talk about Josh's hunt this morning over way too many drinks now, Eliza rises carefully with Nigel cradled against her shoulder.

"I need to put him down," she murmurs, brushing a kiss on Shane's cheek. Her eyes find mine across the room. "Rose, come keep me company?"

I stand without hesitation. Josh gives my thigh a possessive squeeze before his hand slides off. I follow Eliza down the quiet corridor to Nigel's nursery, leaving behind the noise of our two drunk men.

She settles into the rocking chair by the window, unlacing the front of her dress. Nigel latches quickly, tiny fists kneading her breast.

Eliza stares down at him for a long moment, then lifts her gaze to me. "Do you…feel anything strange when you're around him?"

My stomach tightens. I lean against the mantel, arms folded. "Why would you ask that?"

She strokes Nigel's dark hair, lips pressed thin. "There's something off. I can't explain it. I just…have this really bad feeling," her voice cracks on the last word.

I step closer. "How so?"

Eliza shakes her head, frustration flashing across her face. "I don't know. I always feel so drained when I'm with him. Like…" she swallows hard.

"Like…?" I urge. I'm sure she wouldn't bring this up if she thought it was exhaustion from being a new mom.

"Like how he drained his twin's life."

The words hang heavy between us. I open my mouth, close it again. Nothing I can say feels safe or kind enough.

Nigel makes a small, contented sound, eyes closed, utterly innocent, but the dark cloud engulfs him.

Eliza's eyes shine, teary, when she looks up at me. "I'm scared, Rose."

I reach out, rest my hand on her shoulder. "Don't be," I whisper, "we'll figure it out."

She nods, but the fear doesn't leave her face or her energy.

I tell Josh about Eliza's exhaustion, the dread in her voice, and her comparison to the lost baby on the way home.

His face gives nothing away as he asks me, "What do you think about it?"

"I don't want to dismiss it. There was true fear in her eyes, Josh. She's really worried." I stare at our interlaced fingers resting on his leg. "Could a baby even have power that strong? Could his power be…consumption? Or just draining others of their powers?"

His thumb traces slow circles on the back of my hand and he's quiet, thinking.

Finally, after a few minutes, he says in a low voice, "Nothing is impossible in our world, Rose." He brings my hand to his lips and kisses it. "You and I are proof of that."

"I feel like we should be worried…but I think I'm more curious to see what happens," I say quietly to him.

Josh doesn't add to that, but instead, reaches into his jacket pocket and pulls out a necklace with an upside-down crescent Moon and a red droplet sitting on top. My hand automatically moves to my chest, feeling my own necklace there, and I look at him confused.

"I don't understand," I say, frowning.

"This is what the seer gave you," Josh tells me, making my eyes widen.

"Oh…that's weird," I say, reaching for the necklace. "Finally safe?" I ask, hesitantly.

"I made sure," he says, quietly, watching me examine it. It's a carbon copy of mine. I don't see any difference but granted we are in a dark car right now.

I hold it out to him as I move my hair out of the way and say, "Put it on me?"

He does. The new necklace rests just above the first one.

"How do you feel?" he asks, quietly.

I glance down at the necklaces and say, "Am I supposed to feel different?"

"I was trying to track down the seer who gave it to you, but after what you said in the war room about the necklace protecting you…I thought you'd better have this one too," Josh says, looking at the necklaces. He looks confused too, like he doesn't know what to make of it. Then his hand comes up to caress my cheek, cupping the side of my face. "I don't want you to be around Nathanial."

I lean into his touch. "Do you trust me?"

"Yes," he answers. He didn't even have to think about it.

I raise my gaze to meet his. "Really?"

Josh rests his forehead against mine. "Yes. I trust you."

The words make me spiral but for once, it's not because of him. I don't know if I trust myself these days.

"I just hate the whole thing…" he says, before kissing me. I missed this. These tender moments with him.

"He won't hurt me," I assure him when we break away. "I think he needs me more."

Josh sighs heavily, his fingers lacing with mine again, as he says,

"Don't we all."

68 AGAINST NATURE

Rosella Craving
December 31

My hand lingers on Betty this morning. The frozen surface of the stone makes it look glassy, making my palm stick to it. I do it every winter, forgetting not to touch Betty after it starts snowing.

"Old habits die hard," the High Priestess laughs softly behind me. "I'm surprised you didn't just leave your hand behind one of these winters."

"There's always next year." I turn, grinning as I walk up to her. "How are you? New grandmother and all?"

She hugs me. Her smile is so big, I have the answer to my question. She says, anyway, "He's perfect. Have you met him yet?"

"No, not yet. Letting them have their time with their new baby. I'm sure I'll meet Ryder soon," I reply while we walk into the Sanctum together.

"Yes, I'm sure there will be a party," she winks at me, clearly already planning one. "What brings you out here today?"

"I actually wanted to talk to you about Nigel," I say slowly and catch her eyes dart for a split second.

"What about our future Alpha? Come sit," she says, guiding me to the cushioned seats.

I take a minute to collect my thoughts. "Eliza's worried about him. So am I. I also know your powers aren't appreciative of his energy."

She watches me for a moment before she sighs and says, "He's just a baby. Barely six weeks."

"But his powers, Lady Tiara," I whisper. "It…unsettles mine."

She's quiet and I can tell she wishes she had an answer for me. It's not often people come to the Sanctum and leave without some sort of wisdom or guidance from her.

"He's a baby," she repeats, her voice barely above a whisper.

"Craving twins are either blessed or cursed. What if the curse doesn't end with the death of the twin?" I ask her. "What if…it follows them into this life?"

"It's not a literal curse, Rose—not like if a witch casted it. It's nature," she tries to say, but I don't think even she believes that.

"It's also the Divine, High Priestess," I say, reminding her also.

"We can't..." she starts, glancing around as if someone might overhear us. There's no one here but her and I, but still, she casts a sound bubble. Her eyes shut like the words are just too terrible to say. She says it though, "We can't kill a baby because his powers scare us. Your powers scared us and look at you. You're fine."

"Am I?" I ask. She has no idea what I'm doing with Nathanial—what he wants me to do because of what I'm capable of with my powers.

"Aren't you?" she inquires. When I don't say anything, she sighs heavily. "I just suggest we wait to make a judgement. We decide when he's eighteen."

"When he becomes Alpha?" I question her, crossing my arms. That's the dumbest idea, because then he'll have all the power.

"Sixteen then," she states, referring to our legal age.

I hold her gaze for a moment before asking, "What if it's too late by then?"

She places a hand over mine and says, "A baby deserves a chance. We nurture him to be his best version, like we did with you."

I remain silent and she invites me to do a morning blessing with her. I do, but as I leave the Sanctum, I just know that sometimes nurture isn't enough. There's a reason why we say nature takes its course.

Nature is always more powerful. Pure, but also destructive.

I get into my car when my phone rings. I glance at Cristobal and Franklin in the front seats, before answering it.

"Hi," I greet.

"Are you alone?" Liam asks and there's an edge to his voice that I'm not used to.

"No..."

"You trust who you're with?"

"Yes, why?"

"In case they can overhear," he answers and the way Cristobal's shoulders are too stiff and Franklin's head is tilted slightly toward me, it's obvious they're on alert for whatever Liam says next.

"It's Cristobal and Franklin. You found something, didn't you?"

"After you told me about Three Rivers, I looked into the mistress thing. I couldn't find a connection between the two victims and you, but I found something else. The Cursed One's daughters were called Mistresses," Liam says.

We grow up learning that, it's not news, so I tell Liam, "Yes, I know that—"

"But there was someone before them whose name translates to the Mistress and it's the earliest record I've found so far," Liam cuts me off to finish what he was saying.

"Who?" I ask.

"She was considered a goddess and had a very strong following in ancient Greece. She was called Despoina."

My blood runs cold. "Isis."

The climb feels endless. My breath clouds in the frozen air as the fog thickens with altitude. Pine trees are everywhere, thicker as I get farther away from Cravenhold. Their branches are heavy with the fresh snow we got last night. By the time I reach the crest where Nathanial's cabin is, I'm panting in wolf form.

He's always teleported me here, I've never had to make the journey up myself until today.

The cabin sits on the peak, smoke curling from the chimney and I sigh with relief as I shift to human form. Well, at least he's here and I won't have to wait for him.

Before I can reach for the door, it opens and Nathanial looks genuinely surprised to see me.

"Rose? Come in, come in," he says, stepping aside to let me, "I would've met you at Cravenhold. You didn't need to come out here."

The warmth from the fireplace hits me welcomingly, before I lean in to hug Nathanial, keeping things normal so he's not alarmed.

He wraps his arms around me. "Everything alright?"

"Yes, I just needed to talk to you," I tell him, pulling away as he watches me warily.

"Sit, let me get you something warm to drink," he says, shaking his head before disappearing into the small kitchen. I take a look around. There isn't much to see, but I still take it in. The cabin is simple, minimal—completely opposite of the life he portrays to the public and even us. Most people don't know Nathanial spends most of his time at court up here. It's not a space unfamiliar to me now or else I would've wondered the same thing.

I sit down on one of the two armchairs as he returns. He hands me a steaming mug. The scent of buttered rum and cinnamon floods my senses. I don't take a sip and let the heat spread through my palms as I hold the cup.

"Now," he says, settling into the other armchair, "what brings you all the way up here that couldn't wait?"

I meet his warm gaze over the rim of the mug as I lower it. "What do you know about the Mistress?"

That gets his attention. His smile fades, the warmth in his gray eyes goes out as they turn darker. Suddenly, it's colder in here even though the fireplace is blazing.

"Where did you hear that?" he asks me and even his voice sounds different. I want to say that he calls me his little mistress, but Nathanial's always been careful when he uses that, so I have to be equally careful now.

"I know Mother Isis was referred to as Despoina in Greece a long time ago, so I was—" I intentionally leave out reading it in a book and Three Rivers because Shane asked us to. Nathanial has not made an attempt to restore my recent memories by kissing my forehead.

"Where did you hear it, Rose?" he repeats, his tone sharper.

"Does it matter," I tell him, pointedly. He doesn't appreciate that, but I stand my ground. I have to or else I'm not going to get any answers from him.

Nathanial sighs, before standing up to come and give my forehead a kiss. I take a deep breath. That was easier than I expected. Nathanial reaches for a throw and places it on me and sits back down.

"What does she have to do with me? How am I like her?" I ask now that I've gotten the sign. "You call me your little mistress…"

"I don't know," he says and I don't buy it for a second. I give him a *yeah, right* look and he exhales heavily. "I can't predict the future, Rose. I don't know who you will become."

"The Mistress doesn't sound like the best thing *to* become," I say.

"You look a lot like her," Nathanial says, quietly, "you have black hair and gray eyes, but your face…it's almost identical."

"I'm not her," I reply, annoyed. Once upon a time, it would've been the highest compliment, but now, I don't know what's what anymore.

"No, no you're not. Your power, I felt it when you were young. Isis was similar—not the same power as your darkness—but the sheer energy in you. Your ability to harness true, great power…I haven't seen it in a really long time."

"Why me?" I ask. "Why is all this happening? My powers, me being a Warrior…Lilith raising an army of the dead, the Mistress…"

I've known Nathanial all my life. I've seen him in various situations. I know his facial expressions, the way his face moves at any given time.

I've never seen fear on his face until this moment.

"Nature is stepping in," he says and it's ironic that I just had this conversation with Lady Tiara.

I stare at him. "This all feels very *against* nature…"

"Things beyond you or me are at play. When nature steps in, the Divine is close behind—well, at least the Heavens."

I let his words settle, processing all he's just told me. Nature, Divine, the Heavens…what is he talking about?

"You're not making any sense…" I trail off, hoping he'll stop being so cryptic. "I don't understand what all that has to do with Isis or me. What did Isis do when she was the Mistress?"

Nathanial pales if that's possible. "We do not speak of the things she did."

"Well, maybe we should," I insist. Enough with the secrets. When he gives me a warning look, I sigh, "Maybe it's time. I don't believe in coincidences—not in our world. Why do you call me your little mistress and is it somehow tied to what she was doing back then?" Divine, I sound like a journalist.

He doesn't say anything, but stares into the fire as if he's replaying thousands of memories. "Immortality is not for everyone," he tells me absently.

"What does that mean?"

"It means she lost sight of the bigger picture, and I didn't have the heart to kill her."

"Because she disagreed? What does losing sight of the bigger picture mean?" I push.

Nathanial's eyes flash, startling me. "It means she turned against everything we stand for."

"She became a Sisterhood of Sin?"

"My dear child," Nathanial laughs dryly, "there are far worse fates than becoming Lilith's minion. No, what Isis turned into was something entirely different."

"Nathanial," I press, "please, just tell me!"

"Isis always did what was best for her people," Nathanial starts and I make note that he says *her* people. He continues, "At least, that was how it started. Somewhere along the way, she started making deals and not prayers. That taste of power and worship is a dangerous drug. Even more when it's mixed with fear—and control."

"I know she sacrificed herself over and over to protect us from Lilith," I say, watching him. He is a good storyteller, always has been, but every story has some truth to it.

Nathanial nods. "That remains to be true. Isis turned herself into the only entity that could go up against Lilith."

"What did she become, Nathanial?"

"A demon," he answers. "Isis became a demon."

I sit back, letting the words linger. I've never met a demon, nor do I have any experience with any. I know there are absolutely evil demons, and some that are more…morally flexible, for the right price of course.

I lean forward. "If Isis became a demon, Nathanial, why are we trying to wake her up then?"

Nathanial takes a moment, before he looks simply tired. "I haven't been completely honest with you."

"No shit," I say before I can stop myself. Anger flashes in his eyes for a brief second, before I say, "I've done everything you've asked of me. All the time. I deserve to know what my powers are being used for. Don't you have any faith in me?"

He reaches for me but rethinks it and rests his hands on his knees. "I'm going to give a memory I took from you back…if that's okay with you?"

I don't think he realizes how ridiculous that permission sounds. "I mean, you didn't ask before taking it, I'm sure, so what difference—"

"Rose," he cuts me off and I sigh, exasperatedly.

"Yes, please give me the *one* memory back," I say, the sarcasm coming out heavily.

Then he does reach for me. His hand comes up to cup the side of my face, before Nathanial kisses me on the lips. Images of the vampire castle rush in, a meeting with the other monarchs, and oh Divine—The Cursed One is there? And Zak Xandelskye? I gave him my blood and I drank his—I *am* the Mistress of Darkness.

Nathanial pulls away.

I sit with the memory, remembering who I was in it.

I knowingly helped Zak open a portal to another realm. Was what came out of the victims in Three Rivers what entered our world from that realm?

Is that why my face was drawn over and over? Why they called me the Mistress of Darkness—because my blood and power was used to bring them here? Because they answer to me?

It's meant to fuel Isis after we wake her—but at what cost?

And Nathanial.

Why would I ever let him use me like that? Why didn't I protect my powers better? My dad always told me to protect my powers above all. Nathanial sliced my arm without my final say so. He just took my blood.

Right now, Nathanial takes my hand into his as tears slip out of my eyes from red-hot fury. He says, "I know you're confused, so let me explain."

"So you can lie some more?" I ask, my voice is too calm for the rage thrashing inside me.

"So you can understand."

"Tell me then." I demand.

"Opening the portal serves more than one purpose. Lilith wanted the portal, but Aradia just wanted her sister, and I…" Nathanial says.

"You what? What do you want? You have everything," I say, so disappointed in him. This man had the world, still does, what more can someone like him want?

Power.

It's always power.

You can never have enough of it.

He cups my face and wipes my cheeks again. "You. I want you at your full potential. I need you to wake up Isis."

"Why? That doesn't answer why we're waking a demon up," I circle back.

"It's true that Isis can defeat Lilith, but Isis and you together…Lilith will never come back. It's never happened—two Mistresses, one of light and one of darkness working together against Lilith."

I don't buy it. If that were the case, none of this would be hidden.

Shane was right to keep Three Rivers a secret from Nathanial. But now, I don't know who to trust.

"And then what?" I ask him, swallowing the lump in my throat.

"Then Isis will die too. Not go to sleep again. If Lilith is gone, so will she—their souls are merged in that way. It has to do with the deal Isis made to become a demon," Nathanial sighs, tucking a strand of my hair behind my ear, "and then you take Isis's place."

"As the Mistress of Light?" I question. I'm so confused, my head hurts. This is why I always hated politics. "I thought that was Aradia. She is the Mother of the Sisterhood of Light."

"Mother—not Mistress. That was always Isis for her original powers, before she became a demon."

"So how am I taking her place? That's not balancing nature."

"You'll be my queen," Nathanial answers. "You are the Mistress of Darkness. You are the only one whose powers counter mine. The only one."

He's lost his damn mind. I lean away and look at him fully. "You trained me to wield my powers so I can help wake Isis. So she and I can defeat Lilith, and I understand Lilith dying will kill Isis, which is why I am supposed to become the Eternal Queen. Become immortal. I understand how the balance of nature works. I also understand opening the portal because Isis needs…food…when she wakes, but you never said anything about being *your* queen."

How is being his queen beneficial to anything? I don't have to become his anything to be the Eternal Queen. He needs me more than I need him.

Why am I everyone's other half? Josh and I having our unique gold Mating bond, then Zak saying our powers are incomplete without each other's, and now Nathanial?

Nathanial or his powers don't do anything for me.

"You never wondered how Josh is your Mate when his powers do not come close to yours? He's powerful, basilisks are, but not like you. Nowhere near you," Nathanial says, hitting a sore spot.

I did question it, especially when Nathanial kept thinking Josh is hiding something. I just hoped Josh and my powers somehow would come together—the Divine chose us.

"Your Mating bond isn't real, Rose. It was a ruse. Josh hadn't matched with anyone, so I used that opportunity to cover your true bond."

Is he really saying what I think he's saying?

I stare at Nathanial. He wants me to think *he's* my Mate? How stupid does he think I am? I need to get the fuck out of here, right now.

A small part of me wonders if Josh knew something I didn't? If Nathanial fucked with his mind to think I'm not his Mate too. Is that why Nathanial didn't erase Josh's mind the night we went to the Old Tower? Josh said manipulation magic doesn't work on basilisks—I don't have a way to verify that.

No. I know what happened the night I shifted. I know Josh and my bond is very different—but I also know it's real. I know what I felt my whole life, and I know what I saw during my transformation. Nathanial is trying to make me question my own Mating bond like Josh has our entire lives. Nathanial is damn powerful, but even he can't fake the Divine's work.

There is *no* doubt.

Josh is mine and there's no way this fucking asshole is going to make me think otherwise.

Then Nathanial asks me, "Why do you think Josh won't Mark you?" I freeze. He really knows where to hurt someone. I turn my face away from Nathanial, but he turns it right back to say, "Because you're not his to Mark."

Lies.

I don't believe him.

"This is what you've always wanted—to be mine, right?" he watches me and I can't hide under his scrutiny. I'm disgusted with myself for ever letting him touch me in anyway—for even thinking that was an honor. For thinking that made me special, when I was always fucking special.

If Nathanial's gone this far, I have to let him think I believe him. I have to see how much further he's willing to go for whatever his true agenda is. There might be some truth in what he's told me today, but it's not the whole truth.

"Why not just tell me from the beginning?" I ask and he gives me a sad look.

"Because you won't remember this either."

Then Nathanial kisses me again.

69 REALITY

Rosella Craving
December 31

Nathanial was wrong.

I remember every memory Nathanial has ever taken from me the second he kisses me again. Every. Single. One.

I've done horrible things.

My magic…my hands…it's like I don't even recognize myself, but at the same time, I feel restored…

Nathanial teleports me to Cravenhold and I quickly go home. The house is quiet, no lights are on except the one I flip in the entryway. Exhaustion drags at my bones from the run, from everything pulling me in too many directions. I kick off my shoes and head straight for the bathroom, stripping as I go.

Hot water cascades over me in the shower, washing away the day. I stand under the spray longer than necessary, letting it pound against my shoulders.

Once I'm out and dressed for the rest of the day, I decide to have a conversation with Josh's aunt.

"Tell me about the necklaces," I telepath to Mina, knowing she can communicate with me—knowing she has answers.

"You found another," she states, unfazed.

"I know of three now. Two are with me, the third is yours. Are there more?" I ask, praying no.

"No, just the three. Tell me how you got the first one?" she asks and I have no choice.

"Someone put it up for auction at my Veyara Gala. I felt a pull—a need to have it, so Josh bid five drops of blood on it for me," I answer. My chest tightens at the memory and what he gave for it. He said he can never love a murderer like me, so why would he do that?

Mina is quiet for some time. I wait patiently after I text Vanessa to cancel my day.

"Only Helena or her descendent could give you the

necklace," Mina's thought is soft in my mind, like she's gently trying to break bad news to me. ***"She made sure of that. If anyone else touched it before you did, they'd die."***

"What are you saying exactly? Please, just give it to me straight," I plead, not having the bandwidth to decipher more horrors.

"The first necklace belonged to Helena. Cedric had originally made it for her. Then she duplicated it into two more. She charmed them with very powerful protective magic. Very unique and…specific. While the necklaces are meant to protect their wearer, not just anyone can touch them, much less wear them. No one can wear all three unless they're of the Deveraux bloodline—and you," Mina answers me and suddenly I feel like I just got propelled into another terrifying mess. I rummage through my vanity to find the picture Josh let me keep from Coilspire of Helena and him.

My eyes go straight to the gold chain around Helena's neck, and the crescent Moon pendant Josh's tiny hand is fisted around, pressed against her chest. Why didn't I notice this when I first saw the picture? It's small in the photo but it's not hidden.

"Why me? And Deveraux bloodline?" I ask Mina, frowning. I don't recognize the name.

"You, because you're Mated to her son and she recognized your powers for what they are," Mina answers, kindly.

"Which is what?" I ask, afraid of her answer because of what I've been doing with Nathanial. What I've done.

"Purification," she answers and I take a sharp breath of air, but she continues before I can ask her more. ***"I'm not Helena's twin. I'm her triplet. She made three necklaces, one for each of us Deveraux sisters."***

"The seer—the witch who gave me the second necklace. But she couldn't be your twin…she looked elderly," I think to Mina.

"Possibly. Deveraux witches are similar to your changelings. We can take on any form as we wish. It's why I'm Isis's decoy." There are no emotions in her thought as she tells me this. How do we not know of Deveraux witches? Seems like there should be a top clearance level file on them if they can take on different forms.

I have so many questions, but I ask the most pressing one. ***"How do I remember everything now?"***

"Helena's necklace, the first one, is meant to protect your memories—your mind. If anyone tried to take your memories or erase them, they wouldn't be able to," Mina explains. That makes sense to why I woke up remembering Mina and what happened in the Old Tower. She continues, ***"The second necklace, worn with the first, activates when someone tries to take your memories. Not only does it protect, but it gives the wearer all their stolen memories back. You remember things that go back to your childhood now, don't you?"***

My mind is racing.

"Yes, too much," I think to her. ***"Why did Helena do this? How did she know…?"***

"The third necklace is the most powerful. It protects the mind, the soul, and the body when worn with its sisters. It gives the wearer the ability to channel all three of our powers—dead or alive," Mina concludes. ***"Helena added you into the mix later—she broke her own rule to do it the night her son died."***

"Noah," I telepath, taking a sharp breath. ***"I still don't remember that night. You said if my memories were erased then I'd get them back."***

Why would Helena break her rules for me if I killed her son? It doesn't make any sense. Josh said my memory from that night was wiped, so why don't I remember killing his brother like he believes.

Mina takes a moment before responding. ***"Nathanial tried to erase your mind, so you'd only get back the memories he took. If you don't remember something you're supposed to, it just means he wasn't the one who took that memory from you."***

I look over at the vanity in my room, at my reflection and ask Mina, ***"Are you telling me there is more than one person fucking with my mind?"***

"I'm so sorry, Rose…you are a very, very powerful being. Nathanial has always been afraid of you, but he's not the only one scared of losing power," Mina replies as my lips quiver and tears start to spill.

"Is…is Josh in on this? Is he one of them?" I ask, starting to feel lightheaded. I think about our duel in Coilspire where he said he didn't want to control me.

"I don't know. I just know if you got the necklace at your Gala, then it's impossible that Helena gave it to you. It had to

be—"

"Josh," I answer. ***"But why go through the whole act? Why not just give it to me? Why put it up for auction and pretend to spill blood for me?"***

He spilled nothing. It was all a lie.

"Only he can answer those questions," she thinks to me, then adds, ***"just remember…Mating bonds are sacred."***

"How are Cedric and Helena Mates? Were they truly?" I demand to know with more right than I really have around this, but I have to get to the bottom of it. They're my Mate's parents.

"Mates are sacred," Mina repeats, ***"They were challenged, they defended their Mating bond until the end, I'm assuming."***

"But…she was a witch and he…"

"Loved her," Mina answers, sadly and my chest tightens at the rawness of her emotions through the mind link. ***"You want to know how Josh is a shifter,"*** she says.

"He said she was sired," I answer.

"I see. I haven't seen Helena since we were little girls. She had Cedric give the necklace to me, so I wouldn't know anything about that."

"How are Nathanial and Helena connected?" I ask, holding my breath.

Mina pauses, then thinks to me, ***"Before I was in the Old Tower, it was Helena's burden to be Isis's sacrifice."***

"Sacrifice?" I instantly remember the memory Nathanial showed me. It wasn't Helena in it.

"I think it's time you found my sister and talk to your Mate, Veyara."

It's the first time she's ever addressed me by any title and she chose that one.

"Mating bonds might be sacred, but that doesn't mean they're safe," I send my thought to her. ***"How can I ever trust him? He lied about giving me the necklace."***

"You won't know if you don't ask. You are the Mistress of Darkness, use your powers," Mina thinks and I shudder at my other title. ***"Nathanial doesn't know the necklaces' powers. He can never know."***

"I understand. I'll play my part, but for how long? And why? What is all this for?" I ask, sensing that she's ready to end this conversation.

"You'll know. You've always known what to do. I'll see you soon," she telepaths before I feel her connection sever.

Shane's playing the piano, an old song he wrote before he became Alpha, when I find him in the atrium.

He stops playing when he sees me and smiles. "Hey, Rosie. What's going on?"

"Something happened," I telepath to him. You never know who's listening.

"Go on," he prompts, responding in the same manner.

I bite my lip and sit down beside him on the bench. ***"Can I trust you?"*** I ask him and use my powers as he answers.

"Of course, you can, you know that. I know it's hard to see it sometimes, but everything I've done is to protect you. It was my last promise to Dad."

He's telling the truth and I rest my head on his shoulder. ***"I thought I could trust Nathanial and Josh too."***

"What happened?" he asks as he continues to play softly.

So I tell my brother everything.

I tell him about the light Josh and I saw before we went to explore the Old Tower, leading us to Josh's aunt. Shane listens quietly and frowns when he learns Nathanial knocked me out. But I don't stop there.

I tell him everything Mina's just told me—about Helena, the necklaces, and their powers. I tell him about my quick trip to Romania, the jaguar shifter I killed on my birthday, and every time I couldn't remember using my powers.

I tell him how I'm not good. I tell him my hand in it too—the darkness in me that was drawn to everything Nathanial wanted.

By the end of it, Shane is pale.

"I'm so sorry," I say out loud.

"Rose," he cups my face like he used to when I was younger. "What Nathanial did…he—"

"Don't say it," I shake my head, lowering his hands. The look in his eyes says everything but I refuse to be a victim. It doesn't matter that I didn't remember. When I did remember, the times Nathanial did give me my memories, it awoke the darkness in me—a darkness that slept when my memory was erased.

Shane can't understand that I was a willing participant in all of it.

I'm no victim.

"What did Josh have to say about his aunt?" Shane asks me through our mind link. I blink at the change of topic.

"He didn't know he had one," I sigh and play a key on the piano. ***"He did tell me his mom was a witch and she was sired. Did you know?"***

"Yes, of course, it's not a secret. It's just not talked about." Shane exhales deeply. ***"Does he know about your recent discoveries?"***

"He wasn't home, so not yet," I answer.

"But you're going to tell him?" Shane asks, watching me and I can't tell if he wants me to or not. I know the two of them haven't been on the greatest terms lately, though they seemed fine on Yule.

"Yes. I'm tired of the secrets between us," I reply.

Shane agrees, nodding. He thinks to me, ***"I'll look into all this."***

"No," I shake my head, ***"no, you can't. Nathanial clearly wanted this quiet. If you start snooping..."***

"Don't worry about me, but you should talk to Josh," he suggests and my stupid heart clenches. Shane adds telepathically, ***"And Rose, stop using your powers."***

I frown. ***"Why? You've never let me use my powers—"***

"Because it will kill you," Shane looks at me and the plea is clear in his gray eyes. ***"If you exhaust yourself, your power will latch on, and it will kill you."***

"No," I think to him, my thought firm and sure. ***"My powers would never hurt me."***

"Rose, please—you don't know—there was a reason why..." he cuts himself off and I frown at him. Shane realizes his slip up and sighs heavily. ***"Please, for me. Stop using your powers. And talk to Josh. Make him talk to you. He'll fight—but you're his Mate. He needs you just as much as you want him."***

I have nothing to say. I don't know what to think or do right now, so I give my brother a nod and a kiss on the cheek before leaving.

"Can we talk?" I ask Josh through our bond.

Josh and I have a lot to go over but Shane's last words keep replaying in my mind, making me pause and not jump to any conclusions just yet.

As I exit the Palace, I glance over in the direction of the Hunter Residence and notice the flag is down. He's not here and I vaguely remember he mentioned needing to leave with Devaughn to visit one of the Prides. I guess our talk will have to wait.

Despite all that I learned and what Josh has done, I am confident about one important detail…Josh is a lot of things, but he's not a villain.

Because *I'm* the villain.

Once I'm seated in the car and the door closes, I open the burner number app and call the only number saved on it.

He picks up on the first ring but before he can say anything, I speak. "Remember how you always wanted to play with me?"

70 DEAL WITH THE KING

Rosella Craving
December 31

Josh comes home with the largest bouquet of red peonies. I stare at him, mouth slightly ajar at the shock. I try to remember if it's a significant date for us, but I come up blank. It's New Year's Eve, but we've never spent it together, much less celebrated it. I walk up to him hesitantly.

"What's all this?" I ask.

"For you." He hands the flowers to me, saying, "Divine, you are a sight for sore eyes," then he pulls me in for a kiss.

Beta Warrior Josh Hunter bought me my favorite flowers for the first time.

I smile as we pull away and look up at him. "You got me flowers."

"Yeah—truce?"

"We're fighting?" I counter, unaware.

"Aren't we always?" he chuckles, kissing my forehead and heading for the kitchen.

I follow him absently. My eyes are devouring the bouquet. I glance at him and ask, "Did Shane say something to you?"

He pulls out a bottle of bloodwine and frowns. "No…? Why?"

I shake my head as I set the flowers on the kitchen counter. It already has a pretty vase, which is great, because I wouldn't know where to find one here. I look back at him and say, "Just wondering why you got me flowers."

"I'm going to make sure you always have fresh flowers," he says, unscrewing the Crimson Merlot and I can't help the smile that spreads on my face.

"My dad used to say that to Mom all the time," I tell him softly.

He winks. "I know. I remember."

This is already a perfect night, and I don't want to ruin it by talking about all that we need to, but we have to talk. I don't want another day to go by where there's a mountain of secrets threatening our relationship.

"I ordered takeout. It should be here soon," he says, pouring the bloodwine into two glasses.

We've been ordering takeout since the chef is on vacation and Josh is very selective on who prepares his homecooked meals. It's not like he can get poisoned, but I'm not complaining.

"Long day? Did you learn anything on your visit?" I ask him. He, Devaughn, and Daniel have been trying to track the Sisterhood of Sin Covens that have been attacking the Prides and doing Lilith's biddings. Witches are not easy to find.

"Nothing too helpful. Just more violent attacks," he grunts, but doesn't go into it.

The food arrives just then, and we have dinner together. It's nice to do something so normal. It's all I ever wanted with him—normalcy.

After we wrap up dinner and Josh starts to open another bottle, I go up to him and wrap my arms around his waist from behind. Nathanial's words just make me angrier the more I think about it and have been weighing heavy on me.

"Hey," Josh says softly, raising his arm to pull me around so he can look at me. His dark lashes frame his intense but concerned eyes. "What's going on?"

"What did I say during the truth serum session?" I ask, quietly.

Josh looks surprised by the question before his gaze drops. "Rose, let's—"

I lace my fingers with his, and push, "Please? Just tell me."

"I don't want you to hate me…" he says quietly.

"More than I already do?" I ask, teasingly, trying to keep this lighthearted.

He gives me a blunt look, before his hands are on my hips and he props me up on the countertop. He gives me another glass of bloodwine and I take it from him, locking him in with my legs.

He kisses me so softly that my eyes flutter close involuntarily. When we break away for air, he says, "You said you wanted to run away from all this. To live in a house in the clouds." He smiles at that.

Coilspire. It was always the house in the clouds for me.

"What else?" I ask, gently. "That's not so bad."

His thumb traces my bottom lip. "That you want to be mine, but you'll never be."

Oh.

I don't look at him. That sounds more like it.

"It's not true," he says, his voice low and I can feel his intense gaze on my face.

I meet his eyes. "Of course it is. I was under the truth serum."

"It's not *my* truth." He kisses me again, and telepaths, ***"You are and always will be mine."***

"Promise?" I think back, relishing the pressure of his lips moving with mine.

"With every breath I take, sweetheart."

"Do you think we're Mates?" I send the thought to him.

Josh breaks away and glares at me. "What the fuck kind of question is that?"

I don't doubt that we're Mates, but I hate to admit Nathanial's words triggered me. I don't believe Nathanial—that's just stupid. But why *won't* Josh Mark me? Why did he spend four years trying to replace me? A lot of Mates can't stand each other, I mean, look at my uncle and aunt, but that doesn't mean they go out trying to completely replace them. It's why open relationships exist and are common for shifters. But Josh took it to the next level.

He keeps doing it at any given chance.

Honesty might not be his strongest attribute, but I want to be truthful. At least with what I can be honest about.

"I went to see Nathanial today," I start and Josh stares back at me. It's almost as if he's holding his breath. I take a drink of the bloodwine—a big drink.

Josh pries the glass out of my hand and puts it down. "And seeing him made you question our Mating bond?"

"No…I've never questioned our Mating bond, but it is making me wonder why you have. He said some…insane things," I tell him.

"Like what?" Josh nearly growls at me. I reach for the wine glass, but Josh pushes it further, before he tilts my chin to him, forcing me to focus.

"Like we're not Mates, that he took advantage of you not being bonded to cover up the truth of him and I being Mates—he said that's why you won't Mark me…" I trail off, and I'm not sure if I want to look away from Josh or watch him closely for his reaction.

Anger—that's his initial emotion. Then he reins it in and shuts his eyes, starting to pull away from me, but I hold onto him.

"Don't…please…" I whisper. I need him close. "Don't leave."

Josh wraps me in his arms and holds me. He presses his lips to my forehead and says, "You know he lied to you, right?"

"Of course," I say, "but—"

"That is not why I won't Mark you. I told you why I won't in Coilspire and I meant that," Josh wipes away the tears from my cheeks that started falling. His touch is so different from Nathanial's when he did the same thing earlier.

"But you said it was all training…that you can't love a mur…can't love me…"

"What do you think?" Josh asks before he grabs the bottle instead of his glass and takes a swig.

I keep one of our hands connected as I say, "I think you want to hate me but you're falling for me, and you don't know how to deal with both being true at the same time."

Josh stares at me before taking another drink.

Yup.

This time when I reach for the glass, he doesn't stop me.

"What else did he say?" Josh asks. I finish the wine in my glass, then take the bottle from him and pour myself another. I look at my Mate and tell him everything else I learned today.

"You're fucking mine." It's the first thing he says.

Then he kisses me, roughly, angrily, biting my bottom lip as if he has to prove his point. He carries me to the couch before gently placing me down and sitting beside me. My lips are swollen from the kiss and his looks the same.

"I want to explain the necklace," he starts and I'm surprised I don't have to push him for answers. Still, I blink and give him my black eyes. He doesn't falter seeing them as he says, "Yes, the one at the auction was my mother's. I did slip it in as an auction item—my mom had specific instructions."

I frown at that.

He takes a deep breath and lets it out slowly. "It's not that she didn't think you were worthy—Hell, she adored you. She needed to be sure she was right. She wanted you to be drawn to it, called to it, and I thought the auction would be a good way to see that—especially with all the drugs in your system. I wasn't sure if you would be able to, and if you didn't it would've been fine. I would've still bid on it."

"You were buying it from yourself. It didn't matter how much blood it cost," I piece together. He'd outbid anyone if they tried.

"It was a foolproof plan," he says, before he reaches for a book on the coffee table. Except it's not a book, it's a mini safe that pricks his finger before opening. He takes out a vial of blood and hands it to me.

"I don't need your blood, Josh…" I push his hand away.

He insists, placing it in my palm anyway. "You never know when you'll need it. Keep it on you."

"Nathanial and I had a plan," he continues and I sit up. What the fuck does that mean? He reaches for my hand, like he needs to touch me as he says the next words. "I was angry after Noah died—you'll understand when I Mark you. Even with your memories gone, that wasn't good enough. I knew he wanted your powers."

I don't want him to continue.

I'm terrified of what he's going to say next.

"I didn't…I couldn't want you, so I told him—"

"Stop," I cut him off, placing my free hand on his lips. His gray eyes clash with mine and he lowers my hand.

"I have to tell you," Josh whispers as terrified tears run down my face. "I fucked up a lot—and I know you won't ever be able to forgive me, or trust me, but I have to tell you."

"I don't want you to," I cry.

I'm the Mistress of Darkness, but this is what's scaring me?

Josh thinks Nathanial wants me for my powers so he can train me to use me, but I wasn't entirely honest with him. I left out the parts where Nathanial and I were…intimate. We never had sex from the memories I got back from him, but we did cross lines.

"I told him I'd stay out of his way. I didn't care what he wanted with you. But then you shifted," Josh's breath comes out shaky. "I saw our cords connect the first time. I was old enough to remember it. On your first shift though…it was hard to dismiss that."

"Then what happened?" I ask, quietly, urging him to go on.

"When he tried to erase your memory in front of me in the Old Tower, I realized he was up to something else. He called you his little mistress," Josh says, his eyes fixed on me.

I didn't tell him about that. I didn't know how—I'm not actually Nathanial's mistress—not in the normal sense of the word. Did he take advantage of the word, yes, but I think it has more to do with the Mistress of Darkness than anything intimate.

I break away from looking at him and focus on our joined hands. "I…I didn't know what I was doing—I didn't remember—"

"I know," he says, squeezing my hand.

"What did you get out of your plan with Nathanial?" I ask him and for the first time tonight, Josh hesitates.

"I got him off my back," he replies quietly, almost ashamed to admit it. "I stopped being his focus and he started confiding in me when he started believing I really wanted nothing to do with you. He might've tried selling us the story that we weren't Mates, but he knew we were. After the Old Tower, hearing what he called you—I did what snakes do best."

I raise my brows. "You switched up on him. Why?"

"He lied," Josh answers simply. "Shane didn't want you using your powers. Nathanial did. The way I saw it was that he'd train you to be powerful. You were my Mate, at the end of the day you'd be the Veyara. My Veyara. The deal was your powers. Not you. Never you."

I stare at him. "Why?" I repeat.

He frowns deeply, his eyes stormy, captivating. "You're mine and I don't share."

I don't say anything. I just sit silently with him and take in all that he's said. He is telling the truth. I know he is especially with how I'm overwhelmed with the smell of cinnamon rolls fresh out of the oven and the forest after a rainstorm. My heart beats faster, but I still have more questions.

"Did you know about the powers of the necklaces?" I ask quietly.

"No…my mother just told me to give hers to you. I didn't even know she had sisters, or that there were other necklaces until the seer gave you the box. I guess that wasn't for me to know," he answers. He doesn't seem upset by it, having faith in his mother's plans.

"Mina said I should find her sister…can you help me?" I look at him and there's surprise written all over his face. His eyes soften and he seems happy that I asked him to help me.

"I won't stop until I find her. At least we know she probably doesn't look like the seer and more like my mom, so that might give us better luck now," he says, then Josh pulls me onto his lap.

I look at my handsome Mate and run my fingers through his hair. He closes his eyes, taking in the feeling of my touch. When he opens them again, I say, "I left one thing out."

He frowns slightly. "Which is?"

"You were there in Romania—when Nathanial took me there before my birthday to exchange blood and powers with Zak Xandelskye. You came later," I say and he goes still under me. I cup his face in my hands. "You…you've known this whole time that I was the Mistress of Darkness."

Josh just stares back at me, not moving a muscle.

He didn't do anything when he was there. He came in and watched Nathanial draw my blood. He was given a vial of it, and then he left. No words were exchanged. He wasn't surprised by the occupants of the room, nor were they of his arrival. It was all very strange.

"Like I said, Nathanial and I had a deal," Josh says quietly.

"Where's the blood?" I ask him.

"Safe," he answers, and I can tell that's all he'll say on it. I know he's not lying. I know I'm going to need to trust him on this.

My arms come around him, and I kiss his lips softly, before saying, "Thank you." I pull back and add, "For the flowers, I mean. Finding your seer aunt is the least you can do after subjecting me to a big, bad man."

If a basilisk can feel guilty, that emotion washes over Josh's face, before it's gone in a flash. "Yeah? Maybe I can just take you away forever and actually lock you up in Coilspire."

"He didn't like it when you did that the first time," I tell Josh.

"I know. It's why I did it. I didn't particularly like him calling my Mate his little mistress," Josh replies, darkly, before burying his face in my neck. He inhales deeply as if relieved.

I feel the swipe of his tongue before he bites down gently and sucks. My eyes roll to the back of my head as I arch into him while his cock shifts against me, hardening.

"Funny how I'm trying to piece my memories together, but keep uncovering things linked to you," I say, running my hand through his thick black hair again. "See, it pays to be friends with me."

Josh's head comes up instantly and he gives me a wild look like he's never heard of the word.

"Friends?" he questions.

I shrug. "I'd say we're becoming friends." Josh's eyes narrow before he rolls them. He lets out a humorless laugh. I cross my arms. "I'm a great friend! You'd be lucky to have me as a friend. Ask Daniya and Mariella if you don't believe me."

He glares at me. "Rose. I have no intentions of being your fucking friend."

"Your loss," I grumble, very aware of his dick completely hard now.

"Not when our love story's going to be of legends."

Oh…

"You can't say things like that…" I tell him, hating how the butterflies flutter with happiness at his words. It's terrifying.

He smirks. "Why? Afraid you'll actually fall for me? Your Mate?"

"Yes," I whisper.

He pauses, not expecting me to admit it. His hand comes up to the side of my neck. "I think it's a little too late for that, my Veyara," then he presses his lips to mine, and adds, "for the both of us."

71 SWEET AND SALTY

Rosella Craving
January 1

Fireworks light up the Cravenhold skies.

Josh and I stand on our balcony, taking a break from continuous sex to drink blood and watch the light show.

"You never sent me pictures," Josh brings up.

"I don't have them anymore," I tell him, leaning against the concrete rails.

"What?" he snaps at me.

I sigh heavily. "Josh, you said I failed. It was training and you could never want all of this with me—I deleted the pictures since they meant nothing…"

The words are hard to say and the cold look on his face doesn't help. Josh turns and heads into our room before returning with my phone.

He thrusts it to me and says, "Unlock it."

"Rude. Say pretty please," I mumble, taking the phone. He doesn't say anything, not that I expected him to. I unlock it and give it back to him.

He goes through it before letting out a deep breath. "Oh, thank the Divine."

"What?" I ask, frowning.

"You didn't permanently delete them," he answers, still messing with my phone.

"What are you doing?" I ask, reaching for it back.

"Creating a shared folder with me. I don't trust you with my pictures," he says, waving me off.

"*Your* pictures?" I ask, dumbfounded.

"Shh." He dismisses me.

I roll my eyes and turn to watch the fireworks. It's not for another five minutes before he comes up beside me.

"Are you really okay with everything I told you?" he asks quietly.

I glance at him, my hair falling over on one side. "Do I have a choice when we're stuck together? Are you okay with me being the Mistress of Darkness?"

He lets out a laugh. "Do I have a choice? I don't mind us fighting though."

"What? Why?" I frown. "I hate fighting with you."

"Yeah, but the make-up sex is fucking great," he groans, clearly getting flashbacks.

I shove him, my cheeks heating. Josh laughs and wraps his arms around me. On a more serious note, I ask, "And what about me still not remembering what happened when Noah died?"

He pauses before pressing his lips to the back of my head. "I won't lie. It's a little disappointing, but maybe it's for the best. Maybe it's meant to stay in the past."

Shane said my memories weren't wiped, that it's just what they told Josh. Shane also lied about that. The more I think about that night, the less clear it is. I can't even remember the alarm going off even though I know it did.

I know something's not right and I know my brother might just be trying to protect me, but I need to get to the bottom of it, one way or another.

"I just have one question," I say, turning my head a little to look at him.

"Hm?"

"Was any of it real?" I whisper because if I say it out loud, I just might break. I don't know if he hears me because he's quiet for some time.

Josh turns me, running his hand through my hair, and says, "Your eyes. Switch them." My heartbeat quickens as my eyes switch. He cups my face and tells me, "Everything between us from the reunion was real. Everything I said that morning after we got back from Coilspire—I…"

His brows furrow like he can't find the right words. Like he's struggling to admit something. His hands drop from my face, and he closes his eyes because he can't admit it.

He needs you just as much as you want him, Shane told me.

I stand on my tiptoes and press my lips to his. He's surprised by it, but his hands rest on my hips, kissing me back.

"I'm getting all my memories back. For us," I promise him telepathically.

He breaks away from the kiss and looks at me. "What if it destroys us instead?"

I give him an offended look. "Are you challenging our Mating bond?"

"What if it does more harm than it's worth?" he asks. "Getting your memories back…it's not easy."

I cup his face in my hands. "I know, but how can it not be worth it? I just hope you'll be with me to figure it out."

"I meant what I said at Yule. I'm on your side. By your side," he says, his voice coming out rough.

"I'm holding you to that…I don't want to do this alone," I whisper.

Josh catches my lips with his, picking me up as the fireworks continue to crackle around us. ***"You won't be alone."***

We make out under the stars and the fireworks for a little longer before it starts to get too cold. Josh carries me back to bed and I wait for him to join me as he takes off his gray sweats. His cock stands proud and I bite down on my lip.

Josh slides in beside me, his body warm and welcoming. His arms wrap around my waist, pulling me against him. I burrow into his chest, inhaling him—safe, happy, mine.

Our lips meet softly before we kiss, both deepening it, tongues dancing in embrace. My hand trails down his chest, over the hard planes of his stomach, and lower until I wrap my fingers around his hard and patient cock. He groans into my mouth, hips shifting closer. I stroke him slowly, feeling him pulse at my touch, and the sound he makes lights me up inside.

I break away from his lips, trailing kisses down his body as I slip under the blanket before he can protest. I settle between his legs, the darkness warm and intimate. My mouth finds him, lips closing around the tip, sucking gently as my tongue swirls, tasting his precum. He hisses, fingers tangling in my hair.

I trace lower to the base of his cock, curious and teasing. I brush against the slit between his shaft and balls, and he tenses hard, hand pulling my hair in warning.

"Rose—" he grits out, trying to pull me back.

I surface just enough to peek up at him from under the covers. "Does it hurt?"

"No," he says, breath ragged, and cheeks flushed. Is he…blushing?

"It's...sensitive. Like after I come."

Ahhh. I nod, dipping back down. My mouth envelops him again, sucking deeper now, tongue pressing gently against the head before sliding lower. Fuck, he's so big. I coax at the slit with careful fingers, rubbing soft circles, feeling it open just a little.

"Fuck, sweetheart," Josh groans, "I love that mouth of yours."

I keep at him, mouth sliding down his length while my fingers press and tease that sensitive slit, feeling it pulse under my touch. His hips strain, breaths turning ragged, and I don't let up, sucking harder until he's right on the edge.

"Rose—fuck," he gasps, fingers tightening in my hair. "Don't stop, baby, I'm so close—"

He comes hard, spilling into my mouth, hot and salty-sweet. I swallow immediately as my neck and collarbone is hit with more cum. His dick was in my mouth—there's no way…

I pull back just enough to catch my breath, wiping my chin with the back of my hand and see cum oozing from the slit like the tip of his cock.

"Well, that's progress," I say, my voice scratchy, a small proud smile tugging at my lips as I look up at him.

Josh has collapsed against the pillows, chest heaving, skin flushed and slick with sweat. He's utterly spent, eyes closed as if he's piecing himself back together.

I slip from the bed, grab a cloth in the bathroom, and clean the mess from my neck and chest, rinsing it away before returning to him with a clean, damp towel. I crawl back under the covers, and he takes the towel from me, cleaning himself quickly. He tosses the towel straight into the hamper.

I raise an eyebrow. "Impressive."

He smirks, "There was a reason I insisted on the hamper staying right there."

I laugh, then ask nervously, "How do you feel…?"

"That's never..." He trails off, turning his head to look at me, wonder and exhaustion mixing in his gaze. "I didn't know that was possible."

I lean in, kiss his cheek softly. "Nothing's impossible in our world. Even good things."

He holds my eyes for a long moment, then his hand slides into my hair, gripping possessively, pulling me to him. His mouth claims mine, deep and unhurried, and I melt into it.

Josh lifts my leg over his hip and lines his cock to my entrance.

I break away from the kiss to say, "We still have to talk about being married."

He teases the tip with my wetness, before easily slipping inside me, burying himself. "Fuck," he groans with me, before asking, "what…what's there to talk about?"

"Um…that you're my husband—" I get cut off by him thrusting into me. I lock my legs around him, and say, "And that I'm your wife and—" He thrusts again, but this time with much more force, making me moan out. He's trying to distract me.

"That's right. You're my wife," he says, possessively, and picks up speed, making me cry out. My nails scratch at his back as he keeps going.

"That's not what—"

"Quiet, my Veyara. Your Beta is pleasuring you into the new year," he orders, before I cry out in pleasure as he sinks his teeth into my breast.

Vanessa and I arrive at the caves the same time Mariella and Cristobal do. I push aside the curtain of ice-crusted ivy and lead Mariella inside as Cristobal and Vanessa follow us. The tunnel swallows us quickly, walls narrowing to rough stones that scrape my fingertips. The spotlights help us navigate the twists and turns and avoid slickness from the rain and snow.

"Sorry, I know it took a while to get you the test subjects but hopefully it'll do," I tell my best friend as I look ahead.

We round a corner, and the space opens to iron-barred cells and rusted chains dangling from walls. This was the old dungeon once when Cravenhold was first established, before the bigger dungeon was built on the southeastern side. These forgotten cells have been the perfect place to keep my personal prisoners. Uncle Edward took Shane, my cousins, and me down here a long time ago to explore. I continued to come back.

Chains rattle ahead, soft at first, then sharper as our footsteps near. Moans drift and Mariella's steps begin to falter.

I look at her. "It's okay. If this makes you uncomfortable, Vanessa can take you back."

Mariella looks at Vanessa and I think seeing that Vanessa isn't disturbed by any of this, it helps Mariella relax. "No, I'm fine."

"Okay." I don't argue and we step forward.

There are eight women shackled to the far wall, wrists bound above their heads in heavy iron. Black hoods cover their faces, gags stuffed tight behind the fabric so no one can hear them—not that anyone would ever be so deep into the caves. Their bodies tremble in the last couture outfit they chose to wear before being brought here. They twist at our approach, chains clinking like warnings.

Mariella gasps, her free hand flying to her mouth. "Rose…why? Who are they?"

I shrug, letting go of her to cross the cold floor. "They were delusional enough to think they could be me."

One of them jerks harder at my voice, a choked sound escaping her gag. The newbie. I reach the nearest—tall, with curves that once turned heads—turned Josh's head. I cup her chin through the hood, tilting her face up.

"Just showing them how wrong they were," I murmur, thumb pressing into her cheek.

Mariella steps closer, eyes wide in the spotlights. "I don't understand."

I sigh, releasing the woman. She slumps against her chains, breaths ragged. "These are the girls who chased Josh. Actively. Frequently. Throwing themselves at him, spreading whispers about their little conquests." My voice hardens. "I'll settle the score with him eventually—he knows that. But I couldn't let *them* run around, proud and boasting they'd bedded the Beta."

Mariella's gaze shifts from me to the bound figures to Vanessa, assessing the situation now. The cries quiet as if they sense the shift.

"Trust me, they had it coming," Vanessa tells Mariella, her brown eyes narrowed as she comes to stand by my side. She was with me at the tea party. She heard how proud they were. I saw the disgust on her face. It's why I trust her with this even though Cristobal wasn't so sure.

He looks bored out of his mind right now. He likes the chase better, when he gets to capture and bring them here.

I meet Mariella's golden-brown eyes. "Will they do?"

She nods slowly, then firmer. "They'll do perfectly."

"Good. We can set up a full workstation for you here and Vanessa or Cristobal can accompany you, so you're not alone down here."

"Of course. Thank you, this will be helpful for what I'm doing," Mariella nods, eyeing the girls again.

"Just so you know, my blood is poisonous. And Mariella?" I say to get her attention.

"Yes?"

"If you accidentally kill them, that's okay. But do not let them escape."

"You scare me sometimes," Cristobal thinks to me, but I hear the humor in his thought.

"Please, I learned it from you," I telepath him back.

Franklin is the more responsible, serious one. He knows about this and he doesn't entirely approve, which is why he's standing outside, guarding. Cristobal was always a little more unhinged. I'd like to think my father knew what he was doing when he assigned them to be my bodyguards. I never thanked Josh for letting them back on my detail.

I glance at the prisoners before saying to Mariella, "Have fun, I'm going to leave you to it," then to Vanessa, "stay with her."

Vanessa nods as Cristobal escorts me out of the caves.

My phone goes off with a notification from the third-party texting app as soon as we exit. I look at the message quickly. It's followed by a drop pin location. I click on it and see that it's in New York, but also four and a half hours away. It's 1 PM right now.

"Change of plans," I tell my bodyguards as Franklin comes into view, sending the location to our trio group chat, before looking at the message again.

LMC: *Time to play*

72 IZABELLA CRAVING

Josh Hunter
January 1

I enter the war room with Devaughn as the blaring alarm rings throughout Cravenhold. My gaze sweeps the room, taking in the faces amid the chaos.

All the Warriors and Crescents are here—except Crystal and Azura. Crystal's at home with the new baby and Azura's due any day now, completely on bedrest. I instantly notice that my own Mate isn't here.

"Where are you?" I telepath her. She was supposed to be training with Vanessa, who is here and going over footage with Antonio. Her eyes catch mine and I give her a questioning look. She shakes her head—either not knowing where Rose is or not willing to tell me.

"Where is she?" I telepath Vanessa.

"She had an errand to run outside Cravenhold. Cristobal and Franklin went with her," Vanessa responds and I clench my jaw. I pull out my phone and open the tracker app to see her car in the mountains heading northwest.

I look up to find Eliza's sharp blue eyes locked on me from across the room. I haven't seen her at one of these meetings since Rose's transformation, and the way she's looking at me immediately puts me on edge.

I don't know what it is about Eliza, but the woman has a way of getting under my skin when she's all business. Maybe it's her Luna powers or just knowing she'd do anything to protect Rose—even from me. I'm not surprised to see the Luna here right now though.

Shane's watching me too, his jaw tight, his dark hair falling into his eyes. "Where's Rose?"

"She'll be here," I reply, covering for her. I telepath her again, ***"Rose. Where are you?"***

"Do you trust me?" she responds this time.

"Should I?" I reply as my skin feels tight. I don't like this.

"Yes," she answers and I crack my neck in an attempt to relieve the growing tension there.

I focus on the far wall, where a single security camera fills the screen—a clear feed from one of the Cravenhold gates—not one we use often. It's a forest gate. I watch as a girl appears, her face hauntingly familiar. She looks exactly like the last time any of us saw her, six years ago. The resemblance is undeniable—the same dark hair, the same high cheekbones, and the same fierce glint in her eyes. She looks just like Rose, except younger, like she hasn't aged a day.

"No fucking way…" Eliza breathes as she takes a step closer to the screen. James appears on it. One of his units had called it in ten minutes ago as the girl breached one of our outer perimeters.

Security guards and border patrol shifters surround her, their movements tense and weapons drawn. She's held in place, her expression defiant but scared.

I move for the door.

"Where are you going?!" Shane calls after me.

"Hold her. I'm coming," I telepath to James as Devaughn follows me out.

I glare at him, but he shakes his head and says, "Moral support. I'm not here to stop you."

"I don't like it out here. Too open. I'm taking her to the dungeons," James tells us and I feel the other Warriors linked in.

"Don't fucking bring her in," Devaughn replies to him.

"It's too fucking open. We already had the Sin Coven breach us once," James answers. He's not wrong, but he's not right either.

This could be a Trojan horse.

Devaughn, Vanessa, Shane, Eliza, and I meet James in the dungeon. Crystal joins us a few minutes later.

"Babe, what are you doing here?" Devaughn frowns.

"I'm not missing this. The baby's with my sister. He'll be fine," she pushes his hands away and goes to stand with Vanessa and Eliza.

"Just waiting for Zevraiel," I tell them as I text the angel. Dead rising is their fucking department.

Vanessa speaks quietly, her voice rough, like she's forcing the words out. "This is impossible, right? She was dead. Rose killed her. We all know this."

"That's what we thought," Shane says.

"The Divine's punishing us…" Crystal's voice is just above a whisper. Out of all of us, she hated this the most. Crystal wanted no part in it. She hated what we did, hated the blood oath we took to cover it up. This is her worst nightmare.

This is all of our worst nightmares coming to life.

Noah wasn't the only one who died six years ago. His Mate did too. Now Izabella Craving is back.

73 PLAYTIME

Rosella Craving

January 1

Cristobal slows the SUV as the two-lane road turns uneven, tires jarring against potholes and scattered gravel. The warehouse ahead is old, abandoned, with cracked windows and boarded doors.

But there are two black SUVs already parked, waiting.

Cristobal leans forward with his hand braced against the seat in front of him. "I don't like this," he mutters, dark eyes scanning the lot.

"It's fine," I answer softly, even though I'm really confused as to why I'm here, but I tell my bodyguards again, "Remember, this is off the books."

Cristobal pulls in front of the two SUVs, before he turns the engine off. Franklin doesn't hesitate, stepping out first. His shoes crunch against the gravel, scanning the area as he buttons his suit jacket. He opens my door as Cristobal rounds the SUV to come to stand close by me.

At the same moment, the doors to both of the SUVs swing open. Bodyguards dressed similar to mine step out. Then Liam does too.

He's dressed in a long black coat buttoned tight against the evening chill, leather gloves catching the dying light. His blond hair is a mess as usual, his usual smirk plastered on his face as he nears.

"Veyara," he says, closing the distance with unhurried strides. He bends just enough to brush his lips against my cheek, a formal greeting that's foreign to me.

Up close, his eyes linger on me, scanning every inch as if cataloging changes the past months might've caused.

"You look good, little wolf," he flashes me a grin, openly checking out my outfit. There's nothing to see. I'm in my Warrior uniform which is what I wore to the caves. I didn't go home to change when Liam texted.

I smile back. "So do you."

This place isn't our usual rendezvous spots. Not an underground, neon-lit, sultry club or a hotel room.

"Finally playing out your fantasy of letting me kidnap you then?" he asks me, raising a brow.

"Well, you kidnapped someone—wasn't me," I smirk at him, before nodding to the warehouse. "He's in there?"

"Yeah, fucking pain in the ass," Liam says.

Franklin and Cristobal stay close as Liam guides me inside. I stay close to him, our footsteps echoing.

"Heard the Veyara Gala was an event not to be missed," he says, making small talk.

"It was a fun night," I smile at him, not really wanting to talk about one of the best nights I've had with Josh with Liam, so I ask him, "how was your Samhain?"

He stops just long enough for the dim light to catch his handsome profile, "Isn't that why we're here?"

One of his men pushes open a heavy steel door. The hinges scream, and the scent of rust and old water floods my senses.

Liam goes in first, and I follow as I take in the scene before me.

There's a vampire boy in a school uniform gagged and tied to a chair in the center of the room. Light brown hair falls over his forehead, caramel eyes burning more fury than pain in them. Silver shackles bite into his wrists and ankles, glinting faintly where they cut the skin. Around him, a ring of black salt marks the floor and a pentacle is scrawled beneath him.

Recognition flickers in his eyes as I approach, slipping my hands halfway into my pockets, my blue Warrior cape flying behind me. I cross the ring of black salt, my heeled, pointed-toed, leather boots scrape against the concrete as I come to stand beside Liam.

"Hello, Zak," I say to him.

Liam flicks a hand, and one of his guards steps forward to rip the gag from Zak's mouth. The boy coughs, then smirks, black blood at the corner of his lips.

"Oh, you're so fucking dead, Liam," Zak growls at his prince.

The Xandelskye family are proud Soul Snatchers—they're leaders of the Soul Snatchers. Zak's grandfather is the one who married The Cursed One like they mentioned in Romania. Zak is his prodigy.

Zak has some answering to do.

Liam's gloved hands flex once before he strips them off, exposing pale fingers that look deceptively delicate. He shrugs off his coat and drops it into his guard's hands. Then he rolls his black sleeves up, revealing the forearms I used to grip, veins and muscle shifting beneath his skin. In this moment, he looks every bit the deadly vampire mercenary he's known to be.

"We need to talk. You lied to me," I say to Zak, narrowing my eyes.

"Everyone lied to you, bitch. Wake up!" He rolls his eyes.

Liam doesn't hesitate as he steps over the black salt barrier, his shoes grinding the ring as he crouches low in front of Zak. I don't think I've ever seen Liam's eyes so icy gray. Then Liam stands and punches Zak in the face, the sound echoing in the space around us.

"Why don't you tell the Veyara exactly what you were up to on Samhain?" Liam says to Zak.

Zak just spits right in Liam's face.

The tension spikes through the room, my security shifting, Franklin's hand tightens on his weapon. Liam just wipes the spit away with the back of his hand, unbothered. That calm makes my stomach knot tighter. Liam isn't playing games. He doesn't even seem to be enjoying this like the sadistic killer I've heard he can be.

"I'm not saying shit," Zak sneers, silver chains rattling as he pulls against them. Liam grabs him by the throat, just hold him there.

Zak only laughs, "Kinky."

Liam punches him again.

Zak laughs again, even with black blood running down his mouth. His caramel eyes lock on mine. "Did you miss your sister, Veyara?" Zak asks, mockingly.

"Sister?" I ask in return, confused, staring at Zak before looking at Liam, "What does that mean?"

Zak throws his head back, laughter booming in the space, "Oh, this is fucking rich—I thought you were Nathanial's favorite. He didn't tell you shit!"

This time it isn't Liam's fist that cracks across Zak's jaw, it's mine. The vampire boy slumps against his chains, still laughing, though black blood smears his teeth.

When I turn back to Liam, his face is carved from stone, unreadable. My chest tightens as I take him in like this—every inch a killer.

But so am I.

"What you're about to hear," Liam says, calmly but his tone is gentler for me, "will shock you."

"It's toooooo laaaaaaaaate," Zak sings behind me. "She's already there."

"Be straight with me, Liam," I say, ignoring Zak. I'm tired of being in the dark not knowing what is going on. I asked to kidnap Zak so I could ask him some questions, not for Zak to be tied up and still have the upper hand. I cross my arms and ask Liam, "What sister is he talking about?"

His eyes soften, and he takes a slow breath, "First, I need to be honest with you."

"You've always been honest with me," I say, stepping closer to him.

He has. He's never sheltered me from the truth, never sugar-coated anything. He's always treated me like I was worth knowing everything, that I wasn't too young or too naïve.

He's never questioned my decisions and he's the only other person, aside from Cristobal and Franklin, who really knows me. Liam also would never put me at risk or danger.

It's why I trusted him with this—despite knowing I shouldn't be having secret meetings with an ex-lover as the Veyara, and especially not after things just got back on track with Josh.

A small smile ghosts across his lips. He looks at Zak briefly, then his focus is back on me. "When vampires drink each other's blood during sex, they create a mind link that lasts until one of them dies—like how shifters communicate telepathically. But it's more…it's frowned upon," Liam starts as he walks up to me, "but being part of the First Family, when I drink someone's blood, anyone's, I gain access to all of their memories."

"I know that," I remind him, softly, "you told me the first time."

He nods, the faintest curve of a sad smile tugging at his lips. "I know, I remember."

I do too. The night we decided to explore it—for him to drink from me while we had sex or after—any time, really. Liam made sure I knew what I was getting into, what it meant and how it'd affect me. How addicting will it be…I can't help but look at his lips, craving his bite one more time.

Liam's voice pulls me back. "What I didn't tell you," he says slowly, "is that I also have access to memories that have been suppressed. Even wiped. Memories or experiences aren't so easily removed from our beings. They are a part of us, live in our bones, so even when the mind is made to forget, the body and soul still remember. Which is why when I drink someone else's blood, I know everything there is to know about a person. Past, present, and forgotten."

A chill runs down my spine. My hands feel cold even as my pulse races. I take a step closer to him and ask, "What are you saying?"

Can he give me my memories back?

"Hold on," Zak interrupts and from the corner of my eye I can see he's eerily still, "you two are a *thing*?"

The words barely register and neither Liam nor I pay Zak any attention. I can't look away from Liam.

He keeps his eyes on me as he says, "You were a twin, Rose."

74 GHOSTS

Josh Hunter

January 1

The angel, Zevraiel, joins us. He teleports in right as we're walking to Izabella's cell. Crystal flinches at his sudden presence, edging closer to Devaughn.

Zevraiel is a large man with black hair that's cropped short and magnificent pitch-black wings that he doesn't care to ever hide. His eyes are black holes—not dark brown, black. I've never understood how Nephilim are born with purple eyes when the angels who sire have black ones. Maybe it's the magic, or the biogenetics of an angel and another species procreating.

"Thank you for coming so quickly," Shane says to him as we go through the series of security to get to the vault-like cell Izabella is kept in.

"Where is it?" Zevraiel asks, turning those black eyes on me, since I'm the one who called him. I've never seen him have any emotion really. It's like he's made of stone. Even vampires have more reactions and tells.

It's interesting that he keeps referring to Izabella as *it.*

As if reading my mind, he says, "The dead don't come back to life. Whatever is in your dungeon, it's not what it was when it was alive. You can't treat it as such."

"So why raise the dead?" Eliza questions no one in particular.

"Oh, there are benefits to raising the dead," Zevraiel says. "When the dead come back, while they don't have any powers, they are…a different kind of vampire. They feed on magic."

"If they don't have powers or the ability to perform magic, why would they feed on it?" James glances at him over Vanessa's head.

He attempts to walk beside me but it's not working so I hang back, respecting his wings. Besides, this dungeon hallway is not wide enough.

"So the one who raised them can channel it from them," Zev answers.

"They're conduits," I exhale.

"Yes," he replies.

"Are they dangerous?" Shane asks, looking back at him. I'm tall, but standing next to Zevraiel makes me feel uncomfortable. He has at least eight to ten inches on me. He has to be over seven feet and the wings don't help. He's not hard to miss.

"They can be," Zevraiel answers, "whoever raised them has direct access to them at all times. They're merely puppets—they just look very real."

"Fuck," Shane mumbles. Devaughn and I exchange looks. Trojan fucking horse.

"It's not every day I get a message that someone's back from the dead. Even in my world," Zevraiel comments.

"Is necromancy not real then?" Crystal looks at the angel curiously. She would be, being a strong healer.

"It is real. It just isn't what most believe it to be. It's a very advanced level of spirit magic—not many have the capability to possess it."

"What does it entail? How does one come to wield it then?" I ask, curiously, thinking of what Rose told me about Zak Xandelskye.

Zevraiel glances at me before he says, "Someone who's been kissed by death, but brought back immediately. It's a little more than a coma—the body flatlined—but the soul was pulled back."

"Kind of like if you were drowning and someone pulls you out of the water?" Eliza questions.

"If you had drowned, someone pulls you out of the water, and resuscitates you, yes," Zevraiel answers, "but even then, not all spirit users can do it."

"There aren't many amongst the vampires—are there witches who practice it?" Devaughn asks, frowning.

No one answers.

James places his palm on a digital reader. I hear it prick him before the vault door unlocks and we step through.

It's dark in here, aside from the strip of blue light guiding us. It's quiet too.

"Shane?" a quiet child's voice echoes down the narrow hallway and we all freeze. I've made my way to the front of the group and Shane glances at me. I shrug.

"Shit's creepy as fuck," Devaughn telepaths me and I can't agree more.

She speaks again. "Shane, get me out of here! I don't like it!"

"Fuck, she sounds the same," Vanessa says, under her breath.

Rose and Izabella were almost identical twins—Rose has gray eyes while Izabella had pale blue, and Izabella's voice is just a bit deeper. There was always an edge to Izabella's voice, but she was always sick which made her voice raspy.

Suddenly, I get the urge to see my Mate. Anxiety courses through me as we near the cell.

Shane walks up to the bars of a cell where a small girl is already standing and waiting for us.

"I don't like this at all," Devaughn telepaths me and I glance at him, before looking at the girl in front of us. She looks just like Izabella did, but like she spent days in the woods. Her black hair is matted and tangled. Her gray dress looks new, just dirty. She could use a shower with all the dirt on her pale skin. Izabella was always pale with her magic depletion.

"Please, Shane," she chokes out a sob, keeping her eyes on Shane. "Please let me out."

Shane maintains his emotionless expression, but his eyes narrow slightly.

Zevraiel takes a step toward her, and we give him the space. Izabella's eyes widen and she retreats into the cell.

"Who raised you?" Zevraiel asks. She huddles into the farthest corner of the cell, shrinking down, and tucking her knees close to her chest before covering her ears to block out any sound.

"Who. Raised. You." Zevraiel repeats.

"Mistress. I want my Mistress," she starts mumbling and I look at Shane.

"You're not in the position to make any demands, little girl," Zevraiel replies. "Who sent you here?"

"Mistress! Mistress! Mistress! Mistress! Mistress! Mistress!" Izabella starts repeating and with each time, her voice rings louder.

"Who is your Mistress?" Zevraiel asks and I take a step closer.

"Mistress! Mistress! Mistress! Mis—"

"Who is your Mistress?"

She looks up and starts screaming.

Zevraiel doesn't stay long after the screaming, but he does say he'll ask around and keep his ears open for anything Lilith related. Lucifer's not a fan of his daughter—to put it lightly. Zevraiel said the angels will assist in any way they can.

He also said to keep Izabella in the cell and, if we decide to let Rose see her, to make sure Rose isn't alone with her. That was never going to happen anyway. I don't care how powerful Rose is.

"Have Crystal strengthen protection on everyone," Shane says to Eliza, then fixes his stern gaze on me. "Can I trust you to make the right calls where Rose is involved?"

I stare back at him. Can he? Should he? It's what the Elders were afraid of from the beginning with two Warriors in a Mating bond. If it ever came down to picking the fate of the world or Rose, can he trust me to do my duty to serve and protect shifterkind?

The silence is deafening and the answer is obvious.

Mating bonds are sacred.

There's nothing above a Mating bond.

"That's not fair," Eliza says, cutting in and Shane turns his hard look from me to her. She doesn't falter. "You know he will. Rose is your sister—and you've done a lot of off the record things to protect her. She's his Mate. You might be blood bound to her, but he's soul bound."

I'm never going to tell her, but I respect her for putting Shane in his place.

My phone lights up with a text message. I look at it and my face hardens. My friends give me questioning looks.

"Is it her?" Shane asks me.

"No…but I have to go," I tell them, and leave before they can ask any more questions.

"Get the jet ready," I telepath to Cole.

75 RECKLESS BEHAVIOR

Rosella Craving
January 2

"That's impossible," I whisper, staring into Liam's gray eyes.

"It's true," Zak says, sounding almost bored, like all of this is an inconvenience to the Xandelskye heir.

I keep my attention on Liam. "I don't have a twin. I think I'd know if I did."

Unless my twin died like Eliza's baby…

Oh my Divine.

Liam closes the distance between us. His cold hands take mine into his, and only then do I realize my hands are trembling. I can't stop shaking. He's so close to me as he asks, "Have I ever lied to you?"

"No," I answer automatically. He never has.

"Her name was Izabella. She was born with a magical deficiency. Her magic was…depleting. Nothing anyone did helped. Her condition had no cure because it was curse-born," Liam tells me gently, "you were the stronger twin, she was the weaker."

The words crush me. My chest caves as the truth presses down on me. My mind goes to Shane and Eliza's babies.

"I killed her, didn't I?" I whisper, very aware of Zak watching me right now. "The weaker twin always dies at the hands of the stronger," I repeat to Liam what I told Josh when Eliza lost one of the twins. "That's why my powers are so strange, why I'm so strong. The curse of the twins…it promises this."

My mind races to the conversation Josh and I had at the dock right after we learned about the miscarriage. We were talking about the curse of the twins, and I told him about their powers. Josh asked me, *powers like yours?*

I knew he was keeping something from me that night. I knew there was more to it when he mentioned my power. It was in his eyes.

Liam shakes his head gently, pulling me in. His arms wrap around me, and for a moment I let myself be comforted—though the shock doesn't allow me to truly feel anything. I don't know how to process all this right now.

They're telling me I have a sister I have no recollection of. How do you erase a whole person? I remember Noah even if I don't remember the circumstances around his death. I don't remember having a twin at all. Is that why Shane's so against me using my powers?

"It's *why* you're the Mistress of Darkness," Zak says.

"You were close to her," Liam murmurs against my hair, continuing, "best friends. It broke you to see her in pain. It was making her do strange things until one night she killed someone. She wasn't herself and everyone knew it—she knew it. Izabella asked you to end it for her. A mercy death."

"A mercy death?" I choke out, shaking my head and asking him. "When—how old was I? I have no memory of any of this...how?"

Liam strokes my cheek. "You were both twelve."

The number slices through me as if he took a knife to my heart. My eyes widen as my hand flies up to cover my gasp, "Did—did I kill Noah Hunter?"

Liam looks at me with such sad eyes, but before he can answer, Zak groans dramatically, "That's all touching. Really. Can we wrap it up?"

I look at him, then at Liam, composing myself. I'm here on a mission. I can't let Liam's kidnapping of the Xandelskye heir be for nothing. This could start a war if it gets messy. I ask Liam, "What does my twin have to do with Zak?"

Liam's expression darkens, every inch the killer again. His jaw clenches, "*Zak* resurrected Izabella on Samhain."

The words steal the air from my lungs. I stare at him, not sure if I even heard right. "Can we do that? Resurrect people?"

"It's black magic," Liam's voice is clipped, grim.

"To you," Zak mumbles through his split lip that's not healing thanks to the silver shackles.

"Why?" I turn to Zak and ask. "Why would Zak do that?"

Liam's gaze shifts to the tied vampire. "That's why we're here, Veyara. To figure out why." Liam leaves me to return inside the circle. His voice is calm, but it cuts like a blade as he speaks to Zak, "The Veyara's all caught up. Now it's your turn to talk."

"Is that what you used our power for?" I ask Zak, frowning. No one told me anything about resurrection. I thought we were waking

Isis and opening portals.

Zak spits more black blood onto the concrete floor. The sound is wet, ugly, and it makes my powers itch. His caramel eyes move from Liam to me.

"Go to Hell," Zak sneers at us, chains rattling as he shifts his weight. "I'm not telling you shit."

Liam doesn't flinch. He crouches slightly, leveling with Zak, and says in a tone so soft it gives me chills, "Then guess you're coming with me."

Liam moves before I can blink. His hand snakes out, clamping around Zak's jaw with bruising force. I hear the sharp crack as Liam wrenches his head sideways until bone snaps. Zak lets out a strangled sound, then laughter bubbles through it.

Liam tilts Zak's head back into place with casual precision, then sinks his nails into Zak's shoulder. Even worse than an original's fangs are their claws. Vampires don't have claws, but Liam and his brothers…their claws are just as deadly as their fangs. Their claws don't carry any addictive poison. Their claws are pure weapons.

The sound is obscene. Zak's groan caught somewhere between pain and a hiss. I don't know why but my heart lurches. He's fucked up, but he's still just a kid…

Liam's voice is low, terrifyingly calm as he retracts his monstrous nails. "I'll heal you. And then I'll do it again. As many times as it takes. The choice is yours."

Zak coughs, spits more black blood onto the floor, then laughs again, weaker this time. "Fuck you and your shifter slut."

My power acts as a punch and slams into Zak's stomach, brutally. Zak jerks against the chains, choking on blood, gasping like a drowning man. Liam doesn't stop me and I don't look around—I'm utterly focused on Zak, predator locked on prey.

"Talk," Liam says flatly.

Zak wheezes, his grin distorted by the swelling already appearing on his face. "Not a chance."

I strike again, a sharp punch to the ribs. The crack echoes. Zak groans, sagging in the chains, and then Liam sinks his nails in again, Zak screams again. Zak's body jerks, but then the wounds vanish, healed by the same person that caused them.

"You'll heal," Liam says, his tone smooth, almost soothing, "and then I'll start again. I don't make empty promises, Zak."

But Zak holds out for hours. I actually start getting a little worried.

"Tell us why you brought Izabella back," I ask him. "Why her? Why not someone else's dead sibling?"

Zak is a wreck. His head hangs heavy, his face a ruined canvas of split lips, bruised cheeks, blood dried thick around his mouth and chin. His eyes are shut, lashes clumped together from sweat and blood. He trembles against the chains, whether from fear or pain, I can't tell.

I crouch in front of him, close enough that the scent of his blood burns my nose. My hands hover, then settle lightly over his ribs, over the torn skin that Liam had shredded moments ago. I gently press my hand to his side and let my darkness into him, purifying his wounds. Zak shudders under the touch, a soft groan slipping out as the agony dulls.

When his eyes flicker open, hazy caramel through swollen lids, I meet them without flinching. I try in a gentler tone. "Tell us what we need to know," I say softly, my voice more a whisper than a command, "if you don't, Liam won't stop. He'll break you, heal you, and do it again. You've seen what he'll do. You haven't seen what I can do and trust me, Zak, you don't want to."

His lips twitch into a weak sneer, but it doesn't hold.

I stroke his jaw gently. "It doesn't have to be that way. You can end this. Just tell us why you brought Izabella back and what you needed my power for. How exactly did you open the portal?"

Zak swallows, his throat working, the sound audible in the quiet. He shakes his head slightly, but it feels more like hesitation than refusal.

"You can make this stop. Right now. Just say it, Zak. Tell us and it's over," I murmur, lowering my voice to almost nothing.

His breath shudders out, shallow and broken. For the first time, the mocking light in his eyes dims, replaced by something almost innocent—childlike.

Behind me, I can feel Liam's presence like a storm barely restrained, his silence more dangerous than his blows. He's letting me try this even though I'm undoing all our work.

Zak finally lifts his head a fraction, lips parting, his voice hoarse, "You...you don't understand what you're..."

I lean in closer, my hand still warm against his chest, steady and sure even though my heart hammers. "Then make me understand. Why did you bring her back? Spirit is your magical ability. Are you a necromancer?"

I still want to know how he has black blood.

Zak lets out a broken rasp of laughter, though his head tilts toward me as if he can't help it. "Necromancer…guess at this point you could call me that."

Liam's voice drops low, dangerous, "Why, Zak?"

The boy's smirk curdles into something bitter, losing any of that innocence I just saw. He snaps, "Because this world is shit! And it's time for a new one."

For a moment, silence spreads through the warehouse. I feel Liam's eyes on me, disbelief tightening the air between us. Zak can't be serious.

"Aren't you like fourteen?" Liam asks him, sounding as confused as I feel, "What of this shit world have you even seen?"

It's a valid question, especially coming from someone nearly a thousand years old. If Liam told me he wanted the world to change and that it was time, I would've listened to what he had to say. But Zak?

Zak's eyes burn with conviction now, his voice rising with venom, "Aren't you tired of it? Living in the shadows, in secret, like you're ashamed of what you are? When we're the superior species?" he jerks against the silver shackles, the chains groaning. "Everyone's been lying to us. To all of us." His gaze lands on me, sharp enough to cut. "You've been lied to your whole life, Rose. Your powers—" he spits the word like a weapon, "—are a gift. You could fucking overthrow Nathanial if you wanted to."

I stare at him. Overthrow Nathanial? Isn't he working with the monarchs?

Zak turns his glare to Liam, "And you—you should be the true king. How long will you wait? You're fifth in line, but you're the only one who's ever seen the world for what it should be." His teeth flash bloody. "Join me. Both of you."

The blow comes fast. Liam's fist slams into Zak's cheek, snapping his head back. Blood sprays out.

"Stop trying to recruit us, dumbass," Liam snarls, voice rough with loathing, "tell us why you resurrected Izabella."

Zak coughs blood, but he's still smiling, savage and taunting, "It was never about Izabella, why the fuck would it be?" he rasps. His gaze slides back to me, "It was always about Rose, the Mistress of

Darkness."

My pulse hammers so loud I can barely hear anything else.

Liam's fangs drop, his voice coming out a growl, "What do you mean?"

Zak licks the blood off his lip, savoring the moment. "Her power isn't dark—but it could be. It's ancient, older than any of you," Zak says to Liam, then turns to me. "Isis can only be awakened when there is a set of female Craving twins—one of them stronger than the other. I needed your power yes, but I also needed your blood as a connection to Izabella to raise her. Raising Izabella provided us with that opportunity again. Bringing her back also opened the portal Lilith wanted. It's a chance for you to be even greater if you know how to work with it."

"Why? Why would anyone do that—for me? Who are you working for?"

"Like I said, it's time for a change," Zak repeats.

"What kind of change? What do you want with Rose?" Liam demands.

Everything Zak is saying aligns mostly with what Nathanial told me. Nathanial just left out the part where we were bringing back my dead twin—and the fact that I even had a twin. Why would Nathanial do that? What's it to him if I knew that piece of information? Why not just tell me and erase my memory of it? But he did neither.

Zak just leans back, chains rattling, and smiles with bloodied teeth, before he says to me, "Mates are sacred, aren't they?"

I narrow my eyes at him. "You're a vampire. You don't believe in Mates."

Liam's voice is low, as he says, "Vampires can have Mates." I turn to look at him, and he sighs heavily, explaining, "Vampires don't have Mates the way shifters do. But—" his throat works, his eyes never leaving mine, "—on occasion, two vampires can be. It's rare, but it can happen. It's why I've never taken a wife."

We talked about this. If he was ever married or wanted to take a wife like his brothers had. He never committed to the idea. He never showed any lack or desire for more with anyone. Liam was always so easy to be with, to talk to, to escape with—I always wondered why he didn't want to take a wife and have that all the time. Without the sneaking around.

The thought never occurred to me that maybe he was waiting for his Mate.

It's bittersweet to think about Liam with someone else—a true Mate. I know he has other female friends to keep up his very single, very playboy, very reckless reputation—that's never bothered me, not like how it did when Josh was with others.

I know what Liam and I have is different from his flings. I know if I ever needed him, he'd drop everything and come. I know he'd kill for me. I know he loves me, probably more than I can ever love him. But a true Mate would be different.

I love Liam enough to want that for him. I know I will never be able to give him that, he knows it too. Still, through all of it—even knowing I was bound to Josh—Liam has never treated me as expendable. Never treated me like less. Never made me feel replaceable.

Which is why I will always believe him. Trust him.

Zak watches us both, through the mess of blood and bruises. "You can't stop the inevitable," he says finally. "The world as you know it—it's already over."

The words echo through the warehouse, and the silence that follows feels heavier than the chains on him. It's exactly the same thing Nathanial said.

"Gag him," Liam orders flatly. His men move without hesitation, shoving the gag back between Zak's bloody teeth. The boy growls against it, eyes burning, but his words are muffled now, strangled into silence as one of the guards injects him with something. Zak goes limp.

Liam doesn't spare him another glance. He brushes past, his hand closing lightly around my own, guiding me toward the warehouse doors. Our security fall into formation instantly.

"Let's get out of here," Liam says to me. "I'm staying at a cabin not too far." I hesitate, and he notices the pause and turns my face to him, his fingers chilly against my chin. "Hey, just to talk this out."

"I don't know, Liam…if they notice I'm gone for too long—"

"You'll be back before Sunrise. I'll teleport you if I have to," he assures me.

I give him an amused smile. "All three of us? Franklin's a big guy."

Liam snorts, a small spark of the man I'm used to, slipping through. "I said teleport, not carry, but I can do that too."

I let out a laugh even though it feels so wrong after what we just learned inside. I turn to my bodyguards. "Let's go," I say to them, my phone pinging with the location.

76 FOUR

Rosella Craving

January 2

The cabin is larger than I expected, tucked in the woods like something out of a painting, smoke curling lazily from the stone chimney. It smells like the woods, even inside.

I take it in with a slow sweep of my gaze, wondering how Liam even knew a place like this existed in the Middle of Nowhere, New York. Before I can ask, he answers, like he always does when my thoughts are too loud.

"I own it," he says casually, slipping my coat off and hanging it on the rack by the door. "If it wasn't so out of the way, I would've brought you here."

I almost smile. Of course, Liam would have a hidden cabin in the woods, a place to disappear when the weight of being who he is gets too heavy.

"It's…cozy," I say, stepping in further. Even though it's warm, I get goosebumps so I rub my arms.

He gestures toward the couch. "Get comfortable. You've had a crazy night."

I lower myself onto the worn leather, the cushions sighing beneath me. I look around, my eyes searching.

Across the room, Liam pulls a dark bottle from a cabinet and uncorks it with ease. The scent hits immediately, making my throat suddenly very dry for it. It's bloodwine. He pours two glasses and brings them over, setting one gently in front of me before sinking into the armchair beside me.

The distance between us is intentional. Not too far, but not close either. It reminds me that things are different now, that they *have to be.*

I cradle the glass, watching the flames in the fireplace dance. For a moment, I don't know whether I should drink, if it's such a good idea to drink with him right now.

I lift my eyes to him, to the man who knows too much about me, who's seen more of me than anyone else. Yet here he sits, in an armchair instead of beside me, holding himself back in a way that aches—but I love that about him. I know he won't let me cross any lines if that's not what I want. Things are different now than they were in Romania.

"I don't know where to even begin," I admit softly, my voice barely above the crackle of the fire. "Who else knows about Izabella being back? How long have you known about it?"

Liam's elbows are braced against his knees, staring into the fire as he decides to tell me. Then his head turns to me and he says, "My nephew, Jules. Jesse Zeviyanta. And Elena Montenaj—she saw Zak bring Izabella back," he exhales, "and a whole swarm of Soul Snatchers who put him up to it. From what Elena said, all the Soul Snatcher leaders were present Samhain night."

"You haven't told your brothers?" I ask, curiously.

"Not until we know more. You know Darren, he's…serious," Liam sips his wine.

"All of your brothers are serious," I tell him thinking of the meeting in Romania where I met them all for the first time.

Liam lets out a laugh, giving me an amused look. "They're not serious, Rose. They're ancient."

I laugh and Liam joins in. It's true. Jerome and Jarrod are as old as Theron Daevryn, going back thousands of years.

When the laughter dies down, I say, "Zak's story aligns mostly with Nathanial's. I believe him. He wasn't lying. But I don't understand why Lilith would want me to be powerful. I know why Nathanial does."

Liam nods, a dark, cold look taking over his features. There's history there. He knows The Cursed One personally.

His gaze cuts to mine, so sharp it nearly steals my breath. "You need to be careful. Lilith wouldn't just do something that helps you be more powerful unless she had a plan for you."

Zak said so as much.

Overthrow Nathanial.

It makes sense if Nathanial wants to raise Isis to kill Lilith. I recall the meeting with the monarchs, and Nathanial was careful with his words. He never said Isis would die killing Lilith. He just mentioned she would, so I could be the Eternal Queen. Does Lilith think she's helping him take down his own wife? Does she think Nathanial is on her side?

Nathanial has only ever been on one side—his own.

"I knew about the portal," I say to Liam.

"I know. I drank your blood in Romania," Liam says. He drags a hand through his blond hair. He looks…tired. It's a rare look for him and I've only seen it a handful of times on nights we did nothing but talk in bed.

"Do you know what he's talking about? I didn't know we believed in such things…"

"I don't believe in multiverses. No evidence of it. So the only thing I can think of is the world between…"

My pulse quickens as I ask, "Purgatory?" The phrase tastes wrong on my tongue.

He shakes his head. "No. It's different. A realm…not unlike where spirits linger. But it isn't the same, they walk parallel to us—or that's what's believed."

I wait, silently begging him to keep going, but his jaw tightens instead.

"I need to look into it more," he admits, voice low. "Elena suggested something—something disturbing. I thought she was reaching. But now…" his eyes shadow. "I can't rule it out."

Fear prickles down my spine from just his tone. "What was it? Can I help?"

He studies me, long enough to make my breath hitch, before answering. "For now—look into your family history. Anything that stands out. Look into the curse of the twins. Hell, look into all the curses."

Craeven Curses. The book that caught my eye at Coilspire.

I sigh and reach for the chains around my neck, before pulling the necklaces out. I hold up one of the pendants and ask him, "Do you know what this symbol means?"

Liam leans forward and shakes his head. "Should I?"

I shrug, "Thought I'd ask. It's probably not related."

Maybe I'm just being paranoid, thinking everything's connected. Maybe it is.

"I know this was a lot," Liam starts.

"Is there any way I can get my memories back?" I ask, barely above a whisper.

His expression twists with sorrow, the predator in him dimmed by something painfully human. "We can memory-walk. But the amount of my blood you'd have to drink will—"

"—it'll kill me," I finish for him, my stomach dropping. Vampire blood is poison to shifters—especially if it's drunk straight.

The silence between us is heavy, broken only by the faint crackle of the fire. His words turn inside me as his gaze holds mine like it always has—truthful, unflinching, devastating.

There has to be another way.

My head is spinning with everything that's come to light since yesterday. I swallow hard and force the words out before they choke me. "Did I kill Noah Hunter?"

Liam frowns. "No. No—Rose, you did not kill Noah," Liam tells me, looking disturbed that I even asked. "Noah's death…was tragic and unfortunate."

Why would Josh accuse me of it then? If I didn't kill Noah, why is Josh convinced that I did when everyone keeps saying I didn't?

Then there are Zak's taunts echoing in the back of my mind—his conviction, his rage, his certainty that the world as we know it is already done.

"Maybe…maybe Zak's right," I sigh, taking a sip of the wine.

"Say what now?" Liam's head snaps toward me.

"Not in the way he said. But in our own way," I lift my chin, though my heart stutters in my chest, "maybe it *is* time for a change. Because this?" My voice softens, frays. "Living in the dark, fighting the same war with humans, being bound by secrets and curses—is ridiculous."

The dangerous words hang between us.

Liam doesn't answer. Not at first. His silence is thick, stretching too long. His gaze drifts away, toward the window where the night presses against the glass and snow sits around the edges. I wonder what he's thinking. Maybe of the centuries he's had to live and endure in the dark. Centuries of hiding in plain sight—constantly reinventing himself.

Something inside me aches at the distance, needing to comfort him. Slowly, I reach across the narrow space, my fingers brushing his arm in quiet comfort.

He exhales, like he was holding his breath until I broke the moment and touched him. His other hand moves and cold fingers lace with mine.

"Where'd you go?" I ask, softly.

He meets my eyes and gives me a soft smile. "Too many lifetimes," he murmurs, "we'd be here all night."

I squeeze his hand. His gaze drops to our joined fingers, and we sit like that for a while, the fire popping quietly while the snow taps against the windowpanes.

When I finally speak again, my voice is too quiet. "Why didn't you tell me before…about Izabella?"

His jaw tightens. Then he turns his armchair, bringing it closer to me until he cups my face with a gentleness that hurts more than the comfort he's trying to provide.

"Because it didn't matter before." His eyes are soft and honest. "Izabella was dead. You didn't need the burden of knowing you killed your sister, even if it was mercy. You couldn't cope with it after she passed. That's why your memories were…" he swallows, thumb brushing the edge of my jaw. "They were taken."

"I know," I tell him and he pulls back, but his hands come down to hold mine.

"You know?" he asks, watching me.

I nod. "It's been a crazy few months." I hold up the necklaces again and tell him, "These helped. I'm still figuring it all out. I have most of my memories back, except for the night Noah Hunter died and Izabella's existence—but then I guess I won't know how many other memories are really missing…"

Liam is quiet as he focuses on my necklaces again. I don't see any flicker of recognition on his face, just curiosity.

"Liam?" I ask. "Who took my memories?"

He still doesn't say anything.

"Tell me, Liam." My voice sharpens, desperate for answers. I know it's not fair to ask him, knowing I'm putting him on the spot. This isn't his problem, but he's the only person who won't lie to me. "Who did it?"

His eyes close for the barest second, as if the truth is too much. "Rose…"

"Don't," I cut him off, my voice breaking. "You've never lied to me. Don't start now."

"I won't lie to you, but I don't want to hurt you either."

"Please Liam," I say to him, pleading. "I need to know. I have to get my memories back. I want you to…"

For a long, aching moment, he doesn't move. Then at last, his voice breaks with each word heavy as he speaks. "Your parents thought it was best for you because of how much you were hurting."

"My parents did this to me? They took my memories from me?" I ask, shocked and confused. The thought never even occurred to me.

Liam hesitates before shaking his head. "No." His hold on my hands tightens, but I don't let him look away. He genuinely looks like he's in pain as he says, "It took four Warriors to do it."

The air in my lungs feels strangled. "Which four?"

His eyes flicker with sorrow, as though saying it aloud will break me. His voice is so quiet as he says, "You know which four."

"I need to hear it," I whisper, tears already rolling hot down my cheeks.

Liam exhales, his hands falling away from me as the names slice me apart. "Shane. James. Devaughn. And—"

A door to one of the rooms opens, startling me. I look up and find Josh standing on the other side before he says, "And me."

77 FOR US

Rosella Craving

January 2

I stare at my Mate. I felt the bond tug the second I walked into the cabin, but I thought there was no way he could be here.

How is he here?

Josh and Liam are both watching me. I don't know what to even say right now.

"Izabella is at Cravenhold," Josh supplies, causing Liam to look at him.

"What? Why?" Liam asks him.

"I don't give a shit about Izabella!" I exclaim, standing up, my eyes focused on Josh. "How are you here?"

Josh narrows his eyes slightly, before he walks up to us. "I'm sorry, did I interrupt date night with your lover?"

I stare at him.

The crazy thing is—I don't feel guilty at all. One, Liam and I weren't doing anything wrong tonight. Two, good, he finally knows.

Liam stands up, ignoring both of us, and goes to pour a stiffer drink than the bloodwine we've been having.

"You've been here this whole time," I say to Josh.

"Yes," Josh answers as he comes to stand right in front of me. He's inches away and he's…calm. I don't feel the heat that usually radiates off him when he's angry. Even his face is relaxed.

"How…?"

"Who's Mate did you think you were?" he asks me. "Do I need to remind you who the fuck I am? I always know where you are. *Always.*"

I inhale sharply. He has a tracker on me. Mating bonds are natural trackers, but I don't think that's what he's referring to, especially since he hasn't Marked me yet.

"How are you *here?*" I emphasize, staring into his gray eyes. I don't know how to feel about any of this. I just found out he helped wipe the memories of the one night he's been holding over me. What the fuck?

"Liam and I were supposed to interrogate Zak Xandelskye," Josh says to me and my eyebrows rise.

"Liam and you?" I ask slowly.

"But then you said you wanted to play," Liam cuts in. He's made himself a drink and is sitting on the edge of a couch.

"So I thought it'd be best if you went instead," Josh continues.

"Hold on," I blink, looking between the two men, "what is this?"

Liam clicks his jaw and drops his gaze, while Josh watches him before turning back to me. He looks at me too, like he's reading me.

"Liam and I've been working together for four years," Josh answers me and my mind starts spinning.

Four years. *Four years?!*

That's before Liam and I met.

I look at Liam. "We didn't meet accidentally, did we?"

"Rose—"

"There's a way to get your memories back," Josh cuts him off, and I tear my eyes away from a conflicted Liam. I can't deal with that right now.

"How?" I ask. I have to get my memories back. I have to know what happened, and then I'll deal with this mess.

"Is that what you want? Are you sure?" Josh asks.

I frown. "Of course. I told you. I'll do anything…"

Josh looks at Liam, who doesn't give anything away. Then Josh leans in and kisses my forehead and says, "Sit down and I'll tell you."

"You've known this whole time…" I say quietly as we sit.

Josh reaches for my hand, and I try to pull away, but he won't let me. He holds up a finger to me, sternly. "Stop. You're going to have to trust me, if you want your memories back."

I stand down as Liam joins us, sitting on the armchair beside Josh. I look away from him. It doesn't escape me that he chose to sit next to Josh instead of me.

"There are a few steps. As Liam said, the amount of his blood that you need to drink will kill you, but—" Josh reaches into his jacket pocket and brings out a vial of blood. The same vial he was given in Romania. "If we inject this into you, it'll…encourage your memories to come to the surface."

"How the Hell did you steal that from the Royal lab?" Liam asks Josh.

Josh gives him a blunt look. "I never gave it to the lab. They got a sample of something, but it wasn't Zak and Rose's blood though," Josh smirks and Liam rolls his eyes as if this is *normal* between them.

Are they…friends?

I don't know what they see on my face but they both mask their looks and become more serious. Josh continues, "Zak and your blood's been infusing for some time now. Now, I don't know how much Mariella told you because I asked her to keep this quiet—but when you told her your blood's poisonous, it helped her with this too. Since Zak is a vampire—"

"If you inject me with both of our blood, Liam's blood won't be poisonous to me. I get it," I sum it up. He was taking forever to get to the point. Mariella's been reporting back to him. Of course she has. Is there anyone I can trust?

"You won't be completely immune, but it won't kill you—and that's where I come in," Josh says. His thumb involuntarily caresses the back of my hand and I stiffen. "As you drink Liam's blood, I'll be healing you through it the entire time."

"How long will it take?" I ask frowning. Healing magic requires a lot of energy from us.

"However long it takes," he replies.

"Won't that drain you?" I ask him. He can't do that. Why would he do that?

Josh cups the side of my face. His touch makes me lean into slightly. His hand is warm and comforting. I'm still so confused but he's not mad. I'm confused why he's not mad, but at least he's not mad at me.

"Don't worry about that. I can handle it," he replies, going back to holding my hand.

"Knowing all this," Liam says, looking at me. He's wearing a nonchalant, almost cold mask that I don't recognize. "Do you still want to do this?"

I nod. "Yes. I have to."

Josh and Liam exchange looks before Josh nods and Liam says, "Alright, let's do this."

"We can do it in one of the bedrooms," Liam tells me as I take my uniform top off, revealing a lacy black tank top that makes Josh clench his jaw and Liam look away from me.

"Here's fine," I say, firmly, sitting down on the couch before holding my hand out to Liam.

He hesitates but takes it, his chilled touch familiar but strange now, and it's not because Josh is watching. Liam sits down beside me before Josh gives me a bottle of blood.

"Drink that first," Josh says. He kisses my head as I do. I finish it and then lay my head on Liam's lap.

"I'm ready," I tell them as my heart races.

"No, you're not. No one can be ready for this." Liam looks down at me, sadly. "Please, rethink it. We can always do it another night. More planned out."

"I have to do this now, Liam. I'm sorry it had to be you to do it," I reach up to stroke his handsome face. His blond hair falls into his eyes and he looks so, so sad. I hate that I'm doing this to him, but he's my only hope.

"I'm sorry too," he whispers.

Josh pulled up an armchair and is sitting next to me. He takes the vial of Zak and my blood out and transfers it to a syringe before pushing it into my veins.

Everyone holds their breath. Nothing happens. Nothing burns, or stings, or feels strange. Josh takes one of my hands into his and rests the other hand on my thigh.

"I'll be right here. We'll do it together, okay?" Josh tells me, quietly.

I nod and take in his handsome face. For the first time, there's so many emotions in his eyes. I want to kiss him…but there's too much between us—too many secrets.

"Ready?" Liam asks me.

I keep my eyes on my Mate and ask Josh, "Why?"

He frowns, looking confused, "Why…what?"

"All this? The secrets. Why not just tell me everything after I shifted? You and Liam working together, you and Nathanial…all the girls…what's even real with you…?" I ask. I have to know why he did all this?

He breaks our eye contact and is quiet but doesn't let go of my hand. I give it a squeeze. He sighs heavily. "There's nothing I can say that'll make anything okay right now. Trust is not easy for me…"

"You trusted Liam…"

"Nathanial wasn't in Liam's head…there's a lot you still don't know…" Josh says.

"Let's take it one step at a time, okay?" Liam tells me and I look up at him. He gives me a small smile. "I'm sorry you feel blindsided…and we'll talk, but we can't cover years worth of information in one night."

He's right. I'm hurt that Liam and I weren't…what I thought we were, but he has my memories. I need my memories.

I just nod and relax back on his lap.

"We'll do this together. I'm not leaving you," Josh telepaths to me. I take in a deep breath before nodding.

Liam places his wrist in my mouth. "Eyes on me, little wolf, okay?"

I give him a slight nod, before my fangs come out and I pierce his wrist. A part of me hopes that since Josh is my Mate and he's immune to poison, but also Zak's blood didn't kill me—that this will be fine.

It is not fine.

The second Liam's blood touches my tongue and flows down my throat—splitting, searing pain travels through my body, like someone's pouring lava in me. It's hot, burning, like I'm drinking acid. He pins me down, his vampiric strength locking me in place as my legs kick against the couch. My arms try to push him away, trying to pry him out of my mouth. Josh's healing magic surges through me, but it's not nearly enough. I need to scream, I have to scream, but I can't.

"You have to keep drinking," Liam tells me. "Or this pain will be for nothing. We've got you."

I know he's right, but I can't. I can't keep drinking. My stomach is on fire, my entire body feels like I'm burning alive.

I can't do this. I can't.

"You're so close to knowing the truth, baby," Josh's voice is in my mind and like the night of my transformation, it's the beacon I reach for. His hand tightens around mine. ***"I'm so sorry. You can do this. Please…"***

I think about Josh and how I have to get to the bottom of what happened to Noah—if I had a hand in his death. Shane being terrified of me using my powers stems from somewhere, and I have to know. I have to know what really happened that night.

So I force myself to keep drinking as tears flow down the sides of my face. I keep drinking Liam's blood, this poison for the truth.

For me. For Josh. For us.

I feel Liam stroking my hair faintly as his blood flows down my throat—then my brain *explodes.*

And.

Everything.

Goes.

Black.

78 SECRETS BETWEEN US

Josh Hunter

January 2

I've never been this nervous in my life.

Burning pain courses throughout my entire body, starting in my throat as Rose starts drinking Liam's blood. My grip on her hand tightens, but I swallow down the pain as she thrashes.

As a basilisk, I'm immune to poisons, any and all kinds, except vampire blood. Rose, as my Mate, is equally immune. Zak's blood in her, his spirit magic, is supposed to help with her memories—not the pain. If I wasn't using my magic, this would be so much worse, but even with it…she's being tortured.

Fuck, fuck, fuck!

The pain gets worse, bordering agony I've never felt before. My entire body is on fire. It feels like someone skinned me alive, dunked me in acid, then rubbed salt into every inch of me. I breathe through it knowing Rose is actually feeling this. I feel my powers threaten to spill out. I've never lost control and I can't right now.

"You good?" Liam asks me, watching me carefully.

"Yes," I answer through gritted teeth.

He doesn't push me. He knows better by now.

Rose continues sobbing through her pain. Her body jerks like she's being electrocuted from the inside out. Her fingers claw at my hand, nails digging in deep enough to draw blood, but I don't let go.

Her muffled screams rip through the room, raw and broken. I grit my teeth so hard I taste my own blood.

One hour becomes two. Sweat soaks through my white shirt, sticks my hair to my forehead. My magic is starting to fade too as I pour everything I have into her. Every time she convulses, I feel it in my own veins like fire. My vision keeps tunneling, black spots dancing at the edges. I'm shaking. Not trembling—full-body tremors I can't hide anymore.

Liam's eyes flick to me every few minutes, but he doesn't say shit. Rose's cries eventually turn into these hoarse, shattered whimpers that are somehow worse. Then her body goes limp, unable to endure any more pain. She's just…done.

Liam moves first, easing her head off his lap and laying her down on the wide leather couch. Her skin's clammy, lips stained dark red with his blood. Chest rising and falling too shallow, too fast. I hate how small she looks right now.

I cup my mouth. The look on her face is of utter distraught. Tears stain her rosy cheeks while her mouth is covered in blood from Liam forcing her to keep drinking. I sit down on the couch and gather Rose in my arms, needing to hold her—feel her. I don't know how she managed to warm her way into my frozen heart, but she did.

She's burning up. I tuck her head under my chin and let my healing magic flood out again, slower this time.

Liam walks over to the kitchen. He pours a glass of blood and brings it over to me. "You need it."

I take it with one hand, keeping the other locked around Rose. It takes the edge off the fatigue clawing in.

"Something stronger," I tell him. Divine, my voice sounds like gravel.

"Something stronger," I tell him. Divine, my voice sounds like gravel.

Liam raises a brow but doesn't comment. He goes to the cart, unlocks the bottom cabinet with the biometric scanner, because of course he has a goddamn biometric lock on his liquor, and pulls out the Macallan thirty-year infused with AB neg. He brings the bottle to me with no glass.

"All yours," he says, handing it off, before sitting down on the armchair.

I take a swig. Fire races down my throat, explodes in my chest, burns all the way to my fingertips. I need the burn. Need something to drown out the echo of her screams still rattling around in my skull.

I look down at Rose. Her breathing's steadier now, but she's still out cold. Face slack. Lashes dark against too-pale cheeks. Her make-up is completely ruined. My thumb brushes a strand of hair off her forehead before I can stop myself. She's fucking beautiful, even like this.

"Did it work?" I ask. The words come out quieter than I mean them to.

Liam crouches down, elbows on his knees, studying her for a long second.

"Can't be sure till she wakes up," he says finally.

I shift Rose a little higher in my arms, settle my back against the couch so she's draped across my lap instead of half on the leather. My hand finds hers again, smaller, colder now, and I lace our fingers together.

"She's going to have questions," Liam says, quietly.

That's not what I'm worried about. Of course, she's going to have questions. She's been in denial about killing Noah this entire time and now she's going to wake up remembering how bloody her hands got six years ago. She felt guilty for killing those assholes who attacked her—how will she feel knowing she killed her best friend? Her sister too.

I brush back strands of her hair again.

Liam narrows his eyes slightly. "You wanted me to do this two years ago. You sent me to distract her that night instead of going yourself. We should've done it then."

Of course he's going to bring that up. Of course, he's going to hold that over me. Getting to know Rose, falling for her over these past few months, made me realize I truly don't deserve her. Watching her dance with Liam, even for just one song, seeing the genuine smile on her pretty face for him, killed me. The way she laughed so easily with him, the way I never made her laugh...that should've been the worst of it. But it was the way her eyes shone when she looked at him…eyes I only ever wanted on me—want on me. Her eyes always gave everything away even when her face didn't. Her eyes always held so much.

Liam was never supposed to fall in love with her. But when I realized they were seeing each other, I told Liam to give her the memories back. He said he never wanted to hurt her like that, that she couldn't take it. It pissed me off. I didn't want her to remember because it was the right thing. I wanted her to remember so I could hate her without guilt.

"You said you didn't want to be the one to hurt her with this," I remind him.

Liam sighs heavily, rubbing his forehead and glancing at my Mate. "Not remembering was hurting her more."

"Sir," Cole walks in through the front door. "We have company."

Liam and I glance at each other before I ask, "Who else did you tell?"

"No one." He frowns.

"Sir, it's the Alpha," Cole informs me.

"Fuck," I grit my teeth just before Shane walks in but he's not alone. I stop using my magic on Rose. Serpents aren't supposed to have healing magic.

"You told them?" Liam asks me as I cover Rose with the blanket he tosses me.

"What are you doing here?" I look at my best friends, jaw tight.

"I think the question is what are you doing with the vampire prince?" Shane asks stepping closer. "You think I wouldn't know when my sister was distressed?"

"You followed me?" I snap, glaring at them.

"You ran out in the middle of Izabella returning from the dead," James states, crossing his arms over his chest. "We were curious what could possibly be more important than that."

"Yeah, about that…what's going on?" Liam asks me, then looks at the boys. "I thought Jules told you weeks ago she was raised?"

James, Devaughn, and I look at Shane, unaware of that piece of information. It does explain why Shane had such a calm reaction to her being back. Shane comes to sit down on the armchair next to me.

"Izabella walked up to the front gates of Cravenhold earlier tonight," Shane ignores our inquisitory looks and answers Liam.

"By herself? Where is she?" Liam asks, his frown deepening.

"The dungeon," I answer Liam briefly before focusing on Shane. "Why did you follow me?"

How long has he been following me?

"You think I trusted your ass after the shit you've been pulling with Rose?" Shane adds as he looks down at her sleeping form.

"Don't you dare start. You've known everything I've been doing and why," I say to him lowly. Shane's not innocent in any of this. He's just hiding behind the protective big brother role and justifying his actions with it.

"What happened?" Devaughn asks, quietly looking at Rose. Her brows are furrowed as if she's having a bad dream. "Why are we here?"

Suddenly, I'm too damn exhausted for this.

In that moment, Rose begins to stir, then her eyes open. Those beautiful, soft gray eyes focus on me before panic sets in them.

She starts thrashing and fighting, screaming nonsense as we try to hold her down. Shane grabs her feet to keep her from kicking while I lock my arms around her. Liam comes up from behind the couch, and when she sees him, betrayal flashes over her face as she starts crying.

Liam looks just as broken, and it takes everything in me to not punch the asshole. Yes, Liam and I had a plan.

But *Liam* went off script.

Liam fell in love with my Mate.

"Hey," I cup her face, making her look only at me. The confusion and fear in her eyes make my chest tighten. She's terrified. What is she scared of? "It's just us. We're here for *you*, sweetheart."

How we got here doesn't matter right now, but the rest is true.

Rose starts shaking her head, then scans the room until her eyes land on Shane. She pulls her legs back and he hesitantly lets her go, seeing that the fight's left her body. She turns into me, curling so small into a ball on my lap. I hold back the relief I feel, because I know this night is far from over.

I can tell Shane is communicating with her telepathically, and I wish I never told her to strengthen her shields. I wish I could let myself in right now and listen. Despite going through what she did tonight, her mental shields are solid. Whatever Shane says to her makes her body go slack. She glances at Liam, then back to me, before wrapping her weak arms around my shoulders and pulling me into her.

Her soft cheek presses against mine as I feel her breath on my ear. She smells like the home she promised me and all I want to do is take her back to Coilspire.

But then she whispers, "I'm so sorry."

EPILOGUE

Rosella Hunter
January 8

You stand on the edge of a grand unraveling.
War is coming. But the war inside of you has yet to break.
You've turned yourself into a vision of control.
But you were never meant to be kept in a box, even by your own hands.
Bonds will break—they must.
And when they do, it will scorch everything they touch.
Things are not as they seem and when the fire is lit, only you can put it out.
What you cling to now will not weather the storm.
The ending is unavoidable, but you are the spark for a new world.
You must embrace the truth of who you are.

I recall the seer's reading from Mabon as I watch Shane go off on another nighttime boat ride. Josh left for Coilspire from Liam's cabin and didn't return to Cravenhold with us. I haven't heard from him since.

I stare at my hands. I've been doing that a lot since the cabin. I just can't look at them the same anymore.

The things my hands did. The people my hands held. The lives my hands will destroy.

Bonds will break—they must.
And when they do, it will scorch everything they touch.

That didn't mean at all what I thought it did—and now I know why the seer called Josh the Son of the Heavens and the Skies. I finally understand why Josh refused to believe I was innocent—why he fought everyone, why he believed I was guilty, why he never fought to clear my name…and why Shane never said a word.

Some truths are just too dangerous. Some truths need to be covered with lies and manipulation. Some truths tilt worlds and break them.

I look up to the night sky. To the Heavens. To the Divine.

The stars remember, and so do I.

For now…

Rose and Josh's story will continue in the second installment of their duology.

Coming soon.

ACKNOWLEDGEMENTS

To my parents—I hope you never read this book. Or at least…not certain chapters. Thank you for letting me keep my head in the clouds and loving me anyway. For accepting that this is who I am—a dreamer, a storyteller, someone who builds entire worlds and refuses to come down from them.

To my author-sanity lifeline and friend, S.N. Yusuf—Thank you for the endless chats, the shared chaos, and not letting me lose my mind by myself. Writing this book connected us, but your friendship kept me going. You not only helped me survive self-publishing, but you also taught me so much about the indie author world. I'm so grateful our paths crossed.

To Lauren, Sarah, Marie, and Destiny—My Alphas through plot twists, rewrite, meltdown, and indecisive moments. Thank you for letting me give you creative whiplash. You are such a big part of how *As Worlds Tilt* became what it is.

To my incredible PA, Nicky at Bones and Belladonna—Thank you for guiding me through release season and helping me get Rose and Josh out into the world. It's been such a pleasure having you in my corner and on my team.

To Danielle, Breanna, Jodie, Ashley, and Karla—Your excitement for this world has been contagious. Every message, every reaction has meant more than you know. You are everything an author hopes for in a reader.

Ryann and Tabitha—You gave me a bigger vision for *As Worlds Tilt* right when I needed it most. You reignited my excitement for the future of my books and opened new doors for what Rose and Josh can become. Thank you for helping me dream even bigger.

And finally, my street and ARC team, and everyone I've met through this book community—Thank you for supporting me, inspiring me, laughing with me, crying with me, and coming along for the ride. This journey has been brighter because of you. You mean more than I can ever fully put into words.

ABOUT THE AUTHOR

Tasneem Alam writes contemporary dark romantasy that blends emotional depth with intricate supernatural worldbuilding. Her stories center on complex relationships, shifting power dynamics, and the lasting impact of legacy, identity, and choice. With layered characters and interconnected series, she explores how the drive for the truth collides in worlds that mirror our own.

She lives in California and continues to expand her fictional universe while connecting with readers who are drawn to stories that challenge, provoke, and resonate long after the story is over. When she's not plotting the next story, she can be found binge-watching shows, spending time with her family, or laughing too hard with her best friends.

www.ingramcontent.com/pod-product-compliance
Lightning Source LLC
LaVergne TN
LVHW091248110826
845146LV00002BA/455

* 9 7 9 8 9 9 5 5 4 4 2 1 0 *